Haunted Teachers

True Ghost Stories

ALLAN ZULLO

Troll

To my good friend Nick Griffis,
who teaches literacy not from a book
but from the heart.

Copyright © 1996 by The Wordsellers, Inc.

Published by Troll Communications L.L.C.

All rights reserved. No part of this book may be reproduced or utilized in any form or by any means, electronic or mechanical, including photocopying, recording, or by any information storage and retrieval system, without written permission from the publisher.

Cover design by Tony Greco & Associates.

Cover illustration by Kersti Frigell.

Printed in the United States of America.

10 9 8 7 6 5 4 3 2 1

CONTENTS

Does a ghost haunt your teacher?

Ghosts have haunted all sorts of people, such as doctors, lawyers, parents, kids—and even teachers! In schools new and old, teachers have reported seeing phantoms that often appeared to be the spirits of former teachers.

In some cases experts were called in to investigate these so-called hauntings. Usually, the experts walked away baffled. All they knew for sure was that something weird had happened that couldn't be fully explained.

This book is a creepy collection of stories about phantoms—especially ghostly teachers—who have haunted teachers and students in the classroom, on the playground, and at home. These eerie tales are inspired, in part, by real-life cases taken from the files of noted ghost hunters. The names and places in the stories are not real.

Does the spirit of a teacher haunt your classroom? Is your teacher spooked by a ghost? You might think so after reading the startling stories in this book!

THE PHANTOM RIDER

Is that a horse I hear galloping? Connie Hall looked up from her desk and walked toward the window of her second-floor classroom. The teacher, who had stayed late after school to mark papers, peered out into the darkness but failed to see anything unusual.

The sound of horse hoofs rumbling across the school property grew louder. She opened the window and stuck her head out. *Judging from the noise, the horse should be right outside, but I don't see it,* thought Connie. *What would a horse be doing around here? This is a well-developed suburb. There certainly aren't any horses nearby.*

Connie was about to return to her desk when she heard a faint voice utter in despair, "Where is my school? Where are my children?"

The teacher poked her head out the window again and yelled, "Hello, who's out there?"

For a brief moment in the moonless night, she spotted

something moving away, beyond the range of the blue security light that shined on the playground below. *I wonder what that was,* Connie thought. *Maybe someone was riding a horse after all. Oh, well, I better get back to grading my papers.*

It wasn't unusual for the seventh-grade teacher to work alone at night in her classroom at Fletcher Middle School in the town of Mercer. Single with no kids, the slightly overweight 42-year-old woman had devoted her life to her profession since her divorce ten years ago. She put in more hours than any other teacher in the school. And it paid off. Her students always scored higher than the county average on aptitude tests because Connie had a knack for inspiring them. She projected a warmth about her that made kids instantly like her. She flashed a ready smile and made each student feel special. Kids called her "Hugger" Hall because of her penchant for hugging her students. "You're never too old to hug or get hugged," she'd say.

Often Connie would stay after class and then join friends for dinner at a nearby barbecue restaurant. She would return to the school and take care of all the things that teachers must do when they aren't actually teaching. Around 9 P.M., she would go to the fitness center for a workout that never seemed to shed any pounds.

Connie had forgotten about the horse incident until one evening several weeks later when she was decorating her classroom for Halloween. Once again she heard a horse galloping by the school. This time it sounded as if the horse had slowed to a canter near the playground. Connie saw nothing out the window. But she wasn't satisfied, so she walked down the stairs and went outside, locking the door behind her.

I definitely heard a horse snorting, she told herself. *I'm not imagining this.* As she turned the corner of the building, she expected to see the horse, but the playground was empty. Connie stood still for a minute listening to the sounds of the night. Cars rumbled past the front of the school, and a siren screeched in the distance. Nothing unusual.

Connie unlocked the door and walked back into the school. As she started for the stairs, she caught a glimpse of a figure in gray clothes striding down the hall.

"Hello," said Connie. "Who's there?"

The person kept walking away from her, stopping at every classroom door as if looking for someone or something.

"Yoo-hoo! Hello?" Connie shouted. Still no response.

In the darkened hallway Connie could barely make out that the person was a woman with wavy blond hair, wearing a wide-brimmed hat and a long cape. When the woman reached the end of the corridor, she simply vanished.

Connie stood stunned for a long minute before running to the end of the hallway. *How could she disappear like that?* the awed teacher asked herself. *That's impossible!* Connie checked the last two classroom doors on either side of the corridor, but they were both locked. *Who was she? Where did she go? How did she get in here—and more importantly, how did she get out?*

Connie felt a chill squirm across her back. She pulled her button-down sweater tightly around her neck and headed for the stairs. Then she heard the horse gallop off. Connie quickly rushed to the back entrance, flung open the door, and caught a brief glimpse of a figure in gray, riding on a horse into the darkness.

The next day Connie questioned all the teachers and staff and learned that no one had been in school the night before. After she told the janitor, Mr. Blythe, what had happened, he chuckled and said, "Sounds like you have a ghost on your hands."

"What makes you say that?" asked Connie.

"A few years ago another teacher, whose name I can't remember, said she saw a woman in gray on a horse galloping outside the school one night. The maintenance man back then, George Raines, said it was probably the Phantom Rider. Well, I never heard tell of such a thing. It seems that once in a great while, a ghostly woman and her horse like to ride past our school. I don't pay much attention to this stuff, but maybe you were given the privilege of seeing the Phantom Rider herself."

"That's a little hard to swallow," said Connie. "I never heard about this legend before. But maybe I'll do a little research—just for fun, of course."

At the library she found a book on local legends that mentioned the Phantom Rider this way:

"She often rides through the night on a palomino stallion in north Mercer. She wears a gray cloak that floats behind her, and her blond hair streams in the wind. Both hands grasp the reins as she comes out of the past, is visible only briefly, and vanishes into the darkness as if all the legions of another world are in pursuit."

When Connie read the description of the phantom, her heart began to race and her mouth grew dry. *That describes exactly the person I saw in the hallway! Could the Phantom Rider be real?*

Connie eagerly searched the shelves but found no other books containing information about the legend. She yearned to see the phantom again, and wondered if she ever would. Connie didn't have to wait long.

Working late one night alone in the classroom, Connie was reading papers from her students about the effects the Civil War had on the area. She was extremely pleased with the quality of the reports—including one about a young banker named Charles Waldrop who headed a local Confederate militia. One day he encountered a squad of Union soldiers and, while on his trusty steed, let them pursue him through the woods and past the schoolhouse. As the Yankees rode by the school, members of the rebel militia stuck their guns out of the school windows and fired away, killing all six enemy soldiers. Waldrop had lured them past the school on purpose and led them straight into a Confederate ambush.

While she read, Connie became aware of a distant sound. *The galloping horse! I hear it whinnying. The phantom must be back!* The tiny hairs on the back of the teacher's neck stood up. Connie was on her way to the window when her body jerked from surprise.

Standing in the doorway was a woman whose wavy blond hair flowed from under a battered Confederate hat. A long gray cape hid most of an ankle-length dress and her black high-top button-down shoes.

"You startled me," said Connie. "Who are you and how did you get in here?"

The woman, in her early 20s, didn't speak. Connie noticed the woman's face looked extremely pale, her drawn eyes hollow and sunken cheeks tear-stained. Her thin lips had fallen in an expression of sorrow and bewilderment. *With makeup, different clothes, and a smile, she could look really pretty*, thought Connie. *She's obviously troubled.*

"Where are my children?" the woman whimpered.

"Perhaps if you tell me who you are and the names of your children, I might be able to help you."

"My students. I'm looking for my students."

"Are you a teacher?"

The woman nodded.

"Where?"

"Here."

"You must be mistaken," said Connie. "I teach here at Fletcher, and I know everyone on the faculty. Who are you?"

"Sally Foster," replied the woman. "Help me find my students," she said pleadingly. Sally stepped back into the hallway out of Connie's sight.

"Wait, don't go." Connie scurried out into the hallway. Sally was gone. Connie ran down the stairs and stood in the front of the lobby, expecting to hear footsteps or a door close. But all was quiet until she heard the galloping of a horse heading off into the night.

What just happened here? Connie asked herself. *Could she be the strange woman I saw in the hallway? Long cloak, hat, blond hair. Why, she could be the Phantom Rider! How exciting! But if so, why is she haunting this school? And who are the children she asks about? I must find the answers, or I'll never be able to rest.*

Connie was too pumped to read any more papers. Her whole body shook from excitement over seeing what she now believed was a ghost. She gathered her things and drove to the fitness center, hoping the workout would calm her down.

That Saturday Connie went to the county historical society. She scoured dusty old books and yellowed papers from the Civil War days.

She discovered that the school where the rebel troops had hidden and ambushed the Yankees was situated on Miller Road, a mile (1.6 km) north of the city dam—the exact location where Fletcher Middle School now stood. What she learned next really jolted her: The last person to teach at the school was named Sally Foster.

There's no denying it, thought Connie. *I saw the ghost of Sally Foster! Oh, I hope I meet her again, to find out why she's haunting our school. She's so anguished. Maybe if I spoke with her, I could help ease her torment. And I do so want to know why she's looking for her students.*

Night after night Connie waited in her classroom, hoping to encounter the spirit from the past. A week went by without any sign of Sally or her horse. One evening, in frustration, Connie drew Sally's name in big bold letters on the blackboard and shouted, "Sally Foster, where are you?"

"Help me, please."

Connie whirled around and saw Sally standing in the middle of the room. "Sally, you've come back. How can I help you?"

"My school, my students. Where are they?"

"Sally, they're not here. That was a long time ago. What happened to you? Why are you dressed like a rebel soldier?"

Sally clutched at her cloak as if it offered protection against the heartache of the past. Slowly she began to walk around the room, gingerly touching the students' desks and lightly fingering the cabinets and countertops.

"I loved teaching," said Sally. "That's all I wanted to do with my life. Teach, get married, and have children. That's not asking so much."

She smiled for the first time. "I taught in the most beautiful little schoolhouse you can imagine. Whitewashed every summer. I taught 14 children, all wonderfully sweet and delightfully energetic. I loved them all. Do you know where they are? I've been looking for them."

"No, Sally, I don't." Connie was afraid to tell Sally that they had died long ago; that more than 130 years had passed.

"I don't suppose you do," Sally murmured. She strolled toward the front of the room. "Where is the wishing well?"

"We don't have a wishing well."

Sally shook her head. "Everything has changed, yet nothing has changed."

"What about the well, Sally?"

"In the schoolyard was a wishing well. That's where I met my sweetheart, Charles Waldrop."

"The banker who headed the local Confederate militia?"

"Why, yes, do you know him?"

"I know of him."

Sally twirled around once and threw her head back. "Charles was so handsome. He and I would spend hours by the wishing well. It was said that if you wished hard enough before you drank from the well, your wish would come true. We wished to be married and spend the rest of our lives together. But then the war between the states broke out and ruined everything.

"One day, the Yankees were advancing on the town. Charles came to the schoolhouse and told me to take the children and run for the hills, that it wasn't safe to stay in the school."

"I read about how the rebels ambushed the Yankees at the school," said Connie.

Sally nodded. "The children and I were running deep into the woods when we encountered a platoon of Yankees. The children panicked and ran in all directions. I tried to keep them together but it was no use. I grabbed four little ones and took them with me. The Yankees found us and held us briefly before they let us go on our way.

"Eventually, I returned the four little ones to their homes. But I had to find the other children. I ran back toward the school. I had reached the wishing well when I noticed that the Yankees now occupied the schoolhouse, not the rebels. And then I saw . . ." Sally began to cry.

"Sally, what's wrong?"

"It's so hard to talk about it." Her arms were folded tightly across her chest, and her head hung low as she continued. "I saw Charles's dead body. After the ambush, Charles was caught by the Yankees. Rather than surrender, he tried to shoot his way to freedom. But the Yankees shot him to death. The soldiers draped his body over his horse, a beautiful palomino named Charger, and brought him back to the schoolyard.

"It took all that was within me to keep from crying out in grief. But I held my tongue and remained crouched behind the well. Charles's horse was tied up not more than ten yards (9.1 m) away from where I hid. I waited for my chance and sneaked up to Charger and whispered for him to stay calm, which he did. And then, in a flash, I untied him, hopped on, and rode off with Charles's body right out from under the noses of those bluecoats!"

A smug grin spread across her pale face. An instant later, her expression changed to sorrow. "I was riding off not knowing at first where I was going. I simply wanted to be with my beloved. I soon arrived at his parents' house. And there we all sat and wept.

"Later that night I had to make sure the rest of the children—my students—had safely returned to their houses. I donned Charles's hat and cape—to feel close to him—and rode Charger into the woods where I last saw the children fleeing. I don't remember much after that. Shots rang out. I felt a sharp pain here." Sally untied the cape and pointed to a spot below her neck.

Connie gasped at the sight of a dark red bloodstain on Sally's blouse running from her collar down to her waist.

"You were shot!" cried Connie.

"Evidently. Charger was felled too. I don't know what happened after that or where I went, because it was so dark, so very dark. I kept looking for my children, those sweet young things who were put in my care. I kept searching and searching and couldn't find them. And then I went back to the schoolhouse—only it wasn't there. I have lost my beloved, my school, and my students. Do you know where my children are? Help me find my students, my school. Help me." And then Sally slowly faded away.

"Come back, Sally. Come back." Then Connie heard the galloping horse. She knew that Sally's ghost had left.

The teacher's knees began to wobble, and she slipped into a student's desk to steady herself. The last few minutes had been the most extraordinary of her life. *I was talking face-to-face with a ghost! She was right here in my classroom. A teacher who lived in the last century, who has never been able to rest in peace, spoke to me! I have to know more about her.*

Connie returned to the county historical society and searched for more information on Sally Foster and Charles Waldrop. She didn't find anything and was about to give up. As she reached for a directory, she accidentally knocked a shoe box off the shelf. When it hit the floor, several letters fell out. She put them back in the box and was placing it on the shelf when she noticed that an old letter, folded in fourths, had slipped under a table.

She picked it up. Curious, Connie opened it. Dated January 5, 1918, it was from Douglas Waldrop. *Waldrop?* thought Connie. *Could he be related to Charles?* The letter was addressed to Miss Hannah Tripp of Mercer, who Connie later learned was a local author. Hannah had been gathering material for a book on local legends when she unexpectedly died in 1920. The shoe box contained Hannah's notes and research material. *I absolutely have to read this letter,* Connie said to herself.

My Dear Miss Tripp,

You asked if I had any knowledge of a supposed Phantom Rider who gallops on a magnificent palomino near Miller Road. The answer is yes. I have firsthand knowledge which you are free to use any way you wish.

I am near 70 years old now, but what I am about to tell you is as clear to me as when it happened back in 1861 when I was 11 years old.

My older brother Charles fought for the Confederacy and led the Yankees into a deadly ambush at the schoolhouse in Mercer. Unfortunately, he was killed hours later. Meanwhile, his fiancée, the schoolteacher Sally Foster, was leading her students to safety when they encountered a battle. Panic broke out and the children scattered in all directions. She tried to round them up but couldn't.

Sally, a marvelous woman with smarts to match her bravery and beauty, managed to retrieve Charles's body and his palomino Charger from the grasp of the Yankees and return to our home. There, we mourned our loss.

Later that same day, in Charles's hat and cloak, Sally rode on Charger to find her missing students. Tragically, she and Charger were slain by enemy bullets. Her fatal ride was unnecessary, for all the children had arrived home safely.

The Yankees were so angered by the ambush that they burned the schoolhouse to the ground. They left nothing. They even carted off the stone from the school's foundation to help build a wall from which to fire upon the Confederates.

Two days later Charles and Sally were buried side by

side. The night after their funeral I was walking home from the cemetery. In the distance came pounding hoof beats. On and on they came, past the church, past the graveyard, and on toward the schoolyard.

In the moonlight I saw something I could not believe. For it was Charger, and upon him was none other than Sally Foster herself, wearing my brother's Confederate cavalry cape and hat.

I had never seen such an awesome sight. The hoofs scarcely seemed to touch the ground. Charger came to a stop directly in front of me. While the horse stood motionless, the wind and dust swirled up in a cloud, and I heard Sally Foster ask, "Where are my children? Where is my school?" Charger reared up, and then they sped off into the night.

I thought my grief from the death of my brother and his fiancée (of whom I was most fond) had caused me to see things. Surely, what I saw could not have been real, I told myself. But an astounding incident that happened the following month convinced me otherwise.

One night I had sneaked up upon a Union campsite next to where the school once stood. Suddenly there was a hue and cry. The sentries yelled that a Confederate soldier was fast approaching from the east on a horse. The sentries ordered the horseman to stop, and when their call was not obeyed, they raised their rifles and fired. A salvo of bullets flew from a dozen guns. Yet the horse and rider did not fall, but continued to advance. To the soldiers' astonishment, they saw that the rider was a woman. I was even more amazed, for the horse was Charger and the rider was Sally

Foster! As she reached the perimeter of the camp, she shouted, "Where are my children? Where is my school?" Charger reared up and then galloped right through the camp before being swallowed by the darkness. The men stood in silence, unable to fathom what they had witnessed. Even I, who had observed the specter weeks earlier, found it hard to believe.

I have not seen Charger and Sally—whom people now call the Phantom Rider—since. But over the years I have heard of others who claim to have seen her. It's always by the spot where the school once stood. Sadly, I suspect she is doomed to roam the area forever, looking for her students and her school.

So, if anyone should ask you if the Phantom Rider is a legend, tell him no, it is not a legend. Tell him it is absolutely true.

Very Truly Yours,
Douglas Waldrop

Connie's hand trembled when she put down the letter. Now it became crystal clear to her why Sally Foster had made those ghostly appearances at Fletcher Middle School. It was also apparent what Connie must say the next time she saw Sally.

About a week later, alone in her classroom, Connie heard the galloping horse. Within a minute Sally Foster appeared in the back of the room.

"I'm so tired, so weary," Sally moaned. "Do you know where my children are? Do you know what happened to my school?"

"Yes, I know the answers, Sally. Your students all made it safely home. No harm came to them. They grew up and are gone now."

"And my school? Why can't I find my school?"

"I'm sorry to tell you this, Sally, but it was destroyed. The soldiers burned it down."

Sally began to weep. "My whole life was tied up in that school—the children, the wishing well, my fiancé. All gone, all gone. Now what shall I do?"

"Sally, it's time for you to move on. You don't need to haunt this place anymore. It's a different school, with new students and teachers who love them very much. There's nothing more for you and Charger to do here. Your search is finally over."

Sally didn't say a word. She seemed deep in thought. Finally, she said, "Yes, perhaps you're right. Charger and I can rest now." The anguish that had been etched in her face was replaced by a peaceful glow. "We can rest," she repeated as she faded away.

Connie ran to the window and looked down onto the playground. The security light shined on Sally Foster, who sat tall and straight atop her sturdy palomino. The horse reared up, pawing at the air with its front legs as if in happiness and relief. Then he and his mistress galloped off into the night never to be seen again.

CURSE OF THE EGYPTIAN BONE

Middle-school teacher Carter Sexton was grading papers at his desk early one morning when student Kyle Phillips entered the otherwise empty classroom. Kyle was holding a paper bag.

Carter looked up from his desk. "Morning, Kyle. I'm sorry to hear of your grandfather's death. Are you okay?"

"Yes, Mr. Sexton, thank you. I'm fine."

"What's in the bag?"

"My grandmother gave this to me yesterday. It belonged to Grandpa Stan, and now that he's gone, she wanted me to have it. I thought that because we were studying about bones and stuff, I'd share it with the class." He gently pulled out a glass case shaped like a bell that fit over a wooden base. Inside the case was an oddly shaped bone.

Suddenly, sweat burst from Carter's forehead. His heart began beating like a jackhammer. *No, it can't be!* he told himself. *It's not possible. That was destroyed years ago.*

This must be different. It can't be the same one.

"Mr. Sexton, is something the matter?"

"I'm fine, Kyle," the teacher replied in a shaky voice. "May I?"

Kyle placed the case in Carter's shaking hands. The teacher was so nervous he had to set the case down on his desk. He lifted the glass cover and picked up the bone. A wave of nausea swept over him. He put it down and gulped. Then he looked at the faded, partially torn label on the base. "Sacrum from an Egyptian princess, found in 1951 by Zel—" The rest of the label was missing.

Carter buried his face in his hands and muttered to himself. "I don't understand. How is it possible?"

"Mr. Sexton? You're acting a little weird."

A look of terror flared up in the teacher's eyes. He clutched Kyle's arm and said, "We must destroy this bone at once!"

"What are you talking about?" snapped Kyle as he quickly scooped up the bone and put it back in the glass case. "It's mine. It's been in my family for years."

"No, Kyle, it's not yours. This bone belongs to an ancient Egyptian princess—one whose ghost is bent on revenge. The bone is cursed. We must destroy it before it destroys us and, possibly, this school!"

Carter asked Kyle to sit down and listen to the incredible story of the curse of the Egyptian bone.

In 1951, when Carter was six years old, his parents, Alex and Zelda Sexton, left him in the care of relatives and went on a vacation to Egypt. Zelda taught science at Wilson High;

Alex taught geography at Jefferson Junior High. Every year during spring break, they traveled to an exotic locale.

In Egypt they visited the tomb of the boy king Tutankhamen, the Temple at Luxor, the Sphinx, and other famous ancient sites. They also rode in the desert of the Valley of the Kings on the backs of camels.

Knowing of their adventurous spirit, their local guide, Anwar, took them to unusual places that most tourists never got the chance to see. "How would you like to visit a tomb that even the archaeologists don't know about yet?" Anwar asked them.

"We'd love it!" Zelda declared.

"It was discovered by tomb robbers," Anwar said. "Unfortunately, they stole everything of value inside, but there is still much to see."

"Oh, this is so exciting!" said Zelda.

Anwar lit a torch and led the Sextons to the tomb's entrance and down dozens of tiny steps carved out of solid rock. The corridor was so narrow and tight that Alex's broad shoulders touched both sides of the walls. When they reached the main chamber, the Sextons both gasped. There, on a stone slab, lay a skeleton amid scraps and twists of winding cloth.

"I believe this skeleton was once a princess," said Anwar. "See the drawings on the wall. As you know, the ancient Egyptians tried to preserve bodies of those from the upper classes into mummies. They believed that the dead lived on in the next world, and that the body had to be preserved forever so it could serve that person."

"It doesn't look like their embalming method worked too

well on this body," said Zelda, scribbling in her notebook. "It's just a skeleton."

"You must remember that this skeleton is over 3,000 years old. The tomb robbers unwrapped the mummy looking for gold and jewelry inside. When the body was exposed to the air, it decayed, leaving only the bones."

After about ten minutes of examining the tomb, Anwar suggested they leave. Reluctantly, the couple followed Anwar up the narrow steps and out of the tomb into the sunlight.

"That was fantastic, Anwar," said Alex. "This definitely was the highlight of our trip. I can't wait to tell our students back home about it."

"Would you excuse me for a moment?" Zelda said. "I want to go down there again for just a second to take a few more notes. I'll be right back." She ducked into the tomb and returned a minute later.

At the hotel in Cairo later that evening, the Sextons were getting ready for dinner when Zelda walked over to Alex and smiled. Both her hands were behind her back.

"I know that look on your face, Zelda. What's up?"

"I have a confession to make," she revealed. "I took a little souvenir from the tomb." She held out her right hand. In her palm lay a strange-looking bone. "It belonged to the skeleton of the princess." It was the sacrum—the triangular-shaped bone from the lower part of the spinal column that is attached to the pelvis.

"Zelda!" exclaimed Alex. "How could you?"

"I couldn't help it. It was a once-in-a-lifetime opportunity, and I wanted a souvenir. I couldn't resist. It was like the skeleton was begging me to take it. Don't be angry with me."

"I'm not, darling." Alex picked up the bone and examined it in his hand. He smiled and said, "This will make an excellent conversation piece."

"And think of our students. What a fascinating learning tool this will be when discussing ancient Egypt and its pyramids, tombs, and mummies."

"Won't Carter be surprised. He can take it to school for Show and Tell."

"Oh, I do miss our son. Someday he'll understand its significance."

When the Sextons returned home, they showed the bone from the princess's skeleton to Carter. But because he was only six years old, he didn't fully grasp its importance.

The Sextons invited several friends over to their house to tell them about their trip to Egypt. The couple showed them photos of the Great Pyramid and the Sphinx and other Egyptian ruins.

"And now for our prized possession from the trip," announced Zelda. "Ta-da!" She lifted up a bell-shaped glass case and removed the bone, which was resting on a wooden base. Then she excitedly explained how she had obtained it. One by one, the guests examined the sacrum, oohing and aahing at holding a 3,000-year-old bone.

After the artifact was passed around, Alex gingerly placed the bone in the glass case and put the case on a small table in the dining room. The Sextons and their guests soon turned to other topics as they sipped coffee in the living room.

About an hour later, they heard a crash in the dining room. Zelda dashed into the room and cried out, "Oh, no! Not the Venetian vase!" Pottery shards from an expensive antique vase that once stood on the floor lay scattered under the dining room table. "You'd think a firecracker went off inside the vase the way the pieces are strewn," she said.

As she picked up the pieces under the table, she was startled to see the bare feet of her son across the floor. "Carter?" She stood up and stared at the little boy, whose eyes were nearly shut. "Are you sleepwalking again?"

"No," he mumbled, shaking his head.

"Did you break this vase?"

"No, Mama."

"Then how did it break?"

He shrugged.

"You had nothing to do with it? It just broke on its own?"

Carter opened his eyes and extended his arms, looking for a hug from his mother. "I didn't do it, Mama. I was walking in the room, and then the thing went boom. I didn't touch it."

Zelda hugged her son. "Sweetheart, I believe you."

"I wonder what caused this," said Alex as he studied the scene. "Even if Carter was sleepwalking and accidentally hit it, the pieces of pottery wouldn't have scattered this far."

"Carter, what are you doing up?" Zelda asked her son.

"I couldn't sleep because of the lady," he replied.

"What lady?"

"I don't know. She had a funny hat, sparkly things around her neck and arms, and blue pajamas."

Zelda looked at Alex. "Do you know what he's talking about?"

Alex shook his head. "He's obviously been dreaming." He took Carter from Zelda's arms and said, "Come on, Sport, let's put you back to bed. You were dreaming."

The next morning Alex and Zelda flipped a coin to see who would be first to take the bone to school. Alex won, so he brought it to Jefferson Junior High to show off to his students. They gazed at the sacrum as he explained how the ancient Egyptians embalmed the body and turned it into a mummy by wrapping it in oils and special linen.

Later that afternoon Alex placed the bone in his desk drawer. He had promised to let another teacher borrow it for classes the next day. As Alex left the classroom, he closed the door and locked it, shaking the door handle to make sure it was secure.

When he returned the next morning, he took one look and became furious. "What is this, a joke?" he muttered under his breath. "If it is, I don't find it funny."

The students' desks had been stacked in such a manner that they formed a pyramid all the way to the ceiling. His desk was lying upside down in front of the pyramid.

"The sacrum!" Alex rushed to his desk, opened the drawer, and pulled out the glass-encased bone. "Thank heavens, it's not broken."

Principal Joseph Trillen joined Alex in examining the room for clues to the culprits. "I fear that students somehow have made a copy of the master key to the classrooms and can get in here at will," said Alex. "The windows were locked from the inside and there's no forced entry, so they couldn't have come in any other way."

"Why did they stack the desks in a pyramid?" asked Mr. Trillen.

"It could be because I talked about Egyptian mummies yesterday," said Alex.

Pointing to the upper portion of the blackboard, the principal asked, "What about these hieroglyphics?"

In large, neat print, someone had written Egyptian symbols across the blackboard. "I didn't notice the hieroglyphics before," said the teacher, surprised at the writing. "I can't be sure, but when I came into class this morning, I don't think they were there."

"What are you saying? That someone came in after you did this morning and wrote them?"

Alex shook his head. "Of course not. I'm surprised I didn't notice them before, that's all. I guess it's because I was so shocked at seeing the pyramid of desks. Still, it's awfully hard to believe I didn't notice them."

"What do the hieroglyphics mean, Alex?"

"I don't know. At first glance they appear genuine. Whoever went to all this trouble at least learned something about ancient Egypt."

Alex copied the symbols on a piece of paper to show Zelda later. After enlisting the aid of bewildered students, who helped dismantle the pyramid and put the desks back into rows, Alex handed the sacrum over to geography teacher Betty McDonald. At the end of the day, she returned the bone to him.

"How did your students like the sacrum?" asked Alex.

"Oh, they enjoyed it," Betty answered. "But the strangest thing happened. At every one of my classes, I pulled down the roll-up map to point out where Egypt was. And then the moment I started talking about the sacrum, the map snapped up on its own. That never happened before."

"This seems to be a day of strange things," he said.

Alex brought the Egyptian bone home with him that night and told Zelda about the incidents at school.

"Obviously, what happened in your classroom was a nasty prank," said Zelda. "What happened in Betty's classroom was probably a coincidence."

Alex showed her the hieroglyphics he had copied off the blackboard. "I'll see if I can find someone at the college who can read them," she said. She took the glass-encased sacrum and set it on the kitchen counter.

Late that night, Carter ran into his parents' room and jumped on their bed. "Mommy, Daddy, I saw the lady again."

"Who, Carter?" asked Zelda.

"The lady from the other night," the little boy replied. "The one with the funny hat and sparkly things."

"Did she do or say anything to you?"

"No, she was in her blue pajamas and floated over my bed and looked down at me. How can she float in the air like that, Mommy?"

"Carter, it's just a dream," said Zelda. "Would you like to spend the night with us?"

The little boy nodded and snuggled between his parents. He was about to doze off when they all heard a thud.

"What was that?" Zelda asked fearfully.

"It came from the kitchen," Alex said. He threw on his robe and ran down the stairs. The sacrum's glass case had fallen off the kitchen counter and onto the ceramic tile floor. The bone had rolled out and was resting against a chair several feet away. The impact should have shattered the glass case, but, remarkably, the glass and the bone were not broken.

When he returned to the bedroom, Alex told Zelda, "I'm baffled. There is no earthly reason why the glass case fell off the counter by itself and that it didn't break."

The next day Zelda took the sacrum to her school to show her students. She described in detail the tomb it came from. She told them everything except how she had taken it from the skeleton of the ancient Egyptian princess.

After the final class of the day, Zelda placed the glass-encased bone on top of her desk. She left the room, locking the door behind her. When she returned the next morning, she opened the classroom door and let out a scream of anguish.

"Look at this room!" Zelda cried out to the other teachers who had rushed to her side when they heard her shriek. "It looks like someone came in here with a bulldozer! This is terrible!"

Teachers gasped with astonishment when they peered inside. Every desk—all thirty of them as well as Zelda's—had been smashed to smithereens. Posters and maps had been ripped off the walls.

"Oh, my! The sacrum!" Zelda dove into the mess, shoving aside splinters, books, and papers. Minutes later, she shouted, "Eureka! This is amazing!" Amid the rubble, she held up the glass case. Incredibly, it was not damaged. Neither was the Egyptian bone. "Look, everyone. The only thing not damaged in this whole room is the sacrum!"

Suddenly, her eyes caught a series of Egyptian hiero-glyphics on the blackboard. She got to her feet and walked over to it. "I didn't write this."

She reached into her purse and pulled out the copy of

hieroglyphics that had been written on the blackboard in her husband's classroom. They were identical to the ones on her blackboard.

The police were called to investigate the vandalism— the worst in the history of Wilson High. They believed that the vandalism at Wilson and the prank at Jefferson were definitely connected.

Meanwhile, Zelda called a friend of hers, Dr. Miller Gaston, a professor of archaeology at a nearby college, who had worked on several sites in Egypt. He hurried to Zelda's classroom and examined the hieroglyphics on the blackboard. After comparing them with those in a little book of his, he let out a low whistle.

"Zelda, this might be more serious than you think."

"What do you mean, Miller?"

"The hieroglyphics say, 'Be warned. You will be cast into the darkness for eternity.' Zelda, this appears to be a death threat!"

That night at home, Alex paced back and forth, staring at the glass-encased bone. "Look at the facts, Zelda," he said. "Our vase in the dining room mysteriously explodes. Desks are formed into a pyramid in my classroom. I receive a hieroglyphic death threat on the blackboard. The sacrum's display case unexplainably falls off the kitchen counter— and doesn't break. Then everything in your classroom is smashed—except for the sacrum and its glass case. And you receive the same death threat."

"What are you saying, Alex?"

"I'm saying that the bone is cursed."

"That's ridiculous!"

"Is it? It makes sense to me. We're being punished because you stole the sacrum from the skeleton."

"The curse of the mummy?" she asked with a sarcastic laugh. "Give me a break, Alex. Have you been reading comic books instead of *National Geographic*?"

"How else do you explain everything that's happened to us since we brought back the sacrum?"

"As a science teacher, I believe there's an explanation for everything. Our classrooms were obviously targets of vandals, that's all."

"Vandals who can break into classrooms without any forced entry?" Alex scoffed. "Vandals who know ancient Egyptian hieroglyphics? I tell you, this bone is haunted or cursed—or both!"

"Mommy, Daddy, are you fighting?" called Carter, who was sitting on a step near the top of the stairs.

"Oh, sweetheart, I'm so sorry if Mommy and Daddy were talking too loudly," said Zelda as she raced up the steps and hugged her son. "We were just having a discussion. We didn't mean to wake you."

"Oh, you didn't. The lady did."

"The one you've seen before in your dreams?"

"Uh-huh," he replied. "She was floating over my bed, and this time she was laughing."

Alex took Carter from his mother and said, "Carter, I want to show you some pretty pictures in a book, okay?"

Zelda whispered to her husband, "Alex, what are you doing?"

"I have a hunch about this lady," he replied as he carried Carter downstairs into the den. Alex pulled out a book about

Egypt and, with Carter on his lap, began flipping through it. "Aren't these pretty pictures, Carter?"

The little boy nodded. After more pages and pictures, Carter let out a squeal. "Hi, lady!"

"Carter, do you know her?" asked Alex as they stared at the color drawing. It showed a typical Egyptian princess wearing a rounded headdress, a gold necklace and matching bracelets, and a flowing blue dress.

"Yes, Daddy. She's the lady who floats in my room."

"Are you sure, honey?" asked Zelda.

Carter nodded. "See the funny hat and the sparkly things and her blue pajamas? That's what the lady wears."

Alex turned to Zelda and through clenched teeth hissed, "We have to get rid of the sacrum."

"No," she snapped back. "I will not."

"What more proof do you need that this bone is cursed?"

"There is no such thing as a curse, Alex!"

"Zelda, you must send the bone to Anwar in Egypt and have him put it back with the rest of the skeleton."

"I will do no such thing!"

"Then get it out of this house!"

"Your imagination is running wild."

"How's this for imagination?" Alex stormed over to the case, took out the bone, opened the front door, and hurled the sacrum against a stone wall. The bone shattered into five pieces.

"Alex! How could you!" Zelda ran outside and scooped up the pieces. She gently placed them back in the glass case. Then she put the case in the trunk of her car.

The next day, she took the broken bone to school. After

seeing that new desks had been delivered to her classroom, she visited the art department and asked teacher Jim Williams if he could repair the sacrum. "No problem," he assured her. "I have the perfect kind of glue that will hold these pieces together. The bone should be ready by the end of the day."

When the final class was over, Zelda walked into Williams's art room. He was gone, but the fixed sacrum was sitting inside the glass case. When an art student entered the room, Zelda asked, "Do you know where Mr. Williams is?"

"Oh, Mrs. Sexton, didn't you hear?" said the student. "Mr. Williams was rushed to the hospital a couple of hours ago. He was found on the floor, unconscious."

Zelda hurriedly returned to her room, put the sacrum on her desk, and then drove to the hospital. By the time she arrived, Jim had been admitted for a head injury. She went to his room and saw that his head had been bandaged. "Jim, what happened?"

"The craziest thing," he replied. "I had just finished gluing the bones back together when—now, this is going to sound ridiculous—I saw, or rather I imagined I saw, a young woman dressed in ancient Egyptian clothing floating above me. I was so startled by this vision that I leaned back in my chair. It tipped over, and I hit the back of my head on the counter behind me. I was knocked out. A student found me and by the time I came to, I was in the emergency room getting 12 stitches in my head. They're keeping me overnight to make sure I haven't suffered a concussion."

"Oh, you poor dear." Zelda reached over and held the teacher's hand. "Did you say you saw an Egyptian?"

"Yes. While I was mending your Egyptian bone I was imagining what the princess looked like. All of a sudden, this image appeared. It was like nothing I had ever seen before. I mean, it was so real. Not transparent or smoky. Now isn't that just the craziest thing you ever heard?"

"No, Jim, it isn't. I'm so sorry."

"Why? It's not your fault."

Oh, yes it is, she said to herself. *Alex was right. I need to get rid of the sacrum once and for all.*

Zelda headed back toward school. Twice on the return trip, she had to pull off to the side as fire trucks sped by. *My, there must be a big fire,* she thought. As she neared the school, she saw billowing clouds of white and gray smoke rising above the trees. *Oh, it couldn't be. Not the school. Oh, not the school!*

When Zelda turned the last corner she was stopped by a police officer. "Officer, what's going on?" she asked.

"Wilson High is on fire," he said. "You need to clear the lane for the fire trucks. It looks like a bad one."

"But I'm a teacher at Wilson!"

"Look, ma'am, there's nothing you can do."

Fighting back tears, Zelda parked the car and ran up to a crowd of spectators who were watching the flames lick out of a second-story window. In horror, the teacher realized that the fire was blazing in her classroom. *That bone!* she told herself. *That haunted bone! It's to blame for all this! I never should have taken it!*

"Zelda!" shouted English teacher Harriet Lane. "Isn't this just tragic?"

"How did it happen, Harriet?"

"No one knows. The fire started on the second floor. Thank goodness it happened at the end of the day after the students had left. I don't think anybody got hurt. What do you suppose caused it?"

"A vengeful ghost," muttered Zelda.

"A what?"

"Nothing, Harriet, nothing."

The fire, smoke, and water caused thousands of dollars of damage to classrooms on the first and second floors. That meant the school would be closed for several weeks until the completion of repairs.

The next day Zelda returned to the school and met with fire investigators who were sifting through the charred rubble looking for the cause of the blaze.

"All we know for sure is that the fire definitely started in your classroom, Mrs. Sexton," said Captain Mark Plano.

"I was in there for just a second at about 4 P.M.," she said. "Everything was fine then. When I left, I locked the door behind me."

"It was a tremendously hot fire. I'm sorry that everything in the room was destroyed."

"Hey, everybody," yelled fireman Stan Phillips, who had been poking around the burnt remains of Zelda's classroom. "Look what I found!" He blew ashes and soot off the object and then held it up for all to see. "It's a glass case with a bone inside. And it's not damaged! The glass didn't even melt."

"Well, Mrs. Sexton, I stand corrected," said Captain Plano. "Obviously not everything was destroyed in the fire after all." Turning to Phillips, the captain yelled, "Hey, Stan, bring it over here."

As the firefighter walked toward them, he announced, "The label says, 'Sacrum from an Egyptian princess, found in 1951 by Zelda Sexton.'"

Phillips tried to hand it over to Zelda. "Here you go, Mrs. Sexton."

Zelda froze. Her eyes grew wide with fear, and her lips began to quiver.

"Mrs. Sexton, this is for you."

"I don't want it!" she screeched. "I don't want to even touch it!" Zelda pleaded in a cracking voice. "I beg of you, destroy it! Get rid of it! Please, just get rid of it!"

And then she darted off, crying hysterically.

"Apparently your grandfather Stan, the firefighter, didn't destroy it," said Carter as he and Kyle stared at the bone in the glass case.

"Grandpa kept it," said Kyle. "I guess he thought your mom was upset because of the fire, and that's why she acted the way she did."

"Your grandfather had the sacrum for more than 40 years and nothing bad happened to him? No tragedies? No unexplained accidents? No bizarre incidents?"

"Just a normal life, nothing out of the ordinary. Why, did more bad things happen to your parents?"

"My mother was never the same after the fire. Her health declined, and she died seven years later. Dad became a sad and lonely man and lost interest in teaching. He was killed in a car accident in 1965."

"I'm sorry, Mr. Sexton."

"Kyle, please believe me. Now that I've touched the

sacrum, I'm convinced the Egyptian's spirit will be revived—because I'm the son of the woman who stole the bone. This is a dangerous spirit who was outraged at having her skeleton violated. She summoned up a vicious power to act through the bone and do terrible things to those connected with my mother. It's fortunate your grandfather was spared. We may not be so lucky. We can't take the chance. Do you understand?"

"Yes, sir."

Minutes later, Carter—armed with a hammer, a can of gasoline from the trunk of his car, and a lighter—and Kyle, who carried the bone, walked to a vacant lot behind the school. There, Carter cleared a small circular area and lined it with rocks. Then he smashed the bone to bits with the hammer, put them inside the circle of rocks, poured gasoline over them, and lit a fire. When the flames died out, he buried the ashes.

"That should put an end to the bone and the curse," declared Carter, wiping his hands.

"Mr. Sexton?"

"Yes?"

"She's not there now, but I saw a strange-looking young woman staring at us from the corner of the lot. She had a rounded hat, a gold necklace and gold bracelets, and a powder-blue dress. She reminded me of an Egyptian princess."

THE GHOSTLY FRIEND

Teacher Rick Hayden strode into his fifth-grade class wearing a top hat, white shirt, string tie, and black suit. He had a fake black beard, a big nose made out of putty, and a large mole on his cheek.

The students broke out in applause. Every month, Rick would dress up in costume and pretend to be a historical figure such as George Washington, Benjamin Franklin, or Paul Revere. Then he would conduct class as if he were that person and answer kids' questions in character. It made history so much more fun that way.

"Good morning, ladies and gentlemen," he announced. "I presume you know who stands before you."

"K-Mark, the Discount Magician," shouted Tim from the back of the room, cracking up the rest of the students.

"I know not of whom you speak," Rick replied. "However, it may take a magician to save your hide from

40

being thrown into the stockade. Now again, I ask you, who am I?"

"Abraham Lincoln!" they shouted in unison.

Rick doffed his hat and bowed. "At your service." He pulled out a piece of paper and cleared his throat. "It is November 19, 1863, and I am in Gettysburg, Pennsylvania. I am standing at the site where a fierce battle raged four months ago between the Union and Confederate troops. The bloody conflict lasted three days and marked a turning point in the Civil War. General George Meade's Northern army battered Robert E. Lee's Southern force. More than 40,000 brave soldiers were injured or killed. I am here to deliver a speech at ceremonies dedicating the battlefield as a national cemetery for those who lost their lives."

Rick cleared his throat and repeated Lincoln's famous Gettysburg Address: "Four score and seven years ago our fathers brought forth upon this continent a new nation, conceived in liberty and dedicated to the proposition that all men are created equal. Now we are engaged—"

DING! . . . DING! . . . DING!

Darn it, Rick thought. *Not another fire alarm. Of all the times to have a fire drill. We just had one last week.* Annoyed, he took off his hat and beard. "Okay, kids, you know the drill. We've practiced it enough times. Single file. Let's go."

Rick opened the classroom door and was surprised to see one of his students, Bernie Goldman, already in the hallway. "Bernie, what are you doing out here?"

"Sorry, Mr. Hayden, I was late for school. My mom's car didn't want to start this morning."

"Okay, we're having another fire drill, so join the others."

41

The students streamed out of their classrooms and into the hall of Jackson Elementary. From there, they marched out of the doors and gathered on the playground behind the school.

Kids from the other classes giggled when they saw Rick Hayden's costume. They weren't surprised. They knew he was the school's coolest teacher, always willing to try zany things to make learning more interesting.

"Aren't your clothes a little out of style?" fourth-grade teacher Madelyn Keane kidded him. "Or are you trying to make a fashion statement?"

"Yes, these clothes are out of style, and yes, the statement I'm making is, thank goodness we don't have to dress up like this these days."

Principal Harold Tumway walked out to the playground, held up a megaphone, and said, "Everyone did an excellent job of evacuating the building in record time. Fortunately, there is no fire. It was a false alarm. You can return to your rooms now."

Before they began to move, however, a speeding car screeched around the corner and went into a skid. Now totally out of control, the car careened across the street and plowed through the bushes in front of the school. It then slammed into the building with such force that bricks and glass flew in all directions. The car finally came to a stop in the middle of a classroom—Rick Hayden's classroom.

"Stay here, kids!" Rick ordered. Then he and several other teachers dashed to the wrecked classroom. They shoved aside splintered desks and broken cement blocks to reach the smashed-up car. They pulled out the driver, an elderly man who, although badly shaken, had avoided serious injury thanks to his car's air bag and safety belt.

"I thought I was hitting the brakes," he mumbled. "I must have been stepping on the gas instead."

After other teachers escorted the driver to the school clinic, Rick and Mr. Tumway surveyed the damage in the room. Half the desks were busted and the front wall had collapsed.

"What a mess," groaned the principal.

"Mr. Tumway, if we hadn't had that fire drill, my students would have been right here in class. I would have been standing where the car is now. I shudder to think what could have happened. Some of my kids could have been killed."

"And you could have been too," said the principal. "Maybe I shouldn't be so angry over the fire drill."

"What do you mean?"

"Rick, it appears that someone—a student, no doubt—pulled the alarm. He or she should be found and punished. But yet this prank undoubtedly saved injury and possible death."

"Any idea who did it, Mr. Tumway?"

"No. But we do know that the alarm pulled was the one right outside your classroom. Were any of your students out of class at the time the alarm went off?"

"Yes. Bernie Goldman, the transfer student who joined us about a month ago. I saw him in the hall just as we were leaving the room. He told me he was late because his mom had car troubles."

"I think we should have a little talk with Bernie."

Rick hoped that Bernie hadn't done it because he liked him. The student, who had moved from California to Portland, Oregon, with his divorced mother at the start of second marking period, made friends quickly. He always had a compliment for everyone and enjoyed kidding around.

Bernie's eyes were big and gray like the color of a battleship. His ever-ready smile was kind of quirky—the left side of his mouth always seemed to be grinning. One of the reasons Rick liked Bernie was that the student's features reminded Rick of a good friend from childhood.

During lunch hour, Bernie was questioned by Mr. Tumway and Rick. Staring straight into their eyes, the student politely but steadfastly denied pulling the alarm. "I understand why you might suspect me," Bernie told them, "but I didn't do it."

"Do you know who did?" asked Rick.

For the first time during questioning, Bernie avoided making eye contact with them. He bowed his head. "I can't say."

"You *can't* say or you *won't* say?" asked Mr. Tumway, as he frowned and leaned toward the student.

"It's not what you think," Bernie replied, his voice beginning to squeak. "I don't know anything. Besides, shouldn't you be happy that the alarm went off? Who knows how many kids could have been killed otherwise."

"That's not the point, Bernie," said the principal. "Please don't hide anything from us. That makes you as guilty as the person who did it."

"It's not like I saw a student do it. Honest. It's no one."

Actually, it was someone—or rather something. But it would be several days before Rick Hayden learned the startling truth.

Rick loved teaching at Jackson Elementary because the faculty and administration were dedicated to making it the best school possible. He always had good feelings about it, because he used to attend Jackson when he was growing up. Back then, it was an eight-room building. But ten years earlier it had been remodeled and made much larger, with two dozen classrooms, a media center, gym, and cafeteria. Rick got a big kick out of teaching at Jackson because among his students were children of friends he had grown up with.

In the four years he had taught there, nothing unusual had ever happened—until the car crash. It would take two weeks for workers to repair the damage and get new desks in his classroom. During that time, Rick held class in the cafeteria.

It was difficult to teach his students there, especially around 11:30 A.M. when everyone was getting hungry and smelling the food cooking in the kitchen. But Rick made the most of it. Each day he'd pick a student to arrange the tables any way he or she wanted for class—into diamonds, rectangles, or circles.

One day, while Rick was teaching punctuation, Bernie raised his hand. "Mr. Hayden, it's stuffy in here. Could I open a window, please?"

"Sure, Bernie."

Bernie hurriedly opened several windows before a brisk

cold breeze blew papers off the table. "Bernie, please!" shouted Rick. "One window is okay. But not any more. We're getting blown away here—and it's cold."

Bernie paid no heed and continued to open all of the ten windows. "Bernie, did you hear me? Close them. Close all of them!"

Just then screams echoed off the cafeteria walls: "Get out! Hurry! Get out! Gas!" As the hacking and coughing kitchen employees rushed out the door, one of them yelled at Rick, "Get the kids out! Now!"

Rick quickly hustled the students out of the cafeteria. He soon learned that a new employee had accidentally mixed two cleaning liquids, causing a chemical reaction that triggered a dangerous gas.

After the bucket of cleansers had been removed and the cafeteria aired out, Mr. Tumway told Rick, "It was a good thing the windows were opened. The gas could have made you and your students very sick. Just out of curiosity, why were the windows opened in the first place? It's so chilly outside."

"Funny you should ask. Bernie Goldman asked to open a window, and then he furiously opened all of them right before the gas accident. It was like he knew."

At the end of the day, Rick asked Bernie to stay after class. "Bernie, did you have a premonition—a feeling in your gut—that there was going to be a gas hazard?"

"No, Mr. Hayden. I wanted some air, and I figured why not open all the windows so others could enjoy it."

"Bernie, tell me the truth."

"Okay. Caitlin called me a wimp because I said it was

cold in the room. You know how she is, never wearing a sweater or jacket in the winter. So I opened all the windows to freeze her out. I'm sorry, Mr. Hayden. But it turned out to be a lucky break, right?"

Rick nodded halfheartedly. He was convinced that Bernie was not telling the whole truth. But there was nothing more the teacher could say.

Rick's classroom was repaired just in time for the Jackson Open House, where parents and students would meet with the teachers on a one-to-one basis. Bernie and his mother, Maddy, were the last appointment of the night for Rick. While Bernie passed the time in the computer room next door, Rick talked with Bernie's mother.

"Bernie is a bright boy, Mrs. Goldman," said Rick. "For a new student, he's made quite a few friends."

"I was worried about him when I moved back to Portland," she said.

"Oh, you're from here? Bernie never mentioned that."

"I lived in Portland only a short time," Maddy explained. "I married Bernie's father here in 1983. But he was killed in an auto accident six months later. I was pregnant with Bernie, so I moved to California, where my folks live. About two years later I remarried, and my husband adopted Bernie. Unfortunately, we divorced last year. Then, when my company offered me a position back here, I decided to come. This may sound funny, but I wanted to be near my one true love—Peter."

"And Peter is?"

"Peter Lender, my first husband, Bernie's father. He's buried here in town."

"Peter Lender? I went to school with a Peter Lender. And he died in a car accident in the early 1980s! It has to be the same guy!" Then it dawned on Rick. "Bernie's gray eyes and that crooked smile—they reminded me of Peter!"

"I'm sorry, but I don't believe Peter ever mentioned you," said Maddy.

"We grew up together and attended Jackson Elementary. We were the best of friends. But then he moved to the other side of town, and we went to different schools and lost touch. I went off to college and taught in Iowa for several years. I didn't learn about Peter's death until a year after it happened. I didn't even know he was married. Imagine that. Bernie is Peter's son."

"It's a small world. Bernie thinks the world of you, Mr. Hayden."

"Well, I liked Bernie the minute I met him. Now I know why. He has Peter's genes."

Rick noticed a pained expression on Maddy's face. "What's wrong, Mrs. Goldman?"

"Bernie has been acting a little strange since we moved to Portland. He says he dreams about his real father. I've even heard him talking to Peter—well, obviously he talks to *himself,* not to Peter. And Bernie keeps asking questions about Peter. He insisted on having a photo of Peter in his room. He never did before."

"It's normal for a boy to wonder about his birth father. Bernie wasn't ready to ask those questions before. Now with the move to Portland, he's ready to learn as much as he can about Peter."

"I suppose you're right."

"Mrs. Goldman, did Bernie mention to you about why he opened all the cafeteria windows before the gas mishap, or if he had anything to do with the fire alarm right before the man crashed his car in my classroom?"

"No," she replied. "Why do you ask?"

"Never mind. Forget I even mentioned it."

"I certainly will," she snapped. "You make it sound like *he* had something to do with those incidents." She abruptly stood up and stormed out of the room. After she summoned Bernie from the computer room, the two walked past the teacher.

As Mrs. Goldman glared at the teacher, Bernie, who was not aware of any conflict, told him, "I locked the computer room, Mr. Hayden."

"Thank you, Bernie. Good night."

Rick returned to his desk to work on a lesson plan. But he couldn't concentrate. *Darn it, I never should have brought up those two incidents with Mrs. Goldman. That wasn't smart. Now I've angered her. Still, I can't help but wonder if Bernie wasn't somehow involved in both those accidents. I hope not. He's Peter's son, of all people.*

About ten minutes later Bernie entered the classroom. "Mr. Hayden, my mom's car won't start. Do you think you could take a look at it?"

"Of course, Bernie." The two went outside, where Rick tinkered with the engine. "It's a faulty starter switch, Mrs. Goldman. I think I can fix it to get you home, but you'll need to buy a new one."

"Thank you," she said curtly.

Just as the engine roared to life, Bernie tapped Rick on

the shoulder. "Mr. Hayden, you'd better check out the computer room. Um, I'm not so sure I locked it. Maybe you should go there."

Something in Bernie's voice made Rick believe there was cause for concern. The teacher hurried back inside. As he walked down the hallway, he noticed light coming from underneath the computer-room door. Then the light went off.

He reached the door and discovered it was unlocked. He quickly opened it and flipped on the light. Two figures ducked behind a desk. "Who's in here?" Rick said. No one answered. Then he noticed that two computers had been unplugged. The cords were wrapped around the monitors as if they were ready to be moved. "Whoever is in here better come out right now!"

Suddenly two high-school-age boys wearing black jackets and stocking caps pulled down low over their faces jumped up from behind a desk and rushed for the door. But before they could run past Rick, they both fell in a heap. They had been tripped up by a cord that mysteriously had been stretched across the aisle.

"*Ow*, my ankle," grimaced one of the teens.

The other boy was pressing his hand against his bloody forehead. "I think I busted my head. Willy, come on, let's make a run for it!"

"I can't, man. My ankle. I think I broke it. Besides, there are two of them."

"Huh?" said Rick. He turned around. There in the doorway stood Bernie. "Bernie, what are you doing here?"

"I don't know. I thought maybe you might need some help."

"Go to the hall phone and call 911. I think we have a couple of burglars here."

By the time police arrived, the teens had confessed to Rick that they had planned on stealing two computers and selling them. As the intruders were led away, Rick turned to Bernie, who was standing next to his mother, and asked, "Bernie, you didn't have anything to do with this, did you?"

"Oh, no, sir. I didn't. Honest."

Mrs. Goldman glared at the teacher and said, "How dare you suggest that my son was involved in a burglary?"

"Forgive me, Mrs. Goldman." Turning to her son, he asked, "I'm curious, Bernie, how did you know that there might be trouble?"

"I just . . . um . . . I don't know."

"Bernie, are you psychic?"

"Uh, no, sir. I just happened to be around at the right time, I guess. Just like you were a long time ago." Bernie covered his mouth, knowing he said something he wished he hadn't.

"Huh? What do you mean, Bernie?"

Mrs. Goldman grabbed Bernie by the arm. "Come on, Bernie, let's go. I don't like Mr. Hayden's questions. To think you would have anything to do with a burglary or that you are psychic. That's crazy!"

That night Rick couldn't sleep. He kept thinking about Bernie and Peter Lender. Rick dug out an old photo album and thumbed through it, looking for a picture of Peter. He soon found a photo of himself and Peter in Cub Scouts.

It's uncanny, he thought. *Bernie's eyes and smile are exactly the same as Peter's. They look so much alike.* Rick's mind drifted back to those carefree days when he and Peter were kids, always trying to outdo one another: Who could climb the tallest tree, dive off the highest part of a cliff into a water-filled quarry, soar the farthest off a bike ramp.

And then Rick thought about the time he had saved Peter's life when they were 12 years old. They had gone down to the river to swim. A rope had been tied to a sturdy branch of a tall oak on the bank. The boys swung from the rope far out over the water and then dropped into the river.

After about an hour of splashing into the water, Peter climbed past the branch holding the rope. At 40 feet (12 m) up, he shimmied his way out onto a branch until it began to bend.

"Come on up and join me, Ricky, or are you chicken?"

"I'm not chicken, Peter."

"Squawk! Squawk!" Peter replied, mockingly. All of a sudden the branch snapped. "Uh-oh." Peter was now dangling in the air, hanging on to the broken half of the branch.

"Hold on, Peter! I'll get you!"

It was too late. The broken branch twisted off, sending Peter crashing through the tree. To his horror, Rick saw Peter bang his head against another branch before plunging into the river.

Peter's unconscious body slapped the water before disappearing under the surface. Rick dove in and frantically swam in circles, searching for his best friend. "Peter! Peter!" he cried out. The water was too murky to see more than a couple of feet under the surface. Desperately, Rick paddled here and there, bobbing, diving, hoping against hope that he would find his friend. Suddenly, he felt Peter's arm. Rick pulled Peter up until his head was out of the water and dragged him to shore. There, Rick turned him on his side until water came out of Peter's mouth. Then Rick gave him mouth-to-mouth resuscitation.

Seconds later Peter began coughing as he slowly regained consciousness. He opened his eyes and then gagged, "Ricky, get your lips off me, man!"

"You're alive!"

"Of course I'm alive," Peter said between coughs, "although I don't feel so good. My lungs hurt and my head aches." Peter sat up and rested against the trunk of a tree. "Hey, thanks for saving my life. I'll never forget it."

"No sweat, man. You'd have done the same for me."

"I owe you big time. I'll pay you back someday."

That happened back in 1969, Rick recalled. *Peter died in 1983 when he was only 26 years old. What a shame he never got to see his son born.* Rick slammed the photo album shut. *Wait a minute! Could Bernie be Peter reincarnated? It has to be! Remember what Bernie said tonight? He said he happened to be around at the right time, "just like you were a long time ago." How could he possibly have known that I saved his father's life? His own mother didn't even know I was Peter's friend until tonight, and I didn't tell her about the near-drowning. This is amazing! This is incredible!*

The next day, after class, Rick questioned Bernie. "Last night you mentioned that I happened to be at the right place at the right time a long time ago. What did you mean by that?"

"Nothing, Mr. Hayden, nothing," answered Bernie, his

eyes growing wide from surprise. "It just slipped out. Can I go now?"

"Bernie, do you believe in reincarnation?"

"Mr. Hayden, I don't think you should be asking me a question like that. My mom would be really upset."

"I'm sorry, Bernie. You're right. It's just that you remind me so much of your father. We were good friends as kids. And I saved his life once. I know it sounds crazy, but I thought maybe you are really Peter reincarnated."

"You're way off, Mr. Hayden, way off!" Then Bernie, looking terribly frightened, rushed out of the room.

Rick pounded his desk in frustration. *What's the matter with me? How could I let my emotions cloud my judgment like that? I should know better than to discuss such things with a student. But if he's not Peter reincarnated, why is he always around when I'm about to face trouble?*

The next morning Bernie came to class early. "I'm sorry about yesterday, Mr. Hayden."

"You have nothing to be sorry about, Bernie. I was out of line. I apologize."

"I'm so confused, that's all. Things have been happening to me, and I'm trying to sort it all out. But this reincarnation stuff, you can forget about it. I'm positive I'm not my dad."

"How can you be so sure?"

Bernie hesitated for a moment before saying, "Because I've seen him."

The classroom door burst open, and several chattering kids filed into the room. Bernie immediately turned away from the teacher and walked over to his desk. Rick stared at him, not knowing what to say or think.

Throughout the morning in front of his class, Rick stumbled over his words, totally distracted by Bernie's astounding statement. The teacher couldn't wait to talk to him again alone. At recess Rick looked for Bernie and was told the student was last seen in the front of the school.

When Rick reached the front, he stopped and stared at a young man in his twenties with big gray eyes, curly black hair, and a crooked smile. The man, who stood about 100 yards (91.5 m) away, was waving at him.

No, it can't be, Rick thought. *I haven't seen him since the summer I graduated high school. But it has to be him.* Rick rubbed his eyes and looked again. "Peter? Peter Lender, is that you?" Rick shouted.

The man didn't say a word. He continued to wave, only this time more frantically. Terror filled his eyes, his mouth turned into a grimace.

"What?" shouted Rick. "You want me to move?"

Rick started walking toward him when he heard a loud splat behind him. A barrel of hot tar that workers were using to repair the school's roof had accidentally tipped over and fallen two stories off the ledge. The hot tar hit the ground right where Rick had been standing seconds earlier.

"Are you okay down there?" one of the workers hollered.

"Yeah, I'm fine," said Rick, extremely grateful that he hadn't been burned to death by the tar. When Rick turned around to look for the man who resembled Peter, he spotted Bernie standing in the man's place.

"Mr. Hayden, that was a close call."

"Bernie, where's the man who was standing here?"

"I didn't see anybody."

"You had to have seen him," Rick snapped. "He was right here just a few seconds ago." Rick grabbed Bernie by the shoulders. "Bernie, look at me. Now tell me the truth. Where is he?"

Tears welled up in Bernie's eyes. "He's gone."

"Who was he?"

"My dad," Bernie blurted. "I mean, his ghost."

Rick dropped his hands from the boy's shoulders. "That was Peter's ghost I saw just a moment ago?"

Bernie nodded. "I started seeing him shortly after my mom and I moved here. First, he was kind of ghostly, you know, like I could see through him. I thought I was dreaming or something. But then he started becoming clearer and clearer, and he talked to me and said he was my father. I thought I was going crazy. So I asked my mom for a picture of my real dad, and when she showed me, I knew it was him."

"Why didn't you tell me before?"

"It was supposed to be our secret. Besides, I just can't go around telling someone that I saw my father's ghost. Even you."

"But now I've seen him."

"He's been around the school for a while now. He stays close by to protect me—and you."

"Me?"

"Yes. He said you once saved his life, and he wanted to return the favor."

Rick walked back and forth, trying to let Bernie's astonishing words sink in.

"The fire alarm?" asked Rick.

"My father's ghost pulled it. I saw him do it when I was in the hallway. I didn't know why he pulled it at the time. But then we all saw what happened next. He saved a lot of lives—probably yours too."

"And you couldn't tell Mr. Tumway or me who really pulled the alarm without sounding crazy."

Bernie nodded. "Then in the cafeteria my father's ghost motioned me to open all the windows. It didn't make sense, but he looked very upset, so I opened all the windows."

"The gas accident, of course. Then did he tell you to alert me about the burglars in the computer room?"

"Yes. I saw him outside the school, pointing at the window to the computer room. Then he went into the room. He was the one who flicked on the light and scared the burglars. After you arrived, he tripped them when they tried to rush by you. They gave up when they saw you and him. He was behind you. When you turned around, I arrived, and my dad's ghost had gone."

Rick continued to walk back and forth. "So it was Peter's ghost who saved my life today by waving me away from the spot where the hot roofing tar fell."

"That's right, Mr. Hayden. I think he's paid you back a few times over for saving his life, don't you think?"

"Peter always said he would return the favor someday."

"I guess my dad was a man of his word—even after his death."

TIME OF DEATH

Myra Rivera brushed back the long, silky black hair from her face as she typed away at the computer. The popular 16-year-old student had taken a part-time job in the administration office of Buncombe High School because her father had been laid off from his job. She performed clerical duties for three hours every morning from 7 to 10 A.M. before attending classes the rest of the day.

When school secretary Faye Nelson entered the office, Myra looked up from her desk and said, "Good morning, Mrs. Nelson. There's a gold bracelet on your desk. I found it in the hall a few minutes ago."

"Thank you, Myra." Mrs. Nelson examined it closely. "This is definitely an expensive item. Thanks for turning it in."

"No thanks are necessary. I did what anybody would do."

"If only that were true. You're about as honest as they come, Myra."

After examining the bracelet with a magnifying glass, the secretary made a phone call. Then she walked over to Myra and handed her the bracelet. "It belongs to Miss Jennings. Would you please return it to her? She's in Room 308."

"Sure, Mrs. Nelson."

"Hmm," said the secretary. "Isn't 308 the homeroom of the coolest guy in school?"

Myra blushed. "I don't know who you're talking about," she replied with a wink.

"Scott Morris," said the secretary. "I understand he's quite a catch. I also understand he's going out with one of the prettiest girls in school. You still don't know who I'm talking about, hmm?"

Myra giggled. "Now that you mention it, I do seem to recall him." The truth was that Myra and Scott had been a twosome since the beginning of the school year. *This is great*, Myra thought. *I don't have to wait until the end of the day to see him. I'll write him a little note and try to slip it to him when I give Miss Jennings her bracelet.*

Myra took the valuable piece of jewelry and walked out of the office and into the looming halls of Buncombe High, the oldest school in the city. Opened in 1932, the building had awed tens of thousands of students over the years.

As Myra walked on the brown ceramic tile floor, she remembered how scared she had felt two years earlier during orientation for incoming freshmen. Buncombe High appeared so big, cold, and frightening. The thick cement block walls seemed better suited for prison cells than classrooms. The hallways were so high that the ceiling lights cast a dull, dreary light on the students below. The slamming lockers, dropped books, shuffling feet, and loud chatter echoed off the walls, making the corridors as noisy as traffic tunnels.

Despite all its faults, Buncombe High had something no other school in town had—a cherished history. Its legacy was so strong that members of the school board, all of whom had attended Buncombe when they were growing up, refused to consider closing the school.

The governor of the state had attended Buncombe. So had two major-league ballplayers, an NBA star, three Broadway actresses, and hundreds of doctors, lawyers, and public officials. There was no way they were going to tear this school down. It held too many fond memories.

Myra climbed the stairs to the third floor. Then something unusual happened. On her way to Room 308, she heard a woman crying in Room 303, the science lab. She knew there were no classes in that room this early in the morning. Curious, Myra pressed her ear against the door and listened. Someone definitely was sobbing.

What should I do? Myra wondered. *Maybe someone needs my help. Maybe it's a student with a personal problem who's found a place to be alone. Her crying sounds so heartbreaking. I've got to go check.*

Myra opened the door and stepped inside—and entered a bizarre world, a world where seeing was not necessarily believing.

Her eyes, ears, and nose immediately sent convincing

warning signals to the brain that nothing was normal and everything was strange.

A quick glance around the room left Myra totally baffled. There was no crying woman. More puzzling, the room no longer looked like the science lab. There were no lab counters with stools, no Bunsen burners, no glass tubes and jars of chemicals locked in huge cabinets. Instead, this room had rows of uncomfortable, straight-back wooden seats, each with a right-handed arm that flared out into a small square upon which to write.

As she cautiously walked toward the back of the room, Myra noticed the air—thick, stale, and almost stifling, as if in a closed-up attic. Her nose twitched from a strong musty odor, triggering a coughing fit.

Myra spotted two framed black and white photographic portraits hanging on the wall, each of a different smiling middle-aged man. At the bottom of each frame was a brass plate. One said "President Franklin Delano Roosevelt." The other said "Governor Cyrus Pickens." *Why are these photos here?* she wondered.

A hand-scrawled note pinned to a nearby bulletin board announced, "Hey, kiddos, don't forget the big dance Saturday night! Toots Bigelow and his Swing Band play the rowdiest, swellest music in town!"

Swing band? thought Myra. *What's a swing band?* Also pinned on the board was a newspaper headline that read: "Jesse Owens Wins Fourth Gold Medal." *Who's Jesse Owens?* Underneath it, a handwritten note in flowery penmanship said, "Mr. Owens believed in himself when no one else did and look what he accomplished. Set your sights high, and you too can win a gold medal in life!"

Thumbtacked next to a red and black Buncombe Bulldogs pennant was this neatly lettered sign in red paint: "Don't forget the BIG game against Central High! Bite 'em, Bulldogs!" *Bite 'em, Bulldogs? That's so lame! And where's Central High? I never heard of it before.*

It soon dawned on Myra that total silence had engulfed the room. She didn't hear a thing. She glanced at her watch. By now, on the P.A. system, Jill Repulski would be reading the morning announcements. A tardy kid or two would be making a mad dash to his or her homeroom. A media specialist would be pushing the overhead projector cart, its wheels making a clickety clackety sound down the hall.

But it was quiet—deathly quiet—in Room 303.

The silence finally was shattered by a woman's crying—the very reason Myra had entered the room. She turned toward the front. To Myra's surprise, a rail-thin woman was slumped over the teacher's desk, weeping. Her body heaved with every sob.

I can't tell who she is, thought Myra. *Her hair is funny, all piled up on top of her head, like an old-fashioned hairdo. I wonder who she is.*

"Are you, okay, Miss?" asked Myra.

The woman didn't respond. She continued to bawl. *She's obviously crying from heartache, not from pain,* Myra told herself. *I can't stand here like an idiot, I'd better do something. Maybe I should sneak out and leave her in peace. No, maybe I should go up and put my arms around her.*

But a slight fear was holding her back. Nothing made sense; neither the room, the silence, nor the strange woman.

Soon Myra's compassion overcame any misgivings. She crept forward, cleared her throat, and asked softly, "Pardon me, Miss, but can I help you?"

The woman ignored her. A half minute later, the woman sat up. For the first time Myra, who was ten feet (3 m) away, got a good look at her. The puzzled student had never seen her before.

The woman appeared to be in her early forties. The weeping had turned her pale blue eyes bloodshot and had flushed the cheeks on her otherwise milky white skin. She was wearing a long-sleeved white blouse with a lacy collar— the kind that women wore many years ago. She gently fingered an oversized green book with the face of a bulldog in bright yellow on the cover.

"I don't mean to bother you, Miss, but I heard you crying, so I came in to see if I could help," said Myra.

The woman continued to ignore Myra. She pulled a handkerchief out of her right sleeve and dabbed her wet eyes. "I don't want to leave," she whispered before her mouth twisted into another cry. She uttered the words with such sadness that it brought tears to Myra's eyes.

"Miss? Oh, Miss?" Myra said in a louder voice. When the student still received no recognition, she waved her arms to attract attention. Nothing. *The woman acts like I'm invisible. Obviously, she doesn't want me around. I guess I'd better go. Besides, this room gives me the creeps.*

As Myra started to walk away, a band struck up music, and young voices began singing, "For she's a jolly good fellow . . . for she's a jolly good fellow . . ."

What's going on? Myra walked over to the open window

and gazed outside. Down below on the front lawn of the school—known as the quad—about two dozen students in marching band uniforms were playing their instruments while hundreds of other singing students looked up at the window where Myra was standing.

What's wrong with this picture? she wondered. *The uniforms maybe? Our marching band wears snappy red and black uniforms with white-billed caps. These band members are wearing dorky black uniforms and funny red caps. And look at the students. The girls are wearing skirts below their calves! And the boys look ridiculous in their baggy pants and white socks and black shoes.*

Hey! Where's the shopping center across the street? Where's Rick's Deli? Berry's Record Shop? Cards 'n' Stuff? It's a vacant field! Youngman Avenue isn't a two-lane street that dead-ends just past the school. Why is there a baseball diamond where the gas station should be? Those cars in the street look so old—like from a gangster movie. Is this a movie set? Or is this what it's like when you lose your mind?

Myra closed her eyes, hoping that when she opened them, everything would return to normal; that the kids outside would have familiar faces, the shopping center would be across the street, and Youngman Avenue would be a busy four-laner that stretched for miles. She opened her eyes, but it remained the same weird scene from the past.

Nothing makes sense. I don't understand. Now Myra was beginning to panic. Shaking her head, she backed away from the window and then turned around. The sobbing woman was gone. "Miss? Where are you?" *This is too freaky for me. I've got to get out of here now!*

Myra bolted for the door and ran out into the hall. She began walking in a daze, her mind whirring with a million thoughts, none of which came close to explaining what she had just seen. She kept strolling aimlessly in the hall when . . . *Oh my gosh, what if I've stepped back in time? What if I'm trapped in a time warp? I've got to get back to the present!*

She glanced at her hand and noticed she was holding the bracelet she was supposed to return to Miss Jennings. *I forgot all about the bracelet. What if I go in her room and it's not the same? If Miss Jennings isn't there? If the class isn't there? If Scott isn't there? Oh no. Not Scott!*

Myra took a deep breath, closed her eyes, and with a quivering hand, opened the door to Room 308. *Oh, please, please, please be there, Miss Jennings.* She opened her eyes. *Oh, thank goodness! Thank goodness.* Myra leaned against the door jam and gave a big sigh of relief. *Yes, there's Miss Jennings!* Myra scanned the classroom. *There's Scott! I'm back in the present!*

"Myra, are you all right?" Miss Jennings asked. "You look terribly ill."

"I'm not feeling well, Miss Jennings," replied Myra, trying to calm herself. "But I feel a whole lot better than I did just a minute ago."

"Do you need to sit down? Do you need some water?"

"I'm not sure what I need. I'm just so shaky. Would you excuse me, please?" Somewhat fearfully, Myra walked over to the window and peeked outside. She smiled. There was Rick's and Berry's and the gas station.

"Myra, why are you looking outside?"

"I wanted to make sure everything was . . . uh . . ." *You can't tell her the real reason.* "Uh. I thought it was raining. It's not."

Several kids in the class began to laugh. Miss Jennings turned to Scott. "Scott, why don't you escort Myra to the school clinic."

"Sure, Miss Jennings," said Scott, popping out of his seat.

As he started to lead Myra out of the classroom, she turned to the teacher and said, "Oh, I almost forgot. Here's the bracelet you lost. Uh, I'm really glad you're here, Miss Jennings."

The teacher cocked her head and gave a quizzical smile. "Thank you, Myra. Now promise me you'll go straight to the clinic."

"Yes, the clinic. I will."

Myra clutched Scott's arm as they walked into the hall and then she burst into tears.

"Myra, what's wrong?" he asked.

"You'll think I'm stark raving mad if I tell you. And what's really scary is that I'm beginning to think I really am loony."

"Well, tell me anyway."

Myra described the crying woman, the changed science lab, and the outside scene from the past. To Scott, the story sounded so ridiculous, so unbelievable, that he didn't want to hear any more for fear that his girlfriend was mentally ill. But he also could tell from the look in her eyes that she was extremely frightened.

"Am I going crazy, Scott?"

"Why don't we take a look in Room 303, okay?"

"I don't want to go back in there."

"You don't have to, Myra. I'll go."

Myra put her ear to the door, wondering if she would hear the crying woman. But there was silence. She moved back until she was pressed against the opposite wall in the hall. "Go ahead, Scott," she said. "I'll stay out here."

Scott hesitated for a brief moment and then flung open the door. Gingerly, he stepped inside and looked around. He walked over to the window, took a glimpse outside, and then left the room, closing the door behind him.

"Well, what did you see?" Myra asked anxiously.

Scott put his arm around her shoulder. "Myra, I didn't see what you saw. The science lab looks the same. I didn't see anyone inside, and when I looked out the window, everything seemed normal."

Myra moaned and tears sprang up. "See? That proves it. I'm crazy!"

"It doesn't prove a thing, Myra. You're far from crazy. You're the most sane person I've ever met in my life. There's an explanation for this."

"But what is it?"

Scott answered by shaking his head and shrugging.

"Scott, you positively, absolutely can't tell anyone about this."

"Okay, Myra, I won't. What are you going to say to the school nurse?"

"I'll tell her I'm coming down with the flu."

"We have to figure this out, Myra. Meet me after class in the school library. We'll launch our own investigation."

No matter how hard Myra tried to shove the experience out of her mind, she couldn't—not an incident this astounding. She was so obviously distracted that teachers in each of her classes asked her, "What's the matter?" She put on a fake smile and replied, "Nothing."

After the final period she met Scott in the school library, where he had already gathered several books.

"Look at this," he said, pointing to a chronicle of United States history. "I think I've pinpointed the year. You mentioned you saw a newspaper clipping of Jesse Owens. He was a great African-American track star who won four gold medals in the 1936 Olympics in Berlin, Germany. He really showed up Adolf Hitler, the Nazi dictator, who thought blacks were inferior.

"Also, you said there were pictures of Governor Pickens and President Roosevelt. Well, they both held office in 1936. Does that year mean anything to you? Maybe you read about it, and it stuck in your mind?"

"A total blank, Scott. The year means nothing to me."

Scott pushed another book in front of Myra. It was a pictorial year-by-year almanac. He flipped the pages to the 1930s. "Look at these cars and the way people dressed. Is this what you saw when you looked out the window?"

"Yes!" she cried out. "Yes! Those are the same kinds of cars I saw. And the clothes. Scott, do you think I entered a time warp?"

"That's pretty far-fetched, Myra, but who knows?"

"So who was the woman? And why would students be singing, 'For she's a jolly good fellow'?" Myra snapped her fingers. "The yearbook, of course!" She soon found the aisle where the entire collection of the *Buncombe Barker* was shelved. Each book had its own distinctive design and color. "There it is, the 1936 *Buncombe Barker!*" she whispered excitedly.

She pulled it out and then clutched Scott's arm. "This looks exactly like the book the woman was holding when I saw her. It's the same size, and the cover was green and had a yellow bulldog on it just like this."

She plopped to the floor with the book on her knees and began flipping slowly through the pages. "I got a good look at her. If she's a teacher, I should find her in here."

She turned the first few pages and then stopped, stabbing her finger at a full-page photo. It was shot from a third-floor window, down onto the quad where students had gathered for a rally. "Look at this photo, Scott. What do you see across the street?"

"Nothing but a baseball diamond."

"Right! That's what I saw from virtually the same vantage point in Room 303!" Myra's heart was beating faster. Each new clue boosted her confidence that she wasn't crazy. But each new clue only added to the mystery.

Trying hard to stay calm, she continued to flip through the pages until she reached a section on the teachers. She took a deep breath and said, "Well, here goes." Her eyes carefully scanned the English teachers, the math teachers, and then the science teachers.

Moments later she sucked in air and threw her left hand over her mouth. Pointing with her right hand to the photo of a middle-aged woman, Myra exclaimed, "That's her! That's the teacher I saw crying in the room!" She read the caption.

"Her name is Clara Mills. My gosh, Scott, I saw Clara Mills's ghost!"

"Is there anything else about her?" asked Scott.

Myra thumbed through the index and found two other references for Miss Mills. Page 42 showed a photo of her with members of the Science Club. Page 65 featured the results of a poll. Students had voted on an assortment of subjects from "favorite tune" to "favorite gathering place." Miss Mills had been chosen "favorite teacher."

"This is starting to make a little sense," said Myra. "Miss Mills was a science teacher. I saw her in the science lab even though it didn't look like one. And since she was the students' favorite teacher, that could explain why the kids were singing 'For she's a jolly good fellow.'"

"Unfortunately, it doesn't explain the big questions. Why did you see her in the first place? And why did everything look like it was back in time?"

"Maybe we'll learn more about her by looking at other yearbooks." They discovered that every year since the school opened in 1932, Miss Mills had been voted "favorite teacher."

"Do you notice anything different about her photos from 1932 to 1936?" Scott asked.

"She got a lot thinner."

"Right. See how healthy she looks in 1932? By 1936 she's nothing but skin and bones. I bet you she lost 30 or 40 pounds."

Myra pulled out the 1937 yearbook, which had only one mention of Miss Mills. It was on page 1.

Myra turned to the page and blurted, "Oh, Scott, no!"

In the center of the page, bordered in black, was a photo of Miss Mills. Below were the words:

IN MEMORIAM
"FAVORITE TEACHER OF THE YEAR"
CLARA MILLS
1895-1936

The 1935-36 school year ended on a tragic note when Clara Mills, who was voted "favorite teacher" every year since Buncombe High opened its doors, died of heart failure in her classroom on the final day of school.

Miss Mills had planned to retire because of failing health. A special surprise ceremony was to be held for her but, sadly, she died minutes before it began.

Miss Mills was much loved and will be sorely missed.

This yearbook is dedicated in her memory.

"Do you believe this?" Myra exclaimed. "I must have seen Miss Mills right before she died!"

"You mean, 60 years *after* she died," Scott reminded her. "You saw her today."

"Do you suppose we could find someone who remembers her?"

"Let's try the school board," he said. "All of the members

used to be students here at Buncombe High."

After doing a little research, they discovered that one of the board members, Lyndon Farwell, attended Buncombe High in 1936. Unable to take the yearbook home with them, the two teens made a photocopy of a page containing Miss Mills's photo. Then they visited the home of Mr. Farwell and showed him the picture.

"Do you remember Miss Mills?" Myra asked the 74-year-old board member.

"I surely do," replied Mr. Farwell. "I had her for only one year, 1936, when I was a freshman. What a wonderful teacher she was. Bright and cheery. She taught us much more than science. She taught us the power of positive thinking. She convinced every one of us that we could achieve great things, that anything was possible if we believed in ourselves. She motivated us and challenged us and made us not only better students but better people. Everyone loved her."

"What happened to her?" asked Scott.

"She had cancer. But her spirit was strong, and she never talked about her illness. She lived to teach. When I had her for a teacher, she was ailing pretty badly. But she refused to rest or take time off. She kept teaching. It was her way of staying alive. She made it all the way to the end of the school year."

Tears began welling up in the old man's eyes. "I'll never forget her final day. We students had signed a yearbook especially for her. In fact, one of the teachers found former students who had graduated and got them to sign it too. We were going to present it to her on the last day of school as a surprise.

"We gathered outside on the quad, and the band was playing, and we were singing, 'For she's a jolly good fellow.' She was supposed to come to the window. But she never came. One of the teachers went to get her, and he found her slumped over her desk, dead. I can't begin to tell you the shock and hurt we felt when we learned she had died. The kids walked around in a stupor."

"The yearbook," said Myra. "Did you give her the yearbook?"

"I'm sorry to say we didn't. We had it outside to give to her at the ceremony but by then she was dead. She had no family. So they decided to keep it in her classroom. Someone built a cabinet, and the signed yearbook was placed there for posterity, you know, as a remembrance to her."

"But," said Scott, "it's not there now."

"It's been so long," said Mr. Farwell. "Sadly, at some point over the years, probably during one of the school's many remodeling phases, the cabinet and book were removed because no one knew any better."

Scott stared at Myra and murmured, "Looks like we've hit a dead end."

"I guess you're right," she sighed.

"I wish you could find the yearbook that all of us students signed," said Mr. Farwell. "It was a wonderful testament to a wonderful teacher."

"We don't know where else to look."

Mr. Farwell paused a minute. "Say, I just thought of someone you should see. Guido Foggia. He was the janitor at Buncombe for about 40 years. He retired many years ago. Maybe he knows what happened to it."

Later that day, they visited Mr. Foggia, a spry 86-year-old, who proudly told them he still walked a mile around the neighborhood every morning and read at least one book a week. "So what brings you young folks to my doorstep?" he asked.

When they explained their reason for seeing him, his mouth dropped at the mention of Miss Mills's name. "This is so spooky! I saw her two days ago!"

Scott held up Miss Mills's photo. "You saw this Miss Mills two days ago?" he asked in a disbelieving voice.

"I'm old, but I'm not senile. I know what I'm saying. Yes, it's the same Miss Mills in your photo."

"But how?"

"The other day, out of the blue, I came back from my walk and there she was—as lifelike as can be. I thought I was having a stroke. But she truly appeared to me. Well, I guess it wasn't her, but her ghost. She looked so real. All she said was, 'I've come for my yearbook.'

"I knew immediately what she was after—the yearbook that everyone had signed. It had been kept in a special cabinet for years. When the school was remodeled in 1960, the cabinet was removed and got accidentally busted. I rescued the yearbook and brought it home for safekeeping. They were supposed to find a new place for it, but somehow we all forgot about it. For years it stayed in my bookcase along with all the other yearbooks I had from 1932 to 1975, when I retired as the school's chief maintenance man. There's a nice story and picture of me in the 1975 yearbook."

"Let's get back to Miss Mills's ghost," Myra said.

"After she mentioned the yearbook, she just disappeared. I pinched myself real hard to see if I was awake. I was. So I go over to the bookcase and—if I'm lying, I'm dying—the yearbook is gone!"

"Gone?" Scott exclaimed.

"Gone. You can see the space between the books on either side where it used to sit on the shelf. Go figure."

"Mr. Foggia," said Myra, "I'm going to reveal something that I haven't told anyone except for Scott. I saw Miss Mills too." Myra then described her stunning experience in the science lab. "When I last saw her, Miss Mills was holding the 1936 yearbook!"

Mr. Foggia grunted knowingly. "You know what I think? Miss Mills's spirit had been searching for that yearbook for years. When she found it, she returned to her room—the one place she loved the most. This time, she got to read all the marvelous comments written about her in the yearbook. That's why she was crying."

"Why did I see and hear things from 1936?" asked Myra.

"It was probably the most intense moment of Clara Mills's life. Her ghost was reliving the moment when you walked into the room. You unknowingly tapped into her ghost's memory."

"I get it," said Myra. "But now it's become my memory too—one I will carry for the rest of my life."

DEAD MAN'S SHADOW

The horrible vision appeared without warning.

Sixth-grade teacher Mike Kerr was discussing grammar with his class when he developed a headache. It started out as a dull pain in the back of his neck and crept its way up and over his skull before sliding down his forehead.

Suddenly an image began to appear in his mind. Gradually it came into focus until he saw in vivid and frightening detail the anguished face of a bearded man— a man hanging from a rope around his neck!

Mike closed his eyes, but the appalling mental picture remained as clear as if he were staring at the man in real life. The vision lasted about ten seconds before it faded away, leaving Mike so jolted that he had to lean against his desk to keep from falling.

"Mr. Kerr, Mr. Kerr," called out Stacy Reingold, one of his students. "Are you all right?"

"I'm sorry, class," mumbled the teacher. "I'm not feeling well. I have a splitting headache. Uh, turn to chapter 10 and start reading. I'll be right back."

He staggered to the bathroom, looked in the mirror, and saw that all the color had gone out of his cheeks. He splashed cold water on his face and shook his head. *What was that all about?* he wondered. *What just happened to me?*

Mike Kerr was enjoying his first year of teaching sixth grade at Reynolds Elementary. It was challenging but rewarding because he had a good group of students. Besides, he was living in his favorite locale—in the beautiful foothills of Virginia. His parents had been raised there before they moved to Massachusetts, where Mike grew up.

By early spring Mike had become one of the most popular teachers in school. Shortly before his thirtieth birthday, he joked with his students that they should shower him with gifts—ones that cost no money—to cheer him up because he was starting to feel "old."

On the morning of Mike's birthday, student Todd Fisher arrived in school with what he thought was a great present for his teacher. Todd wasn't the best student; he was lucky if he pulled B's and C's. He tried—maybe not hard enough—but at least he made an effort. He was a good kid who stayed out of trouble and displayed a great sense of humor.

"Here, Mr. Kerr, this is for you," said Todd, beaming. Then he placed an old, chipped, dusty brick on the teacher's desk. "Happy birthday."

"Thank you, Todd," said Mike, as he picked up the brick. "Um, what is it?"

"It's a brick."

"Yes, I know it's a brick. Does it have any significance? Or does this symbolize my effectiveness as a teacher?"

"Yes, uh, I mean no. What I'm trying to say is, it does have some significance. My dad owns a demolition company, and this brick comes from the very first schoolhouse here in Rockton. My dad tore it down last year. I thought maybe since your kinfolk probably went to that school, you'd like to have a brick from it. Maybe use it as a paperweight or something. I took one for myself and keep it in my room."

Mike lifted the brick and turned it gently in his hand. He looked at Todd and smiled. "This is a wonderful gift, Todd. Thanks. I'll keep it here on my desk to hold down all the A-plus homework I'll be getting from you."

"A feather paperweight would work just as well for the number of A's I get in homework."

Mike laughed and gently placed the brick near one corner of his desk.

Other students brought their teacher presents, including homemade cookies and a set of baseball cards. It seemed like it was going to be a wonderful birthday—until the vision appeared.

Mike tried to forget about it. But he couldn't. That's because the same headache, followed by the same intense vision, struck him every day for a week. It would hit without warning, while working a math problem on the blackboard, or calling on a student, or inserting a video in the VCR for a science film. Day after day, the mental snapshot would flash in his brain, remain for several seconds, and then vanish.

Mike needed all the concentration he could muster to get him through each day without cracking. But the strain was beginning to show. *I don't get it,* he told himself. *I'm not under any stress. I'm in excellent health. So why am I getting headaches? Why this particular vision? What does it mean? How do I make it stay away?*

Mike was in the middle of an astronomy lesson when the latest vision appeared. "Excuse me, class," he said, turning away from them so they wouldn't see him grimace. Once the vision faded away, he faced the students again.

"Now then, where was I? Oh, yes, who can name, in order, the two planets between the earth and the sun? Todd?"

"What, me?" squeaked Todd. Mike noticed a look of sheer terror spreading across the student's face. The boy gulped and broke out into a cold sweat. Now this was not a difficult question. Even if it was, it shouldn't have caused such a reaction in Todd. "Todd, are you all right?" asked the teacher.

"Mr. Kerr, I don't feel well. May I be excused so I can go to the bathroom?"

"Sure, Todd."

At the end of the day, Mike asked Todd to stay after class. "Is something wrong, Todd? I've noticed these last few days that you seem, well, preoccupied. Is something on your mind? Is everything okay at home?"

"Things are cool at home, Mr. Kerr. I guess I must be coming down with the flu. I've been getting a lot of headaches lately."

"Me too, Todd. Still, you looked scared today when I

asked you a question in class. That's not like you, even when you don't know the answer."

Todd lowered his head and didn't say a word. His eyes welled up with tears. "Mr. Kerr, I think I need some help. I think I'm sick in the head."

Mike led the student to a desk, and they both sat down. "What's wrong, Todd?"

"I've been seeing things in my mind—bad things. Every day a picture pops into my mind. It's awful. It's of a man hanging from a rope by his neck."

Mike sat stunned. *This is incredible. Poor Todd is seeing it too.* The teacher leaned forward and asked, "Did this man have a beard?"

"Yes, he did. How did you know that?"

"I'm not sure." *Don't reveal too much yet,* Mike told himself. *You don't want to scare Todd. His vision and mine must be connected in some manner. I wonder if other kids in the class are seeing the same thing, although they don't act like they do.*

"Am I going crazy, Mr. Kerr?"

"No, Todd. There has to be an explanation. I'll help you get to the bottom of this."

"You won't tell anyone, will you? Otherwise, they'll think I'm nuts."

"I'll keep it quiet. When did you first start seeing the vision?"

"About a week ago."

That's when mine started, thought Mike. *What's the connection?* "Todd, did anything happen back then, anything unusual you can recall?"

"No. Baseball practice started, but I didn't get hit in the head with a ball or anything like that."

Mike walked over to his desk and looked at his calendar for the previous week. He picked up the brick and moved it to get a better look. Teachers' meeting on Monday night. Basketball Tuesday night. Birthday on Wednesday. Date with Jan on Friday night. "Todd, try to remember exactly when you first saw the vision."

"I was riding my bike home from my dad's office. I had stuffed a couple of bricks from the old school in my backpack when I first saw that man in my mind."

Mike looked back at his calendar. *The brick! Todd gave me a brick the next day on my birthday—the day I first started seeing that terrible image!*

"Todd, let me investigate this matter. I don't understand why you should suffer from this vision, but I promise to try to put an end to it."

"Thanks, Mr. Kerr. I don't want to see this man anymore. He's too scary."

After Todd left, Mike picked up the brick and held it in his hand. He examined all six sides as flecks of red chips and dust came off in his hands. The side that had been exposed to the elements had several coats of paint on it. For an instant, Mike thought that side felt warmer than the others, as if it was giving off energy.

Suddenly, like a bolt, Mike was hit again with the vision of the hanged man. This time it was more intense than ever. The man's bloodshot eyes seemed so big and full of terror, anger, and despair. The image remained seared in his mind several seconds longer than usual. It didn't start to fade until Mike let go of the brick, which then fell with a thud on top of his desk.

"It's got to be the brick!" Mike exclaimed to himself.

He drove straight to Fisher Demolition, the firm owned by Todd's dad, Harvey. Mike had no idea what he was going to say or learn. He just knew he needed to go there.

After exchanging pleasantries with Harvey in the company office, Mike told him, "Your son was thoughtful enough to give me a birthday present—a brick from the old schoolhouse you tore down."

"That's my boy. Always trying to butter up the teacher," Harvey said with a laugh. "I'm just joshing you, Mr. Kerr. So, what do you want, more bricks?"

"No, I'd like some information. Were the bricks used for anything after the school was torn down?"

"No, we just dumped them out back for use later as fill. Some people who had gone to that school took a brick as a memento. I probably should have sold the bricks to them, but what the heck, I'm a nice guy."

"This is going to sound really weird, Mr. Fisher, but I was wondering if there's any kind of link between the bricks from the schoolhouse and the hanging of a man."

"Well, there sure as shooting was."

"What?" Mike gasped, squeezing the arm of his chair. "There was?"

"Yep. Haven't you heard about the dead man's shadow?"

Mike shook his head.

"Gosh, everybody in town knows about that. It's the strangest thing that's ever happened here in Rockton. And you didn't know, huh? I guess because you're kind of new to the area, although you have kin who were raised here and—"

"Mr. Fisher, please," interrupted Mike. "I've got to know. What's the story?"

"Let's grab us a soda and sit outside a spell, and I'll tell you all about the dead man's shadow."

In 1875, Del Kincaid, a bearded husky mountain of a man, became the area's first male teacher. The men in town couldn't figure out why this burly, 6-foot 4-inch (2-m), 220-pound (100-kg) former lumberjack would want to be a school-teacher. But they didn't dare kid him to his face because Kincaid had a quick temper and wasn't afraid to unleash it.

In school he demanded the kids sit up in their chairs, address him as "sir," stay quiet in class, and do all their homework. He wouldn't put up with any antics or excuses. If they behaved, he rewarded them with extra playtime and cookies that his girlfriend would make. If they misbehaved, he made them stand in the corner for an hour. If they were really bad, he ordered them to clean the outhouse behind the school.

Only one boy, Randall Turnipseed, ever received the outhouse punishment—twice. He and Kincaid were at odds throughout the youth's years in school. The two never got along. Randall complained that the teacher "had it in for me from the get-go." Kincaid claimed that the boy was "incorrigible—a disruptive influence on the others."

For the most part, the parents liked Kincaid and the job he was doing instructing their children. And the kids respected him.

Over summer vacation in 1880, the teacher took a job helping the local blacksmith. One day, a miner named Tom Worthy—one of the roughest men in town—complained to Kincaid about the job he did shoeing Tom's horse. One word led to another and Worthy, who was about Kincaid's size, sucker-punched the teacher, knocking him down. Kincaid got up, but when he noticed that two of his students outside were watching him, he put down his fists and dusted himself off.

Clearly the teacher was fuming mad, but he held his anger because of the boys. Turning to them, he said, "Fighting might end a conversation, but it doesn't solve anything. I will resolve this matter my way. Now, go on, boys. Scat!"

Worthy never returned home; only his horse did. That evening, his family went searching for him. They discovered his body shortly before sunset, lying by a bridge. He had been stabbed with his own knife. Although Worthy had several enemies, suspicion immediately fell on Kincaid.

Sheriff Wiley Boone, a close friend of Worthy's, went to the teacher's house later that night and roused him out of bed to question him. Kincaid denied any knowledge of Worthy's murder, but Boone didn't believe him—especially when the sheriff noticed bloodstains on a shirt that was draped over the chair.

"Del, where were you between 6 P.M. and 9 P.M.?"

"After work, I went rabbit hunting and then came home," the teacher replied.

"Where did you get the bloodstains on your shirt?"

"From cleaning the rabbit I caught."

"Where's the rabbit?"

"I ate it."

The sheriff was convinced that Kincaid had committed the crime, but he still didn't have enough evidence—until a witness stepped forward. Randall Turnipseed, the boy who couldn't stand Kincaid, walked into the sheriff's office the next day and said, "I heard about the murder, sir. I know who killed Tom Worthy!"

"Well, spit it out, boy. Who's the killer?"

"Mr. Del Kincaid."

"How do you know that?"

"Last night, I was out coon hunting, and I saw Mr. Kincaid and Mr. Worthy arguing by the bridge. The two began wrestling, and the next thing I know, Mr. Worthy is sprawled by the side of the road, dead."

"Why didn't you come forward last night, boy?"

"I thought Mr. Kincaid saw me, and I was afraid he'd come after me."

Sheriff Boone and a deputy marched over to the blacksmith's shop where Kincaid was working. "Del," Boone said, "you're under arrest for the murder of Tom Worthy."

"I told you I didn't do it."

"We have a witness. Now are you going to come peacefully?"

"Yes, I have nothing to hide."

Kincaid was locked in jail while the sheriff tried to piece together the evidence needed to prove that the teacher was the murderer. Day after day, Sheriff Boone questioned Kincaid, trying to coax a confession. But Kincaid would angrily reply, "I haven't killed anyone, and whoever says

I did will have to face the consequences of the truth."

A few weeks later Kincaid was brought to trial. Witnesses described instances where they saw the teacher's temper, which in the excitement of a murder trial, became greatly exaggerated. Then his boss and two of his own students described the scene that took place when Tom Worthy knocked Kincaid down.

Next, Randall Turnipseed took the stand. He described in detail how Kincaid had waited for Worthy by the bridge and then ambushed him. In the course of the fight, said the boy, Kincaid grabbed Worthy's knife and stabbed him several times. Some of Randall's testimony didn't match the evidence.

First, Worthy had been stabbed only once. For the murder to have happened at 8 P.M., as Randall claimed, Kincaid, who left the blacksmith's at seven-thirty, would have had to gallop his horse for nearly thirty minutes in order to reach the bridge, yet no witnesses saw him gallop out of town. Also, Randall was known to tell tall tales. Even though the judge suspected the boy was probably not all that truthful, the testimony was allowed to stand.

Finally, Sheriff Boone took the stand and held up the bloody shirt that Kincaid was wearing the night of the murder. "This clinches it for me. The man is guilty, plain and simple, of murdering my friend, who was a decent father and good husband."

After the state presented its case, Kincaid testified on his own behalf. "Yes, I had words with Tom Worthy the afternoon of his death. Yes, he punched me. But other men in town have traded words and fists with Tom at one time or another. Any one of them could have had a score to settle. And although I disliked the man, I certainly didn't want to see him dead."

He gazed around the courtroom and continued. "After work, I went rabbit hunting nowhere near where Tom was killed. And then I went home. I did not murder Tom Worthy—and that's the truth!" His voice rang full and sharp; his eyes blazed with fervor.

The prosecutor wasn't swayed. In his closing argument, the attorney faced the men in the jury box. (Women were not permitted to serve on juries back then.) "Gentlemen of the jury, it's obvious who killed Tom Worthy. We have a motive—a man who seeks revenge after being humiliated in front of his own students. We have a witness—a boy who saw the murder with his own eyes. And we have physical evidence—a bloody shirt. Can there be any doubt in your mind who committed this crime? In the name of all that's decent, in the name of the victim, I implore you to find Del Kincaid guilty of murder."

The jury took less than an hour to reach its verdict. After the twelve men returned to the courtroom, Kincaid stood at the defendant's table and stared at them. Then he held his breath as the jury foreman said, "We, the jury, find the prisoner, Del Kincaid, guilty of the murder whereof he stands charged."

A shudder rippled through Kincaid's massive body, and his lips quivered in disbelief. Members of the audience broke out in shouts, causing the judge to rap his gavel sharply.

The judge turned to Kincaid and asked, "Have you anything to say before I pronounce the sentencing?"

"Yes, your honor," replied Kincaid, his neck muscles straining from anger. Staring at the faces of the witnesses who testified against him, he bellowed, "I have not killed anybody. Those who say I did are liars. I will haunt this town until each and every liar takes his final breath." Kincaid slumped back in his chair.

The judge cleared his throat and said, "It is the judgment of this court that the prisoner, Del Kincaid, be sentenced to death. He is to be remanded to the Common Jail of this county and there remain until the twenty-first day of August, whereupon he is to be taken by Sheriff Boone from the jail to the place of execution between the hours of ten o'clock in the morning and two o'clock in the afternoon, and there be hanged by the neck until dead. It is also the order of the court that all of Del Kincaid's property be sold at auction to help pay for the cost of this trial. Court is adjourned."

Kincaid kept shaking his head in protest as he was led away by the deputies to await his doom.

On the day of Kincaid's execution, buggies and wagons full of families from neighboring towns and counties began arriving in Rockton. They had come to watch the murderer hang.

When Sheriff Boone went to Kincaid's cell to escort him to the gallows, the lawman was surprised at how calm the condemned man acted. "It's time, Del," said the sheriff. "You're not going to give me any trouble today, are you?"

"No, Sheriff. I've never given you cause."

"Well, you don't seem as upset as I'd expect of a man about to be hanged."

"Oh, I'm plenty upset, Sheriff. And I intend to let everyone know that I've been falsely accused."

Moments later Kincaid sat between the sheriff and a deputy in a horse-drawn wagon that slowly rolled through the throng of onlookers. Kincaid remained expressionless, tuning out the jeers and comments from the crowd.

A few hundred yards ahead in the town square stood the wooden gallows that had been built solely for Kincaid's execution. With his hands tied behind his back, Kincaid was led to the top of the platform. He looked around at the huge crowd that had gathered to see him die. Then he gazed across the street at the red brick schoolhouse— the building that had brought him so much satisfaction as a teacher. *It should never have come to this,* he thought. *I should be in that schoolhouse, teaching, not facing my death. I belong in the classroom. How can they do this to me?*

"Do you have any last words?" the sheriff asked him.

"Yes," he said quietly. Turning toward the crowd, he shouted, "I am an innocent man—and my soul will not rest. It shall find a way to prove to this town that I'm going blameless to the gallows." Tears trickled down his face, causing his beard to glisten in the hot afternoon sun.

Sheriff Boone then placed a black hood over Kincaid's head, slipped the noose around his neck, and tightened it. At exactly 1 P.M., Del Kincaid was hanged.

Satisfied that justice had been done, members of the crowd went their separate ways, leaving the town square empty. Randall Turnipseed was one of the last to leave the area. He watched as the deputies lowered the body of his former teacher and placed it on the horse-drawn wagon.

Randall started to walk away when he glanced at the schoolhouse. Suddenly he felt sick to his stomach. He blinked once, then again and again. *No, it can't be!* he thought. *It must be my imagination!*

There on the south side of the schoolhouse wall—the one facing the gallows—loomed a mysterious shadow. It was the unmistakable, life-sized form of a burly, bearded man hanging from a rope by his neck!

Randall closed his eyes and rubbed them. When he opened them, he saw the same eerie scene. Although faint enough that it could easily be missed by passersby, it was clear enough to anyone who looked at it closely.

Randall walked several yards to his left and then several yards to his right, trying to study the shadow from different angles. But it looked the same no matter where he stood. He grabbed the arm of a friend who had been walking by.

"Henry, look!" Randall said, pointing to the south wall. "What do you see?"

"The schoolhouse."

"No, look at the wall. The shadow."

Henry gave a whistle and gasped, "It looks like a shadow of the hanging!" Turning to several other passersby, Henry shouted, "Hey, everybody, look at the shadow on the wall!"

A murmur spread throughout the town square. People spilled out of the stores and buildings; buggies turned around; men on horseback galloped back. Within an hour the square was once again thick with people buzzing about the strange sight.

"It's a haunting!"

"It's Kincaid, all right. It would take a man as large as him to cast such a big shadow."

"That Kincaid fellow is getting his revenge on us."

"No. Del is telling us he's innocent."

"Maybe it's an illusion."

As night fell, the shadow disappeared. But to everyone's astonishment, it returned at daybreak—and stayed all day. Sheriff Boone immediately tore down the gallows, but that had no effect on the shadow. In fact, nothing did. It appeared every day—rain or shine—on the side of the brick wall.

Men, women, and children from miles around flocked to Rockton to see the bizarre dead man's shadow. Sheriff Boone, the mayor, and many other townspeople were upset and embarrassed by the spectacle. "We can't expect our children to attend a school with the shadow of a dead man on it," said the mayor.

Volunteers tried to scrub the shadow off the red brick wall. When that failed, they tried to cover it up with white paint. But the shadow remained. Then they tried painting the wall black. It still did no good. The shadow showed up as a lighter shade of gray. Finally, with the new school year rapidly approaching, officials came up with the solution. They transplanted ivy from the homes of several volunteers and covered up the entire south wall. That way, the dead man's shadow could no longer be seen.

"I'm blown away by this story, Mr. Fisher," Mike blurted. His hand was shaking so much he couldn't finish his drink. "Are you sure this Del Kincaid had a beard?"

"That's what they say."

"So what happened when you tore down the school? Did you see the shadow?"

"No, we didn't. But you're getting ahead of me. You see, there's more to the story. You know how kids can be. Even though the ivy covered up the wall, every year or so, kids would strip the ivy and get a glimpse of the shadow. This went on for years.

"But then when the kids pulled the ivy down one day back in 1898, the shadow was plum gone. It had disappeared, and it never came back."

"Why?" asked Mike.

"I'll tell you what I think. Remember Randall Turnipseed, the boy whose testimony hung Del Kincaid? Well, after he grew up, he fought in the Spanish-American War in 1898 and was seriously wounded. He was brought back to Rockton, but he never recovered. On his death bed, he gave a confession. He said that he never saw Del Kincaid at the bridge. In fact, Randall wasn't anywhere close to the murder scene. He had been sore at his old teacher and, figuring that Del was guilty anyway, the boy lied on the stand. He simply got caught up in all the excitement of a murder trial. Know what's really odd about this? The same year Randall died, the shadow disappeared on the side of the schoolhouse wall and it never returned."

"That's astounding!" said Mike.

"Yes, but there's a sad note to this story," said Harvey. "The Turnipseeds never told the Kincaid family about Randall's confession."

"What a terrible injustice. So how did you come to know about it?"

Harvey hemmed and hawed before he replied softly, "Randall Turnipseed was Todd's great-great uncle on his mother's side."

Mike shook his head in amazement. *Now everything is beginning to make sense,* he thought. *If Todd is connected to the schoolhouse bricks through an ancestor, maybe I am too.* Shaking Mr. Fisher's hand, Mike said, "Thanks so very much, sir. I've got to run."

"Where are you going?"

"Into the past, Mr. Fisher, into the past."

Mike raced straight to his great aunt Helen, who was born and raised in Rockton. Although she had never seen the shadow herself, she confirmed the story because her father was there the day of the hanging. At Mike's request, she showed him the family tree she had put together over the years. He studied it but found no indication of anyone related to Randall, Kincaid, or the sheriff.

"I thought I had it solved," he moaned.

Aunt Helen reached over and held his hand. "Michael, I have something to tell you. The family tree is not complete. There is a name missing."

"Whose?"

"Del Kincaid. He was your great-great-great uncle. He so shamed our family by committing murder that he was disowned by everyone. I didn't include his name in the family tree."

Mike's head was reeling. *I'm related to Del Kincaid after all. That's the missing link. Now I know why Todd Fisher and I have been seeing the vision of a hanged man.*

The next day, the teacher asked Todd to bring his brick

to school before class. Then Mike put the two bricks side by side on the desk and told the boy the story of the dead man's shadow.

"Todd, I think I have this figured out. We're both having visions of Del Kincaid, the teacher who was put to death on the testimony of Randall Turnipseed. You're related to Randall; I'm related to Del. He was wrongly convicted, and that's why he haunted the schoolhouse with his shadow. Somehow his ghostly energy was revived when you and I— descendants of those involved in the trial—touched these bricks from the schoolhouse."

"So what do we do now?" asked Todd.

"Let's take our bricks and follow me."

They climbed to the top floor of the school and then onto the roof. When it was clear below, they dropped their bricks and watched them smash onto the concrete below.

"I'm pretty sure your headaches and those terrible visions won't be back," the teacher said. "Just don't touch any more bricks from the old schoolhouse, okay?"

"Okay, Mr. Kerr."

"He was innocent, you know."

That night, Mike paid another visit to Aunt Helen. He took out her family tree and grabbed a pen. "It's time we made this family tree more accurate," Mike declared. Then he wrote in the name of Del Kincaid.

Neither Mike nor Todd had those terrible headaches or visions again.

THE MYSTERIOUS TAPPER

"Don't spill any of the water," Remy Burlingame whispered to his roommate, Sean Leicester, as they sneaked down the darkened third-floor hall of Hedley Academy's dormitory.

"I'll be careful," Sean promised.

When they reached the door to the room of fellow students Timothy Barclay and George Figg, Sean set down a bucket of water. He dipped a sponge in the bucket and made a watery trail to the next-door room of Barry Jacoby and Lee Savoy.

Remy and Sean then carefully leaned the bucket of water at an angle against Timothy and George's door.

"Ready?" whispered Remy.

Sean nodded and knocked on the door. The two boys then sprinted lightly down the hall to their own room. They had left their door slightly ajar and kept the room light off so they wouldn't be detected.

Sleepily, Timothy Barclay opened his door, which swung inside, causing the bucket of water to spill into the room. "What the . . . who did this?" Seeing the trail of water lead to his next-door neighbors, Timothy marched over and pounded on their door. "We'll get even with you!"

"Huh?" Barry mumbled. "What are you talking about? It's one in the morning. Go back to sleep."

"Don't rest easy," hissed Timothy. "You'll get yours!"

Meanwhile, in their room down the hall, Remy and Sean buried their heads in their pillows to smother their laughter.

"Nicely done," said Remy.

"Now we've got Timothy and George at war with Barry and Lee."

"Aren't we the *best* practical jokers in school?" Sean said smugly. He pulled out his notebook and marked off two more names on his list of victims. "We've got everybody at least once this term, except for our prize target—Winston Campbell."

Sean, a 14-year-old from Manchester, England, had been at Hedley Academy in London since he was 11. A good student and athlete, Sean loved practical jokes. His main targets were snobby kids who thought they were superior to others. But everyone was fair game. He was so cool that few students realized he was the culprit. He never admitted his role in the jokes and kept a straight face when confronted by victims. He once pretended to be a target himself to avoid being a suspect. He had walked down the hall with whipped cream on his head, complaining someone had sabotaged his cricket cap.

Sean's roommate and partner-in-crime was Remy, a boy who hated being called by his full name of Remington Bedford Burlingame III. Remy shared Sean's delight at having fun at others' expense. He owned a huge collection of fake insects, eyeballs, and human organs, which he enjoyed planting in victims' food, beds, and closets.

Remy didn't act like the stuck-up rich kid he could have become. Give him a T-shirt and torn jeans to wear rather than the school-required blazer and khaki pants, and he would be happy. It didn't matter that his parents were millionaires. The 13-year-old, who had recently enrolled at Hedley, was just one of the guys.

In their darkened room, the roomies were still laughing over the prank when Sean said, "Hey, do you hear dripping water?"

"Yeah, it sounds like it's in our room." Remy turned on the light. "Oh, no!" A water pipe that extended across the ceiling was leaking—as bad luck would have it—directly onto their desks. "My homework!" he moaned. "It's soaked!"

Sean scrambled over to his desk. "My notes from world history class. They're ruined!"

Knowing they couldn't get any maintenance help at this time of night, they tied towels around the leaky joints and set wastebaskets on their desks to catch the drips. Then they turned off the light and went to bed.

TAP . . . THUD . . . TAP . . . THUD . . . TAP . . . THUD.

"Shhh, do you hear that?" asked Sean. He opened the door and looked up and down the hallway. He saw no one. Yet the tapping sound continued.

"What is it?" asked Remy.

Sean closed the door. "Oh, my gosh," he said worriedly. "It's Gerald Rathburn limping on his cane!"

"Gerald Rathburn? The old headmaster? But he's been dead for years."

"It's his ghost!"

"Come on. You don't really believe that old story," said Remy.

TAP . . . THUD . . . TAP . . . THUD . . . TAP . . . THUD.

"When he gets really ticked off, he haunts the hallways of this school. He must be mad at us over our pranks," said Sean.

"Tell me you're making this up," said Remy, beginning to sound scared.

"I wish I was." Sean's eyes got big, and he hopped into bed, throwing the sheets over his head.

Remy turned on the light. He was looking warily around for the ghost when he heard muffled noises coming from under Sean's sheet.

"Sean, are you crying?"

Sean popped his head up and burst out laughing. "I really had you going, didn't I?"

Embarrassed that he had fallen for Sean's joke, Remy fired a pillow at his roomie. "There's no such ghost."

"Of course there isn't," said Sean. "It's just an old legend."

"So what was that noise?"

Sean's smile left. "I don't know. Maybe," he added with a mock look of horror, "it really *was* the ghost of Gerald Rathburn!"

Gerald Rathburn was a brilliant but eccentric scientist who founded the boys' boarding school in 1873 and named it after his father, Hedley, a noted British philosopher. Gerald believed that students needed to learn the basics, but he also encouraged them to engage in unique and offbeat studies that intrigued them. Among the subjects—which have since been rejected by scientists as nonsense—were phrenology (the study of a person's character by analyzing the shape of the head), numerology (the study of how one's personal numbers such as birth dates can predict the future), and alchemy (the study of changing elements into gold through chemistry).

Rathburn also was fascinated by mummies. He wanted to preserve corpses of famous people and turn them into permanent memorials for display in sealed glass cases. Not surprisingly, most people thought his idea was crazy—and many were convinced he was too.

Nevertheless, Rathburn continued to study mummies of ancient Egyptians, the Mayas of Central America, and the Incas of South America. By the turn of the century he had become an expert and wanted his own corpse preserved for generations to admire. He even wrote in his will exactly how he wanted his wish carried out.

Shortly after he died in 1912, Rathburn's body was preserved according to his directions and placed in a sealed box with a glass front. The display case was then put in the back lobby of the school, where it had remained ever since for visitors to see.

Rathburn physically resembled Benjamin Franklin and

struck a commanding pose seated in one of his favorite chairs. His expression was neither mean nor friendly; more of a no-nonsense yet kindly look. He was dressed in tan breeches, a black coat, white ruffled shirt, white gloves, white stockings, and black shoes. Across his knees rested "Tapper," the name he gave his walking stick. He needed it in the last third of his life because of an arthritic knee that caused him to limp.

"I know it's only a legend, but has anyone ever claimed to have seen Rathburn's ghost?" Remy asked Sean.

"Apparently years ago students who got in trouble saw him," Sean replied. "As a prank they had dismantled the headmaster's car and then reassembled it in the hallway of the administration building. Supposedly Rathburn's ghost was so angry that he made an appearance and scolded the students."

TAP . . . THUD . . . TAP . . . THUD . . . TAP . . . THUD.

"There's that tapping noise again," said Remy. The boys stepped into the hallway. "It's definitely in the hallway."

"And it's getting louder, like it's coming toward us."

"What is it, Sean?"

"I really don't know."

"I feel a chill."

"Yeah, me too. A cold draft. Let's go back inside."

They didn't give the tapping noise much thought the next night. They were too intent on completing their final practical joke of the term.

"I've been waiting for months to do this," said Sean as they tiptoed to Winston Campbell's door shortly after midnight. "Everyone at school knows that Winston is a class-A jerk. He thinks he's so perfect. And the way he tries to get in good with the headmaster makes me sick. He even has a room to himself."

"Yes, it stinks!"

They both laughed because that was exactly what they were going to make happen in Winston's room. Carrying a straightened coat hanger and a capsule of sulfur—a chemical element that smells like rotten eggs—the boys reached Winston's door. Sean spit out the bubblegum he was chewing and stuck it on the end of the coat hanger before lightly attaching it to the capsule. Next, he eased the capsule under Winston's door. With a flick of the wrist, Sean left the capsule under a rug in the center of the room and pulled out the hanger.

"There," he whispered to Remy. "When Winston wakes up and steps on the capsule, he'll break it, and his whole room will stink to high heaven!"

Remy then bent the end of the hanger to form a hook. He shoved it under the door until he hooked the leg of a table. Remy began moving the table in a jerking fashion so the books on top of the table fell off.

Soon the boys heard Winston mutter, "Huh? What's going on?" He turned on a light and stumbled over to the table. "How did this happen? Oh, pee-uuu! Oh, *gross!*"

The boys, trying their best to keep from laughing out loud, quietly dashed back to their room. As they fled the scene, they heard Winston coughing, "Oh, what stinks? This is sickening!"

Once inside their room, the jokesters slapped each

other's hands in celebration for a mission accomplished. Sean got out his notebook to check off the name of the latest victim. He flipped through the pages. "Oh no," he groaned. He turned them back and forth. Then he pounded his fist on the cover and winced.

"Sean, what's wrong?"

"My hit list is missing! I can't find it!"

"How did that happen?"

"This morning on my way to English class, my notebook fell out of my hand. Actually, it felt like someone had yanked it away from me, but no one was around. Papers scattered in all directions. I was positive I had picked them all up. Obviously I didn't." He put his hands to his head and moaned. "If someone finds the hit list, we're marked for revenge!"

Suddenly, the roomies started gagging.

"Yuck!" choked Sean, holding his nose. "The stench in here is terrible!"

"Quick, open the window before I barf!"

"What did you do, Remy?"

"It wasn't me! I thought it was you!"

"Help me with this window. It's stuck." Grunting and groaning, the two boys tried to open it but failed, so they rushed to the door. At first it wouldn't budge, but finally they managed to open it. They staggered into the hallway and took several deep breaths.

"Did someone stink bomb us?" Remy asked.

"Could very well be."

Once the stench left their room, the boys searched everywhere but found no clues to the cause of the smell.

Sitting on his bed, Sean scratched his head and said, "Somebody knows. Somebody is getting even with us."

"Who?"

TAP . . . THUD . . . TAP . . . THUD . . . TAP . . . THUD.

"There's that noise again," said Sean. "Let's try to find out who or what it is."

They followed the strange tapping as it moved to the end of the hallway. It led them down the stairs and out the front door of the dormitory. As they stepped outside, the boys hesitated. It was against the rules to leave the dormitory this late.

"We've got to follow it," Sean declared.

"This is so weird," Remy whispered with a shudder. "It's . . . unearthly."

TAP . . . THUD . . . TAP . . . THUD . . . TAP . . . THUD.

The tapping continued on the sidewalk all the way to the back entrance of the administration building, where the door was slightly ajar. The boys cautiously stepped inside the lobby. Groping in the darkness, they blindly followed the tapping for another few seconds. But then the noise stopped. The boys stood still, waiting for the tapping to continue. Suddenly the lobby lights went on. Remy let out a yelp.

They were standing right in front of the glass case containing Gerald Rathburn.

"Shhh!" Sean ordered. "Do you want to get us in trouble?"

"Sorry, I just got spooked by the old man. Say, did he always have a scowl?"

"I don't think so," replied Sean. He stepped closer and studied the face of the long-dead headmaster, whose lips clearly formed a nasty frown. "That's really odd. I don't remember him looking so angry."

"Come on, Sean, let's get out of here. He gives me the creeps."

"You know what else is strange? That tapping noise led us to Rathburn. I wonder why."

Remy gave a shiver. "You don't think —"

"Look!" said Sean, pointing at Rathburn's lap.

"What? I don't see anything."

"Exactly. His cane—what did he call it? Oh yeah, Tapper—is *gone!*"

Remy gulped. "Do you suppose what we heard was Tapper?"

Before Sean could answer, the burglar alarm went off, and the outside floodlights came on. The panic-stricken boys bolted out the door and raced across the yard back to their dorm and up the steps to their floor.

When they got to their door they couldn't get in. "It's locked!" cried Remy, as he frantically searched his pockets. "Where's the key?"

"I don't have it. I thought you did."

Just then Winston Campbell stepped from his room into the hallway. "Hello, lads. What are you doing up in the wee hours of the morning?"

"We heard a noise out in the hallway," explained Sean. "When we went to investigate, we got locked out."

"Are you sure it wasn't something terribly smelly that got you up?" asked Winston, his eyes glaring suspiciously. As he headed toward the bathroom at the end of the hall, he turned around and asked, "By the way, do you two always sleep with your clothes on?"

"Great," Remy whispered to Sean. "Of all the people to have spotted us, it would be Winston Campbell. Do you think he suspects us?"

Sean glumly nodded. "He probably does, but we've got a bigger problem. Someone might have seen us running from the administration building. And now Winston can say that he saw us in our street clothes in the hallway at the time the burglar alarm went off."

After they plopped down on the floor of the hallway, Remy felt something under him. He scooted over and whispered excitedly, "Look! Our key. It must have fallen out of my pocket somehow."

When they entered their room Sean cautioned, "Don't turn on the lights. If one of the teachers was alerted by the alarm, he might be keeping an eye on the dormitory to see if anyone is up."

The boys hopped into their beds, but Remy couldn't sleep. His mind relived the strange events of the night: the lost list, the stench, the tapping, the opened administration door, the remains of Gerald Rathburn, the scowl, the missing cane, and the room key that mysteriously showed up. And he wondered why the alarm went off as they left the building, but hadn't sounded when they entered it.

Remy rolled over in his bed and suddenly felt an object jab him in the back. He leaped out of bed with a frightened yell.

"What is it, Remy?"

"There's something in my bed! Quick! Turn on the lights!"

Sean flipped on the switch, and the two boys stared in disbelief. Lying on Remy's bed was a walking cane.

"That looks like Gerald Rathburn's cane!" Sean exclaimed. "What's it doing *here*?"

"How should I know? It's in your bed."

"You know I didn't take it."

"Wait a minute," said Sean, nodding his head. "Someone is setting us up. Someone very clever."

"He's going to an awful lot of trouble. What will we do now?"

"Let's sleep on it."

"Yeah, right. Like I'll get any sleep tonight."

The next morning the boys hid the cane above the water pipe in their room and went to breakfast in the mess hall. After finishing their meal, the entire student body waited for morning announcements, which were usually read by a classmate.

But today Headmaster Desmond Guthrie stepped to the microphone. "Gentlemen, I have disturbing news to report," he said. "Apparently, at least two persons tried to break into the administration building shortly after midnight last night. We are taking an inventory to see if anything was taken.

"What is even more upsetting to me is that a member of the faculty saw two persons running from the administration building toward the dormitory. Unfortunately, his view was blocked by the bushes so he couldn't see if anyone actually went into the dorm. If anyone has seen or heard anything, it is your duty to report it to me at once. Dare I say that I sincerely hope that the persons involved in this break-in have no connection to this fine school."

Remy and Sean stared wide-eyed at each other before both looked over to Winston, who glanced at them with a raised eyebrow and a hint of a grin.

Later, as the students filed out of the mess hall, Sean whispered to Remy, "Don't panic. Let's think this out."

Remy bowed his head and gazed at the ground. "They're going to discover that the cane is missing," he moaned. "And then Winston is going to squeal on us, and then they're going to find the cane in our room, and my life as I now know it will be over. And the worst thing about it is that I didn't do anything wrong."

"Maybe they won't notice the cane is gone."

"You saw it was missing right away," said Remy. "We could go to Headmaster Guthrie and tell him the truth."

"Which is . . . ?"

"We heard a strange tapping noise in the hallway, and we followed it outside to the administration building, and . . . oh, right, the story sounds so bad even I'm having trouble believing it."

"Remy, if they conduct a search of the rooms and find the cane, our goose is cooked."

The rest of the day the boys fretted over their fate, wondering when they would be caught and then punished for something they didn't do.

After class the boys hurried back to their room. Sean climbed on his desk and reached for the cane, which he had left on the overhead water pipe. "Remy, it's gone!"

"They must know! Oh, man, we're goners."

"I wonder what they're waiting for. Why doesn't Guthrie put us out of our misery?"

"Sean, I guess we better go and see him."

"Yeah, okay, although I'm still not clear on what we're going to say. The truth is going to sound so bizarre."

Remy reached for the door and turned the handle. "Hey, help me with the door handle. It's stuck."

"Here, let me try." Together they tried to open it. But nothing worked. They pounded on the door, attracting the attention of one of the other boarders.

"What's wrong, lads?" asked Timothy Barclay as he walked by their room.

"We're stuck," Sean replied. "Could you try to push on your side and see if we can get the door open?"

"Hey, fellows," Timothy shouted to others on the floor. "It seems Remy and Sean are stuck in their room and can't get out."

"What a shame," said George Figg.

"Yes, it's a pity." Talking to Remy and Sean through their door, Timothy said, "Well, lads, since you probably won't be joining us for dinner, do you mind if we eat your dessert?"

"Hey, don't leave!" shouted Remy, pounding on the door. "What about us?" Turning to his roommate, he said, "I bet those guys figured out a way to lock us in. They're getting even for all the practical jokes we played on them."

Sean tried to open the window. But it remained stuck— just as it did the previous night. "I don't believe this. We're trapped!"

TAP . . . THUD . . . TAP . . . THUD . . . TAP . . . THUD.

"Sean, the tapping noise!"

"It sounds like it's here in this room!"

"It's awfully cold in here. What's happening?"

"I don't know. It's like an invisible person is in the room with us. If this is a practical joke, it's the best one ever."

"Sean, what if it's not a practical joke? What if it's the ghost of Gerald Rathburn? What if the legend *is* true? The tapping sound could have been his ghost walking with his cane. Maybe he's really mad at us. Don't forget, we saw the scowl on his face. It has to be him!"

Walking around the room like a frightened animal in a cage, Sean declared, "Then I'm never going to pull another practical joke as long as I live! I just want to get out of here!"

Suddenly their door unexplainably creaked open. The boys paused briefly in wonder and then bolted out of the room. They raced down the hall, out of the dormitory, and made a beeline for the administration building.

"Headmaster Guthrie," Remy said breathlessly as the two boys barged into his office. In a rapid-fire voice he babbled, "We were the ones in the administration building last night. We heard a strange tapping sound in the dorm and followed it here and the door was open and we went inside and we saw Gerald Rathburn's face had a scowl and his cane was missing only we didn't take it and then the alarm went off and we ran out of the building and we're innocent . . ."

"Slow down, lad, slow down," ordered Guthrie as he leaned against his desk. "What are you jabbering about?"

Remy and Sean tried to calm down while explaining everything that had happened to them over the last few days.

When they finished, Guthrie wrinkled his nose, folded

his arms, and grinned. "Boys, you are victims of your own imaginations. There are simple explanations for almost all of this. First, we've been having problems with our water lines. Air was getting into them and making a knocking sound that you mistook for tapping.

"Second, I learned what happened last night. There was no break-in. Our maintenance man Henry had disengaged the alarm system because of an electrical short in the basement. He had left the door to the back entrance open while he went to fetch a tool. He turned on the power right after you walked in, so the lights went back on. Unfortunately, he forgot about the alarm system and set it off. As for Tapper and Rathburn's scowl, let's go see."

They walked across the hall and examined the glass case containing the old headmaster. The boys were stunned by what they saw. Tapper was sitting across Rathburn's lap as it had for decades.

"Obviously, the cane is there," said Guthrie. "Now, Remy, look at his face. You're not going to tell me that's a scowl, are you?"

"No, sir. It's his usual expression. I must have been mistaken."

"I can't explain why you got trapped in your room or smelled a bad odor, although I have a pretty good idea," Guthrie said. "We know that you two have been pulling pranks on your fellow students. Sean, someone found your hit list. I suspect that your classmates were paying you back."

"I guess you're right, sir," Sean said sheepishly. "We've learned our lesson."

"Good," said the headmaster. "But apparently there is one lesson you haven't learned—obeying curfew. Since you violated it, you two are confined to your quarters for the weekend. That is all."

After leaving the office, Remy turned to Sean and said, "You and I both know the tapping wasn't caused by water pipe problems. Not everything that happened was from the boys pulling practical jokes on us."

"Grow up, Remy. Of course it was them. And I wouldn't be surprised if Guthrie was in on the cane joke. You had me believing Gerald Rathburn's ghost was to blame. There is no ghost. It's just a legend."

Remy smiled weakly. "I suppose you're right."

As they walked past Gerald Rathburn's display case, Remy grabbed Sean's arm and spun him around.

"What is it, Remy?"

Remy, wide-eyed and speechless, pointed to Gerald Rathburn's face. The shocked boys could plainly tell that the no-nonsense yet kindly expression of the old headmaster had changed. This time, the dead man's thin lips had formed a sly smile.

HEROINE
FROM THE BEYOND

T he stocky man with the neatly trimmed beard looked like a combat soldier as he walked ramrod straight in a crisp, freshly ironed camouflage uniform and army boots. His reflector sunglasses hid his eyes. His lips, pressed straight across, gave no hint of his feelings except that he was a no-nonsense kind of man.

His companion, a woman, whose brown hair was pulled back into a ponytail, was also dressed in the same camouflage outfit and army boots. She seemed ill at ease, her eyes constantly darting back and forth. Wiping her sweaty palms on the sides of her pant legs, she walked so close to the man that their shoulders touched. It was as if she sought his protection.

They were marching down the hall of Oakville Elementary with grim-faced principal Mrs. Marion Penney and nervous school secretary Willow Elkins. The four of them headed into the cafeteria, where more than 100 students and teachers were waiting for a school bus safety demonstration to begin.

With the three women standing off to the side, the stone-faced man strode to the front of the room and asked, "Is everyone here?"

"They're all here," said Mrs. Penney in a strained voice.

"Good." Then he whipped out a deadly-looking automatic pistol from the back of his waist, held it over his head, and fired five rapid shots in the air.

The students and teachers were so stunned that for a full second after the final shot tore into ceiling, the entire room remained silent. Then screams and cries of terror exploded like a thunderstorm.

The man ripped off five more rounds in the air and then yelled, "Quiet!" Children covered their ears, whimpered, and dove into laps of each other and their teachers. The man flashed an evil smile. Then he took off his glasses and said, "Now that I have your attention, let me introduce myself. My name is Gary Gillis. I am about to be the most wanted man in the country. And you are my captive audience—and I do mean captive."

Gary Gillis first appeared in tiny Oakville, Wyoming, five years earlier. He had been hired as a security guard at the town's only factory, a maker of sports jackets. But people quickly grew to distrust him because he was such a gun freak. He had more weapons and rifles than the entire police department. And he was always disturbing neighbors by shooting target practice even though it was illegal to use firearms within the city limits. He was fired after only four months on the job because he had a habit of twirling loaded guns in the presence of children.

He soon left town after he became a suspect in the accidental shooting of a hiker. The police released him because they didn't have enough evidence to charge him.

"I've been harassed by everyone here in this burg," Gillis told his landlord. "I'm moving out of this dirtbag town. But someday I'll be back to leave my mark—a mark that will remain forever!"

Gillis worked at odd jobs around the state while his wife, Donna, a country singer who could barely carry a note, tried in vain to build a career. Meanwhile, Gillis began plotting his revenge on Oakville.

"Donna, I have it all figured out," he gleefully told his wife. "We're going to bleed the town of all its cash."

"How, Gary?"

"We'll seize the elementary school and hold everyone hostage. I'll demand that the police give us two million dollars in unmarked bills and a helicopter to take us to safety in the mountains. If the cops try to mess with me, I'll blow up the school."

"Gary, you're crazy!"

"Crazy and soon to be very rich. Are you in or out?"

"The bomb is just a threat, right? You're not really going to harm the children, are you?"

"As long as the cops do as I say."

"They wouldn't dare do anything foolish that could hurt the kids. Count me in, Gary."

For months Gillis read pamphlets from antigovernment

groups known as militias on how to build bombs. Then he gathered the supplies and set off several homemade test bombs in the countryside.

Finally, it was time to carry out his vile kidnapping scheme.

Gillis and his wife loaded his arsenal of guns and rifles into the back of a stolen van. Next, the couple carefully placed a shopping cart full of the necessary parts and ingredients for the bomb into the van. Then, dressed in camouflage gear, they pulled up to Oakville Elementary at precisely 1:30 P.M.

The two walked into the school office, where secretary Willow Elkins asked sweetly, "May I help you?"

"Yes, I would like to speak to the principal, please," said Gillis politely.

"Mrs. Penney is on the phone."

Gillis pulled out an automatic pistol and pressed the barrel against her forehead. "Call her out here right now," he ordered. "Tell her it's urgent."

Wide-eyed with fright, Willow managed to squeak, "Mrs. Penney, come here, quick!"

The 50-year-old principal could tell from Willow's voice there was a problem. She hung up the phone and dashed out of her office only to face a steel-barreled gun aimed at her head.

"I am here to collect a ransom from this town," hissed Gillis. "Now do as I say and maybe, just maybe, I'll let you and the children live. The lives of everyone in this school depend on you. Do you understand?"

Mrs. Penney nodded weakly.

"Get on the intercom and tell everyone to meet in the cafeteria immediately. Tell them you had forgotten about a school bus safety demonstration that was scheduled for 1:30, and that the experts are here now. Tell them they have five minutes to assemble."

Donna, who was keeping an eye on the doorway, added, "And make sure you sound normal."

Mrs. Penney did what she was told. Then the two terrorists led the principal and the secretary to the cafeteria, after first making sure all the classrooms were empty.

Once everyone had gathered, Gillis let his gun do the talking—and for the first time the students and teachers realized they were being held hostage by a madman.

When Gillis fired his weapon into the ceiling, eight-year-old Amber Taylor and classmate Emily Berringer burst into tears. The two girls, who were only 20 feet (6.1 m) from the gunman, threw themselves into the nearest adult lap.

As screams and cries swirled in the air, mixing with gun smoke and falling pieces of the ceiling, Amber and Emily felt warm arms wrap protectively around them. The girls looked up and stared into the gentle green eyes of a freckle-faced, auburn-haired woman in her twenties.

"I don't want to be here," Amber whimpered.

"I want to go home," cried Emily. "I'm scared."

The woman held them tighter and began rocking them. "Try to stay calm, girls. I'm here, and I won't let anything happen to you or your friends."

"Who are you?" asked Amber. "I've never seen you before."

"My name is Caroline Benton. I'm a teacher's aide."

Her calm voice and sweet manner brought comfort not only to Amber and Emily but to other third graders who were nearby. "Children," Caroline told them, "we'll get through this. Trust me."

"Promise?" asked fourth-grader Danny Malone.

Before Caroline could respond, Gillis waved his pistol over the crowd. "You are all my hostages!" he announced. "We're going to be here awhile, so let's move all the tables and chairs to one side and you kids can sit on the floor."

After the hostages did what they were told, Gillis said, "Okay, now for the rules: I will not tolerate any back talk from any kids or grown-ups. If I get angry, I will have to punish you with this." He patted his gun. "No one will be allowed to leave for any reason. I'll let only one person come and go on my orders—and that's your principal. She will act as a go-between for me and the police. If she doesn't do exactly as I tell her, you all will die. You see, children, I am going to be hooked up to a bomb. One false move from anyone and it's ka-boom!"

Children burst out crying again. "I want to go home!" . . . "Me too." . . . "I don't want to die." . . . "You're mean!" . . .

Gillis loaded another clip into his gun and fired off several more rounds into the air. "Quiet! Next time I won't aim for the ceiling!"

On his command, Donna left the cafeteria and returned moments later with the shopping cart that contained Gillis's homemade bomb. He gently slipped his hand into a looped string that was attached to the bomb. If anyone tried to jump him, all he had to do was jerk his wrist. The string

117

would then pull out a piece of wood that had been wedged into a clothespin, which acted as the trigger for the bomb. If the jaws of the clothespin snapped shut, two metal screws at the tips of the clothespin would touch, completing an electrical circuit. Once that happened, the bomb would explode, killing everyone in the room, including the two kidnappers.

Turning to Mrs. Penney, Gillis said, "I want you to call the police. Tell them I'm armed and dangerous, and that I'm rigged to a bomb. I want two million dollars in unmarked bills and a fully fueled helicopter with a pilot to take me and my wife out of here. The deadline is 4:30 P.M."

"Do you realize what you're doing psychologically to these children?" Mrs. Penney said. "They'll be scarred for life."

"Hey, they're bargaining chips," he replied. "The faster I get the money and the chopper, the quicker this ordeal ends and no one gets hurt. Now move!"

In the crowd of squirming, whimpering children, Emily wiped her runny nose on the back of her trembling arm and told Caroline, "He's a nasty man."

"Yes, he is," agreed Caroline, running her fingers softly through the little girl's hair. "Most adults are kind and caring. Unfortunately, there are also some very bad people. Usually, they have serious problems and need help. That's what this man needs."

"And so do we," pouted Amber.

"I think I'm going to get sick," groaned Danny Malone. Caroline quickly went to comfort Danny, and then rushed from one child to another, trying to calm their fears.

Within minutes of Mrs. Penney's 911 call, state, county, and city police—their sirens blaring—surrounded the school. Tearful, panic-stricken parents, who had learned that a terrorist held their precious children, rushed to the scene. They, along with TV crews and reporters from local and national news organizations, were kept out of harm's way by police barricades.

"Gary Gillis," came a voice from a bullhorn outside. "This is Captain Deery. Send Mrs. Penney outside so I can give her a cellular phone to take back to you. Then you and I can talk and resolve this situation before anyone gets hurt."

Gillis glared at the principal. "Go outside and tell them I won't talk to any cop. I won't bargain with them. I want the money and the chopper or this school blows sky high."

When Mrs. Penney left the room, Caroline stood up and grabbed Gillis's attention. "Sir, the children are about to panic. Can I at least organize some activities for them to keep their minds off this terrible situation?"

"Yeah, good idea," he said. "But no funny stuff."

Caroline walked over to the other teachers. "We need to keep the children entertained as best we can. We must remain calm for their sake. If we keep our heads, we'll all get out of here alive."

"Who are you?" asked fourth-grade teacher Becky Stevens.

"Caroline Benton, teacher's aide."

She returned to the third-graders and heard Bradley Sanders whimpering, "This is the worst birthday ever."

"It's your birthday today?" Caroline asked.

After he nodded and told her his name, she stood up and shouted, "Can I have your attention, please."

"Hey, lady, you're not running the show," growled Gillis as he fingered his gun.

Caroline gave him a sarcastic grin and again addressed the students. "It's Bradley Sanders's birthday today, so let's all join in singing 'Happy Birthday.'" She threw her arms out, flashed a big smile, and began singing. The children quickly followed, breaking the tension.

Then, like a butterfly, Caroline flitted about the room, seeming to know by instinct who needed a hug, a word of encouragement, a kiss on the cheek. She boldly demanded from the kidnappers crayons, paper, chalk, a video cart from the media room to show cartoons on the VCR, and other things to keep the kids occupied.

While most adults were afraid to open their mouths, Caroline continued to speak up. They were convinced Gillis would kill her. But, amazingly, he agreed to her demands and ordered Donna to fetch the supplies.

During the siege Gillis sat on a chair in the front. On his left was a table covered with assault weapons and automatic pistols. On his right was the shopping cart containing the bomb, which was still connected to him by a string. To make the bomb even more deadly, Gillis had placed next to it a large open jug of gasoline.

About two hours into the kidnapping, the stench from the gasoline was making most everyone sick and light-headed. Caroline hurried to the back of the room and began opening the windows.

"Who gave you permission to do that?" Gillis shouted in annoyance.

"We have to open them because of the gasoline fumes," said Caroline. "We're getting sick from the smell."

"Well, I'm getting sick of you," he growled.

Caroline ignored him and continued opening the windows.

"I've had about enough of you and your mouth," he snarled, lifting up his gun as the teachers and students gasped. "One little squeeze of the trigger, and I can end your life."

"You already have—"

"Gary Gillis!" said Captain Deery over the bullhorn. "We need more time to collect the money."

Looking at the principal, Gillis said, "Tell them I'll give them an extra hour. That's it. If my demands aren't met by five-thirty, we all die!"

In the third hour of the tense takeover, Gillis's confidence began to wither and Donna's nerves were tattered. The games and distractions no longer eased the minds of the children, who were getting increasingly tired, cranky, and scared.

After hours of trying to keep their spirits up, Caroline took a break. She gnawed on her lower lip and frowned. Then she walked over to teacher Becky Stevens.

"The bomb is about to go off," Caroline whispered.

"How do you know?" Becky asked.

"I just do. You must believe me. Get your students to the back of the room. Have them keep low and face the windows. Tell them we're going to have a group hug. Stay with them and keep them sitting on the floor. Everything will be all right."

"Caroline, you have been wonderful. I don't know how we would have made it this far without you."

"Please, we don't have much time. Move those kids to the back now." Caroline then cornered the other teachers and urged them to do the same thing.

"Hey, what's going on?" Gillis asked suspiciously as he noticed the students crowding toward the back.

Caroline stood up and strolled along the far wall toward the front of the cafeteria. "The children are going to have a group hug to lift their spirits," she told him.

"It could be their last one if the cops don't hurry up with the money," he grumbled. Then he looked at his wife and said, "Donna, get over here. I have to go to the bathroom. I'm going to transfer this string from my wrist to yours."

"Do you *have* to?" she whined.

"Yes. Now we have to be very careful, or the bomb will go off." Slowly he wiggled his wrist out of the loop. Then he delicately placed it on her right wrist.

Just as Gillis was about to walk away, Caroline smashed into a cafeteria cart loaded with clean plates. The impact sent the plates crashing to the floor. The unexpected noise caused Donna to jerk her hand. Her sudden movement yanked the string, which pulled out the wooden wedge from the clothespin trigger.

A split second later a deafening boom rocked the room and echoed off the walls. Then another even more thunderous roar shook the cafeteria as the gasoline ignited and a huge orange fireball mushroomed up from the shopping cart. Fingers of fire shot toward the hostages, followed by choking, blinding smoke.

Bedlam erupted. Voices, young and old, shrieked in panic and fear. "I can't breathe!" "I can't see!" "Help me!" "Over here!" "Get out!" "Ouch! Get off me!" "Help!" Screaming, frantic children stumbled in all directions, banging into walls and each other. Students trampled over one another in a desperate rush to escape. But in the thick, searing smoke, no one could see where to go.

"This way, children!" yelled Caroline as she grabbed two, then four, then as many as her spread-out arms could touch. "Get down on the floor! Cover your mouth and nose! Now crawl as fast as you can to the doorway. Follow me."

On her knees, Caroline groped in the stifling, choking smoke and shoved children out the side door. Then she scrambled to the back of the room where the windows had been blown out by the blast. She grabbed children and swiftly lifted them through the shattered windows.

The heat and deadly smoke had left several children lying on the floor. In the darkness and confusion, Caroline reached the children and dragged them to a teacher, who handed them to an adult on the outside.

"Help! I can't see!" cried Amber Taylor from a dark corner. Caroline scooted through the smoke until she found the little girl. "You'll be fine, Amber," Caroline said. "I'm here for you." Lifting the girl in her arms, Caroline carried her to safety.

"Help me! Help me!"

Caroline recognized the terror-stricken voice. "Emily, where are you?"

"Over here," the girl replied, gagging in the smoke. "I can't move. I'm trapped!"

"Stay calm, honey. I'll find you. Keep talking."

"Hurry! I'm hurt, and it's hard to breathe!"

Caroline finally reached Emily, who was trapped under a table that had been crushed by a fallen steel beam from the ceiling. "I'm here, Emily."

"Get this off me!"

With superhuman strength, Caroline shoved aside the beam and lifted the table. She carried the girl to safety.

Outside, black smoke continued to pour out of the cafeteria's shattered windows. Hysterical parents broke through police lines to join rescue workers who were pulling children to safety.

Wild-eyed students, with soot-blackened faces streaked white with tears, spilled out of the windows. Each small child raced to the nearest adult. They broke down sobbing as they embraced—even when they weren't related. "Gee," said Bradley Sanders, "I didn't know so many people loved me!"

Teacher Becky Stevens, her face cut from flying debris, carried dazed and bleeding children to waiting ambulances. Paramedics loaded slightly injured and shocked students into school buses and cars and rushed them to the emergency room.

Firefighters soon doused the blaze and cleared the smoke out of the cafeteria. "Everybody is out," Fire Chief Ike Lewis announced to Mrs. Penney, who had gathered with the teachers. "We found only two bodies inside—the two kidnappers."

Mrs. Penney clasped her hands together. "No children?"

"That's right, ma'am," said the chief. "Just the two criminals."

"It's a miracle!" Becky shouted.

"I'll say," Lewis added. "It was a good thing the windows in the cafeteria were opened. That helped vent much of the bomb's explosive force."

"Caroline Benton opened those windows right before the bomb went off," Becky told Mrs. Penney.

"Who is she?" asked the principal.

"You know, Mrs. Penney. She's the teacher's aide, the one who kept everyone calm, who spoke up to the kidnappers."

"She's not a teacher's aide. I assumed she was a new parent—one whom I hadn't met yet."

"That's odd, because she definitely told us she was a teacher's aide," said Becky. "If it wasn't for her, many of our kids could have been killed in the blast. She warned us that the bomb was about to explode and told us to go to the back of the room. It blew up minutes later, and then she rescued a lot of children. She was a heroine."

As Becky talked, her eyes kept searching the crowd, trying to find Caroline. Soon Becky went up to the other teachers and asked if they had seen Caroline. They all shook their heads. When she asked them if Caroline was their aide, again they said no. "We thought she was your aide," said a teacher.

Later that evening, the entire town was filled with a sense of wonder and gratitude. No children had been killed or even seriously injured. Only a few needed stitches for cuts caused by flying glass and debris.

Everyone was accounted for—everyone except Caroline Benton.

Becky Stevens checked the hospital and area clinics to see if Caroline had been treated, but none had any record of her. Becky was determined to find Caroline. *How hard could it be?* she thought. *This town has a population of only 5,000. Surely, someone must know who she is.* Becky talked to parents and students, but they had never heard of her before the hostage crisis.

So Becky went to the local newspaper, *The Oakville Weekly Herald,* and asked reporter Mitch Walker to write a story about Caroline's heroics and ask the public's help in trying to find her.

"That name sounds familiar," he said. "Let me check our morgue—that's newspaper talk for clippings of past stories—and see if we've written about her."

Minutes later Mitch returned with a clipping. "Well, I found a story about Caroline Benton."

"Oh, that's terrific!"

"Sorry," he said, "but it can't be the same Caroline."

"Why is that?"

"Here, read it yourself." He handed her the clipping, dated August 15, 1991. It read:

HIKER SHOT TO DEATH
Victim of Stray Bullet From Target Practice

A 22-year-old woman who was visiting Oakville died from a gunshot wound last week near the base of Newbury Mountain.

Police believe she was struck by a stray bullet

from reckless target shooting in an area where guns are not allowed.

Caroline Benton, who was studying for her master's degree in elementary education at the University of Wyoming, was hiking with out-of-town friends on Newbury Trail. Her friends told police they heard someone shooting at a metal target nearby when they saw Miss Benton fall down unconscious. They raced to the nearest phone and called for an ambulance. Miss Benton was pronounced dead on arrival.

An investigation revealed that the stray bullet hit a rock on the trail and split. A ricocheting bullet fragment struck Miss Benton, killing her instantly.

Sheriff's deputies combed the area looking for the person who was illegally shooting target practice. They questioned former security guard Gary Gillis, but he denied being in the area that day. His wife Donna claimed he was home at the time of the shooting.

"We will probably never know who did it," said Sheriff Matt Wisner. "It was a tragic accident. We can only hope that the person who so recklessly was shooting near the hiking trail will come forward. Meanwhile, our investigation is continuing."

Becky was so stunned by what she read that she let the clipping slip out of her hand. As it floated to the floor, she murmured, "This is astounding."

"What is?" asked the reporter.

"The coincidences are staggering. This woman had the same name, apparently the same age and same interest in elementary education as the Caroline Benton I'm looking for. And both met up with Gary Gillis. Now what are the odds of that happening?"

"My calculator doesn't have numbers that high," said Mitch. "You know, the police were absolutely convinced that Gillis killed that woman, but they simply couldn't prove it."

"Wait a second!" said Becky, her voice rising with excitement. "Caroline said something really odd during the kidnapping. When Gillis threatened to kill her, she said, 'You already have.' But she was interrupted when the police shouted something to Gillis. I wonder, was that the end of her sentence, or did she have more to say?"

"I don't follow you, Becky."

"Now here's another question for you, Mitch. Caroline Benton warned us that the bomb was going to explode soon. How did she know that? Or did she plan on causing it to go off? After she was sure the children were in the back, she knocked over a cart of plates that caused the kidnappers to jerk and set off the bomb. She was no more than ten feet (3 m) away from the kidnappers, yet she wasn't killed—at least not in the cafeteria."

"Now I see where you're coming from," said Mitch. "But if you're right, that means —"

"The heroine of the Oakville Elementary hostage crisis was the ghost of Caroline Benton!"

Penguin Education

The Economics of Marx

Edited by M. C. Howard and J. E. King

Penguin Modern Economics Readings

The Economics of Marx

Selected Readings of Exposition and Criticism

Edited by M. C. Howard and J. E. King

Penguin Books

Penguin Books Ltd,
Harmondsworth, Middlesex, England
Penguin Books Inc.,
625 Madison Avenue, New York, New York 10022, U.S.A.
Penguin Books Australia Ltd,
Ringwood, Victoria, Australia
Penguin Books Canada Ltd,
41 Steelcase Road West, Markham, Ontario, Canada
Penguin Books (N.Z.) Ltd,
182–190 Wairau Road, Auckland 10, New Zealand

First published 1976
This selection copyright © M. C. Howard and J. E. King, 1976
Introduction and notes copyright © M. C. Howard and J. E. King, 1976
Copyright acknowledgements for items in this volume will be
found on page 269

Made and printed in Great Britain by
Hazell Watson & Viney Ltd, Aylesbury, Bucks
Set in Monotype Times

Contents

Introduction

Current dissatisfaction with capitalist society has been reflected in an upsurge of criticism of orthodox economic theory (see, for example, Hunt and Schwartz, 1972). Parallel with this has come a revival of interest in Marxian economics. Marx's economic writings are notoriously heavy going for those trained in the neoclassical tradition. His concepts, categories and perspectives are fundamentally different, his output monumental, and his style often obscure. These readings are intended to serve as an introduction to the study of Marx's political economy, and in particular to guide the reader of Marx's own work.

Part One consists of Sowell's centenary appreciation of *Capital*, a wide-ranging and provocative survey of the field. Part Two deals with the more general theoretical foundations of Marx's economic theory. Meek (Reading 14) is one of the few modern economists who have shown any great interest in these theoretical underpinnings, and the remaining readings in this section consist of extracts from Marx himself. They are taken from *Capital*, from the *Critique of Political Economy*, and from the newly-translated *Grundrisse*.

Part Three contains four readings on the labour theory of value. Dobb (Reading 15) and Sweezy (Reading 16) outline the basic elements of Marx's theory of value and exploitation. Shoul (Reading 17) shows how Marx's detailed exposition of the labour theory of value emerged from his critique of classical political economy, while Seton's article (Reading 18) is an important contribution to the debate on the famous 'transformation problem'.

Part Four deals with Marx's theory of capitalist economic development. Harris (Reading 20) discusses Marx's growth theory, and draws an interesting parallel with modern analysis. Heertje (Reading 22) and Meek (Reading 21) consider aspects of Marx's theory of technical change, and its implications for the future of capitalism itself. Tsuru (Reading 19) complements Sowell's discussion of economic crises, showing how Marx developed a theory of the trade cycle as an endogenous and inevitable feature of capitalist economies. Part Five contains Avineri's perceptive analysis of Marx's theory of imperialism, seen in terms of the impact of capitalism on non-capitalist economies.

These readings represent only a small sample of modern discussion of Marx's economic theory. A somewhat larger sample is given in the suggested further reading, where some suggestions are also made on reading

Marx in the original. The interpretation of Marx's ideas, and the appraisal of their merits, remain highly contentious, and the reader should not be surprised to find conflicts of opinion on important issues between the readings. The rest of this introduction outlines some of the major issues raised in the readings, and assesses the modern relevance of the economics of Marx.

1 Theoretical underpinnings
The materialist conception of history

Marx's view of historical development is important for three inter-related reasons. Firstly, it emphasizes the importance of the 'mode of production' and is therefore directly relevant to our understanding of economic history and the operation of economic structures. Secondly, it is only in these terms that Marx's theory of human freedom can be understood, and this theory in turn underlies his criticism of the capitalist economic system. Thirdly, Marx's view of history very largely explains his method of economic inquiry.

Consequently Reading 2 presents one of Marx's own summaries of the materialist conception of history. This is only a summary of a complex theory, and more detailed statements can be found in *The German Ideology*, *The Poverty of Philosophy* and the *Grundrisse*. Thus, although Reading 2 is the best and most complete short exposition it is incomplete, and leaves implicit many important questions.

Read on its own, this passage can lead to the view that for Marx the 'forces of production' are the dynamic of history, and are in some sense independent of human action. Such an interpretation would, however, be incorrect. Marx takes the forces of production to be an index of productive development, which in turn reflects the development of human needs. These latter, in turn, develop endogenously from the system of social relations in operation. History is therefore a process of continuous creation and satisfaction of men's needs through the development of production. This process occurs, Marx argues, in such a way as to lead to a dialectical sequence of stages, which he outlines in Reading 2. These are not necessarily the same for all societies (see Reading 23).[1]

In most cases social change takes place through class conflict, for production generally takes place in a class society. Marx argues that in certain periods men's developing needs and productive power come into contradiction with the class relations of production; that is, with the method by

1. See also Hobsbawm (1964). Marx, in fact, divided history into a number of different typologies of developmental stages at various points in his work, both in the light of his increasing historical knowledge and as aids to the analysis of specific problems.

which production is organized (for example, in capitalist commodity production, through private ownership of capital and the employment of wage labour). The forces of production, which stem from men's historically developing needs, cease to be efficiently operated and developed within the class relations of the society within which they originally arise. To achieve this a new set of relations is required.

Thus the dominant class, whose power and privileges rest on the existing relations of production, becomes an obstacle to progress and is replaced in the course of social conflict by another system of class relations which allows the further development of social production. However, with the progressive development of the forces of production a new contradiction between the forces and relations of production becomes manifest in a new class struggle.

As Marx points out in Reading 2, social classes may not realize the historical significance of what they do, and with a change in the mode of production almost all aspects of society are changed. He argues, however, that the class struggle in capitalism between the proletariat and the bourgeoisie was unique, in that the proletariat would become conscious of its historical significance, and its victory would lead to a classless society of 'free individuality', thus ending this form of dialectical development (see below, pp. 17–18).

The nature of Marx's economics

The above is presented in terms of general laws of historical development. Marx maintains, however, that each of the economic stages to which these general laws relate develops in a specific manner which can be revealed only through empirical science, and in particular through economics. In other words the laws of economic development of each such stage are specific to its own economic structure; *they stem from the particular social relations of production by which it is defined*. Any general laws such as those arrived at by Marx in Reading 2 must therefore be based on an intensive study of specific stages.

The role of economics, Marx argues, is to analyse these systems of economic relationships: to inquire how they originate, operate and develop, both qualitatively and, whenever possible, quantitatively; in the case of capitalism, for example, to discover how they govern its specific laws of distribution, rate of profit, relative prices, and so on.

Important methodological rules of analysis follow from such a view. These are outlined in Reading 3. Since for Marx the historically specific social relations of systems of production are the fundamental determinants of economic phenomena, he argues that economic analysis must afford them explicit and prime place. Failure to observe this principle would lead to distortions in logic and in empirical validity. We see in Reading 3 that Marx takes to task his predecessors and contemporaries on precisely these grounds. His more developed critique in *Theories of Surplus Value* shows that this principle underlies virtually all of his specific criticism of other systems of economics.

Thus there is for Marx no strict distinction between economics and sociology. The definition of economics, of its area of study and its method, are conceived sociologically in terms of the social relations of production. This is, of course, very different from the position taken by neoclassical economists, who abstract from such historically specific social relations, presumably in the belief that they are secondary factors.

The definition of capitalism and its method of analysis

Most of Marx's own substantive economic theory concentrates on capitalism; Reading 4 shows exactly what Marx conceives this historically specific economic system to be. In accordance with the above, its historical specificity is defined by the particular social relations which exist between the main economic actors.

Firstly, there is a separation of the producers from the means of production, which are owned by a minority class. Consequently the producers cannot 'work for themselves', but are *compelled by their economic situation* to work for this class. Secondly, the means of production must, when combined with the producers, be capable of producing output in excess of the necessary consumption requirements of the producers. Without this, the owners could not exploit the producers and receive an income arising from their ownership. Thirdly, the two classes, owners and producers, must interact through periodic exchange, thus giving rise to the system of 'wage labour'. Finally, the subjective aim of the owners must be the unlimited acquisition and accumulation of wealth. The system is not a capitalist one if they employ wage labour solely to service their own direct consumption requirements. Marx's meaning here can be seen even more clearly from Reading 5. In Marx's view capitalist motivation is not a direct and free expression of a 'natural' economic impulse, for such a pattern of action is not even characteristic of other economic actors in capitalism, let alone of actors in pre-capitalist economies.

In order for such a system to arise, relations of personal dependence (for example, slavery and serfdom), which prevent producers from 'freely' disposing of their labour power, must generally have been eradicated; producers separated by some historical process from ownership of the means of production; productivity sufficiently developed; and social conditions arisen which create and sustain the capitalists' motivation. At various stages in his work Marx analyses the historical development of these conditions in Europe, and outside Europe. His economic analysis of capitalism itself is concerned with determining how relative prices, income distribution and dynamic laws of economic development are determined by this specific network of social relations once it has been historically established.

The exact method by which Marx's theory is constructed requires some comment. We see from Reading 2 that Marx outlines a particular scheme of historical stages marking progress in economic development. He carries out his analysis of the historical origins of capitalism in the West largely in these terms, dealing with certain aspects of the decline of feudalism and the emergence of capitalist relations of production, as outlined in Reading 4. His analysis of capitalism itself, however, is largely carried out within an alternative framework which Marx believes is more suitable for highlighting the crucial aspects of its operation. He reorganizes the typology of economic formations found in Reading 2 into three stages, which are presented in Reading 6.

Here the non-commodity-producing economic relations of pre-capitalist forms are telescoped together into the first stage: that based on relations of *personal dependence*. The commodity-producing aspect of all societies is divorced from their actual and historical contexts in the second stage. By commodity production Marx refers to production for exchange on a market by independent producers or groups of producers (see Readings 9, 14 and 19). The third stage is the same as that to which the typology of Reading 2 leads: socialism-communism.

The first stage is relatively straightforward. Pre-capitalist economic formations are quite clearly predominantly based on relations of personal dependence. Slaves are dependent on *particular* slave-owners, serfs on *particular* feudal lords. Thus it makes theoretical and historical sense to consider them as a whole.

The second stage, however, might not on first sight seem to live up to this standard, for the historical relations depicted by it are extremely diverse, covering as they do *elements* of most pre-capitalist formations, as well as of capitalism itself. Marx, however, wishes to concentrate attention on relations of commodity production as such, not only because he sees capitalism as the most developed type of this general form of production, but also because many of its crucial specific properties develop historically from, and can best be developed theoretically out of (and in contrast to) pre-capitalist commodity producing systems. What Marx does, therefore, is to redivide the second stage into pre-capitalist commodity production and capitalist commodity production, building up from the former his model of the latter.

To this end pre-capitalist commodity production is made into an 'ideal type', which Marx terms 'simple commodity production'. It incorporates certain historical elements of pre-capitalist commodity producing systems in their pure form, as they are never found in reality. They are transformed and exaggerated in a certain way to make for a logically precise and consistent whole designed for the purpose of constructing models of capitalist commodity production (see Reading 14; also Meek, 1973).

The characterization of the third stage in terms of 'free individuality', and its relationship to the second, requires an understanding of Marx's theory of human freedom, which we deal with below (pp. 15–18). Before we do so, however, it is instructive to look into the nature of Marx's economic concepts.

The nature of Marx's economic concepts

Sweezy (Reading 16, p. 142) emphasizes the most important point when he says that Marx 'enforces a strict requirement that categories of economics must be social categories, i.e. categories which represent relations between people'. He rightly notes the contrast with orthodox theory in this respect. Such a methodological requirement clearly fits in well with Marx's view of history, and his conception of economics, which we have outlined above. Since Marx concentrates in his own analysis on capitalism, and approaches the study of capitalism via simple commodity production, we need to be particularly aware of the concepts applicable to these forms. Here we deal with Marx's concept of value, and later explain the derived categories of surplus value and capital.

The difficulty in coming to terms with these concepts is that they refer simultaneously to social relations and to things. The specific nature of economic relations in all commodity producing systems is such that they are also and simultaneously relations between commodities. Marx's concepts, then, apply not only to social relations, but also extend to the things through which these relations operate. In commodity production the social character of production is expressed through the exchange of commodities (see Reading 8).

Production is social precisely because the producers work for each other by embodying their labour in things which they then exchange for other, similarly produced things. If we abstract from the physical characteristics of commodities, these exchanges can thus be seen to be exchanges of labour. It is to this social relation that the concept of 'value' applies. It has not only a qualitative dimension, but can also be expressed as a quantitative magnitude when the amounts of labour are measured in 'socially necessary' units (see Sowell, Reading 1, Section 4; also Reading 16). The social property of commodities which we have described thus enables them to serve as bearers of social relations or, as Marx puts it, 'value is a relation between persons expressed as a relation between things' (*Capital*, I, p. 74).

Marx's concept of value is therefore very different from that of orthodox economics, where it is used synonymously with price. Marx *defines* value as the embodied labour content of a commodity. He does maintain, however, that values determine equilibrium prices in commodity-producing economies, though not necessarily in any simple manner (see Readings 14, 15, 18 and below pp. 26–30). It is precisely in this sense that Marx's labour theory of value seeks to determine prices and income distribution in terms of the social relations of production.

The concept of value applies only to systems of commodity production, since it incorporates the social relations specific to this system. Thus, although products in all other types of economy are produced by labour, they are by definition *not* commodities and do not possess value. Nor did Marx consider that it would be useful to change these definitions to make them apply generally. Since prices do not regulate social production in a non-commodity-producing society, there is no need for a theory of value to explain prices.

As we have indicated in our discussion of Marx's concept of value, his definition of economic concepts departs substantially from the meanings given to them in common language. Those of orthodox economic theory, in many cases, do not. This is deliberate on Marx's part: such common expressions reflect the consciousness of social actors in commodity producing systems and this, Marx maintains, is a *false* consciousness expressing scientifically invalid causal relationships. These considerations lead us to Marx's theory of fetishism.

Marx's theory of fetishism

Marx's argument is best approached through his theory of freedom and alienation. In bourgeois society freedom is normally defined as the absence of constraints on individual action. In contrast Marx argues that men are free to the extent that they consciously master and control both nature and their social conditions of existence in accordance with their historically developing needs, both material and intellectual.[2] In these terms Marx characterizes the second stage of his typology (Reading 6) as unfree, and argues that it reflects 'objective' or 'material dependence'. His point is made clear in his theory of economic alienation and fetishism.

This theory of economic alienation[3] has two dimensions. There is an alienation which characterizes commodity production in general, and

2. As we shall see, this becomes identical with conditions which allow individuals freely to develop their individual capabilities in both material and intellectual production.

3. We discuss here only Marx's theory of *economic* alienation. He also deals with the related phenomena of political and religious alienation, particularly in his earlier works. For details, see Further Reading.

one which characterizes capitalism. Corresponding to these are two forms of fetishism (Meek (1973), pp. xi–xiv). The alienation and fetishism characteristic of commodity production in general are outlined in Readings 7, 8 and 9. Marx sees that in commodity production men's own powers become independent forces which control their actions. No communal or social consciousness organizes and regulates production. Instead production is for the market, and economic relations take the form of relations between commodities. The various demands of economic agents translate social requirements into prices and quantities of commodities.

Thus each and every actor responds to social requirements in terms of the prices and quantities of things, that is, through the mediation of material objects over which no one has control. These things, however, are only manifestations of men's collective or social powers of production. The producers, then, are controlled by their own collective power instead of directly dominating the social conditions of their lives through conscious collective regulation. Marx thus describes this situation as one of material domination, in contrast to the personal relations of domination of the first stage and the conscious social regulation of the third (see Reading 6).

The theory of commodity fetishism follows directly from this, by shifting the focus of analysis to the consciousness of the social actors in such a situation. Marx argues that men see the economy as a mechanism operating independently of them, and ruling them as an alien force which is apparently incomprehensible, arbitrary and uncontrollable. They do not see reality as it is, governed by laws which result from the structure of men's social relations.

In capitalism alienation and fetishism are developed still further, as Marx points out in Readings 10 and 11. Not only does capitalism historically extend commodity production to its highest degree; it now also creates capital[4] and capitalistically organized landed property as alien powers to whose demands the producers must submit. All the means of developing production now confront the workers as independent alien objects. Men collectively create capital and landed property, which then become social powers to which they submit and through which they are exploited.

In Reading 11 Marx shifts the focus of his analysis to the consciousness of the actors in such a situation, dealing 'in this case not with the fetishism of commodities as such but with the fetishism of capital and land' (Meek, 1973, p. xiii). Here he is concerned to undermine the ideological mystification created by this form of alienation, especially with regard to the origin of property incomes. Instead of being seen as the result of the historically specific form of social relations, they are regarded as emanating from the nature of material objects themselves.

4. For Marx's use of this concept, see below pp. 23–4.

Marx therefore believed that the appearances of commodity production, both capitalist and pre-capitalist, were illusory. Reality as it appears to social actors is deceptive; and Marx often writes of the true reality as hidden by appearances. The point he is making here is not that behind what we observe is a 'reality' which is 'non-observable' in that it cannot be perceived by the senses. Marx's point is a *sociological* one. For Marx it is the social position of actors within such economic formations which systematically constrains the development of a true consciousness and creates a 'false consciousness' which can be used for ideological purposes. He sees it as the role of scientific economics to penetrate through the fetishism to the reality of social relations, which are expressed in terms of value, surplus value[5] and capital.

However Marx is not concerned with economics for the sake of science alone. He is committed to science because it is the most fruitful way of obtaining knowledge about the world. But he goes beyond this by attempting to expose the social conditions of contemporary man, and in so doing to aid the realization in social practice of his conception of human freedom.

Freedom and revolution

Reading 12 outlines Marx's critique of the bourgeois concept of freedom, and follows clearly from the analysis of the last section. At the same time, however, Marx believed that he saw the potentialities of a free society in the development of capitalism itself. This is so for two related reasons. Firstly, capitalism, more than any other form of economic organization, was physically productive of wealth on a massive scale, and was rapidly developing man's capacity to dominate nature. Secondly, the alienated social conditions of capitalism create the basis for the 'universal development of the individual' (see Reading 13), and through this a basis for the subordination of men's social conditions to their own conscious collective control.

Marx believes that only such universally developed individuals are fully capable of exercising this control. His point would seem to be that individuals cannot consciously dominate their social relationships until they understand them in relation to their needs, and they cannot so understand them until they universally participate in them and thus become universal producers (both materially and intellectually). Only in this situation can society cease to be a mystery confronting individuals as a system of independent alien powers. Capitalism is thus seen as creating the condition for the third stage described in Reading 6, that of 'free individuality'.

Marx's support for proletarian revolution is based on this argument. He sees the working class as the only social agency which has the power, the

5. For Marx's use of this concept, see below pp. 25–6.

interest and the capability to change society in this direction. It has the power because it forms the majority in capitalist society; it has the interest because the contradictions of capitalism[6] lead to a deterioration in its economic and social position as a class; and it has the capability because its own organization as a class increasingly approximates to that of socialism. Thus Marx wrote his economics in the hope that it would hasten the proletariat's conscious decision to overthrow capitalism.

An evaluation

It is impossible in the confines of the space available here to attempt any systematic evaluation of Marx's ideas. This is particularly true of the materialist conception of history, the aspect which has received most critical attention and ideally requires the most detailed consideration. In practice, however, Marx's critique of capitalism in terms of alienation, and his sociological method of economic analysis are more important in any critical assessment of modern capitalism and the orthodox economic theory which seeks to comprehend it. Therefore we limit ourselves to these two aspects of Marx's ideas, and merely point out here that even the greatest critics of the materialist conception of history, like Weber and Schumpeter, have also recognized it as a major contribution to social science.

Marx's theory of alienation seems to us as meaningful and relevant today as it was in Marx's time. There appear to be three limited attempts to answer this critique but, as far as we are aware, no intellectually satisfactory liberal answer has appeared.

Firstly, as we have seen, Marx's critique is based on a view of what men have the potential to become: a view many would regard as somewhat utopian (see, for example, Aron, 1965). Obviously an assessment of Marx's critique can be directly tied to one's view on this question. But to devalue Marx's critique as insignificant on this ground would seem to imply that the alienation characteristic of modern capitalism is a *universal* aspect of the human condition in industrial societies. To admit otherwise attributes some degree of validity to Marx's critique.

Orthodox economists are, in the main, unaware of the question of alienation; those who are apparently aware of it misunderstand Marx's argument (see, for example, Blaug, 1968, pp. 275–6). It is true, however, that a more positive liberal defence of capitalism, held by both economists and other social scientists, rests on the propositions of neoclassical welfare economics (Macpherson, 1972). Yet these propositions cannot be made applicable to either historical or modern variants of capitalism except on the most restrictive assumptions, which are not empirically realistic or even reasonable approximations to reality (see below, pp. 19–21). And, even if

6. On these, see Readings 19–22 and pp. 32–43 below.

they could be established, this defence itself would be of limited relevance against Marx's critique as it is devoid of a utilitarian basis.

Thirdly, there is an answer to Marx embodied in such modern classics as Berlin (1958) and Popper (1945). Berlin's famous essay, which defends the bourgeois conception of freedom (or, as he terms it, negative freedom) against the conception of Marx (and other theorists of what he terms positive freedom), is fatally flawed. It takes the wholly illegitimate position of regarding ideas as independent forces having an autonomous momentum of their own. As such, ideas are divorced from the social and economic structures which in fact give them their historical role, and can be manipulated into any causal factor that prejudice requires. Ideas of 'positive freedom' are seen to culminate in authoritarian and totalitarian social structures. Bourgeois freedom and its social context (capitalism) are in consequence defended by an exceptionally flimsy negative argument. Popper's similar argument falls even more clearly into the same category.

The method of neoclassical economic theory – which is still the dominant theoretical system of orthodox analysis – differs very considerably from that of Marx. However, Marxists who have asserted that neoclassical analysis abstracts from social relations, and attack it on this ground, overstate their case. Neoclassical economics *does* deal with social relationships. It is in fact difficult to conceive of *any* economic analysis which could avoid (at some stage) reference to relations between economic actors. Marxists are objecting to – or rather should be objecting to – the *way* in which neoclassical economics incorporates social relationships, for there is much in neoclassical economics to criticize from the standpoint of Marx's own methodological procedure.

Irrespective of the sophistication of either the model or the theorist, and no matter what particular branch of theory one views, neoclassical analysis rests on three main assumptions. Firstly it is assumed that actors' preferences are exogenous; secondly that actors are rational; and thirdly that interaction takes place in an environment characterized by perfect knowledge.

Presumably few neoclassicals believe that preferences are in fact exogenous to the operation of the economic system, as this is in obvious conflict with sociological research and everyday experience. Often the exclusion seems to be justified on the ground that the theory is 'general', and so must abstract from any particular structure of preferences. *Prima facie* this is a reasonable defence, but it is *not* valid, as the conclusions drawn from this assumption show.

This applies most clearly to neoclassical welfare economics, which assesses the efficiency of economic structures in terms of their fulfilment of preferences. The theoretical recognition of the socially endogenous nature of preferences undermines its logic, for efficiency can be evaluated only if the standards of judgement (the preference structures) are independent of what is being judged (the economic structures). Marx's theory of freedom and alienation is clearly not open to this objection.

The second assumption, rationality, may also be questioned, not only because it is untrue of important areas of economic activity, or because the neoclassical concept of rationality is often empty (as can be seen if one tries to find a case of someone *not* attempting to maximize utility).[7] It is faulty also because the mechanism of this rational orientation is confined to particular kinds of action patterns: namely, to those which result in individual exchange. These, however, are not the patterns which rational action takes in certain crucial economic areas.

Consider, for example, an important point made by Marx which is particularly relevant to the operation of modern capitalism.

> As soon as ... adverse circumstances prevent the creation of an industrial reserve army and with it the absolute dependence of the working class upon the capitalist class, capital ... rebels against the 'sacred' law of supply and demand, and tries to check its inconvenient action by forcible means and State interference (*Capital* I, p. 640; see also Dobb, 1963, p. 23ff).

This is a form of rational action which is *neither* individualistic *nor* involves exchange. But, to be able to deal with it, the theory itself must incorporate the historically specific relations of capitalist economies; it is only in these terms that the capitalist State can be understood (see Miliband, 1969).

This, however, is data from which neoclassical 'high theory' more or less consciously abstracts, but rarely (if at all) brings back into the analysis at the 'lower' level. Overall, rationality may be an appropriate simplifying assumption in the analysis of capitalism at a fairly abstract level, particularly with respect to the ruling class, and Marx himself makes this assumption; but the neoclassical economists, unlike Marx, work with a strangely limited conception that is most unsuitable for studying the actual functioning of economic systems.

The third assumption, perfect knowledge, is crucial for neoclassical theory, as Blaug rightly notes: 'its fundamental theorems rest upon the assumption of perfect certainty' (Blaug, 1968, p. 471). This is sometimes explicitly stated by neoclassical economists,[8] but more often than not is, somewhat carelessly, left implicit. Doubtless it may, in certain contexts, be

7. Or, more correctly, in the absence of perfect knowledge, *expected* utility, which is by no means the same thing.

8. Or it is expressed in terms of assumptions which ensure that the model relates to a world which operates 'as if' there were perfect certainty.

a useful simplification, especially in the analysis of economies which change slowly and are relatively isolated from world history.[9]

In analysing a *capitalist* economy, however, it is extremely doubtful whether it is a useful simplification. The very organization of capitalism, as a multitude of autonomous competing capitals, *creates* uncertainty. The mechanism through which uncertainty operates in a capitalist economy is the expectations of the capitalist – an agent with no explicit place in neoclassical high theory. As such the significance of uncertainty lies primarily in explaining those processes which move the system 'away from equilibrium which are inherent in an individualistic economy, as they were stressed by Marx, by contrast with the tendencies *towards* equilibrium which the Ricardian school had emphasized, and further on the fact that such ruptures of equilibrium themselves play an active and not merely a passive role with regard to the future' (Dobb, 1937, p. 218).

Thus Marx's specification of social relationships is much superior to neoclassical theory, because it relates to the *historically specific* relationships of capitalism. Nevertheless, neoclassical economics might still be defended by the argument that it can solve practical economic problems.

As the examples which we have given indicate, however, neoclassical analysis is weak even according to this criterion. To take another example, neoclassical general equilibrium theory is recognized by its modern frontiersmen to be of very limited usefulness. Its main achievement now seems its rigorous demonstration of *what cannot be said* about the neoclassical fairy-tale world of rational individual actions (see Hahn, 1973, also Harcourt, 1974). This is not very helpful if the appropriateness of such a model is rejected in the first place.

The more simple aggregate forms of neoclassical theory – in terms of the aggregate production function and the aggregate rate of return on investment – appeared more practical until they were undermined by the reswitching and capital-reversing debates of the 1960s.[10] Much the same could be said of the lower-level application of neoclassical theory to particular problem areas, for example, the theory of the firm (Andrews, 1964), the operation of labour markets (Gordon, 1972), and, especially, welfare economics (Graaf, 1957).

There is one practical task, however, in which neoclassical economics

9. Such economic structures have now been destroyed, or are in the process of destruction, largely as a result of the development of capitalism itself (see Reading 23).

10. See Harcourt (1972). It is significant that these problems have arisen precisely because no attention was paid to the principle of historical specificity. As Marx argued in a different, but related, context, the historically specific concept 'capital' should not be confused with the historically unspecific concept 'means of production'. Confusion of these two concepts leads to all manner of logical traps (see *Capital* III, part 7; Bhaduri, 1969).

does excel: namely, apologetics, irrespective of the motivations and the honesty of its proponents. Marx repeatedly emphasized the importance and also the effectiveness of neoclassical economics as an apologia. This remains true today, as Joan Robinson (1971, pp. 143–4) notes:

> Modern capitalism has no purpose except to keep the show going . . . National economic success is identified with statistical GNP. No questions are asked about the content of production. The success of modern capitalism for the last twenty-five years has been bound up with the armaments race and the trade in weapons (not to mention wars when they are used); it has not succeeded in overcoming poverty in its own countries, and has not succeeded in helping (to say the least) to promote development in the Third World. Now we are told that it is in the course of making the planet uninhabitable even in peace time.
>
> It should be the duty of economists to do their best to enlighten the public about the economic aspects of these menacing problems. They are impeded by a theoretical scheme which (with whatever reservations and exceptions) represents the capitalist world as a kibbutz operated in a perfectly enlightened manner to maximize the welfare of all its members.

As a by-product of this apologia, neoclassical theory mystifies what limited sociological content it has by attempting to reduce social relations to the form of relationships between things, and relationships between men and things. In Marx's language, neoclassical theory suffers from fetishism (see also below, pp. 23–4).

All this is not an argument against abstract theory *per se*, or a suggestion that Marx's economic theory provides a feasible alternative theoretical system. Abstract theory has a necessary role in our understanding of the economic world as a coherent whole. Certain aspects of Marx's economic analysis are extremely weak (see below, pp. 35–40), and can certainly be improved. As an orthodox ideology Marxism can also serve a conservative, apologetic function. But Marx does provide crucial methodological groundwork for enabling economists to tackle the crucial problems of the age precisely because these problems result from the structure of social relations. Neoclassical economics' ahistorical method is by the same token an impediment.

2 The labour theory of value
Value

These methodological considerations are crucial in Marx's analysis of the labour theory of value (LTV). As we have already seen (above, pp. 14–15), the theory is historically specific to commodity production. Within this context, Marx poses two questions. Firstly, what is the common social property shared by all commodities, which allows them to be reduced to a common denominator in exchange? Secondly, what determines the actual numerical ratios at which they are exchanged? These two questions represent respectively the 'qualitative' and the 'quantitative' problems of value; they are carefully distinguished by Sweezy (Reading 16).

We have already outlined Marx's answer to the first question (above, pp. 14–15). He defines the value of a commodity as the quantity of socially necessary labour required to produce it. But the Marxian LTV is not, as Sowell suggests, merely a matter of definition. Marx also attempts to solve the quantitative problem of value, and thus to provide an explanation of the actual ratios at which commodities exchange. In its simplest form, the quantitative LTV states that commodities exchange at ratios determined by the quantities of socially necessary labour embodied in them.

Distribution

The closely related question of income distribution may be approached in a similar way. Here the 'qualitative' problem is to explain how income is distributed, that is, to account for the income categories which are observed. Why is it, for example, that in capitalism (and only in capitalism) income is distributed as wages, profits, rent and interest? The 'quantitative' problem is to determine the *size* of the shares in net output which are paid in each category.

At this stage it is necessary to distinguish between the different species of the genus commodity production (see Meek, Reading 14; and above, pp. 13–14). *Simple* commodity production is classless: independent artisans and farmers own their means of production, and market their products themselves. In this case both problems of income distribution are easily solved. Income accrues only to the producers, and in direct proportion to the quantity of labour each performs. The only category of income is income from work; profit does not exist.

In capitalism the means of production are owned by a minority class who employ the producers as wage-labourers. Part of the net output accrues to the owners, and the categories of income distribution differ from those of simple commodity production even if the technical basis of production is identical. It is thus *only* the separation of the producers from the means of production, and the emergence of a propertied class, which alters the categories of distribution. Knowledge of the class structure of society is *all* that is necessary to solve the qualitative problem of distribution.

What Marx argues here is simply that property incomes derive from relations of property ownership. This seemingly innocuous statement is still disputed by many orthodox economists, as indeed is the qualitative LTV. Another form of fetishism is found in the attempts of economists to explain income distribution in capitalism as a result of the 'productivity' of the means of production themselves. This confuses the physical character-istics of *objects* with social relations between *people*. The means of produc-tion are technically productive in any society, but it is only in capitalism that they produce *profit*. Therefore they become *capital* only when they are privately owned by a minority class, and used to employ wage-labour. Thus 'capital is not a thing but rather a definite social production relation belonging to a definite historical formation of society, which is manifested in a thing, and lends that thing a specific social character' (*Capital* III, p. 814). Capital is thus a social relationship between owners and workers, embodied in and concealed by the historically specific nature of the means of production.

The category 'capital' illustrates a general feature of Marx's economic concepts, one which is unique to Marx and not easily comprehended from the viewpoint of orthodox economics. Like 'value', 'capital' refers simultaneously to social relations *and* to things. The specific nature of economic relations in all commodity-producing societies is such that they are also, at the same time, relations between commodities. This is one reason why Marx attributed such importance to commodity production in general, as a mode of production with important characteristics delineating it from other forms of social production (see above, pp. 13–15).

In most pre-capitalist societies the connection between property incomes and class domination is both clear and undeniable (see Marx, Reading 3; and Dobb, Reading 15, Section 1). In capitalism, however, it is hidden by the appearance of free competition and politico-legal equality. No one is openly forced to work, still less to work for nothing, like the feudal serf. Exchange relationships appear to be harmonious, resting on freedom of contract and unconstrained individual choice; the capitalist labour market appears as 'a very Eden of the innate rights of man' (*Capital* I, p. 176). The free wage bargain seems to show that every hour of work is paid for.

Despite this appearance, Marx argues, the reality of capitalist production is essentially similar to that of any class society: those who do not work live off the labour of those who do. Their claim on the surplus product takes various forms: profits to industrial capitalists, rent to landlords, and interest to money-lenders. But the aggregate surplus product stems from the performance of surplus labour, that is, labour over and above that necessary to sustain the worker and his family.

This is the point of departure for Marx's solution to the quantitative problem of distribution. 'Productive' technology is a necessary condition for the existence of capitalism itself: no property incomes, and no pro-pertied class, can exist at very low levels of productivity. It is not, however, a sufficient condition: the working day must be sufficiently long to allow the performance of surplus labour.

Marx argues that the capitalist labour market enforces, firstly, a subsistence standard of living for the worker and, secondly, a working day longer than is needed to produce the subsistence 'wage basket'. The mechanism giving rise to these conditions is the industrial reserve army of the unemployed, which we appraise below (pp. 39–40) in the context of Marx's theory of technical change. The capitalists' share in net output is simply the ratio of surplus to total (necessary plus surplus) labour performed. It will vary directly with the length of the working day, and with the productivity of labour in those industries which, directly or indirectly, produce wage-goods, an increase in which reduces necessary labour-time.

Marx and classical value theory

Marx's comprehensive study of classical political economy made him aware of important problems in the application of the LTV to capitalist society, and in the derivation of a coherent theory of exploitation. He was convinced that not even Ricardo, the most brilliant and consistent of the classical economists, had been able to settle four critical issues. These problems, and Marx's solutions to them, are lucidly developed by Shoul (Reading 17).

It is, firstly, a fundamental and distinctive characteristic of capitalism that labour itself has become a commodity, and is bought and sold in a free labour market. In free competition *all* commodities sell at their values,[11] and this must therefore be true of labour also. But if this is the case, two problems arise. Firstly, the LTV appears simply to replace one problem with another: if the values of commodities depend on the value of labour, on what does the value of labour itself depend? And, secondly, how can a *surplus* value, over and above the value of labour, accrue to the capitalists? How is the existence of property incomes consistent with a free labour market? Taken together, these two problems appear to prove that the LTV cannot be applied to capitalism. Marx's solution was to distinguish between the *activity* of 'labour', and the *commodity* 'labour-power'; it is labour-power, and not labour, which is bought and sold (at its value) in the 'labour market'. The difficulty now disappears, for the 'value of labour' is meaningless: 'as irrational as a yellow logarithm' (*Capital* III, p. 818).

The conflict between the LTV and the theory of exploitation also turns out to be apparent rather than real. The value of the worker's labour-power depends, like the values of other commodities, on the quantity of labour which is socially necessary to produce it; in this case to sustain the lives, and capacity for work, of the worker and his family. Thus, contrary

11. Abstracting for the moment from the third problem, which we discuss shortly.

to the claim made by Harris (Reading 20, p. 199), Marx does have a subsistence wage theory,[12] since this is implied by the postulate that the wage equals the value of labour-power. By working longer than the period required for this purpose, the worker is able to produce commodities with a value greater than that of his own labour-power.

The performance of this *surplus labour* is, as we have seen, concealed by the form of the wage-bargain in a free labour market. The crucial distinction between constant and variable capital is also hidden.[13] Constant capital, which Marx also refers to as 'dead' or 'stored-up' labour, consists of means of production like machinery and raw materials; it merely 'transfers' its value in the course of the production process. Variable capital, which he terms 'living labour', represents labour-power, and *expands* its value through the performance of surplus labour. This produces *surplus value* – the difference between the value of inputs and the value of outputs – and is thus the source of property incomes.

Marx had thus overcome the first two problems in the classical theory of value. The fourth concerned the theory of rent; here Marx's criticism of Ricardo is less well-founded. The LTV applies only to commodities which can be freely produced *and reproduced* by human labour. Land is thus excluded by definition from its domain, and a supply and demand theory of rent is all that is necessary, or possible (see Howard and King (1975), chapter 5, section 2).

The transformation problem

The third problem, which forms the basis of the famous 'transformation problem', is much more fundamental. Surplus value s is produced by the performance of surplus labour, and thus depends exclusively on the amount of labour-power employed; that is, on the quantity of variable capital v employed by the capitalist. If we assume free labour mobility, the rate of exploitation $\frac{s}{v} = e$ will be equal in all industries. But the ratio of means of production to labour $\frac{c}{v} = k$, which Marx terms the organic composition of capital, will normally differ between industries. But the rate of profit r

12. This is not a purely physiological minimum; the value of labour-power has both a natural and 'an historical and moral element' (*Capital* I, p. 171), and thus depends partly on prevailing social conditions.

13. Classical political economy developed a different, and less important distinction between fixed and circulating capital, based on differences in turnover rates rather than on the ability to produce surplus value. Marx's constant capital consists partly of fixed capital (machinery) and partly of circulating capital (raw materials); his variable capital is entirely of the circulating variety.

is simply $\dfrac{e}{k+1}$.[14] If k is not the same in all industries, then either it is true that the commodities sell at their labour values, or r is the same in all industries, but not both.

As Sowell observes, Marx realized the existence of this dilemma well before the publication of the first volume of *Capital* (see Reading 1, p. 65).[15] Ricardo had seen it as a major challenge to the LTV, and one to which he was unable to provide any answer consistent with the LTV. Marx applied to the problem his logical-historical method, and developed a solution which is simultaneously historical and logical (see Meek, Reading 14).

In simple commodity production there is no such problem, since neither capital, nor profit, nor the rate of profit exist, and the equalization of the rate of profit throughout the economy has no meaning. In the early stages of capitalism, intra-industry competition is strong enough to establish an equal rate of profit within each industry, but capital mobility is not sufficiently developed to prevent wide disparities in r between industries.

Only in mature capitalism are the barriers to capital mobility between industries eroded, so that competition equalizes the rate of profit throughout the economy. In contrast with Ricardo, Marx argues that this does not vitiate the LTV. He makes the bold step of asserting that long-run equilibrium prices diverge *systematically* from labour values; and that, precisely because these divergences are systematic, they can be analysed from the standpoint of the LTV itself. Commodities produced under conditions of above-average organic composition of capital will sell at 'prices of production' which exceed their labour values; and conversely commodities produced with a below-average organic composition will sell below their labour values. Only in those industries where k equals the average for the economy as a whole will the price of production equal value. Marx's formulation and solution of the 'transformation problem' was intended to demonstrate that the LTV need only be *modified*, and

14. The rate of profit is the ratio of surplus value to total capital employed; that is,

$$r = \frac{s}{c+v}.$$ Dividing top and bottom by v, we get $r = \dfrac{\dfrac{s}{v}}{\dfrac{c}{v}+1} = \dfrac{e}{k+1}.$

Further problems, which we do not consider, arise if the rates of turnover of capital differ between industries.

15. See, for example, the *Grundrisse*, pp. 435–6, written in December 1857 or January 1858; and, as Sowell observes, numerous places in *Theories of Surplus Value*, again written before the publication of the first volume of *Capital*.

could be used as a coherent basis for a theory of long-run equilibrium price, even in mature capitalism.

Marx's claims were, indeed, even stronger than this. He suggested that the rate of profit is completely determined by the LTV, as a ratio of quantities of embodied labour, and will be unaffected by the transformation of commodity values into prices of production. To substantiate this claim he tried to show that two 'invariance conditions' are maintained: firstly, that the sum of values equals the sum of prices of production; and, secondly, that the sum of surplus value equals the sum of profits obtained by the sale of commodities at these prices of production.

If these two conditions hold, the sum of constant and variable capital ($c+v$) will also be the same in both value and price terms. This will give, with the second invariance condition, a rate of profit identical both before and after the transformation. The economic significance of the invariance conditions is thus greater than their purely mathematical relevance; on mathematical grounds, only one condition is required, and it is a matter of indifference which is used (see Seton, Reading 18, p. 167).

Marx's procedure may be illustrated in an example used by Seton (Reading 18, p. 172). This uses the three Marxian 'departments' of the economy: I produces means of production, II produces wage-goods, and III produces luxuries for capitalists' consumption. When all magnitudes are expressed in terms of labour values, the system is as in Table 1. Here

Table 1 **The value system**

	c	v	s	Value $(c+v+s)$	Organic composition $k = \dfrac{c}{v}$	Rate of profit $r = \dfrac{s}{c+v}$
Department I	80	20	20	120	4·0	20%
Department II	10	25	25	60	0·4	72%
Department III	30	15	15	60	2·0	33%
Total/Average	120	60	60	240	2·0	33%

e is 100% in all three departments, but k varies from 4·0 (in Department I) to 0·4 (in Department II). Thus r ranges from 20% (in I) to 72% (in II). In mature capitalism, competition will ensure that the *average* rate of profit (in our example, 33%) will be paid in all sectors. Following Marx, we may transform labour values into a set of prices of production which equalizes the rate of profit in all three departments at the average level of 33%; these are shown in Table 2.

Table 2 Marx's (provisional) price system

	c	v	Cost-price (c+v)	r	Price of production (c+v) (1+r)	Profit r(c+v)
Department I	80	20	100	33%	133·3	33·3
Department II	10	25	35	33%	46·7	11·7
Department III	30	15	45	33%	60·0	15·0
Total/Average	120	60	180	33%	240·0	60·0

Here the price of production exceeds value, and profit exceeds surplus value, in Department I, where k is greater than the average; and the reverse is true of Department II. But the output of constant capital, which is now 133·3, is greater than the total *input* of constant capital (which remains at 120; input values have *not* been transformed). And the output of wage-goods is less than the input of variable capital. Marx's prices of production cannot, therefore, be equilibrium prices.

It is therefore necessary to transform *input* as well as output values into prices of production (see Dobb, Reading 15, p. 136).[16] Bortkiewicz (1907) provided a method by which this might be done. Seton's article provides formal proofs of the validity and the limitations of the Bortkiewicz procedure; Reading 18 is the definitive statement of this approach to the transformation problem. A full solution to our numerical example yields a ratio of price of production to value of 6:5 in Department I; of 3:5 in Department II; and, since this department has the average organic composition of capital, of 1:1 in III. The correct price system can thus be written in Table 3. Here both invariance conditions are satisfied, and the rate of profit is the same as the average in the value system of Table 1.

Table 3 Correct price system

	c	v	Cost-price (c+v)	r	Price of production (c+v) (1+r)	Profit r(c+v)
Department I	96	12	108	33%	144	36
Department II	12	15	27	33%	36	9
Department III	36	9	45	33%	60	15
Total/Average	144	36	180	33%	240	60

16. Marx appears to have realized that this was necessary, but to have been unwilling or unable to do so (see *Capital* III, pp. 161, 164–5).

Moreover, the requirements for sectoral balance are met: the sums of constant and variable used are equal to the sums of constant and variable capital produced, so that output prices equal input prices. These prices of production, unlike Marx's, are genuine long-run equilibrium prices.

But this example, quite deliberately, illustrates a special case (Seton, Reading 18, p. 172). The organic composition in Department III is equal to the average for the economy as a whole, so that the price of production of luxury commodities equals their labour value. This is clearly a necessary condition, in simple reproduction, for the sum of the surplus values to equal the sum of the profits. If this condition is not fulfilled, then only *one* of Marx's invariance conditions can be satisfied, and the rate of profit in the value system will not be equal to that in the price system. Now there is no reason why the organic composition in Department III should equal the social average. It is thus tempting to conclude that Marx's claims for the quantitative LTV are valid only in this special case when Department III's organic composition is equal to the social average.[17]

Such a conclusion would, however, be quite wrong, as Dobb suggests (Reading 15, p. 138). Following Sraffa (1960), Meek (1967, pp. 161–78) and Medio (1972) have shown that the transformation problem can be reformulated so as to provide a complete solution which does not rest on the existence of an average ratio of means of production to labour in any one sector. A *composite* numeraire can be constructed from fractions of all the 'basic' industries[18] in the economy, and this can be used to transform values into prices, satisfying *both* Marx's invariance conditions. More than a century after Marx wrote Volume III of *Capital*, his claim that a solution can be found to the transformation problem (though not his own solution itself) has been fully vindicated.

An assessment

As Seton's concluding paragraph to Reading 18 suggests, however, this is not by itself enough to rescue the LTV from its critics. The internal coherence of the theory may be secure enough, but is it really *necessary*? This question is discussed, briefly but provocatively, by Sowell, Reading 1, Section 4 (see also Sowell, 1963).

It is clear, firstly, that an ethical condemnation of capitalism is quite distinct from the theory of value, and that Marx neither intended nor

17. Though in the weaker sense in which it is interpreted, as providing merely a theory of relative prices, only *one* invariance condition is necessary, and this conclusion would be excessively critical. See Seton, Reading 18, p. 167.

18. A 'basic' industry is one which produces a commodity used, directly or indirectly, as an input in all other industries. Marx's Department III, for example, produces non-basics.

needed the LTV as a support for his revolutionary perspective. Nor is the theory a necessary condition for the development of an exploitation theory of property incomes, which, as we have seen, can be derived directly from the study of the underlying class relations of capitalist society (see also Dobb, Reading 15, p. 133).

Nor is the quantitative LTV merely a matter of definition, as Sowell seems to suggest. If meaningful statements are to be made about trends in class shares in total net output – a question which plays a vital part in Marx's analysis of economic growth – then some means of *measuring* surplus value is necessary. Sowell overstates his case in arguing that, 'since "surplus value" is simply the difference between wages and the worker's average product, it would remain unchanged under a marginal productivity theory of wages in a perfectly competitive market' (Reading 1, p. 71). We have already seen that the analysis of income distribution in terms of 'factor productivity' is methodologically absurd, and reflects a particularly crude form of the fallacy of commodity fetishism.

The aggregate production function version of neoclassical distribution theory[19] is in any case logically defective. It has been shown that 'capital' cannot be defined independently of prices, and that the rate of profit is equal to the 'marginal productivity of capital' only in the special case where the 'capital–labour ratio' is equal in all industries (Harcourt and Laing, 1971, Part Five; Hunt and Schwartz, 1972, Part Three).

Ironically enough, this case is equivalent to that of equal organic compositions in all industries. As we have seen, Marx's analysis of the transformation of labour values into prices of production can cope with the *general* case in which organic compositions differ; aggregate neoclassical theory, at least, cannot. Aggregate neoclassical theory is thus less satisfactory than the LTV for reasons of methodology *and* internal coherence; and there is nothing to be gained from formulating the theory of exploitation in its terms.

The quantitative LTV may thus be viewed as a useful measuring rod for the valuation of economic magnitudes. As we shall see in Section 3 of this introduction, this is how Marx himself uses the theory. It might still be asked, however, whether the Marxian version of the LTV could not be replaced by a Sraffian formulation in which prices of production are determined directly by commodity and labour input coefficients, without the 'complicating detour' (Samuelson, 1957, p. 892)[20] of labour values. There seems to us to be no compelling reason why this should not be done,

19. There are two other variants of neoclassical theory. The first, based on the concept of the 'rate of return on investment', suffers from similar difficulties. The second, general equilibrium theory, is subject to other difficulties; see Harcourt (1974).

20. See also Samuelson (1971) and (1972) ,where this point is elaborated.

since – as Medio (1972) has shown – the two approaches are formally equivalent, and Sraffa's is the simpler and more elegant.

Sraffa, however, explicitly rejects the notion of the subsistence wage, and leaves open the quantitative question of income distribution. Any realistic appraisal of the evidence on real wages in advanced capitalist countries must result in the conclusion that Marx's equation of wages with the value of labour-power is redundant.[21] This means that there is no longer a Marxian explanation of the size of class shares in net output, and it is notable that Sraffa's disciples have been ready to admit as much.

On methodological grounds, however, both Marx and Sraffa are in substantial agreement. For both it is the relations of *production*, and not the relations of exchange, which play the crucial role in the theory of value. Neither has any truck with utility or marginal productivity, and both attempt to penetrate the appearances of market phenomena to the underlying reality.

Both approaches are subject to one further, very important qualification. In both models it is assumed that there are strong competitive forces tending to equalize rates of profit throughout the economy. The essence of *monopoly*, however, is that capital mobility is impeded, so that rates of profit will *not* be equalized. Sraffa has nothing, and Marx very little, to say about the implications of monopoly, and it may be that the LTV itself (at least in its quantitative sense) is historically specific to the competitive phase of capitalist evolution. Certainly Marx's theory of economic development, to which we now turn, rests on the assumption of generalized free competition.[22]

3 The theory of economic development

The fundamental purpose of Marx's political economy was 'to lay bare the economic law of motion of modern society' (*Capital* I, p. 10). He rejected the implicit assumption of the classical economists that the life-span of capitalism was infinite, and their explicit claim that it would tend to a stable and permanent 'stationary state' with a zero growth rate. Marx's dialectical view of the laws of capitalist economic development is lucidly described by Sowell (Reading 1, pp. 49–55). It led him, not to a mechanistic

21. Unless one is prepared to *define* the value of labour-power as the average wage prevailing at any given time; but this is stretching the 'moral and historical element' in subsistence rather too far, and renders the theory tautological.

22. This is despite the importance which he attaches to the concentration and centralization of capital (see *Capital* I, chapters 25, 32). It should be noted that labour values are independent of demand only if commodity and labour input coefficients are invariant with respect to the level of output of each commodity. But Marx's analysis of the growth of monopoly (*Capital* I, chapters 25, 32) is in terms of 'increasing returns to scale'. Labour values are thus independent of demand, if at all, only in the long run.

'breakdown' theory of economic decay, but to an analysis of the economic contradictions of the system which would transform it from within and eventually lead to its destruction by social revolution.

Marx's account of these contradictions differs in another significant respect from the classical analysis of the barriers to economic growth. Ricardo had predicted a long-run tendency for the rate of profit to fall as a result of diminishing returns in agriculture. The 'niggardliness of nature' represented a *natural* law, in principle applicable to all types of society, which would eventually usher in the stationary state. As we have seen, it is a cardinal feature of Marx's methodology that economic laws must be historically and socially specific. This principle forms the basis of his analysis of the economic contradictions of capitalist society.

Marx's discussion of these problems is scattered throughout his major economic works, and is never integrated into a coherent and systematic whole. It is, however, possible to distinguish two clear strands in his argument. The first concerns the ability of an unplanned capitalist economy to achieve a stable equilibrium growth path. Marx demolishes Say's law, proving (two generations ahead of his time) that generalized over-production is both possible and, in capitalism, highly likely. In conjunction with his analysis of aggregate demand, Marx's theory of economic growth shows how these problems may be induced by 'disproportionalities' in the growth process itself. The second aspect of Marx's analysis of capitalist economic development deals with the nature and effects of technical change. These two lines of thought are developed independently of each other, but are integrated (in an unsystematic and fragmentary fashion) in Marx's account of economic crises. We consider each of these three topics in turn.

Say's law, reproduction and growth

Marx's critique of Say's law is presented by Tsuru (Reading 19). It rests on a clear distinction, made neither by classical political economy nor (in general) by modern orthodox theorists, between three types of economic structure: barter, simple commodity production, and capitalism.

In a barter economy it is inevitably true that 'supply creates its own demand'. Products are exchanged *directly* for each other, without the mediation of money. It is thus impossible to be a 'seller' without also being a 'buyer'. Once commodities are produced, however, the resulting use of money drives a wedge between sale and purchase, and the *possibility* of deficient aggregate demand exists. The circulation process in commodity-producing economies takes the form: COMMODITIES–MONEY–COMMODITIES (C–M–C), rather than a direct exchange of products (P–P). It is now possible for a seller to hold money for a while, instead of making an immediate purchase of other commodities. Thus aggregate demand may be inadequate to allow the sale of all commodities at their values, so that over-production results.

In simple commodity production, however, this is unlikely to occur. Production is undertaken to satisfy the personal consumption needs of the producer and his family, and market sales will normally be made only in order to acquire other commodities. It is only in *capitalism* that over-production becomes very likely. Production is now controlled by capitalists, whose aim is the accumulation of capital rather than personal consumption. Circulation takes the form MONEY–COMMODITIES–COMMODITIES–MONEY ($M-C-C'-M'$). Money capital is used to buy means of production and labour-power, which are converted in the production process into other commodities, of a greater value; the difference between C' and C represents the surplus value which has been produced. This surplus value must be *realized* by the sale of the commodities; the difference between M' and M represents the surplus value in money form.

Thus capitalists' purchases of labour-power and means of production are dependent on the *profitability* of investment. Should it appear to them, for whatever reason, that profitability is threatened, capitalists are likely to hoard money instead of purchasing and employing constant and variable capital. Aggregate demand will then be inadequate to allow the sale of all commodities at their values (or prices of production), and it will prove impossible to realize through the sale of commodities all the surplus value (or profit) produced and contained in them. In these conditions a partial crisis, which might occur in one industry as a result of a disproportionality between different sectors of the economy, may depress capitalists' expectations of profitability and become a *generalized* realization crisis, or crisis of over-production.

Marx's schema of reproduction and accumulation are rigorously examined, and extended, by Harris (Reading 20). They form a highly abstract and deliberately 'unrealistic' piece of formal analysis. Marx ignores the transformation of values into prices of production,[23] and assumes that there is no technical change. Important aspects of capitalist reality are thus set aside, in order that others may be clearly exposed.

Marx's purpose in developing a highly formal growth model is twofold: to show that equilibrium growth in capitalism is not impossible; and to suggest that it is extremely improbable that such a growth path will actually prevail. Instability, Marx argues, is the most probable outcome of the accumulation of capital, even without aggravation by technical change.

23. This is incorporated into the model in Section 4 of Harris's article.

Harris's model, like the majority of Marx's own numerical examples, comprises two sectors rather than the three departments of the analysis of transformation. Department I produces means of production, and is the source of constant capital for itself and for Department II; the latter produces consumer goods, which serve as variable capital and as an outlet for surplus ·value (through capitalists' consumption spending) in both departments. The 'supply' and 'demand' for each type of commodity must be equal if equilibrium is to prevail, either in simple reproduction (with a zero rate of saving and of growth) or in expanded reproduction, where part of surplus value is invested and the growth rate is positive.

The resulting sectoral balance conditions are given by Harris in his equations 8 and 14. They represent a formalization of those implicitly derived, for three departments, in our discussion of transformation (above, pp. 26–30). These conditions may be expressed, as in Harris's equations 8a and 14a, as requiring a definite ratio between the quantity of variable capital in the two departments.

Marx demonstrates the implications of these conditions in his numerical analysis of expanded reproduction (*Capital* II, Chapter 21). If variable capital is not advanced in the required proportions, growth is disrupted by an imbalance between the demand and the supply of each type of commodity. A planning agency could take account of, and avert, such a disproportionality in the levels of output of the two departments. But this is impossible in a competitive capitalist economy in which there is no conscious social regulation of production. In fact, as we have suggested, disproportionality is likely to lead to a generalized crisis of over-production. Thus Marx concludes that, in a capitalist economy, equilibrium growth is a fortuitous and improbable occurrence.

As Harris observes, Marx had in effect produced a more sophisticated, two-sector version of the modern Harrod–Domar theory of economic growth (Reading 20, p. 197). It is a rather constricted model; given Marx's abstraction from the transformation problem, there is no mobility of capital between the two departments, so that the capitalists of each sector can only invest in their own department. Allowance for inter-departmental capital mobility would increase the possibility of stable equilibrium growth. Marx's model, like Harrod–Domar's, also fails to specify the determinants of the capitalists' savings propensities, which must be known in order to calculate the rate of accumulation.

Technical change

Unlike the Keynesian growth models to which Harris refers, however, Marx does not 'explain' the rate of accumulation in terms of the 'animal spirits' of the capitalists; this is an ahistorical evasion of the problem. In competitive capitalism it is technical progress which *compels* the accumulation of capital, and is a major factor in sustaining the subjective preference for accumulation which, as we have seen above, pp. 12–14, is a prominent and unique feature of capitalist society.

Marx makes a clear and important distinction between 'manufacture' and 'modern industry' (see Sweezy, 1968). The former involves an increasing division of labour but a low degree of mechanization, and is characteristic of the early stages of industrialization. 'The end of manufacture is the beginning of big business, of mechanization, and of accumulation of capital' (Heertje, Reading 22, p. 221). These three developments are, in turn, very closely related.

Mechanization brings massive economies of scale, and leads to a rapid increase in both plant size and industrial concentration.[24] The new mechanized techniques must be embodied in new equipment, so that rapid accumulation is a necessary condition for their introduction. This is not a matter of choice for the individual capitalist, but a necessity. Technical progress lowers costs and (eventually) prices, so that continuous innovation and accumulation are a condition for the survival of each capitalist. This is why no actual capitalist economy can exist in a state of simple reproduction, and why the abstraction from technical change is an unrealistic (though heuristically useful) feature of Marx's analysis of expanded reproduction.

Marx's analysis of technical change forms the basis for two of his most important economic laws: the tendency for the rate of profit to fall; and the tendency for the industrial reserve army of the unemployed (RAU) to increase in the course of economic development. Both are analysed on the assumption that realization problems are absent, and that the economy is on an equilibrium growth path. The effects of technical change are thus *logically* (though not, of course, actually) independent of disproportionality and over-production.

The tendency for the rate of profit to decline played the dominant role in Ricardo's theory of economic development, but his analysis assumed the *absence* of technical change. The existence of diminishing returns in agriculture, in conjuction with a Malthusian theory of the subsistence wage, was shown to imply that the rate of profit would fall steadily, probably to zero,[25] and lead to the onset of the stationary state. In so far as

24. Marx terms the former 'concentration' and the latter 'centralization' of capital.
25. He allowed a small risk premium; and technology might be such that, even with diminishing returns, the rate of profit (net of the risk premium) would not fall to zero. See Pasinetti (1960).

technical progress featured at all in Ricardo's model, it was an *offsetting* factor which might allow a temporary respite from the effects of diminishing returns.

Marx's analysis, in contrast, is based on increasing rather than decreasing labour productivity. He treats productivity growth as equivalent to an increase in the quantity of 'dead labour' (constant capital) processed in a given period by each unit of 'living labour' (variable capital); that is, as equivalent to an increase in the organic composition of capital. We have seen that the rate of profit, $r = \dfrac{e}{k+1}$, where e is the rate of exploitation and k the organic composition (above, p. 27). If there is a constant subsistence wage, a productivity increase must raise e, which reflects the share of profits in net output. In order to demonstrate that r will fall as a result of technical progress, Marx must therefore prove that e will rise less rapidly than k.

Meek (Reading 21) shows that Marx recognized the existence of this problem, and that he cannot be criticised for illicitly holding e constant in his analysis. But the actual trend in r depends on the relationship between e and k, which Marx was unable to specify with any precision. Meek's numerical examples show that r may initially *increase* as k rises, and suggest certain conditions under which an increasing rate of profit may be substantial and persistent (Reading 21, pp. 215–16). Even if we assume that technical change *necessarily* increases k (which we shall shortly question), Marx's argument can be treated only as a tentative statement of a potentially important trend.

It is open to a further, more fundamental objection. Marx argues that technical progress leads to a declining rate of profit with a *constant* wage. But this is not possible. A technical improvement must increase either r or the wage; if it leads to a decline in r, the wage must *increase* as a result (Samuelson 1957, 1972; Okishio, 1963). Thus Marx cannot consistently predict *both* a falling rate of profit *and* a constant (still less a falling) wage. This, as we shall shortly see, carries serious implications for his analysis of the RAU.

Meek also observes that Marx failed to prove that technical progress necessarily increases k; that is, to prove that the 'cheapening of the elements of constant capital', which Marx treated as a factor offsetting the fall in r, will not in practice be sufficient to maintain (or even reduce) k as technology changes. Heertje (Reading 22) provides a formal, though partial, foundation for this criticism.

Marx distinguishes between the *technical* and the *value* composition of capital. The former represents a ratio of physical input coefficients (for example machines per man). In Heertje's notation, the sectoral technical compositions are $\frac{b_i}{a_i}$ $(i = 1,2)$.[26] It follows from Marx's definition of technical progress that these must increase, whatever is the form taken by technical change. But the economically relevant concept is that of the value composition, the ratio of the value of constant capital to the value of variable capital. There is no reason to suppose that this must always increase as the technical composition increases.[27]

Heertje assumes a given and equal rate of profit in both departments, so that his analysis is conducted in terms of prices of production rather than values. On this basis he derives formulae for the sectoral and overall organic compositions (Reading 22, p. 225). Section 6 of his article considers the simplest possible case of Marxian technical progress, in which direct labour input coefficients fall while the unit input requirements of means of production remain constant. Since $\frac{b_i}{a_i}$ is increasing, the technical composition is rising in both departments. Heertje shows, however, that this will lead to an increase in k in price terms for the economy as a whole only if labour productivity grows more rapidly in Department II that in Department I. If the reverse is true, the price organic composition will fall.

The limitations of Heertje's analysis are (inevitably) quite severe. In the first place, it might be possible for b_i to rise, so that the quantity of means of production required to produce a unit of output increased in each department; this would be consistent with the existence of technical *progress* so long as a_i declined. Secondly, Heertje assumes that r is constant. This greatly simplifies his analysis, but at a heavy cost: we have already seen that technical change is almost certain to have *some* effect on the rate of profit. As Meek admits of his own numerical examples, 'the problem obviously cries out for mathematical treatment' (Reading 21, p. 215).

To the best of our knowledge there exists no *general* mathematical treatment of the problems encountered here.[28] Any such analysis would be highly complex. It would require the *simultaneous* determination, in the context of technical change, of k, e, r and commodity exchange-ratios, all

26. For the economy as a whole, these must be weighted by the outputs of the two sectors, to give (again in Heertje's notation) $\dfrac{b_1 K + b_2 Y}{a_1 K + a_2 Y}$.

27. Moreover, in a model in which more than one commodity is used as a means of production (constant capital), the technical composition of capital has no meaning at all. The numerator is made up of input coefficients relating to diverse commodities measured in equally diverse units, and the composition of capital can *only* be measured in value terms.

28. Though see Steedman (1971) for a mathematical formulation of Marx's arguments.

in terms both of labour values and prices of production.[29] Without it, however, both Marx's own analysis of the effects of technical progress on the organic composition of capital, and subsequent criticism, must remain inconclusive.

These problems reflect equally on Marx's theory of the RAU. An increase in the value composition of capital means that the rate of growth of constant capital is greater than that of variable capital; the expansion of employment is slower than the growth in the use of means of production. Marx suggests that this will cause increasing unemployment over time which is independent of deficiencies in aggregate demand.

Marx's analysis of the RAU is one of the most central aspects of his theory of economic development. There is an important sense in which it underpins the labour theory of value. For Marx the long-run real wage is maintained at subsistence, not by any Malthusian principle, but by competition between workers in a situation of chronic excess labour supply, which is in turn induced by the growth of the RAU. Take away the RAU and there is no longer a mechanism to equate the wage with the value of labour-power. In a wider context, there is no doubt that Marx considered the RAU as one of the most important factors contributing to the growth of revolutionary class consciousness among the proletariat.

Marx's analysis of the RAU is basically concerned with the long run. He does not deny that cyclical fluctuations in the level of economic activity may result in occasional temporary declines in unemployment in booms (perhaps almost to vanishing point). It is quite clear, however, that he expected the long-run trend in the RAU to be an upward one. Our discussion of the effects of technical progress on the value composition of capital has already suggested that this need not necessarily occur.

Section 7 of Heertje's article takes this criticism further, and shows the conditions which are required if Marx's prediction is to be realized. They closely resemble Harrod's condition for equality between the 'warranted' and 'natural' growth rates. Only if the rate of accumulation is less than the sum of the rate of growth of labour productivity and of the supply of labour-power will the RAU increase; if the rate of accumulation is greater than this, the RAU will contract in the course of economic development.

Let us assume that there is no change in the relationship between the rate of accumulation and the rate of growth of labour productivity (which depends on the nature of technical change and the resulting change in k); and that the rate of growth of labour-power supply resulting from population growth is constant. We then have good reason to suppose that the RAU will in fact *decline* over time. The supply of labour-power does not

29. And, if we allowed *both* commodities to be used as means of production, it would be more complex still.

depend solely on population growth. In the early stages of capitalist development, there exists a vast reservoir of labour-power in the non-capitalist sectors of the economy. The decline of peasant agriculture and independent handicraft production furnishes a constant inflow of newly-created proletarians into the capitalist sector. But the relative importance of this inflow must eventually decline, as the pre-capitalist sector itself declines relatively to the capitalist sector. It then appears that Marx's analysis of the RAU is historically specific to the early stages of capitalist development.

Marx's theory of technical change, then, is suggestive rather than definitive. It cannot be doubted that innovation stimulates accumulation, or that both processes encourage the growth of industrial concentration. The emergence of oligopolistic and monopolistic market structures is thus, as Marx saw, an inevitable feature of capitalist development (see Heertje, Section 9).[30] But it is not certain that technical progress will increase the value composition of capital, nor that any such increase must lead to a growth in the RAU or to a fall in the rate of profit. It is not possible, moreover, for both these trends to prevail at once: an increase in the RAU is a sufficient condition for the real wage to remain constant, and means that innovation will raise the rate of profit; a fall in the rate of profit increases the wage, which must imply a contraction in the RAU. We must conclude that Marx's analysis of the economic contradictions of capitalism comes to rest heavily on his analysis of aggregate demand.

Cyclical crises

We now, therefore, consider Marx's theory of crises. In particular we are interested in the reasons why the possibility of crises which is apparent in commodity production in general becomes an actuality in capitalism. In the light of Tsuru (Reading 19), and of what we have said in the previous section, the crucial problem here is *why* changes in profitability occur which generate excess demand for money and send the system into a slump.

Sowell (Reading 1) shows that there are numerous references in Marx to what we now call random shocks, which trigger off general deficiencies in aggregate demand. Marx goes further than this, however, by arguing that cyclical movements are endogenous and periodic (see, for example, *Theory of Surplus Value* II, pp. 497–8; III, p. 36), although these are 'complicated by irregular oscillations' (*Capital* I, p. 637). Marx did not, then, accept a random disturbance theory of crises as the complete answer, and despite

30. Though it is not true, as Heertje claims, that free competition 'is hardly compatible with the general tenor of Marx's opinion' (Reading 22, p. 230). As we have seen (above, p. 32), the labour theory of value rests on precisely this assumption.

Sowell's discussion of periodicity this does not come out clearly in Reading 1.[31]

Thus for Marx the problem becomes that of finding those factors which through changes in profitability, generate crises as endogenous periodic phenomena. Marx regarded two factors as primarily important: firstly, those encompassed in his theory of the falling rate of profit; and, secondly, a theory of under-consumption. Neither, however, is at all fully developed, and both must be subject to a considerable degree of interpretation.

Contrary to Sowell's argument (Reading 1, pp. 62–4), Marx does refer to the falling rate of profit as a cause of crises (see, for example, *Capital* III, p. 242). Although the law is of a long-run nature, its operation is neither smooth nor regular (*Capital* I, pp. 613, 632–3; III, pp. 249, 263). Thus, although Marx's argument about the falling rate of profit is primarily worked out on the assumption of an equilibrium growth path, in linking it to crises he implies that capitalists react *as if* they experience realization difficulties, and as a result *actually produce them*; or they react to produce those difficulties in other ways (*Capital* III, pp. 250ff.).

Tsuru's argument in terms of under-consumption (Reading 19, pp. 179–84) clearly follows Marx, although Marx himself rightly saw the limitations of other under-consumptionist views. In the light of the passages in Marx on this aspect of his theory, Joan Robinson (1946, p. 49) has given a succinct summary of what he probably had in mind:

> Combined with the equations of reproduction ... [these passages suggest] that Marx intended to work out a theory on some such lines as this: consumption by the workers is limited by their poverty, while consumption by the capitalists is limited by the greed for capital which causes them to accumulate wealth rather than enjoy luxury. The demand for consumption goods ... is thus limited. But if the output of the consumption-good industries is limited by the market, the demand for capital goods ... is in turn restricted, for the constant capital of the consumption-good industries will not expand fast enough to absorb the potential output of the capital-good industries. Thus the distribution of income between wages and surplus is such as to set up a chronic tendency for a lack of balance between the two groups of industries.

The reproduction models emphasize that the interdependence of capital-good and consumption-good industries is a key factor determining the instability of capitalism, for any disproportionality between them would result in a

31. Sowell emphasizes that Marx's theory was one of 'disproportionality'. This is correct, but, as Marx realized, this does not take one very far. Although a disproportionality must arise at some point in every crisis, it can develop without generating a general crisis of over-production. Thus the real problem is to discover the mechanisms which lead to disproportions sufficiently large actually to generate general crises, and in particular to find within these mechanisms factors which account for the endogeneity and regularity of crises.

change in the profit rate which, if downward, could easily trigger off a general crisis. Marx suggests that it is the volatility of the demand for capital goods which is the primary initiating factor.

Marx's argument as to how a partial crisis can turn into a general crisis, and how a general crisis becomes intensified, is summarized well by Sowell (Reading 1, pp. 61–2). Underlying this argument is Marx's view that money provides the least uncertain store of value, or bridge between the present and the future. Thus, due to the anarchic character of the system, any large disruption becomes intensified rather than resulting in a smooth readjustment path. Sowell also presents Marx's theory of the lower turning-point and the periodicity of the cycle.[32]

There are clearly elements of considerable insight in Marx's theory of crises, as well as important limitations. Considering the limitations first, it is clear that any crisis theory framed in terms of Marx's long-run theory of the falling rate of profit is highly questionable (see Meek, Reading 21; and above, pp. 36–7). Moreover, neither this aspect of Marx's argument nor the theory of under-consumption which he developed give any precise theory of the upper turning-point, and are not at all related to one another. Marx's account of the lower turning-point and of periodicity also seems rather limited in the light of modern theory and of research into the significance of echo effects. However, the more specialized nature of the British economy and the extreme regularity of cyclical fluctuations in Marx's time may mean that they were more significant then than is usual.

Despite these reservations Marx was clearly on the track of the most important causal factors in cyclical fluctuations, and was certainly generations ahead of his time. His refutation of Say's law; his distinction between the 'possibility' of crises and their actual causes and symptoms; the emphasis he gave to endogeneity and periodicity; the key role he attributed to profit and deficiency in aggregate demand; and the special significance which he gave to money all bear witness to his achievements.

An assessment

Overall, then, we can say of Marx's macro-economics that, although it involved path-breaking and highly original elements of analysis, many of its most important propositions are highly questionable. This is certainly true of Marx's theory of the falling rate of profit, but it is especially true of his analysis of the industrial reserve army, which appears crucial to his theory of proletarian revolution as outlined in *Capital*. Marx's theory of crises, moreover, and despite its originality, is of limited relevance when used to demonstrate the contradictory nature of *modern* capitalism.

32. Although Marx does give other reasons besides 'echo effects'; see, for example, *Capital* III, pp. 233–5, 254–5; *Theories of Surplus Value* II, pp. 495–6.

This raises a more fundamental problem inherent in Marx's theory of capitalism: why cannot the capitalist class or its leading sectors agree to use the State to ensure that aggregate demand expands steadily so as to ensure that a high level of economic activity is maintained? The whole tenor of Marx's argument is that this is not possible. But Marx in fact provides no adequate technical or sociological justification for this view. Indeed, his own model of expanded reproduction strongly implies that it is technically possible. And no reason is apparent in Marx's theory of class which would lead us to believe that it was sociologically impossible or even, indeed, unlikely at a certain stage of development.

These criticisms do not imply that there is no place for a radical socialist movement, or that capitalism has no internal contradictions which might form the basis for a mass revolutionary movement. They do, however, suggest that Marx's theory of the specific economic contradictions of capitalism may well be of little use as a guide to contemporary action. The usefulness of his more general method, and of his criticism of capitalism in terms of alienation, is of course another matter (see above, pp. 18–22).

4 Imperialism

Reading 23 by Avineri provides an excellent introduction to Marx's views on imperialism, and very little comment is required to place it in perspective. It should however be pointed out that modern research has shown certain empirical defects in Marx's views on the nature of Asiatic society, which Avineri does not delve into. Moreover, it is obvious that Marx overestimated both the destructive and the constructive impact of Western imperialism on non-Western societies.[33] In particular, and despite Marx's expectations, it has manifestly failed to industrialize the Third World, though imperialism equally clearly created internal forces in those societies which are favourable to industrialization.

Its lack of success in this respect does, however, raise the question of whether or not (and at what speed) 'underdeveloped' economies can industrialize on any significant scale while remaining within the orbit of advanced capitalism, whether they are politically independent or not. This remains an open question; for one view, see Warren (1973).

References

References to Marx are taken from the following editions:

Capital, Volumes I, II and III, Lawrence & Wishart, 1970, 1967, and 1971 respectively.
Theories of Surplus Value, Parts I, II and III, Lawrence & Wishart, 1969, 1969 and 1972 respectively.

33. On all this see Stokes (1973) for a good summary of the Indian experience.

A Contribution to the Critique of Political Economy, edited with an introduction by Maurice Dobb, Lawrence & Wishart, 1971.

The Poverty of Philosophy, International Publishers, 1971.

The German Ideology, Part I, with selections from Parts II and III, edited with an introduction by C. J. Arthur, Lawrence & Wishart, 1970.

Grundrisse, translated with a foreword by Martin Nicolaus, Penguin, 1973.

ANDREWS, P. W. S. (1964), *On Competition in Economic Theory*, Macmillan, (London).

ARON, R. (1965), *Main Currents in Sociological Thought, Volume I*, Weidenfeld & Nicolson.

BERLIN, I. (1958), *Two Concepts of Liberty*, Oxford University Press.

BHADURI, A. (1969), 'On the significance of recent controversies in capital theory: a Marxian view', *Economic Journal*, vol. 79, pp. 532–9.

BLAUG, M. (1968), *Economic Theory in Retrospect*, Heinemann.

BORTKIEWICZ, L. VON (1907), 'On the correction of Marx's fundamental theoretical construction in the third volume of "Capital"', in E. von Böhm-Bawerk, *Karl Marx and the Close of His System* (P. Sweezy ed.), Kelley, 1966, pp. 199–221.

DOBB, M. (1937), *Political Economy and Capitalism*, Routledge.

DOBB, M. (1963), *Studies in the Development of Capitalism*, Routledge & Kegan Paul.

GORDON, D. M. (1972), *Theories of Poverty and Underemployment*, D. C. Heath.

GRAAF, J. DE V. (1957), *Theoretical Welfare Economics*, Cambridge University Press.

HAHN, F. (1973), 'The winter of our discontent', *Economica*, N.S., vol. 40, pp. 322–30.

HARCOURT, G. C. (1972), *Some Cambridge Controversies in the Theory of Capital*, Cambridge University Press.

HARCOURT, G. C. (1974), 'The Cambridge controversies: the afterglow', in M. Parkin and A. R. Nobay (eds.), *Contemporary Issues in Economics*, Manchester University Press.

HARCOURT, G. C., and LAING, N. F. (eds.) (1971), *Capital and Growth: Selected Readings*, Penguin.

HOBSBAWM, E. J. (1964), 'Introduction', to Karl Marx, *Pre-Capitalist Economic Formations*, Lawrence & Wishart.

HOWARD, M. C. and KING, J. E. (1975), *The Political Economy of Marx*, Longmans.

HUNT, E. K. and SCHWARTZ, J. G., (eds.) (1972), *A Critique of Economic Theory*, Penguin.

MACPHERSON, C. B. (1972), 'Politics; post-liberal democracy?', in R. Blackburn (ed.), *Ideology in Social Science*, Fontana/Collins, pp. 17–31.

MEDIO, A. (1972), 'Profits and surplus-value: appearance and reality in capitalist production', in E. K. Hunt and J. G. Schwartz (eds.), *A Critique of Economic Theory*, Penguin.

MEEK, R. L. (1967), *Economics and Ideology and Other Essays*, Chapman & Hall.

MEEK, R. L. (1973), *Studies in the Labour Theory of Value*, Lawrence & Wishart.

MILIBAND, R. (1969), *The State in Capitalist Society*, Weidenfeld & Nicolson.

OKISHIO, N. (1963), 'A mathematical note on Marxian theorems', *Weltwirtschaftliches Archiv*, vol. 91, pp. 287–98.

PASINETTI, L. L. (1960), 'A mathematical formulation of the Ricardian system' *Review of Economic Studies*, vol. 27, pp. 78–98.

POPPER, K. (1945), *The Open Society and Its Enemies*, Routledge & Kegan Paul.

ROBINSON, J. (1946), *An Essay on Marxian Economics*, Macmillan (London).

ROBINSON, J. (1971), *Economic Heresies*, Macmillan (London).

SAMUELSON, P. A. (1957), 'Wages and interest: a modern dissection of Marxian economic models', *American Economic Review*, vol. 47, pp. 884–912.

SAMUELSON, P. A. (1971), 'Understanding the Marxian notion of exploitation: a summary of the so-called transformation problem between Marxian values and competitive prices', *Journal of Economic Literature*, vol. 9, pp. 399–431.

SAMUELSON, P. A. (1972), 'The economics of Marx: an ecumenical reply', *Journal of Economic Literature*, vol. 10, pp. 50–51.

SOWELL, T. (1963), 'Marxian value reconsidered', *Economica*, N.S., vol. 30, pp. 297–308.

SRAFFA, P. (1960), *The Production of Commodities by Means of Commodities*, Cambridge University Press.

STEEDMAN, I. (1971), 'Marx on the falling rate of profit', *Australian Economic Papers*, vol. 10, pp. 61–6.

STOKES, E. (1973), 'The first century of British colonial rule in India: social revolution or social stagnation', *Past and Present*, no. 58, pp. 136–60.

SWEEZY, P. M. (1968), 'Karl Marx and the industrial revolution', in R. V. Eagly (ed.), *Events, Ideology and Economic Theory*, Wayne State University Press, pp. 107–19.

WARREN, B. (1973), 'Imperialism and capitalist industrialisation', *New Left Review*, no. 81, Sept–Oct., pp. 3–44.

Part One
An Overview

1 Thomas Sowell

Marx's *Capital* after One Hundred Years

Thomas Sowell, 'Marx's *Capital* after one hundred years', *Canadian Journal of Economics*, vol. 33, 1967, pp. 50–74.

A recurring lament in commemorations of classic works is that they are so well-known that little remains to be said about them. This is certainly not true of Marx's *Capital*. Its difficult method of presentation, the numerous myths about it which have grown up over the years, and recent tendencies to mathematicize popular conceptions of Marxian economics in lieu of digging into Marx's own writings[1] have together made this work almost as little understood today as it has ever been. Böhm-Bawerk's famous 'refutation' of Marx's 'labour theory of value' continues to be reproduced, along with the economic 'breakdown' of capitalism theory, the 'dialectical' forces at work, and all the old familiar cast of fictitious characters. If one accepts the cynical definition of a classic as a work that everyone talks about and no one reads, there is certainly no more classic work in economics than *Capital*. The hundredth anniversary of its publication seems an appropriate time to re-examine not only the book itself but also the beliefs about it which have acquired a life – almost an immortality – of their own.

In keeping with Marx's intention, *Capital* will be broadly defined to include *The Theories of Surplus Value*, a history of economic thought which he planned as the final volume of this work (Marx and Engels, 1942, pp. 215, 219). A special relevance must also be noted for his *Critique of Political Economy*, the first part of an abortive attempt to write the book that was to become *Capital*.

1 The influence of Hegel

Like most current myths about Marx, belief in a pervasive Hegelian influence on *Capital* is very old, extending back to the lifetime of Marx and

1. There is, of course, nothing wrong with rendering the theories of an economist of the past in a more rigorous or mathematical manner than in the original, where this can be accomplished without doing violence to their meaning. But modernity can never be a substitute for knowing what you are talking about. Surely it is the ultimate in a new concept of scholarship when articles can be written on Marxian economics without a single citation of anything that Marx ever said: Cf. Samuelson (1957), Bronfenbrenner (1965).

Engels, who replied to these beliefs, but whose replies have been largely ignored in later discussion. The belief in Hegel's influence usually takes one of several forms: (1) the view that Marx forced his theories into a thesis–antithesis–synthesis mould, that (2) various Marxian economic or social theories or conclusions depend upon Hegelian assumptions or arguments, or that (3) the 'inevitability' of Marx's results is Hegelian, even if the results themselves are not.

The formula thesis–antithesis–synthesis does not appear anywhere in *Capital*. Indeed, among Marx's published works it appeared only in *The Poverty of Philosophy* as a sarcastic characterization of Proudhon's attempt to be Hegelian (Marx, 1963, pp. 105, 107, 150, 151). Specialists on Hegel have argued that this notion was equally insignificant in Hegel's writings (Mueller, 1958). However, since social change usually represents the incomplete victory of the protagonists of change over its opponents, the theories of anyone who deals with social change can readily be forced into the thesis–antithesis–synthesis mould by commentators. But this is no more peculiarly true of Marxian theories than those of Burke, Mill, Veblen, or Schumpeter.

Numerous Hegelian phrasings and conceptualizations appear in Marxian writings, and more so in *Capital* than in most of his works. The significant question, however, is whether the *substance* of what Marx said was affected by Hegelian doctrines, or whether he simply dressed up his own vision in Hegelian trappings. [2]

The only full-scale attempt by Marx or Engels to explain the connection between their philosophy and that of Hegel was Engels's *Ludwig Feuerbach and the End of Classical German Philosophy*. [3] Here he said that he and Marx took from Hegel the 'great basic thought that the world is not to be comprehended as a complex of ready-made *things*, but as a complex of *processes* . . .' [4] (Engels, 1959, p. 226). *Capital* was Hegelian in the very general sense of emphasizing the dynamics of capitalism – 'the law of

2. For example: 'These three events – the so-called Revival of Learning, the flourishing of the Fine Arts and the discovery of America and of the passage to India by the Cape – may be compared with that *blush of dawn*, which after long storms first betokens the return of a bright and glorious day' (Hegel, 1956, pp. 410–11). 'The discovery of gold and silver in America, the extirpation, enslavement and entombment in mines of the aboriginal poulation, the beginning of the conquest and looting of the East Indies, the turning of Africa into a warren for the commercial hunting of black-skins, signalized the rosy dawn of the era of capitalist production' (Marx, 1906, p. 823).

3. 'We have expressed ourselves in various places regarding our relation to Hegel, but nowhere in a comprehensive, connected account . . . a short, connected account of our relation to the Hegelian philosophy, of how we proceeded from it as well as how we separated from it, appeared to me to be required more and more' (Engels, 1959, pp. 195, 196).

4. Italics in all quotations in this paper are in the original.

motion' of capitalism in Marx's words – rather than its static equilibrium conditions. When it came to specific economic doctrines found in *Capital*, Marx and Engels were insistent that the Hegelian phrasing and conceptualization had nothing to do with the substance of what was presented in this way. To a contemporary reviewer of the first volume of *Capital* who had noted its distinctly Hegelian flavour, Marx replied that his 'method of presentation' differed from his method of 'inquiry', though 'it may appear as if we had before us a mere *a priori* construction' (Marx, 1906, vol. I, p. 25).[5] Engels in *Anti-Dühring* examined several allegedly Hegelian notions from *Capital*, explaining in each case that the conclusion reached derived from the empirical evidence and economic analysis which preceded it. For example:

... what role does the negation of the negation play in Marx? On page 834 and the following pages he sets out the conclusions which he draws from the preceding fifty pages of economic and historical investigation ... (Engels, 1939, p. 145).

Engels concludes:

In characterizing the process as the negation of the negation, therefore, Marx does not dream of attempting to prove by this that the process was historically necessary. On the contrary: after he has proved from history that in fact the process has partially already occurred, and partially must occur in the future, he then also characterizes it as a process which develops in accordance with a definite dialectical law. That is all (Engels, 1939, p. 147).

Marx had made a similar statement of his approach more than a quarter of a century earlier: 'It is hardly necessary to assure the reader conversant with political economy that my results have been won by means of a wholly empirical analysis based on a conscientious study of political economy' (Marx, 1961, p. 15).

This still leaves the question as to why *Capital* should be so Hegelian in its presentation as compared to the *Communist Manifesto* and other Marxian writings. In the early 1840s Marx had used much Hegelian imagery,[6] as might be expected in view of his recent study at the University of Berlin where the Hegelian influence had been dominant. But once having moved away from this method of exposition, why should he return to it a quarter of a century later? Marx provided the answer in his introduction to *Capital*:

5. Marx observed elsewhere that 'to bring a science to the point where it can be dialectically presented is an altogether different thing from applying an abstract ready-made system....' (Marx and Engels, 1942, p. 105).

6. e.g., *Economic and Philosophic Manuscripts of 1844*, *The Holy Family* (1845), *The German Ideology* (1845–6), and articles of the period. For an analysis of the Hegelian significance of these writings, see Marcuse (1954, pp. 273–95).

The mystifying side of the Hegelian dialectic I criticized nearly thirty years ago, at a time when it was still the fashion. But just as I was working at the first volume of *Das Kapital*, it was the good pleasure of the peevish, arrogant, mediocre [*epigoni*] who now talk large in cultured Germany, to treat Hegel in the same way as the brave Moses Mendelssohn in Lessing's time treated Spinoza, i.e., as a 'dead dog'. I therefore openly avowed myself the pupil of that mighty thinker, and even here and there, in the chapter on the theory of value, coquetted with the modes of expression peculiar to him (Marx, 1906, vol. I, p. 25).[7]

Engels (1939, p. 138) declared it a 'blunder' to identify 'Marxian dialectics with the Hegelian . . .' Nor was it merely a question of standing Hegel on his head. The Marxian approach was 'a guide to study, not a lever for construction after the manner of the Hegelians' (Marx and Engels, 1942, p. 473). Hegel was attacked for making the world seem to be ruled by his laws, rather than depicting these laws as empirical generalizations about the world (Engels, 1964, p. 63; 1939, p. 42). This inversion had been noted and satirized by Marx and Engels in the early eighteen-forties (Marx and Engels, 1947, pp. 114-15; see also Marx and Engels, 1956, pp. 78-9). Yet it might seem that there is a suggestion of this Hegelian practice in the 'inevitable' triumph of the proletariat depicted by the *Communist Manifesto* and the 'inexorability' of the end of capitalism depicted in *Capital* (Marx and Engels, 1935, p. 36; Marx, 1906, vol. I, p. 837). However, inevitability in general and the modern Western idea of the inevitability of progress in particular have come from many sources besides Hegel. Moreover, there is a serious question as to the degree of inevitability (if that expression is permissible) in which Marx and Engels believed. In 1863 Marx wrote to Engels that 'the comfortable delusions and the almost childish enthusiasm with which we hailed the era of revolution before February 1848 have all gone to hell' (Marx and Engels, 1942, p. 144). Later in the same year, after rereading Engels's *The Condition of the Working Class in England in 1844*, Marx wrote:

Re-reading your book has made me regretfully aware of our increasing age. How freshly and passionately, with what bold anticipations and no learned and scientific doubts, the thing is still dealt with here! And the very illusion that the result itself will leap into the daylight of history tomorrow or the day after gives the whole thing a warmth and jovial humour – compared to which the later 'grey in grey' makes a damned unpleasant contrast (Marx and Engels, 1942, p. 147).

In 1871 Marx observed: 'World history would indeed by very easy to make, if the struggle were taken up only on condition of infallibly favourable chances' (Marx and Engels, 1942, p. 310). There is no reason to doubt that Marx still considered the communist revolution 'inevitable' in the

7. Marx was, of course, Hegel's pupil only in a figurative sense.

sense that he still retained faith that it would happen, but there is also no reason to believe that he regarded it as a mathematical certainty because of some Hegelian formula which guaranteed 'infallibly favourable chances'.

Contrary to popular belief, Marx had no iron laws for history to follow, nor did he regard history as leading up to communism as the ultimate consummation, after which further development would cease.[8] Likewise, he did not claim that there were predestined 'stages' through which all countries must pass, or that the expected communist revolution was (because of these 'stages') going to occur in the United States before it occurred in Russia. Indeed, Marx said the opposite of all these things. To a Russian writer who had argued that his country must pass through the necessary stages of development, Marx replied that the chapter in *Capital* on which he had based himself 'does not pretend to do more than trace the path by which, in Western Europe, the capitalist order of economy emerged from the womb of the feudal order of economy' (Marx and Engels, 1942, p. 353). He added:

> But that is not enough for my Critic. He feels himself obliged to metamorphose my historical sketch of the genesis of capitalism in Western Europe into an historico-philosophic theory of the *marche generale* imposed by fate upon every people, whatever the historic circumstances in which it finds itself . . . But I beg his pardon. (He is both honouring and shaming me too much.) (Marx and Engels 1942, p. 354.)

Similarly Marx never pretended to develop a theory of differential national propensities to revolution. More specifically, he did not regard the United States as being closer to revolution than Russia. Among the contrasts Marx found between the two countries was that in the US 'the masses . . . have greater political means in their hands' (Marx and Engels, 1942, pp. 360–61) to protect themselves; Engels doubted that 'the evil consequences of modern capitalism in Russia will be as easily overcome as they are in the United States', adding that 'the change, in Russia, must be far more violent, far more incisive, and accompanied by immensely greater sufferings than it can be in America' (Marx and Engels, 1942, pp. 513–14).[9]

8. '*Communism* is the necessary form and the active principle of the immediate future, but communism is not itself the aim of human development or the final form of human society.' This statement in a manuscript left unpublished in Marx's lifetime and printed in Bottomore and Rubel (1956, p. 246) only states succinctly what was clearly implied in his published writings. For example, *The Poverty of Philosophy* closed (Marx, 1963, p. 175) with the assertion that in Marx's society of the future social evolution could take place without political revolution. Engels similarly rejected any idea of 'socialist society' as 'a stable affair fixed once and for all.' (Marx and Engels, 1942, p. 473).

9. This is not to claim that Marx's and Engels's analyses of Russia were always acute. For example: 'A few days ago a Petersburgh publisher surprised me with the news that

None of this, however, was based on any 'law' but only on *ad hoc* judgements.

The fact that Hegel's influence on Marx was largely terminological does not mean that it can be safely ignored. For example, perhaps no single word has led to more misconception of Marx's *Capital* than the Hegelian term, 'contradiction'. This expression does not mean physical impossibility, logical error, or economic deadlock. It refers to internal conflicting forces which transform the entity of which they are part. According to Hegel 'contradiction' was 'the very moving principle of the world' rather than something which was 'unthinkable' (Hegel, 1892, p. 223; see also Marcuse, 1954, p. 143).

It is obvious how this relates to the transformation of capitalism into socialism *via* the opposition of employers and employees, whose relationship to each other was the necessary and defining feature of capitalism. It helps explain the repeated presence in Marx and Engels of metaphors which turn on metamorphoses in nature – the transformation (not paralysis) of natural organisms by their own internal forces, as when a germinating seed bursts its integument (Marx, 1906, vol. I, p. 837) or a caterpillar turns itself into a butterfly.[10] Marx spoke of 'contradictions' in terms of 'conflicting elements' in his *Theories of Surplus Value*, and his use of the term to designate various theories of his own in *Capital* obviously indicates that he was not using it in the conventional sense of logical error.[11]

The importance of the Hegelian meaning of this word must be insisted upon because so many interpreters of Marx have either explicitly or implicitly made the conventional meaning of contradiction the basis for imputing to Marx a theory that capitalism will experience an economic breakdown or classical stationary state because of the contradictions to which he refers.[12] No such theory appears in *Capital*. Those who claim that it does are driven to the farcical situation in which they all quote each

a Russian translation of *Das Kapital* is now being printed . . . My book against Proudhon (1847) and the one published by Duncker (1859) have had a greater sale in Russia than anywhere else. And the first foreign nation to translate *Kapital* is the Russian. But too much should not be made of all this' (Marx, 1934, p. 77).

10. For example, 'like a butterfly from the chrysalis, the bourgeoisie arose out of the burghers of the feudal period . . .,' (Engels, 1939, p. 117). See also Marx (1947, p. 22); Marx (1952, p. 186); Engels (1937, p. 60); a similar metaphor involving the metamorphosis of crabs was also used (Marx and Engels, 1942, p. 485), and reference to metamorphosis in general is even more common.

11. Marx (1952, p. 377) and, for example, chapter 4 of vol. I ('Contradictions in the Formula for Capital') and chapter 15 of vol. III ('Unravelling the Internal Contradictions of the Law' of the falling rate of profit) of *Capital* (Marx, 1906).

12. 'Contradiction' was explicitly cited as the basis for this interpretation in Shoul (1957, p. 626n.).

other and ignore Marx.[13] In *Capital* Marx described economic crises as 'transient' (Marx, 1906, vol. III, p. 588) and 'momentary' (Marx, 1906, vol. III, p. 292) phenomena, and said: 'There are no permanent crises' (Marx, 1952, p. 373n.). This is compatible with Marx's assertion that capitalism begets 'its own negation' (Marx, 1906, vol. I, p. 837). Engels has identified this as an Hegelian expression, and Hegel was quite clear as to its meaning: '... Negation ... resolves itself not into nullity, into abstract Nothingness, but essentially only into the negation of its *particular* content ...'[14] A capitalist economy thus does not annihilate itself as an economy, but rather generates the internal pressures which transform it into a socialist economy.

Another and perhaps even more important instance in which the Hegelian influence in form crucially affected the understanding of the substance of what was said was the discussion of 'value' in *Capital*. Here the presentation followed what Marx called the 'dialectical method' (Marx, 1934, pp. 11–12; see also Marx, 1904, pp. 292–4; Marx and Engels, 1942, p. 204) – proceeding through successive levels of abstraction from the 'essence' to the 'appearance'. The difficulties and misunderstandings this created will be explored in Section 4.

2 Business cycles

Although Marx did not claim that capitalism would be destroyed by a cataclysmic depression, business cycles were very important in his overall picture of capitalism, since it was these 'crises that by their periodical return put the existence of the entire bourgeois society on its trial, each time more threateningly' (Marx and Engels, 1935, p. 29).

A distinction must be made between the general conditions which enable business cycles to occur and specific precipitating factors. Marx made this point in criticizing John Stuart Mill for depicting money and credit as causes of cyclical downturns (Marx, 1952, p. 379).[15] The distinction is particularly important in Marx's case. Since crises were for him a peculiarity of capitalism, he had to show what conditions of capitalism permit crises to occur and, within that framework, what forces actually trigger downturns. The former are obviously the more ideologically important

13. For example, Martin Bronfenbrenner cites Paul M. Sweezy, who in turn cites a number of other economists – not including Karl Marx (Bronfenbrenner, 1965, p. 419; Sweezy, 1956, chapter 11).

14. Quoted in Marcuse (1954, p. 124). Engels (1964, p. 225) cited the same definition of 'negation'.

15. The distinction between the factors making for the possibility of crises and those actually producing them was made repeatedly (Marx, 1952, pp. 331, 383–4, 386; 1906, vol. I, p. 328).

and receive repeated attention as a result. The problem arises when this causes them to be confused with the latter as economic variables.

The problem of capitalism, according to Marx, is that production 'comes to a standstill at a point determined by the production and realization of profit, not by the satisfaction of social needs' (Marx, 1906, vol. III, p. 303). No level of output yet attained – in the economy as a whole or in any particular sector – would be unsustainable or excessive relative to unmet needs (Marx, 1952, p. 394). Thus 'the last cause of all real crises is the poverty and restricted consumption of the masses ...' (Marx, 1906, vol. III, p. 658). Did this mean that a decline in consumption precipitates crises? Emphatically not, according to Marx, who repeatedly asserted in *Capital* that consumption tends to *increase* in the cyclical phase preceding the onset of a crisis (Marx, 1906, vol. II, pp. 86, 362, 475; vol. III, pp. 359, 528, 567). He declared:

It is purely a tautology to say that crises are caused by a scarcity of solvent customers or of a paying consumption ... If any commodities are unsaleable it means that no solvent customers have been found for them ... But if one were to attempt to clothe this tautology with a semblance of a profounder justification by saying that the working class receive too small a portion of their own product, and the evil would be remedied by giving them a larger share of it, or raising their wages, we should reply that crises are precisely always preceded by a period in which wages rise generally and the working class actually get a larger share of the annual product intended for consumption. From the point of view of the advocates of 'simple' (!) common sense, such a period should rather remove a crisis (Marx, 1906, vol. II, pp. 475–6).

Despite Marx's unequivocal statements, the absence of an underconsumptionist or breakdown theory of business cycles has been blamed on the unfinished state of *Capital* at Marx's death (Sweezy, 1956, p. 176). In this connection, however, two important points must be noted:

1. Marx was well aware that he was a sick man who had close calls with death before the first volume of *Capital* appeared.[16] Accordingly he elaborated in letters to Engels most of the important doctrines which he wished to develop in *Capital* (Marx and Engels, 1942, pp. 105–109, 129–33, 137–8, 153–6, 238–45, 266–74). For example, the transformation of values into prices was explained to Engels in 1862, five years before publication of the first volume – a fact overlooked by the literature on Marx's 'change of mind' between volumes I and III (Marx and Engels, 1942, pp. 129–33). Similarly, one of Marx's letters mentioned the business cycle theory which

16. Marx complained of his 'continual relapses' (Marx and Engels, 1942, p. 215) and of having been 'on the verge of the grave' (Marx and Engels, 1942, p. 219) among numerous references to his poor health. See also Marx (1934, pp. 35, 90) and Mehring (1935, p. 275).

he expected to unfold in the later volumes of *Capital*. It contained no suggestion of either 'breakdown' or underconsumption. Rather, Marx noted that Engels's 'Outlines of a Critique of Political Economy' – written in 1843 and featuring disproportionality – was still a valid representation of business cycles as they would appear in *Capital* (Marx and Engels, 1942, p. 232).[17] The discussion of cycles in the posthumous volumes (including *Theories of Surplus Value*) did in fact faithfully follow the pattern of Engels's article, as will be seen below. However more polished and logically complete Marx's cycle theory might have been had he lived to complete it himself, there is no reason to suppose that it would have been fundamentally different from what he left.

2. The *theoretical* incompleteness of *Capital* – as distinguished from its need for re-writing – should not be exaggerated. Engels pointed out that the 'essential parts' of volume III (in which business cycle theory was introduced) were complete in manuscript before Marx turned to the final draft of volume I for publication (Engels, 'Preface' to Marx, 1906, vol. II, p. 9). This is independently confirmed by Marx's correspondence where he asserted that because *Capital* was 'dialectically constructed' he had to see it 'as a *whole*' before he could bring himself to send the first volume off to be printed (Marx and Engels, 1942, p. 204). In 1866 Marx declared the manuscript of the third volume 'finished' though far from a publishable state (Marx and Engels, 1942, p. 205).[18] If Marx had had a theory which would explain the complete and irreparable collapse of the capitalist economy, it is difficult to understand its absence from the 'essential parts' of his business cycle theory or how the manuscript of the third volume could be considered analytically 'finished' without it.

Although neither the elements of Marxian business cycle theory nor their combination is remarkable today, they were far in advance of the economic thinking of his time. While classical economics had made cyclical downturns the result of exogenous forces such as war or governmental interference, (Say, 1846, p. 135; Ricardo, 1953, vol. I, chapter 19; vol II, pp. 306, 415; vol. VIII, p. 277) Marx depicted economic crises as necessary consequences of the working of a capitalist economy. Where the early opponents of Say's law – Lauderdale, Malthus, and Chalmers, for example – had been content to show how it was possible to have 'general gluts', Marx

17. Engels's work had appeared in the *Deutsch-Französische Jahrbücher* in 1844.

18. After Marx's death, Engels noted that 'The third book is complete since 1869–70 and has never been touched since' (Engels, Lafargue and Lafargue, 1959, I, p. 134). This appears to contradict Engels's lament elsewhere that the manuscript of the third volume was 'incomplete' (Engels, in Marx, 1906, vol. III, p. 11). However, the specifics of this lament indicated that it was a literary incompleteness to which Engels referred, or the incomplete working out of theories which were present rather than the absence of theories which Marx had not got around to mentioning at all.

repeatedly scorned the route of showing mere possibilities of crisis,[19] attempting instead to show why they were a necessary concomitant of capitalist conditions.

Origins of crises

Marx saw capitalism as a system of unplanned production for a market coordinated by price fluctuations and expanding rapidly over time. All these features contributed to cyclical fluctuations. Because it was production for a market, rather than for the use of the individual producer himself, there was no necessary connection between the quantities produced and desired.[20] This exemplified the dialectical relationship between necessity and accident:[21] it was necessary that production and wants correspond *ex post* but it was accidental whether they would correspond *ex ante*, price fluctuations being a symptom (and corrective) of the divergence:

The *a priori* system on which the division of labour, within the workshop, is regularly carried out, becomes in the division of labour within the society, an *a posteriori*, nature-imposed necessity, controlling the lawless caprice of the producers, and perceptible in the barometrical fluctuations of the market prices (Marx, 1906, vol. I, p. 391).

Because there was no *ex ante* coordination – or in Marx's terms '*a priori* . . . conscious social regulation of production' (Marx and Engels, 1942, p. 247) – and because the economy adjusts 'after the fact' (Marx, 1906, vol. II, p. 362) price fluctuations were necessary and the prospect of violent price fluctuations from time to time inherent. 'Violent fluctuations of price . . . cause interruptions, great collisions, or even catastrophies in

19. See note 15.
20. 'In conditions in which men produce for themselves, there are in fact no crises, but also no capitalist production' (Marx, 1952, p. 380).
21. Necessity and chance were among the polar opposites which dialectical thinking refused to accept as mutually exclusive in reality. Chance affected the most necessary results and certain necessary relationships could be discovered in the pattern of events which were individually the result of chance. Thus 'dialectics reduced itself to the science of the general laws of motion . . . these laws assert themselves unconsciously, in the form of external necessity in the midst of an endless series of seeming accidents' (Engels, 1959, p. 226). Again, 'chance is only one pole of an interrelation, the other pole of which is called necessity. In nature, where chance also seems to reign, we have long ago demonstrated in each particular field the inherent necessity and regularity that asserts itself in this chance' (Engels, 1955a, p. 322). See also Engels (1964, pp. 38, 223) and Marx and Engels (1942, pp. 484, 518). This doctrine was applied to economics: 'The mutual confluence and intertwining of the reproduction or circulation processes of different capitals is on the one hand necessitated by the division of labour, and on the other is accidental' (Marx, 1952, p. 385). See also Marx (1906, vol. III, p. 220).

the process of reproduction' (Marx, 1906, vol. III, p. 140). In a stationary or slowly growing economy, price oscillations would tend to dampen down to the long-run equilibrium price or cost of production. This could not happen, however, under dynamic capitalism, where the incessant growth of output and demand left no opportunity for the producers to discover the equilibrium quantities of their respective products. There was no 'pre-destined circle of supply and demand' (Marx, 1906, vol. II, p. 86). As Marx had expressed it much earlier: 'This true proportion between supply and demand . . . was possible only at a time when the means of production were limited, when the movement of exchange took place within very restricted bounds' (Marx, 1963, p. 68). The reproduction models in Volume II of *Capital* showed the intricate adjustments necessary for equilibrium even under stationary conditions and then still more so under conditions of dynamic growth. Here not only the inter-related output and consumption of various sectors were considered but also the sporadic formation and liquidation of hoards connected with capital replacement and expansion. Marx concluded: 'These conditions become so many causes of abnormal movements, implying the possibility of crises, since a balance is an accident under the crude conditions of this production' (Marx, 1906, vol. II, p. 578).

The germ of the Marxian theory of the downturn – disproportionality and attendant price fluctuations – had originated in Engels's 'Outlines of a Critique of Political Economy': 'Supply . . . is either too big or too small, never corresponding to demand; because in this unconscious condition of mankind no one knows how big supply or demand is' (Engels, 1961, p. 195).

This is not aggregate supply and demand which are in imbalance, but rather the relations of supply and demand for the respective products of the various sectors: 'The perpetual fluctuation of price . . . daily and hourly changes the value-relationship of all things to one another' (Engels, 1961, p. 196). In this 'state of perpetual fluctuation perpetually unresolved', supply and demand 'always strive to complement each other and therefore never do so' (Engels, 1961, p. 195). This was a direct fore-runner of Marx's later argument:

. . . all equalizations are *accidental*, and although the proportionate use of capitals in the various spheres is equalized by a continuous process, nevertheless the continuity of this process itself equally presupposes the constant disproportion, which it has continuously, often violently, to even out (Marx, 1952, p. 368).

In Engels, as later in Marx, business cycles were seen as a perverse con-firmation of the price allocation mechanism of traditional economic theory:

This law with its constant balancing ... seems to the economist marvellous. It is his chief glory – he cannot see enough of it, and considers it in all its possible and impossible applications ... Of course, these trade crises confirm the law, confirm it exhaustively – but in a manner different from that which the economist would have us believe to be the case. What are we to think of a law which can only assert itself through periodic crises? (Engels, 1961, p. 195).

The same idea appeared in Marx a few years later:

The economists say that the *average price* of commodities is equal to the cost of production; that this is a *law*. The anarchical movement in which rise is compensated by fall and fall by rise, is regarded by them as chance. With just as much right one could regard the fluctuations as the law and the determination by the cost of production as chance ... it is solely these fluctuations, which, looked at more closely, bring with them the most fearful devastations and, like earthquakes, cause bourgeois society to tremble to its foundations (Marx, 1955a, vol. I, p. 87).

Later in *Capital* Marx was in fact to treat the price fluctuations as a law governing the allocation of resources – 'the law of value' (Marx, 1906, vol. I, p. 391; vol. III, pp. 745, 1026; Marx and Engels, 1942, p. 246; Engels, 'Preface' to Marx, 1963, p. 18)[22] – thus linking price theory and business cycle theory as Engels had done.

The relationship of crises to the end of capitalism was also first stated by Engels in the same article:

... as long as you continue to produce in the present unconscious, thoughtless manner, at the mercy of chance – for so long trade crises will remain; and each successive crisis is bound to become more universal and therefore worse than the preceding one ... finally causing a social revolution ... (Engels, 1961, p. 196).

Here as in the later writings of Marx, it was not argued that an economic crisis would itself destroy capitalism, but that it would provoke men to do so. Depressions would be ever-*widening* rather than ever-deepening as popular interpretation has suggested – a point reinforced by another work of Engels in this period, in which the international spread of crises over time was postulated (Engels, 1952).

That all of this was not a mere early aberration of Engels's was indicated by Marx's letter to him in 1868 discussing some points to be elaborated in later volumes of *Capital*. Marx observed that as long as the regulation of production 'is accomplished not by the direct and conscious control of society ... but by the movement of commodity prices, things remain as you have already quite aptly described them in the *Deutsch-Französische Jahrbucher*' (Marx and Engels, 1942, p. 232).

22. For essentially the same analysis without specific use of the term 'law of value', see Marx (1906, vol. I, pp. 114–15; vol. III, pp. 220–21).

Money and credit

Marx recognized that classical economics had admitted 'the glut of the market for particular commodities', that it had denied only 'the *simultaneity* of this phenomenon for all spheres of production, and hence general overproduction' (Marx, 1952, p. 408). For Marx money and credit were the mechanisms which turned partial overproduction into general overproduction. They were not, however, causes of crises – 'both make their appearance long *before* capitalist production, without crises occurring' (Marx, 1952, p. 387) – but rather mechanisms which turn the inherent disproportionalities between sectors of the capitalist economy into a general imbalance between aggregate output and aggregate demand.

While for classical economics money was simply a veil concealing, but not essentially changing, the barter of one commodity for another, in Marx it played a more important role. Through money the barter of one commodity for another 'falls into two acts which are independent of each other and separate in space and time' (Marx, 1952, p. 381). These separate acts 'imply the possibility, and no more than the possibility of crises' (Marx, 1906, vol. I, p. 128). However, Marx did not 'seek to explain crises by these simple *possibilities* of crisis' (Marx, 1952, p. 379) – a method he criticized in John Stuart Mill. What was important was to show why crises developed 'from possibility into actuality' (Marx, 1952, p. 390). In short, Marx rejected a purely monetary theory of depressions, though he acknowledged that particular downturns might originate in purely monetary phenomena. He distinguished monetary crises as 'phases of industrial and commercial crises' (Marx, 1906, vol. I, p. 155) from a purely monetary crisis 'as an independent phenomenon' (Marx, 1906, vol. I, p. 155n.). He admitted such crises empirically but did not deal with them theoretically.

Overproduction in particular sectors generate financial panic in these sectors when money receipts are insufficient to meet fixed contractual obligations when they are due (Marx, 1906, vol. I, pp. 154, 155; 1952, pp. 386, 389). The credit system turns defaults in particular sectors into a general contraction of credit. When there are 'debts due to A from B, to B from C, to C from A, and so,' (Marx, 1906, vol. I, p. 154) – in short, 'an ever-lengthening chain of payments' (Marx, 1906, vol. I, p. 155) or 'mutual claims and obligations' (Marx, 1952, p. 386) – then a monetary crisis develops 'from the non-fulfilment of a whole series of payments which depend on the sale of these particular commodities within this particular period of time' (Marx, 1952, p. 389). A general financial panic ensues: '... in periods of crisis when credit collapses completely ... nothing goes any more but cash money' (Marx, 1906, vol. III, pp. 543, 602; 1904, p. 193). With the shrinkage of credit, aggregate money demand becomes insufficient: 'At a given moment the supply of all commodities may be greater than the demand for all commodities, because the demand for the general commodity, money, exchange value, is greater than the demand for all particular commodities . . .' (Marx, 1952, p. 392). Marx was aware that the insufficiency of demand was an insufficiency only at given prices: 'The excess of commodities is always relative, that is, it is an excess at certain prices. The prices at which the commodities are then absorbed are ruinous for the producer or merchant' (Marx, 1952, p. 393). The lower prices are ruinous because the whole price structure cannot deflate smoothly: 'The fixed charges . . . remain the same, and in part cannot be paid' (Marx, 1952, pp. 390–91). Even commodities which were not among those which had been overproduced 'are now suddenly in *relative* overproduction, because the means to buy them, and therewith the demand for them, have contracted' (Marx, 1952, p. 401). Thus 'in times of general overproduction the overproduction in some spheres is always the *result*, the *consequence*, of overproduction in the leading articles of commerce . . .' (Marx, 1952, pp. 408, 393). Against those who tried 'to argue away the possibility of a general glut', Marx declared: 'For a crisis (and therefore also overproduction) to be general, it is sufficient for it to grip the principal articles of trade' (Marx, 1952, p. 393).

Periodicity

Marx believed that business cycles had a regular period, which was due to a regular replacement life of capital goods. He assumed for illustrative purposes that capital goods lasted ten years on the average, but did not – contrary to popular belief – insist that in fact this was the correct period.[23] Marx assumed that crises themselves spurred investment – presumably in their aftermath – so that much capital in sectors throughout the economy would date from the same time, thus providing 'a new material basis for the next cycle . . .' (Marx, 1906, vol. II, p. 211). However, this part of his theory was left in a very sketchy state – perhaps because periodicity was not essential to his overall picture of the end of capitalism. Engels later argued, after Marx's death, that periodic depressions had given way to a chronic stagnation (Marx, 1906, vol. III, pp. 574n.–5n.; Engels, 'Preface' to Marx, 1963, p. 20n.). However, this view, like their earlier belief in periodicity, was not explored to any considerable extent.

3 The falling rate of profit

It is important to note that Marx referred to the law of the *tendency* – he

23. One may assume that this life-cycle, in the essential branches of great industry, now averages ten years. However, it is not a question of any one definite number here' (Marx, 1906, vol. II, p. 211).

called it 'merely' a 'tendency' (Marx, 1906, vol. III, p. 272)[24] – of the falling rate of profit. After explaining the tendency towards declining profit rates because of a rising capital:labour ratio with a given profit: wages ratio (a truistic conclusion *not* dependent on a labour theory of value), Marx proceeded to elaborate the 'counteracting causes' which in most cases amounted to increasing the profit:wages ratio by one means or another (Marx, 1906, vol. III, chapter 14, *passim*).

Although Marx seemed to suppose that the conflicting forces he described would produce a declining rate of profit as a resultant, this was not a logical necessity from his theory, nor did he claim that it was. His purpose in elaborating this doctrine must to some extent be guessed at, but it does not seem to be an insoluble riddle. The *actual* movement of the rate of profit would be relatively unimportant in Marx's overall politico-economic vision, while the *tendency* was very significant. The primary method of preventing a declining profit rate was by progressively increasing the rate of surplus value – the 'exploitation' of the workers. It was precisely this increasing exploitation of the workers which was to intensify the class struggle and hasten revolution. In this light, whether or to what extent it proved successful in preventing a falling profit rate from materializing seems secondary.

Since increasing exploitation of the workers in Marxian terms did not imply declining real wages, Marx's implicit assumption seemed to be that workers looked upon wages primarily as a relative share as he and Ricardo did.[25] This assumption also underlay his doctrine of the 'increasing misery' of the proletariat, and was a key weakness in this doctrine as a theory of revolution.

It has sometimes been claimed that the falling rate of profit doctrine and the doctrine of the increasing misery of the workers are mutually incompatible, since the relative shares of property and wage income cannot simultaneously decline (Robinson, 1947; Samuelson, 1957, pp. 892–5). It should be noted, however, that the former (even as a doctrine of a materialized tendency) is a doctrine of a falling rate of *net* profit, so that the capitalists' share of gross national product need not decline. The rising capital-intensity of production ('organic composition of capital') means that a

24. Similarly, Marx said that 'the same rate of surplus-value, with the same degree of labour exploitation, *would* express itself in a falling rate of profit . . .' (Marx, 1906, vol. III, p. 248) (emphasis added).

25. Ricardo viewed wages as a relative share only as an analytical device. Marx attributed to Ricardo a social philosophy in which the relative position of the classes was more important than their absolute living standards (Marx, 1952, p. 320). In fact, however, Ricardo's social philosophy made the absolute standard of living more important (Ricardo, 1953, vol. II, pp. 249–50). See also Sowell (1960).

greater proportion of the capitalist's gross revenue would go for replacement and expansion of capital.[26]

Marx's tendency of the falling rate of profit has often been causally linked to his business cycle theory by interpreters. But far from attempting to make secularly declining profits a cause of cyclical depression, Marx was at pains to point out the distinction between a long-run falling profit rate and 'temporary' declines for other reasons (Marx, 1906, vol. III, p. 249). The only causal link between economic crises and the secular profit fall was that the cheapening of capital which accompanies a depression was considered an offsetting factor retarding the long-run decline in profit rates (Marx, 1906, vol. III, pp. 292–3).

In classical economics the theory of the falling rate of profit led to a 'stationary state', which may explain efforts to make Marx's theory end in a 'breakdown' of capitalism. But if Marx had meant this, nothing would have been easier than to have said so somewhere in the three volumes of *Capital*, the three additional volumes of *Theories of Surplus Value*, or his voluminous correspondence with Engels – particularly since he discussed the classical theory of the subject (Marx and Engels, 1942, p. 244).

The consequences of the tendency of the falling rate of profit were much milder in Marx. As a tendency it intensified exploitation and hence presumably the class struggle. As a materialized actuality it hastened the concentration of capital (Marx, 1906, vol. III, p. 283), encouraged speculation (Marx, 1906, vol. III, p. 294), and promoted foreign investment (Marx, 1906, vol. III, pp. 278, 300). Quite possibly Marx did not expect capitalism to last long enough to reach a stationary state.

4 Value

Marx's doctrine of value in *Capital* met two major disasters which continue to obscure his meaning a century later: (1) the heavily Hegelian exposition, which Engels repeatedly and vainly warned against (Marx and Engels, 1942, pp. 220–21; Engels, 1937, p. 125),[27] and (2) the twenty-seven year delay between publication of volume I (where value was

26. 'If a falling rate of profit goes hand in hand with an increase in the mass of profits, as we have shown, then a larger portion of the annual product of labour is appropriated by the capitalist under the name of capital (as a substitute for consumed capital) and a relatively smaller portion under the name of profit' (Marx, 1906, vol. III, p. 288).

27. Similarly in reviewing an earlier abstract of Marx's *Critique of Political Economy*, Engels had described it as '*a very abstract abstract indeed*', and expressed the hope that the 'abstract dialectical tone' would disappear as the work developed (Marx and Engels, 1942, p. 110). Engels was much more cognizant than Marx of the difficulties presented by the Hegelian presentation. Of one of his own early works he said: 'The semi-Hegelian language of a good many passages of my old book is not only untranslatable but has lost the greater part of its meaning even in German' (Marx and Engels, 1953, p. 151).

introduced) and volume III (where its relationship to price was elaborated), which allowed time for his followers and opponents – notably the rising marginal utility school – to harden their positions on a 'labour theory of value' which did not exist.

Here, as in other cases, Marx's argument is not fundamentally difficult in itself, though there are great problems in trying to extricate it from its Hegelian entanglements and interpretative overgrowths which have emerged over the past century from attempts to force his theories into the pattern of traditional economics.

Marx's analysis begins with the basic fact that in a complex economy men 'work for one another' (Marx, 1906, vol. I, p. 82)[28] and when they *appear* on the surface to exchange their products they are in *essence* distributing their labour (including capital as past labour). Although this Hegelian conception was not logically necessary for Marxian economics, it is important for understanding the argument as Marx chose to present it in *Capital*.

'Exchange-value' (price) as the relationship between commodities was repeatedly referred to as an 'appearance' (Marx, 1906, vol. I, p. 95n.), a 'phenomenal form' (Marx, 1906, vol. I, p. 43; 1952, pp. 203, 261), part of the 'surface phenomena' (Marx, 1952, p. 261), etc., connected with but different from the underlying reality of 'value'.[29] Value and surplus value were an 'invisible and unknown essence' rather than 'phenomena which show themselves on the surface'.[30] The opening chapter of the first volume of *Capital* criticized classical economics for not understanding 'the hidden relations existing between value and its form, exchange-value' (Marx, 1906, vol I, p. 95n.), for confusing 'the form of value with value itself' (Marx, 1906, vol. I, 57n.), and for failing to discover specifically how 'value becomes exchange-value' (Marx, 1906, vol. I, p. 82n.). Although 'value' or labour time 'ultimately' regulates prices, 'average prices do not directly coincide with the values of commodities, as Adam Smith, Ricardo and others believe' (Marx, 1906, vol. I, p. 185n.).

In his *Theories of Surplus Value* (written before the first volume of *Capital*, though published later) Marx repeatedly made the same argument

28. Like most doctrines in *Capital*, this appeared also in Marx's earlier writings: 'In principle there is no exchange of products – but there is the exchange of the labour which cooperated in production' (Marx, 1963, p. 78).

29. '. . . exchange value, generally, is only the mode of expression, the phenomenal form, of something contained in it, yet distinguishable from it' (Marx, 1906, vol. I, p. 43).

30. *Capital* (Marx, 1906, vol. III, p. 56) refers to surplus value; value was also considered 'invisible' (Marx, 1906, vol. I, p. 107). Marx (1952, p. 133) referred to 'surplus value in general as distinct from its determinate forms' which were 'determined by quite different laws'.

against Ricardo which Böhm-Bawerk was later to make against him, that profit equalization among industries with different capital–labour ratios was incompatible with prices being proportional to labour-determined 'values'.[31] It was *not* a question of temporary 'accidental deviations of market prices from prices [costs] of production' which were the long-run equilibrium prices, but rather 'the constant deviations of market prices, in so far as these correspond to prices of production, from the real values of commodities . . .' (Marx, 1952, p. 121).[32] Similarly he criticized Ricardo for directly identifying surplus value – the labourer's work beyond his own maintenance requirements – with profits (the justice of these criticisms is irrelevant here).[33]

These were not isolated differences on particular theories, but fundamental methodological differences. In contrast to the usual criticism of Ricardo as too abstract, Marx claimed that 'the opposite accusation would be justified – i.e., lack of the power to abstract' (Marx, 1952, p. 231), at least to do so systematically and consistently. According to Marx, Ricardo 'skips necessary intermediate links and tries to establish *direct* proof of economic categories with each other' (Marx, 1952, p. 202). Classical economics in general was accused of making 'a regular hash' of concepts belonging on different levels of abstraction (Marx and Engels, 1942, p. 227). Marx blamed Adam Smith's inconsistent theories of value on his unconsciously operating on different levels of abstraction, alternately 'penetrating to the inner relations' and then dealing with 'the external phenomena . . . in their outward manifestation . . .' (Marx, 1952, p. 202).

Marx insisted that the method of systematic abstraction and successive approximation was the essence of scientific procedure. He said: '. . . all science would be superfluous, if the appearance, the form and the nature of things were wholly identical' (Marx, 1906, vol. III, p. 951). On the first page of his *Critique of Political Economy* he warned that there would be no 'anticipation of results' which depended upon later stages of the argument. In a later discussion of 'the method of political economy', Marx argued that while it 'seems to be the correct procedure to commence with the real and concrete aspect of conditions as they are', yet 'on closer consideration

31. '. . . if profits as a percentage of capital are to be equal, for example in a period of one year, so that capitals of equal size yield equal profits in the same period of time, then the prices of commodities must be different from their values' (Marx, 1952, p. 133; see also pp. 212, 214, 221, 224, 232, 249, 250, 282; Marx and Engels, 1942, p. 243). cf. Böhm-Bawerk (1896, p. 61 and chapter 3 *passim*).
32. cf. Böhm-Bawerk (1896, p. 76).
33. 'We can see by the example of the Ricardian school that it is a mistake to attempt a development of the laws of the rate of profit directly out of the laws of the rate of surplus-value, or vice-versa' (Marx, 1906, vol. III, p. 59: see also Marx, 1952, p. 231, 282, 329, 342).

it proves to be wrong' (Marx, 1904, p. 292). Thus, though he found 'error' in Hegel, he nevertheless approved the Hegelian 'method of advancing from the abstract to the concrete . . .' (Marx, 1904, pp. 293-4).

Similarly, in a preface to a French edition of *Capital* Marx acknowledged that his 'method of analysis' might make the opening chapters on value 'arduous' for those who were 'impatient to come to a conclusion' (Marx, n.d., p. 21). Only in the third volume of *Capital* did the analysis 'approach step by step' economic entities as they appear 'in the ordinary consciousness of the human agencies in this process' (Marx, 1906, vol. III, p. 38). Here, as he informed Engels, he would consider 'the *forms of appearance* which serve as the *starting point* in the vulgar conception' (Marx and Engels, 1942, p. 245). Vulgar economics was defined by Marx as that which 'deals with appearances only' (Marx, 1906, vol. I, p. 93n.) – prices, profit and other tangible entities – without consideration of the underlying human relationships analysed by classical economics.

Marx was conscious (and proud) of pioneering a new method in economics (Marx and Engels, 1942, p. 232). When Engels pointed out to him how his discussion of value and surplus-value in volume I was likely to be misunderstood by people who were 'not accustomed to this sort of abstract thought' (Marx and Engels, 1942, p. 220), Marx replied:

. . . the *conversion of surplus value into profit* . . . presupposes a previous account of the *process of circulation of capital*, since the turnover of capital, etc., plays a part here. Hence this matter can be set forth only in the third book . . . Here it will be shown whence the *way of thinking* of the philistine and the vulgar economist derives, namely, from the fact that only the immediate form in which relationships appear is always reflected in their brain, and not their *inner connections*. If the latter were the case, moreover, what would be the need for a *science* at all?

If I were to *silence* all such objections *in advance*, I should ruin the whole dialectical method of development. On the contrary, this method has the advantage of continually *setting traps* for these fellows which provoke them to untimely demonstrations of their asininity (Engels, 1937, pp. 126-7).[34]

Marxian value, as will be seen below, was a matter of definition rather than theory. However, it facilitated discussion of substantive theories involving the dynamics of class income distribution and the nature and pathology of resource allocation, including business cycles. The Marxian 'law of value' was a theory of the process by which the economy allocates its working time to the respective products composing its total output

34. It is difficult to escape the suspicion that Marx was overly concerned with 'setting traps', particularly in view of the fact that some of the most important clues as to what he was about – including his stark repudiation of Smith and Ricardo on the labour theory of value – were contained in *footnotes* in the first volume of *Capital*. See Marx (1906, vol. I, pp. 57n., 82n., 95n., 185n.)

(Marx, 1906, vol. III, pp. 220–21). The 'law of value ... ultimately determines how much of its disposable working time society can expend on each particular class of commodities' (Marx, 1906, vol. I, p. 391). The 'law of value' thus serves to 'maintain the social equilibrium of production in the turmoil of its accidental fluctuations' (Marx, 1906, vol. III, p. 1028). If there is optimal, equilibrium allocation of labour, 'then the products of the various groups are sold at their values ... or at prices which are modifications of their values ... due to general laws' (Marx, 1906, vol. III, p. 745), i.e. profit equalization. This was 'the law of value enforcing itself, not with reference to individual commodities or articles, but to the total products of *the* particular social spheres of production made independent by division of labour' (Marx, 1906, vol. III, p. 745). In other words, the main point was not to explain the structure of prices in static equilibrium but rather to explain the dynamic process by which these prices came about, especially since this process produced business cycles as a by-product.

Marx never claimed to have a labour theory of value. Indeed, he charged 'bad faith' in this regard to a critic who 'attempts ... to burden me with all Ricardo's limitations' (Marx and Engels, 1942, p. 234). The opening chapter of *Capital* referred to 'Value as defined' (Marx, 1906, vol. I, p. 45). This was no isolated verbal slip; even earlier (in 1858) while writing the *Critique of Political Economy*, Marx had informed Engels of the 'definition of value' which he intended to use in that book (Marx and Engels, 1942, p. 106), and similar language appeared in Marx's later reactions to criticism of the first volume of *Capital*. For example:

... as for Duhring's modest objections to the definition of value, he will be astonished when he sees in Volume II how little the determination of value 'directly' counts for in bourgeois society. *No form* of society can indeed prevent the fact that, one way or another, the working time at the disposal of society regulates production. So long, however, as this regulation is accomplished not by the direct and conscious control of society over its working time – which is only possible under common ownership – but by the movement of commodity prices, things remain as you have already quite aptly described them in the *Deutsch-Französische Jahrbücher* (Marx and Engels, 1942, p. 232).

The 'second volume' referred to was intended to include Books II and III, each of which was in fact posthumously published as separate volumes (Engels, 1937, p. 127; Marx and Engels, 1942, p. 219).[35] In another comment on his critics, Marx again indicated the definitional nature of 'value':

35. Additional material prepared by Marx and discovered by Engels after his death were enough to 'swell the second volume into a second and a third' (Engels, Lafargue and Lafargue, 1959, vol. I, p. 178).

The nonsense about the necessity of proving the concept of value arises from complete ignorance both of the subject dealt with and of the method of science. Every child knows that a country which ceased to work, I will not say for a year, but for a few weeks, would die. Every child knows too that the mass of products corresponding to the different needs require different and quantitatively determined masses of the total labour of society . . .

The science consists precisely in working out *how* the law of value operates. So that if one wanted at the very beginning to 'explain' all the phenomena which apparently contradict that law, one would have to give the science *before* the science. It is precisely Ricardo's mistake . . . in his first chapter on value . . .

The vulgar economist has not the faintest idea that the actual everyday exchange relations need not be directly identical with the magnitudes of value. The point of bourgeois society consists precisely in this, that *a priori* there is no conscious, social regulation of production . . . And then the vulgar economist thinks he has made a great discovery when, as against the disclosures of the inner connection, he proudly claims that in appearance things look different. In fact, he is boasting that he holds fast to the appearance and takes it for the last word. Why then, any science at all? (Marx and Engels, 1942, pp. 246–7).

Marx's disavowal of any attempt to 'prove' his definition of value was in sharp contrast to numerous critics who have claimed that he had vainly attempted a 'dialectical proof' in the opening chapter of *Capital*.[36] To a contemporary critic who had argued along similar lines, Engels replied that his 'total lack of understanding as to the nature of dialectics is shown by the very fact that he regards it as a mere instrument through which things can be proved . . .' (Engels, 1939, p. 147). In Marx there were no dialectical forces, dialectical theories, or dialectical proofs; there was only a dialectical method of approach – looking at dynamic relationships rather than static conditions, seeking the element of 'law' or necessity in apparently random or accidental phenomena, and reasoning systematically through successive approximations. The discussion in the opening chapter of *Capital* was not an exercise in logic but in popularization. Marx was concerned, as he told Engels, that this material should be at least 'bearably *popular*' (Marx and Engels, 1942, p. 157) or even 'specially popularized for the philistine' (Marx and Engels, 1942, p. 220n.); he was painfully aware that his earlier presentation of the same subject in the *Critique of Political Economy* had been 'in a marked degree non-popular' (Marx, 1934, p. 24).[37]

36. . . . for his system he needed a formal proof. . . . So he turned to dialectical speculation . . .' (Böhm-Bawerk, 1896, pp. 151–2). Böhm-Bawerk made the claim, often echoed since, that Marx had attempted 'a stringent syllogistic conclusion allowing of no exception' (1896, p. 63), that Marx was making 'a logical proof, a dialectical deduction' (1896, p. 131). This 'proof' continues in some unspecified way to be linked to dialectics or Hegelianism. cf. Gordon (1959, p. 471).

37. Despite this, Marx repeatedly dismissed suggestions that his writing was in general difficult to understand (e.g. Marx, 1934, p. 75) and entertained the idea of

The utter failure of Marx's attempt at popularization should not obscure the fact that this was nevertheless what he was attempting.

Marxian value was 'socially necessary labour time' in two senses: (1) the technologically required time to produce a given article, and (2) the aggregate amount of time required to produce the total quantity of the article demanded.[38] While 'concrete' (Marx, 1906, vol. I, pp. 54, 58, 67)[39] or 'individual'[40] labour, consisting of the exercise of a particular skill or vocation by an individual worker, was tangible, the 'socially necessary labour' performed by society through the instrumentality of these individuals was not. It could not be measured *ex ante* but only determined *ex post* by the market (Marx, 1906, vol. I, p. 84; 1904, pp. 47, 63–4). It is the market – 'the act of exchange' – which evaluates the concrete 'labour of the individual' as 'part of the labour of society' (Marx, 1906, vol. I, p. 84)[41] – accepting it only at a discount if too much was expended, either technologically or in terms of demand, and at a premium if insufficient labour was devoted to a particular sector (Marx, 1906, vol. III, p. 221). Because the individual or concrete labour actually performed need not coincide with the socially necessary labour which represents value, Marx and Engels argued that (1) disproportionality crises were inherent in capitalism,[42] and that (2) prices could not be fixed according to labour time under socialism as some other socialists wished.[43]

---

writing an account of Hegelian philosophy which would be understandable by the 'ordinary' person (Marx and Engels, 1942, p. 102).

38. '. . . suppose that every piece of linen in the market contains no more labour-time than is socially necessary. In spite of this, all these pieces taken as a whole, may have had superfluous labour-time spent upon them' (Marx, 1906, vol. I, p. 120); '. . . it is a condition for the sale of commodities at their value that only the socially necessary labour time is contained in them . . . only the labour time which is required for the satisfaction of the social need (the demand)' (Marx, 1952, pp. 398–9). See also Engels's 'Preface' to Marx (1963, p. 15).

39. This contrasted with 'abstract' labour, the labour of society (Marx, 1906, vol. I, p. 67; 1904, pp. 23, 29, 33, 102).

40. This phrasing was used in Marx (1904, pp. 27, 29, 43, 45).

41. '. . . overproduction and many other features of industrial anarchy have their explanation in this mode of evaluation' (Marx, 1963, p. 66).

42. In criticizing Ricardo's adherence to Say's law, Marx said that Ricardo 'forgets' that 'the individual labour, through its alienation, must present itself as abstract, general, social labour' (Marx, 1952, p. 381). Similarly Engels observed: 'The fact that value is the expression of the social labour contained in the individual products itself creates the possibility of a difference arising between this social labour and the individual labour contained in these products.' This led to, among other things, 'crises' (Engels, 1939, p. 338).

43. 'Only through the undervaluation or overvaluation of products is it forcibly brought home to the individual commodity producers what things and what quantity of them society requires or does not require. But it is just this sole regulator that the

Although Marx's economic theories were presented in terms of labour 'value', they could be restated in other terms without distorting their meaning, just as the Keynesian 'labour unit' (which has the same meaning) is not essential to that system. Marx declared that 'even if there were no chapter on value' in *Capital*, the relationships he demonstrated would stand anyway (Marx and Engels, 1942, p. 246). While Marx's actual conclusions stand or fall independently of his value concept, this has been obscured by the tendency to attribute to Marx the views of the Ricardian socialists. For example, the idea that workers should receive the full 'value' of their product was scorned by Marx as 'the utopian interpretation of Ricardo's theory' (Marx and Engels, 1942, p. 246; Marx, 1963, p. 49),[44] and Engels pointed out that Marx 'never based his communist demands upon this', which was 'simply an application of morality to economics' (Engels, 'Preface' to Marx, 1963). Similarly, those who wanted labour values to determine prices under socialism were told that they would have to 'prove that the *time* needed to create a commodity indicates exactly the degree of its utility and marks its proportional relation to the demand . . .' (Marx, 1963, pp. 60–61). Marxian 'socially necessary labour' could logically have been translated into the language of the marginal utility theory had Marx had the flexibility, the time, and the energy to do so.

Even Marxian 'exploitation' does not depend on the labour value definition, although obviously its exposition is facilitated and its plausibility enhanced by this phraseology. However, since 'surplus value' is simply the difference between wages and the worker's average product, it would remain unchanged under a marginal productivity theory of wages in a perfectly competitive market. The crucial assumption on which Marx's results depend is that capital is itself a product of labour rather than an independent source of output or a contribution of its legal owner (Marx, 1906, vol. I, pp. 637–8; 1952, p. 360; 1961, pp. 23–4). Since Marx regarded economics as a study of the relations among men rather than the relations among things, the point was that the Marxian capitalist was left in a

---

utopia in which Rodbertus also shares would abolish . . . we then ask what guarantee we have that the necessary quantity and not more of each product will be produced, that we shall not go hungry in regard to corn and meat while we are choked in beet sugar and drowned in potato spirit, that we shall not lack trousers to cover our nakedness while trouser buttons flood us in millions . . .' (Engels's 'Preface' to Marx, 1963, p. 19). See also Marx (1904, pp. 103–6; 1963, chapter 1). Contrast this with the typical interpretation of Joan Robinson: '. . . Marx believed that, under socialism, the labour theory of value would come into its own' (Robinson, 1957, p. 23).

44. '. . . in no conceivable state of society can the worker receive for consumption the entire value of his product' (Engels, 'Preface' to Marx, 1963, p. 21). '. . . deductions from the "undiminished proceeds of labour" are an economic necessity and their magnitude is . . . in no way calculable by equity' (Marx, 1955b, vol. II, p 22).

personally functionless role similar to that of the Ricardian landlord who grew richer in his sleep. It was no more necessary for Marx to argue that capital as such was unproductive than it was for Ricardo to argue that land was unproductive. Indeed, it would have been a complete contradiction for Marx to have argued that the capitalistic means of production were worthless and then that the key to social construction lay precisely in the collective ownership of these means of production.

5 Summary and conclusions

Marx's *Capital* presented a picture in which 'men work for each other' but in a state of neo-Hegelian 'alienation' in which they perceive their own creations confronting and controlling them: the worker creates capital, but the capital employs him (or disemploys him) according to its necessities rather than his (Marx, 1906, vol. III, p. 230; 1961, pp. 23–4).[45] They do not see their own mutual interchanges of labour, but only their products' mutual relations – 'the fetishism of commodities' – in which the underlying human relations expressed by value and surplus value are reflected and distorted as 'exchange-value' (price) and profit.[46] They see their own individual performances of particular kinds of individual 'concrete' labour, but do not see that society as a whole must perform labour in general in the proper amounts in the respective sectors – 'ab-

45. 'The *alienation* of the worker in his product means not only that his labour becomes an object, an *external* existence, but that it exists *outside him*, independently, as something alien to him, and that it becomes a power on its own confronting him; it means that the life which he has conferred on the object confronts him as something hostile and alien' (Marx, 1961, p. 70). Alienation is not merely an objective situation but also a subjective state of mind induced by it in which the '*human mind stands bewildered in the presence of its own creation*', which it does not recognize as such (Engels, 1955a, vol. II, p. 325). This concept recurred throughout Marx's writings, though the specific Hegelian term 'alienation' was no longer used after the 1840s in most cases: Engels (1955a, p. 323); Marx and Engels (1947, pp. 22–3); Marx (1952, p. 317); Engels (1939, pp. 300, 345). See also Marcuse (1954, pp. 273–87).

46. '. . . a definite social relation between men . . . assumes, in their eyes, the fantastic form of a relation between things. In order, therefore, to find an analogy, we must have recourse to the mist-enveloped regions of the religious world. In that world the productions of the human brain appear as independent beings endowed with life, and entering into relation both with one another and the human race. So it is in the world of commodities with the products of men's hands. This I call the Fetishism which attaches itself to the products of labour, so soon as they are produced as commodities', i.e., products for the market (Marx, 1906, vol. I, p. 83). Value involves 'a relationship between persons expressed as a relation between things' (Marx, 1906, vol. I, p. 85n). The appearance of the value is the exchange-value or price. According to Engels, 'economics deals not with things but with relations between persons, and, in the last resort, between classes; these relations are, however, always *attached to things* and *appear as things*' (Engels, 1955b, vol. I, p. 374). See also Marx (1904, pp. 30–31, 51–2); Engels(1937, p. 45).

stract, socially necessary labour – and that this *ex post* necessity of inter-dependence will assert itself despite *ex ante* independence and the accidental relationship of individual decisions to one another. *Capital* was designated to 'lay bare' these human relationships, external necessities, and the secular tendencies to which they lead (Marx, 1906, vol. I, p. 14; vol. III, p. 62).

When the inherent disproportionalities of capitalism reach sufficient magnitudes, price fluctuations become great enough to precipitate scrambles for liquidity in sectors threatened with bankruptcies; this in turn leads to general monetary contraction and depression. A growing capital:labour ratio in the economy means that the workers' share of gross output (not national income) declines over time, increasing class tensions which eventually erupt into revolution triggered by one of the recurrent depressions which cover increasingly larger shares of the economy as industrial capitalism spreads its dominance over time.

This was the vision which Marx and Engels developed in the early 1840s and which remained substantially unchanged throughout the rest of their lives, despite their recurrent complaints in later years that events – and especially the workers – were not following this pattern (Marx and Engels, 1942, pp. 92, 213, 278–9, 289, 420–21, 461, 463–4).

A critique of the Marxian system is beyond the scope of this paper. What may be more relevant in a centenary retrospect is the question whether *Capital* represented any significant advance in economic thinking. In some ways it was the last salvo of classical economics. Yet Marx was by no means 'a minor post-Ricardian' (Samuelson, 1957, p. 911) – or a Ricardian at all (though the Ricardian *theory* of value was obviously the basis of Marx's *definition* of value).[47] There were a number of significant advances beyond the economic thinking of its time which Marx's *Capital* originated, though it did not 'introduce' them into the mainstream of economics because economics largely ignored Marx and later rediscovered his contribution independently. Among these advances were:

1. The systematic use of successive approximations. Long before Marx wrote *Capital*, Ricardo had been criticized for using his highly abstract models as a basis for direct conclusions about the real world – the so-called 'Ricardian vice' (Jones, 1831, p. vii; Whewell, 'Prefatory Notice' to

47. Schumpeter was one of the few historians of economic thought to note that the Ricardian value theory 'forms no part of Marx's teaching' (Schumpeter, 1954, p. 597), and even he had believed otherwise earlier (Schumpeter, 1950, p. 23). Veblen has pointed out much earlier that despite the resemblance of the Marxian doctrine to 'the labour-value theory of Ricardo', in fact 'the relationship between the two is that of a superficial coincidence in their main propositions rather than a substantial identity of theoretic contents' (Veblen, 1906, p. 587). He also saw what Marx's correspondence later confirmed, that the opening chapter of *Capital* was not an attempt to prove the notion of value (Veblen, 1906, p. 585).

Jones, 1859, pp. xii–xiii).[48] But unlike other critics who devoted themselves to an elaborate and often naïve empiricism, Marx attempted to trace the 'intermediate links' (Marx, 1952, pp 202, 282) between the abstract concepts and the concrete manifestations. While unsparing in his criticism of Ricardian abstractions, Marx also scorned those whose 'lack of a theoretical bent' lead them to 'snatch clumsily at the empirical material before them . . .' (Marx, 1952, p. 133). Here Marx was indebted to Hegel, though he could still with justice claim to be the first economist to apply what he called the 'dialectical method'.

2. The treatment of price theory as essentially allocation and distribution theory. Earlier economists had discussed price theory either as an important subject in itself or as a means of establishing a numeraire for discussing aggregates. Marx established his numeraire by definition as Keynes was later to do. He was not concerned with relative prices in equilibrium as such,[49] but with the dynamic process which tended towards such an equilibrium, and with disequilibrium prices as symptoms of allocational imbalance and harbingers of crises.

3. *Capital* pioneered in business cycle theory, not only in the thoroughness of its treatment, in suggesting specific concepts and hypotheses, but more fundamentally in treating the business cycle as an important problem to be dealt with in and of itself, rather than a subject to be backed into inadvertently by admitting the possibility of temporary depression under certain circumstances.

In Marxian economics, as in other areas, 'Marx' must be understood as merely a convenient way of referring to both Marx and Engels. Engels's priority in developing parts of the Marxian vision should be noted, particularly in view of some attempts to disparage his role (for example, Schumpeter, 1950, p. 39n.). He developed the Marxian theory of crises before Marx and originated the concept of the 'reserve army of the unemployed' (Engels, 1952, p. 82).[50] It was unfortunate that circumstances would not permit his taking a more active part in the writing of *Capital*.[51] With his

48. The term 'Ricardian vice' was, of course, coined much later by Schumpeter (1954, pp. 472–3; 1951, p. 150).

49. He disavowed, for example, any interest in the 'dull and tedious quarrel over the part played by Nature in the formation of exchange value' (Marx, 1906, vol. I, p. 94). See also note 46 above.

50. It should be noted further that although the expansions and contractions of the 'reserve army' have been considered by interpreters to determine wages in the Marxian system (Samuelson, 1957, p. 908), in *Capital* they determine only the direction of cyclical fluctuations of wages, not the level around which the fluctuations take place, and certainly not *secular* changes in wages. '. . . the expansion and contraction of the industrial reserve army . . . correspond to the periodic changes of the industrial cycle' (Marx, 1906, vol. I, p. 699).

51. Engels construed his role of editor of the posthumous volumes of *Capital* very

greater facility of exposition, perhaps *Capital* would have been completed earlier, understood better, and subjected to rational criticism instead of remaining so long a shadowy enigma at which many shafts have been vainly hurled.

References

BÖHM-BAWERK, E. VON (1896), *Karl Marx and the Close of His System*, New York.

BOTTOMORE, T. B., and RUBEL, M. (1956), *Karl Marx: Selected Writings in Sociology and Social Philosophy*, Watts.

BRONFENBRENNER, M. (1965), '*Das Kapital* for the modern man', *Science and Society*, Fall, pp. 419–38.

ENGELS, F. (1937), *Engels on Capital* (L. E. Mins ed. and trans.), International Publishers, New York.

ENGELS, F. (1939), *Herr Eugen Dühring's Revolution in Science*, International Publishers, New York.

ENGELS, F. (1952), *The Condition of the Working Class in England*, London.

ENGELS, F. (1955a), *The Origin of the Family, Private Property and the State*, in K. Marx and F. Engels, *Selected Works*, Foreign Languages Publishing House, Moscow.

ENGELS, F. (1955b), 'Review of "Karl Marx, *A Contribution to the Critique of Political Economy*" ', in K. Marx and F. Engels, *Selected Works*, Foreign Languages Publishing House, Moscow.

ENGELS, F. (1959), *Ludwig Feuerbach and the End of Classical German Philosophy*, in K. Marx and F. Engels, *Basic Writings on Politics and Philosophy* (L. S. Feuer ed.), New York.

ENGELS, F. (1961), 'Outlines of a critique of political economy', in K. Marx, *Economic and Philosophic Manuscripts of 1844* (M. Milligan trans.), Foreign Languages Publishing House, Moscow.

ENGELS, F. (1964), *Dialectics of Nature*, 3rd rev. ed., Progress Publishers, Moscow.

ENGELS, F., LAFARGUE, P., and LAFARGUE, L. (1959), *Correspondence*, Foreign Languages Publishing House, Moscow.

GORDON, D. F. (1959), 'What was the labour theory of value?', *American Economic Review*, May.

HEGEL, G. W. F. (1892), *The Science of Logic* (W. Wallace trans.), London.

HEGEL, G. W. F. (1956), *The Philosophy of History* (U. Sibrée trans.), New York.

---

narrowly – probably more narrowly than Marx had intended, in view of his extensive briefings of Engels and his message relayed through his daughter that Engels should 'make something' of the manuscripts he left (Marx, 1906, vol. II, pp. 1, 11; vol. III, pp. 12, 14). It was out of the question for Engels to have actively collaborated in the writing of *Capital* during Marx's lifetime, despite the latter's desire to make him a co-author (Marx and Engels, 1942, pp. 209–10) since he was busy earning money as a businessman to subsidize Marx. The period between his collaboration with Marx on the *Communist Manifesto* in 1848 and his *Anti-Dühring* in the mid 1870s was largely barren for this reason. Another factor of uncertain weight was Engels's ideological vulnerability during this period because of his occupation. As Engels pointed out to Marx, their enemies among the socialists were certain to say, 'The fellow is sitting in Manchester exploiting the workers, etc.' (Marx and Engels, 1942, p. 188).

JONES, R. (1831), *An Essay on the Distribution of Wealth and the Sources of Taxation*, John Murray.

JONES, R. (1859), *Literary Remains*, John Murray.

MARCUSE, H. (1954), *Reason and Revolution: Hegel and the Rise of Social Theory*, 2nd ed., New York.

MARX, K. (n.d.), *Capital*, Foreign Languages Publishing House, Moscow.

MARX, K. (1904), *A Contribution to the Critique of Political Economy*, Charles H. Kerr, Chicago.

MARX, K. (1906), *Capital*, Charles H. Kerr, Chicago.

MARX, K. (1934), *Letters to Dr Kugelmann*, International Publishers, New York.

MARX, K. (1947), *Wage Labour and Capital*, Foreign Languages Publishing House, Moscow.

MARX, K. (1952), *Theories of Surplus Value* (G. A. Bonner and E. Burns trans.), International Publishers, New York.

MARX, K. (1955a), *Wage Labour and Capital*, in K. Marx and F. Engels, *Selected Works*, Foreign Languages Publishing House, Moscow.

MARX, K. (1955b), *Critique of the Gotha Programme*, in K. Marx and F. Engels, *Selected Works*, Foreign Languges Publishing House, Moscow.

MARX, K. (1961), *Economic and Philosophic Manuscripts of 1844* (M. Milligan trans.), Foreign Languages Publishing House, Moscow.

MARX, K. (1963), *The Poverty of Philosophy*, International Publishers, New York.

MARX, K., and ENGELS, F. (1935), *The Communist Manifesto*, in E. Burn (ed.), *A Handbook of Marxism*, New York.

MARX, K., and ENGELS, F. (1942), *Selected Correspondence* (D. Torr trans.), International Publishers, New York.

MARX, K., and ENGELS, F. (1947), *The German Ideology*, International Publishers, New York.

MARX, K., and ENGELS, F. (1953), *Letters to Americans* (L.E. Mins trans.), International Publishers, New York.

MARX, K., and ENGELS, F. (1956), *The Holy Family*, Foreign Languages Publishing House, Moscow.

MEHRING, F. (1935), *Karl Marx: The Story of His Life*, New York.

MUELLER, G. E. (1958), 'The Hegel legend of "Thesis–Antithesis–Synthesis"', *Journal of the History of Ideas*, June, pp. 411–14.

RICARDO, D. (1953), *The Works and Correspondence of David Ricardo* (P. Sraffa ed.), Cambridge.

ROBINSON, J. (1957), *An Essay on Marxian Economics*, London.

SAMUELSON, P. (1957), 'Wages and interest: a modern dissection of Marxian economic models', *American Economic Review*, December, pp. 884–912.

SAY, J.-B. (1846), *A Treatise on Political Economy* (C. R. Prinsep trans.), Grigg & Elliot, Philadelphia.

SCHUMPETER, J. A. (1950), *Capitalism, Socialism and Democracy*, New York.

SCHUMPETER, J. A. (1951), *Essays of J. A. Schumpeter* (R. V. Clemence ed.), Cambridge (Mass.).

SCHUMPETER, J. A. (1954), *History of Economic Analysis*, New York.

SHOUL, B. (1957), 'Karl Marx and Say's law', *Quarterly Journal of Economics*, November.

SOWELL, T. (1960), 'Marx's "increasing misery" doctrine', *American Economic Review*, March, pp. 111–20.

SWEEZY, P. M. (1956), *The Theory of Capitalist Development*, New York.

VEBLEN, T. (1906), 'The socialist economics of Karl Marx and his followers', *Quarterly Journal of Economics*, August.

Part Two
Theoretical Underpinnings

2 Karl Marx

The Materialist Conception of History

Excerpt from Karl Marx, 'Preface', *A Contribution to the Critique of Political Economy*, Lawrence & Wishart, 1971, pp. 20–22.

In the social production of their existence, men inevitably enter into definite relations, which are independent of their will, namely relations of production appropriate to a given stage in the development of their material forces of production. The totality of these relations of production constitutes the economic structure of society, the real foundation, on which arises a legal and political superstructure and to which correspond definite forms of social consciousness. The mode of production of material life conditions the general process of social, political and intellectual life. It is not the consciousness of men that determines their existence, but their social existence that determines their consciousness. At a certain stage of development, the material productive forces of society come into conflict with the existing relations of production or – this merely expresses the same thing in legal terms – with the property relations within the framework of which they have operated hitherto. From forms of development of the productive forces these relations turn into their fetters. Then begins an era of social revolution. The changes in the economic foundation lead sooner or later to the transformation of the whole immense superstructure. In studying such transformations it is always necessary to distinguish between the material transformation of the economic conditions of production, which can be determined with the precision of natural science, and the legal, political, religious, artistic or philosophic – in short, ideological forms in which men become conscious of this conflict and fight it out. Just as one does not judge an individual by what he thinks about himself, so one cannot judge such a period of transformation by its consciousness, but, on the contrary, this consciousness must be explained from the contradictions of material life, from the conflict existing between the social forces of production and the relations of production. No social order is ever destroyed before all the productive forces for which it is sufficient have been developed, the new superior relations of production never replace older ones before the material conditions for their existence have matured within the framework of the old society. Mankind thus inevitably sets itself only such tasks as it is able to solve, since closer examination will always show that the problem itself arises only when the material conditions for its solution are already present or at least in the course of formation. In broad outline, the Asiatic, ancient, feudal and modern bourgeois modes of production may be designated as epochs marking progress in the economic development of society. The bourgeois mode of production is the last antagonistic form of the social process of production – antagonistic not in the sense of individual antagonism but of an antagonism that emanates from the individuals' social conditions of existence – but the productive forces developing within bourgeois society create also the material conditions for a solution of this antagonism. The prehistory of human society accordingly closes with this social formation.

3 Karl Marx

The Nature of Economic Analysis

Excerpt from David McLellan, *Marx's Grundrisse*, revised edition, Paladin, 1973, pp. 26–32.

The subject of our discussion is first of all *material* production. Individuals producing in society, thus the socially determined production of individuals, naturally constitutes the starting point. The individual and isolated hunter or fisher who forms the starting point with Smith and Ricardo belongs to the insipid illusions of the eighteenth century. They are Robinson Crusoe stories which do not by any means represent, as students of the history of civilization imagine, a reaction against over-refinement and a return to a misunderstood natural life. They are no more based on such a naturalism than is Rousseau's *contrat social* which makes naturally independent individuals come in contact and have mutual intercourse by contract. They are the fiction and only the aesthetic fiction of the small and great adventure stories. They are, rather, the anticipation of 'civil society', which had been in course of development since the sixteenth century and made gigantic strides towards maturity in the eighteenth. In this society of free competition the individual appears free from the bonds of nature, etc., which in former epochs of history made him part of a definite, limited human conglomeration. To the prophets of the eighteenth century, on whose shoulders Smith and Ricardo are still standing, this eighteenth-century individual, constituting the joint product of the dissolution of the feudal form of society and of the new forces of production which had developed since the sixteenth century, appears as an ideal whose existence belongs to the past; not as a result of history, but as its starting point. Since that individual appeared to be in conformity with nature and corresponded to their conception of human nature, he was regarded not as developing historically, but as posited by nature. This illusion has been characteristic of every new epoch in the past. Steuart, who, as an aristocrat, stood more firmly on historical ground and was in many respects opposed to the spirit of the eighteenth century, escaped this simplicity of view.

The farther back we go into history, the more the individual and, therefore, the producing individual seems to depend on and belong to a larger whole: at first it is, quite naturally, the family and the clan, which is but an enlarged family; later on, it is the community growing up in its different forms out of the clash and the amalgamation of clans. It is only in the eighteenth century, in 'civil society', that the different forms of social union confront the individual as a mere means to his private ends, as an external necessity. But the period in which this standpoint – that of the isolated individual – became prevalent is the very one in which the social relations of society (universal relations according to that standpoint) have reached the highest state of development. Man is in the most literal sense of the word a *zoon politikon*, not only a social animal, but an animal which can develop into an individual only in society. Production by isolated individuals outside society – something which might happen as an exception to a civilized man who by accident got into the wilderness and already potentially possessed within himself the forces of society – is as great an absurdity as the idea of the development of language without individuals living together and talking to one another. We need not dwell on this any longer. It would not be necessary to touch upon this point at all, had not this nonsense – which, however, was justified and made sense in the eighteenth century – been transplanted, in all seriousness, into the field of political economy by Bastiat, Carey, Proudhon and others. Proudhon and others naturally find it very pleasant, when they do not know the historical origin of a certain economic phenomenon, to give it a quasi-historico-philosophical explanation by going into mythology. Adam or Prometheus hit upon the scheme cut and dried, whereupon it was adopted, etc. Nothing is more tediously dry than the dreaming platitude.

Whenever we speak, therefore, of production, we always have in mind production at a certain stage of social development, or production by social individuals. Hence, it might seem that in order to speak of production at all, we must either trace the historical process of development through its various phases, or declare at the outset that we are dealing with a certain historical period, as, for example, with modern capitalist production, which, as a matter of fact, constitutes the proper subject of this work. But all stages of production have certain landmarks in common, common purposes. 'Production in general' is an abstraction, but it is a rational abstraction, in so far as it singles out and fixes the common features, thereby saving us repetition. Yet these general or common features discovered by comparison constitute something very complex, whose constituent elements have different destinations. Some of these elements belong to all epochs, others are common to a few. Some of them are common to the most modern as well as to the most ancient epochs. No production is conceivable without them; but while even the most completely developed languages have laws and conditions in common with the least developed ones, what is characteristic of their development are the points of departure from the general and common. The conditions which generally govern production must be differentiated in order that the essential points of difference should not be lost sight of in view of the general uniformity which is due to the fact that the subject, mankind, and the object, nature, remain the same. The failure to remember this one fact is the source of all the wisdom of modern economists who are trying to prove the eternal nature and harmony of existing social conditions. Thus they say, for example, that no production is possible without some instrument of production, let that instrument be only the hand; that none is possible without past accumulated labour, even if that labour should consist of mere skill which has been accumulated and concentrated in the hand of the savage by repeated exercise. Capital is, among other things, also an instrument of production, also past impersonal labour. Hence capital is a universal, eternal natural phenomenon; which is true if we disregard the specific properties which turn an 'instrument of production' and 'stored-up labour' into capital. The entire history of the relationships of production appears to a man like Carey, for example, as a malicious perversion on the part of governments.

If there is no production in general there is also no general production. Production is always either some special branch of production, as, for example, agriculture, stock-raising, manufactures, etc., or an aggregate. But political economy is not technology. The connection between the general determinations of productions at a given stage of social development and the particular forms of production is to be developed elsewhere (later on).

Finally, production is never only of a particular kind. It is always a certain social body or a social subject that is engaged on a larger or smaller aggregate of branches of production. The connection between the real process and its scientific presentation also falls outside of the scope of this treatise. Production in general. Special branches of production. Production as a whole.

It is the fashion with economists to open their works with a general introduction, which is entitled 'production' (see, for example, John Stuart Mill) and deals with the general 'requisites of production'. This general introductory part consists of (or is supposed to consist of):

1. The conditions without which production is impossible, i.e. the essential conditions of all production. As a matter of fact, however, it can be reduced, as we shall see, to a few very simple definitions, which flatten out into shallow tautologies.
2. Conditions which further production more or less, as, for example, Adam Smith's discussion of a progressive and stagnant state of society.

In order to give scientific value to what serves with him as a mere summary, it would be necessary to study the *degree of productivity* by periods in the development of individual nations; such a study falls outside the scope of the present subject, and in so far as it does belong here is to be brought out in connection with the discussion of competition, accumulation, etc. The commonly accepted view of the matter gives a general answer to the effect that an industrial nation is at the height of its production at the moment when it reaches its historical climax in all respects. As a matter of fact a nation is at its industrial height so long as its main object is not gain, but the process of gaining. In that respect the Yankees stand above the English. Or, that certain races, climates, natural conditions, such as distance from the sea, fertility of the soil, etc., are more favourable to production than others. That again comes down to the tautology that the facility of creating wealth depends on the extent to which its elements are present both subjectively and objectively.

But all that is not what the economists are really concerned with in this general part. Their object is rather to represent production in contradistinction to distribution – see Mill, for example – as subject to eternal laws independent of history, and then to substitute bourgeois relations, in an underhand way, as immutable natural laws of society *in abstracto*. This is the more or less conscious aim of the entire proceeding. When it comes to distribution, on the contrary, mankind is supposed to have indulged in all sorts of arbitrary action. Quite apart from the fact that they violently break the ties which bind production and distribution together, so much must be clear from the outset: that, no matter how greatly the systems of distribution may vary at different stages of society, it should be possible here, as in the case of production, to discover the common features and to confound and eliminate all historical differences in formulating *general human* laws. For example, the slave, the serf, the wage-labourer – all receive a quantity of food, which enables them to exist as slave, serf and wage-labourer. The conqueror, the official, the landlord, the monk or the Levite, who respectively live on tribute, taxes, rent, alms and the tithe – all receive a part of the social product which is determined by laws different from those which determine the part received by the slave, etc. The two main points which all economists place under this head are, first, property; secondly, the protection of the latter by the administration of justice, police, etc. The objections to these two points can be stated very briefly.

1. All production is appropriation of nature by the individual within and through a definite form of society. In that sense it is a tautology to say that property (appropriation) is a condition of production. But it becomes ridiculous, when from that one jumps at once to a definite form of property, e.g. private property (which implies, besides, as a prerequisite the existence of an opposite form, viz. absence of property). History points rather to common property (e.g. among the Hindus, Slavs, ancient Celts, etc.) as the

primitive form, which still plays an important part at a much later period as communal property. The question as to whether wealth grows more rapidly under this or that form of property is not even raised here as yet. But that there can be no such thing as production, nor, consequently, society, where property does not exist in any form, is a tautology. Appropriation which does not appropriate is a *contradictio in subjecto*.

2. Protection of gain, etc. Reduced to their real meaning, these commonplaces express more than their preachers know, namely, that every form of production creates its own legal relations, forms of government, etc. The crudity and the shortcomings of the conception lie in the tendency to see only an accidental reflective connection in what constitutes an organic union. The bourgeois economists have a vague notion that production is better carried on under the modern police than it was, for example, under club law. They forget that club law is also law, and that the right of the stronger continues to exist in other forms even under their 'government of law'.

When the social conditions corresponding to a certain stage of production are in a state of formation or disappearance, disturbances of production naturally arise, although differing in extent and effect.

To sum up: all the stages of production have certain destinations in common, which we generalize in thought: but the so-called general conditions of all production are nothing but abstract conceptions which do not go to make up any real stage in the history of production.

4 Karl Marx

The Nature of Capitalism

Excerpt from David McLellan, *Marx's Grundrisse*, revised edition, Paladin, 1973, pp. 129–36.

Various conditions have to originate historically or be present before money becomes capital and labour becomes wage-labour which establishes and creates capital. ('Wage-labour' is here used in the strict economic sense in which alone we need it – we shall later have to distinguish it from other forms of labour for a daily wage, etc. – as labour that establishes and produces capital, i.e. living labour, which at the same time produces both the objective conditions for its realization as an activity, and the objective elements of its existence as labour power, as alien forces opposing it, as values which are independent of it and exist for themselves alone.) The essential conditions are established in the relationship as it originally exists:

1. On the one hand, living labour power is present as a purely subjective existence, separated from the elements of its objective reality; thus it is separated just as much from the conditions of living labour as from the means of subsistence and self-preservation of living labour power; in fact, there is on the one hand the active possibility of labour in all its abstraction.

2. On the other hand there is value, or objectified labour. This must be an accumulation of use values large enough to provide the objective conditions, not merely for the production of products or values needed in order to reproduce or maintain living labour power, but also to absorb surplus labour. In short, there must be objective material for labour.

3. There must be a free exchange relationship (money circulation) between the two sides, founded on exchange values, not on the master–servant relationship. There must be a mediation between the two extremes. This means production which does not deliver the means of subsistence directly to the producer, but arranges it through exchange, and since it cannot gain control of the alien labour directly, buys it by means of exchange from the worker.

4. Finally the side representing the objective conditions of labour in the form of independent, self-sufficient values must take the form of value and have as its ultimate purpose the setting up of values, self-valorization and the creation of money – and not the immediate enjoyment or the creation of use value.

So long as both sides can only exchange their labour with one another in the form of objectified labour, this relationship is impossible; it is equally impossible when living labour power itself is the property of the other side and not something to be exchanged. (This does not entirely rule out the possibility of the existence of slavery at isolated points within the bourgeois production system. But this is only possible because it does not exist at other points of the system and appears as an anomaly in opposition to the bourgeois system itself.)

The conditions in which this relationship originally appears, or which appear to be historical presuppositions of its formation, seem at first sight to have a double-sided nature – the dissolution of primitive forms of living labour on the one hand, and the dissolution of its happier relationships on the other.

The first prerequisite is that the system of slavery or bondage should be abolished. Living labour power belongs to itself, and disposes of its own manifestation of force by means of exchange. Both sides are opposed to one another as persons. Formally, their relationship is the free and equal one of those who exchange. As soon as we consider legal relationships, it appears that this is a mere semblance, and a deceptive semblance, which falls away outside the sphere of legal relationships. What the free worker sells is always only a definite, particular quantity of manifestation of force; and labour power as a totality dominates each particular manifestation. The worker sells his particular power to a particular capitalist, facing him independently as an individual. But it is clear that this is not his relationship to the existence of capital as capital, i.e. to the capitalist class. Nevertheless, as far as he is concerned as a real, individual person, he sees opening before him a vast field of arbitrary choice, and thus formal freedom. In the slavery relationship the worker belongs to an individual, particular owner, whose labour machine he is. In all the force that he can manifest, all his labour power, he belongs to another, and thus is not related as a subject to his own particular manifestation of force or his living act of working. In the bondage relationship, the worker is an element of landed property; he is a chattel of the earth just as cattle are. In the slave relationship the worker is nothing but a living machine, who as a result has a value for others, or rather is a value for others. Labour power seems to the free worker to be entirely his property, one of his elements which he, as a subject, controls, and which he retains in selling it. We shall develop this further in the section on wage-labour.

The exchange of objectified labour against living labour does not suffice to constitute one side as being capital, the other as wage-labour. The whole class of the so-called providers of services, from the shoeshine boy to the king, falls into this category. So also does the free wage-earner, whom we find everywhere to a sporadic extent, in places where either the oriental or the occidental community (consisting of free landed proprietors) dissolves into its individual elements – as a result of increase in population, release of prisoners of war, accidental conditions in which there is impoverishment of the individual and the objective circumstances of his self-sustaining labour disappear, as a result of the division of labour, etc. When A exchanges either value or money, i.e. objectified labour, in order to obtain a service from B, that is, living labour, this can occur:

1. In the relationship of simple circulation. Both, in fact, only exchange use values: one of them, means of subsistence; the other exchanges his labour, which is a service that the first desires to consume either directly (personal service), or by supplying the material by means of which, through his labour, through the objectification of his labour, the second creates use value destined to be consumed by the first. As, for example, when a farmer admits a travelling tailor into his house (as used to happen in the past) and gives him the cloth to make clothes with. Or if I give a doctor money to patch up my health for me. What is important in such cases is the service that they render to each other. *Do ut facias*[1] seems here to be on exactly the same level as *facio ut des*[2] or *do ut des*.[3] The man who makes me a suit out of the cloth for which I have supplied him the material gives me a use value. But instead of giving it at once in the objectified form, he gives it in the form of an activity. I give him a ready-made use value; he transforms it into another one for me. The difference between past, objectified and living, present labour appears here only as the formal difference between the various *tenses* of the work, which at one time occur in the perfect tense, at another in the present. It appears in fact to be a merely formal difference, produced by division of labour and exchange, whether B himself produces the means of subsistence from which he has to exist, or whether he obtains them from A; in which case he does not produce the means of subsistence directly, but produces a suit of clothes instead, for which he receives in exchange, from A, the means of subsistence. In both cases he can only obtain control of the use value possessed by A so long as he gives him an equivalent for it, which in the last resort always comes down to his own living labour, whatever objective form it may assume either before or after the conclusion of the exchange. The suit now not only contains labour which gives it a definite form – a definite form of utility given to the cloth by the movement of labour – but it contains a definite quantity of labour and thus not only use value, but value in general, value as such. But this value does not exist for A, since he has consumed

1. ['I give so that you may do.']
2. ['I do so that you may give.']
3. ['I give so that you may give ']

the suit and is not himself a dealer in clothes. He has, therefore, traded in the labour, not as labour which has value, but as something useful, an activity that creates use value. In the rendering of personal services, this use value is consumed as such, without proceeding beyond the form of activity into that of a material thing. When, as often happens in simple relationships, the person who renders a service does not receive money for it but only immediate use values, the illusion that we are here concerned on either side with values rather than use values at once disappears. But even assuming that A pays money for the services rendered, this is not a transformation of his money into capital, but indicates that it has been made a mere means of circulation, in order to obtain an item of consumption, a particular use value. This act is thus not concerned with the production of wealth, but vice versa, it is an act that consumes wealth. What matters to A is not that labour, as such, definite working time, i.e. value, is objectified in the cloth, but that it satisfies a definite need. A's money is not valorized but de-valorized, during the process of converting it from the form of value into that of use value. Labour is here exchanged not as use value for the value, but as a special use value, as value for use. The more frequently A repeats the exchange, the more impoverished he becomes. This type of exchange is not an act of enrichment for him, nor an act of value creation; it is a devalorization of values that exist and are in his possession. The money that A has exchanged for living labour – either a natural service, or service objectified in a material thing – is not *capital* but revenue. It is money as a means of circulation, in order to obtain use value. Use value has a merely ephemeral form in it, and the money is not used to buy labour which will be retained and valorized. The exchange of *money as revenue*, purely as a means of circulation against living labour, can never establish money as capital, nor labour as wage-labour in the economic sense. There is no need to explain in detail why the consumption or spending of money is not the same thing as producing money. In conditions in which most of the surplus labour is agricultural, and in which the landowner retains both the surplus labour and the surplus product, it is the revenue of the landowner which forms the labour fund for the free worker, the manufacturing worker (we refer here to manufacturing by hand), as opposed to the agricultural worker. This exchange is a form of landowner's consumption; he directly distributes another part of his revenue in return for personal services – often only an illusion of personal service with a lot of retainers. In Asiatic societies, where the monarch is the exclusive proprietor of the surplus product of the land, entire towns exist which are basically nothing more than nomadic camps, because of the exchange of his revenue with 'free hands', as Steuart terms them. In this relationship there is no wage-labour, although it may (it need not) come into contradiction with slavery and bondage, since it is always found in the most diverse forms of social organization. In so far as money arranges this exchange, the fixing of prices is important for both sides (but for A only in so far as he does not wish to pay too highly for the use value of the labour; and not because he is concerned with its value). It makes no essential difference that originally this price is chiefly conventional and traditional; and then little by little becomes determined first economically, according to supply and demand, and later by the costs of production, whereby those who sell these living services can themselves be produced. For both before and after, the price-fixing remains only a formal element in the exchange of pure use values. This price is fixed by other relationships, viz. the general laws in force determined by the dominant means of production, and operating behind such particular acts of exchange. In the ancient world, one of the entities in which this type of remuneration first appeared was the army. The ordinary soldier's pay was kept down to a minimum – it was determined solely by the production costs involved in producing soldiers. But the services rendered by the soldier were paid for out of state revenue, not from capital.

In bourgeois society, all forms of exchange of personal service for revenue come under this heading – from labour for personal consumption (the labour of the cook, the seamstress, the gardener) up to the work performed by all the generally non-productive classes – state employees, doctors, lawyers, teachers, etc., also all menial servants, etc. All these workers, from the humblest to the highest, negotiate the exchange of their services (often compulsory) against a part of the surplus product, against the capitalist's revenue. But no one would ever think that the capitalist, by exchanging his revenue for this kind of personal service – that is, by privately consuming it – sets himself up as a capitalist; rather, he is spending the fruits of his capital. The fact that the proportions in which revenue is exchanged for this living labour are themselves determined by the general laws of production does not alter the nature of the relationship.

As we pointed out in the section on money, it is rather the provider of services who establishes value, converting a use value (a definite kind of labour or service) into value, money. In the Middle Ages, those who were tending towards production and accumulation of money set out from the ranks of living labour, accumulating money, and developing capitalist capabilities for a later period, to some extent in contrast to the ranks of the consuming landed nobility. The capitalist came, in part, from the emancipated serf.

It is not the general relationship that determines whether the provider of services receives a salary, a daily wage or a professional fee, or a civil list pension, or whether his rank is superior or inferior to that of the person paying for the service; this depends on the natural, particular quality of the service rendered. Once capital has established itself as the dominating force, all such relationships are in any case more or less *dishonoured*. However, this loss of the semi-divine character of personal service, and the sublime character that tradition may have conferred upon it, cannot be dealt with here.

Capital, and thus wage-labour, is therefore not constituted by a simple exchange of objectified labour for living labour; from this standpoint they are two different forms occurring as use values of different kinds, one in an objective form and the other in a subjective form. For that there must be an exchange of objectified labour that exists as a value for itself against labour as living use value that belongs to it, as use value for value, not for any particular or special use or consumption.

During the exchange of money for labour or service for direct consumption there is always a real exchange. Quantities of labour are exchanged on both sides, though this is only of formal interest, enabling the particular, special utility forms of the labour to be measured. This refers only to the form of the exchange, and does not constitute its content. In the exchange of capital for labour, value is no measurement for the exchange of two use values, but the content of the exchange itself.

2. At the time when pre-bourgeois conditions were dissolved, free workers were seen to appear sporadically whose services were bought not for purposes of consumption but for production. First of all, this took place on a large scale only for the production of immediate use values, not values. Secondly, it occurred when the nobility for example, employed free workers alongside bondmen, and resold part of the worker's product. Thus the free worker produced value for him; but then only in relation to the superfluity, in order to increase superfluous luxury consumption. Basically this is only a disguised purchase of alien labour for direct, immediate consumption, or as a use value. Besides, in situations where the free workers were multiplying, so that this relationship was increasing, the old means of production – communal, patriarchal or feudal – were disintegrating, and the factors that favoured real wage-labour were being prepared. But in Poland, for example, these free servants may suddenly emerge, and as suddenly disappear, without the means of production being altered.

5 Karl Marx

The Motivation of the Capitalist*

Excerpt from Karl Marx, *Capital*, Volume I, Lawrence & Wishart, 1970, pp. 152–3.

The expansion of value becomes his subjective aim, and it is only in so far as the appropriation of ever more and more wealth in the abstract becomes the sole motive of his operations, that he functions as a capitalist, that is, as capital personified and endowed with consciousness and a will. Use-values must therefore never be looked upon as the real aim of the capitalist; neither must the profit on any single transaction. The restless never-ending process of profit-making alone is what he aims at. This boundless greed after riches, this passionate chase after exchange-value, is common to the capitalist and the miser; but while the miser is merely a capitalist gone mad, the capitalist is a rational miser. The never-ending augmentation of exchange-value, which the miser strives after, by seeking to save his money from circulation, is attained by the more acute capitalist, by constantly throwing it afresh into circulation.

* The footnotes in the original have been omitted [Eds.].

6 Karl Marx

A Three-Stage Typology of Economic Development

Excerpt from David McLellan, *Marx's Grundrisse*, revised edition, Paladin, 1973, p. 78.

Relationships of personal dependence (which were at first quite spontaneous) are the first forms of society in which human productivity develops, though only to a slight extent and at isolated points. Personal independence founded on *material* dependence is the second great form: in it there developed for the first time a system of general social interchange, resulting in universal relations, varied requirements and universal capacities. Free individuality, which is founded on the universal development of individuals, and the domination of their communal and social productivity, which has become their social power, is the third stage. The second stage creates the conditions for the third. Patriarchal and ancient societies (feudal also) decline as trade, luxury, money and exchange value develop, just as modern society has grown up simultaneously alongside these.

7 Karl Marx

The Alienation of Commodity Production

Excerpt from David McLellan, *Marx's Grundrisse*, revised edition, Paladin, 1973, pp. 71–2.

The more production is shaped in such a way that every producer depends on the exchange value of his commodities, i.e. the more the product really becomes an exchange value, and exchange value becomes the direct object of production, the more must *money relationships* develop, as also the contradictions inherent in this money relationship, in the relation of the product to itself as money.

The necessity of exchange and the transformation of the product into a pure exchange value progress to the same extent as the division of labour, i.e. with the social character of production. But just as exchange value grows, the power of money grows too; that is, the exchange relationship establishes itself as a force externally opposed to the producers, and independent of them. What was originally a means to the furtherance of production becomes a relationship alien to the producers. The more the producers become dependent upon exchange, the more exchange seems to be independent of them; and the gap between the product as a product and the product as an exchange value widens.

Money does not generate these antagonisms and contradictions; but their development generates the seemingly transcendental power of money. (We shall have to analyse in detail the effect of the transformation of all relations into money relations: natural taxes becoming money taxes, natural income becoming money income, military service becoming the engagement of mercenaries, and especially all personal services taking on a monetary nature, and patriarchal, servile, bonded and guild labour changing into pure wage-labour.)

The product becomes a commodity; the commodity becomes exchange value; the exchange value of commodities is their inherent monetary property; and this monetary property is severed from them in the form of money, and achieves a social existence apart from all particular commodities and their natural mode of existence. The relation of the product to itself as an exchange value becomes its relation to money existing alongside it, or of all products to the money that exists outside them all. Just as the actual exchange of products creates their exchange value, so their exchange value creates money.

8 Karl Marx

Alienation and Fetishism of Commodity Production

Excerpt from David McLellan, *Marx's Grundrisse*, revised edition, Paladin, 1973, pp. 76–9.

The disintegration of all products and activities into exchange values presupposes both the disintegration of all rigid, personal (historical) relationships of dependence in production, and a universal interdependence of the producers. The production of each individual depends on everyone else's production, just as the transformation of his product into food for himself depends on everyone else's consumption. Prices are ancient; and so is exchange; but the increasing determination of prices by the cost of production, and the influence of exchange over all production relationships, can only develop fully and ever more completely in bourgeois society, the society of free competition. What Adam Smith, in true eighteenth-century style, places in the prehistoric period, puts before history, is in fact its product.

This mutual dependence is expressed in the constant need for exchange, value being the universal intermediary. The economists express it like this: each person has his private interests in mind, and nothing else; as a consequence he serves everyone's private interests, i.e. the general interest, without wishing to or knowing that he is. The irony of this is not that the totality of private interest – which is the same thing as the general interest – can be attained by the individual's following his own interest. Rather it could be inferred from this abstract phrase that everyone hinders the satisfaction of everyone else's interest, that instead of a general affirmation, the result of this war of all against all is rather a general negation. The point is rather that private interest is itself already a socially determined interest, which can only be achieved within the conditions established by society and through the means that society affords, and that it is thus linked to the reproduction of these conditions and means. It is certainly the interest of private individuals that is at stake; but its content, as well as the form and the means of its realization, is only given by social conditions independent of all these individuals.

The mutual and universal dependence of individuals who remain indifferent to one another constitutes the social network that binds them together. This social coherence is expressed in *exchange value*, in which alone each individual's activity or his product becomes an activity or a product for him. He has to produce a general product: *exchange value* or – in its isolated, individualized form – *money*. On the other hand the power that each individual exercises over others' activity or over social wealth exists in him as the owner of exchange values, money. Thus both his power over society and his association with it is carried in his pocket. Whatever the individual form in which activity occurs, and whatever the particular characteristics of the product of activity, they are *exchange value*, that is, a general factor in which all individuality and particularity is denied and suppressed. This is in effect a very different set of circumstances from that in which the individual, or the individual spontaneously and historically enlarged into the family and the tribe (and later the community), reproduces himself directly from nature, or his productive activity and his share in the production are dependent on a particular form of labour and of product, and his relationship to others is likewise determined.

The social character of activity, and the social form of the product, as well as the share of the individual in production, are here opposed to individuals as something alien and material; this does not consist in the behaviour of some to others, but in their subordination to relations that exist independently of them and arise from the collision of indifferent individuals with one another. The general exchange of activities and products, which has become a condition of living for each individual and the link between them, seems to them to be something alien and independent, like a thing.

In exchange value, the social relations of individuals have become transformed into the social connections of material things; personal power has changed into material power. The less social power the means of exchange possess and the closer they are still connected with the nature of the direct product of labour and the immediate needs of those exchanging, the greater must be the power of the community to bind the individuals together: the patriarchal relationship, the ancient communities, feudalism and the guild system. Each individual possesses social power in the form of a material object. If the object is deprived of its social power then this power must be exercised by people over people.

[. . .] The very necessity of first transforming the product or the activity of the individuals into the form of *exchange value* or *money*, that they acquire and demonstrate their social power only in this material form, shows both that: (1) the individuals are now producing only in and for society; and (2) that their production is not directly social, not the offspring of an association that divides the labour among its members. The individuals are subordinated to social production, which exists externally to them, as a sort of fate; but social production is not subordinated to the individuals who manipulate it as their communal capacity.

Nothing, therefore, could be more incorrect and absurd than to presume, on the basis of exchange value and money, the control of associated individuals over their general production as occurred above with the bank issuing vouchers for hours of work.

9 Karl Marx

The Fetishism of Commodities*

Excerpts from Karl Marx, *Capital*, Volume I, Lawrence & Wishart, 1970, pp. 71–83.

As a general rule, articles of utility become commodities, only because they are products of the labour of private individuals or groups of individuals who carry on their work independently of each other. The sum total of the labour of all these private individuals forms the aggregate labour of society. Since the producers do not come into social contact with each other until they exchange their products, the specific social character of each producer's labour does not show itself except in the act of exchange. In other words, the labour of the individual asserts itself as a part of the labour of society, only by means of the relations which the act of exchange establishes directly between the products, and indirectly, through them, between the producers. To the latter, therefore, the relations connecting the labour of one individual with that of the rest appear, not as direct social relations between individuals at work, but as what they really are, material relations between persons and social relations between things. [. . .] To them, their own social action takes the form of the action of objects, which rule the producers instead of being ruled by them. [. . .]

A commodity is therefore a mysterious thing, simply because in it the social character of men's labour appears to them as an objective character stamped upon the product of that labour; because the relation of the producers to the sum total of their own labour is presented to them as a social relation, existing not between themselves, but between the products of their labour. This is the reason why the products of labour become commodities, social things whose qualities are at the same time perceptible and imperceptible by the senses. In the same way the light from an object is perceived by us not as the subjective excitation of our optic nerve, but as the objective form of something outside the eye itself. But, in the act of seeing, there is at all events, an actual passage of light from one thing to another, from the external object to the eye. There is a physical relation between physical things. But it is different with commodities. There, the existence of the things *quâ* commodities, and the value-relation between

* In order to bring out Marx's argument more clearly, the excerpts have been rearranged [Eds.].

the products of labour which stamps them as commodities, have absolutely no connection with their physical properties and with the material relations arising therefrom. There it is a definite social relation between men, that assumes in their eyes, the fantastic form of a relation between things. In order, therefore, to find an analogy, we must have recourse to the mist-enveloped regions of the religious world. In that world the productions of the human brain appear as independent beings endowed with life, and entering into relation both with one another and the human race. So it is in the world of commodities with the products of men's hands. This I call the Fetishism which attaches itself to the products of labour, so soon as they are produced as commodities, and which is therefore inseparable from the production of commodities.

This Fetishism of commodities has its origin, as the foregoing analysis has already shown, in the peculiar social character of the labour that produces them. [. . .]

The mode of production in which the product takes the form of a commodity, or is produced directly for exchange, is the most general and most embryonic form of bourgeois production. It therefore makes its appearance at an early date in history, though not in the same predominating and characteristic manner as now-a-days. Hence its Fetish character is comparatively easy to be seen through. But when we come to more concrete forms, even this appearance of simplicity vanishes. Whence arose the illusions of the monetary system? To it gold and silver, when serving as money, did not represent a social relation between producers, but were natural objects with strange social properties. And modern economy, which looks down with such disdain on the monetary system, does not its superstition come out as clear as noon-day, whenever it treats of capital? How long is it since economy discarded the physiocratic illusion, that rents grow out of the soil and not out of society?

But not to anticipate, we will content ourselves with yet another example relating to the commodity-form. Could commodities themselves speak, they would say: Our use-value may be a thing that interests men. It is no part of us as objects. What, however, does belong to us as objects, is our value. Our natural intercourse as commodities proves it. In the eyes of each other we are nothing but exchange-values. Now listen how those commodities speak through the mouth of the economist. 'Value' – (i.e., exchange-value) 'is a property of things, riches' – (i.e., use-value) 'of man. Value, in this sense, necessarily implies exchanges, riches do not'. (Anonymous, 1821, p. 16). 'Riches' (use-value) 'are the attribute of men, value is the attribute of commodities. A man or a community is rich, a pearl or a diamond is valuable . . . A pearl or a diamond is valuable' as a pearl or diamond (Bailey, 1825, p. 165). So far no chemist has ever discovered exchange-value either in a pearl or a diamond. The economic discoverers of this chemical element, who by-the-by lay special claim to critical acumen, find however that the use-value of objects belongs to them independently of their material properties, while their value, on the other hand, forms a part of them as objects. What confirms them in this view, is the peculiar circumstance that the use-value of objects is realized without exchange, by means of a direct relation between the objects and man, while, on the other hand, their value is realized only by exchange, that is, by means of a social process. Who fails here to call to mind our good friend, Dogberry, who informs neighbour Seacoal, that, 'To be a well-favoured man is the gift of fortune; but reading and writing comes by Nature.'[1] [. . .]

The whole mystery of commodities, all the magic and necromancy that surrounds the products of labour as long as they take the form of commodities, vanishes therefore, so soon as we come to other forms of production.

Since Robinson Crusoe's experiences are a favourite theme with political economists,[2] let us take a look at him on his island. Moderate though he be, yet some few wants he has to satisfy, and must therefore do a little useful work of various sorts, such as making tools and furniture, taming goats, fishing and hunting. Of his prayers and the like we take no account, since they are a source of pleasure to him, and he looks upon them as so much recreation. In spite of the variety of his work, he knows that his labour, whatever its form, is but the activity of one and the same Robinson, and consequently, that it consists of nothing but different modes of human labour. Necessity itself compels him to apportion his time accurately between his different kinds of work. Whether one kind occupies a greater

1. The author of 'Observations' and S. Bailey accuse Ricardo of converting exchange-value from something relative into something absolute. The opposite is the fact. He has explained the apparent relation between objects, such as diamonds and pearls, in which relation they appear as exchange-values, and disclosed the true relation hidden behind the appearances, namely, their relation to each other as mere expressions of human labour. If the followers of Ricardo answer Bailey somewhat rudely, and by no means convincingly, the reason is to be sought in this, that they were unable to find in Ricardo's own works any key to the hidden relations existing between value and its form, exchange-value.

2. Even Ricardo has his stories à la Robinson. 'He makes the primitive hunter and the primitive fisher straightway, as owners of commodities, exchange fish and game in the proportion in which labour-time is incorporated in these exchange-values. On this occasion he commits the anachronism of making these men apply to the calculation, so far as their implements have to be taken into account, the annuity tables in current use on the London Exchange in the year 1817. "The parallelograms of Mr Owen" appear to be the only form of society, besides the bourgeois form, with which he was acquainted' (Marx, 1859, pp. 38, 39).

space in his general activity than another, depends on the difficulties, greater or less as the case may be, to be overcome in attaining the useful effect aimed at. This our friend Robinson soon learns by experience, and having rescued a watch, ledger, and pen and ink from the wreck, commences, like a true-born Briton, to keep a set of books. His stock-book contains a list of the objects of utility that belong to him, of the operations necessary for their production; and lastly, of the labour-time that definite quantities of those objects have, on an average, cost him. All the relations between Robinson and the objects that form this wealth of his own creation, are here so simple and clear as to be intelligible without exertion, even to Mr Sedley Taylor. And yet those relations contain all that is essential to the determination of value.

Let us now transport ourselves from Robinson's island bathed in light to the European middle ages shrouded in darkness. Here, instead of the independent man, we find everyone dependent, serfs and lords, vassals and suzerains, laymen and clergy. Personal dependence here characterizes the social relations of production just as much as it does the other spheres of life organized on the basis of that production. But for the very reason that personal dependence forms the ground-work of society, there is no necessity for labour and its products to assume a fantastic form different from their reality. They take the shape, in the transactions of society, of services in kind and payments in kind. Here the particular and natural form of labour, and not, as in a society based on production of commodities, its general abstract form is the immediate social form of labour. Compulsory labour is just as properly measured by time, as commodity-producing labour; but every serf knows that what he expends in the service of his lord, is a definite quantity of his own personal labour-power. The tithe to be rendered to the priest is more matter of fact than his blessing. No matter, then, what we may think of the parts played by the different classes of people themselves in this society, the social relations between individuals in the performance of their labour, appear at all events as their own mutual personal relations, and are not disguised under the shape of social relations between the products of labour.

For an example of labour in common or directly associated labour, we have no occasion to go back to that spontaneously developed form which we find on the threshold of the history of all civilized races.[3] We have one

3. 'A ridiculous presumption has latterly got abroad that common property in its primitive form is specifically a Slavonian, or even exclusively Russian form. It is the primitive form that we can prove to have existed amongst Romans, Teutons, and Celts, and even to this day we find numerous examples, ruins though they be, in India. A more exhaustive study of Asiatic, and especially of Indian forms of common property, would show how from the different forms of primitive common property, different

close at hand in the patriarchal industries of a peasant family, that produces corn, cattle, yarn, linen, and clothing for home use. These different articles are, as regards the family, so many products of its labour, but as between themselves, they are not commodities. The different kinds of labour, such as tillage, cattle-tending, spinning, weaving and making clothes, which result in the various products, are in themselves, and such as they are, direct social functions, because functions of the family, which, just as much as a society based on the production of commodities, possesses a spontaneously developed system of division of labour. The distribution of the work within the family, and the regulation of the labour-time of the several members, depend as well upon differences of age and sex as upon natural conditions varying with the seasons. The labour-power of each individual, by its very nature, operates in this case merely as a definite portion of the whole labour-power of the family, and therefore, the measure of the expenditure of individual labour-power by its duration, appears here by its very nature as a social character of their labour.

Let us now picture to ourselves, by way of change, a community of free individuals, carrying on their work with the means of production in common, in which the labour-power of all the different individuals is consciously applied as the combined labour-power of the community. All the characteristics of Robinson's labour are here repeated, but with this difference, that they are social, instead of individual. Everything produced by him was exclusively the result of his own personal labour, and therefore simply an object of use for himself. The total product of our community is a social product. One portion serves as fresh means of production and remains social. But another portion is consumed by the members as means of subsistence. A distribution of this portion amongst them is consequently necessary. The mode of this distribution will vary with the productive organization of the community, and the degree of historical development attained by the producers. We will assume, but merely for the sake of a parallel with the production of commodities, that the share of each individual producer in the means of subsistence is determined by his labour-time. Labour-time would, in that case, play a double part. Its apportionment in accordance with a definite social plan maintains the proper proportion between the different kinds of work to be done and the various wants of the community. On the other hand, it also serves as a measure of the portion of the common labour borne by each individual, and of his share in the part of the total product destined for individual consumption. The

---

forms of its dissolution have been developed. Thus, for instance, the various original types of Roman and Teutonic private property are deducible from different forms of Indian common property' (Marx, 1859, p. 10).

social relations of the individual producers, with regard both to their labour and to its products, are in this case perfectly simple and intelligible, and that with regard not only to production but also to distribution. [. . .] The recent scientific discovery, that the products of labour, so far as they are values, are but material expressions of the human labour spent in their production, marks, indeed, an epoch in the history of the development of the human race, but, by no means, dissipates the mist through which the social character of labour appears to us to be an objective character of the products themselves.

The life-process of society, which is based on the process of material production, does not strip off its mystical veil until it is treated as production by freely associated men, and is consciously regulated by them in accordance with a settled plan. This, however, demands for society a certain material ground-work or set of conditions of existence which in their turn are the spontaneous product of a long and painful process of development.

References

ANONYMOUS (1821), *Observations on Certain Verbal Disputes in Pol. Econ., Particularly Relating to Value and to Demand and Supply,* London.

BAILEY, S. (1825), *A Critical Dissertation on the Nature, Measures and Causes of Value; Chiefly in Reference to the Writings of Mr Ricardo and His Followers,* London.

MARX, K. (1859) *Zur Kritik der Politischen Ökonomie,* Berlin.

10 Karl Marx

The Alienation of Capitalist Commodity Production*

Excerpt from Karl Marx, *Capital*, Volume I, Lawrence & Wishart, 1970, pp. 570–71.

[. .] in order to convert money into capital something more is required than the production and circulation of commodities. We saw that on the one side the possessor of value or money, on the other, the possessor of the value-creating substance; on the one side, the possessor of the means of production and subsistence, on the other, the possessor of nothing but labour-power, must confront one another as buyer and seller. The separation of labour from its product, of subjective labour-power from the objective conditions of labour, was therefore the real foundation in fact, and the starting-point of capitalist production.

But that which at first was but a starting-point, becomes, by the mere continuity of the process, by simple reproduction, the peculiar result, constantly renewed and perpetuated, of capitalist production. On the one hand, the process of production incessantly converts material wealth into capital, into means of creating more wealth and means of enjoyment for the capitalist. On the other hand, the labourer, on quitting the process, is what he was on entering it, a source of wealth, but devoid of all means of making that wealth his own. Since, before entering on the process, his own labour has already been alienated from himself by the sale of his labour-power, has been appropriated by the capitalist and incorporated with capital, it must, during the process, be realized in a product that does not belong to him. Since the process of production is also the process by which the capitalist consumes labour-power, the product of the labourer is incessantly converted, not only into commodities, but into capital, into value that sucks up the value-creating power, into means of subsistence that buy the person of the labourer, into means of production that command the producers. The labourer therefore constantly produces material, objective wealth, but in the form of capital, of an alien power that dominates and exploits him; and the capitalist as constantly produces labour-power, but in the form of a subjective source of wealth, separated from the objects in and by which it can alone be realized; in short he produces the labourer, but as a wage-labourer. This incessant reproduction, this perpetuation of the labourer, is the *sine quâ non* of capitalist production.

* The footnotes in the original have been omitted [Eds.].

11 Karl Marx

The Fetishism Attached to Capitalist Commodity Production

Excerpt from Karl Marx, *Capital*, Volume III, Lawrence & Wishart, 1972, pp. 826–31.

In the case of the simplest categories of the capitalist mode of production, and even of commodity-production, in the case of commodities and money, we have already pointed out the mystifying character that transforms the social relations, for which the material elements of wealth serve as bearers in production, into properties of these things themselves (commodities) and still more pronouncedly transforms the production relation itself into a thing (money). All forms of society, in so far as they reach the stage of commodity-production and money circulation, take part in this perversion. But under the capitalist mode of production and in the case of capital, which forms its dominant category, its determining production relation, this enchanted and perverted world develops still more. If one considers capital, to begin with, in the actual process of production as a means of extracting surplus-labour, then this relationship is still very simple, and the actual connection impresses itself upon the bearers of this process, the capitalists themselves, and remains in their consciousness. The violent struggle over the limits of the working-day demonstrates this strikingly. But even within this non-mediated sphere, the sphere of direct action between labour and capital, matters do not rest in this simplicity. With the development of relative surplus-value in the actual specifically capitalist mode of production, whereby the productive powers of social labour are developed, these productive powers and the social interrelations of labour in the direct labour-process seem transferred from labour to capital. Capital thus becomes a very mystic being since all of labour's social productive forces appear to be due to capital, rather than labour as such, and seem to issue from the womb of capital itself. Then the process of circulation intervenes, with its changes of substance and form, on which all parts of capital, even agricultural capital, devolve to the same degree that the specifically capitalist mode of production develops. This is a sphere where the relations under which value is originally produced are pushed completely into the background. In the direct process of production the capitalist already acts simultaneously as producer of commodities and manager of commodity-production. Hence this process of production appears to him by no means simply as a process of producing surplus-value. But whatever may be the surplus-value extorted by capital in the actual production process and appearing in commodities, the value and surplus-value contained in the commodities must first be realized in the circulation process. And both the restitution of the values advanced in production and, particularly, the surplus-value contained in the commodities seem not merely to be realized in the circulation, but actually to arise from it; an appearance which is especially reinforced by two circumstances: first, the profit made in selling depends on cheating, deceit, inside knowledge, skill and a thousand favourable market opportunities; and then by the circumstance that added here to labour-time is a second determining element – time of circulation. This acts, in fact, only as a negative barrier against the formation of value and surplus-value, but it has the appearance of being as definite a basis as labour itself and of introducing a determining element that is independent of labour and resulting from the nature of capital. In Book II[1] we naturally had to present this sphere of circulation merely with reference to the form determinations which it created and to demonstrate the further development of the structure of capital taking place in this sphere. But in reality this sphere is the sphere of competition, which, considered in each individual case, is dominated by chance; where, then, the inner law, which prevails in these accidents and regulates them, is only visible when these accidents are grouped together in large numbers, where it remains, therefore, invisible and unintelligible to the individual agents in production. But furthermore: the actual process of production, as a unity of the direct production process and the circulation process, gives rise to new formations, in which the vein of internal connections is increasingly lost, the production relations are rendered independent of one another, and the component values become ossified into forms independent of one another.

The conversion of surplus-value into profit, as we have seen, is determined as much by the process of circulation as by the process of production. Surplus-value, in the form of profit, is no longer related back to that portion of capital invested in labour from which it arises, but to the total capital. The rate of profit is regulated by laws of its own, which permit, or even require, it to change while the rate of surplus-value remains unaltered. All this obscures more and more the true nature of surplus-value and thus the actual mechanism of capital. Still more is this achieved through the transformation of profit into average profit and of values into prices of production, into the regulating averages of market-prices. A complicated social process intervenes here, the equalization process of capitals, which divorces the relative average prices of the commodities from their values,

1. This is a reference to Volume II of *Capital* [Ed.].

as well as the average profits in the various spheres of production (quite aside from the individual investments of capital in each particular sphere of production) from the actual exploitation of labour by the particular capitals. Not only does it appear so, but it is true in fact that the average price of commodities differs from their value, thus from the labour realized in them, and the average profit of a particular capital differs from the surplus-value which this capital has extracted from the labourers employed by it. The value of commodities appears, directly, solely in the influence of fluctuating productivity of labour upon the rise and fall of the prices of production, upon their movement and not upon their ultimate limits. Profit seems to be determined only secondarily by direct exploitation of labour, in so far as the latter permits the capitalist to realize a profit deviating from the average profit at the regulating market-prices, which apparently prevail independent of such exploitation. Normal average profits themselves seem immanent in capital and independent of exploitation; abnormal exploitation, or even average exploitation under favourable, exceptional conditions, seems to determine only the deviations from average profit, not this profit itself. The division of profit into profit of enterprise and interest (not to mention the intervention of commercial profit and profit from money-dealing, which are founded upon circulation and appear to arise completely from it, and not from the process of production itself) consummates the individualization of the form of surplus-value, the ossification of its form as opposed to its substance, its essence. One portion of profit, as opposed to the other, separates itself entirely from the relationship of capital as such and appears as arising not out of the function of exploiting wage-labour, but out of the wage-labour of the capitalist himself. In contrast thereto, interest then seems to be independent both of the labourer's wage-labour and the capitalist's own labour, and to arise from capital as its own independent source. If capital originally appeared on the surface of circulation as a fetishism of capital, as a value-creating value, so it now appears again in the form of interest-bearing capital, as in its most estranged and characteristic form. Wherefore also the formula capital–interest, as the third to land–rent and labour–stages, is much more consistent than capital–profit, since in profit there will remains a recollection of its origin, which is not only extinguished in interest, but is also placed in a form thoroughly antithetical to this origin.

Finally, capital as an independent source of surplus-value is joined by landed property, which acts as a barrier to average profit and transfers a portion of surplus-value to a class that neither works itself, nor directly exploits labour, nor can find morally edifying rationalizations, as in the case of interest-bearing capital, e.g., risk and sacrifice of lending capital to others. Since here a part of the surplus-value seems to be bound up directly with a natural element, the land, rather than with social relations, the form of mutual estrangement and ossification of the various parts of surplus-value is completed, the inner connection completely disrupted, and its source entirely buried, precisely because the relations of production, which are bound to the various material elements of the production process, have been rendered mutually independent.

In capital–profit, or still better capital–interest, land–rent, labour–wages, in this economic trinity represented as the connection between the component parts of value and wealth in general and its sources, we have the complete mystification of the capitalist mode of production, the conversion of social relations into things, the direct coalescence of the material production relations with their historical and social determination. It is an enchanted, perverted, topsy-turvy world, in which Monsieur le Capital and Madame la Terre do their ghost-walking as social characters and at the same time directly as mere things. It is the great merit of classical economy to have destroyed this false appearance and illusion, this mutual independence and ossification of the various social elements of wealth, this personification of things and conversion of production relations into entities, this religion of everyday life. It did so by reducing interest to a portion of profit, and rent to the surplus above average profit, so that both of them converge in surplus-value; and by representing the process of circulation as a mere metamorphosis of forms, and finally reducing value and surplus-value of commodities to labour in the direct production process. Nevertheless even the best spokesmen of classical economy remain more or less in the grip of the world of illusion which their criticism had dissolved, as cannot be otherwise from a bourgeois standpoint, and thus they all fall more or less into inconsistencies, half-truths and unsolved contradictions. On the other hand, it is just as natural for the actual agents of production to feel completely at home in these estranged and irrational forms of capital–interest, land–rent, labour–wages, since these are precisely the forms of illusion in which they move about and find their daily occupation. It is therefore just as natural that vulgar economy, which is no more than a didactic, more or less dogmatic, translation of everyday conceptions of the actual agents of production, and which arranges them in a certain rational order, should see precisely in this trinity, which is devoid of all inner connection, the natural and indubitable lofty basis for its shallow pompousness. This formula simultaneously corresponds to the interests of the ruling classes by proclaiming the physical necessity and eternal justification of their sources of revenue and elevating them to a dogma.

In our description of how production relations are converted into entities and rendered independent in relation to the agents of production, we leave aside the manner in which the inter-relations, due to the world-market, its conjunctures, movements of market-prices, periods of credit, industrial and commercial cycles, alternations of prosperity and crisis, appear to them as overwhelming natural laws that irresistibly enforce their will over them, and confront them as blind necessity. We leave this aside because the actual movement of competition belongs beyond our scope, and we need present only the inner organization of the capitalist mode of production, in its ideal average, as it were.

In preceding forms of society this economic mystification arose principally with respect to money and interest-bearing capital. In the nature of things it is excluded, in the first place, where production for the use-value for immediate personal requirements, predominates; and, secondly, where slavery or serfdom form the broad foundation of social production, as in antiquity and during the middle ages. Here, the domination of the producers by the conditions of production is concealed by the relations of dominion and servitude, which appear and are evident as the direct motive power of the process of production. In early communal societies in which primitive communism prevailed, and even in the ancient communal towns, it was this communal society itself with its conditions which appeared as the basis of production, and its reproduction appeared as its ultimate purpose. Even in the medieval guild system neither capital nor labour appear untrammelled, but their relations are rather defined by the corporate rules, and by the same associated relations, and corresponding conceptions of professional duty, craftsmanship, etc. Only when the capitalist mode of production[2]

2. The manuscript breaks off here [Ed.].

12 Karl Marx

Critique of the Bourgeois Conception of Freedom

Excerpt from David McLellan, *Marx's Grundrisse*, revised edition, Paladin, 1973, pp. 83–4.

When social conditions are considered that generate an undeveloped system of exchange, exchange values and money, or to which an undeveloped stage of such a system corresponds, it is immediately evident that the individuals, although their relationships appear to be more personal, only relate to each other in determined roles, as a feudal lord and his vassal, a landlord and his serf, etc., or as a member of a caste, etc., or of an estate, etc. In money relationships, in the developed exchange system (and it is this semblance that is so seductive in the eyes of democrats), the ties of personal dependence are in fact broken, torn asunder, as also differences of blood, educational differences, etc. (the personal ties all appear at least to be *personal* relationships). Thus the individuals appear to be independent (though this independence is merely a complete illusion and should rather be termed indifference); independent, that is, to collide with one another freely and to barter within the limits of this freedom. They appear so, however, only to someone who abstracts from the conditions of existence in which these individuals come into contact. (Such conditions are again independent of individuals and appear, although they were created by society, to be the same as *natural conditions*, i.e. uncontrollable by the individual.) The determining factor that appears in the first case to be a personal limitation of one individual by another, seems in the latter to be built up into a material limitation of the individual by circumstances that are independent of him and self-contained. (Since the single individual cannot shed his personal limitations, but can surmount external circumstances and master them, his freedom *appears* to be greater in the second case. Closer investigation of these external circumstances and conditions shows, however, how impossible it is for the individuals forming part of a class, etc., to surmount them *en masse* without abolishing them. The individual may by chance be rid of them; but not the masses that are ruled by them, since their mere existence is an expression of the subordination to which individuals must necessarily submit.) So far from constituting the removal of a 'state of dependence', these external relationships represent its disintegration into a general form; or better: they are the elaboration of the general *basis* of personal states of dependence.

13 Karl Marx

The Potentialities of Capitalist Development

Excerpt from David McLellan, *Marx's Grundrisse*, revised edition, Paladin, 1973, pp. 141–4.

While on the one hand capital must thus seek to pull down every local barrier to commerce, i.e. to exchange, in order to capture the whole world as its market, on the other hand it strives to destroy space by means of time, i.e. to restrict to a minimum the time required for movement from one place to another. The more developed capital is, and thus the more extensive the market through which it circulates and which constitutes the spatial route of its circulation, the more it will aspire to greater extension in space for its market, and thus to greater destruction of space by time. (If working time is not considered as the working day of the individual worker, but as an indeterminate working day of an indeterminate number of workers, all *population relationships* come into this; the basic theory of population is thus also included in this first chapter on capital, in the same way as the theory of profit, price, credit, etc.) We see here the universal tendency of capital which distinguishes it from all earlier stages of production. Although it is itself limited by its own nature, capital strives after the universal development of productive forces, and thus becomes the prerequisite for a new means of production. This means of production is founded not on the development of productive forces in order to reproduce a given condition and, at best, to extend it, but is one where free, uninhibited, progressive and universal development of productive forces itself forms the prerequisite of society and thus of its reproduction; where the only prerequisite is to proceed beyond the point of departure. This tendency – which capital possesses, but which at the same time contradicts it as a limited form of production, and thus impels it towards its own dissolution – distinguishes capital from all earlier means of production, and contains the implication of its own transitory nature. All previous forms of society foundered on the development of wealth – or, which amounts to the same thing, on the development of social productive forces. Therefore ancient philosophers who were aware of this bluntly denounced wealth as destructive of community. The feudal institutions in their turn collapsed under urban industry, trade, modern agriculture (even under individual discoveries, such as gunpowder and the printing-press). With the development of wealth – and of new forces and extended individual trade – the economic conditions upon which the community rested were dissolved. The political relationships corresponding to the different constituents of the community suffered the same fate; as did religion, in which it was seen in an idealized form (and both these rested on a given relationship to nature, into which all productive force can be resolved); and the character and points of view of individual people. The development of science alone – i.e. of the most solid form of wealth, which is both a product of wealth and a producer of it – was sufficient to make this community disintegrate. *The development of science*, of this ideal and at the same time practical wealth, is however only one aspect, one form, of the *development of human productive forces* (i.e. wealth). *Ideally* considered, the disintegration of a particular form of consciousness was enough to kill an entire epoch. In reality, this limitation of consciousness corresponds to a *definite stage of development of material productive forces*, and thus of wealth. Of course, development occurred not only on the old basis; there was development of the basis itself. The highest development of this basis, the point of flowering at which it changes (it is nevertheless still *this* basis, this plant in flower, and therefore it fades after flowering and as a consequence of flowering), is the point at which it has been elaborated to a form in which it can be united with the *highest development of productive forces*, and thus also with the richest development of the individual. As soon as this point has been reached, any further development takes the form of a decline, and any fresh development takes place from a new basis. We saw earlier that ownership of the means of production was identified with a limited, determined form of community and thus also of individuals possessing qualities and a development as limited as those of the community that they form.

This prerequisite itself was, in its turn, the result of a limited historical stage of the development of productive forces, a limitation of wealth, just as much as of the knowledge of how to achieve it. The purpose of this community and of these individuals – as a condition of production – is the *reproduction of these determined conditions of production* and of the individuals who, both as single individuals and in their social differentiations and relations, are the living carriers of these relationships. Capital itself establishes the *production of wealth* as such and hence the universal development of productive forces, the incessant upheaval of the prerequisites present in it, as a prerequisite of its reproduction. Value does not exclude any use value; nor does it include, as an absolute condition, any special kind of consumption or trade. Likewise any stage of development of socially productive forces, trade, science, etc., appears to it only as an obstacle that it seeks to overcome. Its prerequisite itself – value – is established as a product, not as a prerequisite higher than production and transcending it. The limitation of *capital* is that this whole development brings out contradictions, and that the elaboration of productive forces, of general wealth, science, etc., appears in such a form that the working individual alienates himself, relating to the conditions that he has produced not as to the conditions of his own wealth but as to those of alien wealth and his own poverty. But this contradictory form is itself a transitory one, and produces the real conditions of its own termination. The result is the creation of a basis that consists in the tendency towards universal development of the productive forces – and wealth in general, also the universality of commerce and a world market. The basis offers the possibility of the universal development of individuals, and the real development of individuals from this basis consists in the constant abolition of each limitation once it is conceived of *as* a limitation and not as a sacred boundary. The universality of the individual is not thought or imagined, but is the universality of his real and ideal relationships. Man therefore becomes able to understand his own history as a *process*, and to conceive of nature (involving also practical control over it) as his own real body. The process of development is itself established and understood as a prerequisite. But it is necessary also and above all that full development of the productive forces should have become a *condition of production*, not that determined *conditions of production* should be set up as a boundary beyond which productive forces cannot develop.

14 Ronald Meek

Karl Marx's Economic Method

Excerpt from R. L. Meek, 'Karl Marx's economic method', in R. L. Meek
Economics and Ideology and Other Essays, Chapman & Hall, 1967, pp. 93–106.

1

Most of the great 'heroic' economic models of a dynamic character which
have been put forward in the course of the history of economic thought –
those of Quesnay, Smith, Ricardo and Marx, for example – possess certain
important characteristics in common. The model-builder usually begins,
on the basis of a preliminary examination of the facts, by adopting what
Schumpeter has called a 'vision' of the economic process. In other words,
he begins by orienting himself towards some key factor or factors which he
regards as being of vital causal significance so far as the structure and
development of the economic system as a whole are concerned. With this
vision uppermost in his mind, he then proceeds to a more thorough
examination of the economic facts both of the present situation and of the
past situations which have led up to it, and arranges these facts in order on
what might be called a scale of relevance. Their position on this scale will
depend upon such factors as the particular vision which the model-builder
has adopted, his political and social sympathies, and the extent to which
the facts display uniformities and regularities which promise to be capable
of casual analysis in terms of the postulation of 'laws' and 'tendencies'.

Taking the facts which he has placed at the top of the scale as his foundation, the model-builder proceeds to develop certain concepts, categories
and methods of classification which he believes will help him to provide a
generalized explanation of the structure and development of the economy.
In this part of his work he has necessarily to rely to some extent on con-
cept-material inherited from the past, but he also tries to work out new
analytical devices of his own. The particular analytical devices which he
employs – his tools and techniques, as it were – are thus by no means
arbitrarily chosen. To quite a large extent they are dependent upon the
nature of his vision, the nature of the primary facts which they are to be
used to explain, and the nature of the *general* method of analysis which he
decides to adopt. The degree of their dependence upon these factors, however, varies from one device to another. Whereas some of the devices may
be useless or even harmful when the facts to be analysed and the orienta-

tion, aim and general method of analysis of the model-builder are radically different, others may have a greater degree of general applicability. Some may well prove useful when applied to other forms of market economy, and some may even be 'universal' in the sense in which, say, statistical techniques are 'universal'.

With the aid of these devices, then, the model-builder proceeds to the theoretical analysis of the particular economic facts which he has placed at the top of his scale of relevance. He endeavours to give a causal explanation of the uniformities and regularities which he has observed in these facts; he affords these explanations the status of 'laws' or 'tendencies'; and he gathers together these laws and tendencies into his first theoretical approximation. He then takes into account the facts next in order on the scale of relevance, from which he has hitherto abstracted, enquires into the extent to which their introduction into the picture requires a modification of the laws and tendencies of the first approximation, and thus arrives at his second approximation. He may well then proceed to a third, fourth, etc., approximation, progressively taking into account facts which he has placed lower and lower on the scale of relevance; but obviously there must come a time when it is not worth while to proceed any further down the scale. At the point where the basic laws and tendencies begin to be submerged beneath the exceptions and qualifications, he usually stops. The facts further down in the scale of relevance are simply abstracted from.

The final task is to use the model for the purpose of making concrete predictions – a task which is carried out largely by extrapolating the laws and tendencies into the future, on the express or implied assumption that the economic facts will continue to maintain their assumed position on the scale of relevance. The model which finally emerges is therefore compounded of elements not only of the past and present but also of the future.

This description of the model-building process is necessarily somewhat schematic, and I certainly do not mean to imply that all the great model-builders *consciously* adopted this intricate methodological approach. In essence, however, this was the method which most of them did in actual fact adopt, whether or not they were fully aware of what they were doing. It does help, I think, to have this general scheme in mind when we are analysing the economic work of a thinker like Marx – particularly if we are analysing it with a view to discovering whether and in what sense it is still relevant today.

2

The application of this general scheme to Marx's model is easier than in the case of most of the other great models, because Marx was more conscious of what he was doing than most of his predecessors in the field. The key causal factor towards which Marx began by orienting himself was the socio-economic production relation between the class of capital-owners and the class of wage earners. This relation, he believed, gave birth to the main contemporary forms of unearned income and to the possibility of the large-scale accumulation of capital; and this accumulation led in turn to rapid technological progress, which interacted with the capital–labour relation to determine the main features of the structure of capitalism and the main lines of the development of the system as a whole.

This was in effect Marx's 'vision' of the capitalist economic process. With this vision uppermost in his mind, he made a thorough examination of the economic facts both of the past and the present. The most relevant fact appeared to him to be the existence in all forms of class society of a mass of unearned income, which in capitalist society mainly took the form of net profit on capital, rent of land, and interest. Associated with this were certain other important facts or tendencies of a historical character which Marx's study of capitalist development in the past revealed to him – notably the progressive decline in the rate of profit; the increasing subordination of formerly independent workers to the capitalist form of organization; the increasing economic instability of the system; the growth of mechanization with its accompanying changes in the industrial structure; the emergence of various forms of monopoly; the growth of the 'reserve army of labour'; and the general deterioration in the condition of the working class. It is important to emphasize that these facts, by and large, were regarded by Marx simply as the *data* of his problem. As anyone can see by glancing at his *Economic and Philosophic Manuscripts of 1844*,[1] Marx had placed these facts at the top of his scale of relevance long before he came to work out the detailed tools and techniques required to analyse them.

The next stage – conceptually if not chronologically – was the development of Marx's *general* method of analysis, which was intimately associated with his vision of the economic process. Three aspects of this general method are worthy of note in the present connection.

In the first place, Marx had begun, as Lenin put it, 'by selecting from all social relations the "production relations", as being the basic and prime relations that determine all other relations' (Lenin, 1939, vol. 11, p. 418). In *Capital*, where he sets out to deal with 'one of the economic formations of society – the system of commodity production', Marx's analysis is 'strictly confined to the relations of production between the members of society: without ever resorting to factors other than relations of production to explain the matter, Marx makes it possible to discern how the com-

1. An English-language edition of these manuscripts was published by the Foreign Languages Publishing House, Moscow, in 1959.

modity organization of social economy develops, how it becomes transformed into capitalist economy, creating the antagonistic ... classes, the bourgeoisie and the proletariat, how it develops the productivity of social labour and how it thereby introduces an element which comes into irreconcilable contradiction to the very foundations of this capitalist organization itself' (Lenin, 1939, vol. 11, pp. 420–21).[2] In the context of the particular range of enquiry encompassed in *Capital*, it is evident that 'relations of production' must be taken to include not only the specific set of relations of subordination or cooperation within which commodity production is carried out at each particular stage of its historical development (e.g., the capitalist stage), but also the broad basic relation between men as producers of commodities which persists throughout the whole period of commodity production.[3]

In the second place, within the framework of the methodological approach just outlined and in close association with it, Marx developed a highly idiosyncratic method of enquiry – it might perhaps be called the 'logical-historical' method – which was one of the more interesting and significant of the fruits of his early Hegelian studies.[4] The description which Engels gave of this method in a review of Marx's *Critique of Political Economy* in 1859 has not been bettered, and the following extract can be reproduced without apology:

> The criticism of economics ... could ... be exercised in two ways: historically or logically. Since in history, as in its literary reflection, development as a whole proceeds from the most simple to the most complex relations, the historical development of the literature of political economy provided a natural guiding thread with which criticism could link up and the economic categories as a whole would thereby appear in the same sequence as in the logical development. This form apparently has the advantage of greater clearness, since indeed it is the *actual* development that is followed, but as a matter of fact it would thereby at most become more popular. History often proceeds by jumps and zigzags and it would in this way have to be followed everywhere, whereby not only would much material of minor importance have to be incorporated but there would be much interruption of the chain of thought; furthermore, the history of economics could not be written without that of bourgeois society and this would make the task endless, since all preliminary work is lacking. The logical method of treatment

2. Lenin adds that Marx, 'while "explaining" the structure and development of the given formation of society "exclusively" in terms of relations of production, ... nevertheless everywhere and always went on to trace the superstructure corresponding to these relations of production and clothed the skeleton in flesh and blood' (Lenin, 1939, vol. 11, p. 421).

3. 'Commodity production' in the Marxist sense means roughly the production of goods for exchange on some sort of market by individual producers or groups of producers who carry on their activities more or less separately from one another.

4. cf. Meek (1967, p. 156).

was, therefore, the only appropriate one. But this, as a matter of fact, is nothing else than the historical method, only divested of its historical form and disturbing fortuities. The chain of thought must begin with the same thing that this history begins with and its further course will be nothing but the mirror-image of the historical course in abstract and theoretically consistent form, a corrected mirror-image but corrected according to laws furnished by the real course of history itself, in that each factor can be considered at its ripest point of development, in its classic form (Engels, n.d., pp. 98–9).

This then was another important aspect of Marx's general method of analysis. No doubt this 'logical-historical' approach was sometimes carried to excess (for reasons which Marx himself partly explained in his 'Afterword' to the second German edition of *Capital* (Marx, 1954–9, vol. I, pp. 19–20)), but in his hands it proved on the whole to be very fruitful. It was particularly important, as will shortly be seen, in connection with the theory of value developed in *Capital*.

In the third place, and again closely associated with the two other aspects just described, there was the important notion that if one wished to analyse capitalism in terms of relations of production the best way of doing this was to imagine capitalism suddenly impinging upon a sort of generalized pre-capitalist society in which there were as yet no separate capital-owning or land-owning classes. What one ought to do, in other words, was to begin by postulating a society in which, although commodity production and free competition were assumed to reign more or less supreme, the labourers still owned the whole produce of their labour. Having investigated the simple laws which would govern production, exchange and distribution in a society of this type, one ought then to imagine capitalism suddenly impinging upon this society. What difference would this impingement make to the economic laws which had operated before the change, and why would it make this difference? If one could give adequate answers to these questions, Marx believed, one would be well on the way to revealing the real essence of the capitalist mode of production. In adopting this kind of approach, Marx was of course following – and developing further – a long and respectable tradition which had been established by Smith and Ricardo. Marx's postulation of an abstract pre-capitalist society based on what he called 'simple' commodity production was not essentially different in aim from Adam Smith's postulation of an 'early and rude' society inhabited by deer and beaver hunters. Neither in Marx's case nor in that of Smith was the postulated pre-capitalist society intended to be an accurate representation of historical reality in anything more than the very broadest sense. Nor was it intended as a picture of an ideal form of society, a sort of golden age of the past which the coming of the wicked capitalists and landlords was destined rudely to destroy. It was clearly part of a quite complex analytical device, and in its time a very powerful one. I am accustomed to tell my students that it was not a *myth*, as some critics maintain, but rather *mythology*.

This, then, was the nature of Marx's *general* method of economic analysis, in the context of which his other tools and techniques were developed and employed. Some of these were inherited by Marx from his predecessors – the concept of equilibrium, for example, and the particular classification of social classes and class incomes which he adopted. Others were newly developed, such as the important distinctions between abstract and concrete labour, labour and labour-power, and constant and variable capital. As his analysis proceeded, certain other concepts, relations and techniques emerged – notably the concept of surplus value, the distinction between relative and absolute surplus value, the ratios representing the rate of surplus value, the rate of profit and the organic composition of capital, and the techniques associated with his famous reproduction schemes.

In so far as it is possible to distinguish *methods* and *tools* of analysis from the *results* of analysis, then, these were some of the main methods and tools which Marx employed to analyse the economic facts which he had placed at the top of his scale of relevance. The uniformities and regularities which he believed he could detect in these facts were analysed in terms of the relations of production, with the aid of these methods and tools; and causal explanations emerged which were generalized in the form of tendencies and laws, modified in the second and subsequent approximations, and eventually extrapolated into the future in the form of more or less concrete predictions.

3

The most important field of application of Marx's general economic method was of course the *theory of value* elaborated in *Capital*. Indeed, Marx's theory of value is perhaps best regarded as being in essence a kind of generalized expression, or embodiment, of his economic method. In his analysis of value, as Engels noted, Marx 'proceeds from the simple production of commodities as the historical premise, ultimately to arrive from this basis [at] capital'. In other words, he begins with the 'simple' commodity, and then proceeds to analyse its 'logically and historically secondary form' – the 'capitalistically modified commodity' (Marx, 1954–9, vol. III, p. 14). The first part of his analysis of value therefore consists of a set of statements concerning the way in which relations of production influence the prices of goods in that abstract pre-capitalist form of society of which I have just spoken above. The second part of his analysis consists of a further set of statements concerning the way in which this basic causal connection between prices and relations of production is modified when *capitalist* relations of production impinge upon those appropriate to 'simple' commodity production – *i.e.*, when the 'simple' commodity becomes 'capitalistically modified'. This process of capitalistic modification is conceived to take place in two logically separate stages. In the first stage, it is assumed, capital subordinates labour on the basis of the technical conditions in which it finds it, and does not immediately change the mode of production itself. In the second stage, it is assumed, the extension of capitalist competition brings about a state of affairs in which profit becomes proportional not to labour employed but to capital employed and in which a more or less uniform rate of profit on capital comes to prevail. Thus Marx's theory of value can conveniently be considered under the three headings of Pre-capitalist Society, Early Capitalism, and Developed Capitalism.[5] To each of these forms of society there may be conceived to correspond certain basic economic categories and certain basic logical problems. The task of the analysis of value as Marx understood it was to solve these basic problems in terms of the relations of production appropriate to the particular 'historical' stage which was under consideration.

In Volume I of *Capital*, then, Marx proceeds 'from the first and simplest relation that historically and in fact confronts us' (Engels, n.d., p. 99) – the broad socio-economic relation between men as produces of commodities. In so far as economic life is based on the private production and exchange of goods, men are related to one another in their capacity as producers of goods intended for each other's consumption: they work for one another by embodying their separate labours in commodities which are destined to be exchanged on some sort of market. Historically, this 'commodity relation' reached its apogee under capitalism, but it was also in existence to a greater or lesser extent in almost all previous forms of society. If we want to penetrate to the essence of a society in which the commodity relation has become 'capitalistically modified', then, one possible method of procedure is to begin by postulating an abstract pre-capitalist society in which the commodity relation is assumed to be paramount but in which there are as yet no separate classes of capital-owners and land-owners. Having analysed the commodity relation as such in the context of this generalized pre-capitalist society, one can then proceed to examine what happens when capitalist relations of production impinge upon it.

5. A word of caution may be appropriate here, in order to forestall possible criticisms involving the fallacy of misplaced concreteness. The three forms of society mentioned here do not necessarily represent actual historically identifiable forms: they are merely the 'historical' counterparts of the three main stages in Marx's logical analysis of the value problem. In Marx's view, it will be remembered, the course of logical analysis is a *corrected* mirror-image of the actual historical course.

Marx's *logical* starting-point in *Capital*, then, is the commodity relation as such, and his *historical* starting-point is an abstract pre-capitalist society of the type just described. In such a society, great importance clearly attaches to the fact that commodities acquire the capacity to attract others in exchange – i.e., that they come to possess *exchange values*, or *prices*. The basic logical problem to be solved here is simply that of the determination of these prices. For Marx, no solution of this problem could be regarded as adequate which was not framed in terms of the appropriate set of relations of production. And for Marx, too, no solution could be regarded as adequate which did not possess as it were two dimensions – a qualitative one and a quantitative one. The qualitative aspect of the solution was directed to the question: Why do commodities possess prices at all? The quantitative aspect was directed to the question: Why do commodities possess the particular prices which they do? This distinction between the qualitative and quantitative aspects of Marx's analysis of value is of considerable importance, if only because it crops up again in the second and third stages of his enquiry.

In the context of the postulated pre-capitalist society, the answers to both the qualitative and the quantitative questions are fairly simple. The quality of exchange value is conferred upon commodities precisely because they are commodities – i.e., because a commodity relation exists between their producers. The price relations between commodities which manifest themselves in the sphere of exchange are essentially reflections of the socio-economic relations between men as producers of commodities which exist in the sphere of production. And just as it is the fact that men work for one another in this particular way which is responsible for the *existence* of commodity prices, so in Marx's view it is the amount of work which they do for one another which is responsible for the *relative levels* of commodity prices. The amount of labour laid out on each commodity, Marx argued, will determine (in the postulated society) the *amount* of exchange value which each comes to possess relatively to the others. In other words, in a society based on simple commodity production the equilibrium prices of commodities will tend to be proportional to the quantities of labour normally used to produce them. This is a familiar proposition which Marx of course took over from Smith and Ricardo, and *given the particular set of assumptions upon which it is based* it is almost self-evidently true. It is this proposition which is usually abstracted from Marx's analysis and labelled 'the labour theory of value' – a procedure which is of course quite illegitimate and which has had most unfortunate consequences.

Having thus proclaimed right at the beginning the general way in which he intends to unite economic history, sociology and economics in a kind of *ménage à trois*, Marx now proceeds to the second logical stage of his analysis. The 'historical' counterpart of this second stage is a society based on commodity production which has just been taken over by capitalists. The formerly 'independent' labourers now have to share the produce of their labour with a new social class – the owners of capital.[6] But nothing else is at this stage assumed to happen: in particular, it is supposed that capital subordinates labour on the basis of the technical conditions in which it finds it, without immediately changing the mode of production.[7] It is also assumed that commodities for the time being continue to sell 'at their values' in the Marxian sense – i.e., at equilibrium prices which are proportionate to quantities of embodied labour. In such a society, the crucial *differential* is the emergence of a new form of class income, profit on capital, and the basic logical problem as Marx conceived it was to explain the origin and persistence of this new form of income under conditions in which free competition was predominant and both the finished commodity and the labour which produced it were bought and sold on the market at prices which reflected their Marxian 'values'. The conditions of the problem were carefully posed by Marx in such a way as to rule out explanations in terms of anything other than the relations of production appropriate to the new stage.

Qualitatively speaking, the Marxian answer to the problem is obvious enough. The basic feature of the new situation is that a new social class has arisen and obtained a kind of class monopoly of the factor of production capital, the other side of this medal being that labour has itself become a commodity which is bought and sold on the market like any other commodity. The existence of this class monopoly of capital means that the capitalists are able to 'compel the working-class to do more work than the narrow round of its own life-wants prescribes' (Marx, 1954–9, vol. I, p. 309). The produce of this extra or surplus labour of the workers constitutes in effect the profit of the capitalists – or, as Marx calls it at this stage, the surplus value. But once again Marx was not content with an explanation couched solely in qualitative terms: he considered it necessary to derive in addition a *quantitative* explanation from the basic socio-economic

6. At this stage, the existence of a separate class of land-owners is abstracted from – a fact which throws further light on Marx's conception of the relation between the logical and the historical in analysis. The land–labour relation was historically prior to the capital–labour relation. But *under capitalism* it is the capital–labour relation which is primary, and the land–labour relation which is secondary. Since the analysis as a whole is oriented towards capitalism, the logical analysis must in Marx's view proceed from the capital–labour relation to the land–labour relation, and not vice versa.

7. cf. Marx (1954–9, vol. I, pp. 184, 310).

relation between capitalists and wage-earners.[8] The 'law of value' is therefore applied by Marx to the commodity labour – or rather labour-power – itself, the value of labour-power being in effect defined as the amount of labour required to produce wage-goods for the labourers at subsistence level. The surplus value received by any individual capitalist can then be regarded as determined and measured by the difference between the number of hours of work which his labourers perform and the number of hours of other men's work which are embodied in the wage-goods which he is in effect obliged to pay his labourers. This 'law', as Marx noted in Volume I, implies that profits are proportional to quantities of labour employed rather than to quantities of capital employed, and thus 'clearly contradicts all experience based on appearance' (Marx, 1954–9, vol. I, p. 307); but the solution of this 'apparent contradiction' is reserved for a later logical-historical stage in the analysis.

This later stage occurs in Volume III, where Marx deals with commodity and value relations which have become 'capitalistically modified' in the fullest sense. His 'historical' starting-point here is a fairly well developed capitalist system in which the extension of competition between capitalists has made profit proportional not to labour employed but to capital employed, and in which a more or less uniform rate of profit on capital prevails. In this new situation, which Marx speaks of as one in which 'surplus value has been transformed into profit', it is easy to see that the equilibrium prices at which commodities normally tend to sell must diverge appreciably from their Volume I 'values': clearly commodities can continue to sell at these 'values' only so long as the profit constituent in the price remains proportional to the quantity of labour employed.[9] Once commodities come to sell not at their Volume I 'values' but at their Marshallian 'costs of production' (or 'prices of production', as Marx called them) a new logical problem arises for solution – that of the determination of prices of this new type. In particular, the question arises as to whether these Volume III 'prices of production' can be explained in terms of the relations of production postulated as determinants in Volume I (suitably modified, of course, to reflect the transition to the new historical stage), or whether Adam Smith was correct in thinking that an entirely new type of explanation of prices was necessary in the stage of developed capitalism.

Qualitatively speaking, Marx's answer was that the 'capitalistically

8. Or, rather, from the broad relation between men as producers of commodities *as modified by* the impingement upon it of the class relation between capitalists and wage-earners.

9. Given, of course, that what Marx called the 'organic composition of capital' varies from industry to industry – which it does in fact do under developed capitalism.

modified' commodity relation was still of primary importance in determining prices even in this final stage, when actual equilibrium prices obviously diverged appreciably from Volume I 'values'. In a commodity-producing society of the modern capitalist type, the labour–capital production relationship still determined the distribution of the national income between wages and profits – i.e., it determined the total amount of profit available over the economy as a whole for allocation among the individual capitalists. As capitalism developed, changes certainly occurred in the *mode* of allocation of this profit between industries and enterprises, but these changes were logically and historically secondary. The socio-economic production relation between workers and capitalists, determining as it did the proportion of the national income available for allocation in the form of profit, was still in a meaningful sense the primary and determining relation. Given the total amount of profit, and given the amount of capital employed in producing each commodity, the profit constituent in the price of each commodity, and therefore its 'price of production', were automatically determined.

Once again, however, Marx was not content with a mere qualitative statement of this kind: he felt it necessary to translate the socio-economic relations involved in this analysis into quantitative terms. The result was his famous and much-criticized statement to the effect that under developed capitalism 'the sum of the prices of production of all commodities produced in society . . . is equal to the sum of their values' (Marx, 1954–9, vol. III, p. 157),[10] together with the equally famous arithmetical illustrations of this proposition. What these statements and illustrations really amounted to was an assertion that under developed capitalism there was still an important functional relationship between embodied labour and individual equilibrium prices, which may be expressed in the following symbolic form:

$$\text{Price of commodity} = c + v + \frac{c+v}{\Sigma(c+v)}\,(\Sigma s)$$

Here c is the value of used-up machinery and raw materials; v is the value of labour-power; s is surplus value; $\Sigma(c+v)$ is the aggregate amount of capital employed over the economy as a whole; and Σs is the aggregate amount of surplus value produced over the economy as a whole. The formula expresses the idea that the profit constituent in the price of an individual commodity represents a proportionate share of the total surplus value produced over the economy as a whole, the proportion being determined by the ratio of the total capital employed in the enterprise concerned to the aggregate amount of capital employed over the economy as a whole.

10. cf. Meek (1967, pp. 146ff.).

Since all the items on the right-hand side of the formula are expressible in terms of quantities of embodied labour, it can plausibly be maintained that there is still a causal connection, however indirect and circuitous, between Volume I 'values' and Volume III 'prices of production' – i.e., between socio-economic production relations and the prices at which commodities actually tend to sell under developed capitalism.

This causal connection is clearly a rather complex one, particularly when it is borne in mind that for the sake of simplicity I have deliberately abstracted from the complications caused by the existence of different turnover periods for the two elements of capital, and also from the very difficult issues associated with the so-called 'transformation problem'.[11] It is understandable that the above formula should not have appeared very often in popular Marxist writing: clearly no revolution would ever have been achieved if this formula had been inscribed on the red banners. Much more suitable for this purpose was the familiar proposition put forward in the first stage of the development of Marx's theory of value in Volume I of *Capital*. But it must be strongly emphasized that neither the Volume I analysis nor the Volume III analysis, taken by itself, can properly be said to constitute the Marxian theory of value. The theory of value as Marx developed it was a subtle and complex compound of the Volume I and Volume III analyses, and we cut ourselves off from all hope of understanding it if we consider it as anything less.

If this interpretation of Marx's theory of value is correct, it follows that any criticism of the theory based on the assumption that it is a crude and primitive over-simplification is entirely misconceived. The only really valid criticism of it which can be made, I would suggest, is one of precisely the opposite type – that for our present purposes today it is unnecessarily complex and refined. I am thinking here of two aspects of the theory in particular. First, there is the quite extraordinary way in which it draws upon and unites certain basic ideas of sociology, economic history, economics, and (up to a point) philosophy. In Marx's hands, the theory of value is not simply a theory which sets out to explain how prices are determined: it is also a kind of methodological manifesto, embodying Marx's view of the general way in which economics ought to be studied and calling for a restoration of the essential unity between the different social sciences. In Marx's time there was much to be said for the adoption of this line of approach, given certain points of view which were then current in the field of economics. It was indeed vitally important at that time to reassert the essential unity between economics and the other social sciences (particularly sociology) which Adam Smith had established but which the 'vulgar' economists who followed Ricardo had gone far to destroy; and the theory

11. See Meek (1967, pp. 143ff.).

of value had traditionally been regarded as an appropriate vehicle for the promulgation of methodological recommendations of this type. Today, of course, it remains as important as it ever was to call for inter-disciplinary cooperation in the social sciences. But I am not convinced that it would any longer be practicable to achieve that very high degree of integration which Smith and Marx still found possible. Nor am I convinced that the theory of value would any longer be the proper medium for the embodiment of an integrationist methodology. The role of the theory of value (in the traditional sense of a theory of price determination) in the general body of economic analysis is much more modest today than it was in Marx's time, and there is no longer any very compelling reason why a theorist wishing to bring sociology or economic history into his economics should feel obliged to start by reforming the theory of value.

If he *did* decide to start in this way, however, and set out to bring sociology into the picture by demonstrating the existence of a qualitative and quantitative relationship of a causal character between relations of production and relative prices, should he make the quantitative link-up in the particular way that Marx did? This is the second aspect of Marx's theory which I had in mind when stating that it seemed too complex and refined for present-day use. Joan Robinson (1965, vol. III, p. 176) has recently suggested that it was an 'aberration' for Marx to tie up the problem of relative prices with the problem of exploitation in the way that he did. I am not myself convinced that it was in fact an 'aberration': as I have just stated, there were very good reasons, given the particular views against which Marx had to fight, for the adoption of this particular method of tying them up. Today, however, it does seem to me that Marx's method of making the quantitative tie-up between economics and sociology tends to obscure the importance of the infusion of sociology rather than to reveal it. Certainly, at any rate, generations of Marx-scholars have felt that they have proved something important about the real world when they have shown that in some moderately meaningful mathematical sense the 'sum of the prices' *is* equal to the 'sum of the values'.[12] I am now persuaded that this was in some measure an illusion. In my more heretical moods, I sometimes wonder whether much of real importance would be lost from the Marxian system if the quantitative side of the analysis of relative prices were conducted in terms of something like the traditional supply and demand apparatus – *provided* that the socio-economic relationships emphasized by Marx were fully recognized as the basic cause of the existence of the prices whose level was shown to vary with variations in supply and demand, and *provided* that these Marxian sociological factors,

12. See Meek (1967, pp. 143ff.).

where relevant, were also clearly postulated as lying behind the supply and demand schedules themselves.[13]

13. In many cases, of course, Marxian postulates would have to *replace* those commonly employed. A Marxist, for example, in analysing the forces lying behind the demand curve, could hardly base his analysis on the assumption that the consumer acted (in some more or less sophisticated way) so as to maximize the net income or utility he received from his purchases.

Postscript

The article from which the above extracts have been taken was largely a product of the heady *New Reasoner* days of the 1950s, when we were all trying to work out new (or at any rate 'revised') frames of reference for the basic ideas on which we had been brought up. This explains the somewhat schematic character of the piece, which some readers may find a little odd. On the whole, however, I would still claim that Marx's economic theory in general, and his theory of value in particular, make more sense when considered within this frame of reference than when considered within most of the available alternatives.

The most neglected aspect of Marx's economic methodology continues today to be what I called in the article his 'logical-historical' approach, the importance of which I then tended if anything to underemphasize. I now feel, however, that I was wrong to speak of Marx's starting-point (in his theory of value) as being *merely* 'an abstract pre-capitalist society in which the commodity relation is assumed to be paramount'. This formulation underestimates the degree of historical specificity which Marx attached to his 'first' stage in a number of places – not least in the key chapter on the historical tendency of capitalist accumulation in Volume I of *Capital* (chapter XXXII), where he speaks of the 'petty mode of production' in remarkably concrete (i.e. *historically* concrete) terms.

There are only two other points – both relatively minor – which may be worth making. First, my side-swipe at the debate on the transformation problem in the final paragraph now seems a bit misconceived: some of the issues raised in the subsequent discussion of this problem have in fact proved to be of considerable importance. Second, I am no longer sure that the assumption that consumers maximize net utility is quite as unrealistic, in this age of mass advertising, as I made it out to be in the final footnote.

R. L. M.
September 1975

References

ENGELS, F. (n.d.), *Ludwig Feuerbach and the End of Classical German Philosophy*, London.

LENIN, V. I. (1939), *Selected Works*, Lawrence & Wishart.

MARX, K. (1954–9), *Capital*, Foreign Languages Publishing House, Moscow.

MEEK, R. L. (1967), *Economics and Ideology and Other Essays*, Chapman & Hall.

ROBINSON, J. (1965), *Collected Economic Papers*, Blackwell.

Part Three
The Labour Theory of Value

15 Maurice Dobb

Marx's *Capital* and its Place in Economic Thought

Excerpt from Maurice Dobb, 'Marx's *Capital* and its place in economic thought', *Science and Society*, vol. 31, 1967, pp. 527–35.

1

Das Kapital is, perhaps, the most controversial work on political economy ever to have been written. The subject of more and sharper controversy even than was Ricardo's *Principles*, it has probably met with wider extremes of praise and denigration than any other work of its kind. More frequently refuted than most economic theories – and when not being refuted it was as often as not, in academic circles, ignored – it has survived to be accepted over a large part of the contemporary world as the authoritative interpretation of capitalist society. Even in the last decade of the nineteenth century a foremost critic could say that 'Marx has become the apostle of a wide circle of readers, including many who are not as a rule given to the reading of difficult books' (Böhm-Bawerk). Despite the passion his doctrines have aroused, however, there are those among his academic critics who have estimated his intellectual contribution soberly. Joseph Schumpeter, for example, in his monumental *History of Economic Analysis*, says of Marx that 'the totality of his vision, as a totality, asserts its right in every detail and is precisely the source of the intellectual fascination experienced by everyone, friend as well as foe, who makes a study of him'; and elsewhere that 'at the time when his first volume appeared there was nobody in Germany who could have measured himself against him either in vigor of thought or in theoretical knowledge'.

The two concepts that have been the special centres of controversy have been those of property income as surplus value, or the fruit of exploitation, and of the historical development of capitalist society towards revolutionary transformation into socialism. The former could be regarded, perhaps, as a development of the 'deduction theory' of profit to be found in Adam Smith (where it was no more than a surplus theory in embryo, and some would say no more than a hint), or possibly as a more rigorous and systematic version of ideas already current among the so-called Ricardian socialists. The latter concept, in itself an application of Marx's general view of history and of the role of class conflict as the motive force of historical change, sharply contrasted with prevailing views of economic progress, since these, even when tinged as they often were with fears about the approach of a 'stationary state', held no inkling of an historical role for the working class. Such a role was quite foreign to bourgeois conceptions, and its introduction was at once transforming and, to traditional notions, distinctly shocking.

Proper understanding of both these concepts depends on an appreciation of the boundaries of political economy as Marx envisaged them. The tendency of modern economic analysis since the last quarter of the nineteenth century has been to narrow its focus to a study of the exchange process, that is, of the market and of market equilibrium under various hypothetical conditions. In gaining precision of formulation it has achieved a fairly drastic narrowing of scope and of range. Conditions of production have been narrowed and faded down to the assumption of given supplies (or supply conditions) of disembodied productive factors and of given technical coefficients or so-called production functions; and insofar as any kind of process of production appears, it does so implicitly as a unidirectional flow of primary factors into final consumer goods (in terms of which the so-called imputation of prices to intermediate goods and factors – the Austrian school's *Zurechnung* – alone makes sense). Anything to do with property ownership, or any distinction between the propertied and the propertyless, is relegated to the category of social or sociological factors, excluded from the domain of economic theory *per se*, and not affecting the formal structure of that theory (merely affecting, perhaps, the value of some of the variables involved).

As is well known, the shape assumed by a theoretical model is itself a selection of the facts and the events to be studied; hence, however impeccable or elegant its logic, it can represent a biased selection which may distort our vision of the real world, instead of illuminating it. One result of the increasing formalization of economic theory in recent decades has been to render its analysis of market equilibrium almost entirely quantitative in character, leaving little or no room for qualitative *differentia* and certainly no room for *differentia* of a so-called socio-economic kind. What Marx called the 'fetishism of commodities' is thus able to ripen behind this imposing façade to an unnatural degree. It is hardly surprising that a relationship such as 'exploitation' or the characterization of income as a 'surplus' should cease to have any meaning within this context, and that even some sympathetic critics should have dismissed the notions of exploitation and surplus value as moral judgements masquerading as economic concepts.

By contrast, Marx conceived the bounds of political economy more widely than this – as, indeed, was true of classical political economy without, in its case, such explicit formulation. For him the 'social relations of production' were included as well as the 'productive forces' and the conditions of exchange. This followed from his historical approach to the analysis of capitalist production and his historical conception of the mode of production as the basis of a given society and 'the true source and theatre of all history'. Qualitative characterization of relationships was as important as was a solution of the quantitative problem of value and of the derivation of prices from values. From the standpoint of causation, especially of movement and change, such characterization was essential; and a constant preoccupation of his analysis was 'to penetrate through the outward disguise into the internal essence and the inner form of the capitalist process of production' behind the market appearance with which the *epigoni* were content.

If we take the terms 'exploitation' and 'unpaid labour' as a socio-economic description of a relationship (and not *per se* a moral epithet) then it is hard to see how its correctness can be disputed. Few if any would question the description of the income of feudal lords as having its source in the appropriation of a part of what was produced by others – the product of 'a subject peasantry', to use the historian Marc Bloch's phrase. (Marc Bloch says: 'Whatever the source of the noble's income, he always lived on the labour of other men.') Surely, anyone who denied this would be concealing or distorting a major feature of an economy based on serf labour. To apply a similar characterization to property income in a capitalist society is to assert that in this respect it bears a major analogy with previous types of class society, and this *despite* the fact that all economic relationships have a contractual form governed by the market. In other words, owners of capital continue to 'live on the labour of other men', even though politico-legal compulsion to work for a master is replaced by the economic compulsion which a propertyless status involves. Are not those economists the word-jugglers and obscurantists who have sought to deny such a proposition with the aid of various types of 'productivity' theory conjuring their denial by imputing the activities of a machine or the chemical properties of land to the passive *rentier* who happens to be their owner?

Some have supposed, wrongly I think, that the characterization of profit as surplus value is somehow derived from the labour theory of value; the two standing in relation to one another as the premiss and conclusion of a syllogism. Thus, the two theories are sometimes regarded as inheritors of Lockean notions of natural right – the natural right to own the product of one's own labour. This is, I believe, an incorrect interpretation. Rather was it a case (as Marx himself explained it in *Value, Price and Profit*) of reconciling the fact of surplus value with the classical notion that in a régime of free trade and free competition, all things exchanged at their values: a reconciliation which he achieved by separating labour power from labour; the former being a commodity which itself had a value, depending upon the value of what was needed for its replacement, or for subsistence. If there was some premiss from which the notion of surplus value was derived as a conclusion, this was the definition of 'producer' and of 'productive' in terms of human activity.

2

The theory of value of Marx stood essentially in the classical tradition, although in its formulation by different writers of the classical school there were ambiguities and some lack of clarity, as well as the well-known differences between Adam Smith and Ricardo on this matter. There is no doubt that it was Ricardo who stood closest to Marx – an affinity that we can appreciate the more now that we have Ricardo's unpublished and previously unknown paper on 'Absolute and Exchangeable Value'.[1] What this theory of value essentially did was to explain conditions of exchange in terms of conditions of production, and hence in the final analysis to represent the prices of production as determined (in the 'normal case' and under conditions of free and perfect competition) by the amount of labour which their production cost, together with the technical conditions of their production, as expressed in what Marx termed the 'organic composition of capital'. This derivation of exchange relations from conditions of production was, again, wholly consonant with his general conception of history and with the leading role played in this by the mode of production. It was, indeed, a direct application of this historical conception, and represents the organic link between the two that enables one to speak of his economic theory as being in this sense *historical* and illustrates the essential unity of his thought.

It is precisely this claim that the structure of prices can be derived from conditions of production that has evoked the most strenuous denials from economists of the subjective, or utility, school. And the charge that Marx's attempt to demonstrate this (and, hence, his theory of profit as surplus value) foundered on a crucial contradiction was what enabled his leading critic, the Austrian Von Böhm-Bawerk, to proclaim confidently 'the close of the Marxian system', thereby leaving the field open for an explanation of prices and incomes simultaneously in terms of utility (*vide* Böhm-Bawerk's own well-known theory of interest on capital as dependent on the different subjective valuation of present and future goods). In Volume I of *Capital*, as is well known, Marx tackled the problem of surplus value on the assumption that commodities exchange at their values. At this stage

1. Published in Ricardo (1950, vol. IV). The paper is unfinished, its writing having been interrupted by Ricardo's fatal illness and death.

his analysis is concerned only with the most *general* features of capitalism, and it is on these that he fixes attention. Expressing it in modern terminology, one could say that analysis is conducted at this stage at the most macroscopic level. He is not concerned at this stage with individual products and industries, but with the 'social relations of production' which determine how the total product, viewed as a whole, is divided between the classes. It is only in Volume III, at a later stage of approximation, that he concerns himself with more of the detail of the picture – that he introduces conditions affecting the relations between different industries and comes close to *differentia* that become visible and important at a more microscopic level of examination. In particular, he takes account of differences in the technical conditions and in the so-called organic composition of capital in different lines of production, combined with the necessity (given conditions of capital mobility between industries) for a uniform rate of profit on capital, irrespective of where capital is used. Under these conditions, for reasons which are sufficiently familiar, 'prices of production', as the normal (or long-term equilibrium) prices at which products exchange, diverge from values; profit being equalized by a process of 'redistribution of total surplus value' between different branches of industry.

In subsequent Marx-*kritik* it was upon the relation between these prices of production and the values of Volume I that attention came to be focused. The theory of surplus value was constructed on the assumption that commodities exchanged at their values; yet it transpired in Volume III that exchange in capitalist society was on the basis not of values but of prices of production which diverged from values. What then was left of the theory of surplus value and all that was pendant on it? This was 'the Great Contradiction' which, according to Böhm-Bawerk, lay at the core of the Marxian system and was the source of its inevitable dissolution. ('The Marxian system has a past and a present, but no abiding future.') What point was there in speaking of two levels of approximation, or two stages of analysis, if the second could not be derived (given the additional data introduced at this second stage) from the first? This could not be done in the manner indicated by Marx; and if it could not, then Marx's theory provided neither a theory of profits nor a theory of prices; and an explanation both of profits and of prices must be sought elsewhere. It was demonstrably untrue that conditions of production determined conditions of exchange.

In subsequent discussion of this question the problem of deriving prices of production from values (or of the later approximation from the essential data postulated in the earlier approximation) was called the Transformation Problem. This discussion was both intermittent and recondite; it was confined to a mere handful of *cognoscenti*, and was very little known either among Marxists or among non-Marxian economists. But on the outcome of it the force of Böhm-Bawerk's apparently telling criticism of the theoretical structure built up in the three volumes of *Capital*, and especially in the first and third, can be said to have turned. On this issue Böhm-Bawerk (1898), usually so perspicacious, had contented himself with a disdainful dismissal of the particular solution indicated by Marx, and had not stopped to inquire whether the character of the problem was such as to make it likely or unlikely that an alternative solution to it could be found.

It is, indeed, clear that Böhm-Bawerk's method of argument was altogether too simple for the nature of the problem in question, and that he had really no notion of complex determination implied in the proposition that 'the values stand behind the prices of production' and 'determine these latter in the last resort'. It is true that the particular arithmetical examples that Marx uses to illustrate the derivation of prices of production from values are inadequate and incomplete – a fact of which he himself was aware (as evidenced in a passage in Marx, 1923, Teil III, pp. 200–201, 212). [2] Moreover, the simple contention that 'on the average' prices of production and values, profit and surplus value came out equal, was quite insufficient. Like much else in Volumes II and III this was unfinished work, and in this unfinished state it was open to some, at least, of the objections that Böhm-Bawerk, and later, Bortkiewicz, levelled at it. This incompleteness consisted in the fact that only the outputs were transformed into prices of production, while all the inputs (including labour power) continued to be expressed in terms of value. Obviously this is not sufficient: as Marx himself saw, the inputs themselves must also be transformed into price terms (the elements of constant capital and wages as the price of labour power, which itself depends upon the price of workers' subsistence, or so-called wage goods). If inputs are so transformed, both the rate of profits and the prices of output will be affected thereby. It follows that the rate of profit will not be the same (except in a special case) as the rate of profit that was formed out of the surplus value of the value situation (by averaging); and in Marx's arithmetical examples it would be different from the rate of profit with which he constructed his prices of production. But it does *not* follow that the new rate of profit cannot bear a definite relation to the old rate of profit (i.e., of the value situation) and, hence, to the rate of surplus value as defined in the theory of surplus value. Nor does it follow that in this situation of complex interdependence, where output prices depend on input prices and output prices reciprocally influence input prices a single set of magnitudes cannot be found for all the variables which satisfy the postulated conditions. The solution, if it can be found, will be like the

2. cf. also Marx (1906–09, vol. III, pp. 190, 194).

solution to a set of simultaneous equations, and the possibility of finding one will depend, formally, on similar conditions.

It was the merit of Bortkiewicz in the first decade of the present century to have shown that such a solution was, indeed, possible in the simplified case of three sectors or industries, producing respectively elements of constant capital (the Department I of Marx's reproduction schema at the end of Volume II), wage goods and luxury goods consumed exclusively by capitalists (Bortkiewicz, 1907a, 1907b).[3] This he did with the aid of the condition (a condition of so-called simple reproduction) that the outputs of each category were equal to the incomes devoted to their purchase (namely, replacement expenditures on constant capital, total wages, and total surplus value). It was a curiosity of this Bortkiewicz solution that it was independent of the conditions of production of the third sector producing for capitalists' consumption: The solution depended exclusively on the conditions of production in the other two sectors.[4] This, he claimed, was not just a formal result, but demonstrated that profit was the fruit of exploitation (or as he preferred to put it, in the manner of Adam Smith, it had the nature of a 'deduction') and had nothing to do with the productivity of capital. ('If it is indeed true that the level of the rate of profit in no way depends on the conditions of production of those goods which do not enter into real wages, then the origin of profit must clearly be sought in the wage-relationship and not in the ability of capital to increase production. For if this ability were relevant here, then it would be inexplicable why certain spheres of production should become irrelevant for the question of the level of profit.')[5]

This Bortkiewicz solution in terms of three sectors was, in essence, a three-industry, three-product solution. Alternatively it could be thought of as yielding the *average* price of production for each sector and, hence, demonstrating that these average prices could be derived from the *data* of the value situation (i.e., conditions of production measured in terms of labour) while leaving the individual prices of particular prices *within* each sector undetermined. It was intuitively obvious, of course, that if a solution were possible for the three-product case, it could be found in all probability for any larger number of products. For some time, however, an

3. Bortkiewicz's solution had, however, been anticipated (as he himself acknowledged quite handsomely) by the Russian economist W. K. Dmitrieff in a little-known work of 1904 (a 'remarkable work', presenting 'something really new', according to Bortkiewicz). Dr Sweezy (1942) deserves the credit for starting a discussion of this solution among English-speaking readers.

4. Or, more strictly speaking, 'on those amounts of labour and those turnover periods which concern the production and distribution of the goods forming the real wage-rate' (Bortkiewicz).

5. Bortkiewicz (1907b: p. 33 of the English translation); see also Dobb (1955).

actual demonstration of this remained lacking – a lack that may perhaps be regarded as an adverse reflection upon the 'creative Marxism' of Marxist economic thinkers of the period. The first such demonstration (to the knowledge of the present writer) that a more general solution was possible for any number of commodities – for the n-product case – was provided by Francis Seton (1956–7). The conclusion was that his analysis had shown the 'logical superstructure' of Marx's theory 'to be sound enough' – a demonstration that some may think acquires additional conviction from the fact that the writer was at pains to dissociate himself from the implications of Marx's theory of surplus value.[6]

Such a demonstration (worked out, indeed, in its essentials many years earlier) is also implicit in the equations which form the crux of the derivation of prices from conditions of production and the ratio of profits to wages in Part One of Piero Sraffa's *Production of Commodities by Means of Commodities* (see especially Chapter II). The upshot of discussion over more than half a century accordingly is that Marx was quite correct in supposing that prices of production as the actual 'equilibrium prices' of a competitive capitalist economy could be regarded as being determined by the conditions and relations of production, including in the latter the basic exploitation-ratio which in value terms is expressed as the rate of surplus value. The logical structure of Marx's analysis of capitalist production, and the unfolding of this analysis from the level of value theory of Volume I through to the theory of prices in Volume III, remains intact after a century of vehement, sometimes acute but more often far-from-understanding, criticism. And in its qualitative characterization of the essentials of capitalist society and of its driving forces, can there be much serious doubt that it provides an insight that no economic writing of other schools has done?

References

BÖHM-BAWERK, E. VON (1898), *Karl Marx and the Close of His System*, New York.

BORTKIEWICZ, L. VON (1907a), in *Jahrbücher für Nationalökonomie und Statistik*, July; translated as 'Marx's fundamental theoretical construction in the third volume of *Capital*', in E. von Böhm-Bawerk, *Karl Marx and the Close of his System* (P. M. Sweezy, ed.), New York, 1949.

BORTKIEWICZ, L. VON (1907b), in *Archiv für Sozialwissenschaft*, July; translated as 'Value and price in the Marxian system', *International Economic Papers*, no. 2, New York, 1952.

DOBB, M. (1955), 'A note on the transformation problem', in M. Dobb, *On Economic Theory and Socialism*, Routledge & Kegan Paul.

6. He considered a denial of factor contributions other than those of labor, on which the doctrine of surplus value rested, to be 'an act of *fiat* rather than of genuine cognition' (Seton, 1956–7, p. 160).

MARX, K. (1906–09), *Capital*, Charles H. Kerr, Chicago.

MARX, K. (1923), *Theorien über den Mehrwert*, (Karl Kautsky ed.), Dietz, Berlin.

RICARDO, D. (1950), *The Works and Correspondence of David Ricardo*, (P. Sraffa ed.), Cambridge University Press.

SETON, F. (1957), 'The "transformation problem"', *Review of Economic Studies*, vol. 24, pp. 149–60.

SRAFFA, P. (1960), *Production of Commodities by Means of Commodities*, Cambridge University Press.

SWEEZY, M. (1942), *Theory of Capitalist Development*, New York.

16 Paul Sweezy

The Qualitative-Value Problem

Excerpt from Paul Sweezy, 'The qualitative-value problem', in *Theory of Capitalist Development*, first published 1942, reprinted by Monthly Review Press, 1968, pp. 23–34.

1 Introduction

The first chapter of *Capital* is entitled 'Commodities'. It has already been pointed out that a commodity is anything that is produced for exchange rather than for the use of the producer; the study of commodities is therefore the study of the economic relation of exchange. Marx begins by analysing 'simple commodity production', that is to say a society in which each producer owns his own means of production and satisfies his manifold needs by exchange with other similarly situated producers. Here we have the problem of exchange in its clearest and most elementary form.

In starting from simple commodity production, Marx was following a well-established tradition of economic theory, but this should not be allowed to obscure the sharp break which divides his analysis from that of the classical school. In the case of Adam Smith, for example, exchange is tied in the closest possible way to the main technological fact of economic life, namely, the division of labour. According to Smith, division of labour is the foundation of all increases in productivity; it is even the basis of the human economy, what distinguishes the latter from the life of the beasts. But Smith is unable to conceive of division of labour independently of exchange; exchange, in fact, is prior to and responsible for division of labour. The following passage sums up Smith's theory of the relation between division of labour and exchange:

This division of labour, from which so many advantages are derived, is not originally the effect of any human wisdom, which foresees and intends that general opulence to which it gives occasion. It is the necessary, though very slow and gradual consequence of a certain propensity in human nature which has in view no such extensive utility; the propensity to truck, barter, and exchange one thing for another (Smith, 1930, vol. 1, p. 15).

This 'propensity to truck, barter, and exchange', moreover, is peculiar to human beings: 'Nobody ever saw a dog make a fair and deliberate exchange of one bone for another with another dog' (Smith, 1930, vol. 1, p. 15). Exchange and division of labour are in this manner indissolubly bound together and shown to be the joint pillars supporting civilized society. The implications of this position are clear: commodity production, rooted in human nature, is the universal and inevitable form of economic life; economic science is the science of commodity production. From this point of view the problems of economics have an exclusively quantitative character; they begin with exchange value, the basic quantitative relation between commodities established through the process of exchange.

Turning now to Marx, we see at the very outset the difference in approach which marks off his political economy from that of Adam Smith. Marx does not deny the existence of a relation between commodity production and the division of labour, but it is by no means the hard and fast relation depicted by Smith. The difference in points of view is clearly brought out in the following passage:

This division of labour is a necessary condition for the production of commodities, but it does not follow conversely, that the production of commodities is a necessary condition for the division of labour. In the primitive Indian community there is social division of labour without production of commodities. Or, to take an example nearer home, in every factory the labour is divided according to a system, but this division is not brought about by the operatives' mutually exchanging their individual products. *Only such products can become commodities with regard to each other as result from different kinds of labour, each kind being carried on independently and for the account of private individuals* (Marx, 1933, vol. I, p. 49; italics added).

Division of labour is deprived of none of the importance which was attributed to it by Smith, but it is emphatically denied that division of labour is necessarily tied to exchange. Commodity production, in other words, is not the universal and inevitable form of economic life. It is rather one possible form of economic life, a form, to be sure, which has been familiar for many centuries and which dominates the modern period, but none the less a historically conditioned form which can in no sense claim to be a direct manifestation of human nature. The implications of this view are striking. Commodity production itself is withdrawn from the realm of natural phenomena and becomes the valid subject of socio-historical investigation. No longer can the economist afford to confine his attention to the quantitative relations arising from commodity production; he must also direct his attention to the character of the social relations which underlie the commodity form. We may express this by saying that the tasks of economics are not only quantitative, they are also qualitative. More concretely, in the case of exchange value there is, as Adam Smith saw, the quantitative relation between products; hidden behind this, as Marx was the first to see, there is a specific, historically conditioned, relation between producers. Following Petry, we may call the analysis of the former *the quantitative-value problem*, the analysis of the latter *the quali-tative-value problem*.[1]

The great originality of Marx's value theory lies in its recognition of these two elements of the problem and in its attempt to deal with them simultaneously within a single conceptual framework. The same considera-tions, however, account in no small degree for the great difficulty in under-standing the theory which is almost invariably experienced by those brought up in the main tradition of economic thought. For this reason it has seemed advisable to separate Marxian value theory into its two component parts and attempt to deal with them one at a time. Consequently here we shall discuss the qualitative-value problem, leaving the more familiar quanti-tative problem for consideration later.

2 Use value

'Every commodity,' Marx (1911b, p. 19) wrote, 'has a twofold aspect, that of use value and exchange value.'

In possessing use value a commodity is in no way peculiar. Objects of human consumption in every age and in every form of society likewise possess use value. Use value is an expression of a certain relation between the consumer and the object consumed. Political economy, on the other hand, is a social science of the relations between people. It follows that 'use value as such lies outside the sphere of investigation of political economy' (Marx, 1911b, p. 21).

Marx excluded use value (or, as it now would be called, 'utility') from the field of investigation of political economy on the ground that it does not directly embody a social relation. He enforces a strict requirement that the categories of economics must be social categories, i.e. categories which represent relations between people. It is important to realize that this is in sharp contrast to the attitude of modern economic theory. As previously noted, Lionel Robbins says – and in this he is merely formulating the practice of all non-Marxian schools – 'We regard [the economic system] as a series of interdependent but conceptually discrete relationships *between men and economic goods*' (Robbins, 1932, p. 69; italics added). From this starting point, it follows, of course, that use value or utility takes a central position among the categories of economics. But it should not be over-looked in any comparison of Marxian and orthodox economics that their respective starting points are in this respect diametrically opposed. Nor should it be made a matter of reproach against Marx that he failed to

1. Petry (1916). This little book, the only one ever published by its author, who was killed in the First World War at the age of 26, deserves much more attention than it has received. A similar distinction is made in the excellent note on value theory, Lowe (1938).

develop a subjective value theory, since he consciously and deliberately dissociated himself from any attempt to do so.[2]

This does not mean that use value should play no role in economics. On the contrary, just as land, though not an economic category itself, is essential to production, so use value is a prerequisite to consumption and, as Petry (1916, p. 17) correctly remarks, is in no sense excluded by Marx from the causal chain of economic phenomena.

3 Exchange value

In possessing exchange value relative to one another, commodities show their unique characteristic. It is only as commodities, in a society where exchange is a regular method of realizing the purpose of social production, that products have exchange value. At first sight it might seem that even less than in the case of use value have we here to do with a social relation. Exchange value appears to be a quantitative relation between things, between the commodities themselves. In what sense, then, is it to be conceived as a social relation and hence as a proper subject for the investigation of the economist? Marx's answer to this question is the key to his value theory. The quantitative relation between things, which we call exchange value, is in reality only an outward form of the *social* relation between the commodity owners, or, what comes to the same thing in simple commodity production, between the producers themselves The exchange relation as such, apart from any consideration of the quantities involved, is an expression of the fact that individual producers each working in isolation, are in fact working for each other. Their labour, whatever they may think about the matter, has a social character which is impressed upon it by the act of exchange. In other words, the exchange of commodities is an exchange of the products of the labour of individual producers. What finds expression in the form of exchange value is therefore the fact that the commodities involved are the products of human labour in a society based on division of labour in which producers work privately and independently.

Strictly speaking, the concept exchange value applies 'only when commodities are present in the plural',[3] since it expresses a relation *between* commodities. An individual commodity, however, possesses the social quality which manifests itself quantitatively in exchange value. A commodity in so far as we centre our attention on this social quality is called by

2. The best criticism of subjective value theory from the Marxist standpoint, and at the same time a very valuable contribution to the understanding of Marx's value theory, is Hilferding (1904).

3. Marx (1934, p. 853). This is Marx's last economic work, being taken from a notebook dated 1881/2. Marx died in 1883.

Marx a plain 'value'. Late in Chapter 1 of *Capital*, he says: 'When, at the beginning of this chapter, we said, in common parlance, that a commodity is both a use value and an exchange value, we were, accurately speaking, wrong. A commodity is a use value or object of utility, and a value' (Marx, 1933, vol. I, p. 70).

As a use value, a commodity is a universal feature of human existence, present in every and all forms of society. As a value, a commodity is a feature of a specific historical form of society which has two main distinguishing characteristics: (1) developed division of labour, and (2) private production. In such an order – and in none other – the labour of producers eventuates in commodities or, neglecting the universal aspect of commodities (utility), in values.

It is essential to realize that it was this analysis of the social characteristics of commodity production, and not an arbitrary preconception or an ethical principle, which led Marx to identify labour as the substance of value.[4] We must now examine this more closely.

4 Labour and value

The requirement that all economic categories must represent social relations led Marx directly to labour as the 'value that lies hidden behind' (Marx, 1933, vol. I, p. 55) exchange value. 'Only one property of a commodity,' as Petry expressed it, 'enables us to assume it as the bearer and expression of social relations, namely its property as *the product of labour* since as such we consider it no longer from the standpoint of consumption but from the standpoint of production, as materialized human activity . . .' (Petry, 1916, p. 19). In what sense, then, are we using the concept 'labour'?

Labour also has two aspects, the one corresponding to the use value and the other to the value of the commodity which it produces. To the commodity as a use value corresponds labour as useful labour.

The coat is a use value that satisfies a particular want. Its existence is the result of a special sort of productive activity, the nature of which is determined by its aim, mode of operation, subject, means and result. The labour, whose utility is thus represented by the value in use of its product, or which manifests itself by making its product a use value, we call useful labour (Marx, 1933, vol. I, p. 48).

4. In the notes on Wagner quoted above, Marx described his procedure in part as follows: 'What I . . . start from is the simplest social form in which the labour product is found in present society, and that is 'commodity'. I analyse it. and first of all in *the form in which it appears*. Here I find that on the one hand in its natural form it is a *useful thing* alias *use value*, on the other hand the *bearer of exchange value* . . . Further analysis of the latter shows me that exchange value is only a 'phenomenal *form*', an independent method of displaying the value contained in the commodity, and then I proceed to the analysis of the latter . . .' (Marx, 1934, p. 847).

Thus tailoring creates a coat, spinning creates yarn, weaving creates cloth, carpentering creates a table, *et cetera*. These are all different varieties of useful labour. But it would be incorrect to assume that useful labour is the only source of use value; nature cooperates both actively and passively in the process of producing use value. 'As William Petty put it, labour is its father and the earth its mother' (Marx, 1933, vol. I, p. 50).

If, now, we abstract from the use value of a commodity it exists simply as a value. Proceeding in a similar fashion to abstract from the useful character of labour, what have we left?

Productive activity, if we leave out of sight its special form, viz., the useful character of the labour, is nothing but the expenditure of human labour power. Tailoring and weaving, though qualitatively different productive activities, are each a productive expenditure of human brains, nerves and muscles, and in this sense are human labour. Of course, this labour power which remains the same under all its modifications must have attained a certain pitch of development before it can be expended in a multiplicity of modes. But the value of a commodity represents human labour in the abstract, the expenditure of human labour in general (Marx, 1933, vol. I, p. 51).

Thus, what use value is to value in the case of commodity, useful labour is to abstract labour in the case of productive activity. When Marx says that labour is the substance of value, he always means, therefore, labour considered as abstract labour. We may sum up the qualitative relation of value to labour with the following statement:

On the one hand all labour is, speaking physiologically, an expenditure of human labour power, and in its character of identical abstract human labour, it creates and forms the values of commodities. On the other hand, all labour is the expenditure of human labour power in a special form and with a definite aim, and in this, its character of concrete useful labour, it produces use values (Marx, 1933, vol. I, p. 54).

5 Abstract labour

Abstract labour which is represented in the value of commodities is a concept which has an important place in Marx's thinking. It must be admitted, however, that it is not an easy concept to comprehend; and for this reason it seems wise to consider the matter in further detail.

It may be well to remove at once any misunderstandings of a purely verbal character. To many the expression 'abstract labour' suggests something slightly mysterious, perhaps not a little metaphysical and unreal. As should be clear from the last section, however, nothing of the sort was intended by Marx. Abstract labour is abstract only in the quite straightforward sense that all special characteristics which differentiate one kind of labour from another are ignored. Abstract labour, in short, is, as Marx's own usage clearly attests, equivalent to 'labour in general'; it is what is common to all productive human activity.

Marx did not think he was the first to introduce the idea of labour in general into political economy. For example, in speaking of Benjamin Franklin, whom he regarded as 'one of the first economists, after Wm. Petty, who saw through the nature of value', he had the following to say:

> Franklin is unconscious that by estimating the value of everything in labour, he makes abstraction from any difference in the sorts of labour exchanged, and thus reduces them all to equal human labour. But although ignorant of this, yet he says it. He speaks first of 'the one labour', then of 'the other labour', and finally of 'labour', without further qualification, as the substance of the value of everything (Marx, 1933, vol. I, p. 59n.).

And in another connection, he remarks that 'it was a tremendous advance on the part of Adam Smith to throw aside all limitations which mark wealth-producing activity and to define it as labour in general, neither industrial, nor commercial, nor agricultural, or one as much as the other' (Marx, 1911a, p. 298). Ricardo, as Marx was well aware, adopted the same point of view and followed it out with greater consistency than Smith. In this, as in many other cases, Marx started from a basic idea of the classical school, gave it precise and explicit expression, developed it, and utilized it in the analysis of social relations in his own original and penetrating fashion.

It is important to realize that the reduction of all labour to a common denominator, so that units of labour can be compared with and substituted for one another, added and subtracted, and finally totalled up to form a social aggregate, is not an arbitrary abstraction, dictated in some way by the whim of the investigator. It is rather, as Lukács (1923, p. 18) correctly observes, an abstraction 'which belongs to the essence of capitalism'. Let us examine this more closely.

Capitalist society is characterized by a degree of labour mobility much greater than prevailed in any previous form of society. Not only do workers change their jobs relatively frequently, but also the stream of new workers entering the labour market is quickly diverted from declining to rising occupations. As Marx (1933, vol. I, p. 51) expressed it, 'We see at a glance that, in our capitalist society, a given portion of human labour is, in accordance with the varying demand, at one time supplied in the form of tailoring, at another in the form of weaving. This change may possibly not take place without friction, but take place it must.' Under these circumstances, the various specific kinds of labour in existence at any given time and the relative quantities of each become matters of secondary importance in any general view of the economic system. Much more significant is the total size of the social labour force and its general level of development. On these depend the productive potentialities of society, whether the latter be manifested in the production of consumer's goods or in the production of implements of war. This is a conclusion which commands universal assent in the modern world; it flows from such common facts of experience that no one would think of denying it. It is important to observe, however, that in arriving at this conclusion we were obliged to abstract from the differences between specific forms of labour, an abstraction which is inevitably implied in the very notion of a total labour force available to society. We are likely to forget or overlook this only because the differences are *practically* of secondary importance.

In the course of a methodological discussion, Marx emphasizes this point in the following terms:

... This abstraction of labour is but the result of a concrete aggregate of different kinds of labour. The indifference to the particular kind of labour corresponds to a form of society in which individuals pass with ease from one kind of work to another, which makes it immaterial to them what particular kind of work may fall to their share. Labour has become here, not only categorically but really, a means of creating wealth in general and is no longer grown together with the individual into one particular destination. This state of affairs has found its highest development in the most modern of bourgeois societies, the United States. It is only here that the abstraction of the category 'labour', 'labour in general', labour *sans phrase*, the starting point of modern political economy, becomes realized in practice (Marx, 1911b, p. 299).

To sum up, we may say that the reduction of all labour to abstract labour enables us to see clearly, behind the special forms which labour may assume at any given time, an aggregate social labour force which is capable of transference from one use to another in accordance with social need, and on the magnitude and development of which society's wealth-producing capacity in the last resort depends. The adoption of this point of view, moreover, is conditioned by the very nature of capitalist production which promotes a degree of labour mobility never before approached in earlier forms of society.

6 The relation of the quantitative to the qualitative in value theory

We are now in a position to see precisely what is implied in the thesis that abstract labour is the substance of value. A commodity appears at first glance to be merely a useful article which has been produced by a special kind of workman, working privately and in isolation from the rest of society. This is correct so far as it goes. But investigation reveals that the commodity in question has this in common with all other commodities (i.e. they are all values), namely, that it absorbs a part of society's total available labour force (i.e. they are all materialized abstract labour). It is this characteristic of commodities (which presupposes use value and manifests itself in exchange value) that makes of 'commodity' the starting point and central category of the political economy of the modern period.

We have reached these conclusions through a purely qualitative analysis, and it may appear that they have little bearing on the quantitative problem. This, however, is not so. The truth is that the basic significance as well as the main tasks of quantitative-value theory are determined by the qualitative analysis. Here we shall merely indicate the reasons for this, leaving more detailed treatment for later.

From a formal point of view it appears that quantitative-value theory is concerned solely with discovering the laws which regulate the relative proportions in which commodities exchange for one another. This is, indeed, the way in which orthodox theory regards the matter; it is simply a question of exchange value.[5] But for Marx, as we already know, exchange value is merely the 'phenomenal form' behind which hides value itself. The question therefore arises: what, beyond the mere determination of exchange ratios, is the quantitative-value problem? The analysis presented above provides us with an answer.

The fact that a commodity is a value means that it is materialized abstract labour, or, in other words, that it has absorbed a part of the total wealth-producing activity of society. If now we reflect that abstract labour is susceptible of measurement in terms of time units, the meaning of value as a quantitative category distinct from exchange value becomes apparent. As Marx (1933, vol. I, p. 114) stated it, 'Magnitude of value expresses . . . the connection that exists between a certain article and the portion of the total labour time of society required to produce it.'

The main task of quantitative-value theory emerges from this definition of value as a magnitude. It is nothing more nor less than the investigation of the laws which govern the allocation of the labour force to different spheres of production in a society of commodity producers. How Marx carried through this task will be treated later.

Before returning to the further implications of Marx's qualitative analysis, it is well to remark that the two concepts, 'socially necessary labour' and 'simple labour', which have stood in the forefront of nearly every attack on Marx's economics, both pertain to the quantitative aspect of

5. cf., for example, the following statement made by Joan Robinson in the Introduction to her book, *The Economics of Imperfect Competition:* 'The main theme of this book is the analysis of value. It is not easy to explain what the analysis of value is . . . The point may be put like this: You see two men, one of whom is giving a banana to the other, and is taking a penny from him. You ask, How is it that a banana costs a penny rather than any other sum?' (Robinson, 1933, p. 6).

value theory and hence will come up for subsequent consideration. That critics of Marx have concentrated their attention on this aspect of the theory, and at that one-sidedly, is no accident; their attitude towards the value problem has disposed them to a preoccupation with exchange ratios to the neglect of the character of the social relations which lie hidden beneath the surface. Hence lengthy critiques of socially necessary labour, but hardly a word about abstract labour.

References

HILFERDING, R. (1904), 'Böhm-Bawerk's Marx-Kritik', *Marx Studien*, Bd 1.

LOWE, A. (1938), 'Mr Dobb and Marx's theory of value', *Modern Quarterly*, July.

LUKÁCS, G. (1923), *Geschichte und Klassenbewusstsein*,

MARX, K. (1911a), 'Introduction to the *Critique of Political Economy*', in *Critique of Political Economy*, Chicago.

MARX, K. (1911b), *Critique of Political Economy*, Chicago.

MARX, K. (1933), *Capital*, Chicago.

MARX, K. (1934), 'Randglossen zu Adolph Wagner's "Lehrbuch der Politischen Ökonomie"', Appendix to *Das Kapital*, vol. I, Marx-Engels-Lenin Institute, Zürich.

PETRY, F. (1916), *Der Soziale Gehalt der Marxschen Werttheorie*, Jena.

ROBBINS, L. (1932), *The Nature and Significance of Economic Science*, London.

ROBINSON, J. (1933), *The Economics of Imperfect Competition*, London.

SMITH, A. (1930), *The Wealth of Nations*, ed. E. Cannan, London.

17 Bernice Shoul

Karl Marx's Solutions to Some Theoretical Problems of Classical Economics

Bernice Shoul, 'Karl Marx's solutions to some theoretical problems of classical economics', *Science and Society*, vol. 31, 1967, pp. 448–60.

Marx's economic analysis has been viewed alternately as the culmination of, and as the sharpest break with, classical economics. More realistically, it can be viewed as having elements both of completion and criticism of the classical system. Marx's attempts to complete this system appear in his extensions and modifications of Ricardo's 'labour-embodied' theory of value.[1] That Marx at first considered his own work to be a break with classical tradition is evident from his early observation that 'in Ricardo political economy reached its climax, after recklessly drawing its ultimate conclusions . . .' (Marx, 1904, p. 70). However, that Marx was himself a member of the classical school is evident from his detailed critique of Ricardo, which forms the second volume of the *Theorien über den Mehrwert* [*Theories of Surplus Value*]. Despite alternative interpretations by orthodox and neo-Marxist economists, it seems evident that Marx does belong to the school of Ricardo. This is the position taken by Schumpeter in his work on the history of economic theory.[2]

In his earliest work in economics, the *Critique of Political Economy*,

1. The difference between the 'labour-embodied' and the 'labour command' theories of value is presumably well known. Elements of each are included in Adam Smith, who also has two other theories of value: the 'toil and trouble' theory (or a marginal disutility theory of value) and a cost of production theory. By and large, except in the famous 'deer-beaver' society in which the labour-embodied theory operates, Smith's labour theory of value is primarily a labour-command theory. This labour-command theory was later taken over by Malthus, whose debates with Ricardo largely stem from alternative theories of value. These debates, as Ricardo was to point out ultimately, could not be resolved because of differences in the assumptions regarding the source and measure of value. A good critical history of the development of the labour theory of value is found in Meek (1956b).

2. Schumpeter, *Economic Doctrine and Method* (1954a, p. 72). This is the English translation of Schumpeter's *Epochen Der Dogmen und Methoden geschichte* (1912). Schumpeter's later work, including *Capitalism, Socialism, and Democracy* (1942), and the monumental *History of Economic Analysis* (1954b), include separate discussions on Marx, but in both he views Marx as continuing Ricardo's work.

which appeared in 1859, Marx himself clearly outlines what he regarded as the four essential problems that had been explored but left unsolved by Ricardo, problems which provided the basis for the post-Ricardian controversies. These four are as follows:

First: Labour itself has exchange value, and different kinds of labour have different exchange values. We get into a vicious circle by making exchange value the measure of exchange value, because the measuring exchange value needs a measure itself. This objection may be reduced to the following problem. Given labour-time as the intrinsic measure of exchange value, develop from that the determination of wages. The theory of wages gives the answer to that.

Second: If the exchange value of a product is equal to the labour-time contained in it, then the exchange of one day of labour is equal to the product of that labour. In other words, wages must be equal to the product of labour. But the very opposite is actually the case. *Ergo*, this objection comes down to the following problem: how does production based on the determination of exchange value by labour-time only, lead to the result that the exchange value of labour is less than the exchange value of its product? This problem is solved by us in the discussion of capital.

Third: The market price of commodities either falls below or rises above its exchange value with the changing relations of supply and demand. *Therefore*, the exchange value of commodities is determined by the relation of supply and demand and not by the labour-time contained in them. As a matter of fact, this queer conclusion merely amounts to the question, how a market price based on exchange value can deviate from that exchange value; or, better still, how does the law of exchange value assert itself only in its antithesis. This problem is solved in the theory of competition.

Fourth: The last and apparently most striking objection, if not raised in the usual form of queer examples: If exchange value is nothing but mere labour-time contained in commodities, how can commodities which contain no labour possess exchange value, or in other words, whence the exchange value of mere forces of nature? This problem is solved in the theory of rent (Marx, 1904, pp. 71–73).

The theory of wages

Marx's solution to the classical problem of how labour, as itself an exchange value, can be the *measure* of exchange value, without circular argument, rests on his distinction between labour and labour-power. In his view, as expressed by Engels, labour as the *source* of value can no more have a specific value than heat can have a specific temperature (Engels, 1906–09, vol. II, p. 27). But *labour-power*, the capacity to furnish labour and to create value, is itself a commodity whose value, like that of all other commodities, is determined by the labour-time 'socially necessary' for its reproduction, 'under the normal conditions of production' (Marx, 1906–09, vol. I, p. 46), in this case, the labour-time (Marx, 1906–09, vol. I, pp. 189–90)[3] required for the production of the labourer's subsistence.

The concept of socially necessary labour is the foundation of Marx's labour theory of value. Since value appears only as exchange value, commodity production presupposes exchange, although, in the first volume of *Capital*, Marx initially presented the concept of socially necessary labour with reference to production alone. This suggests that the labour-time socially necessary is viewed as objectively given, as a technological datum. Later, in the third volume of *Capital*, Marx relates socially necessary labour-time to conditions of demand as well as of supply.[4] But for him demand is largely a function of supply and plays no independent role.

3. Labour-time is measured in units of average, homogeneous, unskilled labour. Marx, like Smith, Ricardo, and Keynes, averages natural differences, and considers skilled labour (which includes the value added by training and instruction), as a multiple of unskilled. It has been argued that this solution vitiates the labour theory of value since differences can be deduced only from appeal to the market, to another principle of valuation. Marx himself writes that, 'a commodity may be the product of the most skilled labour, a given quantity of skilled being considered equal to a greater quantity of simple labour. Experience shows that this reduction is constantly being made. A commodity may be the product of the most skilled labour, but its value, by equating it to the product of simple unskilled labour, represents a definite quantity of the latter labour alone. The different proportions in which different sorts of labour are reduced to unskilled labour as their standard, are established by a social process that goes on behind the backs of the producers, and consequently, appears to be fixed by custom' (Marx, 1906–09, vol. I, pp. 51–2). The argument that deducing from the market the differences in the values created by labour of different skills represents circular reasoning misconstrues the function of the market in Marx's theory. Marx assumes the existence of the market, but considers that it merely *registers* the magnitude of value already created in production rather than in any way *determining* value. *This problem has challenged the validity of the labour theory of value and Marx's solution has been held to be inconsistent.* Marx deals with this problem in Volume III of *Capital* but not in an entirely satisfactory way. See footnote 4 for further discussion of this problem.

4. Of the relations of demand and supply in determining what amount of labour is socially necessary, Marx writes, 'Every commodity must contain the necessary quantity of labour, and at the same time only the proportional quantity of the total social labour-time must have been spent on the various groups' (Marx, 1906–09, vol. III, p. 745). If there is partial overproduction measured by the 'social need', then, 'too much social labour has been expended in this particular line, in other words, a portion of this product is useless. The whole of it is therefore sold as though it had been produced in the necessary proportion. This quantitative limit of the quota of social labour available for the various spheres is but a wider expression of the law of value, although the necessary labour-time assumes a different meaning here' (Marx, 1906–09, vol. III, pp. 745–6). This passage implies that *demand may act to alter value itself, and not merely to determine prices which may deviate from values*. The argument that the total value of the over-produced commodities would be no more than if there had been an equilibrium level of production appears to involve circular reasoning, to assume what it sets out to prove, i.e., that there is some structure of demand which the operation of the

Also basic to Marx's system is the concept of the commodity, labour-power. As the basis for the twofold nature of other commodities, the nature of the commodity labour-power is held to be twofold.[5] It *is* a use value and *possesses* exchange value. As a use value it differs from other use values in two ways. First, it is a use value in the dual sense that it serves to create both use values and exchange values. Second, and more important, the consumption of its use value not only reproduces its own value, but creates an unpaid surplus value as well.

The distinction between labour and labour-power solved the problem which beset classical political economy at the outset – how, without circular argument, to apply the law of value to the value-producing commodity, labour-power. Adam Smith's difficulties, in addition to the fact that he was forced to limit the 'labour-embodied' theory to the famous 'deer–beaver' society, using both a cost of production and a 'labour-command' theory to explain value elsewhere, led him to explore the possibilities of other measures and determinants of value (Smith, 1937, pp. 47–63, 187). In the Ricardian formulation, the law of value *appears* to be applied to the commodity labour-power (which Ricardo, like other classical writers, doubly confuses with the *person* of the labourer and the *activity* of labour (Ricardo, 1943, pp. 6–7)),[6] insofar as the wages of the worker are

law of value enforces. Marx does not deal with this problem except in passing. However, in his system the structure of demand does implicitly help to determine the magnitude of socially necessary labour. This is because the techniques of production, from which the average quantity of socially necessary labour is deduced, are partially shaped by the particular allocation of resources which a given structure of demand enforces. *Only in the case of constant returns do changes in the structure of demand exercise no influence on the technical coefficients of production, and thus on the quantity of socially necessary labour.* However, for Marx, changes in the structure of demand are of secondary importance, if they involve no more than shifts in consumer tastes, which he considered more a product than a determinant of market phenomena. His basic argument was that demand 'is essentially conditioned by mutual relations of the different economic classes and their relative economic positions' (Marx, 1906–09, vol. III, p. 214) and, therefore, does not play an independent, determining role.

5. Marx considered that his greatest contribution to the labour theory of value was to make really clear the distinction and relations between use value and exchange value. These two aspects of value he ascribed to the twofold nature of labour, 'the pivot on which a clear comprehension of political economy turns ...' (Marx, 1906–09, vol. I, p. 48).

6. Lack of distinction between the activity of labour, the person of the labourer, and the commodity, labour-power, prevails throughout the history of economic analysis. As an example, Schumpeter argues that the labour theory of value must fail because it 'can never be applied to the commodity labour, for this would imply that workmen, like machines, are being produced according to rational cost calculations. Since they are not, there is no warrant for assuming that the value of labour-power will be proportional to the man hours that enter into its "production"' (Schumpeter, 1942, pp. 27–28). The difficulty disappears on recalling the fundamental distinction

set equal to the value of his 'labour'. But this determination of wages actually rests on a demand and supply analysis, based in part on the Malthusian principle of population. In Marx's formulation it rests on the law of value alone.

The theory of capital

Marx's solution to the problem of how, according to the law of value, the value product of a given expenditure of labour-power is greater than the value of that labour-power is provided by his theory of capital. This problem and its solution are related to the first problem, the determination of wages.

Capital is defined by Marx as the value of the means of production in capitalist society. It is divided into (1) *variable capital* (the payment of wages), called variable because its expenditure creates a variable value, a value in excess of its own value, which is itself consumed and reproduced in production; and (2) *constant capital* (the payment for material means of production, which are themselves 'congealed labour'), called constant because its expenditure merely *transfers* its own value to the product, but creates no added value (Marx, 1906–09, vol. I, pp. 232–3).

In classical theory, both in Smith and Ricardo, capital is divided into fixed and circulating capital. This division is not based on the productive role of each type of capital, as in Marx, but on its physical durability. Thus, heavy capital equipment is classified as fixed capital, wage goods as circulating capital (Smith, 1937, pp. 262–3; Ricardo, 1943, pp. 24–5).[7]

between labour and labour-power, which is lost in this quotation, where both 'labour' and 'labour-power' are used to refer to the workman himself. In Marx's analysis, labour, as source of value, is an *activity*, not a *commodity* (as labour-power is), and is not 'produced'. It is labour-power that becomes a commodity in the process of exchange between worker and capitalist. It is not 'workmen' that are reproduced, but labour-power that is consumed and reproduced in the process of production – according to the strictest principle of rationality, i.e., at minimum cost.

7. Fixed and circulating capital in the classical sense are parallel to constant and variable capital in the Marxian sense only in that the use values which reproduce the two kinds of capital are roughly similar. Marx's own distinction between fixed and circulating capital rests on the difference of turnover, or the form of circulation, of these types of capital. Thus, circulating capital is that part whose entire value is consumed in the process of production (whether or not it enters physically as a use value into the product), and whose value therefore circulates in the commodity. Fixed capital is that part whose value enters the commodity and circulates piecemeal, i.e., machinery. Thus, circulating capital consists of all the variable capital (representing labour-power), whose value is fully transferred to the product and circulates in it, and part of the constant capital (that part representing raw materials), whose value is similarly transferred in entirety to the commodity. The fixed capital is the remaining part of the constant capital, that part representing plant and equipment (Marx, 1906–09, vol. II, chapter 8, especially pp. 187–92).

According to Marx, there are basic confusions in the classical theory of capital which vitiate the labour theory of value on which it is allegedly based. First, it confuses capital, as a self-expanding exchange value, with capital as a physical stock of use values. Second, it applies to the sphere of production a distinction appropriate to the sphere of circulation, and the wrong one at that since, according to Marx, fixed and circulating capital should refer to the turnover of value, and not to the durability of use values.

Ricardo accounts for exceptions to the law of value by the difference in the proportions in which the two sorts of capital may be combined (Ricardo, 1943, p. 18). This expression implies that the distinction is based on the productive role of the two kinds of capital. But Ricardo's differences in the degree of durability of capital refer essentially to the form of circulation of capital.

Marx asserts that in the confusion of the circulation and production of values the 'whole secret of the production of surplus value and capitalist production . . . [is] obliterated' (Marx, 1906–09, vol. II, p. 249). According to him, the real problem to be explained is how the individual capitalist 'must buy his commodities at their value, must sell them at their value, and yet at the end of the process, must withdraw more value from circulation than he threw into it at starting . . . *Hic Rhodus, hic salta*' (Marx, 1906–09, vol. I, p. 185). The solution to this problem, the 'secret of capitalist production', lies in the conversion of labour-power into variable capital, where 'the capitalist exchanges a definite given, and to that extent constant, magnitude of values, for a power which creates values, a magnitude of values for a production, a self-expansion of values' (Marx, 1906–09, vol. II, p. 250).

In Marx's system the exchange of labour against capital (which is conditioned on the fact that the labourer is free in a double sense – free to dispose of his labour-power as his own commodity and free of the possession of all other salable commodities (Marx, 1906–09, vol. I, p. 187)), is a double one. The first phase of the exchange is purely formal. It is an exchange of commodities of equal value, of labour-power for money capital (wages). The second phase of the exchange is not so much an exchange as the actual (as opposed to the formal) conversion of labour-power into capital (Marx, 1905–10, vol. I, pp. 412–14). While it is being consumed as a use value, in the process of production, labour-power becomes capital. First it reproduces its own, and then it creates an additional, exchange value. Thus, the quantity of labour-power embodied in the commodity is greater than that which is paid for.

As a result, according to Marx's labour theory of value, the equal exchange of labour-power for wages leads directly to an inequality between the value of labour-power and the value of its product. The labour theory of value leads from the determination of wages to a theory of capital which explains the phenomenon of surplus value.

The theory of competition

Marx's answer to the classical question of how market prices based on exchange values can deviate from values is provided by his theory of competition. The transformation of abstract labour values into concrete market prices in Marx's system is demonstrated by successive stages of analysis more complex than that of classical theory.

The distinction between *natural price* (or value) and *market price* is an old one in economic theory. Adam Smith's natural price, around which market price is held to fluctuate, is arrived at by adding the 'natural', competitively determined, wages, profit, and rent (Smith, 1937, pp. 55–63). At the same time, Smith holds that the 'labour-embodied' theory is valid only in primitive society before appropriation and accumulation have taken place, and that elsewhere value is explained by the 'labour-command' theory. In his determination of natural price Smith abandons both his labour theories of value for a cost of production theory.

Ricardo maintains his labour theory of value (apart from the assertion in Section 4, Chapter I of his *Principles* that capital, as well as labour, determines value) and purportedly rejects the determination of natural price (or value) by supply and demand as a 'source of much error' (Ricardo, 1943, p. 260). Yet, he accepts the result that value is partially determined by competition insofar as the average rate of profit, one of the elements of the value of any commodity, is held to be competitively determined. Thus, Ricardo's natural price *assumes* an average rate of profit, established by the mobility of capital (Ricardo, 1943, p. 50), and not systematically linked, as with Marx, to the surplus value created in production. Like Smith, Ricardo considers market price as a competitive deviation from natural price.

Marx's theory of competition is a sharp critique of Ricardo. His own value and price system includes not the two forms typical of classical economics – natural price (or value) and market price, but three forms: value, price of production, and market price. For Marx the essential distinction which solves the Ricardian contradictions is that between value and price production.

In Marx's formulation, the value of every commodity is resolved into constant capital, variable capital, and surplus value. The ratio, $\frac{s}{v}$, the ratio of surplus value to variable capital, represents the ratio of surplus to necessary labour, the rate of exploitation, or the rate of surplus value

(Marx, 1906–09, vol. I, p. 241). The ratio $\frac{s}{c+v}$, the ratio of surplus value to the total capital, is the rate of profit, which magnitude (given the fact that only v, variable capital, produces surplus value), depends on (1) $\frac{s}{v}$, the rate of surplus value, and (2) $\frac{c}{c+v}$, the ratio of constant to total capital, or the *organic composition of capital*.[8] This organic composition of capital is the *value* expression which reflects the *technical* composition of capital, or the relative proportions of material means of production and labour-power (Marx, 1906–09, vol. I, p. 671; vol. III, p. 172).

Therefore, given equal rates of surplus value, individual capitals of the same size, but of unequal organic composition of capital, yield unequal rates of profit. In developing the labour theory of value, wherein all commodities sell at their values, Marx assumes, as a first approximation, that the organic composition of capital is everywhere equal. However, once unequal compositions of capital and competition are introduced, an average rate of profit, differing from the surplus value yielded by individual capitals, is established. This average rate, when added to the cost price of commodities ($c+v$), produces what Marx (1906–09, vol. III, p. 185) calls *prices of production*. These prices of production deviate from values to the extent that the average rate of profit (to which any given surplus value tends to be reduced via the effect of competition), differs from the surplus value yielded by any given capital. But while individual prices of production deviate from values, total price remains equal to total value (Marx, 1906–09, vol. III, p. 188).

Ricardo's difficulty, according to Marx, arises from his assuming an average rate of profit before establishing its basis, and without investigating its effects in the determination of prices. Thus, the exceptions to the law of value noted in the first chapter of Ricardo's *Principles*, which are attributed

---

8. Marx uses the expression $\frac{c}{v}$ for the organic composition of capital. The expression $\frac{c}{c+v}$ moves in the same direction as $\frac{c}{v}$ but more slowly. It has the advantage of showing the related changes in the organic composition, the rate of surplus value, and the rate of profit. Thus, $\frac{s}{c+v} = \frac{s}{v}(1-\frac{c}{c+v})$. This is the formula used by Sweezy (1942, pp. 66–8). It is derived from Marx's equivalent formula, where $\frac{s}{c+v} = \frac{sv}{v(c+v)}$ (Marx, 1906–09, vol. III, pp. 63–4). Since only v produces surplus value, the greater the rate of surplus value, the higher the rate of profit, and the greater the organic composition of capital, the lower the rate of profit.

to the 'proportions in which the two sorts of capital may be combined' (Ricardo, 1943, p. 18), are held to lead, not to price deviations from value, but to actual changes in value itself. According to Marx, Ricardo identifies something similar to the 'price of production' with value itself, because of his ambiguity with regard to the source of value and his unfruitful division of capital into fixed and circulating capitals. This makes it impossible for Ricardo to distinguish between surplus value produced and profit actually received. Further, Marx argues that Ricardo, having identified the two, where he does link profits with wages (in his chapter 'On profits'), logically enough, deduces all changes in the rate of profit from those in wages or the 'rate of surplus value', forgetting that the rate of profit also depends on the 'organic composition of capital' (Marx, 1905–10, II/I, pp. 37–38).

The Marxian price of production, which deviates from value, is the Ricardian natural price. But, according to Marx, commodities do not actually sell at their prices of production. Inequality in the composition of capital and the existence of an average rate of profit establish prices of production differing from values. Similarly, the inequality in the cost price of competitive sellers establishes differences in the prices of production of the same commodity. The price of production which actually rules depends on the distribution of costs within the industry. (Marx, 1905–10, vol. III, p. 578; 1906–09, vol. III, pp. 213–17).[9]

Inequality of supply and demand for any given commodity leads, in turn, to market prices that deviate from the prices of production (Marx, 1906–09, vol. III, pp. 212–13). In the real world market price appears to be determined by supply and demand alone. But, according to Marx, what supply and demand really do is to determine merely the deviations from prices of production. In this system the price of production, around which market prices fluctuate, is itself derived from value. Thus, at each stage competition establishes deviations from the norm, and at the same time, as in classical theory, tends to reduce these deviations. By successive transformation from one price form to another, Marx's theoretical analysis stresses the determining role of the law of value. Although 'under capitalist

9. Marx's argument that the market price will tend to conform to the price of production which is determined by the distribution of costs within the industry is somewhat confused. He argues that the dominating price will be influenced by the number of firms producing above, below, or at the average cost condition, depending on the demand for the particular product. His conclusions are indefinite because of his failure, typical of the time, to realize that the demand and supply for any given commodities are schedules, rather than discrete quantities. With more advanced techniques Marx would have realized that the ruling price of production would be the marginal price, that which just covers cost for the least efficient producer. Elsewhere, he realizes this and refers to the short-run gains made by the more efficient firms.

production the general law of value enforces itself merely as the prevailing tendency . . .' (Marx, 1906–09, vol. III, p. 190), 'whatever may be the way in which the prices of the various commodities are first fixed or mutually regulated, the law of value always dominates their movements' (Marx, 1906–09, vol. III, p. 208).

The theory of economic rent

Marx's theory of rent, which explains the exchange value of 'mere forces of nature', is, like so much of his theory, both a critique of and a supplement to the theory of Ricardo. The essential differences are in Marx's treatment of rent as but one part of the total surplus value and in his theory of 'absolute' rent.

According to his own labour theory of value, Ricardo is forced to deny the existence of absolute rent. For him, unlike Adam Smith, who develops a kind of absolute rent due to monopoly (Smith, 1937, pp. 145, 155), there is only differential rent (Ricardo, 1943, chapter 2). This differential rent is explained by the bringing of increasingly poorer lands into cultivation, so that successive investments of capital yield diminishing returns. At the margin, however, there is no rent. This is the essence of a theory of rent which was developed earlier by Anderson, West, and Malthus.

In developing his own theory of rent, Marx assumes 'that agriculture is dominated by the capitalist mode of production . . .' (Marx, 1906–09, vol. III, p. 721) and that the 'tillers of the soil are wage labourers employed by a capitalist, the capitalist farmer . . . [who] pays to the landowner, the owner of the soil exploited by him, a sum of money at definite periods fixed by contract . . .' (Marx, 1906–09, vol. III, p. 725).

Marx accepts, with some modification, the Ricardian theory of differential rent, both extensive and intensive. He denies, however, that progress is necessarily from better to worse soils (Marx, 1906–09, vol. III, p. 772). Differential rent is defined as the 'excess of the general regulating price of production of the product of one acre over its individual average price . . .' (Marx, 1906–09, vol. III, p. 844). Like Ricardo, Marx believes that as the rate of profit and the rate of interest fall, the historical tendency is for the price of land, and, therefore, differential rent, to rise (Marx, 1906–09, vol. III, p. 731).

Marx's own contribution to the theory of rent is his theory of absolute rent. He considers rent a deduction from the total surplus value, a deduction made necessary by the private ownership of land. In Marx's system the landlord extracts rent from the capitalists as the latter extracts surplus value from the worker (Marx, 1906–09, vol. III, p. 955). The basis for this payment is the fact that, because of its lower organic composition of capital, agriculture creates a rate of profit above the average. The private ownership of a limited supply of land makes it possible for the landlords to retain the surplus value created in agriculture in excess of the average rate of profit (Marx, 1906–09, vol. III, pp. 883–5). In other words, rent is the difference between the surplus value agriculture creates and the average rate of profit that would obtain if competition were completely effective in equalizing profits between industry and agriculture. However, according to Marx, with the equalization of the organic composition of capital between agriculture and industry, or the increasing productivity of agriculture (which could be expected to move faster than that of industry in the period of late capitalism (Marx, 1905–10, vol. II, part 1, p. 280)), this absolute rent would tend to disappear, leaving differential and monopoly rents as the sole forms. The latter form is explained as the result which obtains when a product is sold above its value, and thus realizes surplus value created in industry (Marx, 1906–09, vol. III, p. 1003).

Marx's contribution to the theory of rent is the explanation of the rent phenomenon by the theory of value, as the latter explains the distinction between value and price of production, rather than, as is the case with Ricardo, merely by the facts of nature. Marx's theory completes the solution of the classical problem of how price can exist without value.

Summary

This brief treatment of Marx's solutions to classical problems omits necessarily many similarities as well as essential differences between the two systems. It says nothing of method, for example, or of the two different views of crises and of evolution. It concerns itself solely with how Marx resolves the basic contradictions which the Ricardian labour theory of value was unable to resolve. Marx's solutions are for problems inherent in this theory of value.

The problem of wages is the problem of how labour can be the measure of value, since its own value must be determined first, and this leads necessarily to circular argument. Marx solves this problem by the distinction between labour and labour-power, arguing that the value of the value-producing and value-measuring commodity, labour-power, is that of the subsistence goods necessary to reproduce this labour-power.

The problem of capital is to explain how labour can produce a surplus value. Marx deals with this problem by distinguishing between variable and constant capital, of which, in his theory, only the variable part produces value and surplus value.

The problem of competition is to show that, contrary to appearances, supply and demand do not determine prices but merely price deviations from value. Marx argues that market prices fluctuate around prices of production, similar to the classical 'natural' prices. Further, he shows how these latter prices do, in fact, deviate from (although they are ultimately determined by) the labour values, to the extent that the organic composition of capital varies, and the profit actually received deviates, from the surplus value created by any given capital.

The problem of absolute rent, the existence of which the Ricardian theory of value denies is possible, is the problem of how exchange value can be attributed to forces of nature. Marx solves this problem by showing that (given a limited supply of land, and the fact that agriculture has an organic composition of capital below that of industry) agricultural products *can* sell at their values, rather than at their prices of production, thus making it possible for the landlords to pocket all the surplus value produced in agriculture rather than just the average rate of profit.

Marx's system was left in an unpolished state, so much so that there has been repeated (and in this writer's view, unnecessary) controversy regarding apparent contradictions, particularly between the determination of abstract labour values of Volume I of *Capital* and the more concrete prices of production of Volume III.[10] However, this is not the place for a full reconstruction of Marx's unfinished work. Rather has the attempt been made here to summarize the way Marx's system 'solves' the main problems he inherited from classical political economy. In this centennial year it seems especially fitting to remind ourselves of Marx's relation to his forerunners.

References

ENGELS, F. (1906–09), 'Preface to the first edition [1885]', in K. Marx, *Capital*, Charles H. Kerr, Chicago.

MARX, K. (1904), *Critique of Political Economy*, Chicago.

MARX, K. (1905–10), *Theorien über den Mehrwert*, Stuttgart.

MARX, K. (1906–09), *Capital*, Charles H. Kerr, Chicago.

MEEK, R. L. (1956a), 'Some notes on the transformation problem', *Economic Journal*, March; reprinted in J. J. Spengler and W. R. Allen (eds.), *Essays in Economic Thought: Aristotle to Marshall*, Chicago, 1960.

MEEK, R. L. (1956b), *Studies in the Labour Theory of Value*, London.

RICARDO, D. (1943), *Principles of Political Economy and Taxation*, London.

SCHUMPETER, J. A. (1912), *Epochen der Dogmen und Methodengeschichte*.

SCHUMPETER, J. A. (1942), *Capitalism, Socialism and Democracy*, New York.

SCHUMPETER, J. A. (1954a), *Economic Doctrine and Method*, New York.

SCHUMPETER, J. A. (1954b), *History of Economic Analysis* (E. B. Schumpeter ed.), New York.

SMITH, A. (1937), *An Inquiry into the Nature and Causes of the Wealth of Nations*, New York.

SWEEZY, P. (1942), *The Theory of Capitalist Development*, New York.

10. This entire controversy, initiated by Böhm-Bawerk, and never until recently satisfactorily resolved, is succinctly summarized by Meek (1956a).

18 F. Seton

The 'Transformation Problem'

F. Seton, 'The "transformation problem"', *Review of Economic Studies*, vol. 24, 1957, pp. 149–60.

The definition of the 'value' of a commodity as the (socially necessary) labour-time expended on its production is the cornerstone of the Marxian doctrine of capitalist exploitation. Yet Marx was well aware that the society of his day did not in fact exchange commodities in proportion to their 'values'. His explanation for this departure from the 'simple law of value' was the presumed tendency of capitalists to shift their resources from one industry to another until the resulting scarcity relationships had established a system of commodity prices which equalized the rate of profit (on cost) in all branches. In this manner labour values were said to be 'transformed' into the Marxian prices of production.[1]

The arithmetic illustration of the transformation process which Marx gave in Volume III of *Capital* (Marx, 1906–09, vol. III, pp. 182–203) has been the subject of a long drawn-out controversy. Böhm-Bawerk, one of the first to call attention to the obvious inadequacies of the exercise, was generally taken to imply that the transformation of 'values' into prices[2] as conceived by Marx was a logical impossibility. Since then a number of authors have come to the defence of Marx with attempts to demonstrate the internal consistency and determinacy of his conception by means of an algebraic treatment of the problem. The latest contribution was made by Mr Meek in a recent issue of the *Economic Journal* (Meek, 1956) to which the reader may be referred for a useful bibliography of the subject.

It appears to me that a rigorous analysis of the transformation problem should pursue two distinct objectives: Firstly, it should establish whether, and under what conditions, the problem admits of a uniquely determined solution; and, secondly, it ought to reveal whether or not this solution possesses certain characteristics which Marx had used in the further development of his system.[3] The three best-known post-Marxian solutions

1. It should be noted that in the Marxian system the 'prices of production' (defined as cost *plus* profit at the average rate) are only the first approximations to actual *market prices*.

2. i.e., 'prices of production'.

3. More particularly, I have here in mind the proposition that prices will exceed 'values' in those branches of production where the 'organic composition of capital' rises above the national average, and conversely.

have concentrated on the first objective without explicit reference to the second. This article attempts to deal with both aspects of the problem in turn.

The principle of equal profitability

The proof of the general consistency and determinacy of the problem has often been described as mathematically trivial. Yet few things can be as obscure and easily misunderstood as mathematical trivialities when they involve economic relationships, and most writers have unwittingly concealed the trivial nature of their solution by seeming to make it dependent on unnecessarily restrictive assumptions. Foremost among these has been the subdivision of the economy into three 'departments' producing capital goods, wage goods, and luxury goods respectively, with the corollary that every physical commodity was not merely unequivocally identifiable as the product of one or other of these, but that its ultimate use in the economy was equally invariable, and predetermined by its department of origin: Capital goods were only 'consumed' by factories, wage goods by workers, and luxury goods by capitalists. It can be shown, however, that the most general n-fold subdivision of the economy, in which each product may be distributed among *several* or *all* possible uses is equally acceptable – and easily handled – as a premiss for the required proof.[4]

Let k_{ij} represent the 'cost input' of industry j's product into industry i (reckoned in terms of labour value) - where the term 'cost input' is taken to cover the portion used for further processing (the usual *technological* connotation of 'input') and the quantity bought out of wages by the workers of industry i for their own consumption. In other words k_i comprises both 'machine feeding' and 'labour feeding' input, and the only element excluded from its purview is the portion of industry j's output which is consumed by capitalists or used for investment purposes. The allocation of this portion (e_j) among consuming industries will not be specified in our model. The structure of the economy can then be represented by a scheme closely allied to the familiar Leontief matrix:

$$
\begin{aligned}
k_{11}+k_{21}+ &\quad \ldots \quad +k_{n1}+e_1 = a_1 \\
k_{12}+k_{22}+ &\quad \ldots \quad +k_{n2}+e_2 = a_2 \\
\cdot \quad\quad \cdot &\quad \ldots \quad\quad \cdot \quad\quad \cdot \quad\quad \cdot \\
\cdot \quad\quad \cdot &\quad \ldots \quad\quad \cdot \quad\quad \cdot \quad\quad \cdot \\
k_{1n}+k_{2n}+ &\quad \ldots \quad +k_{nn}+e_n = a_n \\
s_1 \ +s_2 \ + &\quad \ldots \quad +s_n \quad\quad\ = s
\end{aligned}
\qquad 1
$$

4. Mr May (1948) has preceded me in pointing to the hidden generality of the traditional solutions. It is not clear from his remark, however, whether he merely believed that the *number* of departments could be indefinitely increased or whether he was aware that, in addition, the postulate of invariable use could also be relaxed.

where a horizontal reading shows the allocation of each industry's output according to *destination*, and a column-wise reading the structure of each industry's 'cost-input' according to *origin* (including the residual 'surplus' s accruing to it). The sum of each column must of course be equal to the sum of the corresponding row.[5]

It is now quite easy to show how this system of '*value*' flows can be uniquely translated into *price* terms. If p_i is the price of industry i's product (per unit of labour value), the requirement of equal profit ratios (π) in all industries[6] may be expressed as follows:

$$
\begin{aligned}
k_{11}p_1 + k_{12}p_2 \quad &\cdots \quad + k_{1n}p_n = \rho a_1 p_1 \\
k_{21}p_1 + k_{22}p_2 \quad &\cdots \quad + k_{2n}p_n = \rho a_2 p_2 \\
\cdot \quad \cdot \quad &\cdots \quad \cdot \qquad \cdot \\
\cdot \quad \cdot \quad &\cdots \quad \cdot \qquad \cdot \\
k_{n1}p_1 + k_{n2}p_2 \quad &\cdots \quad + k_{nn}p_n = \rho a_n p_n
\end{aligned}
\qquad 2
$$

where ρ stands for the equalized 'cost ratio' ($\rho = 1 - \pi$). Dividing each equation by the relevant total output a_i, and defining the cost-input coefficients $\kappa_{ij} \equiv k_{ij}/a_i$, this may be written:

$$
\begin{aligned}
(\kappa_{11}-\rho)p_1 + \kappa_{12}p_2 \quad &\cdots \quad + \kappa_{1n}p_n \quad = 0 \\
\kappa_{21}p_1 \quad + (\kappa_{22}-\rho)p_2 \quad &\cdots \quad + \kappa_{2n}p_n \quad = 0 \\
\cdot \qquad\qquad \cdot \quad &\cdots \quad \cdot \\
\cdot \qquad\qquad \cdot \quad &\cdots \quad \cdot \\
\kappa_{n1}p_1 \quad + \kappa_{n2}p_2 \quad &\cdots \quad + (\kappa_{nn}-\rho)p_n = 0
\end{aligned}
\qquad 3
$$

We are thus provided with n homogeneous equations in n unknowns ($p_1, p_2 \ldots p_n$), whose consistency – according to a fundamental theorem in algebra – requires the vanishing of their determinant, i.e.:

5. If the k's of any column (i) were resolved into their constituent portions of technological inputs (c_{ij}) and labour-feeding inputs (v_{ij}) and these were separately summed over all industries of origin (j), the column would reproduce the familiar Marxian value equation: $a_i = c_i + v_i + s_i$, where c_i and v_i stand for 'constant' and 'variable' capital respectively. There are various qualifications to this, notably the existence of a state of 'simple reproduction' in which the e's are wholly absorbed by capitalists' consumption and do not contain an investment element; for the Marxian type of process analysis does not allow the output flows of any period to serve as the input flows of the *same* period, but holds them over for consumption in the *next*. Unless, therefore, each period was exactly like the previous one in all respects ('simple reproduction') the input structure appropriate to the Marxian value equation could not be deduced from the output distribution of the same period (i.e., $k_{ij} \neq c_{ij} + v_{ij}$).

6. For algebraic convenience we define the 'profit ratio' π as the ratio of profit to *total value of output*. Obviously π will be equal in all industries if and only if the Marxian 'rate of profit' (profit ÷ total *cost*) is similarly equalized.

$$\begin{vmatrix} \kappa_{11}-\rho & \kappa_{12} & \cdots & \kappa_{1n} \\ \kappa_{21} & \kappa_{22}-\rho & \cdots & \kappa_{2n} \\ \cdot & \cdot & \cdots & \cdot \\ \cdot & \cdot & \cdots & \cdot \\ \kappa_{n1} & \kappa_{n2} & \cdots & \kappa_{nn}-\rho \end{vmatrix} \equiv \left| \kappa - \rho I \right| = 0 \qquad\qquad 4$$

The consistency condition **4** determines the average cost ratio ρ (and hence the profit ratio π) as a function of the (known) input coefficients in value terms (κ_{ij}).[7] A number of simple propositions concerning ρ, most of which are intuitively obvious may be deduced from the mathematical form of this condition, but need not detain us unduly.[8]

When our solution for ρ (in terms of the k_{ij}) is substituted in (3) the system will determine the n prices p_i but for a proportionality factor. *In other words we can obtain unique solutions for the relative prices in terms of any one commodity* (say n): p_1/p_n, p_2/p_n, .. p_{n-1}/p_n and this is as far as the principle of equal profitability will take us.

7. In the Western literature on input-output schemes the matrix of technological input coefficients is often referred to as the 'technology' of the economic system. The inclusion of 'wage inputs' in the coefficients k_{ij} transforms this matrix into what might be called the 'augmented technology' of the system. Having regard to equation **4** and using well-established algebraic terminology, the average cost ratio may therefore be described as a *latent root* of the 'augmented technology'.

8. The following are the most important characteristics of ρ which flow from its definition as a latent root of **4** (see footnote 7 above):

(1) Although the κ_{ij} are expressed in terms of *labour values*, their replacement by the corresponding *physical* coefficients κ_{ij}^* would not alter the latent root ρ; for it is evident that $\kappa_{ij}^* = \kappa_{ij}\,\lambda_i/\lambda_j$ (where the λs stand for the labour value of the physical units) and that the suggested replacement would merely result in a collineatory transformation of the matrix κ (i.e., $\kappa^* = \Lambda \kappa \Lambda^{-1}$ where Λ is the diagonal matrix of the λs). It is well known that such a transformation leaves the latent roots invariant.

(2) Since none of the elements of κ can be negative, we may deduce further characteristics of κ from Frobenius's theorems on the latent roots of positive matrices (Frobenius, 1908, p. 471). The fact that some of the elements of κ may vanish might necessitate slight modifications in very exceptional cases which will be neglected here; see Frobenius (1912, p 456). A real positive solution for ρ will always exist, and must lie between the smallest and the largest column-sum of κ, i.e., between the smallest and the largest *cost-ratio in value terms*. It follows that in the special case where this cost-ratio is equal in all industries (i.e., all column-sums of κ_{ij} are equal), it must also be equal to the *cost-ratio in price terms* ρ and consequently the average profit ratio will equal the ratio of surplus ($\Sigma s/\Sigma a$).

(3) As the (dominant) latent root of a positive matrix is a monotonically increasing function of each of the matrix elements (Frobenius, 1912, p. 456), the reduction of any input coefficient k_{ij} through technological progress or increased 'exploitation of labour' will *ceteris paribus* reduce the cost ratio and correspondingly increase the average rate of profit.

Postulates of invariance

In order to determine the *absolute* prices (as opposed to price *ratios*) a further as yet unspecified condition is required and this may be chosen from quite a variety of alternatives. Essentially what it amounts to is the selection of a definite aggregate (or other characteristic) of the value system 1 *which is to remain invariant to the transformation into prices*. The Marxian texts contain references and *obiter dicta* which could be made to support a number of mutually incompatible 'invariants', and it will be useful to pass in review the ways in which previous analysts of the transformation problem have differed in their selection.

The Bortkievicz-Sweezy analysis[9] claims invariance for the unit-value of luxury goods (the products of Department III in the traditional three-sector analysis) i.e.:

$$p_3 = 1. \qquad\qquad\qquad \textbf{5a}$$

The postulate is designed to ensure that prices will be expressed *in terms of the value of gold* (a product of Department III) which brings the solution into line with Marxian monetary theory. A closely allied, though so far neglected, alternative might be the invariance of the unit value of *wage goods* (i.e. $p_2 = 1$ in the three-sector analysis) which would appear to be supported by the Marxian notion that even under capitalism 'the worker is paid the full value of his labour' and exploitation (i.e. the witholding of the *surplus*) is concealed by 'commodity fetishism'.

Other analysts have allowed *unit*-values to change, and preferred to claim invariance for value *aggregate*. Thus the Winternitz (1948) approach is based on the Marxian dictum that '*total value equals total price*' i.e.:

$$\Sigma a = \Sigma ap. \qquad\qquad\qquad \textbf{5b}$$

This postulate has of course the advantage of symmetry and claims no special position for any one of the three departments. It is no longer a *single* price but a weighted average of *all* prices that is equal to unity (i.e. equal to value). Immediate expression is therefore given to the Marxian theorem that some prices will *exceed* values and others *fall short* of them – a proposition which the Bortkievicz postulate may in certain circumstances contradict.

As a third alternative, one might claim invariance for the *surplus* rather than for aggregate *output* and postulate the equality of total profit (in price terms) with total surplus (in value terms), as Mr Meek (1956) has done, i.e.:

9. Originally advanced by Bortkievicz and later simplified by Sweezy (1942, pp. 109ff.).

$$\Sigma s = \Sigma s_p = (1-\rho)\,\Sigma ap \qquad\qquad \textbf{5c}$$

This is consonant with the Marxian *façon de parler* that capitalists 'redistribute the surplus' among themselves in proportion to their capital, a process which (if nothing else were involved) ought obviously to leave the sum-total of surplus unaffected.[10]

No doubt the three alternative postulates **5a**, **5b** and **5c** do not exhaust all the possibilities. There may be other aggregates or relationships with perfectly reasonable claims to invariance whose candidacy has not so far been pressed. But the point which concerns us here is that *the principle of equal profitability* **2** *in conjunction with any one invariance postulate will completely determine all prices* $(p_1 \ldots p_n)$[11] and thereby solve the transformation problem. However, there does not seem to be an objective basis for choosing any particular invariance postulate in preference to all the others, *and to that extent the transformation problem may be said to fall short of complete determinacy.*

It should be noted at this point that some of the postulates advanced in recent years do not fulfil the essential function of determining absolute price levels, and may even be incompatible with the principle of equal profitability in all branches. Thus, both Mr Dobb and Mr Meek (1956) have advocated a modification of **5b** which they believe to be more in the spirit of Marxism and postulated the equality of total value with total price *in terms of wage goods* (the products of Department II), i.e.:

$$\Sigma a = \frac{\Sigma ap}{p_2}\ \left(or\ \frac{\Sigma a}{\Sigma v} = \frac{\Sigma ap}{p_2 \Sigma v} = \frac{\Sigma ap}{\Sigma vp}\right) \qquad\qquad \textbf{6a}$$

As may be seen from the bracketed version, this is tantamount to the invariance of the output ÷ wages ratio.[12] It is clear, however, that **6a** says nothing about *absolute* prices; it merely imposes an additional, and supernumerary, condition on the relative prices $(p_1/p_2,\ p_3/p_2\ \ldots)$ *which are already determined by the principle of equal profitability.* Unless, therefore,

10. In the traditional three-sector analysis and *under conditions of simple reproduction*, the postulate **5c** is equivalent to the Bortkievicz postulate **5a**, since the 'surplus' will then consist exclusively of Department III products, i.e., luxuries for capitalists' consumption.

11. If the matrix has several positive latent roots the solution will not be unique, but this eventuality can, I think, be safely neglected.

12. I am not sure if I can follow Mr Dobb and Mr Meek in their insistence that such a postulate is particularly well-founded in Marxian doctrine. Why should we require the invariance of the output ÷ wages ratio rather than that of, say, the surplus ÷ wages ratio? If Marx regarded the 'degree of exploitation' as the critical magnitude in any given capitalist economy, then, surely, it is the relation between the *incomes* of social classes which ought to survive the transformation, rather than that between wages and aggregate *output*.

our basic model **1** obeys certain well-defined mathematical constraints, we cannot postulate **6a** alongside that principle. The same will of course be true of any invariance postulate which involves only price *ratios*, and this debars us equally from claiming invariance for the output–surplus ratio:[13]

$$\frac{\Sigma a}{\Sigma s} = \frac{\Sigma ap}{\Sigma sp_3} = \frac{\Sigma ap}{p_3 \Sigma s} \left(\text{or } \Sigma a = \frac{\Sigma ap}{p_3} \right),$$ **6b**

unless we allow the basic model to depart from generality in a definite manner.

The value model under special assumptions

In our endeavour to assess the degree of determinacy of the transformation problem we have so far based ourselves on the most general model of value flows amenable to mathematical treatment (equations **1**). This generality must be abandoned when we wish to investigate the *characteristics* of the Marxian prices of production as opposed to their *uniqueness* or *determinacy*. We shall therefore begin by recasting our basic scheme into the special Marxian mould of simplifying assumptions. As a first step the n industries will be reduced to the familiar three departments (I = producer goods used in further processing, II = wage goods consumed by workers, III = luxury goods consumed by capitalists), and we shall simplify our notation by writing c_i for k_{i1} and v_i for k_{i2}. The k_{i3}'s must all vanish since luxury goods do not function as 'cost-inputs' (either technological or 'labour-feeding') and equations **1** will therefore reduce to:

$$
\begin{aligned}
c_1 + c_2 + c_3 + e_1 &= a_1 \\
v_1 + v_2 + v_3 + e_2 &= a_2 \\
\qquad \qquad \;\; + e_3 &= a_3 \\
s_1 + s_2 + s_3 \quad\;\; &= s
\end{aligned}
$$ **7**

The columns are now an explicit statement of the Marxian value equations[14] $a_i = c_i + v_i + s_i$ i.e. *total value = constant capital + variable capital + surplus* and certain key concepts of the Marxian system can easily be defined for each of three departments:

$$\omega_i \equiv \text{organic composition of capital} = \frac{c_i}{c_i + v_i}$$

$$\varepsilon_i \equiv \text{rate of exploitation} \qquad\qquad = s_i/v_i$$

13. For simplicity the postulate is here presented in the form appropriate to 'simple reproduction' with three departments.

14. Strictly speaking this is only true in conditions of 'simple reproduction', i.e., when $e_1 = e_2 = 0$ (see Marx, 1906–09, vol. III, pp. 182–203). Under 'expanded reproduction' equations **7** cannot be interpreted in terms of 'value components' at all, but this does not affect the conclusions of this section, since conditions **8** and all subsequent equations remain valid in any case.

The principle of equal profitability **2** will now simplify to:

$$c_1 p_1 + v_1 p_2 = \rho a_1 p_1$$
$$c_2 p_1 + v_2 p_2 = \rho a_2 p_2 \qquad\qquad\qquad\qquad\qquad \textbf{8}$$
$$c_3 p_1 + v_3 p_2 = \rho a_3 p_3$$

A unique solution for relative prices can easily be obtained by the previous method since **8** may be written as:

$$(\gamma_1 - \rho)p_1 + \mu_1 p_2 \qquad + \; . \; = 0$$
$$\gamma_2 p_1 + (\mu_2 - \rho)p_2 + \; . \; = 0 \qquad\qquad\qquad \textbf{9}$$
$$\gamma_3 p_1 + \mu_3 p_2 \qquad - \rho p_3 = 0$$

where γ_i and μ_1 stand for the '*constant-*' and '*variable-*' capital ratios respectively ($\gamma_i \equiv c_i/a_i$ and $\mu_i \equiv v_i/a_i$). The latter are of course no more than simplifications of the general 'cost-input' coefficients κ_{ij}, with the technological and the 'labour-feeding' elements neatly separated thanks to the particular delineation of the three industries. It is only by virtue of this separation that the 'organic compositions of capital' and 'rates of exploitation' enter into the determination of production prices at all and that the Marxian assumptions concerning their role in the transformation process can be analytically tested.

As in the general case (see **4**) the consistency of equations **9** requires the vanishing of their determinant:[15]

$$0 = \begin{vmatrix} \gamma_1 - \rho & \mu_1 & 0 \\ \gamma_2 & \mu_2 - \rho & 0 \\ \gamma_3 & \mu_3 & -\rho \end{vmatrix} = -\rho \begin{vmatrix} \gamma_1 - \rho & \mu_1 \\ \gamma_2 & \mu_2 - \rho \end{vmatrix} \qquad \textbf{10}$$

This furnishes a solution for the average cost ratio ρ, which may be substi-

15. An interesting characteristic of the three department assumption is the fact that Industry III is by definition incapable of contributing 'cost-inputs' to the other two. It follows that its value components cannot enter into the determination of the prices and profit-ratios of Departments I and II and the latter must find their level *regardless of the structure of Department III*. Once this has happened, however, the profit ratio established in I and II must spread to Department III also (since the Marxian equilibrium demands equal profitability everywhere), and this will determine the relative price of luxury goods (given the capital ratios γ_3 and μ_3).

Mathematically, these propositions follow from the two zeros in the last column of the determinant and its consequent proportionality to a *two*-rowed determinant (R.H.S. of **10**). Since the proportionality factor cannot be zero, the latter must necessarily vanish, thus giving a solution for ρ dependent on the structure of the first two departments only. When this is substituted in the first two equations of **9**, the price ratio p_1/p_2 can be determined independently of Department III. Although in the particular case of 'simple reproduction' this independence is destroyed by the functional relationship between the three departments (as Mr May has pointed out), it seems to me real enough in the general case of 'expanded reproduction'.

tuted in **9** to make the system uniquely solvable for the three prices, except for the familiar proportionality factor. The latter, of course, can only be supplied by one or other of a possible range of invariance postulates (such as **5a**, **5b**, or **5c**).

Since, however, there is no objective criterion of selection between these postulates, it might be desirable to look for special assumptions concerning the value system **7** which would make *several* or *all* of them compatible at one and the same time. A specialized model of this sort, if it could plausibly be accepted, would remove the last remaining element of indeterminacy from the transformation problem. Several simple possibilities spring to mind:

(1) Mr Meek assumes that the organic composition of capital in the wage goods industry is equal to the national average i.e. $c_2/(c_2+v_2) = \Sigma c/(\Sigma c + \Sigma v)$. He also retains the usual Marxian assumption of equal rates of exploitation in all departments which, in addition, implies $s_2/v_2 = \Sigma s/\Sigma v$. In this way Department II becomes a simple scale model of the total economy $(c_2:v_2:a_2 = \Sigma c:\Sigma v:\Sigma a)$, and we can replace the value components of the second equation in **8** by the corresponding *total* aggregates without affecting its validity i.e.:

$$(\Sigma c)p_1 + (\Sigma v)p_2 = \rho(\Sigma a)p_2$$

However, as a simple summation of the three equations **8** will show, the left-hand side above must also equal $\rho\Sigma ap$ and it follows that $(\Sigma a)p_2 = \Sigma ap$ or:

$$\frac{\Sigma a}{\Sigma v} = \frac{\Sigma ap}{p_2\Sigma v} = \frac{\Sigma ap}{\Sigma vp} \qquad\qquad \textbf{11}$$

Thus, the invariance of the output ÷ wages ratio which we have rejected as an independent postulate in the general case has now been shown to hold *necessarily* when the value structure of the wage goods industry conforms to the national average. I am not sure, however, that such a radical departure from generality is not too high a price to pay for the rather doubtful orthodoxy which an invariant output ÷ wages ratio would impart to the model,[16] particularly since the determination of the absolute price level is still not achieved and requires a further postulate, such as **5b** or Mr Meek's own **5c**. The only advantage that might conceiv-

16. As Mr Meek correctly points out, the proposed departure from generality is only a *sufficient* and not a *necessary* condition of this invariance. However, the alternative assumptions which might establish it, have no recognizable economic meaning other than the postulation of the invariance itself.

ably accrue would be the possibility of simultaneous invariance for the aggregate output value **5b** and the unit value of wage goods ($p_2 = 1$, a variant of **5a**). But Mr Meek does not exploit this possibility.[17]

(2) Suppose now that it was the *capital goods* industry (Department I), rather than the wage goods industry, which was to be a scale model of the whole economy ($c_1 : v_1 : a_1 = \Sigma c : \Sigma v : \Sigma a$). In that case we can write:

$(\Sigma c)p_1 + (\Sigma v)p_2 = \rho(\Sigma a)p_1$ (by virtue of the first equation of **8**),
and $(\Sigma c)p_1 + (\Sigma v)p_2 = \rho\Sigma ap$ (by simple summation of **8**).

Equating the two right-hand sides and dividing by $\rho p_1(\Sigma c)$, we obtain:

$$\frac{\Sigma a}{\Sigma c} = \frac{\Sigma ap}{p_1 \Sigma c} = \frac{\Sigma ap}{\Sigma cp} \qquad\qquad 12$$

Thus, the 'representativeness' of Department I is seen to imply the invariance of the output–constant-capital ratio.

(3) By an exactly analogous process it can be shown that the assumption of representativeness for the *luxury* industry (i.e., $c_3 : v_3 : a_3 = \Sigma c : \Sigma v : \Sigma a$) would imply the equality $\Sigma a / \Sigma s = \Sigma ap/(\Sigma s)p_3$. In this case, however, we cannot take the further step of deducing any meaningful invariance unless we make the additional assumption of 'simple reproduction' (i.e., $\Sigma s = e_3$ and therefore $(\Sigma s)p_3 = \Sigma sp$). If this obtains, a 'representative' luxury industry will imply the invariance of the output ÷ surplus ratio:

$$\frac{\Sigma a}{\Sigma s} = \frac{\Sigma ap}{\Sigma sp} \qquad\qquad 13$$

In some ways this might be the most satisfactory model of all, as it would enable us to postulate *all three* invariances (**5a**, **5b**, and **5c**) at one and the same time. We could allow 'total price' to equal 'total value', speak of a fixed fund of surplus being 'redistributed among capitalists in proportion to their capital', and at the same time permit money prices to be expressed in terms of the value of gold. The model could thus impart complete determinancy to the transformation problem while satisfying all the Marxian preconceptions as to the characteristics of the solution. It is,

17. It could of course be argued that the postulation of **5b** on top of the other assumptions would have brought his model altogether too near triviality. Incidentally, while Mr Meek is perfectly entitled to his choice of figures departing from 'simple reproduction', it is a little confusing to find that his wage goods industry is contracting, while the other two departments expand. There is nothing *logically* inconsistent in this, but it does seem unnecessarily odd.

however, a very restrictive model and may not commend itself in view of its radical departure from generality.[18]

The deviation of prices from values

No analysis of the transformation problem is entirely satisfactory unless it throws some light on the important Marxian assertion that prices will exceed values ($p_i > 1$) in industries with a higher than average 'organic composition of capital' (non-wage share in total capital), and fall short of them in branches with the opposite characteristic. The importance of this theorem to Marxist ideology, particularly in its newest Soviet setting, derives from its alleged implications concerning the process of industrialization under capitalism and socialism respectively. To the Marxist way of thinking, as Mr Meek has pointed out, the transformation of values into prices is not merely a *logical*, but also a *historical* progress. Thus, in the early stages of capitalism, when this transformation has hardly begun, the rate of profit obtainable in capital goods industries (whose 'organic composition' is held to be relatively high) will not as yet have reached equality with that of consumer goods industries.[19] Capitalists will therefore prefer to invest their resources in the latter until the transformation has gone far enough to equalize the rate of profit everywhere. In Marxist ideology, therefore, the process of capitalist industrialization is bound to begin with the development of light industry (textiles, sugar, etc.), and to delay the take-off of heavy industry (metals, engineering, etc.) until a comparatively advanced stage has been reached. This is held to be an obstacle to the realization of the fastest rate of growth attainable on technological grounds, and to discourage the fullest use of labour-saving

18. As a simple illustration of such a model, we suggest the following figures:

		c	v	s	a
	Department I	80	+20	+20 =	120
Value-system:	Department II	10	+25	+25 =	60
	Department III	30	+15	+15 =	60

The transformation (under the assumptions specified) yields the prices $p_1 = \frac{6}{5}, p_2 = \frac{3}{5}, p_3 = 1$ and we therefore have:

		cp	vp	sp	ap
	Department I	96	+12	+36 =	144
Price system:	Department II	12	+15	+ 9 =	36
	Department III	36	+ 9	+15 =	60

The profit ratio (25%) is now equalized in all departments and both aggregate value (240) and total surplus (60) have remained unchanged. Apart from 'simple reproduction' (*i*th row-sum = *i*th column-sum), this result is made possible by the identical value structure of Department III and the total economy (30:15:15 = 120:60:60).

19. The 'rate of exploitation' being assumed equal everywhere.

methods even when capitalism has reached maturity (owing to the inevitable 'over-pricing' of means of production). Thus, in the Marxist view, society is cheated of the fruits of technological advance by the capitalist requirement of equal profitability, and the claims of socialism as a speedier engine of industrialization and greater liberator from human toil can be more plausibly advanced to the extent that it can dispense with this requirement and start the process from the opposite end of heavy industry.

While it would be out of place to enter into the metaphysics, or even the logic, of this argument, it is obviously desirable that we should test the validity of its premiss in the context of the transformation problem. At first sight the truth of the Marxian theorem may seem fairly obvious, particularly when we recall that it is the function of prices so to re-value each commodity that an initially equalized surplus $\div$ *wages* ratio ('rate of exploitation') is replaced by a universally valid surplus $\div$ *total cost* ratio, — a process which would seem to require over-valuation wherever the wage component in total cost is relatively small (i.e., organic composition of capital is high), so that producers can be, as it were, compensated by the price system for the smaller proportion of resources which they can directly apply to extracting surplus from labour. Further reflection, however, will show that the conclusion is only obvious if we neglect the effect of the universal price transformation on the *cost structure* of each industry, as Marx had done in his famous (and inconclusive) arithmetical example. As soon as input effects are taken into account, as they surely must be for complete consistency, the Marxian theorem is far from obvious and requires special proof. The issue has, I believe, been shirked by those analysts who attempted explicit algebraic solutions for the prices of production, and who were evidently deterred by the extreme complexity of the mathematical expressions emerging in the process. Yet the clear recognition of important features of a solution would often be more desirable than its explicit rendering, particularly when the latter is bound to be so cumbersome as to defeat the very object of explicitness. Fortunately it is possible to give the required proof without recourse to an explicit solution.

The principle of equal profitability **8** obviously requires that:

$$\frac{c_i p_1 + v_i p_2}{a_i p_i} = \frac{(\Sigma c)p_1 + (\Sigma v)p_2}{\Sigma ap}$$

for all i (= 1, 2, 3). If, in addition, we postulate that 'total price equals total value', i.e., $\Sigma ap = \Sigma a$, the condition reduces to:

F. Seton 173

$$\frac{\gamma_i p_1 + \mu_i p_2}{p_i} = \gamma_0 p_1 + \mu_0 p_2 \qquad\qquad \textbf{14}$$

where the γs and μs are the constant- and variable-capital ratios of the departments (c_i/a_i and v_i/a_i) and of the economy as a whole ($\gamma_0 \equiv \Sigma c/\Sigma a$ and $\mu_0 \equiv \Sigma v/\Sigma a$), and it follows at once that any absolute price p_i can be expressed in terms of the single price ratio ($p_1/p_2 \equiv p$):

$$p_i = \frac{\gamma_i p + \mu_i}{\gamma_0 p + \mu_0} \qquad\qquad \textbf{15}$$

Now it is clear that the Marxian assumption of an equal 'rate of exploitation' implies a definite dependence between the γs and the μs. For if the ratio of capitalists' to workers' incomes is equal everywhere, so is the ratio of workers' to *total* income $\lambda \left(\equiv \dfrac{v_i}{a_i - c_i} = \dfrac{v_i}{1 - \gamma_i} \right)$, and it follows by substitution in **15** that:

$$p_i = \frac{\gamma_i(p - \lambda) + \lambda}{\gamma_0(p - \lambda) + \lambda} \qquad\qquad \textbf{16}$$

It is obvious, therefore, that *provided* $(p - \lambda)$ *can be taken to be positive*, prices will exceed values ($p_i > 1$) if, and only if, the capital ratio γ_i exceeds the national average γ_0. But since λ is equal in all branches, this can only be so if the organic composition of capital $\left(\omega_i = \dfrac{\gamma_i}{\gamma_i + \mu_i} \right)$ is also in excess of the national average. The converse ($p_i < 1$) will of course apply wherever γ_i falls short of γ_0 (and therefore ω_i of ω_0).

Hence, all that remains to be done in order to prove the truth of the Marxian theorem is to establish that $p - \lambda$ will of necessity be positive, i.e., that the price ratio of the first two departments (p_1/p_2) must exceed the equalized wage ratio λ. This somewhat surprising lemma may be demonstrated as follows:

Since the L.H.S. of **14** remains equal, whether $i = 1$ or 2, we must have:

$$\phi(p) = \gamma_2 p^2 - (\gamma_1 - \mu_2)p = \mu_1 \qquad\qquad \textbf{17}$$

Let us now reproduce the geometric shape of the function $\phi(x)$ for the alternative cases A ($\gamma_1 < \mu_2$) and B ($\gamma_1 > \mu_2$):

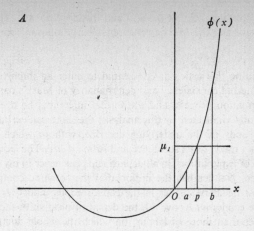

A

$\phi(x)$

μ_1

$O\ a\ p\ b$ x

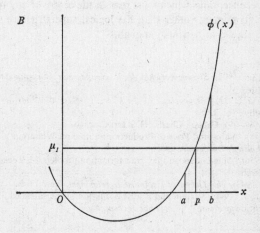

B

$\phi(x)$

μ_1

O $a\ \ p.\ b$ x

In either case it is easily seen that whenever (for a positive *a*) $\phi(p)$ is larger than $\phi(a)$, *p* must itself be larger than *a*, and conversely in the case of $b(>p)$. It follows, in particular, that *p* will exceed or fall short of λ, depending on whether $\phi(p)$ is larger or smaller than $\phi(\lambda)$. But $\phi(p)$ must *always* exceed $\phi(\lambda)$; for:

$$\phi(p) = \mu_1 \qquad\qquad = \lambda(1-\gamma_1)$$
$$\text{and } \phi(\lambda) = \gamma_2\lambda^2-(\gamma_1-\mu_2)\lambda = \lambda(\lambda-\gamma_1)$$

Since $1 > \lambda$, we must have $\phi(p) > \phi(\lambda)$ and therefore $p > \lambda$.[20] Thus $p - \lambda$ is always positive and the Marxian theorem clearly follows from 16, i.e.:

$$p_r \gtreqless 1, \text{ if } \gamma_i \gtreqless \gamma_0, \text{ i.e., if } \omega_i \gtreqless \omega_0. \qquad \textbf{18}$$

In concluding this article it is essential to enter an important *caveat*. While the internal consistency and determinancy of Marx's conception of the transformation process, and the formal inferences he drew from it, have been fully vindicated by this analysis, the same can certainly not be said of the body of the underlying doctrine, without which the whole problem loses much of its substance and *raison d'être*. The assumption of equal 'rates of exploitation' in all departments has never to my knowledge been justified. Neither has the notion that the 'organic composition of capital' must needs be higher in the capital goods industries than elsewhere in the economy. Above all, the denial of productive factor contributions other than those of labour, on which the whole doctrine of the surplus rests, is an act of *fiat* rather than of genuine cognition. It is these doctrinal preconceptions which must remain the centre of any reappraisal of Marxian economics, rather than the logical superstructure which our analysis has shown to be sound enough.

References

FROBENIUS, G. (1908), *Sitzungsberichte der k. preussischen Akademie der Wissenschaften*, vol. 1.

FROBENIUS, G. (1912), *Sitzungsberichte der k. preussischen Akademie der Wissenschaften*, vol. 1.

MARX, K. (1906–09), *Capital*, Charles H. Kerr, Chicago.

MAY, K. (1948), 'Value and Price of Production: a note on Winternitz's Solution, *Economic Journal*, December.

MEEK, R. (1956), 'Some notes on the "transformation problem" ', *Economic Journal*, March.

SWEEZY, P. (1942), *The Theory of Capitalist Development*, New York.

WINTERNITZ, J. (1948), 'Values and prices: a solution of the so-called "transformation problem" ', *Economic Journal*, June.

20. I am indebted to Professor H. G. Johnson for an alternative proof which is not dependent on visual aids, and *pro tanto* more rigorous:

Equation 17 must have one positive and one negative root (since their product is $-\mu_1/\gamma_2$), of which only the former is economically relevant. We can therefore write:

$$p = \frac{\gamma_1 - \mu_2}{2\gamma_2} + \sqrt{\left(\frac{\gamma_1 - \mu_2}{2\gamma_2}\right)^2 + \frac{\mu_1}{\gamma_2}}$$

By virtue of λ being equal to $\mu_i/(1 - \gamma_i)$, this transforms into:

$$p - \lambda = \left(\frac{\gamma_1 - \mu_2}{2\gamma_2} - \lambda\right) + \sqrt{\left(\frac{\gamma_1 - \mu_2}{2\gamma_2} - \lambda\right)^2 + \frac{\lambda(1 - \lambda)}{\gamma_2}}$$

It follows at once that as long as $\lambda < 1$, $p - \lambda$ must be positive.

Part Four
The Theory of Economic Development

19 Shigeto Tsuru

Business Cycle and Capitalism*

Excerpt from Shigeto Tsuru, 'Business cycle and capitalism: Schumpeter vs Marx',
Annals of the Hitotsubashi Academy, vol. 2, 1952, pp. 139–44.

Marx concerned himself principally with the basic analysis of the dynamics of capitalist society – a subject matter which is much wider in scope than the majority of modern economists would care to deal with. The fact that his theory of crises evolved itself on this wide base as pertaining, not to accidental abnormalities, but to the normal course of economic development is the reason for our special interest in the contribution of Marx.

Although Marx placed a great deal of emphasis on the phenomenon of crisis, or the periodical breakdown, he was hardly less articulate in speaking of recurrent 'industrial cycles', by which, there seems to be no question, he meant what we have since become accustomed to call 'the business cycle', But if we figuratively represent the unfolding of a theory as consisting of a hierarchy of levels of abstraction ascending from the most abstract base of essentials to the height of manifoldly concrete phenomena, Marx would place the phenomenon of business cycles nearer the top. Between this latter and the basic characteristics of capitalism he would make intervene numerous steps of approximation only a few of which he attempted to elucidate. If at all, his contribution lay nearer as regards the base than as regards the top. In other words, the direction of his approach is *from capitalism to business cycles*. It is his methodological prescription that the general conditions of cyclical phenomena be demonstrated as developing out of the general conditions of the capitalist mode of production. How then does Marx formulate the defining characteristics of capitalist society?

Toward the end of the third volume of *Capital* we find him summarizing such characteristics into two foci (Marx, 1906–09, vol. III, pp. 1025–7):

(1) The prevailing and determining character of its products is that of being *commodities*;
(2) The production of *surplus value* is the direct aim and determining incentive of production.

These we may take as our starting point and try to pursue their necessary

* For reasons of space, those parts of Tsuru's article dealing with Schumpeter, and comparing Schumpeter with Marx have been omitted [Eds.].

implication in the direction of further concretization. By way of caution, it may be remarked that the two italicized expressions above must be registered in our mind in their specific Marxian context. Marx would maintain that under all stages of society's development human labour confronts itself with nature and man-made means of production to produce the means of consumption, but that the institutional form which this confrontation takes differs according to different stages of history, and that *commodity* is a product of human labour taking one particular institutional form. Likewise with the concept of *surplus value*. Marx would say that beyond a certain stage in the development of productivity human labour is capable of producing surplus above the goods necessary for his subsistence, but that the form which the surplus assumes and the way in which it is distributed differs according to different stages of history, and that *surplus value* is one particular institutional form of such a surplus occurring in one stage of society's development.

Of the two characteristics mentioned above, the first provides background for what Marx calls 'the possibility of crisis'. The commodity production as such pertains not solely to a capitalist society; but by acquiring a *prevailing* and *determining* character, it forms a general background for the basic elements of capitalistic economic transactions. The implications of the commodity production may best be elucidated in its contrast to the barter economy.

Barter economy can schematically be decomposed into a unit process of P_1-P_2; that is to say, the Product 1 is *directly* exchanged with the Product 2. The latter is the aim achieved by parting with the Product 1. Further, the connotation is reversible; for the person who parts with the Product 2, the Product 1 is the end. The commodity economy, on the other hand, calling forth by its very nature the prevalent use of the general value form (money), splits this simple process of P_1-P_2 into two, i.e. C_1–M and M–C_2 (in which C denotes a commodity and M money). M appears to be only an intermediary. But let us scrutinize what this implies. The producer of C_1 now produces it for the market where he expects to exchange it for money. He has no idea who wants it and how much of it is wanted. Communal decision or social consideration no longer shapes or supersedes his individual policy. The external world outside him presents itself only in the shape of a demand curve, as it were. Still it remains that his aim is definitely to acquire C_2. The movement which was started by the entrance of C_1 into the market cannot come to rest until it ends in the acquisition of C_2 by the producer of C_1. But once he sells his C_1 for M, he is under no compulsion to buy C_2 immediately, nor from the person to whom he sold C_1. He can bring M home, wait for a few months, go to a neighbouring town, and buy C_2 with M. In other words, M 'splits'[1] the process of C_1–C_2 both *temporally* and *spatially*. And if the interval of time between the two complementary phases of the process, C_1–M–C_2, becomes too great, if the cleavage between the sale and the purchase becomes too pronounced, the essential unity of the process asserts itself convulsively by producing a crisis. Thus arises the first possibility of crises.[2] Further elaborations on the first possibility are added as Marx makes more concrete his discussion of money; for example, the function of money as 'a means of payment', i.e. the function of acting as the measure of value and the realization of value at *two different* moments, strengthens and concretizes the possibility. However, we shall not here pursue the chain of complications which follow this starting point; instead, we turn now to the second basic characteristic of capitalism and its relation to the phenomenon of crisis.

The second characteristic, the production of surplus value as the direct aim and determining incentive of production, can be telescoped into the unit movement of capitalist production schematized by Marx as:

$$M–C–C'–M' \quad (M' = M + \Delta M).$$

A capitalist starts with money capital, M, buys means of production, C, (including labour power), manufactures his product, C' and sells the same in exchange for M'. Unless M' is larger than M, the movement loses its basic *raison d'être*; in fact, the maximization of ΔM in relation to M is its direct aim. The movement starts with M and ends with M', quantita-

1. In using the transitive verb for M, we commit an oversimplification. C_1 appears from the backstage of workshop into the stage of the market, where plenipotentiary M directs it hither and thither. After it undergoes a metamorphosis into M, it makes an exit again into the backstage never to come back. But M constantly reappears on the stage, and seems to string a series of commodities into a chain *ad infinitum*. Thus the 'continuity of the movement is sustained by the money alone ... the result of the circulation of commodities assumes the *appearance* of having been effected, not by means of a change in the form of commodities, but thanks to the function of money as medium of circulation ... money seeming to set passive commodities in motion, transferring them from the hands in which they are not use-values into the hands in which they are use-values. Although, therefore, the movement of the money is merely an expression of the circulation of commodities, it seems as if, conversely, the circulation of commodities were only the outcome of the movement of the money' (Marx, 1928, vol. I, pp. 94–5). This point is especially important, because the fetish illusion of M being the culprit for all the evils of the exchange economy and the consequent advocacy of monetary measures as necessary and sufficient stems out of the failure to realize the importance of the context within which alone M can operate. The root, Marx would say, lies in the commodity economy itself.

2. Marx stresses the point that it is as yet only a possibility and warns against J. S. Mill's attempt to explain crisis by its possibility.

tively different but qualitatively identical. This permits the goal M' of the process $(M-C-C'-M')$ to become immediately a new starting point, making it possible structurally to satisfy the self-perpetuating tendency for aggrandizement through the successive repetition of the process. Then there arises the possibility of treating such successive series of unit processes over time, each of which is conditioned by the specific time of turnover, as being composed of two unbroken series of M and M' which connect each point of time with a specific value of ΔM. The unity of the process C_1-M-C_2, achieved through having as an objective a consumers' good which by its very nature drops out of economic circulation, is now shattered. The apparent unity in the process of $M-C-C'-M'$ is an abstraction, having no longer a restraining force as a unit process, because it is in the very nature of M, which is the goal of this process, to remain in circulation to fulfil its function of increasing its own value.

It is an essential aspect of capitalistic specificity, according to Marx, that the determining consideration which governs its (capitalism's) unit process is the uninterrupted expansion of ΔM, and *not* the satisfaction of social needs.[3] Therefore, the conditions which promote or hinder the success of such expansion constitute the subject matter of essential significance. This may be divided into two aspects which are 'separable logically as well as by time and space' (Marx, 1928, vol. III, p. 216); namely, (1) the conditions of the *production* of surplus value and (2) those of its *realization*. The first is concerned with the process of production itself while the second is the problem of sale.

(1) The conditions of the production of surplus value are in the main technological and permit the direct improvement at the hand of individual capitalist. The determining motive of capitalist production finds its expression in the constant effort on the part of individual capitalists to improve the technique of production. From the standpoint of society as a whole, the limitation to the production of surplus value lies in the number of working population and the level of technological knowledge. But the objective consequence of this 'capitalistic' (in Böhm-Bawerkian sense) development, abstracting for the moment from the problem of effective demand, is the falling tendency of the rate of profit. This is visualized by Marx as an immanent *tendency* rooted in the capitalist mode of production itself. If the pursuit of the aim of profit maximization leads necessarily to the greater and greater use of machinery, if this in turn finds its expression

3. *cf.* 'The expansion or contraction of production . . . is determined by profit and by the proportion of this profit to the employed capital . . . instead of being determined by the relation of production to social wants. The capitalist mode of production comes to a standstill at a point determined by the production and realization of profit, not by the satisfaction of social needs' (Marx, 1928, vol. III, p. 303).

inevitably in the falling tendency in the ratio of ΔM to the employed capital, a vicious circle is already evident. The falling tendency naturally evokes reactions to counteract it – reactions which are not necessarily free of boomerang effect. But once the tendency becomes actuality, and the rate of profit does fall, the motive power of the system receives a setback and the process of accumulation suffers. It is evident, if such is the case, that expansion can neither be smooth nor go on indefinitely

(2) The conditions of the *production* of surplus value, however, are only one side of the shield. The conditions of its *realization* must now be examined. It is characteristic under capitalism that claims on goods are derived not as a function of status as in a feudal society, nor as a function of actual needs as in the economy of an individual family, but as a function of factor payments which are contracted or expanded in accordance with the ebb and flow of profit-seeking activities of capitalists. It is a corollary of this capitalistic specificity that the aggregate size of such claims emerges as a result of atomistic decision on the part of individual capitalists and thus cannot be controlled directly as an aggregate. In the eyes of individual capitalists in whose hands lies the all-important decision as to the expansion or contraction of economic activities the conditions governing the realization of their surplus value appear in the guise of a natural law standing outside their control.

Thus the inherent tendency in capitalism to expand production and to improve productivity both in the interests of profit maximization, while incidentally exerting a relatively downward pressure on cost-factor payments, is confronted with a basis of realization which it is no single capitalist's business to expand except incidentally to his action in pursuance of profit maximization. Therefore, this inherent tendency leads inevitably to frantic competition among capitalists for markets who expend a huge sum as selling cost and burst out of the bounds of a national economy, seeking forever the expanding market abroad.

Such a reasoning forms a background for Marx's famed dictum (Marx, 1928, vol. III, p. 568):

The last cause of all real crises always remains the poverty and restricted consumption of the masses as compared to the tendency of capitalist production to develop the productive forces in such a way that only the absolute power of consumption of the entire society would be their limit.

In short, we have, on the one hand, the tendency, partaken by each capitalist independently, to enlarge the production of C' regardless of the fall in the value of the product and of the size of ΔM contained in C'; while, on the other hand, each capitalist seeks not only to preserve the value of the existing capital but also to expand it by realizing all the ΔM

he produces. Herein Marx finds the basic contradiction of the capitalist mode of production which tends constantly to upset the harmonious development of production. Capitalist production is continually engaged in the attempt to overcome this barrier of harmony, but it is inherent in it that it overcomes it only by means which again place the same barrier in its way in a more formidable size. The solution, therefore, has to be forcibly brought about by a breakdown which through the destruction of values and the disemployment of resources works toward the restoration of the objectively balanced relations. The *inevitability* of crisis is thus unfolded out of the second of the basic characteristics of capitalism.

References

MARX, K. (1906–09), *Capital*, Charles H. Kerr, Chicago.
MARX, K. (1928), *Capital*, Allen & Unwin.

On Marx's Scheme of Reproduction and Accumulation*

Donald J. Harris, 'On Marx's scheme of reproduction and accumulation', *Journal of Political Economy*, vol. 80, 1972, pp. 505–22.

1 Introduction

The scheme of reproduction occupies a central place in Marx's economic analysis of capitalism (Marx, 1967, vol. 1, chapter 23; vol. 2 chapters 20 and 21). With it, he sought to show the structural relations which prevail in the economy as a whole, focusing on the interdependence between different sectors of production and on the distribution of the total value produced among the classes of society. In simple reproduction, these relations were displayed in their simplest form. In the scheme of expanded reproduction, he went on to introduce the problem of capital accumulation. The latter, though incompletely worked out in a set of sketchy notes and numerical examples, has been shown to be capable of a solution yielding the path of accumulation over time.[1]

It is worth returning to the scheme in order to clarify, after some restatement, the nature of the theoretical solution it offers to some of the central issues raised in recent theories of growth and distribution.[2] Of particular interest are questions concerning the possibility of steady growth in a capitalist economy and the determination of the rate of profits.

In examining the analytical structure of the scheme, it seems useful to work within the particular assumptions and analytical categories Marx used, and the model discussed here is accordingly developed on this basis. It is, of course, possible to recast the analysis with techniques of modern theory which have the advantage of exposing more clearly certain technological and price relations which are not dealt with in the Marxian system of classification.[3] The points at which this needs to be done will be indicated

---

* For helpful comments and discussion I am indebted to Joan Robinson, Wilhelm Krelle, Amit Bhaduri, Bob Rowthorn, Prabhat Patnaik, and David Levine. Responsibility for errors and interpretation is, of course, mine.

1. See Robinson (1951), Naqvi (1960), and Krelle (1970). Other analyses and interpretations of the scheme can be found in Morishima (1956), Sweezy (1956, chapter 5 and 10), Tsuru (1956), and Lange (1959, 1969).

2. For a review of these issues, see Harcourt (1969).

3. For one not-so-recent attempt to do this, see Samuelson (1957). Since then, the puzzles concerning the relation between technology and valuation have reemerged in a

as we go along. The present procedure is, nevertheless, a necessary preliminary to any full-scale investigation of the content of Marx's ideas in this area.

2 Value and distribution

The setting of the analysis is a system in which commodities are produced by commodities ('means of production') and labour. The technology is assumed to be viable in the sense of permitting a positive net product above the replacement of commodities used up in production. Under capitalism, this net product is distributed as wages to workers and profits or surplus value to capitalists.[4] Throughout the present discussion the argument is confined to conditions of competitive equilibrium.[5] For simplicity, technology is also assumed to be constant.

To proceed, a well-known difficulty in Marx's analysis must first be got out of the way. This has to do with the relation between *prices of production* and *labour values*.[6] Many of the riddles connected with this have already been cleared up (see Seton, 1957; Sraffa, 1960; Morishima and Seton, 1961). We know that in equilibrium, under competitive conditions, when there is a uniform rate of profit the relative price of each commodity (in terms of any numeraire) is such as to cover wage costs plus profit at the going rate on the value of the capital employed. These are the prices at which commodities and means of production are exchanged in the market. With a constant technology, labour measured in homogeneous units (say, one hour of work by an average man) per unit of output of each commodity is constant. Output can be valued in labour time, that is, in terms of the amount of labour directly and indirectly required to produce it. If hours worked per week or per year are constant, then the *value* in this sense of a unit of output is constant.

Relative prices of commodities correspond to labour values if the technology is such that the value of means of production employed per worker and the time pattern of production are uniform in all lines of production, or if prices are calculated using a notional profit rate equal to zero. Other-

---

different light (see 'Symposium', 1966; Bhaduri, 1969). An important unpublished study by Morishima, 'Marx in the Light of Contemporary Economic Analysis', came to my attention when the present paper was in final draft for publication.

4. Profits and surplus value are used interchangeably in what follows with no regard to the different categories in which surplus value is paid out.

5. For Marx this would be an equilibrium only in the sense that minor perturbations are averaged out so as to be able to focus on more fundamental relations, not in the sense that it is capable of maintaining itself indefinitely. The mechanism of the business cycle, an integral feature of the analysis, is left out of the present account.

6. For discussions of this problem, see Sweezy (1956, chapter 7), and Meek (1967, pp. 143–57).

wise, prices depart from labour values. Under certain assumptions, all of them well founded in the Marxian theory of value, a unique relation may be shown to exist between them (cf. Seton, 1957; Morishima and Seton, 1961). There is, however, no *general* rule by which the latter can be transformed into the former. The problem is compounded in the presence of joint production due to fixed capital and when technology is changing.

All of this concerns only the *logic* of the problem and leaves open the related question of the significance of transformation of values into prices as an actual *historical* process.[7]

It could be argued, of course (and this is perhaps closer to Marx's position), that the concept of *values* and that of *prices* are both equally relevant, each in its own sphere. Values offer an objective basis, independent of the market, for assessing the amount of the social product above the value of wages which is appropriated by the owners of the means of production, and hence for analysing the outcome of class relations in the society.[8] Surplus value in this sense represents an amount which the worker puts into the production process but which he does not get back. It is 'unpaid labour'. Contrary to a 'vulgar' interpretation, this makes no normative judgement about which class deserves or should get that amount. Prices, on the other hand, enter into the actual relations of exchange, where they perform the role of distributing the surplus among the capitalists at an equal rate, the competitive rate of profit, on the amount of capital which each owns. Going from the value system to the price system makes it possible to see exactly what this role is. In this way, the analysis in terms of values provides the foundation for the theory of prices.

The question remains as to what determines the rate of profit (or the wage rate) and hence the distribution of the net product between owners of means of production and workers.[9] Once the rate of profit (or the wage rate) is determined, relative prices are, of course, given by technology and distribution. We can consider the scheme of reproduction from the point of view of the answer it provides to this question which lies at the heart of the issues raised in recent theories of growth (cf. Harcourt, 1969).

3 The scheme

The scheme of reproduction collapses the economy into two departments or sectors, Department I, producing means of production (machines and

7. On the latter, see Meek (1967, pp. 154–7).

8. Compare the role of the concept of 'standard commodity' in Sraffa's (1960) system.

9. Given the rate of profit, the wage rate can be determined as a function of technology and the rate of profit. Contrariwise, the rate of profit can be determined as a function of a given wage rate and the technology. On this and the fundamental concept of a wage–profit relation (or 'frontier'), see Sraffa (1960).

raw materials), and Department II, producing consumption goods. Production takes one period, the same in each department, and the means of production to be used up in a single period.[10] Gross output of each department covers replacement of means of production ('constant capital' $= c$), wages advanced to the workers at the beginning of the period ('variable capital' $= v$), and surplus value, s, which goes to the capitalists. In this and the next two sections we follow Marx in measuring all magnitudes in terms of labour values. Thus:

$$\text{I: } c_1 + v_1 + s_1,$$
$$\text{II: } \frac{c_2 + v_2 + s_2}{c + v + s} = \text{total value.} \qquad\qquad 1$$

The *organic composition of capital*, regarded as a given constant,[11] is

$$k_i = \frac{c_i}{v_i} \qquad\qquad 2$$

(where $i = 1, 2$). The *rate of exploitation* is the ratio of surplus value to wages:

$$\varepsilon_i = \frac{s_i}{v_i}. \qquad\qquad 3$$

Marx tended to assume

$$\varepsilon_1 = \varepsilon_2 = \hat{\varepsilon}, \qquad\qquad 4$$

that is, the rate of exploitation in both departments is equal to a given constant. By definition, the rate of net profit is the ratio of surplus value to the value of capital, the latter consisting of the value of means of production plus the wages advanced. Thus:

$$r_i = \frac{s_i}{c_i + v_i} = \frac{\varepsilon_i}{1 + k_i}. \qquad\qquad 5$$

If the rate of exploitation is to be the same across departments, the rate of profit, defined in this way, must differ in accordance with a difference

10. These are obvious simplifications which get away from complications due to different time periods of production for different commodities and the existence of fixed capital. Similarly, current capital models commonly treat the production period as uniform and assume a fixed rate of depreciation of capital goods (cf. Samuelson, 1962). The present approach amounts to assuming that this rate of depreciation is unity. For a more general treatment of these matters, see Sraffa (1960) and von Neumann (1945).

11. Marx expected that this ratio would tend to rise over time due to technical change. Such considerations are ruled out here by the assumption of constant technology.

in the organic composition of capital. For the rate of profit to be uniform, the rate of exploitation must differ, and this would contradict **4**. The two rates can be uniform only in the special case that the organic composition of capital is uniform.

Actually, the difficulty here is only apparent.[12] What is needed is to recognize that a uniform rate of profit has no meaning in the system of labour values, only in the system of prices. Under competitive capitalism, the formation of a general rate of profit takes place in the market (that is, 'within the sphere of circulation') through the effort on the part of each capitalist to expand his money profits. Thus, it is the rate of money profits which tends to uniformity among different industries in the long run. Prices adjust to accommodate the difference in profits, calculated at this uniform rate, corresponding to a difference in the quantity of capital. In the price system, the ratio of profits to wages then differs between departments in accordance with the difference in the ratio of capital to labour. A restatement of the problem along these lines will be considered below in Section 6. Meanwhile, as will become clear, the equilibrium dynamics of the system can be set out by continuing to deal in terms of labour values. In so doing there is no presumption that commodities are sold at their values.

How does this system move through time, and what are the economic relations which then prevail within it? Abstracting from technical change, we find that the answer depends on what is done with the surplus. Workers do not save, perhaps because there is no margin between the wages they get and the 'necessaries' of consumption. Only capitalists save, and their saving out of the surplus appropriated in one period provides additional capital in the next period. Marx considers two cases: simple reproduction, and expanded reproduction. We consider each in turn.

4 Simple reproduction

In simple reproduction, by assumption, all surplus value (as well as wages) is consumed, net accumulation is zero, and the economy reproduces itself on the same scale from one period to another. For the flows between departments to balance, purchases by one from the other must match sales. Demand for output of Department I comes from its own purchases for replacement of constant capital plus those of Department II:

$$c_1 + c_2 = c_1 + v_1 + s_1. \qquad\qquad \textbf{6}$$

Demand for output of Department II comes from expenditure on consumption by capitalists and workers in both departments:

12. The issue was raised by Robinson (1947, p. 15; 1951, p. 17).

$$v_1+s_1+v_2+s_2 = c_2+v_2+s_2. \qquad\qquad\qquad 7$$

The balancing condition is

$$c_2 = v_1+s_1, \qquad\qquad\qquad\qquad\qquad 8$$

which can be seen to imply, after dividing by v_2 and substituting from 2, 3, and 4:

$$\frac{v_1}{v_2} = \frac{k_2}{1+\varepsilon_1}. \qquad\qquad\qquad\qquad 8a$$

This case, chosen for its simplicity, thus isolates a critical property of the system. According to 8a, the amounts of variable capital used to hire labour in each department must bear a definite relation to each other depending on the value of k_2 and ε_1. This is the only relation which ensures that the capitalists in each department realize an amount of surplus value at the appropriate rate on the value of the wages advanced while the economy simply maintains the same scale of operation from period to period. It is, so to say, the equilibrium condition of the system and determines a unique allocation of labour between the two departments. Employment being thus determined, output produced in each department is also determined. The distribution of the product between capitalists and workers conforms to the independently given rate of exploitation.[13]

There is, however, no guarantee that the capitalists, taken together, would advance just the right amount of wages and in the right proportions. There is therefore no guarantee that the system could achieve equilibrium.

5 Expanded reproduction

In expanded reproduction, net accumulation is positive. In each period the capitalists invest a certain proportion, say α_i, of their surplus carried over from the previous period. This amount goes to provide additional means of production in each department (Δc_i) plus the additional variable capital (Δv_i) needed to hire the extra labour to work with the extra means of production at the same organic composition of capital.

13. At this point the limitations of Marx's system of classification become apparent. All of the relevant magnitudes are expressed in terms of value aggregates and as such can provide only the conditions for aggregate equilibrium. To translate them into physical terms such as output or employment we need to know the technical coefficients of production and the prices, but these are not specified. All we know about the technology is the overall 'organic composition of capital'. For the same reason the system as it stands is incapable of showing the *quantitative* relation between the accumulation of means of production and the growth of output. To say this is not to deny the richness of Marx's *qualitative* analysis of the relation between capital accumulation, technical change and 'the productive power of social labour'.

A problem concerns the allocation of investment between departments. Marx treated this by assuming that capitalists in each department reinvest their surplus in the same department. This is not a very satisfactory assumption, and it will be relaxed in the next section.[14] Meanwhile its implications can be easily worked out.

Investment in each department is:

$$I_i = a_i s_{it-1}, \qquad\qquad 9$$

and its allocation between variable and constant capital is:

$$I_i = \Delta c_i + \Delta v_i,$$
$$\Delta v_i = \lambda_{vi} I_i, \qquad\qquad 10$$
$$\Delta c_i = (1 - \lambda_{vi}) I_i.$$

It follows from 9, 10, and 3 that

$$g_{vi} = \frac{\Delta v_i}{v_{it-1}} = \lambda_{vi} a_i \varepsilon_i, \qquad\qquad 11$$

$$g_{ci} = \frac{\Delta c_i}{c_{it-1}} = (1 - \lambda_{vi}) \frac{a_i \varepsilon_i}{k_i}, \qquad\qquad 12$$

which give the growth rates of constant and variable capital in terms of the proportion of investment allocated to each, the saving propensity of the capitalists, and the rate of exploitation. Constancy of the organic composition of capital requires $g_{vi} = g_{ci}$. From 11 and 12 this leads to

$$\lambda_{vi} = \frac{1}{1 + k_i}. \qquad\qquad 13$$

Since k_i are given constants, the proportions λ_{vi} are fixed. The growth rates are therefore fixed.

In each period, the increment in means of production and variable capital represents additional demand for the output of both departments over that which prevails in simple reproduction. For the flows between departments to balance in this case requires

$$v_1 + s_1 = c_2 + \Delta c_2 + \Delta c_1, \qquad\qquad 14$$

14. The assumption that investment of surplus is restricted to the department (or business) in which the surplus is appropriated seems contrary to the assumption of competition which requires free mobility of capital between departments. Moreover, as Robinson (1951, p. 17) pointed out: 'This is a severe assumption to make even about the era before limited liability was introduced, and becomes absurd afterwards.' For a recent attempt to work with a similar assumption concerning investment behaviour in a two-sector model, see Inada (1966).

which, after a little manipulation, leads to

$$\frac{v_1}{v_2} = \frac{k_2(1+g_{v2})}{1+c_1 \; k_1 g_{v1}}. \qquad \textbf{14a}$$

We thus have again a determinate solution for the equilibrium allocation of labour between departments.[15] In this case, as compared with simple reproduction, it is governed in addition by the growth rate of variable capital in both departments.

For a constant proportional allocation of labour between departments consistent with **14a**, outlay on labour should grow at the same rate in each. This requires, according to **11** and **4**:

$$\frac{\lambda_{v1}}{\lambda_{v2}} = \frac{a_2}{a_1}. \qquad \textbf{15}$$

But from **13** we have

$$\frac{\lambda_{v1}}{\lambda_{v2}} = \frac{1+k_2}{1+k_1}. \qquad \textbf{13a}$$

Therefore an equilibrium with balanced growth of both departments exists only if

$$\frac{a^2}{a_1} = \frac{1+k_2}{1+k_1}. \; 16 \qquad \textbf{16}$$

The meaning of this solution is clear. The capitalists individually invest an amount of their surplus every period, each in his own department, such as to maintain the given proportion between constant and variable capital. Equilibrium for the system as a whole requires that the amounts invested in hiring labour in the two departments be proportional. In general, these two quantities of investment can be consistent only if **16** holds. But since a_i and k_i are independently determined parameters, there is nothing to

15. For the solution **14a** to be economically meaningful, it is required that $1+\varepsilon_1-k_1 g v_1 > 0$, implying $v_1+s_1-\Delta c_1 > 0$, which says simply that net output of Department I must exceed its own requirements for net investment in means of production.

16. This particular coincidence is the basis of the numerical solutions which have been obtained for Marx's scheme (cf. Robinson, 1951, p. 19; and Naqvi, 1960). In Marx's example (1967, vol. 2, pp. 596–601), the rate of exploitation is the same and the organic composition of capital different; so he has to choose $a_2/a_1 = (1+k_2)/(1+k_1)$ $= 3/5$ to obtain a solution. The condition **16** could be derived more directly by noting that, as a matter of definition, the growth rate of total capital in each department is $g_i = a_i r_i (i = 1, 2)$. Equating these rates and using **4** and **5** gives **16**.

ensure that this condition would, in fact, hold. An equilibrium therefore might not exist.

Even if an equilibrium were by chance to exist, there is no reason why the growth rate of employment corresponding to it should equal that of the available labour force. The rate of unemployment, then, has to be introduced as an additional variable. Indeed, in Marx's analysis, 'the reserve army of the unemployed' plays a central role in the dynamics of the system.

6 A restatement of the scheme

One meaning which it is possible to give to Marx's assumption that the rate of exploitation is given is that this refers to the ratio of the total amount of surplus value to the total wage bill for the system as a whole.[17] A given size of this ratio is enforced by the nature of class relations in the whole society, and competition ensures that the amount of profits thus determined is shared out among the capitalists in equal proportion to the capital which they own. Prices include profits at this uniform rate and the ratio of profits to wages varies from one line to another, reflecting differences in the value of capital measured at those prices.[18]

The mechanism by which this comes about is the unceasing quest for profitable investments on the part of each individual capitalist and freedom of entry into all lines of production. The existence of such a mechanism would imply furthermore that one must abandon as well the assumption that each capitalist invests his surplus only in his own business.[19]

Accordingly, we proceed to modify the previous model by substituting for 4

$$\mathscr{E}' = \frac{s_1' + s_2'}{v_1' + v_2'},$$

4a

where the primes indicate that the variables are to be interpreted in price terms, not in value.[20] We also have

17. This interpretation, in some respects, follows that of Robinson (1969, p. 66).

18. The argument here does not seem to be inconsistent with Marx's conception of a *uniform* rate of exploitation. In value terms, the rate of exploitation of equal labour may still be equal wherever such labour is employed. Indeed, this must be so if competition exists in the labour market so as to ensure equal pay for equal work. But, in the actual relations of exchange, prices enter to redistribute the surplus from capitalists with a lower ratio of capital to labour to those with a higher ratio. This creates the appearance, which Marx was concerned to dispel, that profit is due to capital and the thriftiness of capitalists rather than to the nature of the social relations.

19. See note 14.

20. Some characteristic of the value system must be assumed to remain invariant to the transformation of values into prices (cf. Seton, 1957). It would be consistent with the present approach to take $s_1 + s_2 = s_1' + s_2'$.

$$\varepsilon_i' = \frac{s_i'}{v_i'}. \tag{3a}$$

Recognizing that the organic composition of capital measured in terms of prices would now depend on the profit rate, we should write for **2**:

$$k_i' = \frac{c_i'}{v_i'} = k_i'(r).^{21} \tag{2a}$$

The rate of profit is:

$$r = \frac{s_i'}{c_i' + v_i'} = \frac{\varepsilon_i'}{1 + k_i'}. \tag{5a}$$

This can be rewritten as

$$\varepsilon'_i = (1 + k_i')r = \varepsilon_i'(k_i', r). \tag{5b}$$

The rate of profit must adjust to uniformity between sectors in a manner consistent with the given rate of exploitation. This implies, after substituting into **4a** from **3a** and **5b**:

$$\frac{v_1'}{v_2'} = -\frac{\hat{\varepsilon}' - \varepsilon_2'(k_2', r)}{\hat{\varepsilon}' - \varepsilon_1'(k_1', r)}. \tag{4b}$$

These constitute the fundamental relations of the scheme as restated. We examine the operation of this system by considering first the case of expanded reproduction, assuming that capitalists are free to move their capital between departments.

The aggregate amount of investment is:

$$I' = \sum_i a_i s'_{it-1}, \tag{17}$$

21. Given the matrix of coefficients representing the technique of production, a difference in the rate of profit as between two equilibrium states entails a difference in the pattern of prices and hence in the value, at those prices, of the means of production. When there is a choice of technical methods of production, the technique used is also likely to be different when the rate of profit is different, causing thereby a difference in both the physical quantities and the prices. In general, the organic composition of capital measured in prices therefore depends on the rate of profit. It is independent of the rate of profit only when the quantity of means of production (measured by the embodied labour component) per worker happens to be the same for all commodities, for if it is the same at one rate of profit it must then be the same at every other rate. For reasons made clear by Sraffa (1960, chapter 3), the function representing the relationship between value of capital and rate of profit would not necessarily be of any particular shape. Its shape depends on the specific features of the technology.

and this total is now allocated as follows:

$$I' = \Delta c_1' + \Delta v_1' + \Delta c_2' + \Delta v_2',$$

$$\Delta c_i' = \lambda_{ci} I', \tag{18}$$

$$\Delta v_i' = \lambda_{vi} I'.$$

The growth rates of constant and variable capital therefore become:

$$g_{v1} = \lambda_{v1}\left(a_1\varepsilon_1' + a_2\varepsilon_2'\frac{v_2'_{t-1}}{v_2'_{t-1}}\right),$$

$$g_{v2} = \lambda_{v2}\left(a_1\varepsilon_1'\frac{v_1'_{t-1}}{v_2'_{t-1}} + a_2\varepsilon_2'\right),$$

$$g_{c1} = \lambda_{c1}\left(\frac{a_1\varepsilon_1'}{k_1'} + \frac{a_2\varepsilon_2'}{k_2'}\frac{c_2'_{t-1}}{c_1'_{t-1}}\right), \tag{19}$$

$$g_{c2} = \lambda_{c2}\left(\frac{a_1\varepsilon_1'}{k_1'}\frac{c_1'_{t-1}}{c_2'_{t-1}} + \frac{a_2\varepsilon_2'}{k_2'}\right).$$

Substituting g_{v1} and g_{v2} into **14a**, interpreted in price terms, gives the balancing condition for purchases and sales between departments, and by setting $v_1'/v_2' = v_1'_{t-1}/v_2'_{t-1}$ we get the stationary solution:

$$\frac{v_1'}{v_2'} = \frac{k_2' + (k_1'\lambda_{v1} + k_2'\lambda_{v2})a_2\varepsilon_2'(k_2', r)}{1 + [1 - (k_1'\lambda_{v1} + k_2'\lambda_{v2})a_1]\varepsilon_1'(k_1', r)}. \tag{20}$$

For constancy of the organic composition of capital, set $g_{vi} = g_{ci}$, which gives:

$$\frac{\lambda_{ci}}{\lambda_{vi}} = k_i'. \tag{21}$$

Checking now the time paths of v_1' and v_2' we find from **19** that $g_{v1} = g_{v2}$ if:

$$\frac{\lambda_{v1}}{\lambda_{v2}} = \frac{v_1'_{t-1}}{v_2'_{t-1}}. \tag{22}$$

In general, the system is, therefore, consistent with equilibrium for arbitrary initial conditions. The allocation of investment according to **21** and **22** determines a steady rate of balanced expansion through capital accumulation. The equilibrium allocation of labour is determined according to **20**. This labour allocation must also be consistent with **4b** so as to ensure a uniform profit rate consistent with the overall rate of exploitation.

The two equations 4b and 20, together with 2a, determine the rate of profit as the root of:

$$-\frac{\mathcal{E}'-\varepsilon_2'(k_2',r)}{\mathcal{E}'-\varepsilon_1'(k_1',r)} = \frac{k_2'+(k_1'\lambda_{v1}+k_2'\lambda_{v2})a_2\varepsilon_2'(k_2',r)}{1+[1-(k_1'\lambda_{v1}+k_2'\lambda_{v2})a_1]\varepsilon_1'(k_1',r)},\qquad 23$$

provided that $\varepsilon_2' \neq \varepsilon_1'$. An equilibrium solution may or may not exist, or there may be many, depending on the exact form of the functions and in particular on relation 2a. The modifications introduced evidently impart greater flexibility to the solution.

Even if an equilibrium exists in this case, there is again no reason for the growth rate of variable capital corresponding to it to equal that of the available labour force. Furthermore, there is no guarantee that an equilibrium, even if it exists, could be achieved.

Analysis of the cases examined in Sections 4 and 5 in terms of this alternative scheme is straightforward. All we have to do is to reinterpret the conditions for equilibrium in the light of the new relations 2a, 4b, and 5b.

In the case of simple reproduction we get, instead of 8a:

$$\frac{v_1'}{v_2'} = \frac{k_2'(r)}{1+\varepsilon_1'(k_1',r)}.\qquad 8b$$

This must be equated to 4b which, together with 2a, then determines the rate of profit as the root of:

$$\frac{k_2'(r)}{1+\varepsilon_1'(k_1',r)} = -\frac{\hat{\varepsilon}'-\varepsilon_2'(k_2',r)}{\hat{\varepsilon}'-\varepsilon_1'(k_1',r)}.\qquad 24$$

In the case of expanded reproduction, with capitalists in each department reinvesting in the same department, 14a becomes:

$$\frac{v_1'}{v_2'} = \frac{(1+g_{v2})k_2'(r)}{1+\varepsilon_1'(k_1',r)-g_{v1}k_1'(r)}.\qquad 14b$$

Equating this to 4b determines the equilibrium rate of profit. From 11 and 12, taking account of 5b, we find that equilibrium with balanced expansion requires simply

$$a_2 = a_1,\qquad 16a$$

which is different from the condition 16 obtained in Section 5. It is very simple to go on from this to show that, in equilibrium, the rate of profit is equal to the rate of growth divided by the capitalists' saving propensity, a result which is well known from recent growth theory. That it provides no additional information should be obvious.

It is interesting to consider the reason for the difference between the conditions **16** and **16a**. This difference can be explained as follows. Equilibrium requires that total capital in each department grow at the same rate. *In the system of labour values,* the same rate of surplus value is appropriated in each department. When, by assumption, the surplus appropriated in a given department has to be reinvested there, **16** says that growth can be balanced only if the capitalists reinvest relative amounts of their surplus equal to the relative value of their capital. *In the price system* however, some of the surplus value appropriated is redistributed between departments by the price mechanism so as to equalize the rate of profits. This transfer of surplus between the capitalists compensates for the difference in the value of their capital. For growth to be balanced, it is then only necessary that capitalists reinvest the same proportion of their profits. This is what **16a** says. The difference between the two conditions reflects the fact that one group of capitalists gains at the expense of the other due to the role of prices and competition.

Furthermore, it now becomes easy to see why greater flexibility is gained when we drop the assumption that capitalists reinvest only in their own department. With both capital and surplus value free to move between departments, the condition of equalization of profit rates together with the investment-allocation conditions is all that is necessary for balanced expansion of the system.

7 Conclusion

Robinson (1951, p. 19) remarked with reference to her numerical solution of Marx's scheme: 'This model bears a strong family resemblance to Mr Harrod's warranted rate of growth.' Both the similarity and the difference between Marx and Harrod should now be apparent.

For both, abstract equilibrium relations are significant not in themselves but for what they say about possible sources of disturbance or 'crises' in concrete situations. Harrod's conditions identify two such sources: (1) a discrepancy between the amount of investment required for steady growth (the warranted rate of growth) and the amount which the capitalists actually plan to invest (the actual rate of growth), and (2) a discrepancy between the warranted rate and that made possible by growth of the labour-force and technical progress (the 'natural' rate) (see Harrod, 1948). Both of these can be logically derived from Marx's scheme.[22]

As we have seen, when the capitalists are assumed to invest only in their own business, the actual rate of growth might not equal the equilibrium

22. This is not to say that Marx himself formulated the problem exactly in this way or that he anticipated it. Sometimes the logical implications of an argument can only be set out with the benefit of hindsight.

one, except by accident. If the capitalists move their capital freely between departments an equilibrium can exist. In neither case does the equilibrium growth rate necessarily correspond to that of the labour force.

But Marx's analysis pinpoints another difficulty arising from the possibility of an imbalance between demand and supply at the level of individual sectors. This follows immediately when the *ex post* magnitudes in the equilibrium relations **8** and **14** are viewed in *ex ante* terms. That *partial* overproduction in this sense could give rise to a state of *general* overproduction was an explicit element in Marx's attack on Say's law (cf. Shoul, 1957).

It would have been natural to go on from this to ask: What is there to ensure that accumulation takes place at the appropriate rate? This is the problem of investment demand. An answer was found by later writers such as Lenin, Hilferding, and Rosa Luxemburg to lie in the growth of capital export and imperialism. Marx himself does not appear to have given much weight to the problem of investment demand; he tended to assume that competition would force the capitalists to reinvest their surplus in order to survive in the competitive struggle. The problem was to become a central element in Keynes's analysis of 'effective demand'.

As to which causal factor is the more important in explaining crises, the formal relations set out here are completely neutral. One cannot deduce from them support for either 'underconsumption' or 'disproportionality' as the primary cause of crises (cf. Sweezy, 1956, chapter 10). To choose between these different causes, if indeed a choice must be made, requires additional information about the particular behavioural relations which operate in the system. One must, as it were, 'look for the concrete social conditions of accumulation' (Luxemburg, 1951, p. 119).

Similarly, nothing can be deduced from the preceding analysis as to which department has priority in determining the equilibrium position of the system.[23]

As far as the theory of distribution involved here is concerned, it is evident that the crucial concept is *the rate of exploitation*. Regarded here simply as an exogenous constant, it was taken by Marx to be a function of the social relations operative under capitalism, in particular, the forces underlying the class struggle.[24] Once the rate of exploitation is given in this

23. Luxemburg (1951, p. 125) seemed to assign such priority to Department I as does much of subsequent Marxist literature. Priority of Department I in determining the long-run growth rate of the economy can be deduced from a condition of specificity of means of production in different departments plus restrictions on foreign trade (see the model of G. A. Feldman elaborated by Domar (1957)).

24. In particular, Marx (1968, p. 226) wrote: 'But as to *profits*, there exists no law which determines their *minimum*. We cannot say what is the ultimate limit of their decrease. And why cannot we fix that limit? Because, although we can fix the *minimum*

way the rate of profit can be derived from it, hence the corresponding prices.[25] In this sense the system is closed and internally consistent. Though as a theory of distribution the formulation is incomplete,[26] the essential

---

of wages, we cannot fix their *maximum*. We can only say that, the limits of the working day being given, the *maximum* of profit corresponds to the *physical minimum of wages*; and that wages being given, the maximum of profit corresponds to such a prolongation of the working day as is compatible with the physical forces of the labourer. The maximum of profit is, therefore, limited by the physical minimum of wages and the physical maximum of the working day. It is evident that between the two limits of this *maximum rate of profit* an immense scale of variations is possible. The fixation of its actual degree is only settled by the continuous struggle between capital and labour, the capitalist constantly tending to reduce wages to their physical minimum, and to extend the working day to its physical maximum, while the working man constantly presses in the opposite direction. The matter resolves itself into a question of the respective power of the combatants.'

25. How does the wage rate fit into all this? Unlike Malthus and Ricardo, Marx did not have a subsistence theory of the wage rate. The point is that labour power, being a commodity, has a value, the wage rate, which is equated to its cost of production. For Marx (1968, p. 211) this cost was equivalent to 'the value of the necessaries required to produce, develop, maintain and perpetutate the labour-power'. These 'necessaries' included also a 'historical and moral element'. That the wage rate is driven down to this level is the result of competition in the market for labour and the operation of the 'reserve army of labour', not of any law of population growth. The present analysis takes the rate of exploitation as given and shows the rate of profit consistent with it in a state of reproduction. Once the rate of profit is determined, the wage rate comes out in the wash (see note 9). The question, then, is thrown back from what determines the wage rate to what determines the rate of exploitation. To have both the wage rate and the rate of exploitation independently given would make the system overdetermined. From a strictly formal point of view, we could just as well have started from a given *value* of labour power specified in terms of the labour value of the physical bundle of 'necessaries' entering into the wage. The logic of the analysis would be equally clear-cut. The difference is that, in this case, we should have to take account of the possibility that the commodity composition of this bundle may vary with the distribution of the product. To take the wage as given in terms of an arbitrary commodity would have no definite meaning independent of prices when the wage consists of a heterogeneous collection of commodities. The rate of exploitation, being a ratio, value per unit of value, can well be taken as given independently of the price system. Sraffa (1960, p. 33) claims a similar significance for the rate of profit as the independent variable. But the rate of exploitation has the additional significance of expressing directly the social relation between classes. The rate of profit, on the other hand, expresses a relation between the capitalists: the rate at which each shares in the surplus accruing to the class as a whole and which is brought into uniformity by the forces of competition. In the context of investment decisions, the rate of profit is also a measure of *expected* capitalist income. Which of these possibilities one chooses is not a matter of logic but of the theory that goes with it and the concrete reality to which the theory is intended to apply.

26. It is incomplete because it takes as given that which is itself to be explained, namely, the share of profits in net product. This is a legitimate procedure as the first step in any scientific analysis. To say that the rate of exploitation is 'given' is, in this

feature of the approach is that the laws governing distribution are given by forces outside the system of prices and technology, the investigation of which is viewed as a matter of *political* economy.

That the model is highly aggregative (though less so by virtue of its two departments than the currently fashionable one-commodity model) is thus understandable. Indeed, from the standpoint of Marx's chief interest in the overall division of net product and his emphasis on the primacy of the rate of exploitation, it could not be otherwise. The question of relative prices of commodities is a decidedly subsidiary one. Moreover, as we have seen, prices can be introduced without altering the underlying conception. The 'transformation problem', nevertheless, points to the need to have a correct formulation of the relation between prices, technology and distribution.[27]

In the versions of expanded reproduction presented here, given the saving propensity of capitalists and workers and a particular rate of exploitation, there is no room for the rate of accumulation to adjust. It is this feature which explains the inability of the equilibrium rate of accumulation to coincide with the growth rate of the labour force. This is the exact reversal of the situation in Keynesian growth models where the distribution of income is viewed as adjusting to accommodate the rate of accumulation independently given either by the 'animal spirits' of capitalists or by the 'natural' growth rate (see Robinson, 1956; Kaldor, 1960, pp. 251–300; Pasinetti, 1962). A situation closely related to the Marxian conception can however be found in Robinson's concept of an 'inflation barrier'.[28]

In Harrod's model the rate of accumulation is fixed by a uniform saving rate and given ratio of capital to income; but there is nothing to determine the distribution of income.[29] The neoclassicals introduce the idea of substitution among different methods of production (an idea not developed systematically by Marx) and hope by this means to find a theory of distribution through profit-maximizing calculations leading to equality of the rate of profit and the 'marginal product of capital'. The logical difficulties in this approach have been exposed in the recent debate on reswitching of techniques (Harcourt, 1969; 'Symposium', 1966).

---

sense, not a mere definition but an expression of certain structural conditions in society which remain to be explained by attention to specific historical conditions.

27. That Marx himself was aware of the problem and subsequently returned to it is made clear by Meek (1967, pp. 143–57).

28. See Robinson (1956, pp. 48–50) and Harris (1967). Robinson suggests elsewhere (1965, pp. 32–4) that the Marxian conception might be more powerful than the Keynesian one in explaining particular phases in the historical development of capitalism. cf. also Kaldor's discussion of 'the first stage of capitalist evolution' (1960, pp. 294–6).

29. This point is developed in Harris (1970).

All of this is, of course, a long way from the actual conditions of modern capitalism where, presumably, different profit rates persist among different industries, monopoly affects price formation, accumulation and technical change go hand in hand, the price level and balance of payments enter the picture, and equilibrium is a spectre. Economic theory still has a far way to go in explaining how these things hang together.

References

BHADURI, A. (1969), 'On the significance of recent controversies on capital theory: a Marxian view', *Economic Journal*, September, pp. 532–9.

DOMAR, E. (1957), *Essays in the Theory of Economic Growth*, Oxford University Press, New York.

HARCOURT, G. C. (1969), 'Some Cambridge controversies in the theory of capital', *Journal of Economic Literature*, June, pp. 369–405.

HARRIS, D. J. (1967), 'Inflation, income distribution and capital accumulation in a two-sector model of economic growth', *Economic Journal*, December, pp. 814–33.

HARRIS, D. J. (1970), 'Growth Theory without the aggregate production function', Workshop Paper EME 7021, Social Systems Research Institute, University of Wisconsin.

HARROD, R. F. (1948), *Towards a Dynamic Economics*, Macmillan, London.

INADA, K. (1966), 'Investment in fixed capital and the stability of growth equilibrium', *Review of Economic Studies*, January, pp. 19–30.

KALDOR, N. (1960), *Essays on Economic Stability and Growth*, Free Press, Glencoe, Ill.

KRELLE, W. (1970), 'Marx as a growth theorist', Workshop Paper EME 7028, Social Systems Research Insistitute, University of Wisconsin.

LANGE, O. (1959), *Introduction to Econometrics*, Pergamon, New York.

LANGE, O. (1969), *Theory of Reproduction and Accumulation*, Pergamon, New York.

LUXEMBURG, R. (1951), *The Accumulation of Capital*, Routledge & Kegan Paul.

MARX, K. (1967), *Capital*, vols. I and II, International Publishers, New York.

MARX, K. (1968), 'Wages, price and profits', in K. Marx and F. Engels, *Selected Works of Marx and Engels*, International Publishers, New York.

MEEK, R. (1967), *Economics and Ideology and Other Essays*, Chapman & Hall.

MORISHIMA, M. (1956), 'An analysis of the capitalist process of reproduction', *Metroeconomica*, December, pp. 171–85.

MORISHIMA, M., and SETON, F. (1961), 'Aggregation in Leontief matrices and the labour theory of value', *Econometrica*, April, pp. 203–20.

NAQVI, K. (1960), 'Schematic presentation of accumulation in Marx', *Indian Economic Revue*, February, pp. 13–22.

PASINETTI, L. (1962), 'Rate of profit and income distribution in relation to the rate of economic growth', *Review of Economic Studies*, October, pp. 267–79.

ROBINSON, J. (1947), *An Essay on Marxian Economics*, Macmillan, London.

ROBINSON, J. (1951), 'Introduction', in R. Luxemburg, *The Accumulation of Capital*, Routledge & Kegan Paul.

ROBINSON, J. (1956), *The Accumulation of Capital*, Irwin, Homewood, Ill.

ROBINSON, J. (1965), 'Piero Sraffa and the rate of exploitation', *New Left Review*, May–June, pp. 28–34.

ROBINSON, J. (1969), 'Value and price', in *Marx and Contemporary Scientific*

Thought, Publications of the International Social Science Council no. 13, Mouton, The Hague.

SAMUELSON, P. (1957), 'Wages and interest: a modern dissection of Marxian economic models', *American Economic Review*, December, pp. 884–912.

SAMUELSON, P. (1962), 'Parable and realism in capital theory: the surrogate production function', *Review of Economic Studies*, June, pp. 193–206.

SETON, F. (1957), 'The "transformation problem"', *Review of Economic Studies*, vol. 24, pp. 149–60.

SHOUL, B. (1957), 'Karl Marx and Say's law', *Quarterly Journal of Economics*, November, pp. 611–29.

SRAFFA, P. (1960), *Production of Commodities by Means of Commodities*, Cambridge University Press.

SWEEZY, P. (1956), *The Theory of Capitalist Development*, Monthly Review Press, New York.

SYMPOSIUM ON PARADOXES IN CAPITAL THEORY, (1966), *Quarterly Journal of Economics*, November, pp. 503–83.

TSURU, S. (1956), 'Appendix A', in P. Sweezy, *The Theory of Capitalist Development*, Monthly Review Press, New York.

VON NEUMANN, J. (1945), 'A model of general economic equilibrium', *Review of Economic Studies*, pp. 1–9.

21 Ronald Meek

The Falling Rate of Profit

R. L. Meek, 'The falling rate of profit', in R. L. Meek, *Economics and Ideology and Other Essays*, Chapman & Hall, 1967, pp. 129–42.

1

The purpose of this essay is to clear up a point of some importance which for many years now has bedevilled arguments about Marx's 'law of the falling tendency of the rate of profit'.

The way in which Marx's theory is usually described, by both friends and foes alike, is something like this:[1] Take c (*constant capital*) to represent the value of used-up machinery, raw materials, etc., calculated in terms of units of embodied labour. Take v (*variable capital*) to represent the value of labour-power, also calculated in terms of units of embodied labour. And take s (*surplus value*) to represent the excess of value which the labour-power employed by v produces over and above its own value. Then the *total value* of an individual commodity, or of the output of an individual enterprise over a given period of time, or of the output of the economy as a whole over a given period of time, can be expressed in the familiar general formula:

Total value $= c+v+s$

Now define the ratio c/v as the *organic composition of capital*; s/v as the *rate of surplus value* (or, alternatively, the *rate of exploitation*); and $s/(c+v)$ as the *rate of profit*.[2] It can then easily be shown, by simple manipulation of these ratios,[3] that the rate of profit is connected with the rate of surplus value and the organic composition of capital in the following way:

$$\text{Rate of profit} = \frac{\text{Rate of surplus value}}{1+\text{Organic composition of capital}}$$

1. cf. Meek (1967, pp. 107–8).
2. If we take the rate of profit to be $s/(c+v)$, we are of course assuming that the elements of both c and v are turned over once during the period in question, so that $c+v$ also represents the *stock* of capital. This assumption is highly unrealistic, but since the complications which result from its removal do not affect the substance of the following argument we may ignore them.
3. Rate of profit $= s \div (c+v) = \dfrac{s}{v} \div \left(\dfrac{c+v}{v}\right) = \dfrac{s}{v} \div \left(1+\dfrac{c}{v}\right)$

It follows logically from these definitions that *if the rate of surplus value remains constant* a rise in the organic composition of capital will bring about a fall in the rate of profit. And this, it is claimed, is what Marx said would actually happen with the development of capitalism over time. As capitalism developed, machinery would be more and more substituted for labour; the organic composition of capital would therefore tend to rise; and the rate of profit would therefore tend to fall. There were of course certain 'counteracting influences' (e.g., rises in the 'intensity of exploitation' and falls in the value of 'elements of constant capital') which would retard the fall in the rate of profit, but the effect of these would not be sufficient to offset the effect of the rising organic composition of capital. At any rate in the long run, the rate of profit would fall.

It is around this version of Marx's theory that most of the recent controversy has centred. Two points of criticism in particular have been raised.

(*i*) The rate of profit will fall when organic composition rises *only if the rate of surplus value remains constant*. But in actual fact, it is argued, the postulated rise in organic composition will normally bring about a rise in productivity, which will affect (*inter alia*) the industries producing wage goods. As organic competition rises, the value of the elements of variable capital will tend to fall. Therefore, unless real wages rise in proportion to the rise in productivity (which Marx generally assumes will not in fact happen), the rate of surplus value is likely to rise when organic composition rises. And this rise in the rate of surplus value cannot legitimately be treated merely as a 'counteracting influence', since it is in fact an integral part of the general process of rising productivity which the postulated rise in organic composition will bring about. Thus, not only is Marx's procedure methodologically unsound, but it also turns out to be very doubtful whether one can in fact lay down any definite 'tendency' for the rate of profit to fall.

(*ii*) The substitution of machinery for labour as capitalism develops, it is argued, does not necessarily lead to an increase in organic composition *measured in terms of value* (*i.e.*, in terms of units of embodied labour). The increase in productivity which the substitution of machinery for labour brings about will reduce the value not only of wage goods but also of capital goods, with the result that organic composition in terms of value may not fall at all, or may fall only very slowly. Once again, it is claimed, it is methodologically illegitimate to treat this 'cheapening of elements of constant capital' as a mere 'counteracting influence', since it is in fact an integral part of the general process of rising productivity. And when this 'cheapening of elements of constant capital' is put together with the cheapening of elements of variable capital, it becomes quite impossible to make any generalizations at all concerning the direction in which the rate of profit will tend to move.

In the remainder of this essay, I shall try to sort out the elements of truth and the elements of falsity in these two criticisms.

2

Let us begin by considering the charge that Marx relegated the rise in the rate of surplus value, which the postulated rise in organic composition would bring about, to the status of a mere 'counteracting influence'.[4] If one looks carefully at the items which Marx considers under the heading 'Increasing Intensity of Exploitation' in his chapter on 'Counteracting Influences' in Volume III of *Capital*, one sees that they are in fact confined to certain means of the intensification of labour, the lengthening of the working day, etc., which are not essentially connected with the rise in organic composition and the consequent rise in productivity which it brings about.[5] And the reason why Marx here excludes the type of rise in the rate of surplus value which *is* essentially connected with the rise in organic composition is very simple: *he has already taken this type of rise into account* in his earlier chapter on 'The Law as Such'. Since this fact has been strenuously denied by many critics, detailed citations must be given.

It is true that in the illustration given at the beginning of the chapter on 'The Law as Such' Marx specifically assumes that the rate of surplus value remains constant as organic composition increases. But even in the paragraph which immediately follows and generalizes from this illustration, we find Marx saying that the rise in organic composition will cause a fall in the rate of profit 'at the same, *or even a rising*, degree of labour exploitation' (Marx, 1954–9, vol. II, p. 209; my italics)[6] – a form of words which is repeated several times in his subsequent exposition.[7] Two pages further on, having pointed out that 'what is true of different successive stages of development in one country, is also true of different coexisting stages of development in different countries', he proceeds to show how 'the difference between ... two national rates of profit might disappear, or

4. In this section, I shall be leaning heavily on an important and unduly neglected article, Rosdolsky (1956).

5. There are certain aspects of intensification, Marx explains, which do not affect the relation of the value of constant capital to the price of the labour which sets it in motion. 'Notably, it is prolongation of the working-day, this invention of modern industry, which increases the mass of appropriated surplus-labour without essentially altering the proportion of the employed labour-power to the constant capital set in motion by it' (Marx, 1954–9, vol. III, p. 228).

6. By a fateful mischance, the vital words which I have italicized were omitted from the well-known Kerr edition of Volume III (Marx, 1909, p. 249).

7. e.g., on pp. 211, 216 and 282 of Marx (1954–9, vol. III).

even be reversed, if labour were less productive in the less developed country', so that the value of labour-power was higher and the rate of surplus value accordingly lower (Marx, 1954–9, vol. III, p. 210). And this section of the chapter concludes with an illustration in which the rate of profit is shown to fall even though 'the unpaid part of the labour applied may at the same time grow in relation to the paid part' – i.e., even though the rate of surplus value rises owing to 'the greater productivity of labour' (Marx, 1954–9, vol. III, p. 212).

In the next section of the chapter, where Marx deals with the increase in the *mass* of surplus value which accompanies the accumulation of capital and the fall in the rate of profit, the question of the fundamental relation between organic composition and the rate of surplus value is not discussed, for the simple reason that it is not relevant. But even here Marx goes out of his way to point out that the mass of surplus value will grow if there is 'a drop in the value of wages due to an increase in the productiveness of labour' (Marx, 1954–9, vol. III, p. 215).

In the short section which follows, dealing with the question of the mass of profit contained in each individual commodity, we once again come face to face with the problem of the effect of a rising rate of surplus value. In spite of the rise in organic composition, says Marx, 'the mass of profits contained in the individual commodities may nevertheless increase if the rate of the absolute or relative surplus-value grows'. But this, he suggests, can be the case 'only within certain limits'. For a reason which I shall discuss below, he argues that 'the mass of profit on each individual commodity will shrink considerably with the development of the productiveness of labour, in spite of a growth in the rate of surplus-value' (Marx, 1954–9, vol. III, p. 221). And four pages further on, after Engels's interpolation on the question of the effect of differences in turnover periods on the rate of profit, Marx again returns to the same problem. He admits that 'considered abstractly' the rate of profit may remain the same or even rise, if the increase in the productivity of labour exercises its effects in certain ways upon the value of elements of constant and variable capital, but he argues, for the same reason as before, that 'in reality . . . the rate of profit will fall in the long run' (Marx, 1954–9, vol. III, p. 225).

It is quite clear, then, on the evidence of the chapter on 'The Law as Such' alone, that Marx was well aware of the fact that a rise in organic composition was likely to bring about a rise in the rate of surplus value, and that this fact was very relevant to the question of the behaviour of the rate of profit. And in subsequent chapters the point is made even more explicitly. In the chapter on 'Counteracting Influences', for example, Marx says that 'the tendency of the rate of profit to fall is bound up with a tendency of the rate of surplus-value to rise', because the rise in productivity associated with the rise in organic composition will lower the value of labour-power. 'The rate of profit', he argues, 'does not fall because labour becomes less productive, but because it becomes more productive. Both the rise in the rate of surplus-value and the fall in the rate of profit are but specific forms through which growing productivity of labour is expressed under capitalism' (Marx, 1954–9, vol. III, p. 234). In the chapter on 'Exposition of the Internal Contradictions of the Law', again, in a passage which most of the critics have either missed or misinterpreted, Marx repeats the point that the development of the productivity of labour shows itself not only in an increase in organic composition but also in a rise in the rate of surplus value. And once again, for the same reason as before, he argues that 'the compensation of the reduced number of labourers by intensifying the degree of exploitation has certain insurmountable limits' (Marx, 1954–9, vol. III, p. 242).[8]

What, then, was Marx's reason for believing that it had these 'insurmountable limits'? Why, in other words, did he believe that the downward pull on the rate of profit exercised by the rising organic composition of capital would be greater, at any rate 'in the long run', than the upward push exercised by the rising rate of surplus value? This problem is first raised in Volume I of *Capital*, a few pages before Marx embarks upon his study of relative surplus value. They key passage here is as follows:

The compensation of a decrease in the number of labourers employed, or of the amount of variable capital advanced, by a rise in the rate of surplus-value, or by the lengthening of the working-day, has impassable limits. Whatever the value of labour-power may be, whether the working-time necessary for the maintenance of the labourer is 2 or 10 hours, the total value that a labourer can produce, day in, day out, is always less than the value in which 24 hours are embodied ... The absolute limit of the average working-day – this being by nature always less than 24 hours – sets an absolute limit to the compensation of a reduction of variable capital by a higher rate of surplus-value, or of the decrease of the number of labourers exploited by a higher degree of exploitation of labour-power.

This 'palpable law', says Marx, 'is of importance for the clearing up of many phenomena, arising from a tendency (to be worked out later on) of capital to reduce as much as possible the number of labourers employed by it ...' (Marx, 1954–9, vol. I, p. 305).

It is this point which is emphasized in Marx's discussion of the law of the falling rate of profit in Volume III. 'Even a larger unpaid portion of the smaller total amount of newly added labour', he writes in the chapter on 'The Law as Such', 'is smaller than a small aliquot unpaid portion of the

8. Mr Rosdolsky (1956) has unearthed a number of passages in Marx's *Theories of Surplus Value* in which the point is made even more clearly.

former larger amount' (Marx, 1954–9, vol. III, p. 222).[9] A further example is given in the chapter on 'Exposition of the Internal Contractions of the Law': 'Two labourers, each working 12 hours daily, cannot produce the same mass of surplus-value as 24 who work only 2 hours, even if they could live on air and hence did not have to work for themselves at all' (Marx, 1954–9, vol. III, p. 242). As organic composition rises, less labourers than before will be employed with a given capital, and even if the rate of surplus value rises considerably the total mass of surplus value which that capital yields must necessarily (at any rate after a certain point) fall below its original level. This means that the rise in the rate of surplus value can compensate the effect of the rise in organic composition upon the rate of profit only within 'certain insurmountable limits'.

It is clear, then, that the first of the two criticisms described above is somewhat wide of the mark. In arguing that the tendency of the rate of profit was to fall as organic composition increased, Marx definitely did *not* assume that the rate of surplus value would remain constant. On the contrary, he fully recognized that a rise in organic composition would normally be accompanied by a rise in the rate of surplus value. He argued, however, that this rise in the rate of surplus value would not prevent the rate of profit from falling 'in the long run', and he adduced in support of this argument the reason just outlined.[10]

Marx can, however, be justly criticized for a certain lack of rigour in his argument. In some contexts he speaks of the falling tendency of the rate of profit in terms which suggest that he believed that it would tend to fall more or less continuously as organic composition increased.[11] In actual fact, however, all that his own argument as it stands really allows us to say is that as organic composition increases and the number of men employed with a given capital diminishes, there will eventually come a point beyond which no conceivable rise in the rate of surplus value – not even a rise to infinity – could possibly prevent the mass of surplus value produced by the given capital (and thus the rate of profit) from falling below its original level.[12] It is true, of course, that in the real world the

9. cf. Marx (1954–9, pp. 211–12 and 224–5), where the same point is clearly implied.

10. In his *Theories of Surplus Value*, as Mr Rosdolsky (1956) points out, Marx adduces certain additional reasons for his belief that the rise in the rate of surplus value will not be sufficient to prevent the rate of profit from falling. For one thing, the increase of productivity in agriculture will probably be less than its overall increase; and for another, the workers will probably enforce a rise in real wages as productivity increases. It has to be emphasized, however, that in the sections of *Capital* dealing with the falling rate of profit the reason outlined in the text is the only one which is mentioned.

11. See, e.g., Marx (1954–9, vol. III, p. 209).

12. If we start from a situation in which X men are employed with a given capital, the rate of surplus value being R, then the point in question will evidently be reached when the number of men employed with the given capital has fallen to $RX/(R+1)$.

rate of profit will probably begin to fall before this point is reached, since the rate of surplus value obviously cannot in fact rise to infinity.[13] But it is clear that under certain conditions (e.g., if we start from a situation in which the rate of surplus value is low), the rate of profit may not in fact begin to fall below its original level until the number of men employed with a given capital has been very substantially reduced. Marx's 'long run', in other words, may be very long indeed. And it is also clear that in the intervening period, under certain conditions which are by no means as exceptional as Marx seems to have believed, the rate of profit may well *rise* above its original level.[14] Marx's argument as it stands in *Capital* requires a certain amount of modification and elaboration before anything like a 'law of the falling tendency of the rate of profit' can properly be based on it.

3

The second criticism described above is rather more justified than the first. It is true that Marx *mentions* the 'cheapening of elements of constant capital' in his chapter on 'The Law as Such', but his references are purely incidental. For example he mentions, as an exception to the rule that the rate of profit will fall in spite of the increased rate of surplus value, the case where 'the productiveness of labour uniformly cheapens all elements of the constant, and the variable, capital' (Marx, 1954–9, vol. III, p. 222); and in another place he admits that the rate of profit 'could even rise if a rise in the rate of surplus-value were accompanied by a substantial reduction in the value of the elements of constant, and particularly of fixed capital' (Marx, 1954–9, vol. III, p. 225; cf. p. 243). But it does seem fair to complain that whereas the fall in the value of elements of *variable* capital is in effect taken into account by Marx in his basic chapter on 'The Law as Such', the fall in the value of elements of *constant* capital is treated merely as one of the 'counteracting influences'.

13. The point at which the rate of profit will in fact begin to fall below its original level can be defined in various ways, none of them particularly helpful except in a formal sense. Suppose that in an initial situation 1, the organic composition of capital is O_1, the number of men employed with a given capital is X_1, and the rate of surplus value is R_1. Suppose that in a later situation 2, the organic composition of capital is O_2, the number of men employed with the given capital is X_2, and the rate of surplus value is R_2. The rate of profit in situation 2 will have fallen below its level in situation 1 if $(O_1+1)/(O_2+1) < R_1/R_2$, or alternatively, if $X_1/X_2 > [R_2(R_1+1)]/[R_1(R_2+1)]$. These formulae, like that given in the previous footnote, are only valid if the length of the working day remains unchanged.

14. If, for example, we start from a situation in which the number of men employed with a given capital is 20 and the rate of surplus value is 1, and move to a situation in which the number of men employed is 15 and the rate of surplus value is 3, it is obvious that the rate of profit will rise.

I am not sure, however, whether this procedure involves quite such a grave methodological sin as some of Marx's critics have suggested. What Marx in effect does, in his chapter on 'The Law as Such', is to assume that the increase in the *mass* of constant capital relative to variable which takes place as capitalism develops does in fact reflect itself in some increase (though not necessarily a proportionate increase) in the *value* of the constant capital relative to that of the variable.[15] The effect of this *given* secular increase in value composition, he argues, will eventually be to lower the rate of profit, in spite of the rise in the rate of surplus value which will normally accompany it. Then later, in his chapter on 'Counteracting Influences', he reminds us of the fact (which he has already elaborated at considerable length in the first part of Volume III) that the 'cheapening of elements of constant capital' may well retard the decline in the rate of profit. This is at any rate one way of going about the job, and only a purist could really take exception to it on methodological grounds.

The main criticism which can properly be made of Marx's treatment of the problem is that nowhere does he precisely define the conditions under which the rate of profit will fall with a rising organic composition of capital, if we assume that this rising organic composition is associated with a lowering of the value of elements not only of variable but also of constant capital. As his argument stands, all he really says is (a) that there are certain 'insurmountable limits' to the extent to which the cheapening of elements of variable capital can offset the effect of a rising organic composition upon the rate of profit; and (b) that cases where the cheapening of elements of constant capital causes the rate of profit to rise or remain constant, although 'abstractly' possible, are very unlikely to be met with in practice. This is clearly not enough to support the general conclusions which Marx draws. In the next section of this essay, therefore, an attempt is made to provide a set of simple illustrations in which various different assumptions are made about, for example, the functional relation between increases in organic composition and increases in productivity, and on the basis of which a number of generalizations are made about the conditions under which the rate of profit will in fact fall.

4

What we shall do, in effect, is to imagine the average organic composition of capital over the economy as a whole gradually increasing from a fairly low level to a fairly high one. We shall halt the process at various stages, and examine what happens to the rate of profit when we make various

15. Marx's reasons for making this assumption are well described by Mr Rosdolsky (1956).

assumptions about the effect of the rise in organic composition upon productivity.

Case 1: As our first case, let us start with a situation in which technical conditions are such that over the economy as a whole the average 100 of capital employs 20 men. We assume that the length of the working day is 8 hours, and that the daily wage (equal to the value of labour-power) is 4, whence it follows that the rate of surplus value is 1. Taking one day's operations as our basis, the situation will be as follows:

c	v	s	
20	80	80	**1**

The 20 men will produce a total of 160 new value, of which 80 represents their wages and 80 the surplus value accruing to the capitalist. Organic composition is $\frac{1}{4}$, and the rate of profit is 80 per cent.

In this initial situation, 20 men are employed in conjunction with 20 constant capital – i.e., constant capital per man employed is 1. Let us now suppose that technical innovations are introduced which raise constant capital per man from 1 to $2\frac{2}{3}$. In other words, at the current prices for wage goods and capital goods (which we assume for the moment to be unaffected by the technical innovations, for every $2\frac{2}{3}$ spent on constant capital, 4 will be spent on wages. This means that the average 100 of capital will be divided between 40 constant and 60 variable, 15 men being employed. The situation will be as follows:

c	v	s	
40	60	60	**2A**

The rate of surplus value will remain at 1, but organic composition will rise to $\frac{2}{3}$ and the rate of profit will fall to 60 per cent.

Now it is very probable that the increase in organic composition from $\frac{1}{4}$ to $\frac{2}{3}$ will raise productivity, in both the wage-goods and capital-goods industries. Let us assume that the increase in productivity is such as to reduce the value of all elements of constant and variable capital by $\frac{1}{4}$. This means that the elements of constant capital which cost 40 in situation **2A** can now be bought for 30, and that the 15 men who require to be employed in conjunction with this amount of constant capital can now be obtained at a wage of 3 per day instead of 4 – i.e., for a total expenditure of 45 instead of 60. The organic composition of the average 100 of capital will not change as compared with situation **2A**, since the values of the elements of both constant and variable capital have been reduced equally, but both the mass of constant capital and the number of labourers employed will increase by $\frac{1}{3}$ as compared with situation **2A**. 20 men will now be employed with the average 100 of capital, creating in the day's operations 160 new value, of which 60 will represent their wages and 100 the surplus value accruing to the capitalist. The situation will be as follows:

c	v	s	
40	60	100	**2B**

The rate of surplus value will rise to $1\frac{2}{3}$, and the rate of profit will rise to 100 per cent.[16]

Now suppose that further technical innovations are introduced which, at current prices, raise constant capital per man to $4\frac{1}{2}$. In other words, for every $4\frac{1}{2}$ spent on constant capital, 3 will be spent on wages, so that the average 100 of capital will be divided between 60 constant and 40 variable, $13\frac{1}{3}$ men being employed. The situation will be as follows:

c	v	s	
60	40	67	**3A**

Now assume that another increase in productivity, such that the elements of both constant and variable capital are reduced in value by a further $\frac{1}{4}$, follows the technical innovations. The wage will now fall to $2\frac{1}{4}$, and $17\frac{7}{9}$ men (as compared with 20 in situation **2B**) will be employed with the average 100 of capital. The general situation will be as follows:

c	v	s	
60	40	102	**3B**

The rate of surplus value will rise to $2\frac{11}{20}$, and the rate of profit will rise to 102 per cent.

Finally, suppose further technical innovations which raise constant capital per man to 9, and assume that the consequential increase in pro-

16. If the increase in productivity had affected only the elements of variable capital, reducing their value by $\frac{1}{4}$ but leaving the elements of constant capital unaffected, the average 100 of capital would have been divided between 47 constant and 53 variable, with a rate of profit of 88 per cent. If on the other hand the increase in productivity had affected only the elements of constant capital, reducing their value by $\frac{1}{4}$ but leaving the elements of variable capital unaffected, the average 100 of capital would have been divided between 33 constant and 67 variable, with a rate of profit of 67 per cent. Clearly the role played by the cheapening of elements of variable capital in retarding 'the falling tendency of the rate of profit' is much more important than that played by the cheapening of elements of constant capital. The reason for this is fairly obvious: under given technical conditions, a cheapening of elements of variable capital not only increases the number of workers employed with a given capital, but also increases the proportion of unpaid to paid labour time. A cheapening of the elements of constant capital, on the other hand, although it also increases the number of workers employed with a given capital, has no effect at all on the proportion of unpaid to paid labour time.

ductivity reduces the values of the elements of constant and variable capital by a further $\frac{1}{4}$. The **A** and **B** situations, before and after the change in productivity, will be as follows:

c	v	s	
80	20	51	**4A**
80	20	75	**4B**

In the final situation $11\frac{23}{27}$ men will be employed, the rate of surplus value will rise to $3\frac{3}{4}$, and the rate of profit will fall to 75 per cent.

In relation to our problem, the relevant comparisons are of course between situations **1**, **2B**, **3B** and **4B**. Calling these four situations simply **1**, **2**, **3**, and **4**, we may summarize our results as follows:

	Organic Composition	Assumed reduction in value of c and v	Rate of surplus value	Rate of profit (%)
1	$\frac{1}{4}$	–	1	80
2	$\frac{2}{3}$	$\frac{1}{4}$	$1\frac{2}{3}$	100
3	$1\frac{1}{2}$	$\frac{1}{4}$	$2\frac{11}{20}$	102
4	4	$\frac{1}{4}$	$3\frac{3}{4}$	75

On the assumptions of our first case, then, the rate of profit rises during the first three stages, but falls at the last stage.

Case 2: Using the same method of procedure, and halting the process at the same stages, we now take a case where we start with a rate of surplus value of 1, as before, but where the increase in productivity associated with each move from one stage to the next is assumed to reduce the value of the elements of constant and variable capital by $\frac{1}{8}$, instead of by $\frac{1}{4}$ as before. The result is as follows:

	Organic composition	Assumed reduction in value of c and v	Rate of surplus value	Rate of profit (%)
1	$\frac{1}{4}$	–	1	80
2	$\frac{2}{3}$	$\frac{1}{8}$	$1\frac{17}{60}$	77
3	$1\frac{1}{2}$	$\frac{1}{8}$	$1\frac{3}{5}$	64
4	4	$\frac{1}{8}$	2	40

The increase in productivity associated with the rising organic composition of capital is in this case too small to prevent the rate of profit from falling continuously.

Case 3: We now take a case where the rate of surplus value in the initial stage is $\frac{1}{2}$, and where each move is assumed to reduce the value of the elements of constant and variable capital by $\frac{1}{4}$. The result is as follows:

	Organic composition	*Assumed reduction in value of c and v*	*Rate of surplus value*	*Rate of profit (%)*
1	$\frac{1}{4}$	–	$\frac{1}{2}$	40
2	$\frac{2}{3}$	$\frac{1}{4}$	1	60
3	$1\frac{1}{2}$	$\frac{1}{4}$	$1\frac{27}{40}$	67
4	4	$\frac{1}{4}$	$2\frac{11}{20}$	51

The rate of profit begins by rising, and falls only at the last stage; but even at the last stage it remains higher than it was in the initial stage. (Compare case 2.)

Case 4: We now take a case where the rate of surplus value in the initial stage is $1\frac{1}{2}$, and where each move is assumed to reduce the value of the elements of constant and variable capital by $\frac{1}{4}$. The result is as follows:

	Organic composition	*Assumed reduction in value of c and v*	*Rate of surplus value*	*Rate of profit (%)*
1	$\frac{1}{4}$	–	$1\frac{1}{2}$	120
2	$\frac{2}{3}$	$\frac{1}{4}$	$2\frac{1}{3}$	140
3	$1\frac{1}{2}$	$\frac{1}{4}$	$3\frac{9}{20}$	138
4	4	$\frac{1}{4}$	$4\frac{19}{20}$	99

The rate of profit begins by rising, but falls at an earlier stage than in case 3.

Case 5: We now take a case where the rate of surplus value in the initial stage is 1, and where each move is assumed to reduce the value of the elements of constant capital by $\frac{1}{8}$ and of variable capital by $\frac{1}{4}$. The result is as follows:[17]

17. In cases 5 and 6 the actual organic composition at each stage, when the effect of the increase in productivity has been taken into account, will be rather different from that shown in the first column of the tables. In these two cases readings of organic composition are taken at the 'A' stages, whereas readings of the rate of surplus value and rate of profit are taken at the 'B' stages.

	Organic composition	Assumed reduction in value of c	and v	Rate of surplus value	Rate of profit (%)
1	$\frac{1}{4}$	–	–	1	80
2	$\frac{2}{3}$	$\frac{1}{8}$	$\frac{1}{4}$	$1\frac{37}{80}$	93
3	$1\frac{1}{2}$	$\frac{1}{8}$	$\frac{1}{4}$	$2\frac{5}{9}$	92
4	4	$\frac{1}{8}$	$\frac{1}{4}$	$3\frac{13}{18}$	67

Case 6: Finally, we take a case where the rate of surplus value in the initial stage is 1, and where each move is assumed to reduce the value of the elements of constant capital by $\frac{1}{4}$ and of variable capital by $\frac{1}{8}$. The result is as follows:

	Organic composition	Assumed reduction in value of c	and v	Rate of surplus value	Rate of profit (%)
1	$\frac{1}{4}$	–	–	1	80
2	$\frac{2}{3}$	$\frac{1}{4}$	$\frac{1}{8}$	$1\frac{9}{32}$	82
3	$1\frac{1}{2}$	$\frac{1}{4}$	$\frac{1}{8}$	$1\frac{27}{44}$	71
4	4	$\frac{1}{4}$	$\frac{1}{8}$	2	46

In this case the initial rise in the rate of profit is relatively small as compared with case 5, and the fall, when it occurs, is much more drastic.

This problem obviously cries out for mathematical treatment (which the present writer is not equipped to provide), and it would obviously be unsafe to come to any very firm conclusions on the basis of a mere half-dozen examples of the type given above. But the following tentative generalizations may perhaps be made.

(*i*) In all the cases considered, except number 2 (where the assumed rise in productivity is very small), the rate of profit begins by rising above its original level, and the direction of its movement does not change until the process of rising organic composition has got well under way. If we start from a fairly low level of organic composition, then, I think it can possibly be said that on Marx's premises the 'tendency' of the rate of profit is first to rise, and then some time afterwards to fall.[18]

(*ii*) The initial rise in the rate of profit will be higher and the point of downturn will be later (a) the lower is the rate of surplus value in the

18. cf. the conclusions reached by Dickinson (1956–7).

situation from which we start; (b) the greater is the rise in overall productivity associated with the rising organic composition; and (c) the greater is the rise in productivity in the wage-goods industries relatively to that in the capital-goods industries.

5

In conclusion, one important point must be emphasized. The fact that the 'tendency' just described appears in Marx's model does not of course mean that it will necessarily appear in the real world. It is true that Marx built his model in an endeavour to explain a *real* tendency for the rate of profit to fall which had apparently shown itself before his time[19] and which he undoubtedly believed would continue to show itself in the future. But such a model, because of the complexity of the processes actually involved, can in itself really do little more than draw attention to the main determining factors and the general manner of their interaction; and it can be used for purposes of prediction only (a) if the assumptions of the model are true of the real world, and (b) if the subsidiary determining factors abstracted from in the model do not exercise any significant influence. And these are two very big 'if's' indeed. For example, it is assumed in Marx's model that real wages remain constant as productivity increases, and that the effect of increasing productivity in the capital-goods industries is merely to retard, and not actually to prevent, the secular increase of organic composition in value terms. In a world in which these assumptions are not valid, and in which, in addition, certain factors abstracted from in the model (the intensification of labour and the prevalence of monopoly, for example) have become significant, it is virtually impossible to predict how the rate of profit will in fact behave.

We should not be too disappointed, then, if the statistics we gather do not in fact show a 'falling tendency of the rate of profit'.[20] The main value of Marx's model in the present-day world is two-fold. In the first place, it provides us with a conceptual framework within which certain problems relating to the long-term behaviour of the rate of profit may perhaps be usefully considered. And in the second place, it keeps before our eyes the extremely important fact that changes in the rate of profit depend not on

19. It is quite possible that such a tendency had not in actual fact revealed itself in the preceding period. It is true that the rate of profit on *commercial* capital in the earlier stages of capitalist development was higher than the rate of profit on *productive* capital in the later stages. It is also true that the rate of interest on loans *for personal consumption* in the earlier stages of capitalist development was higher than the rate of interest on loans *for productive purposes* in the later stages. But it is not logical to deduce from these facts alone (as many contemporary economists did) that the tendency of the rate of profit on productive capital is to fall.

20. cf. Gillman (1958, *passim*).

technical factors alone, but rather on the interaction of these with sociological factors.[21]

Postscript

If I were rewriting this article today, I do not think I would wish to withdraw any of the points of substance, but there are two or three places in
which I would try to make their presentation a little clearer. The main
passage which now seems to me to lack sufficient clarity is that on pp.
207–9, where I describe Marx's reason for claiming that a rise in the rate
of surplus value can compensate the effect of a rise in the organic composition of capital upon the rate of profit only within 'certain insurmountable limits'. Since there is still a great deal of misunderstanding of this
matter in the current literature, it might be worth while to give here a
simple illustration of Marx's point.[22]

Suppose we start off in year A with a situation in which over the economy
as a whole each unit of capital (each 100, say, or each 1,000 or 10,000)
employs 20 men. The length of the working day, let us assume, is 12 hours,
and the 'value' (in Marx's sense) of a day's labour power is 8 hours.
Under these circumstances, each man employed will produce a surplus
value of 4 per day, so that the total amount of surplus value yielded per
unit of capital will be 80 per day.

Suppose now that we move to a later year B in which each unit of
capital employs 10 men instead of 20. It does not necessarily follow that
the amount of surplus value yielded per unit of capital will fall below its
previous level: the effect of this particular rise in organic composition
could conceivably be compensated by an increase in the length of the
working day, or by a reduction in the value of labour power. If, for example, the length of the working day were increased from 12 to 16 hours
(the value of labour power remaining at 8), or if the value of labour power
were reduced from 8 to 4 (the length of the working day remaining at 12),
surplus value per unit of capital would remain at the same level as before
– i.e. 80 per day.

But if the number of men employed with each unit of capital continues
to decrease, there must come a point beyond which full compensation of
this type is no longer possible, so that surplus value per unit of capital
(i.e., roughly, the rate of profit) must necessarily fall. Suppose, for example,
that we move from B to a later year C in which each unit of capital employs only 3 men. It can easily be shown that the effect of *this* rise in
organic composition upon the rate of profit could *not* conceivably be

21. cf. Meek (1967, p. 112).
22. This illustration is similar in essence to the very abbreviated one used by Marx
himself in *Capital* (quoted above, p. 208).

compensated. For suppose – to take the extreme case – that the length of the working day were increased to its absolute maximum of 24 hours, *and* that at the same time the value of a day's labour power were reduced to its absolute minimum of zero. In spite of this, surplus value per unit of capital would necessarily fall to 72 per day.

What this illustration shows is that on Marx's assumptions the possibility of compensating the effect of a rise in organic composition upon the rate of profit by a rise in the rate of surplus value (however caused) has certain impassable limits.

R. L. M.
September 1975

References

DICKINSON, H. D. (1956–7), 'The falling rate of profit in Marxian economics', *Review of Economic Studies*, vol. 24, pp. 120ff.

GILLMAN, J. (1958), *The Falling Rate of Profit*, New York.

MARX, K. (1909), *Capital*, Volume III, Charles H. Kerr, Chicago.

MARX, K. (1954–9), *Capital*, Foreign Languages Publishing House, Moscow.

MEEK, R. (1967), *Economics and Ideology and Other Essays*, Chapman & Hall.

ROSDOLSKY, R. (1956), 'Zur neuren Kritik des Marxschen Gesetzes der fallenden Profitrate', *Kyklos*, vol. 9, no. 2.

22 Arnold Heertje

An Essay on Marxian Economics*

Arnold Heertje, 'An Essay on Marxian economics', *Schweizerische Zeitschrift für Volkswirtschaft und Statistik*, vol. 108, 1972, pp. 33–45.

1 Introduction

In this essay we propose to discuss some aspects of Marxian economics in the light of modern economic theory. In particular, we want to lay stress on the types of technical change implied in Marx's thinking. In order to arrive at some rigour of the analysis we shall start from a model developed by Samuelson (1957), which has been used to harmonize neoclassical and Marxian conclusions to some extent. Although we do not base our considerations on the view that a capitalist economic system adjusts itself to technical change in the smooth way, as Samuelson assumed, we employ his model as a starting point for our analysis. The plan of the paper is as follows. In Section 2 we describe the main features of Samuelson's model. Section 3 is devoted to a compact synopsis of Marx's opinions on technical change. In Section 4 we describe in short Marx's position with respect to the compensation theory of labour. In Sections 5 and 6 we study the relations between the accumulation process, labour productivity and the organic composition of capital. Types of technical change are discussed in Section 7. Section 8 is devoted to an analysis of the relations between technical change and the labour market. Then we make some remarks on the impact of technical change on the market form. In Section 10 some conclusions are formulated.

2 Samuelson's model of Marx

Following Samuelson's interpretation of Marx, we introduce two industries I and II. Industry I produces homogeneous capital goods called K and Industry II produces homogeneous consumption goods called Y. Production in both industries requires homogeneous labour $L_1 + L_2 = L$ and capital goods $K_1 + K_2 = K$. We restrict ourselves to the case of simple reproduction. We assume that the production functions are of the Leontief

* I would like to express my gratitude to Prof. Dr P. Hennipman, who suggested several improvements of an earlier draft, and to Dr J. B. Polak who corrected my English.

type and that the capital stock adjusts itself to the fixed quantity of labour L.

So we deal with the following set of relations:

$$L_1 = a_1 K \qquad K_1 = b_1 K$$
$$L_2 = a_2 Y \qquad K_2 = b_2 Y$$

Where (a_1, a_2, b_1, b_2) are technical coefficients, all > 0. The system can be summarized by:

$$a_1 K + a_2 Y = L$$
$$b_1 K + b_2 Y = K \qquad\qquad 1$$

Now K and Y can be expressed in terms of the given quantity of labour L.

$$Y = \frac{1-b_1}{a_2(1-b_1)+a_1 b_2} . L$$

$$K = \frac{b_2}{a_2(1-b_1)+a_1 b_2} . L \qquad\qquad 2$$

Samuelson now introduces a price system (p_1, p_2, w, r), where p_1 is the price for capital goods, p_2 the price for consumption goods, w the wage rate and r the rate of interest. Assuming perfect competition the following price relations hold:

$$p_1 = (wa_1 + p_1 b_1)(1+r);$$
$$p_2 = (wa_2 + p_1 b_2)(1+r). \qquad\qquad 2'$$

For the relation of p_1 and w we find the following expression:

$$\frac{p_1}{w} = \frac{a_1(1+r)}{1-b_1(1+r)}. \qquad\qquad 3$$

It is also possible to calculate the real wage rate w/p_2 from the model.

Now the following money flows can be calculated for the two sectors:

$$p_1 K = (wL_1 + p_1 K_1)(1+r);$$
$$p_2 Y = (wL_2 + p_1 K_2)(1+r). \qquad\qquad 4$$

Samuelson proposes to interpret $p_1 K_1$ as the Marxian constant capital C_1 and $p_1 K_2$ as the Marxian constant capital C_2. Furthermore, it has been suggested that we consider wL_1 and wL_2 as the Marxian variable capital V_1 and V_2 respectively, so that the surplus values S_1 and S_2 are the differences between the receipts of industry I or industry II and the sum of the constant and variable capital $C_1 + V_1$, or $C_2 + V_2$ respectively. For S_1 and S_2 we get:

$$S_1 = (C_1 + V_1) r;$$
$$S_2 = (C_2 + V_2) r. \qquad\qquad 5$$

As we shall make extensive use of the concept of the 'organic composition of capital' we derive an expression for it in terms of Samuelson's model. Let us define the organic composition of capital as C_i/V_i, we then have:

$$\frac{C_1}{V_1} = \frac{p_1 K_1}{wL_1} = \frac{a_1(1+r)}{1-b_1(1+r)} \cdot \frac{b_1}{a_1} = \frac{b_1(1+r)}{1-b_1(1+r)}; \qquad 6$$

$$\frac{C_2}{V_2} = \frac{p_1 K_2}{wL_2} = \frac{a_1(1+r)}{1-b_1(1+r)} \cdot \frac{b_2}{a_2} = \frac{a_1 b_2(1+r)}{a_2[1-b_1(1+r)]}; \qquad 7$$

$$\frac{C}{V} = \frac{C_1+C_2}{V_1+V_2} = \frac{p_1 K}{wL} = \frac{a_1(1+r)}{1-b_1(1+r)} \cdot \frac{b_2}{a_2(1-b_1)+a_1 b_2}$$

$$= \frac{a_1 b_2(1+r)}{\{1-b_1(1+r)\}\{a_2(1-b_1)+a_1 b_2\}}.$$

The condition for the equality of the organic composition of capital in both sectors reads $a_1 b_2 = a_2 b_1$.

Some of the typical conclusions of Marx are consistent with this model of Samuelson and others are not. The next sections give some attention to this matter.

3 Technical change in Marxian economics

In the sketch Marx gives of the development of manufacturing which can be conceived of as the starting point for industrial capitalism, the influence of the changes in the structure of production on the division of labour has been made clear repeatedly. Marx illustrates the interwovenness of the relations that characterize the continuously changing conditions of production by looking at the division of labour as a consequence of dynamics. As soon as manufacture reaches a certain size, it becomes the typical form of the capitalist mode of production, but at the same time its own narrow technical basis conflicts . . . *mit den von ihr selbst geschaffnen Produktionsbedürfnissen*'[1] (Marx, 1872, Bd I, p. 343).

Manufacture creates the field of application for the construction and production of machines: '*Dieses Produkt der manufaktormässigen Theilung der Arbeit produzierte seinerseits – Maschinen*'[2] (Marx, 1872, Bd I, p. 383). The end of manufacture is the beginning of big business, of mechanization and of accumulation of capital. Each movement, even the smallest one, is a fundamental change. Capital '. . . *muss die technischen und gesellschaftlichen Bedingungen des Arbeitsprozesses, also die Produktionsweise selbst*

1. '. . . with the production needs which it itself has created' [Eds.].
2. 'This product of the manufacturing division of labour produced for its part-machines' [Eds.].

Arnold Heertje 221

umwälzen, um die Produktivkraft der Arbeit zu erhöhen . . .[3] (Marx, 1872, Bd I, p. 321). We note that Marx, in order to explain the main lines of the evolution and to relate them to micro-economic details, devotes much more attention to the factual aspects of machinery than his predecessors. It seems as if Marx uses a magnifying glass in order to improve the position of the telescope. His description runs from tools to automatic systems and leads to the conclusion that the technical basis of big business is the production of machines by machines. The new type of division of labour depends on the nature of the machines. Machinery overthrows the old system of division of labour. In the manufacture the workman was a tool, '*in der Fabrik dient er der Maschine*'[4] (Marx, 1872, Bd I, p. 444). The accumulation of capital consists of the transformation of surplus value in dead production factors and living labour. The first category Marx calls constant capital, the second category he calls variable capital. Surplus value only springs from variable capital. The composition of constant and variable capital in Marxian terminology is the 'organic composition of capital'. Marx starts from the assumption that the organic composition of capital remains constant, so that '. . . *eine bestimmte Masse Produktionsmittel oder konstantes Kapital stets dieselbe Masse Arbeitskraft erheischt, um in Bewegung gesetzt zu werden . . .*'[5] (Marx, 1872, Bd I, p. 637). The demand for labour then is in proportion to the growth of capital. In this case it is possible that the demand for labour is greater than its supply, so that '. . . *die Arbeitslöhne steigen*'[6] (Marx, 1872, Bd I, p. 638). Although this situation may be considered favourable for the workmen, it does not bring to an end '. . . *das Abhängigkeitsverhältnis und die Exploitation*'[7] (Marx, 1872, Bd I, p. 643). As long as the increase of wages does not slow down the rate of accumulation, the increase of wages may continue. As soon as pessimistic profit expectations play their part, however, the wage increase and its effect disappear together. The capitalist mechanism '. . . *besiegt also selbst die Hindernisse, die er vorübergehend schafft*'[8] (Marx, 1872, Bd I, p. 645).

Marx now considers the case in which the '*bösartige Voraussetzung*'[9] (Marx, 1953a, p. 293) that the organic composition of capital remains

3. '. . . must revolutionize the technical and social conditions of the labour process, that is, the mode of production itself, in order to raise the productive power of labour' [Eds.]

4. 'in the factory he serves the machine' [Eds.].

5. '. . . a specific quantity of means of production always requires the same quantity of labour power to set it in regular motion' [Eds.].

6. '. . . wages rise' [Eds.]

7. '. . . the dependency relationship and the exploitation' [Eds.].

8. '. . . thus itself overcomes the obstacles which it temporarily creates' [Eds.].

9. 'Malicious supposition' [Eds.].

constant, does not hold. Capitalism always produces a phase in which the accumulation of capital implies a permanent change in the organic composition of capital. These changes are related to the increase of labour productivity: '*Die Masse der Produktionsmittel, womit er* [the labourer] *funktioniert, wächst mit der Produktivität seiner Arbeit*'[10] (Marx, 1872, Bd I, p. 647).

As a consequence of the increase of labour productivity constant capital increases and variable capital declines, so that the organic composition of capital rises. The accumulation goes hand in hand with the concentration of more capital in the hands of many individual capitalists. On this footing large-scale industries can be built in order to raise the productivity of labour again. This type of concentration is limited by the rate of growth of the '. . . *gesellschaftlichen Reichtums*'[11] (Marx, 1872, Bd I, p. 650) and is also characterized by a uniform distribution of capital over many capitalists, who as producers compete with each other. Concentration in this sense should be clearly distinguished from centralization: '*Es ist Konzentration bereits gebildeter Kapitale, Aufhebung ihrer individuellen Selbständigkeit, Expropriation von Kapitalist durch Kapitalist, Verwandlung vieler kleinerer in wenige grössere Kapitale*[12] (Marx, 1872, Bd I, p. 651). Centralization is not limited by the growth of production and accumulation. Competition expels the producers who hesitate to introduce new methods of production because they are not able to lower their prices, a price cut being made possible by an increase of labour productivity. Labour productivity does not only depend on improved technology but also on the scale of production. '*Die grösseren Kapitale schlagen daher die Kleineren*'[13] (Marx, 1872, Bd I, p. 651). This again implies a fundamental change in the structure of production, because the centralization indicates the period in which large-scale industry came up in order to deal with big projects, such as the construction of railways.

Centralization embodied in the form of innovations, increases the social power of capital. During the process of accumulation, the capitalist has been modified from a powerless object to a subject with power.

4 The labour market

Marx underlines the well-known opinion of Ricardo: 'Machinery and labour are in constant competition' (Ricardo, 1817, p. 479). Marx also

10. 'The quantity of means of production with which he works grows with the productivity of his labour' [Eds.].

11. 'Social wealth' [Eds.].

12. 'It [centralization] is the concentration of already created capitals, the sublation [*Aufhebung*] of their individual independence, the expropriation of capitalist by capitalist,the transformation of many smaller into a few larger capitals' [Eds.].

13. 'Thus the larger capitals beat the smaller' [Eds.].

distinguishes between sudden and evolutionary forms of mechanization, but in both cases labour is on the wrong side of the table. The kind of optimism one finds in the different types of the compensation theory is not shared by Marx. If labourers thrown out of industry A can find work in industry B, this is due to new investment, but not to a change in the existing structure of capital. Only new capital formation can create employment. If accumulation takes place with a constant organic composition of capital, the demand for labour rises. These periods are periods of rest in capitalistic development, but with the progress of accumulation they become shorter, the organic composition of capital augmenting as a consequence of the increase of labour productivity and centralization becoming more important. The industrial reserve army increases while the substitution of capital for labour overcompensates the demand for labour due to accumulation, to '*Luxusproduktion*' and to the use of labour in unproductive jobs. Wages going down, the demand for consumption declines, which again weakens the motive to invest. ' *Die Akkumulation von Reichtum auf den einen Pol ist also zugleich Akkumulation von Elend, Arbeitsqual, Sklaverei, Unwissenheit, Brutalisierung und moralischer Degradation auf dem Gegenpol, d.h. auf Seite der Klasse, die ihr eigenes Produkt als Kapital produziert*'[14] (Marx, 1872, Bd I, p. 671).

5 Accumulation, labour productivity and organic composition of capital

Let us try to study more carefully the relations between accumulation, labour productivity and the organic composition of capital. To this end we start from the stationary variant of Samuelson's model, which makes clear the Marxian division of the economy in two sectors and defines Marxian concepts in a straightforward way. Our procedure does not imply a judgement on the adequacy of Samuelson's model as a good description of Marx' theory.

In the following table the data we need for our investigation are summarized. For each sector we have calculated labour productivity, the capital–output ratio and the organic composition of capital. The quantities have also been determined for the economy as a whole. We shall consider the rate of interest as a constant.

Now, Marx starts with the assumption that during the process of accumulation the organic composition of capital remains constant. Let us first assume that the partial organical compositions of capital are equal. In terms of the model this means $a_1b_2 = a_2b_1$, and the organic composition

14. 'The accumulation of wealth at one pole is thus also the accumulation of misery, torment of work, slavery, ignorance, brutalization and moral degradation at the other pole, that is, on the part of the class which produces its own product as capital' [Eds.].

	Sector I	Sector II	Total
Labour productivity	$\dfrac{1}{a_1}$	$\dfrac{1}{a_2}$	$\dfrac{1-b_1+b_2}{a_2(1-b_1)+a_1b_2}$
Capital–output ratio	b_1	b_2	$\dfrac{b_2}{1-b_1+b_2}$
Organic composition of capital	$\dfrac{b_1(1+r)}{1-b_1(1+r)}$	$\dfrac{a_1(1+r)b_2}{a_2-a_2b_1(1+r)}$	$\dfrac{a_1b_2(1+r)}{\{1-b_1(1+r)\}\{a_2(1-b_1)+a_1b_2\}}$

of capital everywhere in the economy then is $\dfrac{b_1(1+r)}{1-b_1(1+r)}$. The constancy of this expression then means that the technical coefficient b_1 is a constant. In other words the capital–output ratio of Sector I remains constant. Now, it seems reasonable to assume that Marx had in mind that the capital–output ratio of Sector II, the input coefficient b_2, remains constant. In this particular case a constant organic composition of capital implies constant capital–output ratios. With respect to the coefficients a_1 and a_2, we still have a choice. Again, it seems probable that Marx considered these labour input coefficients as constants, but it is by no means necessary to make this assumption. It does not contradict the Marxian assumption of a constant organic composition of capital to suppose that labour productivity in both sectors increases at a uniform rate k, so that $a_1(t) = a_1(o)e^{-kt}$ and $a_2(t) = a_2(o)e^{-kt}$ with $k > 0$. In this situation we are confronted with technical change which does not affect the partial and total organic composition of capital. Assuming a constant rate of growth, in Marxian terminology a constant rate of accumulation, it depends on the ratio of this rate and k whether labourers are thrown out or not. It appears that Marx did not reflect on this case, as according to him a constant organic composition of capital combined with the given rate of accumulation provokes an increasing demand for labour. To this end the assumption is necessary that all coefficients (a_1, a_2, b_1, b_2) remain constant.

Let us now suppose that the partial organic compositions of capital are not equal, so that $a_1b_2 = a_2b_1$ does not hold. In that case all four coefficients enter in the expression for the total organic composition of capital. The most simple procedure would be to assume that all coefficients remain constant, that is all capital–output ratios and productivities of labour remain constant. Then there is no question of technical change. However, it is possible to introduce several types of technical change which do not alter the organic composition of capital. A first case may be to assume a uniform increase of labour productivity in both sectors with a rate k. This type of technical change does not affect the three capital–output ratios, and the situation on the labour market again depends on k and the rate of accumulation.

A second interesting case may be that the coefficients a_2 and b_2 decline at a uniform rate k, viz. $a_2(t) = a_2(o)e^{-kt}$ and $b_2(t) = b_2(o)e^{-kt}$.

This second type of technical change, which only refers to the second sector, also does not effect the partial and total organic composition of capital. Labour productivity in Sector II rises, while it remains constant in Sector I. The capital–output ratio in Sector I remains constant, but this ratio declines in Sector II, which is also the case with the ratio for the whole economy. Unemployment may arise in Sector II depending on the rate of accumulation and the rise of labour productivity.

So far the conclusion can be drawn that technical change can be distinguished from accumulation. Some types of technical changes are compatible with the Marxian assumption of a constant organic composition of capital, others are not. Finally, it is shown that the constancy of the organic composition of capital does not necessarily imply that the capital–output ratio is also constant.

From this point of view it is not correct to state that Marx assumed a constant capital–output ratio,[15] although it should be added that Marx did not reckon with types of technical change that influence the capital–output ratios. That the identification of a constant capital–output ratio and a constant organic composition of capital may lead to confusion can be illustrated by means of a treatment of the typical Marxian case of a changing organic composition of capital.

6 Increase of organic composition of capital

In the Marxian literature an increase of the organic composition of capital and an increase of the productivity of labour are twins. Our procedure now is to assume an increase of the productivity of labour and to analyse whether an increase of the organic composition of capital can be derived from this assumption.

Now, the first difficulty we encounter regards the choice of the input coefficient we want to alter. The expression for the productivity of labour contains all four technical coefficients, so from a formal point of view we could choose at will one of these. However, it hardly needs emphasis that the Marxian way of thinking obliges us to consider the change of the coefficients a_1 and a_2, which determine labour productivity in Sectors I

15. See, for example, Güsten (1965). Even Robinson (1964b, p. 83) agrees that in Marxian analysis '... technical progress normally takes forms which raise the ratio of capital to output'.

and II. Let us assume again that the relations $a_1(t) = a_1(o)e^{-kt}$ and $a_2(t) = a_2(o)e^{-kt}$ with $k > 0$ hold, and that b_1 and b_2 remain constant.

We first consider the case in which the organic composition of capital in both sectors is equal, so that $a_1 b_2 = a_2 b_1$. The organic composition of capital then equals $\dfrac{b_1(1+r)}{1 - b_1(1+r)}$. It follows immediately that the rising productivities of labour do not influence the organic composition of capital. So, we have to conclude that Marx did not mean this state of things. Of course, this does not imply that it is not a real case.

Let us now assume that the organic compositions of capital in the two sectors differ from each other and that also labour productivities in the sectors increase at different rates, so that rate $a_1(t) = a_1(o)e^{-kt}$ and $a_2(t) = a_1(o)e^{-lt}$ with $k > 0$ and $l > 0$.

The expression for the total organic composition of capital now reads:

$$\frac{a_1(o)b_2(1+r)}{\{1 - b_1(1+r)\}\{a_2(o)(1-b_1)e^{(k-l)t} + a_1(o)b_2\}}$$

The condition for a rising organic composition of capital is $k < l$. If the increase of labour productivity in Sector I is smaller than the increase of labour productivity in Sector II, the implied type of technical change indeed happens to coincide with a rising organic composition of capital. An interesting feature of this typical Marxian case is that the partial organic composition of capital in Sector I remains constant, while that in Sector II rises. We should add that at one stage Marx creates the impression that he considered a rate of growth of labour productivity in Sector I higher than that in Sector II to be the normal state of things: '*Aber auf einem gewissen Höhepunkt der Industrie muss die Disproportion abnehmen, das heisst die Produktivität der Agrikultur sich relativ rascher vermehren als die der Industrie*'[16] (Marx, 1953b, Bd II, p. 280).

Now, we are in a position to understand the incorrectness of the view that '*Marx erwartete, dass der technische Fortschritt zu einer fortwährenden Zunahme des Kapitalkoeffizienten führen werde*'[17] (Güsten, 1965, p. 109). While the assumptions introduced are fully in accordance with the Marxian hypotheses, the conclusion can be derived that the capital–output ratios remain constant.

The situation on the labour market again depends on the rate of accumulation on one side and the values of k and l on the other side. If unemployment occurs it will be first in Sector II. Marx assumed that in the

16. 'But at a specific peak of industrial development the disproportion must decline, that is, productivity in agriculture grows relatively faster than that in industry' [Eds.].

17. 'Marx expected that technical progress would lead to a continuous increase in the capital coefficients' [Eds.].

long run unemployment resulting from the rise in labour productivity is higher than the number of labourers which find employment as a consequence of the demand for labour which follows from accumulation. This position is based on the supposition of '. . . a given trend rate of accumulation' as Steindl (1969, p. 252) justly observes.

7 Technical change and the labour market

In this section we shall study the effects of accumulation and rising productivities of labour on employment more carefully, explicitly assuming a growing economy. The essence of Marx's employment theory concerns the interchange between the given quantitative rate of accumulation and the qualitative nature of accumulation. The fact that a constant organic composition of capital is compatible with a change in the technical structure of the economy can warn us not to relate the number of unemployed exclusively to a change in the organic composition of capital, as is done by Gottheil (1962). Although Marx did not assume qualitative changes in the case of a constant organic composition of capital, we should nevertheless specify the type of technical change in order to derive precise conclusions in case of a rising organic composition of capital.

Let us assume that labour productivity in Sectors I and II obeys the laws $a_1(t) = a_1(o)e^{-kt}$ and $a_2(t) = a_2(o)e^{-lt}$, with $k<l$, so that the organic composition of capital rises. The supply of labour grows at a constant rate n in both sectors according to $L_1(t) = e^{nt}$. $L_1(o)$ and $L_2(t) = e^{nt}L_2(o)$. A given rate of accumulation m is assumed so that $K_1(t) = e^{mt}K_1(o)$ and $K_2(t) = e^{mt}K_2(o)$. Furthermore the Leontief type production functions are assumed and initially everybody is at work, so that $L_1(o) = a_1(o)K(o)$ and $L_2(o) = a_2(o).Y(o)$.

We introduce a measure of employment, being the ratio between the demand for labour and its supply. For Section I we find:

$$\mu_{\text{I}} = \frac{\dfrac{a_1(o)}{b_1}K_1(o)e^{(m-k)t}}{\dfrac{a_1(o)}{b_1}K_1(o)e^{nt}} = e^{(m-k-n)t};$$

and for Sector II:

$$\mu_{\text{II}} = \frac{\dfrac{a_2(o)}{b_2}K_2(o)e^{(m-l)t}}{\dfrac{a_2(o)}{b_2}K_2(o)e^{nt}} = e^{(m-l-n)t}.$$

The condition for full employment in Sector I reads $m = k+n$ and for

Sector II $m = l+n$. As $k < l$ in Sector II unemployment emerges if there is just full employment in Sector I. Both sectors show unemployment if $m < k+n$, the rate of accumulation being too small to provide employment for everybody.

Marx's theory of unemployment rests on two basic postulates. In the first place on a given rate of accumulation and in the second place on a special type of technical change that does not affect the technical coefficients b_1 and b_2, so that the capital–output ratios remain constant. With other types of technical change, such as a decrease of the coefficients a_2 and b_2 or b_1 and b_2, less pessimistic conclusions can be derived, depending on the influence of those types of technical change on the rate of accumulation m and the so far given rate of interest r. The distinction between embodied and disembodied technical change then also becomes necessary.

8 Types of technical change

It seems useful to classify the types of technical change we meet in Marxian economics, according to modern criteria. The two types of technical change that are a natural consequence of Marxian reasoning are the well-known Harrod-neutral technical change and the even better known Hicks-neutral technical change. The combination of constant capital-output ratios, a constant rate of interest and declining coefficients a_1 and a_2 corresponds to Harrod's definition of neutral technical change (Harrod, 1948, pp 24ff.) The conclusion may be drawn that Marx assumed most of the time Harrod-neutral technical change. This is especially striking in his theory of employment. As is well known, Harrod-neutral technical change is labour-augmenting and compatible with a growth of labour supply. Unemployment therefore is the result of the given rate of accumulation of capital and the labour-augmenting type of technical change. We have tried to make clear that the Marxian assumptions are also compatible with another type of technical change, viz. a uniform decline of the coefficients a_2 and b_2 of Sector II. Now, we are confronted with Hicks's (1932, p. 130) version of neutral technical change, applied to Sector II. The ratio of the marginal products of labour and of capital remains constant if a_2 and b_2 decline at a uniform rate.

Putting aside for a moment the case of Hicks-neutral technical change, the conclusion may be drawn that Marx's theory is a consistent piece of analysis if Harrod-neutral technical change is assumed. The important implication then is a spread of technical change over the economy, which changes in different ways the labour coefficients a_1 and a_2. It is natural to look at the Marxian theory of capitalism as '. . . a mere accident of technique' (Robinson, 1964a, p. 144). In this connection also Blaug may be quoted, who states that Marx's theory '... results in a theory of economic growth in which investment prospects dry up not because there have been too few labour-saving improvements but because there have been too many' (Blaug, 1960). So far Samuelson's model produces results which are to a large extent compatible with Marx's conclusions.

At this point of our essay it seems appropriate to call attention to a wider concept of technical change implied in Marxian economics. According to Marx accumulation brings about a refinement and a revaluation of the division of labour, it stimulates large-scale production, it leads to concentration and in the end to centralization. Samuelson's model can be used, as we have tried to make clear, to grasp both the case of a constant and that of a rising organic composition of capital. To this end it is a highly elegant and useful model. However, it is not suited to describe the effects of technical change in the narrow sense of the word on technical change in a broader sense. The model describes the role of technical change given a certain structure, but not how this structure is broken down by technical change. It needs no emphasis that it is highly ambitious to think of a model that is capable of describing and perhaps of forecasting the influence of technical change on the structure of the economy. Nevertheless, it is the main task of economic theory in our day.

9 Technical change and market form

One aspect of such a model may be brought to the fore, viz. the influence of technical change on the market form. Samuelson explicitly assumed perfect competition reigning everywhere in the economy. It is not difficult to produce quotations of Marx's work that seem to justify this assumption (e.g. Marx, 1904, Bd III, p. 173). To us it seems highly questionable whether Marx actually had in mind a market form in which the individual producer has no power at all with respect to price setting. In this whole system the concentration of power on the side of the capitalists plays so important a role, that the idea of powerlessness in case of perfect competition is hardly compatible with the general tenor of Marx's opinion. Marx's description of market processes is more in line with oligopolistic market forms. In particular in this respect we think of Marx's proposition that the innovations are introduced under the influence of competition, a phenomenon which is accompanied by heterogeneity insofar as there are pioneers and followers. Such a pattern of behaviour is more compatible with oligopoly, of which also quality competition is an aspect, than with the uniform world of perfect competition, in which no initiatives are being taken. Meek (1967, p. 108) also observes that '... social polarization is accentuated by the growth of monopoly'.

But even if one would like to hold that Marx started from perfect competition, one cannot deny that the monopolization of the relations of production is essential to his theory of accumulation. The causes that are responsible for large scale production are not randomly distributed, but are deeply rooted in the technique of production and its changes. To a certain extent Fellner (1957, p. 17) did recognize this as he accounted for a '. . . degree of monopoly power' in his Marxian model.

Of course, a formalization of Marx's theory in which the relation between technical changes and the power structure on the market, especially on the side of the producers, is accounted for is hampered by the fact that instead of one theory we are confronted with a whole set of oligopoly models. The supply of oligopoly models is differentiated with respect to the methods used, the type of maximizing behaviour, the weapons of competition considered and the interpretation of empirical data. This circumstance however is no foundation for the illusion that Marx is being integrally dealt with by formalizations that are based on perfect competition.

10 Conclusion

It is hardly possible to evade the conclusion that Marx was the first economist who saw and foresaw the significance of technical change for economic development (Sweezy, 1968). This conclusion is hardly weakened by the fact that most of the time he assumed a specific type of technical change.

That the refinement of analysis makes room for the opinion that technology has a complex and not a uniform character is a confirmation of Marx's intuition more than a contradiction of the internal logic of his system. Nevertheless it is true that the forecasts of the industrial reserve army, the decline of real wages and the rate of profit have to be corrected in view of other types of technical change in the narrow sense of the word. The analysis would undoubtedly have to go into the details of embodied technical change and would also have to reconsider the assumption adhered to in this paper, that the rate of interest r is constant during the accumulation. Again it should be stressed that technical change in the broad sense changes the power structure of producers among themselves and of entrepreneurs and labourers. This last development, which also biased Marx's forecast on the decline of the real wage rate, has perhaps been provoked by Marx himself. The influence of different types of power structures in society on the main economic quantities is by no means clear. From Marx we can learn that for the analysis of such a problem the study of the concrete features of technology and technical change is essential.

Postscript (1976)

The analysis given above can be illustrated by means of wage–interest curves. The assumption has been made that the new technique is entirely dominant over the old methods of production, viz. there are no interior switch-points of the wage–interest curves. Together with the assumption that the rate of interest (or profit) is given this implies that the application of a new technique provokes a rise in the real wage rate. However, the question of whether the real wage in fact rises depends to a great extent on the situation on the labour market, and it should not be forgotten that the whole apparatus based on wage–interest curves forms an open system that can be closed via different routes. Since the supply of labour depends on population growth, the assumption of the latter is essential. The demand for labour depends on the actual rate of accumulation of capital, and if this rate is relatively low its negative effect on the real wage will more than counterbalance the positive effect of a new technique. (For a further elaboration see my forthcoming book *Economics and Technical Change*, London, 1976.)

References

BLAUG, M. (1960), 'Technical change and Marxian economics', *Kyklos*, vol. 13.

FELLNER, W. J. (1957), 'Marxian hypothesis and observable trends under capitalism, a "modernised" interpretation', *Economic Journal*.

GOTTHEIL, F. M. (1962), 'Increasing misery of the proletariat; an analysis of Marx's wage and employment theory', *Canadian Journal of Economics and Political Science*.

GÜSTEN, R. (1965), 'Bemerkungen zur Marxschen Theorie des technischen Fortschrittes', *Jahrbücher für Nationalökonomie und Statistik*, vol. 178.

HARROD, R. F. (1948), *Towards a Dynamic Economics*, London.

HICKS, J. R. (1932), *Theory of Wages*, London.

MARX, K. (1872), *Das Kapital* (Bd I), 2nd ed.

MARX, K. (1904), *Das Kapital* (Bd III), 2nd ed., Hamburg.

MARX, K. (1953a), *Grundrisse der Kritik der politischen Ökonomie*, Berlin.

MARX, K. (1953b), *Theorien über den Mehrwert*, 5th ed., Berlin.

MEEK, R. (1967), *Economics and Ideology and Other Essays*, London.

RICARDO, D. (1817), *The Principles of Political Economy and Taxation*, London.

ROBINSON, J. (1964a), 'Marx and Keynes', in J. Robinson, *Collected Economic Papers I*, Oxford.

ROBINSON, J. (1946b), 'The model of an expanding economy', in J. Robinson, *Collected Economic Papers I*, Oxford.

SAMUELSON, P. A. (1957), 'Wages and interest: a modern dissection of Marxian economic models', *American Economic Review*.

STEINDL, J. (1969), 'Karl Marx and the accumulation of capital', in D. Horowitz (ed.), *Marx and Modern Economics*, London.

SWEEZY, P. M. (1968), 'Karl Marx and the industrial revolution', in R. V. Eagly (ed.), *Events, Ideology, and Economic Theory*, Detroit.

Part Five
Imperialism

23 Shlomo Avineri

Karl Marx on Colonialism and Modernization

Shlomo Avineri, 'Introduction', *Karl Marx on Colonialism and Modernisation*,
Anchor Books, New York, 1969, pp. 1–31.

Marx is usually considered a European thinker, primarily interested in the
impact of industrialization on Western society; yet his message of salvation
is universal. While his theories draw on the Judaeo-Christian philosophical
tradition and the Western historical experience, their resonance today
seems to be strongest in the non-European world. With China and Cuba as
the most radical exponents of a Marxist world view, Marxism seems almost
to have become a weapon wielded by the underdeveloped nations against
the developed and industrialized ones.

An understanding of Marx's views on the non-European world is thus
of both theoretical and practical relevance: while posing a challenge to
our understanding of Marxism as a political philosophy, it also confronts
us with one of the major issues of contemporary politics. It is furthermore
a subject that has been almost totally neglected until quite recently.[1] That
most of what Marx had to say about the non-European world has not been
said in his principal theoretical writings, but is scattered in numerous
newspaper articles and in his correspondence, might also have been one of
the reasons for the relative neglect of this aspect of his thought among his
admirers and critics alike.

1

The general tone of Marx's views on the non-European world is set in *The
Communist Manifesto* (1848); significantly for the development of Marx's
further thoughts on the subject, the discussion centres round the impact
of European capitalist expansion on non-European civilizations. The
Manifesto does not, on the other hand, discuss non-Western historical
developments prior to European penetration, and the non-Western world
thus appears for the first time in the *Manifesto* when its structure is already
heavily undermined by expanding European, bourgeois civilization.

1. For the recent literature, see Karl A. Wittfogel (1957, chapter 9) and George
Lichtheim's brilliant critical essay (1967). See also the articles by Ferenc Tokei, Jean
Chesnaux, and Maurice Godelier in the special issue of *La Pensée* of April 1964
devoted to '*le mode de production asiatique*'.

The capitalist mode of production is, for Marx, the first historical mode of production that is carried by its own momentum towards embracing the whole world within its net of productive relations. The need for expanding into the non-European world is thus an immanent feature of bourgeois society. Since it is the most revolutionizing force in history, it will also, according to Marx, ultimately undermine the very conditions for its own existence and further functioning. 'The bourgeoisie,' Marx writes, 'cannot exist without constantly revolutionizing the instruments of production ... The need of a constantly expanding market for its products chases [it] over the whole surface of the globe ... [It] has through its exploitation of the world market given a cosmopolitan character to production and consumption in every country.'[2]

It is this dialectical end-result that enables Marx to sing, tongue in cheek, the praises of the bourgeoisie. For Marx, the bourgeoisie

draws all, even the most barbarian, nations into civilization. The cheap prices of its commodities are the heavy artillery with which it batters down all Chinese walls, with which it forces the barbarians' intensely obstinate hatred of foreigners to capitulate. It compels all nations, on pain of extinction, to adopt the bourgeois mode of production ... to become bourgeois themselves. In one word, it creates a world after its own image ...

The bourgeoisie has subjected the country to the rule of the towns. It has created enormous cities, has greatly increased the urban population as compared with the rural, and has thus rescued a considerable part of the population from the idiocy of rural life. Just as it has made the country dependent on the towns, so it has made barbarian and semi-barbarian countries dependent on the civilized ones, nations of peasants on nations of bourgeois, the East on the West.

The implications of such an approach are far-reaching, for they enable Marx to dissociate moral indignation and social critique from historical judgement. This is also Marx's method in approaching the phenomenon of capitalism: he is careful not to mistake a condemnation of the social evils inherent in capitalism for a romantic search after the idyllic pre-industrial times. It is true that capitalism is the most brutalizing and dehumanizing economic system history has ever known; after all, there have been few critiques of capitalism more outspoken than Marx's *Economic and Philosophical Manuscripts* and *Das Kapital*. Yet to Marx, capitalism is still a

2. It should be recalled that it was Hegel who has been one of the first European thinkers who tried to find the theoretical connection between colonial expansion and the internal workings of the modern economic system. In his *Philosophy of Right*, Hegel (1821, §256) says: 'This inner dialectic of civil society (*bürgerliche Gesellschaft*) thus drives it – or at any rate drives a specific civil society – to push beyond its own limits and seek markets, and so the necessary means of subsistence, in other lands which are either deficient in the goods it has overproduced, or else generally backward in industry, &c.'

necessary step towards final salvation, since only capitalism can create the economic and technological infrastructure that will enable society to allow for the free development of every member according to his capacities.

Marx's views on overseas European capitalist expansion is thus an extension of his dialectical understanding of the potentialities of capitalism in general. Capitalist society is universalistic in its urges, and it will not be able to change internally unless it encompasses the whole world,[3] it is this that determines Marx's and Engels's attitude to the concrete cases of nineteenth-century European expansion in India, China, North Africa, etc.

But before discussing Marx's views on these particular cases, a preliminary question has to be answered: What was, according to Marx, the nature of the society (or societies) European expansion has been destroying in Asia and Africa? In the *Manifesto* Marx refers in an undifferentiated yet characteristic way to 'barbarians', 'semi-barbarians', 'nations of peasants', 'the East'. Compared to Marx's careful analysis of European society and history, this is primitive and certainly unsatisfactory. It is even surprising within the context of the *Manifesto*, since its appeal is, after all, predicated upon a philosophy of history for whose universal applicability the strongest possible claim is made throughout the whole document.

The Preface to *A Contribution to the Critique of Political Economy* (1859) is the only one of his published major theoretical writings in which Marx explicitly relates the socio-economic conditions of the non-European world to his general philosophy of history. The short paragraph in which he does this begs several basic theoretical problems, which have bedevilled Marxism ever since. In discussing the stages of economic development, Marx strongly brings out the dialectical tensions inherent in every historical period: 'No social order', Marx maintains in a passage that has become classic, 'ever disappears before all the productive forces, for which there is room in it, have been developed; and new, higher relations of production never appear before the material conditions of their existence have matured in the womb of the old society.' He then goes on to specify the stages of historical development:

In broad outline we can designate the Asiatic, the ancient, the feudal, and the modern bourgeois methods of production as so many epochs in the progress of the economic formation of society.

Three of the four modes of production mentioned here had been already discussed by Marx in the *Manifesto* – the ancient, the feudal, and the bourgeois; the Asiatic mode of production is a new one, and its introduction

3. For a fuller description of the implications of this universalistic nature of capitalism, see Avineri (1968, pp. 150–73).

raises a number of questions. On the most obvious level, one cannot but be aware of the discrepancy between the analytical and historical nature of the three familiar modes and the mere geographic designation of the Asiatic one.

Secondly, while it is obvious from the structure of the Marxian system that the three familiar modes are dialectically related, the 'Asiatic' mode of production seems to stand apart from the others. It is a central theme in Marx's theory of history that feudalism grows out of the internal tensions of the ancient, slaveholding society, just as Marx devotes a great amount of historical study to show how capitalism emerged out of the womb of the internal disintegration and structural change (*Aufhebung*) of feudalism; and socialism, too, is to Marx a consequence of the inner mechanisms of the capitalist system. Each successive stage stands, both historically and conceptually, in a dialectical relationship to the one preceding it and makes no sense except in that particular context. Yet the Asiatic mode of production does not fit into this systematic exposition; nowhere in the passage quoted, or in any of his other writings, does Marx imply that the Asiatic mode of production is integrated into the dialectical series of the other modes; obviously the ancient mode did not grow out of the Asiatic, nor does Marx show how the Asiatic mode develops internally into any of the other ones. Despite the explicit dynamism of Marx's dialectical model, it seems to be an uneasy combination of two sets of disparate elements: a sophisticated, carefully worked out schema describing the historical dynamism of European societies, rather simple-mindedly grafted upon a dismissal of all non-European forms of society under the blanket designation of a mere geographic terminology of the 'Asiatic mode of production', which appears static, unchanging, and totally non-dialectical.

Marx never really admits this discrepancy, and the systematic difficulties implied in the series of Asiatic–ancient–feudal–bourgeois modes of production never come to the surface in his theoretical writings. Yet time and again he warns his disciples not to overlook the basically *European* horizons of his discussions of historical development. In a letter written in 1877 to the Russian socialist journal *Otechestvenniye Zapiski* he warns readers not to 'metamorphose my historical sketch of the genesis of capitalism in Western Europe into an historico-philosophic theory of the general path every people is fated to tread'. In the same letter he expressly limits the historical scope of *Das Kapital* to Western Europe: 'The chapter on primitive accumulation [in *Das Kapital*, Bd I] does not pretend to do more than trace the path by which, in Western Europe, the capitalist order of economy emerged from the womb of the feudal order of society.'

Marx is thus faced with the acute awareness that his theory of economic development is applicable to the West alone: in so far as the non-European world is being changed in the direction of capitalism, this occurs, as pointed out in the *Manifesto*, because of the impact of Western bourgeois society, not as a consequence of an internal development of the Asiatic mode of production or through the agency of internal social forces. Yet despite this Marx does include the Asiatic mode of production in his model of the 'progress of the economic formation of society'.

2

But what *is* the Asiatic mode of production?

In his *Critique of Political Economy* Marx does not discuss it, except to point out that an analogy exists between ancient Roman and Teutonic forms of common property and various forms of Indian village communes.

Yet by the time Marx wrote his *Critique of Political Economy*, he had already studied economic and social conditions in Asia in some detail. Marx's interest in Asia dates from 1853, when the parliamentary debates about the renewal of the East India Company charter drove him to an extensive study of the Company's history and Indian social conditions in general. At that time Marx was the regular London correspondent of the *New York Daily Tribune* and covering the British scene made it imperative to discuss Indian – as well as Chinese and Middle Eastern – affairs at considerable length.

The first hint that Indian studies were leading Marx to some novel conclusions about the nature of non-European society is included in a letter to Engels of 2 June 1853. Here he comments on François Bernier's studies of India and then goes on to point out what is to him the unique feature of social conditions in Asia:

Bernier correctly discovers the basic form of all phenomena in the East – he refers to Turkey, Persia, Hindostan – to be the *absence of private property* in land. This is the real key even to the Oriental heaven.[4]

It is this absence of private property in land that makes the historical process in Asia so different from European historical developments. Each of Marx's successive European modes of production – ancient, feudal, bourgeois – is predicated upon different yet always existing and widely diffused forms of private property in land. Asia is different, and following some suggestions by Engels, Marx tried to work out the institutional implications of absence of private property in land in India. Marx (1853a) says:

There have been in Asia, generally, from immemorial times, but three departments of Government: that of Finance, or the plunder of the interior; that of War, or plunder of the exterior; and, finally, the department of Public Works.

4. The same view is reiterated in Marx (1858b), also Marx (n.d., Bd III, chapters 20, 37, 47).

Climate and territorial conditions, especially the vast tracts of desert, extending from the Sahara, through Arabia, Persia, India and Tartary, to the most elevated Asiatic highlands, constituted artificial irrigation by canals and waterworks the basis of Oriental agriculture ... This prime necessity of an economical and common use of water, which, in the Occident, drove private enterprise to voluntary association, as in Flanders and Italy, necessitated in the Orient where civilization was too low and the territorial extent too vast to call into life voluntary association, the interference of the centralizing power of Government. Hence an economical function developed upon all Asiatic Governments, the function of providing public works.

It is evident that Marx is quite perplexed by the phenomenon he is trying to explain: the parallel with Flanders and Italy points to other alternatives besides centralized government irrigation, so an explanation in purely geographic terms does not offer a wholly satisfactory solution. Marx must be aware of this when he obliquely refers to civilization being 'too low' in the Orient as an independent variable responsible for the failure to achieve the kind of voluntary organization that emerged in at least partially comparable European conditions.

The centralizing Oriental state power goes hand in hand with a unique social structure, again very different from anything known to Europe: 'The whole Indian Empire, not counting the few larger towns, was divided into *villages*, each of which possessed a completely separate organization and formed a little world in itself.'

These villages, Marx goes on, are based on property held in common by the villagers: and it is this common ownership of land that is to Marx the mainstay of what he calls Oriental despotism. Though Marx is aware that this description does not fit Chinese conditions very well, he maintains that common property in land was at least the background of the present Chinese land system; and in any case, he argues, both Indian and Chinese villages are based on a peculiar union of agriculture and manufacture, which makes each village into a self-sufficient and self-contained microcosmos, autonomous, autarchic, inward-looking, cut off from the outside world and hence capable of serving as the basis of conservatism, immobility and stagnation.

Some of the harshest lines ever written on the Indian village community and on Indian life prior to British penetration have come from Marx's pen. Far from using Indian village communism as a paradigm for future communist society, Marx did the contrary. He discusses (Marx, 1853a) the fatal impact of British commerce on the social fabric of Indian society; he then remarks:

Now, sickening as it must be to human feeling to witness these myriads of industrious patriarchal and inoffensive social organizations disorganized and dissolved into their units, thrown into a sea of woes, and their individual members losing at the same time their ancient form of civilization and their hereditary means of subsistence, we must not forget that these idyllic village communities, inoffensive though they may appear, had always been the solid foundation of Oriental despotism, that they restrained the human mind within the smallest possible compass, making it the unresisting tool of superstition, enslaving it beneath traditional rules, depriving it of all grandeur and historical energies. We must not forget the barbarian egotism which, concentrating on some miserable patch of land, had quietly witnessed the ruin of empires, the perpetration of unspeakable cruelties, the massacre of the population of large towns, with no other consideration bestowed upon them than on natural events, itself the helpless prey of any aggressor who deigned to notice it at all. We must not forget that this undignified, stagnatory, and vegetative life, that this passive sort of existence, evoked on the other part, in contradistinction, wild, aimless, unbounded forces of destruction, and rendered murder itself a religious rite in Hindostan. We must not forget that these little communities were contaminated by distinctions of caste and by slavery, that they subjugated man to external circumstances instead of elevating man to be the sovereign of circumstances, that they transformed a self-developing social state into never changing natural density, and thus brought about a brutalizing worship of nature, exhibiting its degradation in the fact that man, the sovereign of nature, fell down on his knees in adoration of Hanuman, the monkey, and Sabbala, the cow.

One of the underlying assumptions characterizing such a view of Indian society is that it is devoid of internal mechanisms of social change. Conflicts can be locally resolved, no foci for supralocal interest articulation exists; there is a total hiatus between social forces and governmental action. It is further significant that while Marx postulates primitive communism as a universal initial stage of development, in Europe it always managed to develop further into a higher mode of production, whereas Indian village communism remained stagnant. Consequently, Marx deduces that Asian society has no history in the Western sense. Marx (1853b) categorically states:

Indian society has no history at all, at least no known history. What we call its history, is but the history of the successive invaders who founded their empires on the passive basis of that unresisting and unchanging society.

Marx (1862) expressed a similar view on China in an article discussing the Taiping Rebellion:

The Oriental empires always show an unchanging social infrastructure coupled with unceasing change in the persons and tribes who manage to ascribe to themselves the political superstructure.

It would be beside the point to try to pass judgement on the adequacy of Marx's contention that Asia has no history: it could certainly be argued that Marx's knowledge of Indian and Chinese History was minimal, though his notebooks at least point in another direction. The ultimate judgement of Marx's view on the subject would obviously depend on the meaning we attach to the concept of history, and such an investigation cannot be undertaken here. What is significant is that this was Marx's view, that for him Asia had no history, a view that is quite startling coming from Marx. Stated bluntly it implies that Marx is aware of the fact that his philosophy of history does not account for the majority of mankind since it is relevant only to the European experience. This may be hubris, but in that case Marx shared it with many of his contemporaries, whatever their political coloration.

The notion that Asia has no history is not, of course, of Marx's own making. While many eighteenth-century authors saw China as a model society, where order, stability, and obedience have been successively achieved through Oriental wisdom, Marx followed Hegel in rejecting such a view of the Celestial Empire as misleading romanticism. To Marx as to Hegel history means man's process of changing his environment; where there is no change, there is no history, and man remains a pure natural being. A society not undergoing change is basically outside the pale of history and of human interest. In his *Lectures on the Philosophy of History* Hegel (1956, pp. 105–6) had this to say about the Orient:

On the one side we see duration, stability – Empires belonging to mere space as it were [as distinghished from time] – unhistorical history . . . The States in question, without undergoing any change in themselves, or in the principle of their existence, are constantly changing their position towards each other. They are in ceaseless conflict, which brings rapid destruction. This history too is, for the most part, really *unhistorical*, for it is only the repetition of the same majestic ruin.

More specifically, the lack of historical development in China and India is reiterated by Hegel (1956, pp. 116, 139) time and again:

With the Empire of China History has to begin, for it is the oldest . . . and its *principle* has such substantiality that for the empire in question it is at once the oldest and the newest . . . China and India lie, as it were, still outside the World's History . . .

India, like China, is a phenomenon antique as well as modern; one which has remained stationary and fixed.

Viewed within this tradition, Marx's analysis of the features of Indian and Chinese society thus consists of two ingredients: the basic notion of Oriental societies as unchanging, stagnant, and hence unhistorical is Hegelian; to this is added the specifically Marxian explanation of the stationary nature of society in Asia in terms of its unique mode of production, based on common property and giving rise to Oriental despotism.

Yet by adopting the Hegelian typology of Oriental society, Marx found himself confronted with a problem of the philosophy of history that was absent, to a large degree, in the original Hegelian schema. Since each of the Hegelian historical 'Worlds' (the Oriental, the Classical, and the Germanic-Christian) represents a moment in the progress of the idea of history rather than a mere period of history or a temporal phase of historical development, there is no intrinsic necessity within the Hegelian system for these 'Worlds' to grow one out of another and to succeed each other in time. China can thus coexist in time with the modern Germanic, Western civilization, just as it coexisted with the world of antiquity two millennia ago. Yet Marx's philosophy of history is predicated upon the dialectical nature of the process of production, which is always changing and subverting its own conditions of existence and thus always leading towards new forms of social organization.

It is now obvious that the 'Asiatic mode of production' by its own nondynamism and non-changing nature does not have these dialectical elements of internal change built into its own system. To use Marx's pet phrase, out of *its* womb there arises no new, more developed society. It is what it was and there is little in Marx's own description of it to suggest that it can change by its own momentum. Marx's concept of the Asiatic mode of production thus poses a serious challenge to the assumption that Marx developed a philosophy of history universal in its applicability. We have already seen that in his discussion of Russia Marx had been aware that his explanation of historical development towards capitalism was limited to the Western historical experience; yet this by itself does not postulate an internal difficulty within the Marxian system, since it merely calls for more detailed and more differentiated study of Russian conditions. Marx's writings on India and China go further than this: they clearly indicate that Oriental society has no internal mechanisms of change, that the dialectics of historical development are not operative in Asia. A Chinese 'feudalism' or an 'Indian slave-holding' society never existed according to Marx. The paradox is that the more penetrating Marx's analysis of Asian society is, the graver the difficulties it poses to the internal structure of Marx's philosophy of history.

3

But the problem is not merely one of an internal inconsistency in Marx's philosophy of history. Since Oriental society does not develop internally, it cannot evolve toward capitalism through the dialectics of internal change; and since Marx postulates the ultimate victory of socialism on the prior universalization of capitalism, he necessarily arrives at the position of having to endorse European colonial expansion as a brutal but necessary step toward the victory of socialism. Just as the horrors of industrialization are dialectically necessary for the triumph of communism, so the horrors of colonialism are dialectically necessary for the world revolution of the proletariat since without them the countries of Asia (and presumably also Africa) will not be able to emancipate themselves from their stagnant backwardness.

Marx's view of European – and particularly British – colonial expansion is determined by these dialectical considerations. Consequently, Marx's views on imperialism can be painfully embarrassing to the orthodox communist; there certainly is a deep irony in the fact that while Marx's writings on European industrialization are always the first to be used and quoted by non-European Marxists, his writings on India and China are hardly known or even mentioned by them.[5] The Maoists in particular seem to be totally unaware of them; they certainly make much of their particular brand of Marxism look very much out of touch with Marx himself.

The fundamental Hegelian distinction between subjective motivation and objective historical results is at the basis of Marx's attitude toward European colonial expansion. Just as Marx never reduces the process of industrialization to mere moralistic rhetoric about the money-grabbing greediness of Manchester industrialists, so the motives behind colonial expansion should not be mistaken for its historical significance. History works through agents who are hardly aware of the ultimate import of their actions: this is the crux of Hegel's doctrine of the 'Cunning of Reason' (*List der Vernunft*), and Marx faithfully follows Hegel here, though he substitutes collective groups, as classes, for the individual heroes of Hegel's system. Since the Asiatic mode of production does not create the conditions for its own overthrow, an external agent is needed, and the agent's own motives and rationalizations are irrelevant. Marx (1853a) says:

England, it is true, in causing a social revolution in Hindostan, was actuated only by the vilest interests, and was stupid in her manner of enforcing them. But that is not the question. The question is, can mankind fulfil its destiny without a fundamental revolution in the social state of Asia? If not, whatever may have been the crimes of England she was the unconscious tool of history in bringing about the revolution.

5. Two interesting exceptions have, however, to be noted: Nambooridiripad (1952) and Amer (1958). Both authors suggest a Marxist explanation of social conditions in their respective countries in terms of the 'Asiatic mode of production'. Not surprisingly Ibrahim Amer was imprisoned by Nasser's régime shortly after the publication of his book.

And in Marx (1853b):

England has to fulfil a double mission in India: one destructive, the other regenerating – the annihilation of old Asiatic society, and the laying of the material foundation of Western society in Asia.

The underlying historiosophical assumption behind this is clearly stated by Marx in the same article:

The bourgeois period of history has to create the material basis of the new world – on the one hand the universal intercourse founded upon the mutual dependency of mankind, and the means of that intercourse; on the other hand the development of the productive powers of man and the transformation of material production into a scientific domination of natural agencies.[6]

Marx goes into considerable detail to discuss the various aspects of the impact of Western bourgeois civilization on Indian society. Marx argues that for the first time in its history political unity has been imposed on India by the British sword and strengthened by the introduction of modern means of communication. A European-trained Indian army, 'the *sine qua non* of Indian self-emancipation' has been created by the British – obviously, for their own purposes, but its ultimate impact will transcend whatever aims the British had in mind; this army will be able to ensure that henceforward India will cease 'to be the prey of the first foreign intruder'. A free press has been introduced into India 'for the first time in an Asiatic society'; a new class of British-trained civil servants 'endowed with the requirements for government and imbued with European science' is slowly evolving and last but not least, by abolishing the old system of common-land tenure dependent upon the ultimate domain of the state, the new forms of limited peasant property introduced by the British, 'abominable as they are, involve two distinct forms of private property in land – the great desideratum of Asiatic society'.

Not without malicious irony Marx points out that the intensity of the changes imposed by the British on the land-holding system in India is far more profound than anything done by the French Revolution. European bourgeois civilization, committed to the sanctity of private property, is causing more havoc to established property in land in Asia than all the revolutionary parties in Europe combined: 'Did any revolutionary party ever originate agrarian revolutions like those in Bengal, in Madras, and in Bombay?' And in an article on 'The Annexation of Oude' Marx (1858a) shows how 'by one stroke of the pen', England has upset more property

6. In his less sophisticated yet more brutal style Engels (1848) says the same about the French occupation of Algeria: 'The conquest of Algeria is an important and fortunate fact for the progress of civilization.'

relations in India than were upset in the whole of Europe since the French Revolution. The irony is compounded, Marx points out in a footnote in *Das Kapital*, Bd III, by the fact that the British think that what they were doing in India was duplicating the English land-holding system.

That this social transformation is being carried out by the European bourgeoisie, which is totally unaware of the ultimate consequences of its own acts, only brings out the basic dialectical nature of Marx's analysis. But the integration of India – and to a lesser degree of China as well – into the world market is a two-way road: not only is Asia becoming more dependent on Europe, Europe is also, dialectically, becoming more dependent on Asia.

Thus a reciprocal – though still negative – world community grows out of European colonial expansion. Such an argument is in tune with one of Hegel's central themes in his *Phenomenology of Mind*. In a chapter called 'Lordship and Bondage' Hegel shows how the master–slave relationship develops a dialectical dependence of the master on his slave. While the slave can find satisfaction and self-consciousness in his work and in his knowledge that through his labour he is changing reality, the master, on the other hand, 'just where he has effectively achieved lordship, really finds that something has come about quite different. ... Lordship shows its essential nature to be the reverse of what it wants to be . . . It is not an independent, but rather a dependent consciousness that the master has achieved' (Hegel, 1967, pp. 236–7). Hegel thus postulates emancipation through the realization that the master is, in the last resort, dependent upon the slave.

A similar process is already operating in India according to Marx (1853b):

The ruling classes of Great Britain have had, till now, but an accidental, transitory and exceptional interest in the progress of India. The aristocracy wanted to conquer it, the moneyocracy to plunder it, and the millocracy to undersell it. But now the tables are turned. The millocracy have discovered that the transformation of India into a reproductive country has become of vital importance to them, and that, to that end, it is necessary, above all, to gift her with means of irrigation and of internal communication. They intend now drawing a net of railroads over India. And they will do it. The results must be inappreciable.

This ultimate dependence of Europe on Asia is also implied by Marx when discussing the economic balance of payments regulating the flow of funds from the metropolis to the colonies, and especially to India. It is here that Marx's sophisticated understanding of the dialectics of historical development proves itself so superior to the more linear analysis of Lenin's *Imperialism: The Highest Stage of Capitalism*. Marx also succeeds in bringing out the ultimate contradiction in colonial trade: discussing the consequence of the Indian Mutiny, he says: 'These financial fruits of the "glorious" reconquest of India have not a charming appearance; . . . John Bull pays exceedingly high protective duties for securing the monopoly of the Indian market to the Manchester free-traders' (Marx, 1859a). The dialectical analysis of colonial expansion is thus merely an instance of realizing the internal structural tensions of capitalist society.

4

As early as 1847 Marx argued in *The Poverty of Philosophy* that the relative amelioration in the conditions of life of the British working class should not be discussed separately from what British penetration into India did to the standards of living of those engaged in the Indian home industries. According to Marx, cheap Indian labour enables a small sector of the British working class to raise its standards of living at its expense. But when Marx later discusses the overall economic benefits Britain is reaping from India, he comes out with a far more complex theory than such a simplistic view of 'exploitation'.

In a series of articles on the East India Company Marx arrives at the conclusion that one has to distinguish between the benefits derived from India by the British economy and society as a whole, and the specific benefits derived from India by individuals and groups in England. Marx argues that as far as the British public is concerned, *the cost of administering India exceeds the income derived from it.* Over the decades the constantly growing debt of the East India Company has been paid out of the pocket of the British tax-payer, and these expenses were in excess of all benefits the economy derived from India. Nor did the liquidation of the Company change the picture, and British political rule in India will continue to be deficit-financed in terms of the national economy (Marx, 1859a). The real beneficiary of British rule in India is not the British economy as a whole: it could do better without it; those who benefit from India are several thousand individuals who are either bond-holders of the East India Company or are employed in the various branches of British administration. In an article on 'British Incomes in India' Marx (1857e) discusses in some detail the net of patronage connected with the East India Company and with those Cabinet officers engaged in Indian affairs; for them and for their protégés, India has been a gold mine. In each of the various branches of the Indian administration – clerical, medical, military and naval – salaries in India were disproportionately higher than those paid for comparable positions at home. But since the burden of Indian administration was ultimately borne by the taxpayer in England, and since the gross income all those individuals derived from India was much below the costs of

Indian administration, *British rule in India was, in effect an indirect way of taxing the British people for the benefit of their upper classes*, whose sons, sons-in-law, and cousins were shipped off to India to make their fortunes in the Indian service. By showing that incomes from India, whatever their distribution, were lower than the cost of the administration that collected them, Marx arrives at even a more profound indictment of British imperialism in class terms than is usually attributed to Marxism: ultimately it was Britain, and not only India, that was being exploited for the benefit of the English ruling classes through British rule in India.

Marx's critique of colonial expansion thus avoids a mere moralistic stance and is deeply integrated into his general critique of European capitalist society; similarly, his insistence on the ultimate necessity of colonialism is divorced from his moral indignation of its horrors. This is surely a complex attitude to adopt, and it does not translate well into the necessarily more simple-minded language of political mass organizations, as the ideological writings on the subject by most European and non-European communist theoreticians amply show. The sophistication of Hegelian dialectics cannot be easily adapted to the more prosiac needs of Marxist parties of whatever coloration.

We have already noted how the inner consistency of Marx's European-oriented philosophy of history breaks down when confronted with what he conceives to be the non-dialectical and stagnant nature of the Asiatic mode of production. Consequently, the only impetus for change has to come from the outside, and European bourgeois civilization is thus the external agent of change in non-European societies. The direct corollary of this would be that Marx would have to welcome European penetration in direct proportion to its intensity: the more direct the European control of any society in Asia, the greater the chances for the overhauling of its structure and its ultimate incorporation into bourgeois, and hence later into socialist, society.

It is for this reason that Marx never entertained any doubts that Indian society, because of direct British political and administrative as well as economic control, would be completely overhauled, while the indirect and only sporadic nature of European control over the Chinese market gave Marx cause for doubt whether the obstinate unchanging Chinese society would not, after all, be able to withstand change. Certainly this is one of the paradoxes inherent in Marx's position about colonial expansion, but it has to be squarely faced. In 'Trade with China' Marx (1859b) shows how British direct control over India enabled it to undermine the combination of 'husbandry with manufacturing industry' that had always been at the root of Oriental despotism. 'In China,' he remarks, 'the English have not yet yielded this power, nor are they likely ever to do so.' Consequently, the traditional patterns of consumption prevail in Chinese society: 'Absence of wants and predilection for hereditary modes of dress, are obstacles which civilized commerce has to encounter in all new markets.'

Marx returns to the same theme in *Das Kapital*. In Volume III he again compares the nature of European control over India and China and says:

The obstacles presented by the internal solidity and organization of pre-capitalist national modes of production to the corrosive influence of commerce are strikingly illustrated in the intercourse of the English with India and China. The broad basis of the mode of production is formed here by the unity of small-scale agriculture and home industry, to which in India we should add the form of village communities built upon the common ownership of land, which, incidentally, was the original form in China as well. In India the English lost no time in exercising their direct political and economic power as rulers and landlords to disrupt these small economic communities. English commerce exerted a revolutionary influence on these communities . . . And even so, this work of dissolution proceeds very gradually. And still more so in China, where it is not reinforced by direct political power.

George Lichtheim (1967, p. 75) sees in this passage an indication that in the later part of *Das Kapital* 'we find Marx remarking upon the stability of ancient village communities in a manner suggesting that he saw some genuine virtues in their peculiar mode of life'. From this Lichtheim also infers that in later life Marx somewhat changed his extremely critical analysis of the Asiatic mode of production. There seems however nothing in Marx's language to suggest such a change of heart: all that Marx is voicing in this passage is the view that the European impact, especially in China but also, though to a lesser degree in India, is simply not strong enough: nowhere does he suggest any 'genuine virtues' in the Asiatic mode of production. The only sentiment expressed here is regret that perhaps these village communities are not, after all, going to disappear as completely as he hoped they would – and should. A similar view is reflected in a letter Marx wrote to Engels on 8 October 1858:

The specific task of bourgeois society is the establishment of a world market, at least in outline . . . As the world is round, this seems to have been completed by the colonization of California and Australia and the opening up of China and Japan. The difficult question for us is this: on the Continent the revolution is imminent and will immediately assume a socialist character. Is it not bound to be crushed in this little corner [i.e. Europe], considering that in a far greater territory the movement of bourgeois society is still in the ascendant?

The unchanging nature of non-European society is thus a drag on the progress of history – and a serious threat to socialism. In a letter to Kautsky of 12 September 1882, Engels voices the otherwise misconstrued notion that, come the revolution, the European proletariat will have to take over control of some colonies in order to prepare them for independence. To call this a socialist colonial policy, as has been done by some observers, is missing the point: the point is that European colonialism might not have revolutionized the non-European world enough. While the white Anglo-Saxon dominions will become independent, Engels contends that 'on the other hand, the countries inhabited by a native population, which are simply subjugated – India, Algeria, the Dutch, Portuguese and Spanish possessions – must be taken over for the time being by the proletariat and led as rapidly as possible towards independence'. Engels is sufficiently aware of the difficulties involved, adding that 'how this process will develop is difficult to see'; though he remarks that India may be able to carry through a socialist revolution, he does not seem totally convinced that this is really possible. Nor is Engels entertaining the possibility of national wars of liberation prior to the proletarian revolution in Europe.

Though it is theoretically obvious that once capitalism is introduced from the outside into non-European society, the next step should be a development toward socialism, Marx nowhere makes an explicit suggestion to that effect. This should not be read as if he had doubts about the ultimate feasibility of socialism in Asia; it is a reflection of his reluctance to engage in historical prediction in cases where there are still several intervening stages between present circumstances and what he considered to be the universal trend towards a new form of society. Even in his articles on the Ottoman Empire, where conditions were after all less outlandish, there is little to suggest what kind of future development Marx envisaged for the Middle East. His understanding of the retrograde impact Islam had even on the Christian communities in the Middle East is profound and intriguing: in an article on 'Moslems, Christians and Jews in the Ottoman Empire' Marx (1854) shows how the provisions of Islamic law made the Eastern Christian communities dependent upon their religious leadership; the origins of the theocracy the Greek Orthodox clergy practises over the Christian minority in the Ottoman Empire derive from the political status ascribed to it by the Muslim law regulating the status of non-Muslims in Islamic society. But Marx does not indicate what the forces of change in Islamic society could be; he seems to be aware that, unlike conditions in the Western world, there is no tension between the secular and the ecclesiastical authorities, and the lack of this dialectical relationship contributes to the stagnation that is common to Islamic society, as well as to Oriental society in general. Similarly Engels, in a letter to Bernstein in 1882, voices some doubts about the progressive nature of Arabi Pasha's revolt against the British.

The only instance where Marx suggests the possibility of internal change toward a socialist kind of society in Asia is in a highly ironical and controversial context. Discussing in the *Neue Rheinische Zeitung Revue* of February 1850 some rumours about agrarian unrest in China, he points out that some of the rebels call for distribution of land and even advocate total abolition of private property. He then goes on to remark:

It may well be that Chinese socialism is related to European socialism just as Chinese philosophy is related to Hegelian philosophy. But it is an amusing fact that the oldest and most unshattered Empire on this earth has been pushed, in eight years, by the cotton ball of the English bourgeois toward the brink of a social upheaval that must have most profound consequences for civilization.

When our European reactionaries, on their next flight through Asia, will have finally reached the Chinese Wall, the gates that lead to the seat of primeval reaction and conservatism – who knows, perhaps they will read the following inscription on the Wall: *République Chinoise – Liberté, Égalité, Fraternité!*

The text is more than ambiguous, and in any case it suggests the possibility of a Chinese republican revolution rather than a communist one.[7] But even so, and even if it should be considered more than a *jeu d'esprit*, it is at least intriguing to discover that Marx entertained such possibilities, even if only on a highly speculative level. It also brings out even more strongly the lack of a systematic discussion on his part of the possibilities of socialism in Asian society.

5

If we have concentrated until now on suggesting that Marx's view of European colonialism was far from being a mere moral condemnation of it, this should not be construed to suggest that Marx was oblivious to the basic barbarism that went along with European expansion. Marx's writings on Asia, though far from flattering to anyone who has cherished a romantic image of pristine Oriental purity reigning supreme before the advent of the Western barbarians, abound with criticisms of European hypocrisy in Asia, its double standards, and the wanton cruelty implicit in the introduction of Western commerce in Asian society. 'Civilization mongers' is a pet phrase of Marx in many of his articles on China and India, and nothing could be more scathing than his exposé of the sheer inhumanity of the British opium trade with China, or the cruelties inflicted by the British on India in the wake of the Mutiny. Yet in all this there is no romanticizing of the Asians: Asian society is criticized by Marx no less than its European destroyers, and though the manner of its destruction was horrid, there was to Marx little worth preserving in Indian or Chinese society, which represented for him a barbarian primitive stage of human development that became ossified and sterile.

7. See Lowe (1966).

Marx's attitude toward the Indian Mutiny of 1857 is another instance where he divorces his moral condemnation from his historical analysis. The Foreign Languages Publishing House in Moscow once published several of Marx's articles on the Mutiny under the title: *The First Indian War of Independence, 1857–1859*. No title could be more misleading; though Marx condemned as a matter of course the brutalities of British repression, he had little sympathy with the causes of the revolt and with the totally disorganized and disoriented Indian sepoys who headed it. Even before the Mutiny, Marx discussed the British claim to India not on absolute grounds but only in relation to the possibility of Russian domination, and having to choose between English and Russian rule in India, Marx (1853b) prefers the former.

From the outset Marx saw no chance for the revolt to succeed. He rightly attributed its immediate cause to very trivial – though legitimate – complaints of the Indian soldiers about the way their British officers were disregarding their religious sensibilities in supplying them with cartridges whose paper was said to have been greased with the fat of bullocks and pigs, 'and the compulsory biting of which was, therefore, considered by the natives as an infringement of their religious prescriptions' (Marx, 1857a). Marx obviously could not have much sympathy with such kind of motivation, nor could he have been enthused by the prospect of seeing the Mogul Emperor restored to full powers in Delhi. If the Mutiny signified anything to Marx on a broader historical level, it was certainly a Mutiny in favour of the continuation of the Asiatic mode of production and an attempt to stop the modernizing impact of British rule in India. The Mutiny did, however, cause Marx (1857d) to reflect upon the sociology of revolutionary movements, and his remarks have wider scope:

> The first blow to the French monarchy proceeded from the nobility, not from the peasants. The Indian revolt does not commence with the ryots, tortured, dishonoured and stripped naked by the British, but with the sepoys, clad, fed and petted, fatted and pampered by them.

It is true that Marx later changed his view on how easily the Mutiny would be suppressed; yet he never had any doubts about its ultimate failure. In his first report of the revolt, obviously following the overconfident reactions of the British press, Marx (1857a) concludes that 'the rebels at Delhi are very likely to succumb without any prolonged resistance'. His second article on the Mutiny, reporting the reinstatement of the Mogul Emperor in Delhi, is accompanied by the remark that 'any notion, however, of the mutineers being able to keep the ancient capital of India against the British forces would be preposterous . . . The fall of Delhi may be daily expected' (Marx 1857b). Further developments – the spread of the revolt, the blunders of the British officers, as well as further and more accurate information – proved this prognosis to be obviously wrong, and the Mutiny settled into a lengthy war of attrition. It was, ironically, a long parliamentary speech by Disraeli that convinced Marx that the causes for the Mutiny might be more deep-seated than mere soldierly dissatisfaction: Marx (1857c) always had a grudging admiration for Disraeli, and he was obviously impressed by the speech. Yet he did not change his basic conviction that the Mutiny was doomed and its suppression a mere question of time and adequate British reinforcements.

Analysing the military aspects of the Mutiny, Engels pointed out in several articles written on Marx's behalf that the sepoy army was totally disorganized and unmotivated, utterly incapable of sustained military action and quickly deteriorating into that sort of armed countryside banditry with which Oriental society was only too familiar.

A similar lack of basic sympathy can be discerned in Marx's attitude to the Taiping Rebellion. In an article on 'Chinese Affairs' Marx (1862) recognizes the Taiping Rebellion as another indication of the disintegration of traditional Chinese society under the impact of 'European intervention [and] Opium wars'. But the rebels themselves do not, as far as he is concerned, stand for the wave of the future: most of the article is devoted to a rather horrifying account of the terror and intimidation inflicted on the Chinese population by the Taipings. Marx sees no positive social aims, let alone historical consciousness in the rebels; the Taipings are to him the apostles of 'destruction, in grotesque horrifying form, without any seeds for a renaissance . . . They are an even greater scourge to the population than the old rulers.'

If Marx thus dismisses as regressive two instances of anti-Western outbursts in Asia, he – and Engels – similarly show little patience for attempts at a partial defensive modernization introduced by other rulers in Asia. In an article entitled 'Persia-China' written at Marx's request, Engels (1857) discusses the defeat of the Persian army by an infinitely smaller Anglo-Indian force. This defeat caused some surprise in Europe, since the Persian army had been trained by European instructors and had ample supplies of modern equipment. But for Engels it was nothing but a 'European system of military organization . . . engrafted upon Asiatic barbarity'. In a fascinating sketch almost prefiguring some twentieth-century situations, Engels points out that it is the irregular guerrillas, and not the local standing armies, that offer relatively effective resistance to European incursions: yet even these irregulars have no chance of ultimate victory. But he has no respect whatsoever for attempts to introduce European military techniques into a society that has not yet overhauled its non-Western structure: modernizing just one sector of society – the military –

is never going to work, and such an army proves itself a paper tiger. Again, the analysis seems not to have lost its validity:

> The fact is that the introduction of European military organization with barbaric nations is far from being completed when the new army has been sub-divided, equipped and drilled after the European fashion. This is merely the first step towards it. Nor will the enactment of some European military code suffice: it will no more ensure European discipline than a European set of drill-regula-tions will produce, by itself, European tactics and strategy. The main point, and at the same time the main difficulty, is the creation of a body of officers and sergeants, educated on the modern European system, totally freed from the old national prejudices and reminiscences in military matters, and fit to inspire life into the new formation. This requires a long time, and is sure to meet with the most obstinate opposition from Oriental ignorance, impatience, prejudice, and the vicissitudes of fortune and favour inherent to Eastern courts. A Sultan or a Shah is but too apt to consider his army equal to anything as soon as the men can defile in parade, wheel, deploy and form column without getting into hopeless disorder. And as to military schools, their fruits are so slow in ripening that under the instabilities of Eastern Governments they can scarcely be expected to show any. . . .

The implication is, of course, that in order to be successful, modernization has to be total and change the whole order of society: this cannot be achieved by purely political or administrative reform, but has to be predi-cated upon a prior structural change in socioeconomic relations. Dialecti-cally, European expansion, with its consequent brutal obliteration of the Asiatic mode of production, seems to Marx and Engels the only way to achieve this.

Anyone who has closely followed the main themes in Marx's writings about the non-European world cannot but be impressed by the mastery of detailed knowledge and by the breadth of the historical perspectives implied. It is true that one can criticize Marx on many counts: his under-standing of Chinese society seems less profound than his grasp of Indian affairs, and certainly his central thesis about Oriental despotism being based on the absence of private property in land does not apply to China; yet the combination of agriculture with home manufacture, which he sees as determining the basic autarchy of village communities in Asia, is cer-tainly as true of China as it is of India. Again, Japan hardly figures in his writings, mainly due, one would suppose, to the lack of sources and to the fact that Marx was, after all, covering current events for a newspaper, and Japan was not at that time making headline news; but one wonders how the successful case of defensive modernization in Japan would have affected Marx's judgement of the basic stagnant nature of society in Asia.

Yet with all these reservations in mind, one has to admit that few nineteenth-century thinkers and social theorists grasped as well the long-range implications of European colonial expansion for the socio-economic structure of non-European society: even fewer had a comparable vision of the degree of world historical change brought about by the corrosive influence of Western commerce and the dialectical necessity for modernization and industrialization thus made imperative by European penetration into underdeveloped societies.

But this profound understanding has its limitations as well as its serious handicaps in terms of social praxis. Marx's sole criteria for judging the social revolution imposed on Asia are those of European, bourgeois society itself. Since Marx's socialism is a dialectical outcome of the *Aufhebung*, transcendance, of European bourgeois civilization, he sees little reason to look for autochthonous roots for socialism in non-European society. 'Chinese communism' or 'African socialism' have no place in the universalistic scheme of Marx's socialist theory and make little sense within his philosophy of history.

It is significant that the only instance where Marx has some hesitation about the necessity or desirability of a European victory in a European–non-European confrontation is in discussing the Russo-Turkish conflict. And this again happens not because he sees anything commendable in the Ottoman Empire or in Islamic civilization, but because he fears a Russian victory would greatly enhance the forces of counter-revolution and reaction *in Europe*. For Marx, Russia is the arch-enemy of revolution in Europe, and the Middle Eastern issue is only an appendage to a struggle that is basically European: that it has universalistic implications, does not make it less Europocentric.

Yet even these limitations bring out the unique contribution Marx's discussion on Asia adds to his own theory of society. In Asia state power assumes autonomous proportions; Oriental despotism, to Marx, does not reflect the distribution of economic power in society. It is another instance in which non-European society presents a model different from the traditional Marxian model of the relations between economics and politics, and though this may imply an inner inconsistency it also points to pluralistic elements in the Marxian analysis itself. It may even help to explain some of the idiosyncrasies of Maoist communism in terms of the 'Asiatic mode of production' and Chinese history.

Yet Marx's basic failure to incorporate his insightful understanding of non-European society into the universal framework of his method of historical explanation is plainly visible. The nemesis of this failure is manifest in the contemporary quest for a Marxist interpretation of Asian history, and here the anti-Marxists sometimes join the Marxists in search of a conceptual framework that may not in fact be there. The ludicrous attempt to talk about Chinese 'feudalism' or to explain the Indian caste system in terms of the European medieval guilds has lately been discarded by the Chinese Communists themselves. Yet the idea of overcoming this difficulty by postulating the revolution on the mobilization of the underdeveloped world against the industrialized nations, of discussing future history in terms of a war of the Villages of the World against the Cities of the World – all this is even more absurd when viewed in Marxian terms: it was, after all, Marx who talked about 'the idiocy of village life' as the major epistemological obstacle for agrarian socialist revolutionary movements.

With all his understanding of the non-European world, Marx remained a Europe-oriented thinker, and his insights into Indian and Chinese society could never be reconciled with his general philosophy of history, which remained – like Hegel's – determined by the European experience and the Western historical consciousness. It may well be that a successful incorporation of the non-European world into a comprehensive system of history has ultimately to require the sort of rejection of the Western scale of values that is implied in Toynbee's philosophy of history. But such an approach poses other difficulties, since a reasonable argument could be made that the idea of history itself makes little sense outside the Western tradition.

Despite all this, it would be foolish to suggest that the attempt to make Marx relevant to the non-European world will fail because Marx's own writings give little comfort to such an approach. Such an attempt, forced as it may seem in terms of Marx's social philosophy, may yet turn out to be politically successful. If one looks for analogies, one has only to remember that it was among the Gentiles that the beliefs of the man who was crucified as King of the Jews became historically significant.

The irony of history may thus make Marx into a respectable, even fashionable, subject for academic discourse in a relatively affluent and bourgeois West, while in the non-European world an ideology relating itself to Marxism, yet overlooking most of what he said about the non-European world, may be politically triumphant. All this may have very little to do with the basic theoretical issues raised by Marx in his discussion of both the Western and the non-Western world. But these limitations of Marx may even, dialectically, vindicate his own dictum about man's consciousness being determined by his social existence. Or, as Hegel put it several decades before him, 'every individual is a child of his time; so philosophy too is its own time apprehended in thoughts'.

References

AMER, I. (1958), *Al-Ard wa'l-Fellah, al-Mas'ala al-Ziraiyya fi Misr* [*The Land and the Fellah: The Agrarian Question in Egypt*], Cairo.

AVINERI, S. (1968), *The Social and Political Thought of Karl Marx*, Cambridge.

ENGELS, F. (1848), in *Northern Star*, 22 January.

ENGELS, F. (1857), *Persia–China*, New York Daily Tribune, 5 June.

HEGEL, G. W. F. (1821), *Philosophy of Right*.

HEGEL, G. W. F. (1956), *The Philosophy of History* (J. Sibrée trans., C. J. Friedrich ed.), New York.

HEGEL, G. W. F. (1967), *The Phenomenology of Mind* (J. B. Baillie trans.), New York and Evanston.

LICHTHEIM, G. (1967), 'Oriental despotism', in G. Lichtheim, *The Concept of Ideology*, New York, pp. 62–93.

LOWE, D. M. (1966), *The function of 'China' in Marx, Lenin and Mao*, Berkeley and Los Angeles.

MARX, K. (n.d.), *Das Kapital*.

MARX, K. (1853a), 'The British rule in India', *New York Daily Tribune*, 25 June.

MARX, K. (1853b), 'The future results of British rule in India', *New York Daily Tribune*, 8 August.

MARX, K. (1854), 'Moslems, Christians and Jews in the Ottoman Empire', *New York Daily Tribune*, 15 April.

MARX, K. (1857a), 'The revolt in the Indian army', *New York Daily Tribune*, 15 July.

MARX, K. (1857b), 'The revolt in India', *New York Daily Tribune*, 4 August.

MARX, K. (1857c), 'The Indian question', *New York Daily Tribune*, 14 August.

MARX, K. (1857d), 'The Indian revolt', *New York Daily Tribune*, 16 September.

MARX, K. (1857e), 'British incomes in India', *New York Daily Tribune*, 21 September.

MARX, K. (1858a), 'The annexation of Oude', *New York Daily Tribune*, 28 May.

MARX, K. (1858b), 'Land tenure in India', *New York Daily Tribune*, 7 June.

MARX, K. (1859a), in *New York Daily Tribune*, 30 April.

MARX, K. (1859b), 'Trade with China', *New York Daily Tribune*, 3 December.

MARX, K. (1862), in *Die Presse*, Vienna, 7 July.

NAMBOORIDIRIPAD, E. M. S. (1952), *The National Question in Kerala*, Bombay.

WITTFOGEL, K. A. (1957), *Oriental Despotism*, New York and London.

Further Reading

English editions of Marx's works are many and varied. At the time of writing (January 1974) the following are probably the most easily obtainable in the United Kingdom:

Capital, volume I, Lawrence & Wishart, 1970.

Capital, volume II, Lawrence & Wishart, 1970.

Capital, volume III, Lawrence & Wishart, 1972.

Theories of Surplus Value, Part One, Lawrence & Wishart, 1969.

Theories of Surplus Value, Part Two, Lawrence & Wishart, 1969.

Theories of Surplus Value, Part Three, Lawrence & Wishart, 1972.

Economic and Philosophical Manuscripts of 1844, edited and with an introduction by D. Struik, Lawrence & Wishart, 1970.

The Poverty of Philosophy, International Publishers, New York, 1971.

The German Ideology, Part I with Selections from Parts II and III, edited and with an introduction by C. J. Arthur, Lawrence & Wishart, 1970.

A Contribution to the Critique of Political Economy, edited and with an introduction by Maurice Dobb, Lawrence & Wishart, 1971.

Grundrisse, translated and with a foreword by Martin Nicolaus, Penguin, 1973.

Marx and Engels: Selected Works, Volumes I, II, and III, Progress Publishers, Moscow, 1973 (contains, *inter alia*, three short works cited below: *Wage Labour and Capital; Wages, Price and Profit*, and *Critique of the Gotha Programme*).

1 An overview
Marx

Wage Labour and Capital

Wages, Price and Profit
   Two short pamphlets, written in relatively simple language, and providing a good introduction to the core of Marx's political economy.

Secondary sources

M. Blaug, *Economic Theory in Retrospect*, Heinemann, 1968 (chapter 7).

D. Horowitz (ed.), *Marx and Modern Economics*, MacGibbon & Kee, 1968.

Joan Robinson, *An Essay on Marxian Economics*, Macmillan, London, 1942 (second edition, with new introduction, 1969).

E. Roll, *A History of Economic Thought*, Faber & Faber, 1961 (chapter 6).

J. A. Schumpeter, *A History of Economic Analysis*, Allen & Unwin, 1954 (use index).

2 Theoretical underpinnings
Marx

Economic and Philosophic Manuscripts of 1844
   These were unpublished during Marx's lifetime. Their primary importance is that they contain his early ideas on alienation; they also outline some of his early ideas on economic theory, many of which he was later to modify.

The German Ideology, Part I
   Written in 1845–6, this work was unpublished in Marx's lifetime. It is primarily important as the first systematic statement of the materialist conception of history.

The Poverty of Philosophy
   This was published in 1847 as a reply to Proudhon's 'Philosophy of Poverty'. Its main significance lies in its presentation of the materialist conception of history, but it also contains much of interest on Marx's economic method and early economic ideas (again, many of which he was later to modify).

Grundrisse: Foundations of the Critique of Political Economy (Rough Draft)
   This was a work of self-clarification undertaken in 1857–8. The first full English translation is the Penguin edition of 1973. Its chief interest lies in its clarification of Marx's economic method, of his theory of alienation and fetishism, and many of his more mature ideas on historical development. (Important extracts, mainly centred on Marx's theory of alienation, can be found in *Marx's Grundrisse*, edited by D. McClellan, Macmillan, London, 1971; many of the historical passages appeared in *Karl Marx: Pre-Capitalist Economic Formations*, edited by E. J. Hobsbawm, Lawrence & Wishart, 1964, to which Hobsbawm also provides an excellent introduction.)

Capital, volume I, chapter 1, section 4.
   This is Marx's main discussion of commodity fetishism, partly reprinted here as Reading 9.

Capital, volume I, part VIII.
   This deals extensively with certain historical changes which Marx regarded as crucially important in bringing about capitalist development in Europe. (Also important in this respect are chapters 20, 26, 37 and 47 of *Capital*, volume III.)

Capital, volume III, part VII.
   This highlights important aspects of Marx's economic method, and develops the theory of fetishism as applied to capitalist commodity production. Part of this section is reprinted here as Reading 11. (On these issues see also *Theories of Surplus Value*, Part Three, Addenda.)

Critique of the Gotha Programme
   Written in 1875, this is particularly important in outlining Marx's conception of post-capitalist society.

Two useful collections of extracts from Marx's works are:

T. B. Bottomore and M. Rubel (eds.), *Karl Marx: Selected Writings in Sociology and Social Philosophy*, Penguin, 1963.

D. McLellan (ed.), *The Thought of Karl Marx: an Introduction*, Macmillan, London, 1971.

Secondary sources

H. B. Acton, *The Illusion of the Epoch*, Cohen & West, 1955.

R. Aron, *Main Currents in Sociological Thought: Volume I*, Weidenfeld & Nicolson, 1965; Penguin, 1968.

S. Avineri, *The Social and Political Thought of Karl Marx*, Cambridge University Press, 1968.

R. Blackburn (ed.), *Ideology in Social Science*, Fontana and Collins, 1972.

M. Bober, *Karl Marx's Interpretation of History*, Harvard University Press, 1950.

M. H. Dobb, *Studies in the Development of Capitalism*, Routledge & Kegan Paul, 1963.

M. C. Howard and J. E. King, *The Political Economy of Marx*, Longmans, 1975 (chapters 1, 2 and 8).

E. K. Hunt and J. G. Schwartz (eds.), *A Critique of Economic Theory*, Penguin, 1972.

G. Lichtheim, *Marxism*, Routledge & Kegan Paul, 1961.

A. MacIntrye, *Marxism and Christianity*, Penguin, 1971.

E. Mandel, *Marxist Economic Theory*, Merlin, 1968 (chapters 1–4).

H. Marcuse, *Reason and Revolution*, Routledge & Kegan Paul, 1955.

R. L. Meek, *Studies in the Labour Theory of Value*, second edition, Lawrence & Wishart, 1973 (introduction).

I. Meszaros, *Marx's Theory of Alienation*, Merlin, 1970.

R. Miliband, *The State in Capitalist Society*, Weidenfeld & Nicolson, 1969.

B. Ollman, *Alienation: Marx's View of Man in Capitalist Society*, Cambridge University Press, 1971.

V. Venable, *Human Nature: The Marxian View*, Meridian Books, 1966.

3 The theory of value
Marx

Capital, volume I, chapters 1–2.

The complicated chapter 1 establishes the basis of the labour theory of value, and discusses commodity fetishism, a topic further developed in chapter 2 on the process of exchange. (Part of chapter 1 is reprinted here as Reading 9.)

Capital, volume I, chapters 4–6.

Chapter 4 demonstrates the nature of exchange in capitalism; chapter 5 shows that surplus value originates in production rather than in exchange; chapter 6 analyses the market for labour-power.

Capital, volume I, chapters 7–8; 16–17.

In chapter 7 Marx develops his theory of surplus value, distinguishing in chapter 8 between constant and variable capital; in chapters 16–17 he discusses the determinants of the rate of exploitation.

Capital, volume III, chapters 48–50.

Here Marx applies the concept of fetishism to the analysis of income distribution, attacking on methodological grounds early 'factor productivity' theories of class shares.

Capital, volume III, chapters 8–12.

These chapters give Marx's account of the transformation problem, and his provisional solution to it. They show how the process of competition itself confuses economic agents, and hides the true nature of value and the origins of surplus value.

Theories of Surplus Value, Part One, chapters 2–3.

Here Marx expounds and criticizes the theories of value, and the embryonic theories of surplus value, of the Physiocrats and Adam Smith.

Theories of Surplus Value, Part Two, chapters 10 and 15.

Chapter 10 discusses Ricardo's theory of price, and chapter 15 his theory of surplus value.

Critique of Political Economy, Part I.

A general attack on the classical theory of value, culminating in the passage analysed by Shoul in Reading 17. (The Lawrence & Wishart edition also contains an excellent introduction by Dobb.)

Secondary sources
The classical theory of value

M. H. Dobb, *Political Economy and Capitalism*, Routledge, 1937 (chapters 1–3).

M. H. Dobb, *Theories of Value and Distribution since Adam Smith*, Cambridge University Press, 1973 (chapters 2–5).

M. C. Howard and J. E. King, *The Political Economy of Marx*, Longmans, 1975 (chapters 3–4).

R. L. Meek, *Studies in the Labour Theory of Value*, second edition, Lawrence & Wishart, 1973 (chapters 2–3; chapter 4, section 1).

P. Sraffa, 'Introduction', in P. Sraffa (ed.), *The Works and Correspondence of David Ricardo*, Cambridge University Press, 1951.

Marx's theory of value: Before transformation

M. H. Dobb, *Political Economy and Capitalism*, Routledge, 1937 (chapter 3).

M. H. Dobb, *Theories of Value and Distribution since Adam Smith*, Cambridge University Press, 1973 (chapter 6).

M. C. Howard and J. E. King, *The Political Economy of Marx*, Longmans, 1975 (chapter 4; chapter 5, parts 1–2 and 5).

R. L. Meek, *Studies in the Labour Theory of Value*, second edition, Lawrence & Wishart, 1973 (chapters 4–5).

M. Morishima, *Marx's Economics*, Cambridge University Press, 1973 (chapters 1–6 and 13–14).

Joan Robinson, *Economic Philosophy*, Penguin, 1964 (chapter 2).

T. Sowell, 'Marxian value reconsidered', *Economica*, vol. 30, 1963, pp. 297–308.

P. M. Sweezy, *Theory of Capitalist Development*, Dobson, 1946 (chapters 3–4).

P. H. Wicksteed, 'The Marxian theory of value', in P. H. Wicksteed, *Commonsense of Political Economy*, vol. II, Routledge, 1933, pp. 705–24.

M. Wolfson, *A Reappraisal of Marxian Economics*, Columbia University Press, 1966 (chapters 2–3).

The transformation problem

A. Bhaduri, 'On the significance of recent controversies in capital theory: a Marxian view', *Economic Journal*, vol. 79, 1969, pp. 532–9.

E. von Böhm-Bawerk, *Karl Marx and the Close of His System* (P. M. Sweezy ed.), Kelley, 1966.

L. von Bortkiewicz, 'On the correction of Marx's fundamental theoretical construction in the third volume of "Capital" ', in E. von Böhm-Bawerk, *Karl Marx and the Close of His System* (P. M. Sweezy ed.), Kelley, 1966, pp. 199–221.

P. Garegnani, 'Heterogeneous capital, the production function and the theory of capital', *Review of Economic Studies*, vol. 38, 1970, pp. 407–36.

G. C. Harcourt, *Some Cambridge Controversies in the Theory of Capital*, Cambridge University Press, 1972.

M. C. Howard and J. E. King, *The Political Economy of Marx*, Longmans, 1975 (chapter 5, parts 3–4).

R. L. Meek, *Economics and Ideology and Other Essays*, Chapman & Hall, 1967 (pp. 161–78).

R. L. Meek, *Studies in the Labour Theory of Value*, second edition, Lawrence & Wishart, 1973 (introduction).

A. Mediò, 'Profits and surplus-value: appearance and reality in capitalist production', in E. K. Hunt and J. G. Schwartz (eds.), *A Critique of Economic Theory*, Penguin, 1974, pp. 312–46.

M. Morishima, *Marx's Economics*, Cambridge University Press, 1973 (chapters 7–8 and 12).

P. A. Samuelson, 'Understanding the Marxian notion of exploitation: a summary of the so-called transformation problem between Marxian values and competitive prices', *Journal of Economic Literature*, vol. 9, 1971, pp. 399–431.

P. Sraffa, *The Production of Commodities by Means of Commodities*, Cambridge University Press, 1960.

P. M. Sweezy, *Theory of Capitalist Development*, Dobson, 1946 (chapter 7).

J. Winternitz, 'Values and prices: a solution of the so-called transformation problem', *Economic Journal*, vol. 58, 1948, pp. 276–80.

4 The theory of economic development

Marx

Capital, volume II, chapters 20–21.

Chapter 20 develops Marx's model of simple reproduction, in which net investment is zero. On the basis of this model, chapter 21 allows for capitalists' saving, and analyses 'expanded reproduction'.

Capital, volume I, chapter 25.

This long chapter combines theoretical reasoning and historical evidence on the nature and effects of technical change in capitalist economies. It includes Marx's most systematic account of the growth of the industrial reserve army, and of his wage theory.

Theories of Surplus Value, Part Two, chapter 16.

Marx's critique of the Ricardian theory of the falling rate of profit highlights the crucial methodological differences between Marxian and classical political economy. Marx's own analysis is seen to depend on increasing rather than decreasing productivity, and thus to be bound up with the question of technical progress.

Capital, volume III, chapters 13–14.

These two chapters extend Marx's argument on the falling rate of profit. Chapter 13 shows that technical change increases the organic composition of capital and thus tends to reduce the rate of profit, while chapter 14 discusses the 'countervailing influences' which may weaken or abort this tendency.

Capital, volume III, chapter 15.

Here Marx discusses the relationship between income distribution, aggregate demand, and economic crises.

Theories of Surplus Value, Part Two, chapter 17, sections 6–14.

These notes on Ricardo's theory of accumulation, unsystematic and unfinished as they are, represent Marx's most elaborate exposition of his theory of crises. His refutation of Say's law, and his emphasis on the uniquely crisis-prone nature of capitalism, are lucidly developed.

Secondary sources

Reproduction

A. Ehrlich, 'Notes on Marxian model of capital accumulation', *American Economic Review*, vol. 57, Papers and Proceedings, 1967, pp. 599–616.

E. Evenitsky, 'Marx's model of expanded reproduction', *Science and Society*, vol. 27, 1963, pp. 159–75.

M. C. Howard and J. E. King, *The Political Economy of Marx*, Longmans, 1975 (chapter 6, sections 3 and 6).

W. Krelle, 'Marx as a growth theorist', *German Economic Revue*, vol. 9, 1971, pp. 122–33.

M. Morishima, *Marx's Economics*, Cambridge University Press, 1973 (chapters 9–10).

K. A. Naqvi, 'Schematic presentation of accumulation in Marx', *Indian Economic Review*, vol. 5, 1960, pp. 13–22.

Joan Robinson, *An Essay on Marxian Economics*, Macmillan, London, 1942 (chapter 6).

Joan Robinson, *On Re-Reading Marx*, Students' Bookshop, 1953.

Technical change, the reserve army and the falling rate of profit

M. Blaug, 'Technical change and Marxian economics', *Kyklos*, vol. 13, 1960, pp. 495–509.

M. C. Howard and J. E. King, *The Political Economy of Marx*, Longmans, 1975 (chapter 6, parts 2 and 4).

R. L. Meek, *Economics and Ideology and Other Essays*, Chapman & Hall, 1967, pp. 113–28.

M. Morishima, *Marx's Economics*, Cambridge University Press, 1973 (chapters 11–12).

N. Okishio, 'A mathematical note on Marxian theorems', *Weltwirtschaftliches Archiv*, vol. 91, 1963, pp. 287–98.

P. A. Samuelson, 'Wages and interest: a modern dissection of Marxian economic models', *American Economic Review*, vol. 47, 1957, pp. 884–912.

P. A. Samuelson, 'The economics of Marx: an ecumenical reply', *Journal of Economic Literature*, vol. 10, 1972, pp. 50–51.

T. Sowell, 'Marx's "increasing misery" doctrine', *American Economic Review*, vol. 50, 1960, pp. 111–20.

P. M. Sweezy, *Theory of Capitalist Development*, Dobson, 1946 (chapters 5–6).

P. M. Sweezy, 'Karl Marx and the industrial revolution', in R. V. Eagly (ed.), *Events, Ideology and Economic Theory*, Wayne State University Press, 1968, pp. 107–19.

Crises

B. A. Balassa, 'Karl Marx and John Stuart Mill', *Weltwirtschaftliches Archiv*, vol. 83, 1959, pp. 147–63.

M. Bronfenbrenner, ' *Das Kapital* for the modern man', *Science and Society*, vol. 29, 1965, pp. 419–38.

Fan-Hung, 'Keynes and Marx on the theory of capital accumulation, money and interest', *Review of Economic Studies*, vol. 7, 1939, pp. 28–41.

N. Georgescu-Roegen, 'Mathematical proofs of the breakdown of capitalism', *Econometrica*, vol. 28, 1960, pp. 225–43.

M. C. Howard and J. E. King, *The Political Economy of Marx*, Longmans, 1975 (chapter 6, part 5).

M. Rakshit, 'Reserve army, effective demand and Marxian crisis models', *Arthaniti*, vol. 5, 1962, pp. 1–25.

Joan Robinson, *An Essay on Marxian Economics*, Macmillan, London, 1942 (chapter 6).

J. A. Schumpeter, *A History of Economic Analysis*, Allen & Unwin, 1954 (use index).

H. Sherman, 'Marx and the business cycle', *Science and Society*, vol. 31, 1967, pp, 486–504.

B. Shoul, 'Karl Marx and Say's law', *Quarterly Journal of Economics*, vol. 71, 1957, pp. 611–29.

J. Steindl, *Maturity and Stagnation in American Capitalism*, Blackwell, 1952.

P. M. Sweezy, *Theory of Capitalist Development*, Dobson, 1946 (chapters 8–12).

5 Imperialism
Marx

Karl Marx on Colonialism and Modernisation, edited and with an introduction by S. Avineri, Anchor Books, Garden City, N.Y., 1969.

This largely consists of Marx's journalistic articles on the non-European world, with some relevant extracts from his general theoretical writings and correspondence. (Avineri's introduction is reprinted here as Reading 23.)

K. Marx and F. Engels on Colonialism, Lawrence & Wishart, 1960.

Again, this contains Marx's journalism, but there are more extracts from his theoretical work and his correspondence. The latter includes some of Marx's views on the role of colonies in the genesis of capitalism in the West, which we have not dealt with here.

Pre-Capitalist Economic Formations, edited with an introduction by E. J. Hobsbawm, Lawrence & Wishart, 1964.

This is made up of extracts of Marx's views on historical development, mainly from the *Grundrisse*, which deal in part with Asiatic society. Hobsbawm's introduction is excellent.

Secondary sources

S. Avineri, *The Social and Political Thought of Karl Marx*, Cambridge University Press, 1968 (chapter 6).

M. C. Howard and J. E. King, *The Political Economy of Marx*, Longmans, 1975 (chapter 7).

T. Kemp, *Theories of Imperialism*, Dobson, 1967 (chapter 2).

V. Kiernan, 'Marx and India', *Socialist Register*, 1967, pp. 159–89.

G. Lichtheim, 'Marx and the "Asiatic mode of production" ', *St Anthony's Papers*, vol. 14, 1963, pp. 86–112.

R. Owen and R. Sutcliffe (eds.), *Studies in the Theory of Imperialism*, Longmans, 1972.

E. Stokes, 'The first century of British colonial rule in India: social revolution or social stagnation?' *Past and Present*, no. 58, 1973, pp. 136–60.

D. Thorner, 'Marx on India and the Asiatic mode of production', *Contributions to Indian Sociology*, no. 9, 1966, pp. 33–66.

K. Wittfogel, *Oriental Despotism*, Yale University Press, New Haven, 1957 (chapter 9).

Acknowledgements

Permission to reproduce the readings published in this volume is acknowledged from the following sources:

1 Canadian Economics Association
2 Lawrence & Wishart Ltd
3 A. D. Peters & Co. Ltd
4 A. D. Peters & Co. Ltd
5 Lawrence & Wishart Ltd
6 A. D. Peters & Co. Ltd
7 A. D. Peters & Co. Ltd
8 A. D. Peters & Co. Ltd
9 Lawrence & Wishart Ltd
10 Lawrence & Wishart Ltd
11 Lawrence & Wishart Ltd
12 A. D. Peters & Co. Ltd
13 A. D. Peters & Co. Ltd
14 Chapman & Hall Ltd
15 *Science & Society*
16 Monthly Review Press
17 *Science & Society*
18 *Review of Economic Studies*
19 *Hitotsubashi Journal of Economics*
20 University of Chicago Press
21 Chapman & Hall Ltd
22 *Schweizerische Zeitschrift für Volkswirtschaft und Statistik*
23 Doubleday & Company Inc.

Author Index

Subject Index

Department – *contd*
  II, 28, 35, 188
  III, 28
diminishing returns, 159
disequilibrium, *see* cyclical fluctuations
disproportionality, *see* cyclical
  fluctuations
distribution, 23–5, 84, 198–9, 200
  see also profit: reserve army of
  unemployed
division of labour, 58, 94, 140–41,
  221–2

economic structure, *see* materialist
  conception of history; relations of
  production
economics, 11–12, 17, 83, 142
economics of scale, 36
effective demand, *see* cyclical
  fluctuations
employment, *see* cyclical fluctuations;
  reserve army of unemployed;
  Say's law
England, *see* imperialism
equilibrium, *see* reproduction models;
  transformation
exchange value, 143–4, 148, 153
expanded reproduction, 35–6, 43,
  190–93
  see also reproduction models
exploitation, 25–6, 31, 37, 63, 71, 122,
  131–3, 137, 246–8
  rate of, 26, 63, 156, 168, 188, 193,
  199, 203

false consciousness, 15, 17
  see also fetishism
fetishism, 15–17, 72, 95–103, 105–9,
  132
feudalism, *see* relations of personal
  dependence; stages of production
fixed control, *see* capital
forces of production, 10–11, 79, 111–13
freedom, 15, 17–19, 110

historical materialism, *see* materialist
  conception of history

historical specificity, *see* methodology

ideal type, 13
ideology, 79
  see also fetishism
immiseration thesis, 63
  see also alienation; reserve army of
  unemployed
imperialism, 43, 198, 235–56
income distribution, *see* profit;
  surplus value; reserve army of
  unemployed
India, 243–9, 250–54
Indian Mutiny, 252–3
inevitability, 52–3, 58, 79
invariance postulates, 28, 166–7,
  170–71

Japan, 254

labour, necessary, 25
  socially necessary, 14, 23, 70, 73, 152
  surplus, 24, 26
  types of, 144–7
  wage form of, 86, 91, 104, 151
labour command theory of value, 150,
  153, 156
labour power, 25, 123, 134, 153–4
labour theory of value, 15, 22–32,
  39–40, 49, 64–72, 119–27, 131–76
  see also commodity production;
  transformation; value
law of value, 68, 119–27
  see also labour theory of value
laws, economic, 11, 33, 84, 116
laws of motion, 32, 51–2
logical historical method, 27, 117–18,
  120–24, 127

Malthusian population principle, 36
manufacture, 36, 221–2
materialist conception of history,
  10–11, 18, 53, 79–80, 238–9,
  242–4, 246, 255
  see also methodology

methodology, 13–15, 22, 48–55, 66–7, 69, 73–4, 81–5, 114–27, 142
mode of production, *see* materialist conception of history; stages of production
modern industry, 36, 221–2
money, 42, 61–2, 94, 96–7, 99, 109
  see also capital; commodity production; cyclical fluctuations; Say's law
monopoly, 32
  see also capital

neoclassical economics, 12, 19–22, 132, 134, 200

organic composition of capital, *see* capital
oriental despotism, *see* Asiatic society
overproduction, *see* cyclical fluctuations

petty mode of production, 127
  see also commodity production
physiocrats, 99
prehistory, 80
price of production, 27, 29, 30, 124–5, 136, 138, 157–8, 162, 186–7
  see also profit; transformation; value
production, nature of, 81–5
profit
  falling rate of, 33, 36–9, 41–2, 62–4, 159, 182–3, 203–18
  rate of, 26–7, 157, 193–7, 199, 203
  see labour theory of value; transformation; surplus value
proletariat, 11, 12, 17–18, 39, 247, 249–50

rate of exploitation, *see* exploitation
rate of surplus value, *see* exploitation; surplus value
realization crises, *see* cyclical fluctuations

relations of personal dependence, 12–13, 16, 81–2, 87, 93, 95–6, 101–2, 109–12
relations of production, 11, 79, 116–17, 120–22, 132–3, 135
  see also capitalism; exploitation; materialist conception of history; methodology
rent, 26, 108, 151, 159–61
reproduction models, 34–5, 41, 59, 185–201
reserve army of unemployed, 25, 36–7, 39–40, 42, 74, 193, 224, 227–9, 231
revolution, 17–18, 39, 42, 53, 60, 63, 79, 244, 249–50, 252, 255
Ricardian socialists, 71
Robinsonades, 81, 99–101

Say's law, 33–5, 57, 70, 198
simple commodity production, *see* commodity production
simple reproduction, 30, 35–6, 137, 164, 167–8, 189–90
slavery, *see* relations of personal dependence; stages of production
stages of production, 13, 80, 93
  see also materialist conception of history
stationary state, 32, 64, 132
subsistence wage, 25–6, 32, 199
  see also Malthusian population principle; reserve army of unemployed
superstructure, 79
  see also materialist conception of history
surplus labour, *see* labour
surplus product, 24, 90
  see also surplus value
surplus value, 14, 25–6, 34, 65–7, 71–2, 105–9, 122–4, 131, 133–5, 153, 156, 158–60, 168, 172, 180–82, 186–8, 203
  see also exploitation; profit; transformation; value

More about Penguins
and Pelicans

Penguinews, which appears every month, contains details of all the new books issued by Penguins as they are published. From time to time it is supplemented by *Penguins in Print*, which is our complete list of almost 5,000 titles.

. A specimen copy of *Penguinews* will be sent to you free on request. Please write to Dept EP, Penguin Books Ltd, Harmondsworth, Middlesex, for your copy.

In the U.S.A.: For a complete list of books available from Penguins in the United States write to Dept CS, Penguin Books, 625 Madison Avenue, New York, New York 10022.

In Canada: For a complete list of books available from Penguins in Canada write to Penguin Books Canada Ltd, 41 Steelcase Road West, Markham, Ontario.

The Pelican Marx Library

General Editor: Quinton Hoare, *New Left Review*

Grundrisse
Foundations of the Critique of Political Economy
(Translated with a foreword by Martin Nicolaus)

Early Writings
(Introduced by Lucio Colletti; translated by
Rodney Livingstone and Gregory Benton)

The Revolutions of 1848
Political Writings – Volume 1
(Edited and introduced by David Fernbach)

Surveys from Exile
Political Writings – Volume 2
(Edited and introduced by David Fernbach)

The First International and After
Political Writings – Volume 3
(Edited and introduced by David Fernbach)

TO BE PUBLISHED

Capital (in three volumes)

AMINO ACIDS IN THERAPY

A guide for practitioners that deals with all aspects of amino acid therapy and lists conditions which are particularly responsive to such treatment.

AMINO ACIDS IN THERAPY

A Guide to the Therapeutic Application of Protein Constituents

Leon Chaitow
N.D.,D.O.,M.B.N.O.A.

THORSONS PUBLISHERS LIMITED
Wellingborough, Northamptonshire

THORSONS PUBLISHERS INC.
New York

First published January 1985
Second Impression June 1985
Third Impression 1986

British Library Cataloguing in Publication Data

Chaitow, Leon
    Amino acids in therapy. a guide to the
    therapeutic application of protein constituents.
    1. Amino acids—Therapeutic use
    I. Title
    615'.3137   RM666.A45

    ISBN 0-7225-0998-7

Printed and bound in Great Britain

I dedicate this work to the people I love most, Irene, Max, Alkmini and Sasha, with thanks for their support and affection

CONTENTS

INTRODUCTION

This book is designed to bring to the attention of the healing professions the importance and value of those fractions of protein which, therapeutically speaking, have been largely ignored for far too long — the amino acids. The explosion of research and knowledge in this area, and the paucity of published material, other than in biochemistry textbooks and professional journals, prompted the undertaking of its writing.

As a practitioner who has been involved for some twenty-five years in the use of nutritional measures in the battle against ill health, and in the promotion of optimum health, the use of amino acids is not new to me. They have been creeping into use for some years, but now their value in clinical practice has become very marked indeed; for example, the use of methionine and glutathione in heavy metal toxicities; the use of tryptophan in insomnia, and in some cases of depression; the use of lysine in herpes simplex infections; the use of arginine in certain cases of male infertility; the use of carnitine in a threatened myocardial infarction; the use of tryptophan and phenylalanine in weight control, or of taurine in gall bladder conditions and epilepsy, etc. All have proved of value in their therapeutic applications.

They can be said to be 'curative' only when the condition for which they are being employed is the result of a deficiency of the particular nutrient. They can also be used to ameliorate illness and to support a struggling body in chronic disease in ways that are not curative but which are certainly not injurious and which are often helpful. The underlying cause of any illness must be the prime consideration and any therapeutic supplementation, be it vitamin, mineral, enzyme or amino acid, must be seen as part of that effort, rather than as the sum total of effort required. It will be stressed frequently that individual needs for these, as for all nutrients, will show marked differences from one person to another. There is no standard dosage, and no standard approach to any condition, for it is the patient who is to be considered in his entirety not the symptoms manifested. Emotions, structure and posture, lifestyle, attitudes, behaviour patterns, genetic factors and diet are some of the keys to understanding the causes of ill health, and the promotion of recovery, maintenance and enhancement of health.

Amino acids are just some of the many nutrients that might be indicated in any given individual's requirements. I have found them of value and, if used according to the knowledge derived from research to date, quite safe. If we do no harm to our patients and in addition give their bodies the materials with which to begin to function adequately, then we are fulfilling a positive role in promoting health. I am not a biochemist, and am indebted to those whose work is in the field of research into the minutiae of biochemical activity.

As a practitioner who has employed the methods outlined in the book I have no hesitation in commending them to all who utilize nutritional methods in order to promote health. Knowledge of therapeutic usefulness of amino acids will develop rapidly in the years ahead. Once the basic understanding exists of the interrelationship between amino acids and the various body functions and biochemical processes in which they operate, keeping up to date with new discoveries will present little difficulty. As diagnostic methods, such as amino acid profiles, become available more widely, so will it become essential for all who utilize nutritional methods in therapy to become familiar with these universally valuable substances.

1.

AMINO ACID PROFILE: ASSESSING INDIVIDUAL REQUIREMENTS

It is obvious that if reliable use is to be made of amino acids, in therapeutic terms, some form of test is essential to help the practitioner to ascertain the needs of the patient. Recent developments, notably in the field of high performance liquid chromatography (HPLC), have allowed the development of tests which can be routinely performed to show amino acid levels. These can then be compared with normal or reference ranges in order to assess amino acid disturbances and to allow for interpretive guidelines to be produced.

Since amino acids play such vital roles in the healthy organism and since they have such a major part to play in terms of the structure and function of the body, in both health maintenance and disease, the importance of a test which can aid in the assessment of their relative presence cannot be overestimated. Such a test may be used to discover aspects of the nutritional and metabolic status of the patient, as well as the effects of such factors as stress, trauma, other therapeutic measures (drugs etc.), as well as nutritional supplementation.

It should be recognized that for proper utilization to take place, in terms of maintenance and development of body tissues, as well as in the myriad processes of the body, the amino acids must be present in the correct ratio to each other. If ratios are inadequate, in specific amino acids, the ability for proper protein synthesis will be adversely affected.

Until the recent development of more sophisticated methods,

such as HPLC, the only way in which an amino acid profile could be achieved involved cumbersome, time consuming and expensive methods, such as calorimetric and microbiological tests. HPLC is an analytical method of a degree of sensitivity, speed, reliability and relative cheapness, to allow for quantitative assessment of an individual's amino acid status.

Protein malnutrition is the frequent precursor of amino acid deficiency. Such deficiency-states may be associated with improper diet; failure to digest or absorb adequately; stress conditions; infection or trauma; drug usage; imbalances or deficiencies involving other nutrients, such as minerals or vitamins; age and its associated dysfunctions etc.

Supplementation of appropriate amino acids may result in a restoration of normality in conditions resulting from any of these causes. It should be noted that when there exists an inadequate total calorie intake in healthy individuals, there can result a utilization of amino acids as sources of energy. This can, in turn, result in amino acid deficiency, which will not be normalized by supplementation. For this reason, when dealing with healthy individuals, the evaluation of free amino acid pools in the tissue fluids (usually plasma or urine) requires in addition the examination of the factors which might physically be affecting the energy state of the body, such as stress or the dietary pattern.[1]

As part of the routine examination, and clinical testing of the patient the addition of amino acid profiles can be seen to provide potentially useful information. Among the conditions that can thus be evaluated are inherited or secondary amino acid disorders; hepatic and renal conditions; cardiovascular conditions; disorders of the immune system; musculoskeletal problems etc. It is now becoming clear that the role of amino acid ratios, in a variety of neurological and psychiatric conditions is also of importance. A series of amino acid surveys can be used to indicate the effectiveness, or otherwise, of therapeutic measures, and of the progress, or otherwise, of disease processes. The prognostic value of such methods therefore becomes important. In their survey of the subject of amino acid analysis Dennis Meiss and John McCue[1] discuss an example of information that might be gleaned from routine analysis of this sort.

The synthesis of collagen requires vitamin C-dependent hydroxylation of certain proline and lysine residues, a manganese-dependent glycolysation of specific hydroxylysine residues, and a copper-dependent cross linking through lysyl and hydroxylysyl derivatives. The stability of collagen depends on the hydroxyproline content and on the lysine-hydroxylysyl cross-links.

Any agent or condition that interferes with amino acid uptake or utilization will have deleterious effects on the synthesis and maintenance of collagen in bone and connective tissue. Important factors contributing to this availability and utilization of amino acids involve dietary intake, balanced levels of essential and non-essential amino acids, adequate supply of cofactors for enzyme action (including vitamins and minerals) and caloric status.

Here are some examples of how amino acid analysis might detect improper or disrupted collagen synthesis. A plasma sample that is unusually high in proline and lysine might indicate inadequate conversion of these amino acids. Proline and lysine must be hydroxylated into hydroxyproline and hydroxylysine in order for collagen to have proper strength and structure.

Symptoms of defective synthesis would include pain in limbs and a general weakening of collagen in tendons and bones. The problem could be linked to vitamin C deficiency. Vitamin C is essential for hydroxylating proline and lysine: collagen synthesized in the absence of vitamin C is usually insufficiently hydroxylated and therefore less stable and easily destroyed. The recommended treatment might be vitamin C supplementation. Another analysis of proline and lysine levels at a later date could be used to monitor the effectiveness of supplementation.

A further example is given in this paper which shows another possible way in which collagen levels might be impaired, and the way in which amino acid involvement might be detected.

Unusually high levels of glycine in the plasma and urine may signal caloric or renal deficiency — a serious impediment to proper collagen formation. As in the previous instance, weakening of collagen in tendons and bones would result. When the patient is not getting enough calories, glycine in collagen may be converted into pyruvic acid for use in energy conversion (gluconeogenesis). By increasing the patient's glucose level, proper collagen-glycine levels may be restored.

The causal relationship in these two examples is reasonably clear. Other instances may not prove so clear cut, and expert interpretation of the amino acid analysis may be called for.

Currently available in the U.S.A. are amino acid profiles which, at a cost of little over one hundred dollars, provide the following:

1. A laboratory print-out showing precise levels of thirty amino acids.
2. A comprehensive discussion of these results citing up-to-date literature, for further reference.
3. Any abnormal patterns are treated in detail in that the discussion explains whether they are characteristic of (or coincident with) various pathologies or other metabolic disturbances.
4. A summary of the discussion, emphasizing probable diagnostic considerations, and where appropriate, related mineral and vitamin requirements.
5. There is also a print-out of the physiological role of each amino acid that shows as abnormal in the report.

Minerlab in California, who offer this service, provide collection kits for plasma and urine samples, either of which can be used for the analysis. Plasma is shipped to the laboratory packed in dry ice, which makes the possibility of transatlantic delivery an improbable procedure. The urine sample is required within forty-eight hours of collection and this may well be a possibility if arrangements were made with an airline, or with a firm specializing in rapid document delivery. The urine specimen (twenty-four hour) is collected in a special container to which has been added hydrochloric acid (provided by the laboratory as part of the kit). During the collection period this is refrigerated, and two samples of the well mixed urine-acid mixture are mailed in special containers to the laboratory. It is only a matter of time before a similar facility is available in Europe, but for the present the obstacle of the Atlantic and continental America, remains.

The amino acids reported on in a Minerlab test are as follows: [2]

Alanine; a-aminoadipic acid; a-amino-n-butyric acid; arginine; asparagine; aspartic acid; b-alanine; b-amino-isobutyric acid; citrulline; ethanolamine; glutamic acid; glutamine; glycine; histidine; homocysteic acid; homoserine; hydroxylysine; isoleucine; leucine; lysine; methionine; ornithine; phenylalanine; phosphoserine; serine;

taurine; threonine; tryptophan; tyrosine; valine.

The reference ranges in the assessment and discussion, which is part of the report, represent the most statistically significant ranges which appear in the published literature on the subject. They are only guides and should not be regarded as absolute since research continues, and current beliefs may be modified by subsequent findings.

As with other tests and analysis this is not meant to be diagnostic, but to provide further evidence which, together with all other data available, should assist in the ascertainment of a diagnostic or prognostic finding.

An example from a Minerlab report gives an idea of the assistance such a print-out might be to the practitioner:

> Histidine is low in the urine of this individual. A low urine concentration of this amino acid has been reported to accompany rheumatoid arthritis. Also histidine levels are lower in patients taking salycilates and steroids (Bremer H.J. et al., *Disturbances of Amino Acid Metabolism,* Urbasn and Schwarzenberg, 1981).
>
> Additionally a low histidine level without accompanying low levels of a majority of other essential amino acids may imply a specific dietary deficiency. Optimum metabolism of histidine is dependent upon adequate availability of folic acid.

The development of this type of nutritional profile with its potential for incorporation into the standard clinical procedures of nutritionally orientated physicians, is a major step towards the ideal of being able to predict future patterns of disease long before they manifest. It is certainly evident that disturbances in the levels of and ratios between amino acids and other nutrient factors, if corrected by nutritional manipulation and supplementation at an early stage, may well prevent degenerative states from becoming manifest. Identification of individual requirements by these means is a major part of the task of the practitioner whose aim it is to both prevent ill health and to restore it once it is lost.

Used in this way amino acid therapy is seen to be providing the body with its needs rather than addressing the symptoms of the patient and thus avoids the employment of amino acids, and other nutrients, in a pharmacological manner.

This introduction to the subject is meant to focus attention on an area of nutrition which is growing in importance as research reveals more of its potential. Greater knowledge must come from a thorough immersion in the literature available in this field.

1. 'Amino Acid Analysis: An Important Nutritional and Clinical Evaluation Tool'. Meiss, D., Ph.D, and McCue, J., Ph.D. *Nutritional Perspectives,* Vol 6. No 2, pp 19-24. 1983.
2. Address: Minerlab, 3501 Breakwater Avenue, Hayward, California 94545 ([415] 83-5622)

2.

THE FIRST PRINCIPLES

All the nutrient factors essential for the health of the body are required in their optimum quantities in order for health to be manifest. The optimum quantity of any single nutrient will differ in each individual, depending upon characteristics which are either genetically or environmentally acquired, and which may vary with different conditions such as stress, infection, pregnancy etc.

The complex interrelationship between the essential nutrients of the body are becoming clear as research unravels the mysteries of biochemical activity. An area of current interest is that of the role of the amino acids. Their relevance to health, and their use in a variety of conditions of physical and mental dysfunction, make them an exciting new tool in the hands of the nutritionally orientated physician. It is essential that they be used therapeutically (a) only when there is a demonstrable requirement for their administration, and (b) when they are employed in such a way as to ensure that they are suitably combined with those nutrients with which they are normally associated, in their metabolism, and (c) that they are used in such a way as to ensure that no harm comes to the body through the creation of toxicity or of a nutrient imbalance.

These provisos are applicable to the use of all nutrients, whether they are vitamins, minerals, essential fatty acids or whatever. Because of particular inborn, or acquired idiosyncracies, an individual may have unusual requirements for a nutrient factor, or combination of factors. The assessment of that need is the task of the practitioner. Combined with the isolation of particular nutritional needs is the requirement to uncover the reasons for that particular need, if indeed that is possible, and to remedy the cause of the problem by suitable lifestyle or dietary or emotional alterations and modifications.

The division of nutrients into groups of particular biochemical activity or origin, such as vitamins, minerals, amino acids, etc. must not blind us to the fact that a long chain of activity exists which involves all the nutrient factors interacting. This may break down, or become inefficient, at any point along the chain if any one of the nutrients or their products is not present in its optimum quantity. In all physiological functions there is a level of nutrition relating to each participating nutrient, below which obvious signs of disease will be manifest, in the case of deficiency, and above which obvious signs of toxicity will be manifest, in the case of excess. Between the level of obvious deficiency and patent toxicity, lies an area of function in which there are infinitely varying degrees of normality. At the lowest level, just above deficiency, there will exist signs of sub-clinical dysfunction. Many people spend much of their lives in this state. And since it is demonstrable that individual needs may vary by large amounts (see next chapter) in the case of the amino acids, the level at which a breakdown of function occurs will differ widely. This makes a nonsense of Recommended Dietary Allowance figures, which at the best can be seen to be applicable to a mythical 'average' human who does not exist. Recommended dietary levels and therapeutic dosages of any nutrient can therefore only give a rough guideline, as to whether the needs of the body are going to be met.

It is self-evident that the dietary levels of intake, of any nutrient, is but the first step in a chain of events involving the ultimate safe arrival of the nutrient, or its products, at the site of the particular biochemical activity for which it was destined. The bioavailability of the substance and its ability to be absorbed, transported and utilized at the cellular level are all factors which must be considered if deficiency is suspected. Whatever stage of a nutrient's journey to its biological appointment is inefficient, or disturbed, requires therapeutic attention, rather than that there should be an automatic assumption that deficiency, on the cellular level, necessarily means that there is a dietary inadequacy. Nowhere is this more evident than in amino acid therapy.

Naturopathic methods, and modern clinical nutrition and

orthomolecular methods, are in total accord inasmuch as adequate nutrition is seen to be one of the main essentials for health. The same factors which promote and maintain health are seen to be the factors which will restore it, or allow it to be restored, when health is absent. This is as true for amino acids as for any other nutrient. Unless the correct amount of any of these is present in the correct tissues at the appropriate time there will not exist the possibility for normal function of the body. The reasons for such a relative local deficiency may be different in one person as against another.

Inherited characteristics may determine the requirement of a particular nutrient in quantities far in excess of what is considered normal. This is the basis of genetotrophic theory of disease causation, as promulgated by Professor Roger Williams Ph.D. This will be considered later in more detail. There might be acquired alterations to digestive function, or to the ability of the nutrient to be absorbed. Such acquired absorption and digestive problems, are frequently the result of incorrect feeding programmes in infancy, which may produce damage to these functions that is irreversible.

General nutritional imbalance is also a possible cause of damaged absorption or utilization of nutrients. If the dietary pattern is such as to produce biochemical imbalances or inadequacies of substances which are vital to the processing, transportation or delivery of other nutrients, then that aspect must be dealt with, as a primary consideration. It is also possible that the only factor in a nutrient's inability to find its way to where it should be may be the form in which it is ingested. This can determine its biological availability. The example of orally ingested inorganic iron is clearly such a one. With all these variables, and with the vast and complex interrelation of nutrient factors, one to another, in all their chemical forms as they are swept along in the unending process of the vital life of the body, it is easy to become intellectually overwhelmed.

The ideal to aim for is of coming to an understanding of the body's general nutrient and other requirements, and of being able to identify particular needs. Thereafter the realization that the body is invested with self-regulating, self-healing attributes, which can be enhanced by modification of lifestyle, nutritional patterns, stress levels, etc., and which will then operate to improve overall function and restore health, is to have a sound basis for beginning to unravel the particular needs of any patient. The aim is not to identify nutritional requirements on the basis of 'a particular nutrient for a particular complaint', but to work with the body in its self-regulating efforts (homeostasis), and to attempt to provide the essential nutrient factors, which may be indicated, as part of a comprehensive approach which takes into account all those factors which might be mitigating against the normal working of the organism. As has been stated, there may be a variety of reasons for the self-same symptoms appearing in different people.

It is the causes which require identification, and not the symptoms which require 'curing'. There is every reason to attempt to make the patient more comfortable and to reduce the discomfort and misery of symptoms, but only if the underlying causes are also being dealt with, and if the treatment of the symptoms does not involve either the danger of adding to the body's problems, or of delaying the processes of recovery.

Were the use of nutrients in therapeutic terms to begin to mirror the use of drugs in that they were prescribed purely on a symptomatic basis, without regard to the real needs of the body, then the method would fall into justifiable disrepute. The essential difference would exist in that at least nutrients are elements which are part of the normal economy of the body, which most drugs are not. Nevertheless, they (nutrients) are capable of causing damage, and even death, if wrongly applied, and so the repetition is required of the fundamental principle of nutritional therapy, *that the body be provided with the nutrients it needs, in the quantities dictated by its own unique individuality.* It is on this basis, and this basis alone, that we should move on to attempt to assist the nutritional status of the body in general, and of the amino acids in particular.

Note: The designation of an amino acid with the letter l-(as in l-tryptophan) indicates the naturally occurring form, as found in foods or synthesized by the body. These will not be used in the text as it will be assumed that all amino acids discussed are l-form, unless otherwise stated e.g. d-phenylalanine.

3.

INDIVIDUAL REQUIREMENTS

In his landmark book on the subject of nutrition, entitled *Biochemical Individuality*[1] Roger Williams Ph.D. establishes the known facts relating to variations in the requirements of essential nutrients. This knowledge is re-emphasized and updated by Professor Jeffrey Bland in an overview of clinical nutrition comprising his contribution to the book of which he is also the editor, *Medical Applications of Clinical Nutrition,*[2] and the material contained in this chapter owes much to these two researchers.

There is evidence of variations in amino acid excretion patterns, in urine for example, which shows massive differences between individual amino acids such as lysine, where some healthy individuals displayed excretion levels several times that of others. The same individuals were also shown to have up to ten times the quantity of particular enzymes present in their saliva. Saliva has been used as a means of determining variations in individual make-up, and the degree of such variation, both as to constituents and as to their individual quantities, is profound. Similarly Williams reports that the amino acid composition of duodenal secretions indicates that each individual has a distinctive and relatively constant, pattern of amino acids, both in health and ill health.

Evidence that some pathological states were associated with particular patterns and characteristics, was also noted. In relation to amino acid variations in blood plasma, Williams showed that all individuals tend to maintain a unique, distinctive pattern of amino acid concentration. Studies were conducted to assess human amino acid requirements for the maintenance of nitrogen equilibrium. In a relatively small sample of individuals (about thirty people) it was demonstrated that, in some people, the RDA of amino acids was low by a factor of three. Larger samples of people could be expected to show even greater variations from the norm.

Bland discusses the range of individual amino acid requirements, pointing out that the reported ranges differ by between two- and seven-fold, with an average range of four-fold differences in requirements for particular amino acids. This was in samples of between 15 and 55 subjects. In one small group of college women variations in requirements of amino acids were between three- and nine-fold, with an average in excess of five-fold. Such findings are supported by animal models, and the general conclusion is that RDA of individual amino acids has little practical value, apart from the barest average guideline; and that individual requirements of amino acids, as with all nutrients, are variable to an unpredictable extent. Inborn genetic differences are the main single factor determining these variations. Every stage of any process within the body is capable of being genetically modified to create such variability. It could be that the digestion, absorption, processing into different forms, transportation, storage or utilization of any substance, in any biochemical process, has in some way been modified genetically to produce a unique nutrient requirement pattern. It is this pattern that must be met, within certain limits, in order for health to be enjoyed. It need not be any obvious genetic effect acting directly on the particular nutrient in question, but rather an indirect influence upon it, that creates a need for greater quantities than normal. Any genetic alteration of any of the thousands of enzymes involved with amino acids, in biochemical processes of the body, could result in expressions of imbalance in one nutrient factor or another, including amino acids.

Certainly factors other than the inherited characteristics of the individual can have similar, if less marked, effects. These can include the interaction of those nutrients present, or in short supply, in the diet; stress factors; exercise levels; particular physiological (e.g. pregnancy) or pathological (e.g. fever) states, which also present the body with demands in excess of RDA estimates. Trauma, shock, intense heat and cold, surgery and emotional strain, as well as the use of toxic substances, whether these be in the diet (e.g. alcohol, coffee) or in the environment (e.g. heavy metals in water, or atmospheric pollution) or the use of therapeutic or addictive drugs, may all involve increased demands for essential individual nutrients, sometimes by heroic amounts.

The term 'essential nutrient' may also be considered a variable factor in the light of the evidence of biological individuality. An essential nutrient is generally understood to be one which the body is unable to synthesize for itself, and which it is dependent upon the diet to provide. There are some forty-five such substances including, in adults under normal conditions, eight amino acids. However, under certain conditions some of the amino acids, which are usually considered non-essential, in that the body is able to synthesize them, can become 'essential' and require dietary reinforcement in order to maintain health. Such substances are called 'contingent nutrients' by Bland. This phrase has an elegance which encapsulates their ambiguous role. In certain contingencies they become essential, and recognizing the possibility is an invaluable aid in the effort to assess the particular needs of the individual. It appears that in the young and the elderly the chances of nutrients developing a contingent status is greatest. Arginine is synthesized in young people, but not in adequate amounts to meet the needs of the growth period. It is, therefore, at this time a contingent nutrient, and essential in the diet to maintain health.

There are other times when it is quite reasonable to suppose that the ability of the body to produce adequate quantities of particular non-essential amino acids might be wanting. Bland gives the example of histidine which we can produce in more or less adequate amounts under normal conditions. Since histidine is required in the production of histamine there are many opportunities for the body's requirements to outstrip its ability to produce enough. Such increased demands might occur during chronic illness or the use of particular drugs.

All amino acids are potentially contingent nutrients, under suitable conditions, and so the dividing line between the essential, and the non-essential may become blurred. In normal conditions there is a distinction to be made between those amino acids which can, and those which cannot, be self-produced. What is normal will differ with individuals and the stresses imposed upon them. Williams' concept of genetically originating 'diseases of nourishment', i.e. genetotrophic diseases, is the basis for our understanding of the phenomenon of diversity and individuality as to the needs of each person. The range of augmentation of specific nutrients required to deal with each inborn variation in requirement, in order to normalize, or prevent associated dysfunction and disease, has been estimated by Bland to vary from two-fold, to several hundred-fold, to meet the particular requirements of some people.

The assessment of the particular needs of any individual depends upon a mixture of the scientific analysis of various tissues (hair, blood, urine, etc.) as well as clinical observation and experience. The ideal of comprehensively analysing all the biochemical variables in the tissues and functions of the body, in order to arrive at a definitive conclusion as to the individual's requirements, would involve a battery of tests, frequently expensive, some of which are not adequately developed at this time. An analysis of the individual's diet, and an astute clinical assessment and observation of signs, symptoms and history, together with those tests, profiles, and analyses which are reliable and readily available, provides the best opportunity for identifying particular needs. The establishment of correct dosages of supplemental nutrients is a matter of experience, as well as trial and error. Such error should always err on the side of caution.

At this stage it is only necessary for us to be aware of the certainty that each person possesses variations in needs of all nutrients, and these variations are sometimes extremely marked. It is also pertinent to note a corollary to the above, that there exists a certain possibility that normally non-essential nutrients may be inadequately available, and therefore may be entering the realm of essential substances. Whether this is because of inborn factors or acquired ones is important to establish, since if acquired via the environment there exists a strong chance of removing causative factors. Such a possibility does not, however, present itself readily in genetically acquired idiosyncracies of this sort. In the latter cause permanent nutritional supplementation may be required to maintain health.

1. *Biochemical Individuality,* Roger Williams Ph.D., Texas University Press 1979.
2. *Medical Applications of Clinical Nutrition,* Ed. J. Bland, Keats 1983.

4.

AMINO ACIDS AND PROTEIN

By definition an amino acid is any of a large group of organic compounds which represent the end products of protein hydrolysis. They are amphoteric in reaction, and from them the body re-synthesizes its proteins. Ten of them are considered essential inasmuch as they are required to be present in the diet, at least at some stage of life, when the body is unable to manufacture either adequate amounts, or any at all, for its use. These ten are arginine, histidine, isoleucine, leucine, lysine, methionine, phenylalanine, threonine, tryptophan and valine.

Arginine and histidine are of ambiguous state inasmuch as they may be synthesized by the body, but arginine in young people, during the periods of growth, is required in the diet as well. Histidine is in a similar situation during youth, old age and when degenerative diseases are operating. These two then fall into the contingent category, discussed earlier.[1]

The other essential amino acids, together with a number of non-essential amino acids, such as glutamine and cystine, which have been found to have important therapeutic effects, form the main body of discussion of this book. New amino acids are being discovered, and doubtless therapeutic roles will be ascribed to some of these, and to many of the known but thus far therapeutically non-valuable ones. Our knowledge in this field is in its infancy. However, there are already indications as to the useful application of all of those mentioned above, as well as certain combinations of them.

The use of amino acid profiles, a method which is in its early stages of refinement, will in time enable the establishment of precise roles for all these substances. The possibility will exist for the use of such tests as prognostic indicators. Rather than as a means of diagnosing existing pathology such profiles will enable the foreseeing of trends and indications of impending health problems, which prompt action may be able to forestall.

In considering amino acids in relation to health and ill health there are two main areas to cover. The first looks at particular conditions relating to disorders of amino acid metabolism, resulting in a related pathological state. This will only be considered briefly, since the subject is more than adequately covered in standard medical textbooks. The second area, and the one which attracts the major interest among nutritionally orientated practitioners, is that involving conditions not specifically related to diseases of amino acid metabolism, and yet which appear to respond positively to dietary manipulation which involves the intake of particular amino acids (and other nutrients).

Such conditions as certain forms of depression; insomnia; herpes infections; weight problems; fat metabolism dysfunction; epilepsy, etc. have all been shown to improve, in suitable cases, by the use of appropriate amino acid therapy. Certain physiological functions have also been enhanced by the selective use of amino acids. These include detoxification of heavy metals; modification of free radical activity; enhanced mental function via neurotransmitter stimulation, etc.

The ability of the brain neurones to manufacture and utilize a number of neurotransmitters, such as serotonin, acetylcholine and, it is conjectured, the catecholamines, dopamine and norepinephrine, is dependent upon the concentrations of both the amino acids and choline in the bloodstream. This largely depends upon the food composition at the previous meal.[2] Since the brain is apparently unable to make adequate quantities of amino acids and choline to meet its requirements for neurotransmitter synthesis it is vital that adequate quantities of these precursors are present in the circulation.[3] The role of tryptophan and tyrosine in this process will be considered later. In the current context it is pertinent to simply be aware of the vital role played by amino acids in brain function. It is pointed out that the dry material of the brain comprises more than one third protein,[4] and that stress can create a situation in which non-essential amino acids cannot be adequately produced to meet its needs.[5] A number of researchers have shown that such a situation can result in a range of mento-emotional symptoms, such as depression, apathy, irritability etc. The subsequent imbalance in uric acid levels resulting from incomplete amino acid synthesis, and consequent utilization of free amino acids as fuel by the body, can result in children, in self mutilating behaviour.[6]

A neurotransmitter is a low molecular weight compound, soluble in water, which is ionized at the pH of the body tissues. Neurotransmitters are primarily synthesized in nerve terminals, and are stored to some extent in vesicles in the presynaptic terminus. When depolarization of the presynaptic neuron takes place, neurotransmitters are released coming into contact with specific receptors on the surface of the next, distal, postsynaptic cell. There exist both excitatory neurotransmitters, such as acetylcholine, as well as inhibitory neurotransmitters, such as serotonin, which decreases the likelihood of the postsynaptic cell firing. One postsynaptic neuron might receive stimulation from many thousands of presynaptic neurons simultaneously, somehow determining whether to depolarize or not. The neurotransmitters can be seen as the chemical link whereby one neuron, or a group of these, communicates with another. The importance of the neurotransmitters that are directly related to the nutritional intake of particular food is self-evident.

Some of the vital consequences of inadequate amino acid synthesis are therefore of potentially dramatic import in many current social and medical diseases. Before moving on to look at pathological states resulting from amino acid metabolism defects, it is important that we examine the basic role of protein and the relationship of the amino acids with it.

Protein

Life without protein is not possible. Growth development and function depend upon it, and it in turn depends upon the correct supply of amino acids. Apart from water, the next most profuse substance in the body is the amino acid group. The matrix into which these substances are incorporated is protein. The structure of all amino acids is similar in that a carbon atom, and an amino group (containing nitrogen), and a carboxyl group are always present as is a variable aliphatic radicle, indicated by the letter 'R', in the formula

$$H^3 N - C - C \begin{matrix} R \\ \\ R \end{matrix} \diagdown\diagup \begin{matrix} O \\ \\ O \end{matrix}$$

Those amino acids already present, by virtue of being synthesized in the body, are known as Non- Essential Amino Acids (NEAA) and the others, which must be derived from the diet, as Essential Amino Acids (EAA). Both groups are required, in order for protein synthesis to be completed satisfactorily. If one of the EAA is absent or inadequately supplied, then protein synthesis will not be possible. All the essential amino acids must therefore be present in the digestive tract at the same time. Proteins in foods differ substantially in their composition of amino acids. Those that contain all the EAA are termed complete proteins, and those that do not are called incomplete proteins (vegetable sources). Incomplete proteins can become complete by the judicious combining of appropriate vegetable sources, such as grains and pulses (ratio of 2:1).

Total protein requirements will vary with age, sex, body-type, occupation, stress levels, exercise pattern etc. Protein is required for the formation and maintenance of blood, muscle, skin and bone as well as the constituents of blood such as antibodies, red and white cells etc. Hormones, enzymes and nucleoproteins are all dependent upon protein. Certain racial groups are better able to metabolize the protein in their food than others. Orientals can survive in good health on a lower protein intake than Caucasians of the same age, sex and body-type.

Most amino acids can be converted into other amino acids, thus methionine can be altered to form cysteine; and tyrosine can be formed from phenylalanine. If protein is not able to be synthesized, due to an inadequate presence of EAA, then the body can utilize the remaining amino acids as fuel. However, since the body cannot oxidize the nitrogen portion of the amino acid, there is a degree of residue from such a process. This residue joins the breakdown products of protein in the body as urea or uric acid.

Despite earlier prejudice against the use of incomplete protein sources by vegetarians, it is now acknowledged that this mode of eating provides all that is required for a healthy body, as long as combinations of vegetable protein sources are adequate.

The relative quantities of amino acids contained in any particular food determines its nutritional value. Whilst individual amino acids may be absent from some vegetable sources of protein, there is nothing 'inferior' about the ultimate protein produced when correct vegetable protein combinations are simultaneously introduced into the eating pattern, so as to allow the amino acid 'pool' to contain its correct complement for protein synthesis. Wheat products, which are deficient in the essential amino acid lysine, are moderately endowed with methionine, whereas the reverse is true for legumes. If both were eaten at the same meal the proportions of lysine and methionine would then complement each other.[7]

Absorption of dietary amino acids, for protein synthesis by the liver, occurs from the intestines. Such synthesis is impaired if the EAA trytophan is not consumed at the same meal as the other amino acids.[7] One consequence of protein inadequacy is termed 'negative nitrogen balance'. This occurs when the intake and synthesis of protein fails to meet the overall level of total nitrogen loss via sweat, urine, faeces etc.

It is calculated that whilst 32 per cent of total estimated protein requirement in children should be supplied as essential amino acids, this level drops to only 15 per cent in adults. On a body weight basis adults therefore require 78mg of EAA per kilogram of body weight, whereas children require 214mg of EAA per kilogram of body weight per day. As has been stated, other variables in determining protein requirements may include stress, infection and heat, which can all cause increased nitrogen loss. Increases in muscle mass as a result of intensive exercise or heavy work will also call for increased protein synthesis, and therefore of greater amino acid intake. It is important to realize that calculation of protein requirements are only valid if the body's energy requirements have been met. For if energy intake is not adequate some dietary and/or tissue protein will be oxidized or converted into glucose in the liver to meet energy needs. Efficiency of nitrogen utilization is dependent upon the total calorie intake, and this is in turn a factor in deciding protein requirements.

Studies of nitrogen balance have produced estimates of RDA of protein for different groups. These do not, of course, take into account individual inherited or acquired variables as to requirements for particular amino acids. Whilst standard RDA levels seem to indicate that most people in industrialized countries obtain adequate protein levels, the number of variables (age, sex, occupation, health status, racial group, stress levels etc.) as well as the fact of biological individuality, makes these of questionable value. It is evident from surveys of food intake amongst urban teenagers for example that inadequate protein intake is not uncommon.

In America the intake of protein in healthy adults is estimated to be the equivalent of 90 - 100g per day, which represents between 15 and 17 per cent of the total caloric intake. Minimum protein requirements in an adult are set at 35-40g per day, and the RDA is put at 44-56g per day (in a healthy adult). The excess of protein over actual requirements indicates a more than adequate protein intake according to many nutritionalists. How then can there be the possibility of a deficiency in amino acids? The overall imbalance in nutrient intake, as well as the genetically determined variables in requirement, together create a situation in which particular needs may not be met, even in the face of the veritable deluge of protein. As health levels decline in the face of dietary patterns which bear little relation to the human body's actual needs, and as this factor, together with such elements as stress and pollution further mitigate against normal function, so there develops the possibility of conditions such as pancreatic insufficiency. This phenomenon is of vital importance to our understanding of the aetiology of amino acid deficits.

This subject is dealt with in detail in an appendix to the book *A Physician's Handbook on Orthomolecular Medicine.*[8] It is pointed out that the pancreas is faced with the task of making useful by-products from ingested food and chemicals, as well as buffering against reactions to foods and chemicals. For a variety of reasons the pancreas may be overstimulated, and one such reason is the very fact of excessive protein intake. The proteolytic enzyme production capacity of the pancreas can, like any other function, become impaired through over-use. This is especially true in an organ like the pancreas with multi-purpose functions, all of which may be being overtaxed simultaneously. A variety of factors can mitigate against longterm pancreatic efficiency. These include the assault on it by the monumental amounts of sugar which it is obliged to handle via its insulin production. Evolutionary adjustment to the increase in sugar consumption cannot occur in the short space of time involved in this dramatic change in human nutritional habits. Alcohol also has a direct ability to induce pancreatic insufficiency, as have a wide range of drugs, coffee and cigarettes.[9] Lipid peroxidation is considered another factor in diminishing pancreatic efficiency, and excessive fat intake is therefore a further contributory cause. The first effects of such a pancreatic insufficiency are a reduction in bicarbonate production, leading to symptoms which are frequently dismissed as gastritis. This is followed by reduced enzyme activity and finally aberrant insulin production.

Inactivation of, or insufficiency in the production of, proteolytic enzymes, from the pancreas, such as trypsin, chymotrypsin and carboxpeptidase, can result in poor digestion of proteins into amino acids. A further likelihood is that protein molecules might be absorbed in their undigested forms, which can provoke inflammatory reactions, sometimes in distant tissues and organs. If at the same time the circulating anti-inflammatory enzymes are deficient, as a further consequence of pancreatic exhaustion, then the ability of the body to deal with such inflammatory reactions (allergic or otherwise) will be reduced or absent. The ability of pancreatic insufficiency to interfere with amino acid digestion is, however, our main concern. Should inadequate breakdown of ingested proteins take place, and amino acid deficiency result, despite high levels of first class protein in the diet, the consequences could include difficulty, or inability, on the part of the body to produce adequate enzymes, hormones, antibodies and new tissues. The likelihood would then also exist for excessive demands to be made on a wide range of minerals and vitamins, particularly pyridoxine, zinc and magnesium, leading to deficiencies in these. The immune system's ability to adequately defend the body under such conditions would be severely compromised. Braganza[9] states that pancreatic dysfunction and disease involves the presence of free radical damaged phosphotidylcholine, and free radical damaged linoleic acid. As amino acids such as methionine and glutathione (the tripeptide, see page 88) protect against lipid peroxidation and free radical damage, their importance in such an aetiology is obvious.

We have, therefore, a picture in which the very presence of excessive protein in the diet (a fact of life in many western cultures) is a contributory cause of the deficiency of adequate protein levels within the system due to pancreatic insufficiency. The consequences of proteolytic enzyme deficiency resulting from pancreatic insufficiency, which itself results, in part, from specific amino acid deficiency (methionine etc.), is most important in our understanding of the role of diet in the production of amino acid imbalances and disease such as allergy. Amino acid imbalances acquired via environmental and dietary sources, superimposed upon those acquired by genetical idiosyncracies, thus create requirements of individual nutrients in excess of average, and this is the overall justification for utilizing amino acids and other nutrients therapeutically in the manner discussed in this book.

1. *Medical Applications of Clinical Nutrition,* Ed.J.Bland, Keats 1983
2. 'Nutrients and Neurotransmitters', *Contemporary Nutrition,* Vol.4 No. 12, 1979
3. *Archives of Pharmacology,* 303:157-164. 1978.
4. *Orthomolecular Psychiatry,* Vol.4, No.4. pp297-313, 1975.
5. *Journal of Clinical Nutrition,* 1:232, 1953.
6. *Schizophrenia,* 1:3:1967.
7. *Contemporary Nutrition,* Vol.5, No.1, 1980.
8. *A Physician's Handbook on Orthomolecular Medicine,* R. Williams, D. Kalita, Keats, 1979.
9. *The Lancet,* Vol.11 for 1983, 29 Oct, pp1000.

5.

AMINO ACIDS AND THE
BODY CYCLES

The biochemistry of the body is intensely complex, and in order
to come to terms with amino acid therapy it is necessary to have
a basic understanding of some of the major processes in which
they are involved or which affect them. Two such cycles of activity
are the urea cycle and the citric acid cycle (Krebs cycle).

The major toxic byproduct of amino acid activity in the body
is ammonia, and in order to prevent it from reaching harmful levels
in the system the body undertakes a sequence of metabolic
reactions, which turns the unwanted nitrogenous wastes into urea
for subsequent elimination via the kidneys. The liver is the main
site of this activity. This is called the urea cycle. Were ammonia
to be allowed to reach toxic levels a number of serious consequences
would occur.

The body produces an 'energy carrier' called adenosine
triphosphate (ATP) which is involved in many metabolic processes
concerning carbohydrates and amino acids. The production of
ATP is the result of activity in what is called the citric acid cycle,
or Krebs cycle, in which chemical respiration and oxidative
phosphorylation produce carbon dioxide and bound hydrogen
atoms. This leads to an electro-transfer reaction which results in
ATP. One other product of the sequence of metabolic reactions
in the citric cycle is the formation of alpha-ketoglurate, which is
the primary amino acid receptor. Acting with vitamin B_6, in the
form of the coenzyme pyridoxal phosphate, alpha-ketoglurate
detaches the NH_2 molecule from dietary protein. Thus it

counteracts excess acidity. This cycle of natural combustion of nutrients (citric acid/Krebs cycle) can be severely interfered with by the presence of ammonia, the breakdown product of amino acid activity. By interfering with and depleting the levels of alpha-ketogluterate, ammonia produces a toxic effect which can lead to a wide range of symptoms, such as: irritability; tiredness; headache; allergic food reactions (especially to protein foods); and also, at times, diarrhoea and nausea. It is also possible for mental symptoms to manifest, including a confused state. Alpha-ketoglutaric acid is the precursor of glutamic acid, the principal amino acid contributor to brain energy supplies. In the conversion to glutamic acid from alpha-ketogluteric acid, other amino acids are metabolized by the transaminase enzyme, and pyridoxal phosphate (B_6). When such an exchange is interfered with, for one of a number of reasons, there occurs an amino aciduria. Among the reasons put forward for the development of such a situation are: Vitamin B_6 deficiency; zinc deficiency, resulting in an inability to transform B_6 into pyridoxal phosphate; inadequate alpha-ketogluterase, etc.

It is possible for alpha-ketogluteric acid to be deficient when excessive ammonia is present, and also if the citric acid cycle is interfered with, or if manganese assimilation is not adequate.

Alpha-ketoglutaric acid may be usefully supplemented, in the diet, in cases where an excessive amount has built up, or where there is evidence of impaired citric acid cycle function. It may also be necessary when amino acid transfer is diagnosed as inadequate, and manganese is simultaneously found to be deficient. The therapeutic dose of alpha-ketoglutaric acid is between 500mg and 2500mg daily, together with pyridoxal phosphate (B_6), and a low protein diet.[1] Interruptions in the primary mechanism of nitrogen waste disposal, the urea cycle, can result in a variety of enzymatic deficiencies. It has been found that arginine can positively modulate certain aspects of such interruptions.[2]

Philpott maintains that there is evidence from amino acid profiles that alpha-ketoglutaric acid is the most deficient substance that can be demonstrated in cases of either physical or mental degenerative disease. He sees its involvement in a number of enzyme steps, associated with vitamin B_6, as well as its role as a precursor of glutamic acid, as being profoundly influential in the production of symptoms when it is deficient. The first such symptom to be noted being weakness. He points to the link between the citric acid cycle (energy generation sequence) and the urea cycle (nitrogenous waste disposal sequence) as being aspartic acid. The improvement in alpha-ketoglutaric acid status that might be achieved by supplementing its citric acid precursor, improves citric acid cycle function. Supplementation of aspartic acid would be expected to have a similar effect on the urea cycle, resulting in ammonia detoxification. Philpott bases his comments on the evidence of a large number of amino acid profiles, in cases of physical and mental degenerative disease. He states that the approach of utilizing citric acid and aspartic acid supplementation will more often than not be the correct one in such cases. If, however, reliable amino acid profile testing were available, specific evidence would then be to hand for confirming the requirement for such supplementation. [3] This is obviously more desirable than an arbitrary assumption.

Levine indicates a further ramification which involves the effects of stress on amino acid status. [4] In normal aerobic metabolism thirty-eight molecules of ATP (energy carrier) are produced for each molecule of glucose metabolized. In states of shock, oxygen consumption and supply decreases and acidosis ensues. This results in as little as two molecules of ATP being produced from each molecule of glucose. Low ATP precludes the biosynthesis of protein, and the derangement of amino acid metabolism which follows can result in many complications. Under flight simulation stress it has also been shown that there was raised excretion of basic and neutral amino acids concurrent with a lowered level of acidic amino acid excretion. The result of this for any length of time is the production of an acid state. Whilst dysfunction of the urea cycle may be the result of multiple enzyme deficiencies, it is frequently the result of impairment of the enzyme arginase. This would be indicated by high levels of arginine in the urine. Other defects in the urea cycle might be indicated by excessive amounts of ornithine, or citrulline. Arginase deficiency is usually accompanied by hyperammonaemia, with glutamine levels also elevated. Symptoms would usually relate to the effects of ammonia accumulation on carbohydrate metabolism, and upon the effect on neurotransmitters. Headache, motor problems, hyperactivity, irritability, tremors, ataxia, vomiting, liver enlargement, and even psychosis may occur. A requisite cofactor of arginase is manganese, and deficiency of this can result in increased excretion of arginine via the urine. Lysine and ornithine are inhibitors of arginase, and a diet high in lysine (such as that suitable in herpes infection) may be indicated in such defects of the urea cycle as well as supplementation of essential amino acids (including tyrosine and cystine). [5] A similar pattern of high arginine excretion (together with ornithine, cystine and lysine) may occur in the amino acid transport disorder cystinuria. This possibility can be excluded by determination of plasma arginine, and blood ammonia levels.

1. Pangborn, Jon, Bionostics Inc/Klair Laboratory, Pamphlet.
2. Jay Stein, (editor), *Internal Medicine,* Little Brown, 1983.
3. Philpott, W., Philpott Medical Center, Oklahoma City, Pamphlet.
4. Levine, Stephen. Allergy Research Group, Pamphlet.
5. Stanbury, J. et al. *The Metabolic Basis of Inherited Diseases,* McGraw-Hill, 1983.

6.

DISORDERS OF AMINO ACID METABOLISM

There are a recognized number of disorders relating to amino acid metabolism. It is also generally acknowledged, by even the most conservative of medical experts, that it is reasonable to assume that new inborn errors of amino acid metabolism will continue to be discovered and described, as the overall knowledge of amino acid metabolism develops. Disorders of amino acid metabolism, transport and storage, currently recognized by orthodox medicine do not individually involve large numbers of the population, although their overall combined incidence is substantial. Those diseases which result from amino acid metabolism defects, as a rule, affect mental faculties and result in a reduced life expectancy. Those that involve disorders of transportation and storage of amino acids are associated with a wide range of symptoms. Diagnosis of these disorders requires access to skilled clinical laboratory facilities.

Techniques such as amino acid analysis, simple chromatography and electrophoresis can cope with assessment of amino acid status before transamination. Once this has occurred, however, more complex procedures such as gas-chromatography, mass-spectrometry, and the more recent high-performance liquid chromatography, are required to provide unambiguous identification of amino acid status. Access to this type of diagnostic procedure is outside the scope of most practitioners, and it is therefore in a hospital or clinic setting that such conditions are likely to be assessed and treated.

Our interest in these conditions has two purposes. Firstly, to be aware of their existence and to be alert to them should they come into our care. Secondly, to be aware of the type of ramification possible in the case of total absence of a particular amino acid aids us in our understanding of its possible effects in partial deficiency. The subclinical and early clinical signs of mild deficiency are far more likely to be the subject of clinical attention if the previously discussed mechanisms of pancreatic insufficiency and individual patterns of genetically acquired increased requirement are operating.

Diseases Directly Related to Amino Acids

Glycine	Nonketotic hyperglycinaemia
	Ketotic hyperglycinaemia
Alanine	Lactic acidosis
Valine	Hypervalinaemia
	Maple Syrup Urine Disease (MSUD)
Isoleucine	Propionic acidaemia
	MSUD
Leucine	Isovaleric acidaemia
	MSUD
Methionine	Hypermethioninaemia
Cystine	Cystinosis
	Cystinuria
Serine	Hyperoxaluria II
Threonine	Hyperthreoninaemia
Phenylalanine	Phenylketonuria (PKU)
	Atypical PKU
Tyrosine	Hereditary tyrosinaemia
Tryptophan	Tryptophanuria
Proline	Hyperprolineaemia I & II
Glutamic acid	Pyroglutamic acidaemia
Histidine	Histidinaemia

Arginine	Hyperargininaemia
Lysine	Hyperlysinaemia
Argininosuccinic acid	Arginosuccinicaciduria
Ornithine	Hyperornithinaemia Ornithin aminotransferase deficiency
Citrulline	Citrullinaemia
Homocystine	Homocystineuria
Pipecolic acid	Hyperpipecolicaemia Zellwagers' syndrome
b-Alanine	Beta-alaninaemia

Some Amino Acid Diseases:

Phenylketonuria: This is one of the most studied amino-acidopathies, with an incidence of approximately 1:14000 (USA). It is an autosomal recessive condition, which results from a deficiency of hepatic phenylalanine hydroxilase, which converts phenylalanine to tyrosine. Untreated, the symptoms are: severe mental retardation; hypopigmentation of skin and hair; eczema like rashes; seizures; EEG abnormalities; and microcephaly. The cause of mental retardation is thought to be either direct cerebral toxicity, due to excess phenylalanine, or from the decreased presence of tyrosine, and consequent neurotransmitter deficiency. Dietary treatment, instituted in the first month, can result in IQ levels of close to 100 being achieved, as opposed to the untreated phenylketonuria (PKU) patient, in which an IQ of below 50 and generally around 20 is usual. The diet is maintained at a level low in phenylalanine, at an average daily intake of between 250mg and 500mg throughout childhood. This is continued at least until age eight.

Histidinaemia: Is the result of deficiency of the enzyme histidine-a-deaminase which converts histidine into urocanic acid. Symptoms include mental retardation, in fifty percent of cases, and speech defects. Although dietary levels of histidine can be manipulated to keep blood levels low, this does not produce clinical improvement.

Urea cycle disorders: Nitrogen waste is generated mainly by protein metabolism and is disposed of primarily by the urea cycle, in which free ammonia, or aspartic acid, are processed into urea. The ability to thus deal with nitrogenous wastes can be severely interrupted by a variety of possible factors all of which can result in a constellation of symptoms, including hyperammonaemia; mental retardation; protein intolerance; seizures and coma, and even death, if untreated. Treatment is initially by exchange transfusion, peritoneal dialysis or haemodialysis, to remove ammonia. Protein restricted diets are then instituted. Nitrogen removal is further enhanced by administration of keto acid analogs of EAA, and argenine supplementation. A variety of possible causes exist, and differential diagnosis requires skilled laboratory work.

Branched Chain Amino Acid Metabolism Diseases: These involve the amino acids leucine, isoleucine and valine, and include the best known of this class of diseases, Maple Syrup Urine Disease.

Maple Syrup Urine Disease: This is the result of deficiency of the enzyme keto acid carboxylase which assists in the degradation of all three branched chain amino acids. The name derives from the sweet smelling urine that results. There is a marked accumulation of these amino acids, particularly leucine. In neonates there may be vomiting, lethargy, hypertonicity, seizures, and death. Patients respond to dietary patterns low in these amino acids if instituted early. Variations in this condition include late onset forms, which recur with stress, infection and protein excess. One form responds to thiamin (B_1) therapy at doses of 10mg to 150mg daily.

Other forms of branched chain amino acid diseases are responsive to Vitamin B_{12} and Biotin, whereas all forms require strict dietary control.

Homocystinuria: Results from a deficiency of cystathionine synthetase which catalyzes the conversion of methionine to cystathionine. Symptoms include failure to thrive, light complexion and mental retardation. Life threatening disabilities such as venous and arterial thromboses may occur. Dietary levels low in methionine, and supplemented with cystine, seem effective, as is the use, in some cases, of high dosages of pyridoxine (B_6). (see 'Methionine' page 55).

Retinal Gyrate Atrophy: This condition results from ornithine-a-aminotransfirase deficiency and leads to atrophic degeneration of the retina and choroid, resulting initially in night blindness and subsequently loss of peripheral vision, leading to blindness by the fifth decade. It responds to a diet low in arginine. Low protein dietary patterns stabilize visual function.

Hartnup Disease: This results from transport dysfunction relating to alanine, serine, threonine, valine, leucine, isoleucine, phenylalanine, tyrosine, histadine and tryptamine. These can be elevated five- to ten-fold in the urine. Symptoms include a pellagra-like eczematoid rash of the extremities and face, which is photosensitive. Variable symptoms, such as ataxia tremor, nystagmus, hallucinations, mental retardation etc. These clinical features are episodic and can be produced by stress, infection, sunlight and sulphonamide treatment. There is a marked similarity between the symptoms and those of pellagra, even extending to improvement in skin and neurological abnormalities on the administration of nicotinamide.

As an example of overall amino acid profile distinctions between physically and mentally handicapped children, and normal children, a study carried out in Manchester and reported in *The Lancet* (11, 10-14, 1981) is illustrative. Amino acid excretions were taken from 75 physically and/or mentally handicapped children (epileptics, spastic, quadriplegia or diplegia, Down's syndrome, mental and developmental retardation, psychiatric disorders and congenital cataract) as well as from 59 children classified as normal. Ion-exchange chromatography was used, and showed that abnormally high levels of glycine, taurine and cystathionine were found in the greatest frequency in the handicapped group. In a few there was evidence of high levels of phenylalanine, serine, tyrosine, histidine and asparagine.

The comment of the leader of the research team was that all children who were failing to develop normally should be thus assessed, after high protein dietary loading. Long-term care could possibly be avoided if adequate dietary treatment could be found by such means of identification of individual biochemical factors. Without an understanding of the biochemical defects at work this could not take place.

There is a distinction between those conditions listed above as obviously genetically induced and others, perhaps less marked and yet, which can be influenced by environmental factors such as stress or by infection. Those that lend themselves to a comprehensive approach, which involves the limiting of stress factors and overall health improvement as well as the correction of specific nutrient imbalances, including amino acids, are the large group of conditions which form the major area of discussion in this book. The conditions outlined above are but a sample of the many and varied disorders that involve primarily, or secondarily, some of the amino acids, whether these be EAA or NEAA in variety.

Our attention is now directed towards those individual (or groups of) amino acids, which have a place in the therapeutic repertoire of nutritionally orientated practitioners. These will be considered individually, with indications as to their usefulness in various conditions. Indications will also be given as to other nutrient factors which are useful, or essential, as part of their use. Sources of supply from food will be indicated so that nutrient sources can be suggested from food as well as the use of supplements. It should now be clear to all that the elements we are considering are at least as powerful and vital in their potential for good as the more glamorous vitamins and minerals. They are equally as devastating in their potential for harm when deficient. The amino acids have been a much neglected area of nutritional research and the time for their inclusion in consideration of common problems of health and disease, is now here.

References

Scriver, C.R. and Rosenberg, L.E. *Amino Acid Metabolism and its Disorders,* Saunders, (Philadelphia), 1973.
Stein, J. H., (Editor). *Internal Medicine,* Little, Brown and Co. (Boston), 1983.

7.
INDIVIDUAL AMINO ACIDS:
THERAPEUTIC ROLES

Essential Amino Acids (EAA)

Arginine	These two amino acids are essential in the growth
Histidine	period of life and sometimes in adult life through acquired, or genetic, factors.

Isoleucine
Leucine
Lysine
Methionine
Phenylalanine
Threonine
Tryptophan
Valine

**Non-Essential Amino Acids (NEAA) with
Therapeutic Characteristics**
Proline
Taurine
Carnitine
Tyrosine
Glutamine and Glutamic acid
Cysteine and cystine
Glycine
Alanine
b-Alanine
Gama Aminobutyric acid (GABA)

Asparagine and Aspartic acid
Citrulline
Ornithine
Serine
Glutathione (Cysteine, glutamic acid, glycine)

ARGININE

This EAA, during the growth period, can subsequently be manufactured by the body. It is synthesized from citrulline in a reaction involving aspartic and glutamic acids. It is the immediate precursor of ornithine and urea, and as such is a vital part of the urea cycle in the liver, which is the major route of detoxification and elimination of urea. Proteins such as collagen and elastin, and vital substances such as haemoglobin, insulin and glucagon, all involve arginine's presence. Eighty per cent of the male seminal fluid is made of arginine. Williams[1] reports that whilst not an EAA in adults, it may be required in the diet ('contingent') in certain individuals, and that idiopathic hypospermia has been successfully treated with 8g of arginine administered daily. Williams states: 'It seems reasonable to suppose that certain individuals would be found who would have partial genetic blocks which would make the production of arginine from other amino acids difficult.' Such an individual might have 'idiopathic hypospermia' for this reason (as well as others) and hence, for normal functions, may be said to require arginine. Borrmann[2] reports that arginine is useful in cases of sterility, and that it acts as a detoxifying agent.

Arginine is contra-indicated in cases of herpes simplex infections, according to a number of authorities. [3,4,5] Foods rich in arginine should therefore be avoided by patients with such viral infections (see Lysine section for indications in such cases). Arginine is glycogenic. It is arguably the most important member of the urea cycle in man. In this cycle it is broken down to ornithine and urea, by the action of arginase, which promotes the detoxification of ammonia from the body.

According to Philpott[6] however, arginine is noted for its support of the immune system and that, although the herpes virus can be 'starved' of arginine by a dietary pattern that favours lysine (which competes with it) so can the body itself be starved of arginine.

Long-term imbalance in the diet mitigating against arginine would be harmful to the immunological system and also result in disordered carbohydrate metabolism. Philpott suggests arginine as a chelating agent for manganese, when this mineral is indicated as being deficient. He points to the team of arginine and manganese being suitable as they enter the last stage of the urea cycle in this form, with both having functions beyond their use in this cycle.

The use of parenteral amino acid mixtures in seriously ill or injured people is becoming more widespread, although the precise formulation of the amino acid mixture is still subject to debate. In animal experiments to help formulation of such mixtures it has been found that supplementary arginine minimizes post-wound weight-loss, accelerates wound healing and increases the size and activity of the thymus gland (in both injured and uninjured rats).

Experiments were conducted to assess whether arginine's effect on the pituitary gland was the cause of these benefits, since arginine is known to be a secretogogue of growth hormone. The results showed that beneficial effects on wound healing, as well as on general well-being, of arginine, were dependent upon an intact hypothalamic-pituitary axis. [7] The report concludes: 'We suggest that supplemental arginine may provide a safe nutritional means to improve wound healing and thymic function in injured and stressed humans.' Animal trials have also indicated that dietary arginine reduces hypercholesterolaemia and atherosclerosis. The animals used were rabbits. [8]

The suggested usefulness of arginine in male sterility is mirrored in experiments conducted to assess the effects of arginine deficiency in female rats. Sexual maturity was delayed in arginine deficient rats. Varying grades of arginine deficient diets were fed to groups of rats, and the effects monitored. Those on a diet containing 56 per cent normal dietary arginine reached puberty at the correct time, but ovarian weight and first ovulation rates were low, compared with rats on the higher levels of arginine. [8]

A further important aspect of arginine function is its ability to modulate aspects of the urea cycle, where supplementation may be called for if there is evidence of dysfunction.

Aspartic acid is also of use in such conditions. A variety of functions have been shown to become aberrant when arginine is deficient. Glucose tolerance, insulin production, and liver lipid metabolism, all are affected in such a state. The ability of rats to metabolize lipids was impaired, and livers contained greater concentrations of fats, in those experimental animals on a low arginine diet. As yet these results cannot be translated into predictions of similar effects in humans, but research continues. Relative deficiency in arginine, which might result from a high lysine/low arginine dietary pattern, in the treatment of herpes simplex infection, might be assisted by important findings in trials in which complex carbohydrates were assessed against simple carbohydrates for their relative effects on arginine utilization. By increasing faecal nitrogen loss, and decreasing urinary nitrogen loss, and the need for urea synthesis, arginine deficiency was ameliorated. This trial showed that the addition of guar gum to the diet (but not wheat bran) reduced the possible ill-effects of arginine deficiency. [10]

Patients following a 'herpes' diet, or taking supplemental lysine and reducing arginine rich foods in their diets, should find this of value to help in the avoidance of the possible lowered immune function, predicted by Philpott[6], when arginine is deficient. Diabetics should also benefit by guar gum's ability to provide arginine in relation to glucose tolerance and insulin enhancement. Other effects of arginine as reported in research journals show some of the ramifications of either excess or diminished arginine presence.

A recent report[11] described the case of an infant with carbamyl-phosphate synthetase deficiency. Dietary control revealed that a cessation of growth occured and a distinctive rash appeared when serum arginine was low. The addition of 400mg of arginine daily reversed both the growth cessation and the rash. This was experimentally allowed to recur when arginine was removed from the diet for two weeks. It later became necessary to increase arginine levels to 800mg daily to maintain growth. This report suggested that Bland's contingent state had been reached for arginine, and that it became an essential amino acid in these circumstances due to the defect in the urea cycle resulting from carbamyl-phosphate synthetase deficiency.

There is one research reference to the possible effect of arginine when in excess of normal levels in the serum. [12] Patients suffering periodic catatonic states were found to have elevated levels of both arginine and glutamine. Whether this was a causative factor, or a concurrent phenomenon, is not clear. Major food sources of arginine are peanuts, peanut butter, cashew nuts, pecan nuts, almonds, chocolate and edible seeds. It is found in moderate quantities in peas and non-toasted cereals. Arginine exists in a free state in such plants as garlic and ginseng.

A recent controversial application for arginine has been promoted by a number of American researchers. Basing their recommendation on arginine's known ability to promote growth hormone production, authors Durk Pearson and Sandy Shaw[13] and Earl Mindell[14] suggest that weight reduction, and muscle building, can be enhanced by its supplementation. In Pearson's view, ornithine is also called for in this regard. Mindell states: 'Stimulation of growth hormone in the adult benefits an improved immune response, allowing our bodies to repair themselves more efficiently. In the process, the release of extra amounts of growth hormones in adults can lead to the metabolism of stored fat and the building and toning up of muscle tissue.' The dosages suggested in this particular programme are 2g, on an empty stomach before retiring, and 2g on an empty stomach one hour prior to vigorous exercise. Mindell warns of adverse effects after several weeks of this programme in mature adults, where the first side effects noted are reversible thickening and coarsening of the skin. It should be emphasized that there are no long-term studies in this area of massive supplementation of amino acids and the author of this work reports the above but does not add his voice in support of anything but the short term use of such dosages. (See also Ornithine, page 87).

It is reported[13] that schizophrenics should be cautious in their use of arginine as it may result in aggravation of symptoms as a consequence of methyl donation by polyamines comprising such amino acids as arginine and ornithine, which are known to promote growth hormone release. Doses of over 30mg daily of arginine in anyone who has a history of schizophrenia, is therefore not recommended.

References

1. Williams, R., *Biochemical Individuality,* University of Texas Press, 1979.
2. Borrmann, W., *Comprehensive Answers to Nutrition.* New Horizons, Chicago, 1979.
3. Passwater, R. *Energy Medicine* Vol ll. No.1-11, 1980
4. Kagan, C., *Lancet,* 26 Jan 1974.
5. *Dermatologica* 156:257-267 (1978)

6. Philpott W., *Manganese-Arginine Complex* Klaire Laboratories leaflet.
7. *American Journal of Clinical Nutrition,* 37(5) p786, 1983.
8. *Atherosclerosis,* 43, 1982 p381.
9. *Hormone and Metabolic Research,* (1982) 14(2) pp471-5.
10. *Journal of Nutrition,* 113(1)131-7, 1983.
11. *Am.J. of Diseases of Children* 135(5)437-442, 1981.
12. *Journal of Mental Science,* 104 No 434 pp 188-200, Jan 1958.
13. Pearson and Shaw, *Life Extension,* Warner Books, 1982.
14. Mindell, Earl, Ph.D., *Arginine,* pamphlet, 1983.

HISTIDINE

This is regarded as an EAA in the growth period, but, since healthy adults are shown to be capable of synthesizing amounts adequate to their needs, it is termed a NEAA in adult life. The neurotransmitter histamine is derived from histidine and, as Hoffer puts it:[1] 'It is not difficult to believe that histidine levels will influence histamine levels.' When the acid group is removed from histadine it becomes histamine. Both histamine and histidine will chelate with trace elements such as zinc and copper. Histidine is therefore used as a chelating agent in some cases of arthritis, tissue overload of copper, iron or other heavy metals. Professor Gerber of Downstate Medical Center, New York, utilizes between 1g and 6g daily in arthritic patients. Pfeiffer further notes that both histidine and histamine act as chelating agents (they will attach themselves to other substances, notably trace elements or metals) and that this may account for their usefulness in treating some forms of arthritis, where copper or other metal excess can thus be removed from the system. Pfeiffer maintains that histamine is a neurotransmitter of some as yet unspecified portion of the brain.

Pfieffer and Iliev, of the Brain Bio Center, showed, by accurately assaying tissue histamine content, that they were able to identify two distinct categories of schizophrenia which, together, make up two thirds of those affected. The histapenic patient is extremely low in brain and blood histamine, and is usually over-stimulated. Whereas the hitadelic patient is high in levels of histamine in the blood and brain, and is usually suicidally depressed. Methionine (see page 55) serves as an agent for decreasing histamine. It methylates, and thus detoxifies, histamine. Pfeiffer recommends methionine's use in histadelic patients, together with other substances including calcium lactate, zinc and manganese.[2] Histidine is reported as effective in allergic conditions. It has a vasodilating and hypotensive action via the autonomic nervous system and has been used in cardiocirculatory conditions. It is important in erythropoisis and leukopoisis making it of use in the treatment of anaemia.[3]

Histidine has been found to be necessary for the maintenance of myalin sheaths,[4] and Borrmann reports its usefulness in aiding auditory dysfunction by virtue of its effects on the auditory nerve. Deficiency is said to be associated with nerve deafness.[5] Pearson and Shaw point out that the release of histamines from body stores is a necessary prerequisite for sexual arousal, and histidine supplementation may assist in problems relating to this (together with niacin, and vitamin B_6 which is required for the alterations of histidine to histamine.)[6]

Brekhman reports that as part of the Soviet space programme over 25,000 different chemical substances and compounds have been examined to try to discover effective protective substances against the effects of radiation. Among the standard preparations which are now issued to cosmonauts in this regard as nonspecific pharmacologically protective medicines is histidine (the only other amino acid is tryptophan). Dosages are not stated.[7]

Childhood requirements (RDA) are put at 33mg per kilogram of body weight per day. It is found in animal sources of protein at levels of 17mg per gram.[8]

Note: Since histadelic patients are displaying symptoms resulting from excessive histamine in the system, it is unwise for anyone with symptoms of manic depression to supplement with histidine unless it is established that levels of histamine are within the normal range.

References

1. Bland, J., (editor), *Medical Applications of Clinical Nutrition,* Keats, 1983.
2. Pfeiffer, Carl, *Mental and Elemental Nutrients,* Keats, 1975
3. Kohl, H., *Aminosauren,* Cantor, Aulendorf. 1954
4. *Amino Acids,* pamphlet, Dietary Sales Corporation, Indiana
5. Borrmann, W., *Comprehensive Answers to Nutrition,* New Horizons, Chicago, 1979.
6. Pearson, D. and Shaw, S., *Life Extension,* Warner Books, 1983.

7.   Brekhman, I.I., *Man and Biologically Active Substances,* Pergamon Press, 1980
8.   *Nutrition Almanac,* McGraw Hill, 1979.

ISOLEUCINE

Although the EAA isoleucine has, as yet, not been identified as having particular therapeutic characteristics, Borrmann reports that: 'it is useful in haemoglobin formation,'[1] but he does not elaborate on that remark.

Isoleucine has been identified as one of a group of amino acids deficient in amino acid profiles run on mentally and physically ill patients,[2] as reported by Jon Pangborn Ph.D. and William Philpott M.D. Therapeutic doses of between 240mg and 360mg daily are suggested in combination with the other amino acids found lacking (e.g. valine, leucine, tyrosine, cystine, glutamic acid and ketoglutaric acid). As mentioned in the previous chapter isoleucine is, as one of the branched-chain amino acids, one of the culprits in the acidemias, such as Maple Syrup Urine Disease.

Bland[3] gives the range of isoleucine requirement in normal adults between 250mg and 700mg daily, as against the National Academy of Sciences RDA for an adult of 12mg per kilogram of body weight, which for a 75kg man would mean a daily intake of around 900mg. The isoleucine content of protein, of animal origin, is 42mg per gram of protein.[4]

Major food sources of isoleucine are beef, chicken, fish, soy protein, soyabeans, eggs, liver, cottage cheese, baked beans, milk, rye, almonds, cashews, pumpkin seeds, sesame seeds, sunflower seeds, chickpeas, lentils.[4]

References

1.   Bormann, W., *Comprehensive Answers to Nutrition,* New Horizons, Chicago, 1979.
2.   Philpott Medical Center, pamphlet 'Selective Amino Acid Deficiencies'.
3.   Bland, J., (editor), *Medical Applications of Clinical Nutrition,* Keats, 1983.
4.   *Nutrition Almanac,* McGraw Hill, 1979.

LEUCINE

Leucine is an EAA with no particular identified therapeutic role, apart from its complicity in conditions relating to disorders of branched-chain amino acid metabolism, such as Maple Syrup Urine Disease and multiple carboxylase deficiency. As with isoleucine it was found to be relatively deficient in assessments of amino acid status of groups of mentally and physically ill subjects[1] and is supplemented, together with the other appropriate amino acids (isoleucine, valine, tyrosine, cystine, glutamic acid and ketoglutaric acid) at a dosage of between 240mg and 360mg daily, in divided dosage.

The range of human requirements in health is given[2] as from 170mg to 1100mg daily representing a 6.4 fold possible variation in need. This was derived from a sample of only 31 individuals and so the chances of far greater variations in need existing in the public at large is great. RDA is given as 16mg per kilogram of body weight in adults, which for a 75 kilo individual would require a daily consumption of 1200mg. The level of leucine found in animal protein is given[3] as 70mg per gram. Major sources of leucine in food are beef, chicken, soya protein, soya beans, fish, cottage cheese, eggs, baked beans, liver, whole wheat, brown rice, almonds, brazil nuts, cashew nuts, pumpkin seeds, lima beans, chick peas (garbanzos), lentils, corn.

Of particular interest to nutritionally orientated practitioners are the reports in *The British Journal of Nutrition*[4,5] which indicate that dietary excess of leucine may be a precipitating factor in the causation of pellagra. It was found that when rats were fed on a diet that provided 15g of leucine per kilogram in excess of requirements for a period of seven weeks it led to a significant reduction in concentrations of nicotinamide nucleotides in the blood and liver. This effect was only apparent when the overall diet provided less than an adequate amount of nicotinamide, so that the animals were dependent upon synthesis of nicotinamide from tryptophan to meet all or part of their needs. It was noted that other nutrients and their enzymes were not thus affected by the loading of leucine to the diet. The second report, which confirms the essentials of the first, established the minutiae of the process. It states it thus: 'A dietary excess of leucine led to inhibition of kynurinase and increased the activity of picolinate carboxylase.

Both of these effects would result in a reduction in the rate of metabolism of acroleyaminofuamrate to quinolenic acid and hence to nicotinamide nucleotides. These two effects proved an explanation for the pellagragenic effect of a dietary excess of leucine in animals that are wholly or partly reliant on endogenous synthesis of tryptophan to meet their requirements for nicotinamide nucleotides, and presumably also explains the pellagragenic effect of a dietary excess of leucine in man.'

Rudin[6] points out that among the factors being investigated as causes of pellagra are the presence in corn of an abnormally high leucine/isoleucine ratio. Leucine would seem to be essential, but with potentials for causing harm if other factors permit. The ratio of amino acids to each other is patently important as is the necessity for ensuring overall nutrient status, as evidenced by the fact that leucine excess had no harmful effect if nicotinamide was adequately present, whereas it was able to induce pellagra-like symptoms when the body was obliged to utilize precious tryptophan supplies to manufacture vitamin B_3. The right handed d-form of leucine has been shown to have a similar effect to that displayed by d-phenylalanine (see page 58) in that it retards the breakdown of the natural pain killers of the body, the endorphins and enkephalins. It has, however, not been researched in this regard, as has d-phenylalanine, but may in time be found to be just as useful in chronic pain control.[7]

References

1. Philpott Medical Center, pamphlet, 'Selective Amino Acid Deficiencies'.
2. Bland, J., (editor), *Medical Applications of Clinical Nutrition,* Keats, 1983.
3. *Nutrition Almanac,* McGraw Hill, 1979.
4. *B.J. of Nutrition,* Vol.49, No.3, May 1983, p231.
5. *B.J. of Nutrition,* Vol.50, No.1, July 1983, p25.
6. *Journal of Orthomolecular Psychiatry*, Vol. 12, No. 2, p91-110.
7. Pearson, D. and Shaw, S., *Life Extension,* Nutri Books, 1984.

LYSINE

Lysine is an EAA and it has been found to have therapeutic effects in the viral related disease. Particularly of current interest is its ability to control herpes simplex virus, if the diet is low in arginine. It has also been found to have other therapeutic effects which will be discussed. Lysine cannot be synthesized in the body and the breakdown of lysine is not reversible. It is therefore vital that it is in the diet in adequate quantities. Its deficiency in cereal proteins makes it the limiting factor in rice, wheat, oats, millet and sesame seeds. Insufficient intake leads to poor appetite, decrease in body weight, anaemia, enzyme disorders, etc. It is used therapeutically to enhance the growth of children, and to assist gastric function and appetite.

Lysine and Herpes

Some years ago, before herpes became such a prevelant and talked about condition, a chance observation by Dr Chris Kagan at the Cedars of Lebanon Hospital, Los Angeles, opened the way for its control by means of amino acid therapy. He noted that solutions of herpes virus cultures were always encouraged to grow rapidly by the addition of 1-argenine to the solution. This was based on the research of Dr R. Tankersley, who also found that to slow down growth in a solution containing herpes virus it was necessary to add 1-lysine. On the basis of this the therapeutic application of lysine was attempted. The results were excellent.[1] It was found in one trial that 43 of the 45 patients involved improved markedly. Dosages were from 300mg to 1200mg of lysine daily, at the same time as reducing dietary arginine intake. Patients studied for up to three years on this programme showed complete remission and no side effects. Pain disappeared rapidly, and in all cases no new vesicles appeared. Resolution of existing vesicles was more rapid than in patients' past experience. There was no extension of the initiating lesion in any cases. It was found that within one to four weeks of terminating the use of lysine, lesions returned.

Subsequent experience with this pattern of treatment has shown that providing the balance of lysine to arginine can be kept at the right levels the replication of viral particles can be checked. The failure of the method is almost always the result of inadequate lysine intake, or an excessive arginine intake, and the individual must find the correct balance by trial and error. The mechanism that is thought to operate in this control of viral particles is one in which the structurally similar lysine is absorbed into the virus instead of arginine, which is catabolized by the body. Arginine and lysine compete for transport through the intestinal wall, and if there is a sufficient excess of lysine then it is successful in reducing the intake of arginine, which is required by the virus for replication.[2]

The major food sources containing a high lysine:arginine ratio are fish, chicken, beef, lamb, milk, cheese, beans, brewer's yeast and mung bean sprouts. Foods which contain a high arginine: lysine ratio, and therefore should be avoided, include gelatin, chocolate, carob, coconut, oats, wholewheat and white flour, peanuts, soybeans and wheatgerm.

Most fruits and vegetables have a lysine excess over arginine apart from peas. Vitamin C has a protective effect on body levels of lysine.[3] Dosages recommended are 500mg to 1500mg of lysine daily, spread through the day. Variability will depend upon the overall nutrient balance of these two substances, and biochemical individuality. During acute herpes episodes a minimum of 1500mg of lysine, plus at least 1 gram of vitamin C (with bioflavinoids) should be taken through the day, with special attention to the dietary intake of arginine being kept low.

Lysine therapy is recommended by the Herpes Organisation in the UK, and it is available freely through health food stores and some pharmacists. Other aspects of lysine's applicability to therapeutics include the fact that from it the body forms an amino acid called carnitine which is causing some interest in its role as an agent for transporting fatty acids across the mitochondria, where they can be used as a source of fuel in the generation of energy. If carnitine levels are low within the cells, then there is poor metabolism of fatty acids, thus contributing to an elevation of blood fat and triglycerides. Recent research[4] suggests that there is a rapid conversion, in vivo, of orally-administered lysine to carnitine in humans. This may be impaired in cases of malnutrition. This will be considered further in the section dealing with carnitine (page 75).

Drs Cheraskin and Ringsdorf[5] report that deficiency of lysine results in reduced ability to concentrate. Borrmann[6] reports that it is required for antibody formation, and that deficiency results in chronic tiredness, fatigue, nausea, dizziness and anaemia. The range of human needs[7] is given as between 400mg and 2800mg daily, a seven-fold variation in a sample of 55 people. Adult requirements are given as[8] 12mg per kilogram of bodyweight, which would result in a 175lb individual requiring just in excess of 2,000mg per day. Its availability in first class protein is approximately 50mg per gram.

References

1. Griffith, R., Delong, D.,and Kagan, C., *Dermatologica* No. 156, pp257-267, 1978.
2. Yacenda, J., *The Herpes Diet,* pamphlet, Felmore Ltd., Tunbridge Wells.
3. 'Amino Acids Dietary Sales Indiana and Kagan C.', *Lancet* 1:37, 1974.
4. *Am.J. Clin Ntr.* 37:Jan 1983, pp93-8.
5. *Psychodietetics,* Bantam Books, pp22, 1977.
6. *Comprehensive Answers to Nutrition,* New Horizons, Chicago, p10, 1979.
7. Bland, J., (editor), *Medical Applications of Clinical Nutrition,* Keats, 1983.
8. *Nutrition Almanac,* McGraw Hill, pp236, 1979.

METHIONINE

Methionine is an EAA. It is a methyl donor and is one of the sulphur-containing amino acids. The methyl groups are required for nucleic acid structure, collagen, and each cell's protein synthesis function. Methyl donation in this case occurs with vitamin B_{12}, via the unique molecule S-adenosyl methionine.

Methionine gives rise to the amino acids cysteine and cystine (see page 81). Methionine, as well as cysteine and cystine can act as a powerful detoxification agent, being capable of the removal from the body of toxic levels of heavy metals such as lead.[1] Schauss discusses the use, in such cases, of foods rich in these compounds such as beans, eggs, onions and garlic, but states: 'Since it requires large quantities of these foods to have a significant impact upon the body's toxic metal burden, it is often more desirable to use specific nutritional supplements.'

The sulphur amino acids are also noted as protectors against the effects of radiation.

Methionine is an antioxidant, and as such is a good free radical scavenger.[2] Because it has a methyl group to offer it can combine with active free radicals which are harmful to the system. Studies[3] show that alcohol is one oxidant which can stimulate the release of superoxide radicals. Methionine has shown protective effects against alcohol in this regard and in general. Methionine also aids in the maintenance of the pool of glutathione peroxidase, the powerful enzyme antoxidant (see page 88).

Adelle Davis considered methionine to be 'one of the body's most powerful detoxifying agents'.[4] Pfieffer also notes[5] its ability to detoxify histamine when levels of this are high in schizophrenic patients (histadelic).

Deficiency of methionine can be the cause of choline deficiency, according to Adelle Davis, as it can retention of fat in the liver.[4]

Williams confirms this,[6] saying:'There are certain nutrients, sometimes called lipotropic agents, which are peculiarly effective in promoting the bodily production of lecithin. Three substances of this group are methionine, choline and inositol.' He describes an experiment at Harvard in which it was found that monkeys were afflicted with atherosclerosis as a result of consuming a completely satisfactory diet, with the single exception of methionine deficiency. The blood proteins albumen and globulin, which are connected with antibodies, cannot be synthesized without the adequate presence of methionine.[7] It is thought that choline and folic acid assist methionine in its detoxification activities.

From a therapeutic viewpoint the ability of methionine to eliminate toxic metal loads would appear to be one of its prime uses. As an essential aspect of the body's ability to use selenium, methionine has also shown great importance. It is essential for the absorption, transportation and bioavailability of selenium. In humans seleno-methionine is more readily incorporated into the tissues than other forms of selenium, such as Se-selenite.[8] The range of human needs of methionine is given as between 800mg and 3000mg per day. This represents a 3.7 fold variation in need, based on a sample of 29 individuals.[9]

Daily requirements are given as 10mg a day per kilogram of body weight for all the sulphur amino acids, including methionine.[10]

It is found primarily in the following foods: beef, chicken, fish, pork, soybeans, egg, cottage cheese, liver, sardines, yogurt, pumpkin seeds, sesame seeds, lentils. Dosage, therapeutically, varies from 200mg to 1000mg daily. Note that methionine has a particularly distinctive odour. It is a meaty, sulphurous smell which most people find unpleasant. Methionine metabolism disorders may be indicated in the urine by the accompaniment of excess methionine, with homocystine (which is normally not detected in urine). This may indicate a limitation in the remethylation of homocystine, to form methionine, which reaction would normally complete the sulphur conservation pathway. This could be due to deficient folic acid; or defective folic acid metabolism; or deficient intestinal absorption; or impaired vitamin B_{12} metabolism. Both B_{12} and folic acid are required for enzymatic remethylation of homocystine.[11] A more likely cause of homocystineuria would be an enzyme defect, involving cystathionine B-synthase. Symptoms could include cardiovascular, skeletal and joint changes, ocular and neurological problems, as well as brittle hair, thin skin, fatty changes in the liver and myopathy. Pyridoxal phosphate (vitamin B_6) may be deficient concurrently.

A low-methionine, cysteine/cystine supplemented diet, would be indicated if there was no response to vitamin B_6 supplementation is such a case. In addition betaine supplementation assists in decreasing plasma levels of homocystine in B_6 non-responsive patients.[12] B_6 may not appear responsive if folic acid is depleted,[11] and as a consequence supplementation with B_6, B_{12}, folic acid and magnesium are often indicated to normalize the methionine metabolism in such conditions.

It is vital that the relationship between protein in general, and methionine specifically, with vitamin B_6 (pyridoxine) be understood. Methionine is an anti-oxidant. However its derivative homocysteine is a powerful oxidant. Adequate levels of vitamin B_6 allow this to be reconverted into an antioxidant substance, cystathione. A high meat intake, for example, with an inadequate vitamin B_6 intake would produce just such a situation, as would high methionine supplementation without B_6 supplementation. Cardiovascular disease could well result from such an imbalance of nutrients and consequent free radical activity in the absence of antioxidants.[13]

References

1. Schauss, Alexander, *Diet, Crime and Delinquency*, Parker House, Berkeley, 1981.
2. Passwater, R., *Supernutrition,* Pocket Book, New York, 1976.
3. *Amino Acids,* pamphlet Dietary Sales Corporation, Indiana.
4. Davis, Adelle, *Let's Eat Right to Keep Fit*, George Allen and Unwin, London, 1961.
5. Pfieffer, Carl, *Mental and Elemental Nutrients,* Keats, 1975.
6. Williams, Roger, *Nutrition against Disease,* Bantam Books, New York, 1981.
7. Borrmann, W., *Comprehensive Answers to Nutrition,* New Horizons, Chicago, 1979.
8. *Reviews in Clinical Nutrition,* Vol.53, No.1, Jan 1983.
9. Bland, J., (editor), *Medical Applications of Clinical Nutrition,* Keats, 1983.
10. *Nutrition Almanac,* McGraw Hill, 1979.
11. Stanbury et al, *Metabolic Basis of Inherited Diseases,* McGraw-Hill, 1983.
12. *N. England Med. Journal.* 309 (8):448-453, 1983.
13. Pearson, D. and Shaw, S., *Life Extension,* Warner Books, 1984.

PHENYLALANINE

Phenylalanine is an EAA which has been found to have remarkable therapeutic properties, and which itself gives rise to other amino acids which are the forerunners of many vital substances in the economy of the body.

Deficiency of phenylalanine can lead to a variety of symptoms, including bloodshot eyes, cataracts[1] and, according to Hoffer, many behavioural changes.[2] Hoffer points out that a number of neurotransmitters derive from phenylalanine. It is converted into tyrosine (see page 77) unless the patient is suffering from phenylketonuria (see Chapter 4). This condition occurs when the enzyme which converts phenylalanine to tyrosine is deficient. Children thus affected display psychotic behaviour, and adults typically schizophrenic behaviour.

Tyrosine is converted into norepinephrine and subsequently epinephrine. All the end-products of phenylalanine are themselves converted into other end-products, one of which is adenochrome which is a powerful hallucinogen. Adenochrome was the basis for Hoffer and Osmond's hypothesis of schizophrenia, which led to the use of niacin and vitamin C in its treatment.[3] It can be seen, therefore, that deficiency of phenylalanine can lead to a wide variety of behavioural changes. The direct conversion of phenylalanine to tyrosine, and then to dopamine and on to norepinephrine and epinephrine, indicates the wide range of potential influence that it has. Neither phenylalanine nor tyrosine should therefore be supplemented in individuals taking monoamineoxidase drugs (MAO's).

One of its other roles has been shown to be its involvement in the control of appetite. It has been demonstrated[4] that free amino acids in the gut, especially tryptophan and phenylalanine, trigger the release of cholycystokinin (CCK). It has been found that in man a single high protein meal, or high carbohydrate meal, can increase CCK levels from 700pg to 1100pg/ml within half an hour. It is thought that CCK may induce satiety, and a termination of eating, either by altering gastro-intestinal function (e.g. gastric emptying) or by interaction with central nervous system feeding centres. It is known that CCK effects on satiety do depend upon intact vagal fibres, and it is thought that this route might allow CCK to interact with the amygdala and hypothalamus, via CCK receptors on vagal fibres. Phenylalanine is being employed as an appetite suppressant in obesity. It is taken prior to a meal to initiate CCK release and among its other effects are, frequently, a feeling of greater alertness, increased sexual interest, memory enhancement and, after 24 to 48 hours, an antidepressant effect. Pearson and Shaw[12] suggest that in the use of phenylalanine for weight reduction purposes, between 100mg and 500mg should be taken in the evening on an empty stomach just before retiring. This should only be continued until weight reduction is satisfactorily achieved.

It should be noted that if overall amino acid intake is low (e.g. low protein diet) and phenylalanine is taken in large doses, thus causing amino acid imbalance, there could be an induced tyrosine toxicity. In animal trials it was found that a low protein diet, combined with a level of phenylalanine equal to 3 per cent of the diet, resulted in signs of depression and eye lesions. This level of phenylalanine consumption would be difficult to achieve in man, but the possibility of incorrect use exists.[5]

Recent research reports have shown a new and potentially dramatic use for phenylalanine in the field of pain control.[6] [7]

The form of phenylalanine found in the animal protein diet of man is laevo, or left-handed phenylalanine. That found in plant and bacterial cultures is dextro, or right-handed phenylalanine. This form is converted in the body to 1-phenylalanine. There also exists a so called racemic mixture consisting of equal parts of the d- and 1- forms, which is known as d1-phenylalanine, or more simply DLPA. The original study reporting the pain controlling aspect of DLPA was published in 1978, by Dr Seymour Ehrenpreis and colleagues of the University of Chicago Medical School. At this stage it was d-phenylalanine that was creating interest. Patients were selected on the basis that other forms of treatment had failed. Pain relief in a variety of conditions, ranging from whiplash injury to osteo- and rheumatoid arthritis, was rapid and lasting. There were no adverse effects noted, nor was there any degree of tolerance, i.e. the pain relief did not diminish with subsequent use. Pain relief took from one week to four weeks to reach its optimum level, and frequently lasted for up to a month after the cessation of treatment.

Subsequent work by these, and other, researchers, has led to the combining of the d- and 1- forms, into DLPA which not only provides the pain relieving effect but also supplies the body with its requirements of phenylalanine. The effects on arthritic conditions are especially pronounced, since the majority of cases employing DLPA have found relief. It appears from research that DLPA inhibits enzymes that are responsible for the break-down of endorphins, carboxypeptidase A and enkephilinase enzymes. This appears to allow the pain relieving attributes of endorphins a longer time span for their pain relieving action. This means of course that DLPA (or d-phenylalanine on its own) is not acting as an analgesic, but is rather allowing the endogenous pain control mechanism of the body to act in a more advantageous manner.

It has been noted that patients with chronic pain problems have reduced levels of endorphin activity in the cerebrospinal fluid and serum, and DLPA (or d-phenylalanine on its own) enhance the restoration of normal levels. It is worth recording that DLPA does not interfere with the transmission of normal pain messages, thus the defence mechanism of the body is not compromised. It is only the ongoing, pain-relieving mechanism that is enhanced. DLPA is usually presented in 375mg tablets. The usual dosage is two tablets taken 15 to 30 minutes prior to meals, to a total of six tablets daily. If there has been no improvement within a period of three weeks the dosage is doubled. If there is still no response then the DLPA should be discontinued. However, there is only a small percentage of failure (between 5 and 15 per cent). Relief is usually noted within seven days, at which time dosage is reduced in stages, until, by trial and error, the minimum maintenance dose is reached. Many patients find that a week per month on DLPA provides maintenance of pain relief; whereas others require continued taking in reduced quantities. There are apparently no contra-indications or side- effects reported to date. Since both d- and l-phenylalanine are normal constituents of the economy of the body, there is no reason why there should be any side effects, as long as the overall nutritional status is maintained.

With no contra-indication or side-effects, and with no tolerance or addiction apparent, as well as the ability for DLPA to combine with any other form of treatment, the use of this substance seems to be comprehensively assured. An antidepressant effect is also reported, which should make its use even more attractive.

The normal ranges of requirement of phenylalanine in humans is given as between 420mg and 1,100mg per day. This was in a sample of 38 individuals.[8]

The National Academy of Science requirement is shown as 16mg per kilogram, in adults.[9] This represents some 1,200mg per day in a 75kg man. Rose[10] states the recommended daily requirement to be in the region of 2.2g. The relative difference in the figures given, indicates to some extent just how individualized dosages should be.

Food sources of phenylalanine include soybeans, cottage cheese, fish, meat, poultry, almonds, brazil nuts, pecans, pumpkins, and sesame seeds, lima beans, chickpeas (garbanzos) and lentils. The content of phenylalanine and other aromatic amino acids in first class protein is given as 73mg per gram.[9]

Therapeutic Dosages: A general concensus suggests that depressive states are relieved within a few days by the taking of 100mg to 500mg of l-phenylalanine per day. Caution should be employed in the use of phenylalanine in hypertensive individuals, and low doses (around 100mg daily) should be used at the start of a programme by anyone with suspected high blood-pressure, and a check should be kept on pressure levels.

References

1. Davis, Adelle, *Lets Eat Right to Keep Fit,* George Allen and Unwin, London 1961.
2. Bland,J., (editor), *Medical Applications of Clinical Nutrition,* Keats, 1983.
3. Hoffer, A. and Osmond, H., *How to Live with Schizophrenia,* Johnson, London, 1966.
4. *Reviews in Clinical Nutrition,* Vol. 53, No.3, pp169, March 1983.
5. *Agric. Biology and Chemistry,* Vol. 46, No.10, pp2491, 1982.
6. Bonica et al, *Advances in Pain Research and Therapy* Vol.5, Raven Press, N.Y., 1983.
7. *Proceedings of International Narcotic Research Club Convention,* Ed. E. Leong Way, 1979.
8. Bland, J., (editor), *Medical Applications of Clinical Nutrition,* Keats, 1983.
9. *Nutrition Almanac,* McGraw Hill, 1979.
10. Rose, W., 'Amino Acid Requirements in Man', *Nutrition Reviews,* Vol. 34, No. 10, 1967.
11. *American J. of Psychiatry* 147:622, May 1980.
12. Pearson D., and Shaw,S., *Life Extension,* Warner Books, 1984.

THREONINE

Threonine is an EAA. As yet few therapeutic roles are evident. Threonine (along with lysine) is deficient in most grains and it requires the combining of a pulse which contains threonine (and lysine) with a grain, to ensure a complete protein in vegetarian meals.[1]

Deficiency in threonine results in irritability and generally difficult personality, according to Cheraskin.[2] Williams lists it[3] along with most of the B vitamins, magnesium, ascorbic acid, iodine, potassium, tryptophan, lysine and inositol and glutamic acid as being essential in mental illness prevention and treatment. Borrmann[4] states that threonine is 'very useful in indigestion and intestinal malfunctions, and prevents excessive liver fat. Nutrients are more readily absorbed when threonine is present.' Threonine serves as a carrier for phosphate in the phosphoproteins. A fatty liver, resulting from a low protein diet, will be corrected by threonine which acts as a lipotropic factor.

Research on mice indicates that variations in individual amino acid quantities in the diet can modify the susceptibility of the animal to particular infections. Weaning mice fed on diets which were 75 per cent limited in histidine, or threonine, but not in methionine, were more susceptible to infection by salmonella typhimurium, whereas mice on a diet 75 per cent limited in methionine and threonine were more susceptible to infection by listeria monocytogenes. Replenishment with the limiting amino acid, histidine and threonine, reversed the susceptibility to S. typhimurium. The extrapolation of the type of nutrient imbalance to the human model could indicate ways of minimizing risks for susceptible individuals to specific infections.[7]

The range of human requirements is stated to be between 103mg and 500mg daily. This represents a range of 4.8 fold difference in a sample of 50 people.[5] Daily requirement is stated to be 8mg per kilogram of body weight in adults. Its availability in first class protein is 35mg per gram. This level of requirement would mean that a 75 kilo individual would require 600mg per day.[6]

References
1.   Davis, Adelle, *Lets Eat Right to Keep Fit,* George Allen and Unwin, London, 1961.

2. Cheraskin and Ringsdorf, *Psychodietetics,* Bantam, 1976.
3. Williams, R., *Nutrition Against Disease,* Bantam, 1981.
4. Borrmann, W., *Comprehensive Answers to Nutrition,* New Horizon, Chicago, 1979.
5. Bland, J., (editor), *Medical Applications of Clinical Nutrition,* Keats, 1983.
6. *Nutrition Almanac,* McGraw Hill, 1979.
7. *Nutrition Research* Vol.12, No.3, pp309-317, 1982.

TRYPTOPHAN

Tryptophan is an EAA. Among its many therapeutically significant roles is its essential part in the synthesis of nicotinic acid. In its own right it has been used therapeutically in the treatment of insomnia, depression and obesity.

There are, however, cautionary signals coming from a number of research results, which point to the necessity of tryptophan being used with care. In the indicated areas of use, and in its proper relationship with other nutrients, it is perfectly safe. It is, however, capable of causing marked side-effects when incorrectly employed.

Tryptophan is a nutrient affecting neurotransmitter function; it is converted to 5-hydroxy-tryptophan by tryptophan hydroxylase. This in turn is converted into serotonin, which is a neuro-transmitter. This can stimulate neurons, which amplify the transmission of signals to the cell which the neuron is innervating.[1] A great deal of research has been conducted into the mechanisms whereby brain function is altered in relation to serum levels of the nutrient factors which influence neurotransmitter production. These include tyrosine, which becomes ultimately epinephrine; and lecithin in its pure form of phosphatidylcholine, which becomes the neurotransmitter, choline; as well as tryptophan. It has been found that serotonin levels in the serum influence the individual's choice of food, so that more or less carbohydrate will be consumed. Wurtman,[2] who has researched this area exhaustively, has found that by altering levels of carbohydrate eaten it is possible to increase the levels of serotonin in the brain. Tryptophan levels in the brain, ready for conversion to serotonin, depend upon serum tryptophan levels as well as the ratio between plasma tryptophan and tyrosine, phenylalanine, leucine, isoleucine and valine (large neutral amino acids). Since a high protein meal leaves much less tryptophan free for the passage across the barrier than other amino acids, less tryptophan is carried across the barrier. A high carbohydrate meal which induces insulin release has a marked effect on the five amino acids mentioned because they are circulating as free molecules. Tryptophan is, however, not in this form and is therefore unaffected by the insulin. The ramifications of this effect of food choice on the levels of serotonin have implications for the control of excessive eating.

Animals given a choice between carbohydrate or protein-rich meals not only regulate the amount of calories consumed, but also control the ratio between protein and carbohydrate. Administration of a small carbohydrate-rich meal increases the level of serotonin in the brain, and this in turn increases the amount of protein in relation to carbohydrate eaten at the subsequent meal. If tryptophan is given before a meal a similar result may be anticipated since serotonin levels will rise and reduced calorie intake, via a higher protein, lower carbohydrate meal, will result, voluntarily. The phenomenon of carbohydrate craving, found in many people on a reducing diet based on a high protein diet, may therefore be the result of reduced serotonin, due to the high protein intake.

The symptoms of anxiety, tension or depression, mentioned by many people prior to a carbohydrate snack, and the relief felt afterwards, may be the direct result of relative serotonin lack followed by serotonin thus released into brain circulation.[3,4]

A high protein meal has the opposite effect since plasma levels of the Large Neutral Amino Acids increase proportionately more than tryptophan, thus reducing the amount of free tryptophan available for crossing the blood-brain barrier, and ultimate serotonin production.

The use of this knowledge in constructing nutritional patterns which will encourage self determined weight loss is most important. To recapitulate: by giving a small quantity of carbohydrate prior to the meal it was shown that overall carbohydrate intake decreased voluntarily. If this is accompanied by, or replaced by, the intake of tryptophan then serotonin production is more assured, enhancing the likelihood of a lower carbohydrate, higher protein selection being made subsequently.[5]

Tryptophan's role in certain mental disorders involves its complex relationship with other nutrient factors. The enzyme nicotinamide-adenine dinucleotide (NAD) is required in the brain to perform several vital functions. In schizophrenics there seems to be inadequate NAD in the brain. NAD is formed by the action of Vitamin B$_3$ (niacin) on tryptophan, and if niacin is deficient, inhibition occurs of this transformation of tryptophan. This results not only in inadequate amounts of NAD, but in excessive amounts of tryptophan in the brain. This can lead to perception and mood changes. Pyridoxine is also involved in the tryptophan-niacin interaction. These problems are relatively easily corrected by the supplementation of niacin and pyridoxine.[6]

Enhancement of tryptophan uptake by the brain is reported by the use of vitamin C and pyridoxine in concert with its oral administration.[7]

Cheraskin and Ringsdorf report[8] that there is an inverse relationship between tryptophan consumption and emotional complaints. Increasing the tryptophan intake decreases the number and severity of such complaints. Research carried out showed that of a group of 66 individuals, assessed after several months of tryptophan supplementation, those who had increased from 1,001mg per day to an average of 1,331mg per day showed a remarkable decrease in the number of psychological complaints, whereas those who had not altered their tryptophan intake showed no change. As mentioned previously, niacin is converted from tryptophan, under the influence of pyridoxine. The ratio of conversion is one gram of niacin from 60g of tryptophan. Tryptophan is not richly supplied in the diet, and the amount of tryptophan that can be converted to niacin is therefore not predictable, and certainly does not meet the body's daily requirement. Tryptophan that is not thus converted to niacin or serotonin remains largely bound to albumen in the blood. Tryptophan is also the precursor of 5-hydroxytryptamine which is a vasoconstrictor, utilized in the clearance of blood clots.

Serotonin has been widely promoted as a sleep inducing agent. Its precursor tryptophan was researched in this regard by Dr E. Hartmann of Boston State Hospital. He reported, [9] 'In our studies we found that a dose of one gram of tryptophan will cut down the time it takes to fall asleep from twenty to ten minutes. Its great advantage is that not only do you get to sleep sooner, but you do so without distortions in sleep patterns that are produced by most sleeping pills.' Goldberg and Kauffman state that they replicated Hartmann's results and found that tryptophan did not in any way depress the central nervous system but 'simply allowed the body to do what it normally does under ideal conditions.'[9]

A summary of its effects on sleep was given in a study in California.[10] Firstly it was found that tryptophan was an effective hypnotic when administered at any time of day. Further it was found that it significantly reduced the time of sleep onset without affecting the various stages of sleep. Finally it was shown that tryptophan produces a more relaxed waking state 45 minutes after ingestion and that at this stage sleep may be induced more easily if required. By combining Vitamin B_6 and magnesium with tryptophan there is an enhancement of all the effects described above. A combined supplement of these three factors is available in the UK (*Somnamin* from Larkhall Laboratories).

There have been inconsistent reports as to the efficacy of tryptophan in the treatment of endogenous depression. Broadhurst reported a 65 per cent improvement in thirty two depressive patients, after four weeks of supplementation of 4g of tryptophan daily.[11]

McSweeney reported that a daily intake of 3g of tryptophan together with 1g of nicotinamide was superior to unilateral ECT administered twice weekly when treating unipolar depression.[12] Other trials however[13] have shown less than encouraging results, with negligible antidepressant effects in unipolar depressive patients, and only partial antidepressive effects on bipolar depressive states. Among the reasons presented by researchers for the negative results of these trials is the possibility that numbers involved were too small and that the time of study was too short. It also appeared that there was a maximum level of tryptophan dosage above which efficacy diminished. Higher doses than 6g daily could be influenced by such factors as the induction of liver pyrolase, which affects tryptophan's competition with tyrosine in the blood-brain barrier resulting in reduction of norepinephrine synthesis. This could also result in enhancement of the formation of amines such as tryptamine which could affect serotonin function. The question was also raised as to the relative numbers of unipolar and bipolar depressives in the trials as they might respond differently to tryptophan. The importance of administering tryptophan well away from the consumption of protein meals was also emphasized as being a factor to stress in all future trials. It is not yet clear in what way other antidepressive agents interact with tryptophan.[14]

Buist[15] discusses the differences, which are known to exist, in two subgroups of depressive patients. These can be delineated according to their therapeutic response to various antidepressants, and to their level of a norepinephrine metabolite MHPG. The first group has low urinary MHPG (and therefore low brain norepinephrine) and they do not respond to amitryptaline, but do not show a favourable response to trycyclic drugs (which raise the brain norepinephrine levels, rather than serotonin). These individuals also exhibit mood elevation after taking dextroamphetamine.

The other group has a normal urinary level of MHPG (or it may be high), indicating normal or high brain levels of norepinephrine. They fail to respond to tricyclic drugs, but show a favourable response to amitryptaline which enhances brain serotonin levels, as against dopamine or norepinephrine. These individuals fail to show mood elevation in response to dextroamphetamine. It is to be expected that these two subgroups would respond differently to tyrosine (see page 77) and to tryptophan. Tyrosine raises brain levels of norepinephrine and so would be expected to improve the first group, whereas tryptophan raises serotonin levels and therefore would be expected to improve the second subgroup. By assessing MHPG levels, and previous known response to drugs such as tricyclics, it should therefore be possible to predict which depressive patients would respond to tryptophan.

The lesson to be learned from this is that whilst nutrient substances are part of the overall economy of the body, and whilst in certain conditions they can have therapeutic effects, this does not make them universally applicable in any named condition. Since quite obviously the same manifestation of dysfunction, e.g. depression, can be the result of a variety of instigating factors, and quite probably is the result of several of these, rather than just one. No single nutrient will be the means of resolving all such cases.

The correct use of any nutrient in health or ill health is to provide the body with its needs on a cellular level. If the biochemical requirement of an individual is for tryptophan, then awareness of its physiological and therapeutic roles, as well as of possible complications and interrelations with other nutrients, will enable its safe and successful employment.

There are warnings of one hazard in the use of tryptophan as a supplemented nutrient, and that is in the case of pregnancy. Trials on hamsters[17] have shown quite clearly that, in animals at least, a high intake of tryptophan, combined with a high protein diet, leads to reduced litter size and increased mortality. A recent report on this subject states: 'It is often assumed that a substance is safe for consumption if it occurs naturally within the body. However, such a rationale has limits with respect to tryptophan.' These trials tested tryptophan in relation to normal and high protein intake. Since a low protein diet favours transport of tryptophan to the brain and kidneys, it is to be expected that the effects of supplementation of tryptophan on pregnancy would be even more marked in such cases.

There is as yet no evidence linking tryptophan usage with any human complications of pregnancy. However, the warning is clear that until such time as it is shown to be otherwise the use of tryptophan in women anticipating becoming pregnant should be limited. Tryptophan normally occurs as 1 per cent of the protein intake, whether of plant or animal origin. In the trials quoted the levels given ranged from 3.7 per cent to 8 per cent, which it is claimed is within the range utilized in supplementation for depression and insomnia.

It should be noted that tryptophan is not compatible with monoamine oxidase inhibiting drugs.

Tryptophan can be utilized to assess the adequacy, or otherwise, of body pyridoxine levels (B_6). This is based on the concept that adequate metabolism of tryptophan requires sufficient B_6. Should there be a deficiency, or insufficiency, of B_6 then upon the oral intake of tryptophan there would occur a urinary spill of the tryptophan metabolite xanthurenic acid. With adequate levels of B_6 an intake of between 2g and 5g of tryptophan produces no spillage of xanthurenic acid. In clinical studies between 50mg and 100mg of tryptophan per kilogram of body weight have been used to assess B_6 status. Ideally a 24 hour sample is used, but if inconvenient then the sample is collected for a six hour period following the tryptophan load. If there is an excess of 25mg of xanthurenic acid in that six hour urine sample then B_6 insufficiency is indicated, and 75mg of xanthurenic acid in a 24 hour sample has the same interpretation.[17] In trials, with implications for humans, but conducted on rats, previously non-aggresive rats were placed on a tryptophan deficient diet. They displayed aggressive tendencies after 90 days, which was unrelieved by niacin supplementation (they had also been deprived of adequate niacin). Normality was restored after sixty days either on a normal diet or intraperitoneal tryptophan injection.[17] The range of human needs of tryptophan is between 82mg and 250mg daily in a sample of fifty people.[18]

National Academy of Sciences give the daily requirement for an adult as 3mg per kilogram of body weight, meaning that a 75kg individual would need an intake of 225mg daily. The level of tryptophan found in first class protein (and plant protein) is approximately 11mg per gram.[19] The best sources of tryptophan from food can be found in the following: soya protein, brown rice (uncooked), cottage cheese, fish, beef, liver, lamb, peanuts, pumpkin and sesame seeds and lentils.

Note that vitamin B_6 is essential for the conversion of tryptophan, and pellagra is considered a combined deficiency of niacin, pyridoxine and tryptophan.[20]

Tryptophan update: A recent study at Finland's University of Tampere, Department of Neurology, indicates that tryptophan has potential as a pain reducing agent.

Eleven healthy volunteers were randomly assigned, in a double-blind crossover trial, to either 2g of tryptophan daily, or a placebo. Dietary instructions were that a high carbohydrate, low fat, low protein diet, should be adhered to (to enhance tryptophan uptake in the brain). Pain was induced by a submaximal application of a tourniquet, to produce ischaemic pain, which was assessed before dietary changes; after tryptophan; after placebo. Blood samples were taken to assess tryptophan levels, and the other amino acids which compete with it for uptake. There was a general tendency for pain to be attenuated with tryptophan, and in two subjects remarkable increases in pain tolerance levels were noted.[21]

According to research into the most suitable timing for the taking of tryptophan,[22] one of its main limitations for uptake, and ultimate conversion to serotonin (or niacin), is the competition that it has with leucine, isoleucine, tyrosine, phenylalanine, valine and threonine. Thus, supplementation should be away from protein meals, and preferable together with a carbohydrate meal or snack. The resulting insulin release will ensure that competing large neutral amino acids are taken into the musculo-skeletal tissues, leaving a relatively greater amount of tryptophan in the blood. An hour‑prior to a protein meal is the closest tryptophan should be administered to protein. A snack may be as small as a single biscuit, or preferably a fruit or vegetable juice (e.g. carrot). Vitamin B_6 should be taken at the same time to maximize the serotonergic effect.

Recent research by Dr G. Chowinard of McGill University, Montreal, indicates that the functional usefulness of tryptophan is enhanced by the concurrent supplementation of niacinamide.[23] The ratio suggested is two parts tryptophan to one part niacinamide.

References

1. *Scientific American,* April 1982, pp50-58.
2. *Lancet,* 1 May 1983, pp1145. *American J. of Clinical Nutrition* Vol.34, No.10, p2045, 1982.
3. *Journal of Nutrition,* No.112, p2001, 1982.
4. *Reviews of Clinical Nutrition,* Vol.53, No.3, p169.
5. *Physiology and Behaviour,* No.29, p779, 1982.
6. Philpott and Kalita, *Brain Allergies,* Keats, 1980.
7. Passwater, R., *Super Nutrition,* Pocket Book, 1976.
8. Cheraskin and Ringsdorf, *Psychodietics,* Bantam, 1976.
9. Goldberg, P. and Kaufman, D., *Natural Sleep,* Rodale, 1978
10. *Psychopharmaceutical Bulletin* No.17, pp81-2, 1981.
11. *Lancet* Vol.1 1392, 1970.
12. *Lancet* Vol.11 510-511, 1975.
13. *Psychopharmacologia* (Berlin) 34, pp11-20, 1974.
14. *Psychopharmacology Bulletin* 18, pp7-18, 1982.
15. *International Clinical Nutrition Review,* Vol.3, No.2, 1983.
16. *Life Sciences* 32:1193, 1983.
17. *Bolletino Soc. Italiana di Biologia Sperimenta* 58 (19) 1271, 1982.
18. Bland, J., (editor), *Medical Applications of Clinical Nutrition,* Keats, 1983.
19. *Nutrition Almanac,* McGraw Hill, 1979.
20. Pfeiffer, Carl, *Mental and Elemental Nutrients,* Keats, 1975.
21. *Acupuncture and Electro Therapeutics Research* Vol. 8, No.2, pp156, 1983.
22. *International Academy of Nutrition Newsletter,* November 1983.
23. Mindell, Earl, *Tryptophan,* 1981.

VALINE

Valine is an EAA but thus far little has been ascertained as to its therapeutic value.

In trials to assess the effects of pre-meal intake of amino acids, conducted in 1982, the combination utilized was phenylalanine (3g), valine (2g), methionine (2g), and tryptophan (1g). The results showed 4g of the mixture, in the ratio given, resulted in reduced food intake in 50 per cent of the obese subjects. As described in the section on phenylalanine (page 58) this is thought to be the result of the release of choleycystokinin which induces a feeling of satiety. When combined with the tryptophan-induced presence of additional serotonin, and consequent feelings of drowiness and calm, this is thought to result in a lesser desire for food.[1] What role valine plays in this formula is not clear.

There is a class of patients suffering from hypervalinaemias, or subacute b-aminoisobutyric aciduria, with symptoms ranging from headaches and irritability to 'crawling skin', and delusions and hallucinations. Symptoms may be aggravated by eating high-valine foods or taking of a supplement which contains valine. Treatment is by a low protein diet, and the taking of supplements which excludes valine and methionine and histidine which all provoke the protein-intolerant syndrome which may be part of the complex of biochemical faults in such cases.[2] (Klaire Laboratories produce *Amino Complex 111,* which is available from York Nutritional Supplies in the U.K., and which corresponds to this formulated need.)

Borrmann describes valine as 'useful in muscle, mental and emotional upsets and in insomnia and nervousness'.[3]

The range of human needs is given as between 375mg and 800mg per day in a sample of 48 people, which shows a 2.1 fold variation.[4]

The daily requirements given by the U.S. National Academy of Sciences is 14mg per kilogram of body weight per day in an adult. This indicates a daily requirement of 1,050mg for a 75kg individual. The content of valine in first class protein is 48mg per gram.[5]

Main food sources of valine include soy flour, raw brown rice, cottage cheese, fish, beef, lamb, chicken, almonds, brazil nuts, cashews, peanuts, sesame seed, lentils, chick peas (garbanzos) and lima beans (raw), mushrooms, soybeans.

One of valine's lesser claims to fame is that it is the amino acid that is genetically substituted for glutamic acid in the haemoglobin molecule, resulting in sickle cell anaemia.[6]

References
1. *American Journal of Nutrition,* Vol.34, No.10, p2045, 1982.
2. Pangborn, Jon, Ph.D, pamphlet. Klaire Laboratories, Carlsbad, California.
3. Borrmann, W., *Comprehensive Answers to Nutrition,* New Horizons, Chicago, 1979.
4. Bland, J., (editor), *Medical Applications of Clinical Nutrition,* Keats, 1983.
5. *Nutrition Almanac,* McGraw Hill, 1979.
6. Dixon-George, Bernard, *Beyond the Magic Bullet,* Allen & Unwin, 1978.

PROLINE

Proline is not an EAA but may be synthesized by the body. It is one of the main components of collagen, the connective tissue structure that binds and supports all other tissues. Pauling[1] points out that there is evidence that vitamin C is required for the conversion of prolyl residues or procollagen (the precursor of collagen) into the form that gives collagen its characteristic properties.

The use of proline in wound healing, and in the promotion of improved collagen status, as well as in cosmetic improvement of 'ageing' tissues has been proposed by researchers in California.[2] Hydroxyproline, which the body incoporates into collagen, is readily transformed by the body from proline; it is incorporated into the structure of tendons and ligaments.[3]

Proline is one of the aromatic amino acids, such as phenylalanine and tryptophan.

Supplementation would seem to be indicated in cases of persistent soft tissue strains; hypermobile joints; soft tissue healing requirement, and in lax and 'sagging' tissues associated with age. Combined with vitamin C supplementation it is more effective. Pfeiffer states clearly that the protein collagen is neither properly formed, nor maintained, if vitamin C is lacking.[4]

References
1. Pauling, Linus, *Vitamin C-The Common Cold and Flu,* Freeman and Co, 1976.
2. Levine, Stephen, *Allergy Research Group Pamphlet* Concord, California.
3. Anthony Harris, *Your Body,* Futura, 1979.
4. Pfeiffer, Carl, *Mental and Elemental Nutrients,* Keats, 1975.

TAURINE

Taurine is not an EAA. It is manufactured in the body and is also found in animal protein, but not in vegetable protein. It is a sulphur amino acid derivative.

Its synthesis in humans is from the amino acids methionine and cysteine, primarily in the liver with the assistance of vitamin B_6. Bland states[1] that vegetarians on a diet containing imbalanced protein intake, and therefore deficient in methionine or cysteine, may have difficulty manufacturing taurine.

Dietary intake is thought to be more necessary in women, since the female hormone estradiol depresses the formation of taurine in the liver. Any additional estradiol in the form of medication would increase this inhibition. In animal studies large oral doses of taurine have been shown to stimulate production of growth hormone.

The main interest, until recently, has been in taurine's role as a neurotransmitter in which role it functions with glycine and gamma-aminobutyricacid, two neuroinhibitory transmitters. A further role played by taurine is in maintaining the correct composition of bile, and in maintaining solubility of cholesterol. Several studies have shown that bile acids are secreted, in bile, in a form in which they are conjugated with glycine and taurine. The taurine conjugates are described as 'superior biological detergents'[2]. The data in a recent trial showed that increasing the availability of taurine through dietary means, probably exerts a protective effect against cholestasis, induced by monohydroxy bile acids.

Changes in platelet function are considered to be one possible factor in the aetiology of migraine, and taurine is apparently uniquely concentrated in the platelets. This connection with migraine was established by assessing taurine levels during and after headaches. It was found that taurine levels in the platelets were significantly higher during headache periods. The trial[3] authors proposed that the metabolic platelet defect in migraine involves taurine as well as the tryptophan derivative serotonin.

It is noted by other researchers that taurine is found in the developing brain in concentrations up to four times that found in the adult brain.[4] Since taurine acts as a suppressor of neuronal activity in the developing brain, during the phase when other regulatory systems are not fully developed, it is thought that deficiency of taurine, at this stage, might contribute towards, or predispose the individual to, epilepsy. Taurine has been shown in human trials to have an anticonvulsive effect.[5] Its apparent role is that it normalizes the balance of other amino acids, which in epilepsy are thoroughly disordered. In epilepsy serum levels of over half the amino acids are lowered,[6] whilst serum levels of taurine are high and cerebro-spinal fluid levels are low. Serum zinc has been found to be low in epileptics, and since low serum zinc results in plasma and urine levels of taurine rising this may be part of taurine's association with epilepsy.

Dosage is suggested at one gram a day, not more, followed by daily doses of not more than 500mg, and reducing to 50mg and 100mg a day. High doses are not as effective as low doses repeated infrequently, since taurine accumulates rapidly and is only slowly metabolized. Full spectrum light exposure results in increased levels of taurine being concentrated in the pineal and pituitary glands.[7] Continued exposure to artificial lighting, which is deficient in the ultraviolet portion of the spectrum, might cause this concentration to be reversed, and to impair whatever function taurine performs in the pituitary and pineal glands. Taurine is associated with zinc in eye function, and impairment of vision has been shown with taurine deficiency prior to the development of structural changes.[8]

Taurine has also been shown to have a role in sparing the loss of potassium in heart muscle. It is thought to be the substance regulating osmotic control of calcium, as well as potassium, in heart muscle. This has been shown to be of importance during dieting periods for weight loss. During any stringent dieting programme the addition of sulphur-rich amino acids, such as methionine and cysteine, will ensure adequate taurine and therefore protect the heart muscle from calcium and potassium loss.

Taurine has been found to have an influence upon blood sugar levels, similar to that of insulin.[9] Bland comments[1] upon the ubiquitous role of taurine, which he dubs 'a remarkable accessory food factor'. He points to its possible involvement with muscular dystrophy, where its interrelationship with vitamins A and E is thought to be of importance. He discusses also the link with Down's syndrome children, in which IQ levels are said to have improved with taurine supplementation (along with B complex, C and E vitamins).[10] Should there be a genetic, or metabolic defect in the individual's ability to synthesize taurine, then supplementation could become critical. There are a number of metabolic disorders that can result in taurine levels in urine being high (apart from dietary oversupply of it, or its precursors methionine and cysteine). Impaired renal tubular conservation may be responsible. If other beta amino acids, such as GABA are being normally excreted, then transport disorders can be ruled out. Heart conditions, such as myocardial infarction, or skeletal damage, physical or emotional stress, and diseases involving platelet or leucocyte haemolysis, are all potential causes of increased taurine excretion in the urine. High alcohol consumption, and the use of salycilates may also be implicated, as can a deficiency of zinc, impairing as a result the integrity of cell membranes. Gastro-intestinal pain, acute cholecystitis and cardiac arrythmias, may all accompany high urine levels of taurine.[11]

References

1. *International Clinical Nutrition Review,* Vol.2, No.3, 1982.
2. *Am J. of Clin. Nutrition,* Vol.37, No.2, p221, 1983.
3. *Headache Journal,* Vol.22, No.4, pp165, 1982.
4. *Orthomolecular Review,* Vol.3, No.3, 1983.
5. *Taurine,* Ed. Huxtable, Barbeau, pp1-9.
6. *Epilepsia* 16:245-249, 1975.
7. *Life Sciences,* 22:1789-1798, 1978.
8. *Nature,* 194:300-302, 1962.
9. *Canadian Chemical Process Industry,* 26:569-570, 1942.
10. *Proceedings Nat. Acad. Sciences,* 78:564-578, 1978.
11. Huxtable, R. and Pasante-Morales, H., *Taurine in Nutrition and Neurology,* Plenum Press, 1982.

CARNITINE

Carnitine is synthesized in the liver by humans as well as being a part of the diet in the form of muscle and organ meats. It is not found in vegetable forms of protein. Carnitine is not an EAA.

A number of therapeutic roles have been described for carnitine which is converted rapidly from lysine as well as methionine.[1] The process of conversion is dependent upon adequate vitamin C being present.[2] The supply of carnitine is especially enhanced by lysine ingestion, as compared with other amino acid precursors of carnitine such as threonine and tryptophan.[1]

It is suggested that men have a higher need for carnitine than women. Higher levels are found in serum in men than women, and men have high levels present in the epididymis of the testes. Lysine depletion in animals results in infertility as a result of the loss of sperm motility.[3,4] Bland[2] suggests that although carnitine is not a vitamin it may be an essential nutrient in newborn infants, due to inadequate ability to synthisize it; and in adults with genetic limitations in their ability to convert methionine or lysine to carnitine.

Carnitine has been shown to have a profound involvement in the metabolism of fat, and in the reduction of triglycerides. Oxidation of triglycerides occurs when 1g to 3g of carnitine are administered daily. This is of potential value in conditions as diverse as intermittant claudication; poor hand and foot circulation; myocardical infarction[5] and kidney disease. Carnitine transfers fatty acids across the membranes of the mitchondria, where they can be utilized as sources of energy.

A variety of other conditions have been suggested as being potential beneficiaries of carnitine supplementation, including muscular dystrophy, myotonic dystrophy, and limb-girdle muscular dystrophy, since these lead to carnitine loss in the urine and therefore greater requirements.[6] The application of the use of carnitine to the stimulation of fat metabolism leads to possible benefits in cases of obesity. Since fat is more readily mobilized, and clearance is more rapid, with the use of carnitine, there is every reason to expect that a clinical application in this direction will be forthcoming with further research.

Research in Rome[5] showed that during acute, or chronic, cardiac ischemia, or chronic hypoxia, there occurs an accumulation of free fatty acids and long chain acyl-CoA-esters which can damage the myocardium. Carnitine appears to offer protection by forming esters with these fatty substances. Carnitine has been shown to be deficient in hearts of patients who have died of acute myocardial infarctions, especially in necrotic tissue. If carnitine were available, then, it is postulated, the areas immediately surrounding the necrotic areas could be restored to normal. Carnitine has been shown[7] to be useful in conditions of ketosis in individuals on diets which produce the accumulation of ketone bodies, or fat waste products, in the blood. Such a build up can acidify the blood, resulting in calcium, magnesium and potassium loss, and can indeed be life-threatening. Fat metabolism requires carnitine to be adequately present. It is noted that in scurvy the fat levels of the blood are high,[8] and this is thought to be as a result of the relationship which exists between vitamin C and carnitine. A low level of vitamin C will result in apparent carnitine deficiency.

References

1. *Am.J. of Clin. Nutrition,* Vol. 37, No. 1, p93, 1983.
2. *International Clinical Nutrition Review,* Vol. 2, No.3, p14, 1982.
3. *Clinical Chem. Acta.,* 67:207-212, 1977.
4. *Journal of Nutrition,* 107:1209-1215, 1977.
5. *Lancet,* Vol 1, pp1419-1420, 1982.
6. *Am J. Clin. Nut.,* 34:2693-8, 1981.
7. Earl Mindell, *Carnitine,* 1983.
8. Hulse, J. et al, *Journal of Biological Chemistry,* No. 253, pp1654-9, 1978.

TYROSINE

Tyrosine is not an EAA. Tyrosine is a precursor to thyroid, adrenocortical hormones and to dopamine. Some of the symptoms of its deficiency include low body temperature, low blood-pressure and 'restless legs'.[1] Tyrosine derives from phenylalanine. Tyrosine is capable of producing toxic reactions, in excessive dosages of itself, or of phenylalanine,[2] as has been demonstrated when rats fed a low protein diet, which contained more than 3 per cent phenylalanine, developed lesions on paws and eyes, and had growth rate and food intakes depressed, all of which is identical with tyrosine toxicity. The pigment of skin and hair, melanin, is derived from tyrosine.

Therapeutically tyrosine has been employed to enhance its derivatives (dopa, dopamine, norepinephrine, epinephrine) as well as its ability to alter brain function. Brain tyrosine levels are most conveniently raised by ingestion of pure tyrosine, with a high carbohydrate meal to lower levels of competing amino acids. A high protein meal will increase serum and brain tyrosine to a degree but not enough to effect catecholamine synthesis greatly. Physiologically active neurons are highly responsive to neurotransmitters such as tyrosine (and choline) and will actively synthesize neurotransmitters from these precursors. There are very few side effects resulting from even fairly large doses of tyrosine.[3] Wurtman who has done much research into this area of biochemistry suggests that if neurons are not active the precursor is not used. If the neurons are active however, a particular dose of tyrosine can either reduce blood pressure in hypertension, or increase it in haemmorrhagic shock, by virtue of the provision of the tyrosine for catecholamine synthesis, these active neurons, will then produce the particular physiologically desirable effect.

Tyrosine is reported to help some Parkinson patients, and to aid in relieving some depression cases.[3] The use in depression of such drugs as monoamine oxidase inhibitors and tricyclic antidepressants involves an increase in the brain's levels of monoamines such as serotonin and norepinephrine, either by slowing down their degradation, or by prolonging their action, at the synaptic receptor. The use of neurotransmitter precursors, which can increase the levels of serotonin and norepinephrines is another way of achieving a similar end. The use of their precursors tryptophan (see page 63) and tyrosine can therefore be seen to be a logical step in this direction. Tyrosine has been found to be most effective[4] when there exists a deficiency state. Patients who have previously responded to amphetamines may respond well to tyrosine therapy.

There is evidence that small doses of tyrosine are more effective in increasing brain levels of neurotransmitters, than large doses.[5] Although blood and brain levels of tyrosine will increase with large doses, there appears to be an inhibition of the enzyme tyrosine hydroxylase which converts tyrosine to catecholamines, when large amounts of tyrosine are present.

Research into tyrosine is in its early stages and more will be heard of this powerful substance in human economy.

Note: Tyrosine is not compatible with the taking of MAO drugs (monoamineoxidases).

References

1. Philpott, W., pamphlet on *Selective Amino Acid Deficiencies,* Klaire Laboratories, California.
2. *Agricultural Biology and Chemistry,* Vol.46, No.10, p2491, 1982.
3. *Lancet,* p1145, 21 May, 1983.
4. *Psychopharmacology Bulletin* No.18, pp7-18, 1982.
5. *Biochemical Journal,* Vol.206, pp165, 1982.

GLUTAMINE AND GLUTAMIC ACID

Glutamine is not an EAA although Bland suggests that under certain conditions it may become a 'contingency nutrient' and therefore essential.[1] He points out that glutamine is synthesized in certain tissues for use in others, and that it is the dominant amino acid in serum and cerebro-spinal fluid. It is the only amino acid that easily passes the blood-brain barrier. Glutamic acid can be synthesized from a number of amino acids. It easily loses its amine group, and thus participates as an amine donor in transamination reactions, which are so vital in the process of the formation of NEAA's. When glutamic acid combines with ammonia it becomes glutamine. It is also a major excitatory neurotransmitter in the brain and spinal cord, and is the precursor of GABA, which is an inhibitory transmitter, as well as glutathione (see page 88).

Williams[2] comments that the glutamine derivative glutamic acid does not pass this blood-brain barrier, although it might be in the blood in relatively high levels, and yet infiltrate the brain fluids in only small amounts. Its amide, glutamine, has no such problem, after which it is readily converted into glutamic acid. The function is described by Williams thus: 'The essential and suggestive fact to remember is that glutamic acid is uniquely a brain fuel.' Pfieffer[3] shows that vitamin B_6, via a phosphate reaction in the brain, allows the removal of the acid group from glutamic acid, and the formation of gamma aminobutyric acid (GABA), which is a calming agent, and possibly a neurotransmitter. Glutamic acid is a component of folic acid. It is also a key component of the chromium compound known as the glucose tolerance factor (GTF). The best source of this, for anyone suspected of glucose intolerance, is Brewer's yeast.

Behavioural problems and autism in children have been successfully assisted by Dr Bernard Rimland, of the Institute for Child Behaviour, by nutritional means, which include glutamic acid as a major component.

Glutamic acid, having been converted to that form in the brain from glutamine, is involved in two key roles. Along with glucose it is the fuel for the brain cells.[4] The second function of glutamine is to act as a detoxifier of ammonia from the brain. As it picks up ammonia, glutamic acid is reconverted to its original form of glutamine. Passwater points out[4] that as the brain is able to store relatively small quantities of glucose, it is dependant upon glutamic acid. He states: 'The shortage of 1-glutamine in the diet, or glutamic acid in the brain, results in brain damage due to excess ammonia, or a brain that can never get into "high gear".' Dr William Shive has pointed out that glutamine has a protective role to play in the body's relationship with alcohol. It has been shown to protect bacteria against alcohol poisoning,[5] and when given to rats it decreases their voluntary alcohol consumption. It is the only substance to have this effect. Williams[2] assumes this to be the result of its effect, in the brain, on the appetite centre. Glutamic acid has no such protective effect on bacteria, and presumably doesn't on humans either. Williams suggests between 2g and 4g daily of glutamine, as a treatment for anyone with an alcohol problem. Passwater comments on a case in which glutamine has stopped sugar craving in much the way that it has been shown to stop or reduce alcohol craving. Presumably by a similar action on the appetite centre (in the hypothalamus).

Among other noted areas of usefulness are its application in depression; IQ improvement in mentally deficient children; enhanced peptic ulcer healing; benefits to epileptic children, and applications in schizophrenia and senility (by Dr Abram Hoffer).[6]

Dr H. Newbold recommends that to attain an optimum level of intake 200mg should be taken three times daily for a week, increasing to two capsules of 200mg each three times daily after that, to assess general well-being. The suggested pattern for alcohol problems is 1g three times daily.[7] There are seldom glutamine deficiencies, according to Philpott,[8] but, as Bland explains, contingency status may be reached through excessive demand in relation to genetic factors which lead to suboptimal synthesis in the body.

Pfeiffer discusses the way in which the well-known 'Chinese Restaurant Syndrome' relates to glutamine. Glutamic acid, which is present in monosodium glutamate, combining with a pressor amine such as tyromine, which is commonly found in certain protein foods such as aged cheese, pickled herring etc. produces the headache. Much Chinese restaurant food is also high in salt leading to fluid retention which adds to the problem.[3] Bland notes that sensitivity to monosodium glutamate indicates a need for supplemental pyridoxine.[9] Doses of between 50mg and 100mg daily are suggested.

References

1. Bland, J., (editor), *Medical Applications of Clinical Nutrition,* Keats, 1983.
2. Williams, R., *Nutrition Against Disease,* Bantam, 1981.
3. Pfeiffer, Carl, *Mental and Elemental Nutrients,* Keats, 1975.
4. Passwater, R., *L-Glutamine The Surprising Brain Fuel.* Pamphlet.
5. *J. Biol. Chem,* Vol. 1.214, No. 2, pp503, 1955.
6. *Orthomolecular Psychiatry,* Freeman and Co., San Francisco, 1973.
7. Newbold, H., *Mega Nutrient for Your Nerves,* Berkeley Books, New York, 1978.
8. Philpott, W., *General Amino Acid Deficiencies,* pamphlet, Klair Laboratories, California.
9. Pearson, D. and Shaw, S., *Life Extension,* Warner Books, 1983.

CYSTEINE AND CYSTINE

Cystine is a stable form of the sulphur-rich amino acid cysteine. The body is capable of converting one to the other as required. In metabolic terms they can be thought of as the same.

Apart from methionine, all the sulphur-rich amino acids can be synthesized by the body, from methionine and elemental sulphur. These are taurine, cysteine and cystine. Methionine and cysteine are utilized in the formation of a number of essential compounds, such as coenzyme A, heparin, biotin, lipoic acid and glutathione (see page 88). Cysteine is a vital component of the glucose tolerance factor (along with glycine, glutamic acid, niacin and chromium). Cystine is found in abundance in a variety of proteins such as hair keratin, insulin, the digestive enzymes chromotrypsinogen A, and trypsinogen, papain and also lactoglobulin. The flexibility of the skin, as well as the texture is influenced by cysteine as it has the ability to slow abnormal cross-linkages in collagen, the connective tissue protein. Cysteine will convert cystine in the absence of vitamin C. There is strong caution regarding the use of cysteine by diabetics (see note at the end of this section).

The enzyme glutathione peroxidase contains a large element of cysteine. As a detoxification agent cystine has been shown to protect the body against damage induced by alcohol and cigarette smoking. One report stated that not only was it effective in preventing the side-effects of drinking, such as a hangover, but that it prevented liver and brain damage as well. It also reduces damage such as emphysema, resulting from smoking.[1]

Philpott maintains that for proper utilization of vitamin B_6, cystine or cysteine is essential.[2] The measurement of cystine by 24 hour urine and blood serum studies in a variety of chronic degenerative illnesses, both mental and physical, has been correlated with B_6 utilization disorder in research by Philpott. The results show that low B_6 utilization is produced, at least in part, by low levels of cystine (or cysteine).

The metabolic steps of the formation of these two amino acids is from methionine to cystathionine to cysteine to cystine. In chronic diseases it appears that the formation of cysteine from methionine is prevented. One element in orthomolecular correction of the biochemistry of the chronic disease is therefore the restoration of adequate levels of cysteine (or cystine). Supplementation is one method of short term correction of such a relative deficiency, and Philpott suggests a dosage of cysteine or cystine of 1g three times daily for one month, then reducing to twice daily. As with many amino acids, the end of the meal is the best time for taking them.

It is noted that cysteine is more soluble than cystine and that it contributes its sulphur more readily, and thus achieves better results in some patients. The very presence of the sulphur taste, however, makes its encapsulation desirable. Philpott recommends that B_6 be taken in doses of 50mg three times daily in the form of Pyridoxal-5-phosphate, at the same time as cysteine. These recommendations, as with all others relating to doses, must be seen in the context of biochemical individuality, and therefore subject to large variations in individual patients. It should also be noted that all recommendations assume that an overall assessment of nutrient status is concurrently being undertaken. No single nutrient is seen to be curative in any condition. Levine points to cysteine and cystine being important in stabilizing crosslinks in keratine and other proteins as well as being useful for heavy metal detoxification.[3] This is common to all sulphur amino acids.

People with diabetic tendencies should not use large supplemental doses of cysteine unless under supervision, as it is capable of inactivating insulin by reducing certain disulphide bonds which determine its structure.[5] Pearson and Shaw note[5] that in order to avoid the conversion of cysteine to cystine, with possible consequences as far as the formation of kidney or bladder stones, at least three times the dose of vitamin C should accompany the taking of cysteine supplementally.

References

1. *Nutritional Consultants,* p12, Nov/Dec 1980.
2. Pfeiffer, Carl, *Mental and Elemental Nutrients,* Keats, 1975.
3. Philpott, W., *Philpott Medical Center,* Oklahoma City, pamphlet.
4. Levine, Stephen, Allergy Research Group, Concord California, pamphlet.
5. Pearson, D. and Shaw, S., *Life Extension,* Nutri Books, 1984.

GLYCINE

Glycine is not an EAA. It is utilized in liver detoxification compounds, such as glutathione (of which it is an essential part together with cysteine and glutamic acid). Glycine is essential for the biosynthesis of nucleic acids as well as of bile acids.[1] As a methyl group carrier glycine has an added role in macromolecular biosynthesis. It is methylated as betaine. Glycine is a glucogenic amino acid.

In its own right it has not been shown to have therapeutic applications, but as a major part of a detoxification compound, such as glutathione, it is of profound importance.[2]

Glycine is a major part of the pool of amino acids which are available for the synthesis of non-essential amino acids in the body by means of transamination and amination. It is readily converted into serine. It is a constituent of a number of amino acid compound formulations used as tonic preparations.

Experimental evidence on rats indicates that glycine (in conjunction with arginine) has a useful role to play in promoting healing after trauma.[3] Traumatized rats were fed on diets without, or with, glycine plus arginine, or with ornithine plus glycine. These amino acids occur in particularly high concentrations in the skin and connective tissue, and might be required for repair of damaged tissue. Arginine and glycine supplementation significantly improved nitrogen retention in both traumatized and non-traumatized animals, whereas ornithine was less effective in this role. It is postulated that creatine synthesis, and turnover, results from the enrichment of arginine and glycine, and this produces repair benefits.

Human trials indicate that gastric acid secretion is enhanced by glycine and its homologous peptides.[4] Further trials, on infants, on a variety of different feeding programmes indicate that, after feeding, the sum of plasma-free amino acids increases, and the glycine:valine ratio falls. The type of meal determines how quickly this takes place, and how soon normal levels are restored. Breast feeding, as opposed to formula feeds, produced faster alteration as well as speedier normalization. Studies of plasma-amino acids in infants should therefore take into account when and what the child was last fed, for standardization of results to be meaningfully determined.[5]

References

1. Levine, Stephen, Allergy Research Group Publication, Concord, California.
2. Amino Acids pamphlet, Dietary Sales, Indiana.
3. *Journal of Nutrition,* Vol.111, No.7, pp1265-74, 1981.
4. *Am. J. of Physiology* Vol.242, No.2, ppG85-G88, 1982.
5. *Acta Paediatrica Scandinavica,* Vol.71, No.3, pp385-9, 1982.

ALANINE

This is a non-essential amino acid. The main nutritional function of alanine is in the metabolism of tryptophan and pyridoxine, in which it plays an essential role. In conditions such as hypoglycaemia alanine may be used as a source for the production of glucose, in order to stabilize blood glucose, over lengthy periods.

In trials designed to assess the effect on high cholesterol levels of combinations of different amino acids, alanine was found to have a cholesterol-reducing effect in the serum of experimental animals (rats), when in combination with arginine and glycine.[1] Levels were reduced by 20 per cent when arginine and alanine alone were administered, and by a full fifty per cent when glycine was also added. Alanine is usually included in amino acid compound tablets; where daily intake levels of between 200mg and 600mg daily are suggested.

References

1. *Atherosclerosis,* No.43, pp381, 1982.

b-ALANINE

This is the only naturally occuring b-amino acid. It is found in its free state in the brain. It is a component of carnosine, anserine and of pantothenic acid (vitamin B_5) which is itself a component of coenzyme A. The function of carnosine and anserine (which occur in animal muscle) is unknown.

b-Alanine is metabolized to acetic acid, and in plants and micro-organisms it is formed by decarboxylation of aspartic acid.[1]

Therapeutically it is useful to assist in synthesis of pantothenic acid.

References

1.   Meister, A., *Biochemistry of the Amino Acids,* Academic Press, New York, 1965.

GAMA-AMINOBUTYRIC ACID (GABA)

This is a non-essential amino acid, formed from glutamic acid. Its function in the central nervous system appears to be as a regulator of neuronal activity. It is essential for brain metabolism.

It has been used in the treatment of epilepsy and hyper-tension.[1,2] It is thought to induce calmness and tranquillity by inhibiting neurotransmitters which decrease the activity of those neurons involved in manic behaviour and acute agitation.

Pearson and Shaw[3] point out that GABA may be useful in reducing enlarged prostate problems, by virtue of the stimulation of the release of the hormone prolactin by the pituitary. Doses of 20mg to 40mg daily are recommended (dissolved under the tongue). This is not suggested as an alternative to seeking professional advice in problems of this sort.

References

1.   *Physiology Review,* Vol.39, pp383-406, 1959.
2.   *International Review of Neurobiology,* Vol.2, pp279-332, 1960.
3.   Pearson, D. and Shaw, S., *Life Extension,* Warner Books, 1983.

ASPARAGINE AND ASPARTIC ACID

Aspartic acid is a non-essential amino acid which plays a vital role in metabolism. It is found in abundance in plant protein. It is glycogenic and is active in the processes of transamination and deamination.

It is plentiful in plants, especially in sprouting seeds. In protein, aspartic acid exists mainly in the form of its amide, asparagine. In plants asparagine is therefore in a reversible combination of ammonia and aspartic acid. This is important in the metabolism of plants in order to preserve ammonia. Asparagine serves as an amino donor in liver transamination processes, and participates in metabolic control of the brain and nervous system. It has therapeutic uses in treatment of brain and neural conditions. Aspartic acid performs an important role in the urea cycle where it assists in the formation of carbamyl phosphate and arginosuccinic acid, as well as carbamyl L-aspartic acid, which is the precursor of the pyrimadines. Aspartic acid, as a potassium or magnesium salt, is useful in physiological cellular function. Aspartic acid is used therapeutically in the detoxification of ammonia, and to enhance liver function. [1,2]

According to researcher and author Earl Mindell, aspartic acid increases stamina and endurance in athletes. Its ability to increase resistance to fatigue is thought to be as a result of its role in clearing ammonia from the system. [3] Asparagine also plays an important role in the synthesis of glycoprotein and many other proteins.

References
1. Meister, A., *Biochemistry of Amino Acids,* Academic Press, New York, 1965.
2. Greenstein, J. and Winitz, M., *Chemistry of the Amino Acids,* Wiley, New York, 1961.
3. Mindell, E., *Three Amino Acids for Your Health,* pamphlet, 1981.

CITRULLINE

This exists primarily in the liver and is a major component of the urea cycle. It exists plentifully in plant foods such as onion and garlic. It is formed in the urea cycle by the addition to ornithine of carbon dioxide and ammonia. In combination with aspartic acid it forms arginosuccinic acid, which on further metabolization becomes arginine.

Therapeutically it is used for detoxification of ammonia and in the treatment of fatigue.[1] As a precursor of both arginine and ornithine it is capable of influencing the production of Growth Hormone.

Reference

1. *A Symposium on Amino Acid Metabolism*, John Hopkins Press, 1955.

ORNITHINE

Ornithine is not an EAA. It is a most important constituent of the urea cycle and is the precursor of other amino acids such as citrulline and glutamic acid, as well as proline.[1] Ornithine's therapeutic value lies in its involvement in the urea cycle, and in its ability to enhance liver function. It is used in the treatment of hepatic coma states.[2]

Ornithine is formed when arginine is hydrolyzed by arginase. According to Pearson and Shaw in their controversial book, *Life Extension*[3] Growth Hormone is released in response to supplementation of 1g to 2g of ornithine taken on an empty stomach at bedtime. It is also claimed that the immune system is thus stimulated[4] improving the immune response to bacteria, viral agents and tumour activity. (See also Arginine, page 44.)

Dr Jeffrey Bland comments on this type of approach which he calls 'experimental pharmacology using nutritional factors', saying that, in effect, there is no way of knowing what the long-term impact of such an approach will be. There are no controls, and no follow-ups, and in short the use of such methods, for more than the short term (months only), is to be questioned. Caution should be employed in the use of ornithine by anyone with a history of schizophrenia, who may find a worsening of associated symptoms if this or arginine is utilized excessively.

References
1. *Pharmazie,* Vol.15, pp618-622, 1960.
2. *Symposium on Amino Acids,* John Hopkins Press, 1955.
3. Pearson, D. and Shaw, S., *Life Extension,* Warner Books, 1982.
4. Mindell, Earl, *Ornithine,* pamphlet, 1982.
5. Personal Communication, 1984.

SERINE

This is a hydroxy-amino acid. It has glycogenic qualities and is very reactive in the body, taking part in pyrimadine, purine, creatine and porphyrin biosynthesis. It takes part in a reaction with homocysteine (which is derived from methionine) to form cystine.[1]

Its main use is in cosmetics where it is added as a natural moistening agent, involved in skin metabolism.[2]

References
1. Greenstein and Winitz, *Chemistry of the Amino Acids,* Wiley, New York, 1961.
2. Meister, A., *Biochemistry of Amino Acids,* Academic Press, New York, 1965.

GLUTATHIONE

Glutathione is a tripeptide comprising the three amino acids cysteine, glutamic acid and glycine. The value of this biologically active compound is in the prevention and treatment of a wide range of degenerative diseases.

Its role as a deactivator of free radicals is well established.[1] Free radicals, often the result of peroxidized fats, are immune system supressors, mutagents, carcinogens and encouragers of cross-linkage and thus the ageing process. Prevention and slowing of free radical activity is one of the major contributions of that class of substances which act as antioxidants such as vitamins A,C,E, the mineral selenium and amino acids such as methionine, cysteine and the compound amino acid, glutathione. Since free radicals comprise a separated part of a molecule, with one or more unpaired electrons, they are extremely reactive and can result in cellular damage when they unite with other molecules. Lipid peroxidation occurs when saturated or unsaturated fats are exposed to oxygen. Peroxides result, and one such is hydrogen peroxide. Free radicals are part of the end result of this process. Interaction between free radicals and DNA and RNA can result in genetic alterations within the cell, resulting in biochemical anarchy. The interaction of free radicals with protein structures results in, among other things, the gradual development of cross links in collagen fibre, which is the characteristic sign of ageing. The tissues literally become constricted and tight, interfering with cellular circulation and drainage, and in texture become leathery, contracted and stiff. Glutathione is uniquely qualified to act against free radicals which produce this intensification of the ageing process.[2] This activity is conducted extracellularly by glutathione against free radical activity as well as lipid peroxides, which are deactivated. Intracellularly the activity of a glutathione-related enzyme, glutathione peroxidase, accomplishes the same task. In this enzyme glutathione is combined with selenium.

Trials at the Louisville School of Medicine have clearly demonstrated the connection between ageing and the reduction in glutathione's presence. Comparing young and old animals it showed that glutathione was reduced in all tissues by as much as 34 per cent. Thus the ability to detoxify, as well as ageing through cross linkage of proteins, was markedly different in the older animals.

Glutathione has been shown in trials at Harvard Medical School to have the ability to enhance the immune protective status of certain cells. In trials in which cigarette smoke was introduced into a tissue culture, the usual result of impairment of phagocytic function was inhibited by glutathione.[3]

The possibility that there is a role for glutathione in cancer prevention comes from trials in which glutathione produced regression of aflatoxin B_1 induced liver tumours, when administered in late stages of tumour development.[4] In rats in which this chemical would normally produce 100 per cent liver cancer development, there was a total of over 80 per cent alive and well after two years when glutathione was also administered.

Heavy metal detoxification is a further area in which glutathione has been useful.[5] It is effective in removing harmlessly from the body, lead, cadmium, mercury and aluminium.

Glutathione is found to be helpful in assisting the liver in its detoxification of liver peroxidation. Thus alcohol-produced damage of the liver is thought to be prevented in several ways by glutathione. In the first place there is actual reduction of hydroperoxides, prior to their attacking saturated lipids, as well as the conversion of lipid hydroperoxides into harmless hydroxy compounds. Glutathione also enables the liver to detoxify undesirable compounds to their substrates for excretion, via the bile, through the action of glutathione-S transferases.[6]

Blechman and Kalita point out that, as with any substance within the body, whether this is a vitamin, a mineral, or anything else, it is necessary to determine specific biochemical needs, on an individual basis, and that what assists one person in the progression from ill health towards optimum health may not do so for another.[7] Glutathione appears to be a most promising, naturally occurring, compound with ramifications spreading throughout the processes of detoxification and ageing.

References

1. *Science,* 179;588-591, 1973.
2. *Physiology Review,* 48;311-373, 1968.
3. *Science,* 162, 810, 1968.
4. *Science,* 212, 541-2, 1980.
5. *J. Am. Med. Assoc.,* 187;358, 1964.
6. *Functions of Glutathione,* New York: Springer Verlag, 1978.
7. Kalita, D.and Blechman,S., *The Biochemical Powers of Glutathione,* pamphlet.

8.

THERAPEUTIC USES OF
AMINO ACIDS — A SUMMARY

Arginine
Infertility due to motility problems in sperm.
As chelating agent for manganese supplementation.
Acceleration of wound healing.
Enhancement of thymus activity.
Glucose tolerance enhanced (animal study).
Insulin production enhanced (animal study).
Fat metabolism enhanced (animal study).
Excess may lead to catatonia.
Function of arginine assisted by guar gum.
Modulates aspects of urea cycle.

Histidine
Metabolized into neurotransmitter histamine.
Maintenance of myalin sheaths.
Auditory dysfunction due to neural changes assisted.
Protective against effects of radiation.
Removal of toxic metals from body.
Treatment of arthritis (rheumatoid).
Useful (with niacin and pyridoxine) in problems relating to inadequate sexual arousal.

Isoleucine
Possible involvement in chronic mental and physical illness.

Leucine
As for isoleucine.
Excess may predispose to pellagra (unless nicotinamide levels optimum).

Lysine
Viral control in conditions such as herpes simplex infection (plus low arginine diet).
Production of carnitine.
Concentration enhanced.
Deficiency may lead to fatigue, dizziness and anaemia.

Methionine
Methyl donor in B_{12} metabolism.
Gives rise to taurine and to cystine and cysteine.
Detoxifying agent: removes heavy metals from body.
Antioxidant: protects against free radicals.
Detoxifies against excess histamine (histadelic schizophrenia) in brain.
Detoxifies liver, preventing fatty build up.
Deficiency can lead to atherosclerosis.
Essential for selenium bioavailability.

Phenylalanine
Gives rise to tyrosine and thence to dopamine, norepinephrine and epinephrine.
Stimulates production of cholyscystokinin and thus induces satiety, relevance in obesity and weight control.
d- (DPA) and dl-phenylalanine (DLPA) is powerful, nontoxic, nonaddictive, painkiller, via enhancement of endogenous pain control factors.
Antidepressant.

Threonine
Deficient in grains, and therefore vegetarians may be deficient if diet imbalanced. Personality disorders can result.

Tryptophan
Essential for synthesis, in body, of nicotinic acid (vitamin B_3).
Gives rise to neurotransmitter serotonin.

Influences amount of protein eaten if taken prior to a meal with carbohydrate snack, thus aiding in weight reduction. Lack leads to craving for carbohydrate.

Uptake by brain enhanced by pyridoxine (B_6), and vitamin C. Inverse relationship between level of tryptophan and emotional complaints.

Aids sleep inducement and sounder sleep (combined with B_6 and magnesium).

Antidepressive in some patients (see page 66).

Possible dangers in excess in pregnancy. Affects size and survival of litters in hamster studies, in large doses.

Valine

Part of amino acid combination for obesity control (combination of phenylalanine-valine-methionine-tryptophan in ratio 3:2:2:1, resulted in decreased food intake when 4g taken prior to meals, in 50 per cent of obese women). Excess leads to symptoms such as hallucinations and 'crawling skin'.

Proline

Gives rise to hydroxyproline.

Proline and hydroxyproline essential for collagen formation and maintenance. Useful in all conditions affecting status of supporting structures, and in reducing collagen degeneration with ageing process.

Vitamin C essential for adequate incorporation into connective tissues.

Taurine

Synthesized in body from methionine, or cysteine in liver (mainly). Inhibited by estradiol.

Conjugates with bile salts to maintain solubility of fats and cholesterol.

Reduces possibility of cholestasis.

Deficiency in childhood predisposes to epilepsy. It is a neuro-transmitter.

Used to treat epilepsy.

Relates to zinc levels in serum directly. Taurine in serum rises with low zinc serum, and results in low taurine levels in brain, increasing chances of fits.

Spares potassium loss in heart muscle.
Influences blood sugar levels similarly to insulin.
Claims for enhanced IQ levels in Down's syndrome children (together with other nutrients).

Carnitine
Synthesized from lysine (and methionine).
Vitamin C essential for conversion.
Men have greater need than women. Possible relation to infertility, via inadequate sperm motility, if deficient. Reduces triglyceride levels.
Useful in circulatory disorders such as intermittent claudication.
Protects against myocardial infarctions by removing free fatty acids etc.
Deficient in heart muscles which are involved in myocardial infarction and necrosis.
Potential use in muscular dystrophy etc.
Aids in mobilizing fatty deposits in obesity.
Useful in condition of ketosis.

Tyrosine
Derives from phenylalanine.
Precursor of thyroid hormones.
Precursor of dopa, dopamine, norepinephrine, epinephrine.
Deficiency leads to low body temperature; low blood pressure.
Aids in altering abnormal brain function, in its capacity as neurotransmitter.
Suggested to be useful in Parkinsons disease, and some cases of depression (when tryptophan is not, tyrosine may be useful).
Small doses of tyrosine more effective than large in increasing brain levels of neurotransmitters.

Glutamine and Glutamic Acid
Under certain conditions may become essential nutrient.
Dominant amino acid in cerebro-spinal fluid and serum.
Glutamine (but not glutamic acid) readily passes the blood-brain barrier.
Glutamine readily converts to glutamic acid.
Glutamic acid is 'unique brain fuel'.
Glutamic acid gives rise to GABA, calming agent in brain, and possibly neurotransmitter.

Glutamic acid is component of folic acid.
Glutamic acid is component of glucose tolerance factor.
Useful in treating childhood behavioural problems.
Glutamic acid detoxifies brain of ammonia by reconversion to glutamine.
Glutamine protects against effects of alcohol. Decreases desire for alcohol, and in some cases for sugar.
Aids in peptic ulcer healing.
Useful in depression.

Cysteine and Cystine

Cysteine, together with methionine, is a major sulphur containing amino acid.
It is a major component of glucose tolerance factor (with glycine, glutamic acid, niacin and chromium).
Cystine or cysteine, are essential for adequate utilization of pyridoxine (B_6).
In chronic disease formation from methionine to cysteine is prevented.
Supplementation in chronic disease of cysteine said to be useful.
Removes heavy metal deposits (mercury etc.).
Protects against effects of alcohol and smoking.
Involved in maintenance of hair strength; as well as insulin and enzyme construction.
Texture and flexibility of skin maintained by free radical inactivation.

Glycine

Component of glutathione tripeptide (together with cysteine and glutamic acid).
Takes part in liver detoxification and elimination of free radical particles.
Component of glucose tolerance factor.

Alanine

Reducing effect on cholesterol (animal trials).
Essential in tryptophan and pyridoxine metabolism.

b-Alanine

Assists in synthesis of pantothenic acid.

Gama Aminobutyric Acid (GABA)
Regulator of neuronal activity.
Stimulates prolactin and therefore potentially useful in enlarged prostate cases.
Induces calmness in manic disorders.

Asparagine and Aspartic Acid
Synthesis of glycoproteins.
Amino donor in transamination in liver.
Detoxification of ammonia.
Increases endurance in athletes.

Citrulline
Precursor of ornithine and arginine.
Vital role in urea cycle.
Employed in detoxification and fatigue relief.

Ornithine
Releases growth hormone.
Vital in urea cycle.
Experimentally used in weight reduction.

Serine
Used externally in cosmetics as moistening agent.

Glutathione
This is tripeptide, composed of glutamic acid, cysteine and glycine.
Deactivator of free radicals.
Deactivates lipid peroxidation.
Delays ageing process by virtue of action on free radicals.
Enhances immune function.
Causes regression of tumour development (in animal experiments) as well as exercising protective role against tumour-inducing agents (aflatoxin in rat livers). Detoxifies heavy metals from body

Amino acids (with exceptions such as phenylalanine, see page 58) are best taken supplementally after meals. Since there is competition for uptake it is best that this is normally not a high protein meal. In the case of tryptophan, for example, it is desirable that supplementation is after a carbohydrate meal in order that insulin, thus produced, can depress presence of rival amino acids. The intricacies of amino acid supplementation and dietary manipulation will vary to some extent from one to another. Knowledge of the relationship between the amino acids, their precursors etc., and the means of bioavailability, will assist in the successful manipulation of the local biochemistry, or of the overall biochemistry, to therapeutic advantage.

9.

MAJOR AREAS OF THERAPEUTIC APPLICATION OF AMINO ACID THERAPY

Detoxification of heavy metals:
Methionine, cysteine, cystine and glutathione. (Sulphur containing amino acids).
Histidine.

Counteracting effects of free radical activity:
Methionine.
Glutathione.

Assistance in fatty metabolism:
Methionine.
Taurine.
Carnitine.

Acceleration of wound healing:
Arginine.
Proline/hydroxyproline (collagen-connective tissue regeneration).

Control of viral infection:
Lysine.

Thymus activity enhancement:
Arginine.

Glucose tolerance improvement/enhanced insulin production-utilization:
Arginine.
Taurine.
Glutamic acid.
Cysteine.
Glycine.

Immune system enhancement:
Glutathione.

Rheumatoid Arthritis:
Histidine.

Brain detoxifier (of ammonia):
Glutamic acid.

Brain detoxifier (of histamine in histadelic schizophrenia):
Methionine.

Protection against radiation effects:
Histidine.
Glutathione.
Cystine.

Weight Control — Obesity:
Phenylalanine. ⎫
Tryptophan.   ⎬ Appetite Control and better food selection
Valine.   ⎭
Methionine.
Carnitine (mobilizing fat deposits).

Depression:
Phenylalanine.
Tryptophan.
Tyrosine.
Glutamine/glutamic acid.

Infertility:
Arginine.
Carnitine.

Insomnia:
Tryptophan.

Epilepsy:
Taurine.

Ageing process — skin and soft tissues:
Proline/hydroxyproline (with Vitamin C).
Glutathione.

Ageing process general:
All amino acids.
Glutathione (prevents cross linkage through free radical activity).

Cholestasis:
Taurine.

Circulatory disorders (intermittent claudication etc.):
Carnitine.
Taurine.

Concentration ('brain fuel')
Glutamic acid (derives from glutamine).

Behavioural problems:
Glutamic acid.
Threonine (if deficient).
Tryptophan.
Taurine.

Alcoholism and alcohol induced damage:
Glutamine.
Cystine.

Peptic ulcer:
Glutamine.

Hair Health:
Cystine.

Tumours — (animal study):
Glutathione.

Lipid peroxidation deactivator:
Glutathione.

Myocardial infarction protection:
Carnitine.
Methionine.
Taurine (spares potassium).

Pain control enhancement:
Tryptophan.
Phenylalanine (d- and l- as DLPA)
or d-Phenylalanine.

Chronic disease:
All amino acids.
Isoleucine.
Cysteine/cystine (essential for B_6 utilization).
Phenylalanine.

Parkinson's disease:
Tyrosine.

Muscular dystrophy:
Carnitine (possibly).

Drug damage (protection):
Tryptophan. }
Lysine.   } animal studies
Cysteine/cystine. }

Allergic conditions:
All amino acids.
Specific amino acids according to indications.

10.

SUMMARY OF THERAPEUTIC DOSAGES CURRENTLY EMPLOYED AND CAUTIONS

Arginine
Up to 8g daily (Infertility). Doses of over 30mg not suggested if history of schizophrenia.

Histidine
Between 1g and 6g daily (rheumatoid arthritis). Take with vitamin C.

Isoleucine
240mg to 360mg daily.

Leucine
240mg to 360mg daily.

Lysine
500mg to 1,500mg daily, for maintenance of anti-herpes effect. Up to 3g daily in active stages. Always in divided dosages (plus low arginine diet).

Methionine
200mg to 1,000mg daily (detoxification).

Phenylalanine
Depression: 100mg to 500mg daily for up to two weeks.
Pain: (DLPA) 750mg, (or DPA 400mg) three times daily, 15

minutes prior to meals. (2,250mg daily). Doubled dosage after three weeks if no improvement. If no response after this, cease use. Weight Reduction: 100mg to 500mg, on empty stomach before retiring.

Proline
500mg to 1,000mg daily, with vitamin C.

Threonine
150mg to 500mg daily.

Tryptophan
General: 300mg daily.
Insomnia: 1g, prior to sleep (plus magnesium and B_6).
Depression: 3g (plus 1g nicotinamide).
Pain relief: 2g.
Maximum therapeutic level 6g daily.
Always take separately from competition with protein meals, at least one hour prior to meal.
Add B_6 for increased serotonergic effect.
Absorption enhanced by accompaniment of carbohydrate snack, or juice.
Function enhanced by accompaniment of niacinamide (ratio tryptophan: niacinamide should be 2:1).
Caution in pregnant women.

Valine
In weight reduction: 1g daily, in mixture of phenylalanine, valine, methionine and tryptophan, in ratio of 3:2:2:1. 4g of mixture prior to meals.
General: 250mg to 750mg daily.

Taurine
100mg to 1g daily. In epilepsy start at 1g daily, reducing to maintenance of as little as 50mg daily. High doses are less effective than low.

Carnitine
1g to 3g daily (in alcohol problems). General: 200mg three times daily, increasing after one week to 400mg three times daily (to improve 'brain energy' levels).

Cysteine or Cystine
1g three times daily, for one month, then twice daily (at end of meal) in all cases of chronic physical or mental ill health (with B_6). Cysteine converts to cystine in absence of vitamin C, therefore supplement together in a ratio of 3 parts vitamin C to 1 part cysteine.
Caution in use of cysteine in diabetes.

Glutathione
1g to 3g daily.

Alanine
200mg to 600mg daily.

Gama Aminobutyric acid (GABA)
20mg to 40mg daily dissolved under tongue.

Note: All the dosages described should be seen as rough guides only. The individuality of each patient will determine that requirements differ, and it is on the assumption that these individuals' needs will be met that this information is given.

Note also that many of the amino acids compete with each other for uptake. For example, tryptophan has to compete with the other large neutral amino acids, such as tyrosine and phenylalanine, as well as the branched chain amino acids, leucine, isoleucine and valine, for its uptake. Thus a high carbohydrate meal will encourage tryptophan uptake more successfully than a high protein meal, which would provide competition for it.

Note also that all the amino acids discussed in the work are the laevo(L) form, unless otherwise stated (such as in d-phenylalanine). This indicates a natural form of those amino acids discussed.

Amino Acid Compounds and Combinations
There are a variety of conditions in which it is desirable that a compound, including all, or some, of the essential amino acids, be made readily available to the individual. Many patients have adverse reactions to a variety of protein foods, and restriction of these foods, together with a supplementation of an amino acid compound containing the essential amino acids, as well as other

therapeutically indicated amino acids, in addition, or separately, is a valid approach. The usefulness of such compounds in conditions where the nutritional status may be impaired for one reason or another is also clear. In many cases there is a need for such supplementation in view of general protein impoverishment in the diet, through an inadequate dietary pattern. This may be the result of chronic disease (cancer etc.) or of mento-emotional illness (anorexia) or simply ignorance, poverty or a combination of these factors. Selective combinations of amino acids are also produced to meet the needs, identified in particular patterns indicated by amino acid profiles. These will usually include those amino acids which enhance production of hormones, and other desirable substances, in ill-health, and excludes those which are either seldom, if ever, deficient, or which have the ability to provoke undesirable symptoms in certain individuals. Thus cystine might be included for its detoxifying and anti-free-radical activity, as well as for its contribution of sulphur. Glutamic acid may be included in order to detoxify the brain of ammonia, and to provide an additional energy source for brain cells. Tyrosine might be included in order to aid ultimate production of adrenocortical and thyroid hormones, as well as dopamine.

Cautions
There is no substance which incorrectly employed cannot cause harm, whether this is 'natural' substance such as water, or a supplemental nutrient factor such as an amino acid. The following cautions are meant to guide the safe usage of these valuable therapeutic and preventive agents.
Arginine should not be employed in dosages above 30mg daily in cases of schizophrenia, unless under supervision.
Ornithine should not be employed in dosages above 30mg daily in cases of schizophrenia, unless under supervision.
Arginine intake should be kept low in cases involving herpes simplex virus.
Cysteine should be used with caution in diabetics especially if using insulin.
Cystine should be used with caution in individuals predisposed to bladder or kidney stones.
Cysteine should be used with vitamin C in order to obviate high cystine levels in individuals prone to kidney or bladder stones (3 parts vitamin C to 1 cysteine).

Histidine should be accompanied by vitamin C intake.

Histidine should not be taken by individuals with high histamine levels (histadelics) or individuals with manic depressive symptoms. Women prone to depression or PMT should use histidine with caution.

Phenylalanine should not be taken by individuals taking MAO drugs (monoamineoxidases)

Tyrosine should not be taken by individuals taking MAO drugs.

Methionine should be accompanied by vitamin B_6 to avoid build up of homocysteine.

Phenylalanine should be used cautiously by hypertensives.

Tyrosine should be used with caution by anyone with melanoma.

Tryptophan should not be used by women anticipating becoming pregnant. Trypotophan is incompatible with MAO drugs.

APPENDIX

ESSENTIAL AMINO ACID CONTENT OF COMMON FOODS

(Derived from *Nutrition Almanac,* McGraw Hill, 1979)

Food	Weight (gms)	Protein (gms)	TRP (mg)	LEU (mg)	LYS (mg)	MET (mg)	PHA (mg)	ISL (mg)	VAL (mg)	THR (mg)
Wholewheat bread	23	2.1	29	166	71	37	117	106	113	72
Wholewheat flour	120	15	192	1072	432	240	784	688	739	464
Soya flour	110	45	605	3428	2784	650	2179	2380	2339	1734
Oatmeal (cooked)	236	4.7	76	501	221	86	275	275	319	205
Brown Rice (raw)	190	14.3	159	1233	558	260	717	675	1004	558
Brown rice (cooked)	150	3.8	41	327	148	68	190	179	266	148
White rice (cooked)	150	3	33	258	117	54	150	141	210	117
Wheatgerm	6	1.8	16	110	99	26	58	76	88	86
Cottage cheese	260	44.2	469	4608	3584	1195	2304	2475	2475	2005
Edam cheese	28	7.7	108	775	591	211	429	523	575	300
Parmesan cheese	28	10	140	980	730	260	540	670	720	370

Food	Weight (gms)	Protein (gms)	TRP (mg)	LEU (mg)	LYS (mg)	MET (mg)	PHA (mg)	ISL (mg)	VAL (mg)	THR (mg)
Egg-boiled/raw	50	6.5	102	559	406	197	369	420	470	318
Buttermilk	246	8.9	90	809	678	188	433	515	613	384
Skim milk	64	23	320	2220	1780	570	1095	1461	1575	1073
Yogurt (part skim)	250	4.3	93	842	706	196	450	536	638	400
Fish, Cod (canned)	453	87	870	6609	7655	2523	3216	4435	4611	3742
Shrimp (cooked)	453	92	821	6240	7225	2381	3038	4187	4351	3530
Trout (raw)	453	97	974	7302	8571	2827	3606	6654	6930	5621
Orange	180	1.8	5	—	48	5	—	—	—	—
Peach	100	0.68	4	29	30	31	18	13	40	27
Strawberries	149	1.04	13	63	48	1.5	34	27	34	37
Beef (roast)	453	108	1154	7888	8369	2405	3944	5002	5291	4233
Liver (cooked)	453	120	1354	8398	6772	2167	4515	3786	5689	4334
Lamb	453	80	1525	9075	9543	2884	4832	6131	5768	5421
Chicken (breasts)	358	74.5	894	5438	6630	1937	2980	3948	3800	3204
Almonds	133	25	234	1934	774	344	1524	1161	1495	811
Brazils	167	23	312	1885	740	1571	1030	990	1374	705
Peanuts (roasted)	240	60	800	4432	2592	640	3680	2992	3616	1952
Pumpkin seeds	230	67	1201	5269	3068	1267	3735	3735	3602	2001
Sesame seeds	230	42	711	3461	1256	1382	3181	2052	1925	1548
Walnuts	100	15	175	1228	441	306	767	767	974	589
Lima beans (raw)	100	20	202	1628	1488	250	1212	992	1030	836
Beans (green-cooked)	125	2	28	116	104	30	48	90	96	76

Food	Weight (gms)	Protein (gms)	TRP (mg)	LEU (mg)	LYS (mg)	MET (mg)	PHA (mg)	ISL (mg)	VAL (mg)	THR (mg)
Carrots (cooked)	150	1.35	11	77	62	11	50	54	66	51
Chickpeas dry-raw (garbanzos)	100	20.5	164	1517	1415	266	1004	1189	1004	738
Lentils (cooked)	100	15.6	140	954	898	100	654	540	626	496
Mushrooms (tinned)	200	3.8	12	444	—	266	—	840	596	—
Potato (baked)	100	2.6	26	130	138	31	114	114	138	107
Soybeans (cooked)	200	22	330	1870	1518	330	1188	1298	1276	846
Tomato (raw)	150	1.65	15	68	69	12	46	48	46	54

USEFUL ADDRESSES

Among the chief suppliers of amino acids individually and in various
 combinations in the U.K. are the following:
Larkhall Laboratories, 225 Putney Bridge Road, London SW15 (Tel. 01-870
 0971).
Nature's Best, Freepost, P.O.Box 1, Tunbridge Wells, Kent. (Tel. 0892 34143).
York Nutritional Supplies, 4 Museum St., York. (Tel. 0904 52378).

INDEX